MANDARIN

Books by Robert Elegant

Fiction
CHINA AND THE WEST
Manchu (1624–1652)
Mandarin (1854–1875)
Dynasty (1900–1970)

A Kind of Treason
The Seeking

Non-fiction
China's Red Masters
The Dragon's Seed
The Centre of the World
Mao's Great Revolution
Mao versus Chiang
The Great Cities: Hong Kong

MANDARIN

by

ROBERT ELEGANT

HAMISH HAMILTON
London

M 65532

F

First published in Great Britain 1983
by Hamish Hamilton Ltd
Garden House 57–59 Long Acre London WC2E 9JZ

Copyright © 1983 by Robert and Moira Elegant

British Library Cataloguing in Publication Data

Elegant, Robert S.
  Mandarin.
  I. Title
  813'.54   PS3555.L37
  ISBN 0-241-11122-6

Printed and bound in Great Britain by
Richard Clay (The Chaucer Press) Ltd, Bungay, Suffolk

For
Richard Hughes
who, I sometimes believe,
was present

CONTENTS

Book One
April 11, 1854 – October 21, 1855
THE SETTLEMENT

Page 1

Book Two
April 1, 1856 – November 7, 1856
THE HEAVENLY KINGDOM

Page 125

Book Three
August 24, 1860 – September 1, 1864
THE COLLAPSE

Page 237

Book Four
March 7, 1872 – January 13, 1875
THE RESTORATION

Page 429

BOOK ONE

April 11, 1854 – October 21, 1855

THE SETTLEMENT

CHAPTER ONE

The Garden of Crystal Rivulets
The Summer Palaces near Peking

The young Manchu officer slipped behind the crimson pillars on the highest tier of the Tower of Buddha's Fragrance. He stood at his assigned post in obedience to the regulations of the Great Pure Dynasty. He was none the less uneasy, as apprehensive as if he were skulking for some ignoble purpose rather than carrying out his duties. He assured himself again that he was hidden by the long shadows of the pillars supporting the azure and gold umbrella roof before allowing his eyes to range over the sunset vista of Kunming Lake.

The seventeen arches of the bridge to South Lake Island were mirrored in the placid water, illusorily close from the Mount of Myriad Longevity, the highest eminence within the Garden of Crystal Rivulets. In the east, grotesque in his eyes, shone the white marble facades and the bulbous domes of the Romanesque palaces erected a century earlier by an Italian Jesuit architect for the Chien Lung Emperor, the fourth and greatest sovereign to rule since the Manchus conquered China.

Stealthily, almost furtively, his gaze shifted to the Hall of Jade Billows and the Hall of Joyous Longevity, which spread low under outswept roofs on the foreshore of the lake. When he saw the diminutive Pavilion of Auspicious Twilight between the two massive halls, he started, and, almost against his will, his eyes fixed themselves on the terrace.

Though certain he was unseen, the young officer smiled guiltily. With an effort, he resumed his surveillance of his assigned sector of the Yüan Ming Yüan, the Park of Perfect Radiance which extended for several hundred square miles all for the pleasure of his sovereign, the Hsien Feng Emperor of the *Ta Ching Chao*, the Great Pure Dynasty. The sight he had glimpsed was forbidden to all eyes, above all his, although he had actually been detailed to watch over the Summer Palaces this unseasonably warm April evening.

The low rays of the sun in the west lit two figures framed like puppets on a stage between the scarlet balustrades and the upcurled eaves on the terrace of the Pavilion of Auspicious Twilight. The larger lounged in a rosewood chair, his Imperial-yellow robe thrown back to expose his beige under-robe. A woman sat erect on an ebony stool beside him. The voluptuous form the officer remembered was obscured by the stiff folds of

3

her tribute-silk gown. Across the distance, the white narcissi appliquéd on the plum fabric shone clear in the golden light, as did the stylized *shou* – longevity – ideograms embroidered on her black cuffs.

The Baronet Jung Lu forced his eyes towards the red disc of the setting sun burning through the haze-shrouded clefts of the Fragrant Hills. He would not look again at the woman who had been the companion of his youth. He would not worry the old wound. Above all, he would not allow himself to hope. Fate was a whirligig, constantly spinning, but despite fate's wildest vagaries, she was forever beyond his reach.

Jung Lu shrank into himself behind the crimson pillar. The Emperor could not have sensed his impious gaze, much less his blasphemous memories and his sacrilegious longings. Nonetheless, he shivered in the warm twilight and pulled his cape around his shoulders as if the dusk were suddenly cold. He could discount neither the preternatural knowledge the common people attributed to the Son of Heaven nor, more practically, the sovereign's myriad sources of mundane information. The penalty for *lèse majesté* – in thought as much as deed – was decapitation after prolonged torture.

Unaware of the Baronet Jung Lu's fearful gaze, the Hsien Feng Emperor, the seventh of his line to rule China, watched the transparent stream pour from the square blue and white porcelain wine-pot. It was good to relax in the gentle twilight, for once untroubled by the eunuchs who usually swarmed around him, eager to spare him even the effort of pouring his own wine. In the sanctuary of the Garden of Crystal Rivulets ten miles from his chief residence in the Forbidden City of Peking, he could also escape the Mandarins who constantly pressed for decisions he was loath to take. It was delightful to be alone with the Virtuous Concubine Yehenala, far from the jealousies and the intrigues of a thousand court ladies. For once content, the Emperor sipped from a wine-cup painted with peonies. He must, he cautioned himself, drink sparingly, lest he mar the joys of the night.

Yehenala was not exalted among his hundreds of concubines. The Dowager Empress had designated her for the lowest rank when she was chosen among sixteen other aspirants to share his bed. She was, naturally, avid for promotion, but she was not importunate. Yehenala was only a little more than normally skilled in the arts of love, but her ardour largely compensated for her lack of total refinement. She was, after all, just past eighteen, having entered the Forbidden City three years ago, a year after his own elevation to the Dragon Throne. Yet he was himself not quite twenty-three.

'*Ho chiu* . . .' he commanded. 'Have some wine, and try these plums. The clotted cream's delicious.'

'Truly delicious, Majesty.' Yehenala's tone was as suggestive as the chiming of wind-bells. 'But the wine . . . perhaps not too much, lest . . .'

4

'It will be well . . . glorious, be assured.'

'It is *always* glorious, Majesty, pleasure no other man could give. But this slave hopes the ecstasy will not be dulled by wine . . . only enhanced.'

'The perfect balance,' he agreed magisterially, 'is all important.'

The shadow lifted from the Emperor's brow; the incipient frown no longer marred the dark-ivory skin between his sparse eyebrows. He watched the golden spoon carry the sliced plums dripping with yellow cream to Yehenala's carmine mouth, and he was pleased that she was almost as discriminating a gourmet as himself. She was, besides, almost as ingenious and avid a lover as himself. One could, of course, not equate the amatory skills of a male and a female. They were too different, but she was proficient – for an amateur. Gratified by the spontaneous profundity of his thoughts, the Emperor gave himself to the pleasure of studying his concubine.

Her conversation was provocative, and her movements were so graceful she seemed to float on the six-inch platforms of her flowered-satin shoes. Decorously condescending towards inferiors, she was sometimes wantonly playful towards himself. But she never transgressed the bounds of the deference due the Son of Heaven. He marvelled at the porcelain translucence of her skin, and he was stirred by the averted glance of her level eyes under their moth-antenna brows.

The Emperor sighed in satisfaction and lifted his cup again. But he was suddenly uneasy, as if he were observed even in the Pavilion of Auspicious Twilight, his refuge from his eunuchs and his Mandarins. He set his cup down and peered suspiciously across Kunming Lake.

He saw only the old-gold ripples on the lake and the four-tiered Tower of Buddha's Fragrance silhouetted against the dying sun. He sipped his wine again and caressed Yehenala's shoulder, delighting in the smooth flesh and the delicate bones under the silk robe. His hand slipped down the swell of her breast to the curve of her waist.

The Baronet Jung Lu's fingernails drew blood from his palms. He felt no pain, but only the rage throbbing in his chest. A pink haze obscured his vision, though his eyes were inextricably fixed on the terrace.

'Nala, it's growing cold,' the Emperor murmured. 'Shall we, perhaps? Better go inside and . . .'

The Emperor abruptly withdrew his hand. His ears, tuned all his life to such intrusions, had heard a gentle scratching on the door leading to the bedchamber.

'*Lai*! . . . Come!' His voice was rimed with displeasure. Would they never leave him a moment to himself, he wondered, a single instant undisturbed?

The door was opened by a eunuch whose orange and green robe was scrolled with the five-clawed Imperial Dragons of a personal attendant of the Son of Heaven. His dull eyes cast down and his torso bent, the eunuch

5

shuffled on to the terrace. He sank to his knees and offered a despatch-box of scarlet leather chased with gold.

The Hsien Feng Emperor's fingertips toyed with the elongated brass lock as the eunuch withdrew. Frozen in anger, he stared across the lake beyond the Mount of Myriad Longevity crowned by the Fragrant Tower towards the Hill of Jade Springs with its single pagoda and the hazy Fragrant Hills in the distance.

'Even here!' he said bitterly. 'Even here, there is no rest for Us.'

'Majesty, the cares of state are heavy.' Yehanala was gravely sympathetic. 'But Your Majesty's shoulders are broad . . . immensely broad. And Your Majesty's transcendent wisdom . . .'

'You, too, must read it.' The Emperor mastered his rage and joked. 'We shall, perhaps, require your wise counsel.'

He inserted a two-pronged key into the lock and drew a scroll from a case of yellow silk. Muttering to himself, he broke the seal, unrolled the parchment, and began to read.

'Covering letter from the Ministry of War: Memorial from one Wu Chien-chang, Intendant of Shanghai. Forwarded for Our personal attention because pressing. Submitted with humblest respect and so on and so on . . .'

'The Memorial itself, Majesty?' Yehenala's impatience tested the limits of the privilege her master allowed her. 'What does it say?'

'Ah yes, the Memorial.' Depressed by his martyrdom through the cares of state, the Emperor did not reprimand her impertinence – and thus confirmed her privilege. 'Prepare the vermilion ink. It appears that We . . . always We . . . are again obliged to decide. As if We did not employ hordes of Mandarins to take minor decisions.'

While the Emperor laboriously deciphered the formal language of the despatch, Yehenala ground a red inkstick against a malachite inkstone, dribbling water into its well from the pierced forehead of a miniature green-porcelain tiger. She selected a sable-hair brush from the sheaf in a carved jade brush-holder and twirled the tip in the vermilion fluid. The Emperor waved the brush away and handed her the Memorial.

'Read, Nala,' he commanded. 'Read and weep. It is coming again, the time of troubles. If only We had been firmer . . . as we wished and you suggested.'

Yehenala frowned, pretending to great difficulty in reading the turgid bureaucratic jargon studded with classical allusions. It would be imprudent for her to display greater proficiency in the Officials' Language than her Imperial Lord. By his grace she was permitted to develop her unwomanly bent for scholarship and to read the Memorials submitted by his Mandarins throughout the Great Empire. The intimate knowledge of affairs of state acquired from those despatches had already placed much power in her frail hands.

6

Her frown deepened as she read, and her breath quickened. When she laid the document down, her lips were compressed in resolution.

'The accursed foreign devils!' Her angry forefinger tapped the Memorial. 'The cunning, murderous devils. The time has come . . .'

'Not so fast, Nala,' the Emperor chided. 'We must deliberate.'

'But they've attacked Your Majesty's troops. At Shanghai, the centre of their aggressive . . . their blasphemous intrigues against the Sacred Dynasty. Worse, they're plotting with the rebels. The barbarians incited those scum, the Small Swords, to strike at the Imperial Army. Your Majesty *must* act!'

'It *is* evil, gross evil!' In his distraction, he did not reprimand her imperative tone. 'The barbarians come across the oceans to harass Our sacred domains. And, now, to unite with the Small Swords, the vile secret society with its obscene motto: *Overthrow the Manchus and Restore Chinese Rule*! Next, the oceanic barbarians will combine with those vermin, the Taipings, the so-called Heavenly Kingdom of Great Peace. You know, they practise some barbarian mumbo-jumbo religion, and they call Our Imperial soldiers Imps. Those sons of turtle-bitches cut off their Manchu queues and grow their hair long to show that they are free Chinese. *Free* Chinese! What a contradiction in terms!'

'And the long-haired rebels dare approach Peking itself,' Yehenala goaded. 'Less than two hundred miles from where we sit, those lice who call themselves Holy Soldiers of Great Peace . . .'

'We know, Nala, We know,' the Emperor sighed. 'But Our counsellors advise patience. Manage the barbarians, they say. Do not fight them . . . just yet.'

'The barbarians *are* fighting. They're attacking Your Majesty's forces. If they unite with the Taipings, then . . . I beg forgiveness for my presumption, Majesty . . . but the Sacred Throne will tremble . . .'

'The Sacred Throne already trembles, Nala . . . as you know.'

'Not truly, Majesty. Only a passing tremor, no more. But, if the oceanic barbarians unite with the Taipings, the Sacred Throne *will* tremble.'

'You're right, Nala. We have long thought so. But Our Mandarins counsel prudence. The Empire is enormous, they say, almost the entire world. The barbarians come from small and distant lands, and their numbers are small. Patience, Our ministers counsel, just wait them out.'

'The barbarians' weapons are powerful, Majesty, yet no more than flywhisks beside the might of the Empire. Despite this disgraceful affair at Shanghai, Your Majesty can easily overcome . . .'

'What do you advise, Nala, my little firebrand?' He smiled at her pugnacity.

'War, My Lord, war! We must crush them. And we must split the barbarians from the rebels . . . by shrewd stratagems.'

Yehenala spoke eloquently and bitterly for several minutes. Fired by her

7

passion, the Emperor snatched the vermilion brush from her eager fingers. His hand trembled with anger as he wrote.

Concealed by the darkness under the eaves of Buddha's Tower, the Baronet Jung Lu still watched. In the yellow light of the oil-lamps, the Emperor and the Virtuous Concubine looked even more like puppets. But they were, he knew, flesh and blood. Jung Lu wearily wiped his blood-stained palms on his blue tunic.

CHAPTER TWO

April 12, 1854   *Shanghai*

Clouds obscured the divided city, and rain lanced the Hwangpoo River. The downpour tore with cold ferocity at the straw-mats of the refugees sleeping in the streets of the South City, where the Chinese lived. Infants shrieked in terror of the spirits of the night, and wretched dogs yelped. From the camp of the Imperial Army on the east bank of the Hwangpoo a cannon boomed funereally.

When the winds parted the clouds mantling Shanghai, the City Above the Sea, moonlight skittered on the river, and unlighted junks rolled in the gusts. To the north, lamplight shone warm from pillarred mansions of the European and American intruders. Only guttering lanterns lit the gloom of the Chinese quarter, which stank of sour rice, rotting vegetables, and excrement. Gongs boomed and cymbals clashed in the Imperial Camp to terrify the rebels holding the South City – and to drive away the demons of the rainclouds.

A dark junk bucked across the current towards the west bank of the Hwangpoo, its planks gaping to admit streams of silt when the blunt prow slapped the waves. The stern-oar shrilled in its tholes, and the halyard supporting the matting-sail squealed through its wooden block. When the sail's bamboo battens clattered to the deck, the two men squatting near the prow cocked their heads. Though the storm overwhelmed all other sounds, they feared discovery.

'I pay *nung* allee time *kyong-eow* . . .' The shorter man threw off the straw raincape covering the short jacket and baggy trousers of a respect-able workman. 'I tell you many time more better we wait and come down with silk on steamboat.'

'Aisek, no can do.' His taller companion, who was similarly dressed, replied in the same mixture of pidgin English and Shanghai dialect.

8

'Already, we come late. We *must* come back fast. A sin if no come back this night.'

'I fear to meet the Small Swords or, worse, the Imperial soldiers,' Aisek grumbled. 'A terrible shame after that great stroke of business. Better we come in daylight by steamboat . . . even a week late.'

'And let everybody see us and spoil our business?' the taller objected. 'We have much silk to fill the empty hulls. Rejoice and put away your fears.'

'I rejoice when we reach . . .'

'We're almost there now. And the families wait for us.'

'Let it please God we see them safe tonight,' Aisek insisted querulously.

'*Shmae Ysroel* . . .' Saul intoned the Hebrew prayer, and Aisek joined him. 'Hear, oh Israel, the Lord our God is one!'

The cloud mass descended again, blotting out the moonlight. The junk's prow embedded itself blindly in the sodden riverbank, and the impact hurled them to the deck. They rose hastily, clutched their cloth-wrapped bundles, and dropped over the side into the darkness. Their cloth shoes squelching in the mud, the two men clambered on to the shore.

The boatmen grunted and swore hoarsely as they leaned on their long poles to free the junk from the sucking mud. Despite the wailing of the storm and the clashing of symbols from the Imperial Camp, they were also stalked by fear of discovery. The junk's master-owner, who was called *Low Dah*, the Old Great One, sighed with relief when the prow shook off the clutch of the land and pointed towards the junks rearing at their anchors in the stream. He mouthed soft obscenities of delight at escaping the hidden perils of the Shanghai night. It had been a hazardous voyage from Soochow, the city of brocaded silks and walled gardens, which lay sixty miles north-west across low land seamed with canals and rivers. The green delta of the Yangtze, which he called Chang Chiang, the Long River, was infested with rebels against the Manchu Dynasty and was harried by the Dynasty's predatory soldiery.

Leaving his sons to work the junk, the *Low Dah* stooped into the low cabin to burn incense-sticks before the wooden image of Tien Mu Hou, the patron goddess of sailors. He had been foolish, he knew, to undertake the voyage when the land was torn by battle. Shot-shattered timbers testified both to his foolhardiness and to the intercession of the Goddess, which had preserved his vessel, his sons, and his life. Yet the mad foreigner had insisted even more vehemently than his Chinese companion, who was only a little less mad.

It was lunatic to make the hazardous passage and doubly lunatic to pay ten times the normal rate for the passage. Their madness, which had naturally been irresistible, was his good fortune. He chuckled contentedly as he spilled silver coins from a cotton bag and avidly counted the Maria Theresa dollars.

*

Squalls blinded the two travellers struggling north towards the foreign enclave. The murk also shielded them from watchful eyes in both the Imperial outposts and the rebel-held South City. Not only soldiers and rebels, but all men were their enemies that night, above all, Saul's foreign competitors, who believed he had been confined to bed with a virulent fever for the past two weeks. They must come unseen to Saul's house just behind the Bund lined by the compounds of the great trading houses. Otherwise, their secret journey to Soochow would yield no great profit.

A purpose greater than profit also drove them homeward. Compelled by that higher imperative, the pair loped along the moat of the Chinese city, now held by the rebels of the Small Sword Society. The danger had been when the junk slipped out of Soochow Creek past the steamers and clippers anchored along the Bund, easily evading the Imperial gunboats on the Hwangpoo River. The clouds were opening, and the thunder was diminishing like the footfalls of a retreating giant. Fearing the moonlight, they moved faster. But Saul and Aisek shrank under the illusory shelter of the wall of the South City when a cannon boomed again from the Imperial camp.

The shot rumbled above the thunder and the rain, the roar of displaced air like the crash of a stricken oak. Believing the ball was hurtling directly towards them, Saul and Aisek threw themselves face down in the mud.

The shot struck, rebounded into the air, and fell to earth again. It ploughed through the ground with an immense sucking sound like the oak's groaning when its roots tear free of the soil.

'The Lord is one!' Saul breathed his guttural invocation when the spent ball dribbled past them.

'You said,' Aisek whispered, 'we must above all fear the *foreigners* tonight.'

'They're not as fierce as your countrymen,' Saul acknowledged. 'At least tonight. But the foreigners mustn't find us . . . and wonder where we come from.'

Light glimmered on the battlements above them, flickering as the wind tossed the globular paper-lanterns. Shadow enveloped them, but the next instant the lanterns' rays lit them mercilessly. Saul dug his fingers into the mud and silently prayed to his distant God.

On the wall, men shouted in a harsh dialect Saul could not even identify. Aisek, who could just follow the altercation in Cantonese, burrowed deeper and promised five lengths of brocade to Kwan Yin, the Goddess of Mercy, to bring them safely home.

10

'I tell you I saw it,' a voice rasped. 'I saw someone move.'

'You're mad,' a second voice rejoined. 'There's nothing there. Your eyes are rotted by too much wine.'

The lanterns drifted away, and darkness enfolded them again. Aisek lifted his face from the mud and looked at the cliff of the city-wall above them. Disembodied in the glare, heads covered with scarlet turbans floated above the battlements among a thicket of spears. He frugally revised his promise, resolving to give two lengths of brocade to Kwan Yin. The Goddess had not been tried hard, since it was no miracle to hide them from this desultory search. Besides, Saul's almighty God, in Whom he too believed, was assuredly also taking a hand.

Attracted by the light, the cannon boomed again – and a second iron ball rumbled across the Hwangpoo. Trailing a spray of solid mud, the ball buried itself fifty yards short of the red turbans bobbing on the battlements.

'The Imps aim as well as the Small Swords search.' Scornful in his relief, Saul used the rebels' contemptuous name for the Imperial troops.

'After all, they're your weapons . . . barbarian weapons.' Aisek instinctively championed his enemies because they, too, were Chinese. 'Your people invented them.'

'Not quite, Elder Brother. They're *not* my people, the cannon-makers. No more than they're yours. Neither is *our* people.'

The grey net of clouds was opening to free the pale moon from its meshes. Contemptuous of both the Small Swords and the Imperialists, Saul loped northward. His shorter companion trotting behind, they skirted the clustered hovels of refugees. After a quarter of an hour they came to the edge of the foreign settlement. Only narrow Yangjingbang Creek separated them from the haven where four-square houses arrogantly streamed light.

Saul froze in horror. Silhouetted by the glow, sentries armed with rifles were patrolling the northern bank of the Yangjingbang. The foreigners' normal negligent contempt for their reluctant – and troublesome – Chinese hosts was for some reason replaced by wariness. The boundary had not been guarded when they left Shanghai two weeks earlier.

They had come so far through so many perils. Now, as they gazed at their goal like Moses at the Promised Land, they were on the verge of being discovered. If they were, their hazardous journey would have been in vain.

The long European rifles were a greater peril than any they had already faced. With the cold certainty of despair, Saul knew the foreigners would not miss. Unlike the rebels and the Imperial troops, they would shoot straight. And they would count the lives of two unknown natives hardly worth a challenge before they fired.

Moonlight silvered the narrow ribbon of water, which was as forbiddingly impassable as a broad moat.

*

11

A red smear glistened below the ivory cylinder fixed to the doorpost where the blood of the sacrificial lamb had stained the teak. No larger than a man's thumb, the cylinder glowed in the candlelight spilling from the open doorway. Cloaked by the watery moonlight that had succeeded the storm, the two travellers trudged from Szechwan Road into the compound. Their jackets dripped water, and their cloth shoes were sodden pulp. Saul's ruddy beard was saturated, while Aisek's black goatee was a wet wisp like the tail of a drenched kitten.

A girl of fifteen burst from the doorway, careless of the puddles on the gravel path. Water spurted beneath her high-buttoned kidskin shoes to splatter the hem of her white-silk kaftan. Tawny hair streaming loose beneath a green scarf, her slender form darted towards the travellers.

'Pappa, Pappa,' she cried in lilting English. 'I knew you'd come. I told Mamma, I told her you couldn't, not . . . not tonight . . . not this night.'

Still prattling, the girl hurled herself at Saul and kissed his cheeks.

'Fronah, my dove, let me breathe.' When Saul laughed, his austere features brightened. 'I said I would. And I have.'

'I knew it! I knew it!' The girl burbled to the woman in the orange kaftan, whose oval face was still shadowed by anxiety. 'I told you he would, Mamma.'

'Sarah, you are well?' The tall man embraced his wife and kissed her forehead. 'I'm very sorry I'm late, but . . .'

'Saul, you're back.' His wife was also uncomfortable at displaying their affection. 'I prayed . . . and you've come back.'

'And the house, it's all prepared?' Saul kissed the ivory cylinder before entering the doorway. 'Everything is ready?'

'Of course it is, Saul.' Asperity tinged her voice, though she had known he would ask the superfluous question. 'How could I not?'

'Uncle Aisek!' The squat Chinese man squirmed uneasily in the girl's embrace, though his eyes beamed. 'You said you'd bring Pappa home safe. And you have.'

'Enough, Fronah. You're disturbing Mr Lee,' Sarah commanded, following her husband into the house. 'Leave him be.'

Two Chinese youths in blue long-gowns stepped from the lighted doorway and kneeled on the wet gravel before Aisek.

'Welcome, my father, welcome.' The elder, who was taller and thinner than his brother, spoke in formal Mandarin, the Officials' Language, rather than Shanghainese. 'We were consumed by concern for your safety.'

'Well, I'm back, lads,' Aisek laughed. 'And none the worse, as you see . . . or not much the worse. It all went magnificently. Your grand-mother'll be pleased. Or will she?'

'Of course, Grandma'll be delighted,' the younger said. 'She's been worried, though. Really grousing . . . grousing all the time. Disaster, she

keeps saying, only disaster can come of trafficking with barbarians . . .
total bankruptcy.'

'Dawei, that's no way to speak about your grandmother.' The sting of
the reprimand was assuaged when the father clasped his sons' shoulders. 'If
only your mother were still alive to see this triumph.'

The youths bowed their heads in sympathy with their father's memory of
sorrow. They were actually moved more by his fleeting embrace than by
grief for their mother who had died years earlier. In anger, Chinese of the
middle-class might violate the Confucian injunction against demonstrating
their emotions. But however deeply they felt, fathers and sons rarely
displayed affection, even in private.

*

'The last minutes were the worst.' Saul uncharacteristically began his tale
at the end. 'I almost despaired when I saw those sentries along the
Yangjingbang. Just across the creek was safety . . . and a fortune. But how
to cross it undiscovered?'

'*Pien-jen* . . .' Aisek spoke in the Mandarin his sons preferred, rather
than Shanghainese, and the girl Fronah translated for her parents.
'Deception was the handmaid of triumph.'

After bathing, Saul and Aisek had changed from their coarse workmen's
garments. That clothing had made them inconspicuous during their
journey across the revolt-harried Yangtze Delta to Soochow, and Saul had
concealed his ruddy beard with a bandage that apparently covered an
injury. By disrupting trade the rebellion offered the merchants an unparalleled opportunity. The first bulk silk for the eager markets of Europe and
America would command exorbitant prices. Their new garments were
appropriate to the prosperity they already enjoyed – and to their confident
expectations of great wealth.

Saul wore a white-linen robe clasped with a brocade sash. His feet were
thrust into black-leather sandals with upturned toes, and his grey-silk
turban was tied in the manner of Baghdad. Aisek was dressed with
subdued opulence in a shimmering blue-silk long-gown embossed with *fu* –
prosperity – ideograms. His shoes were dark satin, while his skullcap was
the same glossy black as his hair, whose grey stippling he dyed. Though his
countrymen venerated age, Aisek Lee did not wish to look older than his
thirty-nine years. Aside from the laugh wrinkles around his deepset eyes
and his full mouth, Aisek's round face was unmarked by time.

Actually a year younger, Saul appeared the elder because of the deep
calipers engraved from his mouth to his nostrils. His narrow face and high,
seamed forehead were dominated by a high-arched nose with narrow
nostrils.

Their elbows propped on green-satin cushions, the partners lounged in

13

wide ebony chairs. Their shoulders were draped by purple-striped shawls with white fringes, as were the youths'. His shoulders sloping powerfully and his head a ponderous globe, the Chinese merchant was drawn with curved horizontal brush-strokes. The Jewish merchant had been sketched with straight pen-lines, which extended vertically from his long head to his slender fingers and his narrow feet.

'By deception we triumphed,' Aisek repeated complacently.

'It was a justifiable deception, a *worthy* deception.' Saul defended his honour, which he valued above profit. 'If I hadn't played sick, we couldn't have gone in secret. And where would the ladies of London and New York look for their new silk frocks?'

'Must come to you and me . . . All *tai-tai* must buy silk belong you and me.'

Aisek spoke in their accustomed mixture of pidgin English and Shanghainese, the *lingua franca* of the two families. With the snobbery of youth, Aisek's sons preferred Mandarin, the Officials' Language. They spoke English almost as well as Saul, who had learned that language as a mature man in Bombay, a way-station on his long road to China. Normally he spoke Hebrew to his wife. If the Lees and her parents had difficulty in understanding each other, Fronah would translate, since she spoke the various languages best.

'My mother fears we go bust, but she very wrong,' Aisek exulted. 'We very soon become very rich.'

'Tell us how you got across the creek, Pappa,' Fronah demanded, her light brown eyes sparkling above her delicate cheekbones.

'Well, it was simple, quite simple after that first shock,' Saul replied. 'I saw Dr MacGregor wandering alone with a lantern like a man on a midnight stroll. He was dragging his shotgun by the barrel . . . seemed he almost forgot why he was there. So I called to him. Of course, he knew about our little . . . ah . . . white lie and, you know, he'd helped . . .'

'For squeeze for himself,' Aisek interjected. 'A share of profits . . . a little squeeze . . . for his hospital.'

'Any rate, he got us across the Yangjingbang. And here we are, no one the wiser. No one knows where we went or that the silk's coming down by steamer next week.'

'Saul, it's late,' Sarah interrupted his self-congratulation. 'It's past time for the first cup of wine . . . to celebrate *all* our blessings . . .'

'Our *own* liberation, as well, Sarah,' Saul joked. 'Tonight is truly a joyous occasion . . . for our people and for ourselves. God's mercy and His bounty are endless.'

He was solemn when he rose and glanced round the company self-consciously reclining on cushions. The white-damask tablecloth was set with plates of parsley and lettuce, as well as bowls of salt-water and bowls of nuts and raisins minced with cinnamon. A lamb-shank and several

14

hard-boiled eggs lay on a platter beside three rounds of flat bread. Some twelve inches across, the discs were dark barred by the brazier.

'Blessed art Thou, Lord our God, Ruler of the universe, Creator of the fruit of the vine, Who hast chosen us amidst all peoples and singled us out among all other nations.' Sault chanted in Hebrew and raised his silver winecup. 'Thou hast lovingly granted us, Lord our God . . . this feast of unleavened bread, a joyous festival of holy assembly. The season of our liberation recalls our going forth from Egypt . . . Blessed art Thou, Lord who hast set apart and sanctified Thy people Israel . . .'

Guided by Fronah's whispered translation, the three Chinese joined the Sephardic Jews in the Seder's first cup of wine. They, too, washed their hands in the silver basin presented by a houseboy wearing a white jacket and black trousers tied at the ankles. They, too, took small portions of lettuce and parsley dipped into salt water, the 'bitter herbs' that recalled the cruel days of the Hebrews' captivity in Egypt. They, too, knew that the blood of the sacrificial lamb daubed on the doorpost symbolized the Almighty's instructions to His people when He afflicted the Egyptians with plagues to compel them to release their Hebrew slaves. It is written: *Let every one of you take of the blood of the Paschal lamb and dip a bunch of hyssop onto that blood and mark his door therewith so that the Angel of Death shall know you to be My people and pass you by and spare your first-born.*

Aisek and his sons joined Saul in the ritual invocation: 'Blessed art Thou, Lord our God, Ruler of the universe, Creator of the fruit of the earth.'

The company watched Saul take up one disc of the three *matzah*, which recalled the unleavened bread the Israelites had eaten during their protracted journey to the Promised Land. The Chinese were puzzled when Saul snapped that *matzah* in two and replaced one portion between the unbroken discs. He wrapped the larger portion in a napkin and ostentatiously set it down on the stool behind him.

Saul smiled broadly, and his eyes danced gleefully as Fronah whispered to the boys: 'That's the *afikoman*. You do remember, don't you? You must steal it so Pappa doesn't see. Then you know what to do, don't you?'

The flames in the black-marble fireplace tinged the air crimson as Saul sat again on his broad chair, violating the strict order of the Passover rites. This year, it was all important to bring his guests into communion with his family – and with the Jewish faith. The brandy the celebrants had drunk to warm them flushed their cheeks. Their gestures were lively, though restrained by the reserve of both cultures. Fronah had taken two thimble-cups, and her light-brown eyes glowed. The fire and the lamplight created a haven in the alien Shanghai night, where the storm was rising again.

'Tonight I have changed the order of the Seder,' Saul said genially.

15

'There's no reason not to. A Seder not only recalls our ancestors' flight from Egypt. It's also an occasion for discussion . . . like an old Greek symposium. Our ancestors took a lot from the Greeks. We recline on our left elbows to show our liberty as did the Hellenistic freemen. Tonight, we'll first talk a little.'

'You can *always* talk, my dear.' Sarah was proud of her husband's scholarship, but felt it her wifely duty to curb his occasional pretentiousness. 'This night is no different, but you do talk particularly well tonight.'

'Thank you, my dear.' Saul casually acknowledged – and dismissed – her tartness. 'This night, above all other nights, we are enjoined to remember the trials and triumphs of our people – before the Exodus and during the many centuries since. We are instructed: *Tell your children. Tell your sons and daughters so that they may know – and through knowledge become one with Israel.*'

'You say that every Seder, Pappa,' Fronah objected. 'What's different tonight that makes it *so* different from other nights that are different . . . different from other Passovers? Tell me, Pappa.'

'I shall, Fronah,' Saul agreed indulgently. 'Tonight we are honoured by the presence of the Lee family, Aisek, the father, Aaron and David, the sons. For the first time, they, too, are participating in the joyous festival of their ancestors.'

Sixteen-year-old David Lee, called Dawei in Chinese, glanced at his elder brother. Eighteen-year-old Aaron, otherwise Ailun, was intent on Fronah's translation. His narrow face, the features sharply cut like his deceased mother's, frowned in concentration. David was less absorbed. The interest in his wide-set eyes flickered erratically as his thoughts wandered. His face, almost as round as his father's, mirrored his mood, which oscillated from reverence to mischievousness.

'I am convinced that we are not only of the same people, but the same tribe,' Saul continued. 'You know, Jews came to China centuries before the Christian era. More than 300 years ago, when their descendants were "discovered" in Kaifeng by the Jesuits, the priests of the false Messiah, they bore surnames that seemed wholly Chinese: Chao, Chin, and Shih, among a few others. Lee, too, but Lee is, of course, Levi . . .'

'The *same* tribe?' Aaron murmured.

'Yes, Aaron, the same tribe. As you know, we are called Haleevie. What does Haleevie mean? It's the Hebrew ha-Levi, meaning the tribe of Levi, the custodians of the temples. The spelling we use was adopted when we were in Spain. Since you are also Levis, we are of the same tribe of Israel.'

'How can you be so sure after so many centuries, sir?' David asked.

'Certainty is the Lord God's alone. But as far as human learning takes us, yes, I'm sure. Your father and I have discussed the matter. And we are agreed. That is why you're here tonight to partake in the rites of your ancestors. Though there are, I fear, certain matters . . . certain ways in which . . .'

'Saul, tonight's meant to be joyous,' Sarah interjected. 'Forget your reservation for tonight. Let's celebrate the liberation of Israel . . . and your return . . . without reservations.'

Saul assented readily, as he almost invariably assented when Sarah pressed her point. Apparently docile, his petite wife was usually quiet in company. But her firmly arched nose and her delicately pointed chin showed great determination. When her brown eyes flashed and she spoke emphatically, he listened.

'You're right, my dear,' Saul said. 'No reservations . . . not tonight.'

The reservations Saul suppressed were fundamental. His joy at discovering his kinship with the Lees was diminished by his fear that they might never be wholly one with the community of Israel. Aisek had agreed that his sons should receive instruction in doctrine, though he said his old head could not hold so many new ideas. Still, Saul, who was practical as well as devout, wondered whether it would be wise for Aaron and David to declare themselves orthodox Jews.

Most perplexing was the question of circumcision, the ritual removal of the foreskin required of every male in Israel. The operation could be painful, perhaps dangerous, for an adolescent, but that was not the chief deterrent. Circumcision was abhorrent to the Chinese because it resembled the mutilation of the palace eunuchs, who sacrificed all their parts to the knife. Their abject career could lead to great wealth and power, but they were despised by most Chinese, not only because they surrendered their manhood to ambition or necessity, but because their bodies were not whole. The Confucian ethos required men to preserve intact the bodies that were the inalienable gift of their ancestors. (Mutilating women by binding their feet was another matter.) The eunuchs themselves preserved their 'relicts' in spirits so that they could be buried with them – and rejoin their ancestors, presumably, once again whole men.

Circumcision might, therefore, close to Aaron and David the official career to which they aspired – like all educated Chinese. The Mandarins of the Great Pure Dynasty were a small and privileged class, their ranks replenished not by inheritance but by merit demonstrated through strenuous examinations. A man circumcised, an incomplete man, might not be acceptable to the Mandarinate. Yet millions of Chinese Moslems, unlike a few hundred Chinese Jews, circumcised their sons – and some Moslems served as officials.

Actually the key question was practical. Avowing Judaism might actually be an advantage to the boys in dealing with foreigners, who were eager to befriend – and, of course, convert – Chinese Jews, while holding other Jews at arm's length. But the Chinese would probably not be so welcoming. Moslem Mandarins were tolerated because they had existed in

17

some numbers for some time. Precedent ruled; any practice that had long endured was not only sanctioned, but semi-sacrosanct. In its disarray, the erratically theocratic Empire distrusted innovation above all else. Whether Aaron and David could ever avow themselves practising Jews was a decision, Saul concluded, that must be left to the wisdom of the Lord.

Besides, he should not further postpone the rites of the Seder. Fronah was twisting on her chair, impatient for her moment of glory. He began the formal Narration, the *Haggadah*, which told of the liberation of the Hebrews by their exodus from Egypt to the land of Israel. After removing the eggs and the lamb-shank, Saul raised the platter with two hands to display the *matzah* – and to dramatise the difference between that bread of affliction and the present bounty.

'Behold and see,' he intoned, 'the bread of woe our fathers ate . . . Let all who hunger now partake . . . to celebrate our freedom and the Passover . . . May the wandering tribes this year return to Israel . . .'

As Saul replaced the platter, Aisek mused: 'My father sometimes talked of his grandfather's remembering the Feast of Unleavened Bread. My mother always scoffed, though she was a Chao of Kaifeng before she came to Shanghai to marry. But my mother always scoffs, all honour to her.'

'When the Lord chooses, she will be enlightened.' Saul was impatient of his partner's often repeated grievance.

'She scoffs at everything.' Aisek was not diverted. 'She scoffs at our being Jews . . . hates our joining the Seder. Worse, she hates our partnership . . . claims it's impoverished the family.'

'The Lord will dispose as He pleases,' Saul reiterated.

'She goes around in rags. She hoards every scrap, even the burnt husks from the rice-pot.' Brandy and wine had lubricated Aisek's tongue. 'She sits and keens. She wails and says only her frugality keeps the family alive, because I've wasted our substance in futile ventures with a barbarian. When I tell her of our great coup, she won't . . .'

Sarah passed the crystal carafe, and the red wine flowed into the ancient silver cups reserved for Passover. They were Spanish heirlooms brought from Baghdad when she joined Saul in Bombay sixteen years earlier. She was not sure she liked seeing her treasured cups in the hands of the Lees, though Saul insisted that the Chinese were not only Jews, but distant kinsmen. Still, the boys, especially David, were a delight – even if David did encourage Fronah's wildness.

Sarah Haleevie's pleasure in her daughter was this night unmarred by her intermittent annoyance at Fronah's willfulness. She listened with complacent pride as the girl began the ritual *Mah Nishtannah*. The youngest present always asked the Four Questions to initiate the recollection of history that was a central purpose of the Seder.

Fronah preened herself, smoothing her kaftan over her hips and tossing her head. Though irritated by this display of vanity, her mother remained silent. The girl's oval face was animated, and the resonant Hebrew lingered on her full lips. Her brown hair glinted with ruddy highlights when she dipped her minutely pointed chin for emphasis. Reflected from her white- silk kaftan, the lamplight moulded the pertly rounded tip of her nose.

'Why is this night different from all other nights?' Fronah's tone was grave, but a smile quirked her mouth. 'On all other nights, we eat leavened or unleavened bread. Why this night only unleavened bread? . . . Why this night only bitter herbs? . . . Why do we dip the herbs into salt-water? . . . And why, unlike all other nights, do we eat reclining?'

Unperturbed by his daughter's high spirits, Saul Haleevie explained the symbols of the Hebrews' captivity in Egypt and their escape to the Promised Land: the bitter herbs of bondage, the *matzah* that had fed them during their flight, and the relaxed posture of free men. Twice again the celebrants drank ritual cups of wine before the white-jacketed Shanghai houseboy served the abundant meal that sealed their rejoicing.

'Next year in Jerusalem!' Saul intoned as the rite of the Seder ended. 'Next year in Jerusalem!'

The Lees were puzzled by the riddles, the jokes, and the songs that enlivened the ceremony. Levity had no place in Chinese rituals. But they were pleased to acknowledge – and to honour – the distant ancestors Saul revealed to them. Already the proud heirs of six millennia of Chinese civilisation, they were further exalted by their descent from another people amost as ancient. Antiquity and continuity were the mainsprings of life for all Chinese – even Jewish Chinese.

Though he was deeply moved, Aaron was also disturbed by his kinship with the Haleevies. They were part of the tide of outlanders now sweeping over the barriers the Chinese Empire erected to protect its cultural, spiritual, and economic institutions from adulteration. Less than a score of Jews among some three hundred foreigners in Shanghai were a minute part of that tide of alien commerce and alien doctrines. But every outlander undermined traditional Chinese life. He now sat in a foreign house inside a foreign enclave, whose inhabitants disdained Chinese law and were exempt from Chinese jurisdiction. Worse, the foreigners, who had imposed themselves upon China with cannon, were again taking up arms against the Empire.

Aaron responded passionately to his father's casual question: 'Why were the foreigners patrolling Yangjingbang Creek? Dr MacGregor said the foreigners had clashed with the Imperial forces, but no more.'

'The barbarians call it the Battle of Muddy Flat, making a great joke,' Aaron replied bitterly. 'But it was no joke. The barbarians dared join with the Small Sword rebels to attack His Imperial Majesty's forces. They think they defeated our troops, who were reluctant to smash the barbarians' presumption. Joke they may. But it could come to war again . . . a new war against the barbarians.'

'What started the fighting?' Struck by Aaron's vehemence, Saul did not see David slip from the dining-room.

'No more than has been going on since the Small Swords took the South City half a year ago and our troops besieged them. The barbarians claimed Imperial soldiers curtailed their freedom of movement . . . harassed them and their women. Then, on April the third, the barbarians presented an ultimatum. They demanded guarantees and immunities the government couldn't possibly grant. But they didn't wait. The next day the barbarians brought up their warships, landed troops, marched on Imperial headquarters . . . and swept over it.'

'Swept over it?' Aisek asked. 'Just brushed the troops aside.'

'Virtually, Father. Though I don't think our soldiers fought hard. Probably ordered not to resist. Who wants another war like the war over opium only fourteen years ago? But it *will* come. I'm afraid . . .'

'I am weary,' a lugubrious voice complained. 'I am weary and worn with travelling.'

Aisek and Aaron broke off in astonishment. Although they had anticipated the interruption, the Haleevies were also startled. David no longer wore his long-gown, but his father's discarded travelling clothes. He balanced the *afikoman*, the larger piece of the broken *matzah*, on his shoulder like a heavy burden.

'Where do you come from, traveller?' Fronah asked gleefully.

'*Tsung Ai-chi* . . .' David replied dolefully. 'Out of Egypt. And I am very weary . . . weary unto death.'

'And where are you going, traveller?' Fronah delighted in the by-play. 'Whither go you?'

'To the land of Israel by the grace of the Lord our God,' he answered. 'And when I come to Jerusalem, I shall . . .'

Shrill wailing interrupted David, who turned towards the doorway, where three Chinese women drove the protesting houseboy before them. Two were maid-servants in thigh-length tunics over flapping trousers. The third leaned on their arms, hobbling on bound feet. Her long, green-satin *chi-pao*, narrow-cut like the Manchu riding-coat that gave it its name, was slit to the knee to reveal slim black trousers. Not only her clothing, but her long nails and her white-powdered face demonstrated that she was a lady of a prosperous family.

But her shining hair hung loose from the white band encircling her forehead. Her features were twisted by grief, and her make-up was runnelled by tears. Her soft red mouth wailed, and her hands tore at her clothing. The serving women sobbed convulsively.

'Maylu, what is it?' Aisek Lee demanded of his concubine.

'Lord, your mother . . .' the lady replied. 'Your honoured mother in her venerable age, she has . . .'

'Go on, woman!' Aisek commanded when her sobs muffled her words. 'Speak out!'

'Your thrice honoured mother, Lord. She has passed . . . passed from this world. I found her . . . hanging from a beam. Woe unto our house! Only an hour before, she told me, but I could not believe it. She said she would . . . hang herself. She could not endure living in abject . . . abject, she said . . . poverty. Woe unto our house!'

CHAPTER THREE

Easter Sunday April 16, 1854   *Nanking*

The midday sun burnished the tiles of the ten-tiered pagoda, and a spire of flame blazed on the hill outside Tienking, the Heavenly Capital. The metropolis entwined by a coil of the Yangtze River had been called Nanking, the Southern Capital, since it served as the administrative centre of the Great Ming Dynasty centuries earlier. Renamed a few months ago, it was again the capital of a resurgent dynasty, which had within half a decade conquered almost half of China. The ardent troops of the *Taiping Tienkuo*, the Heavenly Kingdom of Great Peace, were that Easter Sunday of 1854 approaching Peking, the Northern Capital, where the decadent Manchu Emperor kept his Imperial Court.

The light shining from the pagoda pierced the foliage surrounding the palace of the Heavenly King. Behind that leafy screen, the fretwork windows of the Hall of Worship were flung open to entice the meandering breeze. The heat was inequable for mid-April, and the light bathing the congregation was tinctured with the green of the leaves. The intense beam glared on the brass bells of the horns and the oboes played by black-robed musicians beside the altar. Their melancholy minor-key melody burst occasionally into strident gaiety.

The iridescent rays illuminated the Hall of Worship like the sun through a diamond. The light lingered on the tall man in the grey frock-coat who stood before the altar, his small eyes and his beaked nose glowing with fervour in his raw-boned face. The rays lit the worshippers' upraised eyes before casting a golden aura around the figure on the dais at the opposite end of the Hall. When the breeze touched him, five-clawed Imperial dragons cavorted on his Imperial-yellow silk robe and his jewelled

21

headdress glittered. His olive features, snub-nosed and heavy-boned, were stamped with majestic self-confidence, and his robust body was arrogantly erect. He listened patiently to the ringing cadences of the foreign preacher in the frock-coat.

'*Hsiung-ti, chieh-mei* . . .' The American brought a Kentucky twang to his Chinese. 'Brothers and sisters, I say unto you, let us rejoice. This day, above all other days, we should rejoice. The Lamb of God is reborn. Jesus Christ is risen. The Saviour of mankind is risen. Christ is risen. Allelulia.'

'Allelulia! Allelulia!' Children's trebles and women's clear tones accentuated the deep voices of the men seated across the aisle. 'Allelulia! Allelulia!'

The horns pealed unabashedly joyous, and his subjects turned to the golden figure of the Heavenly King. They looked to him as their pontiff, as well as their monarch – and as an incarnate divinity. But the fundamentalist American preacher was reluctant to surrender the attention of a Chinese congregation twenty times larger than any he had previously addressed.

'I say unto you, brothers and sisters,' he declared, 'I say unto you, furthermore, that the Kingdom of God will be built upon earth. The Kingdom of God is, even now and here, abuilding upon this ground on which we stand. There is rejoicing in Heaven, that the great Chinese nation acknowledges the One True God and His Son Jesus Christ. We are all brothers and sisters in oneness with Jesus Christ. Together with all true believers from across the oceans, you will destroy the Manchu idolators and set the rightful Emperor, the Heavenly King, upon the Dragon Throne in Peking. The Lord be praised!'

'*Tsan-mei* . . .' The congregation responded ardently, and the horns pealed again. 'The Lord be praised! Allelulia!'

The women piously lifted their eyes to the carved wooden ceiling, their hands automatically smoothing the calf-length tunics that covered their voluminous pantaloons. The preacher saw again with wonder that all wore flat-heeled cloth-shoes turned up at the tips. Not a single female, not even the wives of the Taiping Princes and the Heavenly King, was disfigured by the tiny bound feet, the maimed 'golden lilies' that were elsewhere the caste-mark of Chinese ladies of rank. Even more remarkably, long hair curled beneath the cloth turbans and the conical straw hats of the robed men. None wore the long braided queue growing from the back of a shaven crown that had been the emblem of Chinese subjugation to Manchu overlords for more than two centuries.

The expression of both men and women were open and confident, unmarred by the deceitfulness most foreigners discerned in the faces of other Chinese. Discarding the queue, the symbol of their degradation by an alien race, these Chinese had regained their dignity and their self-respect. All were gravely attentive when the Heavenly King spoke in a high-pitched, portentous voice.

'The Great God, Our Heavenly Father, has sent Ourself, the Heavenly

King, to rule over you and to subdue the rivers and the mountains to Our dominion. On this joyous day, the day of the resurrection of Our Heavenly Elder Brother, We bring you new tidings of delight, tidings of joyous portent for Our Heavenly Kingdom of Great Peace.'

The wide mouth above the glossy goatee closed. The fleshy lips were briefly still while the proturberant, visionary eyes swept the Hall of Worship. The Heavenly King nodded his approval of the offerings on the scarlet altar-cloth: three handleless teacups chased with gold, three dragon-scrolled ricebowls, and three red-lacquered ducks on blue-and-white platters. Prolonging his pause as tension rose, the Heavenly King resumed just before his followers' concentration wavered:

'We bear witness, direct witness, to the resurrection that came unto Him, our Heavenly Elder Brother Jesus. Did not Our Heavenly Father call Us to His Celestial Domain to reveal His will to Us? Did He not reveal to Us Our destiny, which is to hold dominion over all the land? Did he not reveal to Us that We, too, are his son, the Heavenly Younger Brother of the Lord Jesus Christ? Were We, too, then not reborn?'

'*Shih-di! Shih-di!*' The congregation responded as one. 'So it is! So it is!'

'The Heavenly Father has already given Us dominion over half the Great Empire because We are His Son and because We are virtuous. The people rally to Us because Our troops are virtuous. They know that any soldier of the Taiping who abuses or robs them is immediately executed. And this very day We have received tidings of the inestimable favour Our Heavenly Father has newly bestowed upon Us.'

'The Lord be praised!' The congregation intoned. 'Tell the joyous tidings!'

'So We shall!' The Heavenly King graciously assented. 'Know, then, that the fate of the Manchu demons and Imps is now sealed. They shall all be destroyed . . . wiped from the face of the earth . . . driven down into the eighteen hells that yawn beneath. Not one will ever see even the lowest of the thirty-three Heavens. And the Chinese people shall rule themselves again.'

'The Heavenly Father be praised!' The congregation chorused. 'When, oh King, when?'

'Soon, Our people, very soon it shall come to pass. The outlanders from across the oceans have decisively defeated the Manchus at Shanghai. Already our brothers in religion, our brothers in Christ, the outlanders are now our brothers in arms. Together we shall sweep the Imps from the land. Soon! Very soon!'

CHAPTER FOUR

June 21, 1854

'*Arel* . . .' Saul Haleevie swore in Hebrew. 'Uncircumcised son of a poxed Aleppo whore.'

The coolie vanished around the bend of the alley after spattering Saul with human excrement from the wooden buckets swaying on a bamboo carrying-pole burnished by time and sweat. Fingers pinching their noses, the throng in the tortuous thoroughfare of the Chinese quarter parted before the night-soil coolie's warning hoots. When his passage was recalled only by a trail of malodorous khaki splotches on the cobblestones, the pedestrians coalesced again into a mass.

'Wantchee *play* no can talkee, must no talkee, my friend.' Whispering into his partner's ear in pidgin, Aisek Lee stopped before an open shop-front. 'Suppose talkee, allee damnfool dress-up no use.'

Saul nodded contritely behind the bandage that concealed his ruddy beard and his aquiline nose, so that only his eyes and forehead were visible beneath his grimy head-cloth. He clapped his hand against his jaw, miming the toothache the bandage presumably assuaged, and pretended fascination with the display of multi-coloured fans. Beneath his coarse tunic, sweat dripped cool from his armpits and trickled down his ribs to soak the waistband of his baggy trousers. The early evening was so humid, perspiration would have puddled in his cotton-shoes if his trousers were not tied at the ankles.

Also dressed in the workmen's clothing that had disguised them during their jouirney to Soochow, Aisek was dubious about their foray into the South City, which was held by the rebels called the Small Swords. He had been disconsolate since his mother's death, though he could not retreat into mourning as Mandarins were retired for three years after a parent's demise. A white scarf was knotted around his neck to declare his bereavement, and he brooded sombrely. He knew he was not guilty of his mother's suicide, but none the less reproached himself. A son is absolutely responsible for his parents' welfare, and he had failed his widowed mother.

Aisek was also depressed because the coup that should have brought the partners 30,000 silver *taels*, £10,000 sterling or $50,000 American, had yielded less than a third. Most of their silk was still held in the new inland Imperial Customs House. Generous bribes had, quite extraordinarily, failed to free the goods. Oppressed by guilt and anger, Aisek ascribed their ill-fortune equally to divine retribution and to powerful enemies.

Saul feigned enthusiasm for the showcase of fans and automatically shooed away the horse-flies, whose glittering wings rivalled the brilliance of those small works of great art. The swarm followed an itinerant food-seller, whose carrying-pole supported two boxes holding a charcoal stove, a greasy wok, and uncooked dumplings. The master fan-maker shouted abuse at the cook, the sweat-stains on his grey-cotton gown outlining his armpits and his bulging belly.

'Take your damned slops and your flies elsewhere!' he screamed. One hand gesticulated obscenely. The other whisked a chicken-feather duster over the showcases protruding into the lane to prevent the horseflies' sporting his stock: the silk discs painted with pastel landscapes; the gentlemen's black fans folding on ribs inlaid with mother-of-pearl; and the gauzy ladies' fans stretched on ribs of golden filigree.

'*Dsou-ba* . . .' Aisek urged loudly. 'Let's move on, brother.' Saul complied reluctantly. He was captivated by the exquisite masterpieces, which would command high prices on European markets fascinated by *chinoiserie*. He understood Aisek's anxiety. It would be disastrous if they were unmasked, since dealing with the rebels who held the South City was a capital crime under Manchu law. But his unguarded exclamation in Hebrew had apparently passed unheard amid the constant tumult of hawkers' cries, loud bargaining, and shouted conversation.

The smells were equally overpowering. The stench of night-soil lingering on the heavy air mingled with the tang of vinegar and cooking-oil, the sweet pungence of ginger and anise, and the musky sweat of the ex-huberant throng.

Saul followed Aisek, through a lane reverberating with tinkling silver-smiths' hammers into a small square. In the murky water of an artificial pond, orange carp drifted languidly under the zig-zag bridge to a scarlet tea-house. Mahjong tiles clacked through its open windows, and a falsetto aria accompanied by a two-string violin shrilled beneath its peaked cupolas.

A dragon's head peered over a granite wall, white teeth gleaming and obsidian eyes glittering. The great beast's jagged horns twitched mena-cingly in the heat-rays, and its long body undulated. A wooden gate beneath the stone dragon was guarded by sentries in yellow tunics. They wore no Manchu queues, but lank hair hung beneath their red turbans. Short swords were thrust into their red sashes.

Saul lethargically followed Aisek through the gate, unhappy at calling on the leaders of the Small Swords. But it was necessary to advance the partnership into which Aisek and he had entered two days earlier under British law, which governed British subjects in the foreign enclaves on the China Coast. Their association was also recognised by the Great Pure Dynasty, which, presumably, ruled everywhere else.

Aisek's spirits had lifted only briefly when Saul stressed: 'You won't be just a comprador, working for a foreign principal . . . dealing with the

25

Chinese for a percentage. You'll be a full partner, sharing both profits and losses.'

'The losses are coming faster now – and all my fault,' Aisek replied wryly.

Instead of celebrating their partnership with a banquet, the normally law-abiding merchants were entering the rebels' headquarters in the Yü Yüan, the Garden of Ease built by a Mandarin of the Ming Dynasty centuries earlier.

Some two thousand members of the clandestine Small Sword Society were pledged: 'Oppose the Alien Manchus and Restore the Chinese Ming Dynasty!' Since that slogan had been proclaimed two centuries earlier, the numerous secret societies had altered greatly. Flourishing among the poor, who despaired of legal redress for their wrongs, the brotherhoods of the dispossessed had become extra-legal governments, growing more powerful as the Ching Dynasty's corruption festered. In the enlightened nineteenth century, their rites reached back to ancient superstition, which bound members with blood oaths. The leaders implacably murdered all defectors.

When the Small Swords seized the South City ten months earlier in September 1853, the apprehensive foreign community was hostile. But it had gradually become reconciled to its tumultuous neighbours, and both British sailors and American marines had fought beside the Small Swords at Muddy Flat three months earlier. Yet the consuls who governed the foreign community were still wary because the secret society threatened the stability of commerce. The outlanders had not come to China to champion the oppressed. They had come to trade – and to profit.

Nonetheless, power was its own vindication. The Small Swords were associated with the *Taiping Tienkuo,* the Kingdom of Heavenly Peace, which was a major military and political force. Because the secret society's gory rites offended the Taipings' puritanism, they did not formally accepts its allegiance. But the Heavenly King neither objected to the Small Swords' using his coinage nor repudiated their loyalty – and he rejoiced at their foothold in China's chief port. The failed Mandarin from mountainous Kwangsi Province who proclaimed himself the younger brother of Jesus Christ had already conquered most of South China. The impoverished countrymen had risen in revolt to overthrow the Manchus – and to establish their own *Chinese* dynasty. Since they might succeed, a prudent foreign merchant was well advised to understand them – and to propitiate them.

Saul Haleevie was appalled by the Taiping doctrines, an unstable amalgam of traditional Chinese beliefs, primitive socialism, and Protestant Christianity. He was, however, attracted by their desire to expand trade and their puritanical rectitude, the antithesis of Ching corruption. He reassured himself that the risk was justified as the partners followed their guide along the paths winding among low pavilions.

26

Long-needled spruces shaded ferns curving before creamy magnolias and dark cinnamon trees. Within its granite walls, the five-acre park was truly a Garden of Ease, every shrub, flower, and tree perfectly complementing the bright painted structures among man-made hillocks. Its serenity in the midst of the squalor of the South City further emphasised the abyss between the prodigal luxury of the nation's rulers and the misery of their overtaxed subjects. A rapidly increasing population, hardly checked by recurrent natural disasters, was straining the resources of the Empire that had a century earlier been the wealthiest in the world. The fury of the common people was embodied in the red-turbaned insurgents hurrying through zig-zag corridors under peaked roofs or lounging beside miniature man-made lakes.

Their guide stopped before a pavilion with a sloping roof and led them up shallow steps flanked by stone lions with hyacinth-curled manes. They entered the Hall of Flaming Spring from a terrace whose crimson pillars and fretwork balustrades were weathered by Shanghai's bitter winters and brutal summers.

'*Kuei shang-jen* . . .' The man behind a table strewn with documents, weapons, and food remants spoke with a Cantonese accent. 'The honourable merchants are welcome. You do me much honour by your presence.'

The narrow, flat-nosed face of the formidable Liu Li-chüan, the 'Field Marshal' of the Small Swords, belied his reputed bloodthirstiness. His prominent eyes shone with intelligence, while his wispy beard was more appropriate to a diligent clerk than a ruthless general. Yet he had led the surprise attack that seized the heart of China's chief port, and his manifesto championed the poor by reducing the extortionate price of rice. Profiteers would, he proclaimed, be decapitated.

'*Pi-jen pu* . . .' Aisek replied with Confucian politesse. 'We are unworthy to enter your glorious dwelling. We are vastly honoured to confer with Your Excellency.'

'I am commanded by the Heavenly King to put certain questions to you and your barbarian associate . . . and to make certain proposals.' The young man seated beside the Field Marshal wore a merchant's cotton gown, and a Manchu queue hung from his shaven crown. He was, Aisek concluded from his domineering manner and his brusque disregard for etiquette, one of many secret Taiping agents.

'I await your words,' Aisek replied as brusquely.

'You, I know, are not idolators,' the young man continued. 'You do not worship idols like the French Catholic barbarians. The outlander and I are, accordingly, brothers in Christ. The Heavenly King is therefore convinced we can reach an agreement beneficial to both sides.'

'My partner and I listen,' Aisek replied.

'First, there is a matter of your silk, which is held by the Customs of the diabolical Imps. You've bribed heavily, of course. Corruption prevails

27

everywhere under the Manchu barbarians, though it is punishable by death in the Heavenly Kingdom. My Lord will restore your silk to demonstrate his benevolent intentions.'

'We should, of course, be delighted to secure our lawful goods,' Aisek answered without consulting Saul. 'How can reparation be accomplished?'

'There's only one way.' The envoy's smooth face tightened in contempt for the woolly minded merchant. 'Only one way to deal with the Imps. We'll seize the silks and . . .'

As Aisek translated, Saul's lips twitched in amusement, and he observed: 'It *is* tempting, but it would never work. How would we ship the silks? How explain their coming into our hands? Consul Alcock would never permit it. Not openly flouting Customs regulations. But don't reject his offer outright. Tell him . . . Oh, you know better than I what to say, Aisek. And let him spell out his proposal.'

'We are deeply moved by the benevolence of the Heavenly King.' Aisek threw up a smokescreen of formality. 'Profoundly conscious of the honour, we should like to consider the implications before troubling His Majesty. Certain questions arise . . . But enough of our petty problems. We should be thrice honoured to hear the proposal of the Heavenly King.'

'I can't understand why . . .' The envoy shook his shaven head in perplexity. 'Such a simple matter, but that is, I suppose, the way of merchants. As to His Majesty's proposals, I shall be brief.'

'My partner and I are attentive to your slightest word . . .'

'You know that the Heavenly King considers peaceful trade essential to the welfare of his tens of millions of subjects,' the envoy declaimed. 'He further wishes to strengthen his ties of friendship with his brother in Christ, the merchant Ha-lee-vee . . . as well as his ties to all his co-religionists among the barbar . . . the noble sojourners from across the seas. Is it not good to exchange the goods the Lord God has given unto each of us in different wise so that all benefit and all are drawn together in brotherhood?'

When the envoy paused for translation, Aisek did not tell his Jewish partner that the heretical Chinese Protestant considered himself his brother in Christ. Searching their faces to assess the effects of his eloquence, the Taiping emissary saw only fixed smiles. He nonetheless continued enthusiastically.

'You need goods, I believe. We possess much tea, as well as much silk. We also control the roads and rivers along which those goods must travel . . . even in the territories still not liberated from the Imps. We have porcelains, as well, and certain spices I understand the bar . . . foreigners value highly. At favourable . . . no, not favourable, but just prices. The Heavenly King forbids all profit and all property to his subjects. But the price would be most attractive. You are interested?'

'In principle, of course. As merchants we will trade with all who desire

28

our goods . . . all who offer goods of value. What does His Majesty require of us?'

'It is not what the Heavenly King *requires* of you, but the opportunities he *offers* you.' The envoy leaned across the littered table to emphasise his master's generosity. 'I shall be very frank. Total candour is the proper basis for the long and prosperous relationship My Lord envisages. We have approached you first because we feel a smaller firm like your honoured house can provide a more intimate . . . a more confidential . . . relationship . . .'

Aisek's murmured aside was superfluous, since there were few secrets in Shanghai – and no secrets long preserved. Saul, too, knew that the Heavenly King had asked two major firms, Russells, the Americans, and Jardines, the British, to act for him. Both had reluctantly refused. The mercantile community endorsed that decision, while regretting the lost profits. Most foreigners had not yet decided whether trade with the Taipings, who *might* some day rule all China, could compensate for the wrath of the Imperial Government, which *still* ruled most of China – and was finally moving ponderously to crush the rebellion.

Moreover, the consuls, the *de facto* governors of the foreign settlement, were determined to enforce the letter of their treaties with the legitimate Manchu government. While their foreign ministries waited to choose the régime that offered the greater advantage it was expedient to uphold the *status quo* – and to punish those who aided the rebels. Although the consuls could not prevent adventurers' dealing with the Taipings, that small trade was wholly inadequate to the insurgents' needs.

'My master requires muskets and cannon as well as steamers and machinery to make munitions.' Portentously confidential, the envoy revealed to them what every street loafer in Shanghai already knew. 'We shall, beyond all doubt, triumph. The Lord God, Father of the Heavenly King, has decreed that outcome. But He leaves the manner of victory to the genius of His Beloved Son. We must win quickly to spare the people further suffering. But we cannot win quickly while we oppose the modern weapons the Imps buy from the foreigners with crude pikes, spears and a few ancient guns. We also require foreign experts to train our soldiers. Do you now see the benevolent intentions of the Heavenly King towards yourselves?'

'Our dull wits, regrettably, do not wholly comprehend your profound wisdom,' Aisek prevaricated. 'Though we try your patience, please tell us precisely what arrangements the Heavenly King has in mind.'

'Nothing less than a monopoly on our trade for your esteemed house. You will be our confidential agents, supplying us with everything we need and taking as much of our produce as you wish. What say you to that?'

Saul was greatly tempted. By a single word he could raise his struggling infant business to the level of the heavily capitalised major houses. His

29

small firm was not only more supple than the great houses. Her Britannic Majesty's Consul Rutherford Alcock was not particularly concerned with its actions because it was insignificant. Saul was tempted – and Aisek was eager to reverse the decline of their fortunes. Yet prudence must temper boldness or they could destroy themselves.

Aisek's reply, accordingly, spun a web of words to veil its meaning. They could, unfortunately, not immediately agree, he said, though it would be egregious folly to reject the princely offer. Perhaps they could begin in a small way to test whether they could serve the Heavenly King worthily. Rash haste, he added, would be disrespectful to the Taiping monarch. Even more disrespectful would be failing not to apprise themselves of the full particulars of the relationship His Majesty envisaged.

The Taiping envoy was on familiar ground. Accustomed to negotiating while disclaiming negotiation, he genially spent an hour discussing specifics, but, of course, only hypothetically. Saul and Aisek finally took their leave when the long June twilight had given way to an evening bright with moonbeams.

They were, they knew, committed – *if* they wished to commit themselves. Yet either party could still withdraw without dishonouring itself or wounding the other's self-esteem.

Retracing the cramped alleys of the South City, which still resounded with restless life long after nightfall, Saul reflected that it had been a typical Chinese negotiation. Thrusts and parries had appeared no more than mock fencing, but had actually cut to the heart of the matter. He gloated over the possible profits, but knew he would have felt no exhilaration if there were no risk.

*

Moonlight flowed over the refugee camp between the South City and the foreign settlement, softening the jagged contours of clapboard hovels and smoothing the lines from faces pinched by hunger. Despite their professed benevolence, the Field Marshal of the Small Swords and the Heavenly King of the Taipings were inflicting acute suffering on their common people.

'First, we must see if we can do it,' Saul stressed. 'If we can't, there's no point in thinking about it. First, we must check . . .'

He broke off in mid-sentence. He had dismissed the distant hoof-falls as just another sound in the hectic night, but the drumbeat was drawing close. A detachment of Manchu cavalrymen swept around the refugee camp, careless whether their horses crushed sleepers on the ground or toppled scurrying pedestrians. Emerging from the crush of refugees like leopards bursting from deep grass, five horsemen encircled the partners.

Moonlight glinted on the barrels of their muskets and silvered their round hats. At the command of their leader, who wore the rhinoceros insignia of a lieutenant on his chest, two troopers slide off their rough-haired ponies. Awkward in their rigid-soled felt boots, they approached Aisek. Swords flashed from the scarlet scabbards that flapped against their calf-length yellow tunics. Hook noses bisected the soldiers' flat faces, and their eyes were slits when they raised their swords above their heads. Though pitted with rust, the curved blades gleamed in the moonlight.

Saul was nauseated by the horses' musty reek and the soldiers' acrid sweat. He felt Aisek shiver beside him in the stillness.

'*Ni shih* . . .' The lieutenant's question was an assertion. 'You are Li Ai-shih, a merchant of Shanghai?'

Aisek's face contorted in a grimace, and his head trembled. When he nodded tremulously, Saul saw the face of terror by the gentle moonlight.

'You will accompany us!' the lieutenant commanded.

A cavalryman bundled Aisek on to a horse and mounted behind him. So numbed by fear he could not control his limbs, the merchant sagged in the saddle like a rag doll.

'I can tell you it's a capital charge.' The lieutenant was coldly contemptuous. 'You could lose your head!'

The cavalrymen bore down again on the throng of refugees and vanished behind the camp. Saul stood frozen in the moonlight, deaf even to the receding hoof-beats.

CHAPTER FIVE

July 8, 1854   *Imperial Headquarters near Shanghai*

At daybreak, the smoke of a hundred cooking-fires hung in the still air above the village called Wukwei, which was swollen with mat-shed structures and felt tents. Columns of soot intertwined in a grey spire over the Imperial Headquarters twelve miles west of the foreign settlement. The early morning sun glinted on the flooded paddy-fields extending in every direction to the horizon like an immense circular mirror.

There had been no rain for two weeks, and no breeze stirred the leaves of the few trees that shaded the streams of travellers flowing along the rutted dirt-road from Shanghai: military Mandarins jouncing on thick-bodied ponies, civil Mandarins in gilded palanquins, slovenly files of infantrymen, ramshackle provision-wagons, and farmers whose cart-wheels wailed an endless lament to their wooden axles. The country-

31

side was fully awake at half past five in the morning. All men were eager to get through the tasks they could not put off before the brutal sun sent the temperature above 100 degrees and made every movement a small torment.

Three young people borne in sedan-chairs were marked out by their white-cotton mourning garments. Riding first because he was the eldest, Aaron Lee was preceded by one of the retired Manchu soldiers Saul Haleevie employed to guard his property. His ancient fowling-piece bobbed each time his stolid tread struck the rock-hard ground. The barrels of muskets wavered in the heat-rays above the shoulders of the four elderly Manchus flanking the sedan-chairs. From the second, David Lee reflected that the array of armed might was hardly intimidating. Called Bannermen because of the eight differently coloured corps-flags they had once followed, the veterans were very old. But their weapons were older. A Brown Bess musket manufactured a century earlier armed the oldest Bannerman, who trudged behind the coolies carrying Fronah Haleevie's sedan-chair on their sun-blackened shoulders.

The escorts and the sedan-chairs were necessary for the same reason that the procession included six personal servants and ten coolies carrying water, provisions, and gifts. Attacked by bandits or rebels, the guards might fire, but would thereupon certainly flee on tendon-corded legs. Aaron, David, and Fronah, all robustly healthy, would have preferred to ride horses. But like their guards, the sedan-chairs, though merely plank-seats and footrests slung from bamboo poles, proclaimed them children of privilege and influence.

Fronah was stifled by the coarse mourning-robe she wore over her usual summer kaftan. Though straw-sandals symbolised her grief and her humility, she was delighted to escape the constricting high-buttoned shoes her mother believed a lady's only respectable footwear. She seethed at being assigned to the dusty tail of the procession because she was not only the youngest, but an unmarried female. Nonetheless, she stared under her eyelids at the gaudy officers and the slovenly soldiers, whose shoddy finery and ragged formations were new to her. The farm people were familiar, for she had often talked with them when she evaded her mother's discipline to romp across the countryside with David.

Her light-hearted playfellow was almost as staid as his habitually solemn elder brother. Although he could never attain Aaron's intense dignity, David's normal high spirits were restrained by the gravity of their mission, as well as the white robes they wore to mourn his grandmother – and to evoke sympathy for their grief. His round face was self-consciously impassive, its composure broken only momentarily when a covey of ring-necked pheasants whirred from a rice-field. He hoped Fronah would this once also do as she was told and remain decorously silent.

Some two weeks after Aisek Lee's arrest, Saul Haleevie's threats of foreign intervention and his bribes to venal Mandarins had finally wrung permission from a particularly obstructive Chinese bureaucracy for the prisoner's children to visit him. The permits were granted by the Intendant Wu Chien-chang, the senior Mandarin of Shanghai: Samqua, as he had been known to foreigners when one of the few merchants permitted to trade with them at Canton (before the Opium War of 1839-1842 shattered that restriction). Saul's 'gifts' had recalled to the Intendant the obligation he owed Aisek for helping him buy steam-powered gunboats to deploy against the Taipings. None the less, Samqua contended that he could do no more than grant permission for the visit. He could neither intervene on Aisek's behalf nor reveal the charge until the formal indictment was promulgated.

Saul could not visit his partner, since he was only a business associate. Neither could the concubine Maylu, since she was not a blood relation. However heinous his crime, the prisoner's sons could not be denied the opportunity to console him. Doing so would frustrate their filial piety, and filial piety was the cardinal virtue that sustained the Confucian state. If sons could not comfort their father in his distress, how could the Emperor, who was the father of the nation, be confident of the obedience of his subjects, who were his children?

Though his magnanimity was strained, the Intendant had finally agreed to Fronah's presence as the presumptive bride of the elder son of the accused. Since she was Aaron's *fiancée*, Fronah was no longer a stranger, but already a daughter of Aisek Lee's family. Samqua had lifted his eyebrows quizzically when told of the engagement. But he knew that Saul would offer many more rich presents before the case was settled. An official did not serve his Emperor – or his family – by spurning wealth.

Though Sarah protested, Saul had insisted on the deception, while David and Fronah giggled and Aaron flushed scarlet. The projected marriage also gave the future bride's father legal standing in the matter, and Saul knew he must manage Aisek's defence. The Lee family in distant Kaifeng lacked either the interest or the resources to champion their remote cousin.

Fronah's presence would also demonstrate foreign concern for Aisek's fate, threatening barbarian intervention to intimidate the Chinese bureaucracy. If the barbarian Ha-lee-vee were so deeply concerned for his partner that he would risk his only daughter among the ill-disciplined Imperial soldiers, what other steps might he not take? Sarah had wept, but Saul insisted that Fronah must visit the man she called Uncle Aisek.

A wave of fetid air overwhelmed the smell of cooking-fires and horse-droppings when they came to the square in the centre of Wukwei. The stench of putrefaction did not trouble the lean dogs snapping at each other's flanks as they fought for scraps from the warders' breakfast before the village schoolhouse, which had been converted into a prison for the temporary *yamen*, a senior Mandarin's offices and residence. The weathered plaque above the lintel was inscribed with a quotation from the *Shu Ching*, the ancient *Theses on Government*: CHIN JEN SHAN JEN . . . TO EACH ACCORDING TO HIS MERITS.

Reluctantly setting down the chicken gruel that would further swell his bulk, the chief warder waddled across the square to take their permits with greasy fingers. Although notified of their coming, he was in no hurry to admit them. Aaron maintained stone-faced patience as the warder's black-rimmed fingernail traced the ideograms and the red seal of the Intendant Wu Chien-chang. David grimaced at Fronah behind the warder's broad back, which strained his filthy green tunic above his maroon-leather boots. After submitting to the petty official's questions for some minutes, the youth's cheekbones were red with anger. The normally flighty Fronah mimed resignation to warn David against displaying his anger. He smiled wryly, shrugged his shoulders, and the hot blood left his face.

Feeling the time ripe, Aaron pressed the man's hand. Metal jangled as the warder dropped into the money-pouch on his belt a thousand holed copper coins strung on a cord. He motioned the guard to unlock the door, but held up his hand when they turned to enter.

'Not the young lady,' he rumbled. 'It's not fitting for a young lady . . . even a barbarian.'

Disdaining concealment, David handed over another string of cash. When the plank-door creaked open, putrescence belched from the dark doorway. The guard coughed, and the visitors choked. Eyes watering, they followed the glimmer of the guard's lantern into darkness laced with bright pinpoints where sunlight seeped through holes in the roof.

Fronah stumbled against the massive tree-trunk to which were chained penitents from the Buddhist Hells. Emaciated, contorted, and maimed, most wore only loin cloths stained by excrement and urine. The black pellets of rats' droppings were strewn across the rough flagstones. Fronah retched and turned towards the door, but David's hand on her back pressed her forward.

A prisoner lifted his bony face, revealing empty eyesockets leaking pus. That feeble movement overturned the cracked bowl beside him, and, feeling the water cold against his leg, he began to weep. The guard laughed and kicked the water-bowl out of the blind man's reach.

Aisek Lee occupied a privileged position in the corner of the prison-house. So much and no more had his old business associate, the Intendant Samqua, done for him.

His solid frame, visibly depleted after two weeks, was covered only by torn trousers. Welts left by whips striped his torso, which was splotched with festering flea and lice bites. The manacles welded around his wrists were joined by heavy iron links, and the chain of his leg-irons passed through an iron ring sunk in the stone floor. His round head was twisted awry by a two-foot-square wooden collar, to which was nailed a placard bearing the single ideogram *wu* – abomination.

The flesh had shrunk from his bluff features, revealing the heavy bone beneath the pallid skin, and the deep seams in his cheeks were ingrained with black filth. But his eyes shone when he looked up at them crookedly. A smile briefly lit his face when his sons dropped to their knees. Fronah, too, knelt, feeling tears wet her cheeks.

'Honoured father! Revered parent!' Aaron spoke with intense formality. 'It grieves me profoundly to see you thus unjustly confined. However, you will soon . . .'

'*Dieh-dieh! Dieh-dieh!*' David reverted to the language of childhood. 'Daddy! Daddy! What have they done to you? We've got food and clothes and . . .'

'Must have cost a pretty penny, too.' Aisek comforted his comforters. 'But it'll be all right, lads. With the right pull, everything'll come right. I'm sure . . .'

'Uncle Aisek, Papa says he'll do everything possible.' Fronah interjected. 'He says to remember you're not abandoned. He'll never abandon you. And he sent you this.'

'If only I knew why . . .' Aisek unwrapped the parcel to reveal an ivory cylinder like that fixed to the Haleevie's doorpost. 'But what's this? Some foreign charm?'

'A *mezuzah*, Uncle Aisek. Inside is the prayer of Israel from Deuteronomy. It speaks of the Lord's love for his chosen people and the injunctions He laid upon them. *And those words, He commanded, thou shalt write them upon the doorposts of thine house.* Father says to remember the trials of our ancestors in Egypt and take heart . . . have faith that you too will be freed.'

'Tell your father I'll cherish the *mezuzah* . . . as I cherish his friendship. But, Fronah, how did you come here?'

Aisek smiled as Fronah explained why Saul had insisted she accompany the boys and how he had secured permission. His eyes shone with unshed tears when she concluded.

'I'll not forget this, young lady,' he said slowly. 'Some day, Heaven permitting, I'll repay you and your honoured father. This sacrifice . . . what you have seen . . .'

'Father, I am charged by Uncle Saul to ask if you can possibly think why?' Aaron broke in. 'He has sought everywhere by many means. But no one will tell him the formal charge. And, aside from your talk with the Small Swords, he can think of no reason . . .'

'Nor I, my son. I'm certainly not the only one who's visited the Garden of Ease, but no one else has been arrested.'

'No hint from your gaolers, Father?' David asked. 'We've *got* to find out why . . .'

35

'Of course, lad. I *know* it's vital. Do you think my wits are addled after two weeks?' He regained control. 'I'm sorry, lad, for losing my temper. But there's only this . . .'

Aisek's broad thumb stabbed at the ideogram on the placard tacked to the wooden cangue that twisted his neck. Silent in perplexity for half a minute, he resumed forlornly.

'*Wu* . . . abomination, it says, as you see. I must be charged with a crime so grave it stinks in the nostrils of decent men. But I cannot think what possible . . .'

'There *must* be a reason, Uncle Aisek.'

'A reason? Of course there's a reason. Why else couldn't we shake those accursed silks loose from Customs? Who tipped off the Mandarins about our visit to the Garden of Ease? Someone wants me out of the way. That's the reason. But who? I only know he must be very powerful.'

The guard, who had withdrawn beyond earshot, was pushing through the welter of criminals, his lantern flickering on twitching limbs and vacant eyes in haggard faces.

'You must go now, young masters and young lady,' he warned. 'I've given you a hell of a lot more time than's proper. No, there's no point in offering. I can't. But, thank you anyway. Many thanks for the gift.'

'You'll come back, of course?' Aisek's courage failed for an instant. 'You *will* be back, won't you?'

'Of course, we will, Father.' Aaron did not feel the tears on his cheeks. 'Uncle Saul says so . . . whatever it costs.'

'If I find out anything, I'll be sure to tell you.' Aisek's humour sustained them all. 'I won't keep it secret. But, right now, I can't imagine what charge they can possibly lay. An abomination! What abomination? What possible abomination?'

CHAPTER SIX

February 13, 1855   *Shanghai*

Built tall and wide to attract the elusive breezes of the muggy Shanghai summer, the windows of the house on Szechwan Road were covered by fleece-lined curtains and sealed with strips of paper against the rain that whipped the grimy slush of winter. Coal flamed in the black-marble fireplace of the dining-room, and the white tapers in the candelabra on the mahogany table vied with the oil-lamps on the walls. Touched by the gloom of February, the most melancholy month, the crystal decanters and silver platters on the sideboard glowed sombrely. The lean houseboy pouring tea from a dull pewter tea-pot yawned with jaw-cracking rigour and rubbed his sleep-encrusted eyes.

Just outside the compound, Saul Haleevie knew, the junior clerk was fighting another skirmish in his battle against the sooty fog. Depressed by the dreary morning, Saul dwelt with wry amusement on his mental image of the short figure with stiff arms cocked wide by the lawyers of coats the Chinese wore against the cold. The rag clutched in the small hand with the cracked knuckles and the split nails would polish the three brass-plates on the gateposts until they gleamed. The next day the unending battle would be resumed, for the Chinese were persistent, if not patient.

The plate on the right was the foundation of the house. S. KHARTOON & SONS, it read and beneath in smaller letters: *Head Office for China*. It was Saul's association with the trading firm founded in Bombay half a century earlier by his co-religionist from Baghdad that had brought the Haleevies to Shanghai. His continuing subordination to the Khartoons, Saul now felt, intolerably restricted his enterprise. It was an honour to be associated with the Khartoons, Sarah reminded him when he swore to break away. Only the Sassoons, she added, were bigger.

The brass-plate on the left gatepost read: HALEEVIE AND LEE and beneath simply: *Merchants*. A third plate beside it bore the same legend in ideograms. Affixed nine months earlier, two days after his partner's arrest, those plates were Saul's first assertion of independence. They further proclaimed his commitment to China – and his devotion to Aisek Lee, who still awaited formal indictment in mid-February of 1855.

'She mustn't go tomorrow! Not for the tenth time.' Sarah's normally light voice was emphatic with grievance. 'It's so cold, she'll catch something. Besides, it gets more dangerous all the time. It's not fitting for a young girl . . . all those soldiers. Though she thinks she's already a grown lady. Let Aaron and David go without her.'

'If I could, I would, my dear.' Saul fended her off. 'The first time I couldn't know it would be so horrible . . . so upsetting for her and for you. But, since then, she insists, as you know.'

'Just forbid her, Saul. She'll listen to you, even if she laughs at me. She'll obey her father.'

'Will she, my dear? I wonder!'

Saul's long fingers tapped a hard-boiled egg against the colourful garlands on the black Kiukiang-ware plate. The raw vegetables he liked with soured cream for breakfast were out of season, but he relished the preserved peppers and the pickled cabbage. Perhaps he should not eat the soft pitta bread as well as the rice-gruel old China hands called congee, but he was hardly as stout as the European taipans, who quaffed ale and burgundy with bacon, sausages, and liver for breakfast in summer or winter. Bacon was, of course, forbidden him. Besides, his congee was made with fish, rather than chicken, because the dietary laws forbade eating meat with the soured cream or the milk in his tea. But he needed a good breakfast. The morning was raw, and he expected an arduous day.

'Of course she'll listen to you, Saul.' Sarah stuffed preserved peppers into her pitta. 'A daughter obeys her father, even if she won't listen to her mother.'

Sarah Haleevie felt again the familiar agitation her daughter aroused, a contention between irritation and pride. Though wayward and vain, the girl was unquestionably brilliant. Headstrong and stubborn, she was often loving and kind. She was also ruthlessly cunning when determined to have her own way, which was most of the time. Her father was usually blind to the deceit her mother saw clearly.

'My dear, it's not *that* terrible. Otherwise I wouldn't let her keep seeing Aisek . . . no matter how she sulked. No harm's come to her . . .'

'Yet . . .' Sarah interjected. 'Not yet.'

'. . . and it could go hard with Aisek if she stopped. The Mandarins are used to her visits . . . the threat that, somehow, the British will intervene. You know the Chinese hate change. Any change and they'd read all sorts of meanings into it. It could go very hard with Aisek.'

'You'd sacrifice your own daughter for your Chinese friend?' Sarah's thumb and index finger angrily pleated the cream wool of her kaftan, which had been worked with red-and-green arabesques by Kashmiri needle-women. 'You only make her more obstinate. Like her silly new fad about clothes. I'm fond of Aisek, of course. But all this, it's just Chinese nonsense. It'll go on for a while, then he'll be free. But when something terrible happens to Fronah, she won't . . .'

'He's one of us . . . a Jew, a Levi. And he's in desperate trouble. An abomination, they call it, though they won't say exactly what. I've looked into it. An abomination is the worst possible crime under Chinese law. It could be treason. It could be . . . God knows what. But the punishment is death . . . terrible torture and then death.'

'I thought you were getting somewhere. Didn't you feel he'd soon be free?'

'I'm getting nowhere, I fear. Samqua, the Intendant, talks encouragingly, but that means nothing . . . nothing at all. He wants to keep me hoping, and he wants to drag the case out. After all, he's making a tidy sum. He's milking me, of course, but he's clever. Never demands too much. If I stopped paying him off . . . then, there'd be a quick decision. And Aisek could lose his head.'

'I *am* sorry, Saul. I do like Aisek, *really*. And the boys, it's lovely to have them with us. You know, I never dreamed it could actually end so horribly. You did get Aisek moved, didn't you?'

'To a cell by himself, yes. And he gets decent food as long as I pay ten times its worth. The guards don't beat him any more. He's not tortured to make him confess some unknown crime. They've taken the cangue off his neck. Even struck off his manacles. But, after all, it's his money, paying for all that.'

'How can you say *his* money? It's our money you're pouring out, isn't it? Sometimes . . . the way you turn words around . . . sometimes, you're too clever for me – and for yourself.'

'No, my love, it's *really* his money, not ours. After he was arrested, the Mandarins confiscated everything they could lay their hands on. Aisek's houses, his trade-goods, his art collection, even his furniture. They left him nothing . . .'

'Just what I said. If they took everything, it's our money paying for . . .'

'Not quite, my dear.' Saul smiled. 'I grabbed . . . that's what some people are saying . . . grabbed everything belonging to the partnership. Half, of course, was his. I also moved everything I could from his houses before the bailiffs got there. It was the only way to salvage something for the boys . . . and for Aisek. They can't touch my belongings, you know. We're British-protected, so the Chinese can't touch us.'

Saul no longer marvelled at the extraordinary position foreigners in China had occupied since the Treaty of Nanking ended the Opium War in 1842 thirteen years earlier. Not only was the rocky island of Hong Kong ceded outright to Britain, but non-Chinese were, for the first time, permitted to reside in five Treaty Ports, among which Shanghai was the foremost. The interlopers also enjoyed privileges no other sovereign state granted to aliens.

Saul no longer thought it strange that the property of a Chinese accused of violating Chinese law could be preserved from confiscation by the Chinese authorities because a foreigner fraudulently claimed that property. That anomaly arose from the 'extra-territorial' rights granted the outlanders under duress, the right to govern themselves by their own law, cosily called 'extrality' in the jargon of the Treaty Ports. The foreigners enjoyed complete immunity from Chinese law. As long as a foreigner claimed certain goods as his own, the Mandarins could not touch those goods, though they knew he lied.

Rutherford Alcock, Her Britannic Majesty's Consul, had already told Saul that he would not countenance open defiance of the Mandarins' authority over a Chinese subject. He would, however, block Chinese intervention as long as Saul maintained that the property was his own, since failure to protect *any* British property could imperil *all* British property in China.

The Consul exercised his broad powers with great discretion and great concern for legality. Only after striving for years to work with the Imperial Customs had he finally concluded that trade would wither under the Mandarins' extortions. Only in July 1854, seven months earlier, had the consuls, led by Rutherford Alcock, taken over direction of the Chinese Maritime Customs. With the reluctant acquiescence of the hard pressed Intendant Samqua, foreign commissioners and inspectors now administered the Customs efficiently. Moreover, the dues were scrupulously earmarked for the Chinese government.

The consuls were, therefore, not concerned with the savage blow they had dealt the Empire's sovereignty when the Ching Dynasty's existence was threatened not only by the Taiping rebellion, but by natural disasters and universal corruption. Rutherford Alcock felt he had judiciously buttressed the *status quo*, just as Saul Haleevie felt his evasion of Chinese law justly preserved Aisek Lee's possessions.

'Another thing, my dear.' Sarah broke into Saul's reflections. 'This mock engagement to Aaron. He *is* Chinese . . . even if you insist he's also Jewish. It's a public scandal. You must put an end to it immediately.'

'I can't, Sarah, not yet. Everything I said about Fronah's visits to Aisek applies . . . even more strongly. Samqua's quite happy to be deceived as long as it's profitable for him. But he'd be furious at being shown up. If I take away Samqua's face that way, it would go very hard with Aisek.'

'Aisek! Aisek! Always Aisek! Don't you care what you're doing to your daughter? It's bad enough she makes her own reputation for wildness. But this crazy engagement! How will she ever marry a decent Jewish boy? Mrs Elias was saying the other day . . .'

'Exactly *what* was Mrs Elias saying?' Saul's tone was hard. 'It'll go very hard with young Moses Elias if his wife talks too much. I won't have my employees gossiping about my daughter. You tell Miriam Elias to keep her worries to herself. I'll look after my own family without help from her.'

'Never mind, Saul. It was only a few words, and she won't any more. But you must do something about this ridiculous engagement.' Fearing his rising anger, Sarah retreated with a parting shot: 'But what the Khartoons will say about all this!'

'All what, Sarah?' Saul's self-control was ominous. 'What?'

'Oh, not the engagement. You'll take care of that, I know.' Sarah blundered deeper into the minefield of Saul's anger. 'But the partnership with Aisek . . . and trading on your own. Old Solomon Khartoon won't like it at all. Saul, what are you doing to us? When the old man hears . . .'

'When the old man hears, it'll all be over.' Saul bridled his temper. 'As long as profits don't fall, the old man won't say anything. As long as he gets his porcelains, teas, and silks, he'll be happy. Anyway, Sarah, I'm *not* an employee, but an independent manager. It's agreed I can do business on my own account. I'm not a clerk working for the Khartoons, you know, Sarah. I'm not . . .'

'Of course, dear, you're not.' Sarah soothed him. 'And the rest, I'm sure you'll work it out.'

'Of course I will, Sarah.' Saul was pleased to have postponed the inevitable confrontation with his wife. 'You'll see. It'll all work out well.'

*

The chanting of male voices rolled down the long corridor from the junior clerks' office into Fronah's bedroom on the second storey of the house on Szechwan Road. The iron-bound door that led to the counting-house above the small godown for particularly valuable goods was normally bolted to keep the family and the firm apart. He might live over the shop, Saul declared with patrician hauteur, but he would not permit its bustle to disturb his wife and daughter. Ladies should not merely be untroubled by business, but should be unaware of business. However, the iron-bound door had been unbolted a few months earlier in the cause of hospitality to give Aaron and David Lee easy access from their bedroom to their new schoolroom.

Perched on the yellow-silk counterpane, her bare legs dangling against the organdy frill that concealed the bed's rosewood frame, Fronah listened with half an ear to the rumble of the youths' voices. They were reciting classical texts in the traditional forced rhythm, as they would every day until they took the Civil Service Examinations. Only constant repetition, which was called *pei-shu*, turning one's back to the book, could fix the passages indelibly in their minds. In a few years' time, they would be locked into individual cells for days with rice-cakes, drinking water, paper, ink, and writing-brushes to compose essays that would shape their lives. Obsessive diligence was, therefore, normal among aspirant Mandarins.

Fronah heard their tutor's reedy tenor interjecting comments. The sons of a felon awaiting trial were not welcome at the private Academies of Letters, which prepared young men for the Civil Service Examinations that would open to one in two hundred the door to the honours, wealth, and power enjoyed by Mandarins. Saul had, therefore, found the tutor and provided the impromptu schoolroom. It was, he felt, no particular favour to shelter his partner's homeless sons if he did not assist them towards the career on which their father's heart was set. To be a merchant was fine, Aisek would say, but it was glorious to *tso kuan*, serve His Imperial Majesty as a Mandarin.

A merchant could amass greater wealth than all except a few of the most senior among 40,000 officials who ruled 200 million subjects. A merchant could also exercise great power, providing he did so discreetly. Times were changing, and business men were no longer relegated to a lower stratum of Confucian society beneath officials and farmers, though above despised soldiers. Merchants, like soldiers, were too important in the new order shaped by foreign incursion to be denied respect. Some merchants like the Intendant Samqua could even cross the profound social gulf by purchasing

41

Mandarin's rank from a government desperate for money to pay the armies fighting the Taipings.

None the less, it was better to become a Mandarin through the Civil Service Examinations. Not merchants, but Mandarins were the wealthiest men in China, aside from Imperial Princes and the avaricious eunuchs who were the Emperor's closest associates. Not merchants, but Mandarins were surrounded by almost regal pomp and held thousands of lives in their palms. All Chinese dreamed of the day their sons would put on official robes.

Fronah instinctively understood Aisek Lee's ambitions as she bent her head to allow his concubine Maylu to brush her long hair. Unlike most foreigners, she comprehended the aspirations of the Chinese intuitively. Unlike all other foreigners apart from a few servants, the girl who had celebrated her sixteenth birthday ten days earlier spoke both Shanghainese and Mandarin, the Officials' Language. No one wrote the spoken language, but she could read – and, with effort, write – the elided literary style. She knew the texts Aaron and David were reciting that morning, though she no longer joined regularly in their increasingly abstruse studies. Encouraged by her father, she had studied with them for several years – defying both her mother's head-shaking misgivings and the Chinese suspicion of learned women.

'*Ai-yah, tung-le* . . .' Fronah protested when the bristles bit into her scalp. 'That hurts, Maylu.'

'So tender, Small Lady?' the concubine teased. 'I'll be more careful. Go back to your profound thoughts.'

Fronah gave herself languorously to the caresses of the ivory-backed brush. Red highlights glinted among her chestnut waves in the candle-light reflected from the mirrors on her vanity-table. Fragrant with sandalwood, the bedroom was shielded by violet-silk curtains lined with fleece. The flames in the white-marble fireplace were so hot she wore only a shift scooped low over her breasts. The white lawn tautened when she twisted her body, and her nipples pressed against the light fabric. The hem rucked up, half-exposing the dark triangle between her thighs. Luxuriating in Maylu's slow brush-strokes and Maylu's spiced gossip, Fronah stretched sensually.

'Small Lady, someday you'll delight and madden every man who sees you, and . . .' the concubine whispered lubriciously.

Fronah did not respond to the insinuating flattery, which normally evoked visions of raptures on silken sheets with astonishingly handsome, crisply moustached gallants. Her thoughts veered towards the glorious future she planned, and she reproached herself for not rising earlier to join the boys' lessons. If she were to play the brilliant role she envisaged, she must, she knew, learn as much as she possibly could of Chinese culture, as well as Western culture. But the meanderings of the twelfth-century sage

Chu Hsi on the nature of the observation of nature were too abtruse for her.

'Tell me again, Maylu.' Fronah's thoughts were skittish. 'Do you really, you know you told me last week, with his . . . and your? . . . Do you? Have you really?'

'Not often, Small Lady. But I, perhaps, a few times. Perhaps more than a few times. And the pleasure . . . the exquisite pleasure. I remember once . . .'

Lulled by the slurred accent of Maylu's native Soochow, the city of pleasure, Fronah allowed herself a few more minutes of indolence before the tasks she had set herself for the day. She giggled. Her mother would be horrified if she were able to understand her conversations with the thirty-one-year-old former courtesan who now lived by Saul Haleevie's grace in their household.

Kind despite her occasional asperity, Sarah Haleevie had welcomed the company of another woman, though they had only a few words of pidgin in common. Besides, Maylu was quite respectable. No longer a courtesan, she had taken the place, though not the full status, of Aisek Lee's deceased wife. Concubinage was an honourable state by Chinese law and custom.

Sarah had been pleased when Maylu made herself first useful and then indispensable, though the concubine was, Saul stressed, by no means a servant. Never asserting her own will and never clashing with the mistress of the house, Maylu had brought the twelve servants into line. No longer were the Haleevies plagued by the slipshod work and the excessive squeeze that victimised other foreign households. Since Sarah could not control the evasive houseboys and the sly amahs, the household had before Maylu's arrival never met her standards, which were, quite simply, perfection. Sarah was, therefore, grateful to the Soochow woman.

She was grateful, too, when Maylu taught Fronah Chinese skills in the feminine arts of cuisine, needlework, and painting. All those arts the concubine taught Fronah well. She also instructed Fronah in matters that would horrify her mother. But Maylu's decorous manner, as well as their lack of a common language, concealed the concubine's frivolousness. Aside from her devotion to Aisek and his sons, Maylu was light-minded, and her talk was salacious.

'But no more naughty words. I must talk of serious matters, your mother commands.' Maylu reprimanded herself half-heartedly. 'You know they're saying it won't be long now? The barbarians'll soon attack the South City again.'

'Why now?' Fronah wanted to hear what the Chinese were saying, though she knew from her father that the rebels' provocations – and the Imperial government's promises – had convinced the foreign community that the Small Swords must be smashed.

'It's funny, Small Lady. First the barbarians say they hate the Small

43

Swords. Then they trade with the Small Swords, even smuggle them muskets and cannon. Now, all of a sudden, everything's changed again. The barbarians are hard for an ignorant woman to understand.'

'What else are people saying, Maylu?'

'They say Intendant Wu . . . that bloodsucking devil you call Samqua . . . gave the French much money and soon there'll be a big attack, a final attack. It's very peculiar. The barbarians are all different, but the French are the worst. They're bloodthirsty for their God, their Lord of Heaven.'

'I've told you before, Maylu, it's very simple.' Fronah again strove to enlighten the concubine. 'The French hate the Taipings, while many English love the Taipings. And for the same reason, because they think the Taipings are Protestants. The Small Swords say they belong to the Taipings, even if the Taipings say no, they don't, because the Small Swords worship idols and kill animals in their rituals. Above all, the Taipings hate the creed of the Lord of Heaven, the Catholic religion. Because the Catholics have idols in their churches, and the Taipings hate all idolators. So the French join with the Imps . . . with Samqua . . . to fight the Small Swords, even . . .'

'I'm sorry, Small Lady, it's just too complicated, too much for an ignorant woman. But everyone's saying the big battle'll come soon. The sooner we get rid of the rebels, the better!'

'You want to get rid of the Small Swords, Maylu? I thought you hated the Imps and liked the Small Swords because they're Uncle Aisek's friends. And the Imps, they've done terrible things to him.'

'I do. I hate Samqua and all the devilish Mandarins of Shanghai. If the Emperor only knew, they could never treat my poor man so. But the Emperor is far away. He is so high he can't know the evil things his servants do.'

'The Emperor, you say all the time, is the father of all. How can he *not* know? Anyway, why do you hate the Small Swords?'

'They promised so much, but made the people suffer more. If no Small Swords came to Shanghai, my man wouldn't visit them and wouldn't be captured.' Bored with politics, Maylu reverted to spiced gossip. 'Besides, the Small Swords have women with them, even one woman leader. And you know what *they* do with the men . . . sometimes two or three men at once. They're shameless hussies. They should be wiped out . . . strangled. No, beheaded after slicing with a thousand cuts.'

'Just when I think I understand you, you change completely.' Exasperated by the concubine's inconsistency, Fronah reflected that, at times, all Chinese baffled her – even Aaron and David.

'You don't understand everything, not yet, Small Lady,' Maylu chided. 'You must be patient and study hard. Chinese people aren't like Europeans or Jews, even if my man is Jewish, too. Now, your hair, it's all fixed, just like the picture in your magazine.'

Maylu stepped back to admire her creation, and Fronah darted eagerly to her vanity table. The triple mirrors reflected the 'coiffure for a young lady with long tresses' depicted in her borrowed copy of *The Lady's Gazette of Fashion*. Maylu's hands were deft in Chinese hair-styles, which were as elaborate as Victorian Englishwomen's. Parted from forehead to nape, Fronah's hair was parted again crosswise from eartip to eartip. The front was combed up in a double pompadour, while the back was plaited into many three-strand braids coiled together to hang in plump whirls over her neck. Crowned by a triple bow of mauve velvet, the coiffure was to her eye just like the fashion-plate.

Despite her mother's objections, Fronah had recently given up the flowing hair-do of a Baghdad maiden as too childish – and too alien. But she could not alter the face she studied disapprovingly in the mirror. Sadly the features were not at all like the prim, snub-nosed model with the minute chin and tiny mouth. Her eyes were too large and too brilliant; not only too dark, but too liquid. Unlike the insipid model, whom she thought perfection, Fronah's mouth was wide and generously curved. Her colouring was vivid, and her slender nose was delicately arched. Besides, her face was not plump, but moulded over delicate cheekbones.

She could, Fronah concluded, only do the best with the face God had given her. If she could not move men by her beauty, she would move them by her intelligence, her learning – and the voluptuous body God had also given her.

Sighing, she rose for the ordeal of dressing. Despite her mother's horror, she had ten days earlier, on her birthday, given up the kaftans that made her look so outlandish. Fronah believed the paraphernalia laid out on the bed would transform her into a European gentlewoman or, at least, the semblance of a young English lady. Though the costume was painfully constricting, she had resolved that she would thenceforth wear no other clothes.

Turning modestly so that the concubine saw only her buttocks and her slender back, Fronah slipped her shift off. Maylu handed her a linen chemise with broad straps. Fronah pulled it over her head, careful not to rumple her coiffure. Giggling conspiratorially, Maylu lifted the whale-boned corset that would compress Fronah's waist to seventeen inches.

Fronah shrank as the concubine fitted the black-silk garment with the scarlet ribbons to her hips and bust. While the girl gripped the bed-post, Maylu pulled on the broad laces in back. When Fronah gasped in pain, she deftly tied the laces.

The undergarments proliferated: thigh-length stockings supported by garters adorned with tiny green rosettes; lawn pantaloons that would peep coquettishly beneath the skirts; a cream-linen petticoat under the steel cage that held out her skirts; two more petticoats, one muslin, the other red silk; and a satin corset-cover draped with cream Valenciennes lace.

45

After drawing on pale-grey shoes buttoned above the ankles, Maylu covered Fronah's head with a cloth to protect her hair-do.

Teetering upon high heels and trussed by her undergarments, Fronah looked like a headless woman in a wax-museum. She waited helpless for the concubine to slip over her head the dress confected by Shanghai's leading ladies' tailor. When all the buttons, bows, hooks, and eyes were fastened, Fronah regarded herself with delight in the mirror.

The skirt of dove-grey poplin, which billowed out from her thighs, was gathered by a cord above the hem. Trimmed with black-braid and velvet rosettes, a hussar's jacket hung open over a bodice cut low to show the lace-froth corset-cover. Half an hour's labour had transformed her into a rigid dummy. Even if it had been perfectly cut, which it was not, the dress would have been grotesque on a young girl.

Fronah crowned herself with a bonnet of lilac silk, which was trimmed with black-braid and tied under the chin with lilac ribbons. Finally armoured to sally forth, she momentarily regretted the loose comfort of her kaftan. But she was, she firmly believed, the image of a European gentlewoman. However, she must not only look the part, but speak it.

During her first six years in Bombay, Fronah had acquired the rudiments of not only Hebrew, her parents' mother-tongue, and Gujerati, the language of her birthplace, but the English of the British rulers. She had also acquired a lilting Indian intonation, which the British scornfully called *chichi*. During ten years in Shanghai, her accent and her diction had become even more idiosyncratic. The dozen or so Jews of the Treaty Port did business with all, but met only each other socially. Other foreigners, not convinced that Hebrews really counted as Europeans, did not impinge upon their exclusivity. Fronah had, therefore, grown up with the children of her father's Baghdad clerks and associates. Shaped by their guttural accents, her English was further adulterated by pidgin and Shanghainese. The young girl sounded like a middle-aged *babu*, a pompous Bombay clerk who had been too long in China.

Fronah's speech was now a major obstacle to her determination to break out of the narrow Jewish circle. Though her world was comfortable, even luxurious, the exotic Gentile world was alluring. Though the few unmarried women were in demand, she could not move into that glittering milieu and confidently meet dazzling young men while her speech provoked ill-concealed smiles. Since the English were dominant among some three hundred resident foreigners, and the Americans were numerous – even among the 2,000 or so transient sailors and soldiers – all nationalities except the chauvinistic French habitually spoke English. A continental accent might be intriguing, but a *chichi* accent was a stigma.

Chance – actually providence, Fronah believed – had produced Dr William MacGregor's wife Margaret. Lacking a physician of their own, the Jews patronised Dr MacGregor, though he was attached to the Anglican

London Missionary Society. He was pleased to attend the small Hebrew community. Damned even more certainly than Chinese pagans because they rejected their own Messiah, the Jews required his spiritual ministrations even more than his medical attention. However, William MacGregor, who was as tolerant as he was dedicated, did not proselytise actively.

He was delighted when Fronah confided that she wished instruction. He concealed his disappointment when she explained that she wished instruction in English, not Christianity. William MacGregor laughed and told her he possessed neither the time nor the talent to teach her elocution and reading. Besides, it would be improper for a young lady to study with a gentleman. Fortunately, his wife, one of a score of respectable foreign women in the settlement, had been a teacher at home. That earnest Scotswoman yearned for intellectual employment more satisfying than desultorily studying Chinese, which was itself an eccentric occupation for a gentlewoman. Only the permission of Fronah's father was required.

Sarah Haleevie knew her daughter exposed herself to unimaginable dangers by venturing outside their own secure circle. Saul's Chinese Jews were bad enough, but European Christians she feared in the marrow of her pious bones. Her husband's broader vision saw great advantages to Fronah – and to the House of Haleevie – though he was also wary of the wife of a Christian clergyman. Saul knew that his daughter, despite her wilfulness, was deeply devoted to her Jewish heritage. Quelling his misgivings, he had granted his permission.

Fronah retied her bonnet's lilac ribbons and stepped through the door of her bedroom. Her heart beat erratically under her new carapace – and she winced as the whaleboned corset compressed her breasts and bit her waist with each movement. Exulting none the less in her appearance, she set out for her rendezvous with Margaret MacGregor, convinced that the bony Scotswoman with the carrot hair would open the door of an enchanted world to her.

Margaret just as eagerly awaited Fronah's arrival in the small house provided by the London Missionary Society in the compound of her husband's hospital. Tall and angular, she could not have carried off the elaborate dresses that Victorian couturiers confected for the rounded, ideal female form, even if her husband's pinched finances and the simple manner of life prescribed by their vocation had not required her to wear modest and plain garments. But her secret passion was the newly popular fashion magazines her aunt sent from Edinburgh. She looked forward with equal enthusiasm to teaching the petite Fronah to dress tastefully, yet fashionably, from the resources of Saul Haleevie's apparently bottomless purse and to remoulding Fronah's manners and speech. The ambitious pupil had found a mentor who was just as ambitious.

47

CHAPTER SEVEN

Salvoes of fireworks had resounded throughout the hours of darkness, hardly subsiding as the revellers drifted towards their beds long after midnight. Reverberating among the shacks of the refugees, those barrages bade a joyous farewell to the calamitous year of the tiger and welcomed with hope the year of the hare. The salvoes hailing the Lunar New Year, when every man is granted a fresh start, were particularly gratifying to the dispossessed on February 17, 1855. Bought with coppers hoarded for rice, the exploding fireworks not only vented the refugees' rage at fate, but frightened away malevolent spirits bent on blighting the coming year.

After ritually cleansing their grimy shacks, the women of the refugees had for the first time *not* smeared honey and opium on the lips of the wooden statuettes of Tsao Shen enshrined beside their cooking-stoves to seal the mouth of the Kitchen God before his annual journey to Heaven and prevent his reporting the family's transgressions to the Higher Gods. Some had scourged him with rush-brooms so that he would report the people's fury at the afflictions of the past twelve months. The women had charged the Kitchen God to warn his superiors that their images, too, would be punished if they did not halt their spiteful wickedness.

When the tardy sunrise streaked the grey tile-roofs and the weathered brick-walls of the South City with pink, the barrrages of fireworks rose again to crescendo. When the crimson edge of the sun peeped over the eastern mudflats, all the guns of the Small Swords and the Imperial Army roared a salute to the dawn of the New Year. The dogs tucked their tails into the grooves between their lean haunches and retreated again beneath the shacks. When the cannon thundered and the muskets rattled, the white fog floating off the Hwangpoo was marbled with black-powder smoke.

On the flat roof of the house on Szechwan Road, Aaron and David Lee were holding their fire to salute the full sun. Less provident, Fronah Haleevie darted from parapet to parapet, her long hair streaming behind her. The skirts of the kaftan she had donned in her eagerness to join the raucous welcome to the New Year were gathered in her left hand to keep from tripping.

Each time Fronah paused, a Lucifer blossomed between her fingers to ignite one of the thirty-foot-long string of firecrackers hanging like crimson banners from the parapets. Each densely braided string sputtered, sparkled, and rattled for five minutes before it finally vanished amid pennants of smoke.

The haze veiled the oval South City, which was still dark behind its walls. The eastern district glimmered tentatively, but shadows wreathed the spire of the Tongkadoo, the Roman Catholic Cathedral just beyond the South Gate. Though the western district was still shrouded by night, brightness shone from the open square in the centre to light the baroque tea-house and the Garden of Ease, the headquarters of the Small Swords.

After striving in vain for more than a year to retake the South City, the Imperial forces had finally found an effective ally in the French two months earlier. Though he conceded that French interests in Shanghai were minor and the French community miniscule, French Consul C.N.M. de Montigny had taken the initiative by proposing the erection of a second wall along the northern arc of the Chinese city. Sallying from that fortification, French sailors and Imperial soldiers had been staging attacks on the rebel stronghold.

After a major assault was repelled at the beginning of December 1854, the allies had settled down to a siege of attrition. The first direct intervention by a foreign power in China's civil war dwindled to an inconclusive duel between the quick firing Minie rifles of the French, which were supported by batteries of breech-loading, rifled cannon, and the muskets, matchlocks, and horse-pistols of the rebels, which were supported by a few smooth-bore, muzzle-loading cannon. But the Small Swords, cut off from supplies, were growing hungry in their fortress, which shimmered like a walled city in an old Chinese painting through the veil of smoke that covered the roof of the house on Szechwan Road.

When the sun glowed round and bright as a new copper penny through that veil, Aaron and David touched off the grenades that Fronah's father had forbidden her. The aspirant Mandarins' dignity dissolved into childlike glee. The normally solemn Aaron urged his capering younger brother to toss the giant fire-crackers higher and set off a rocket, which arched across the cloudy sky like a silver-and-orange comet. Young houseboys and amahs joined their own fireworks to the pandemonium, mingling freely with the children of the house. All Chinese were equal, members of one great family – at least on such a joyous occasion. The youths and girls laughed and screamed, their eyes streaming from the acrid fumes, which obscured the Chinese city.

Through occasional rifts in the billowing smoke, the South City glowerd incandescent under clouds of crimson vapour.

The radiance in the Chinese city did not die when the brilliant sunrise gave way to a pale February morning. The eastern district was still luminous under shoals of smoke darker than the grey haze given off by the fireworks. The servants' chatter subsided, and they gazed in astonishment at their families' distant homes. Smoke coiled on the tile-roofs like livid dragons, and leaping flames stained the low-lying clouds sickly pink.

49

'It's burning!' David's words gave reality to their fears. 'The South City . . . it's burning!'

'We can't just stand by,' Fronah cried. 'What can we do?'

'Watch!' Aaron advised with sour realism. 'That's all we can do. Watch!'

'We've got to raise the alarm' David protested.

'Just watch!' Aaron insisted dourly. 'Down below, they already know it's a disaster. When men bring disasters on themselves, what can others do but look on?'

They watched in silence as the fire took hold on the timber buildings and leaped higher. The clouds over the South City were no longer pink, but a slick repellent crimson, and the flames soared to touch those clouds. They watched in horror from the rooftop behind the twin walls that cut off the South City. The spectacle was at once terrifying and fascinating from their safe vantage-point.

The Small Swords attacked while the besiegers were bewildered by the sudden conflagration. Knowing they could no longer defy slow starvation and massed cannon, the insurgents had put the torch to the eastern district just before dawn on New Year's Day, when their enemies were least vigilant. Almost two thousand men wearing red headcloths swarmed out of the gates, abandoning the residents and the refugees to the flames. The rebels' short swords and long spears hacked paths through their enemies' flesh. Most drove desperately towards the Taiping realm, though a hundred-odd struck towards the haven of the foreign settlement.

The watchers on the roof saw the enemies close with each other like animated toy soldiers. The hastily mustered Imperial units shredded beneath the steel blades to allow a wedge of Small Swords through their formation, then drew closer. Again and again, the ranks of the besiegers opened and closed. Sword thrusts were glints of silver, and muskets' reports were orange flares. The scarlet roses of cannon-fire budded, flowered, and withered in seconds. When the French naval batteries belatedly came into action, their muzzles blossomed with giant peonies.

The main column of the Small Swords drove south towards the Catholic village of Zikawei and dispersed into the countryside on foot or in sampans on the silver lacework of canals and streams. Shoals of smoke covered the Imperial troops pouring into the narrow alleys of the South City to take their revenge after the frustrating siege. The wounded and sick rebels trapped in the Garden of Ease behind the baroque tea-house were easier prey than their formidable fellows in the countryside. Besides, there was little profit in pursuing those fierce fugutives, while all the wealth of the South City now lay open to the Manchus' troops.

When the remnants in the Garden of Ease surrendered, the Imperial force rendered them the justice rebellion merited. While fastidious officers fluttered their fans against the smoke, the soot-smeared soldiers did their duty. As each rebel was dragged into the square, an infantryman seized his

50

hair and jerked his head forward. The executioner's two-handed scimitar flashed in the murk, and the rebel's head squelched on the pavement. Some Small Swords still struggled, but most waited stolidly on flagstones already greasy with blood. Standing amid the severed heads, the executioners regretted the rebels' lack of convenient queues. One hard pull and the culprit's neck was stretched out for the scimitar.

The Emperor's troops killed greater numbers and did greater damage that day than the Small Swords had done in a year and a half. More than a thousand civilian men and women arbitrarily charged with rebellion were efficiently beheaded. Hundreds of coffins awaiting burial were pried open so that the corpses could be formally arraigned for rebellion. When rotting heads were severed from mouldering bodies, justice was perfect – and the Imperial Braves could get on with their looting.

Although distance blurred the horror, the shrieks and the stench reached the rooftop in the foreign settlement. However, Fronah and the brothers did not see the grisly finale. Saul had broken into their trance of horror and ordered them off the roof as the soldiers began to slaughter the insurgents captured in the Garden of Ease.

They had, none the less, seen for the first time the reality of the violence amid which they lived. Even David could not muster a defensive jest when Sarah scolded him for encouraging Fronah to watch the bloodshed. For two days, even David wandered subdued through the house on Szechwan Road, which stank of the smoke that filmed its white walls.

CHAPTER EIGHT

February 20, 1855   *Shanghai*

On the afternoon of the third day of the Lunar New Year, C.N.M. de Montigny, Consul of France, jubilantly ordered champagne served in his drawing-room behind walls pocked by bullets. He raised his tulip-glass and sniffed the Dom Pérignon, vintage 1843. Before sipping the golden-amber wine, he twirled his glass so that the bubbles beaded on the sides.

Consul de Montigny had much to celebrate. He had just been informed that the Mandarins would honour their promises made to win French assistance. He had, he confessed to himself, not been wholly confident that the Chinese would keep their word. Since that confirmation would enrage the rest of the foreign community, de Montigny's joy was complete.

The Consul reflected complacently that he had struck a great blow for the glory of France. He had sustained the power of the Holy, Catholic, and Apostolic Church; Chinese converts and their priests were no longer in danger either in the Tongadoo Cathedral just outside the South City or in the Catholic village of Zikawei, where lay the remains of the Ming Chancellor, Dr Paul Hsü, the first great convert to the Faith. The Small Swords, who were allies of the twice heretical Taipings, had been crushed.

He had, further, decisively demonstrated the might, the resolution, and the independence of France in the face of the other foreigners' objections to his allying himself militarily with the Imperialists. He had also cemented the special relationship between himself and the Mandarins, which promised a brilliant future for French trade.

The rewards were, moreover, not all spiritual, intangible, or deferred. The message the Consul had just received formally granted France the district lying between the South City and Yangjingbang Creek. Virtually unsettled, except for the Consulate and the premises of the jeweller Remi, the territory was in itself not particularly valuable. However, since it bordered the Hwangpoo for seven hundred yards, its acquisition more than doubled the previous five hundred yards of French river-front. That wharfage was incalculably valuable.

At little cost in French blood, Consul C.N.M. de Montigny congratulated himself again, he had struck a mighty blow for France, for legitimate rule in China, and for himself. The first foreign intervention in the civil strife of China was brilliantly successful – in the judgement of its initiator.

CHAPTER NINE

February 26, 1855   *The Foreign Settlement*

Her Britannic Majesty's Consul in Shanghai leaned back in his swivel-chair and gazed past Saul Haleevie's shoulder at the traffic on the Bund, the embankment along the Hwangpoo River. He noted with pleasure that the pale afternoon sun had partially dispersed the fog.

'Do believe me, Mr Haleevie, I feel deeply for your evident distress and I respect your devotion to your Chinese associate.' John Rutherford Alcock, Fellow of the Royal College of Surgeons and sometime Inspector of Anatomy for the Home Office, spoke in an agreeable baritone. 'I shall, I assure you, continue my strenuous endeavours on behalf of Mr Aisek Lee, though I am already stretching my authority to its . . .'

'But, Your Excellency, Consul Alcock,' Saul protested. 'For almost a year now, Aisek Lee is still imprisoned . . . and not even charged, even for all your trying. Even for my trying, too, the bribes and . . .'

'Samqua *is* pestilential, I grant you that.' Rutherford Alcock permitted himself an indiscretion. 'But we must work with him. After more than ten years in China, I have, I believe, learned a few things. First, we can only deal with those Chinamen who will, at least, meet us half-way. They are few enough. Second, we Europeans must act together. That, Mr Haleevie, is why I am striving on your behalf for your associate, though properly he has no claim to my protection.'

Despite his own self-confidence, Saul Haleevie was overawed by the tall man with mutton-chop whiskers, who spoke in measured sentences. The forty-six-year-old former military surgeon had already proved himself decisive – and, upon occasion, autocratic – in dealing with the Mandarins. He was also kind, though benevolent might better describe his ponderous goodwill. His manner was avuncular, for he was sincerely concerned for the welfare of not only his own British charges, but the Chinese, as well. None the less, Saul was uneasy in his presence. The British Consul was *primus inter pares*, unquestionably first among the theoretically equal consuls who ruled the foreign settlement.

Intimidated by the Consul's authority, Saul felt his own vulnerability keenly. His robe and turban must appear outlandish to the Englishman in the frock-coat whose high lapels accentuated the lustre of his cravat under the starched wing-collar that framed his square chin. Recalling Fronah's desire to speak in the understated yet precisely emphatic manner of the English, Saul was acutely conscious of his own failings. The guttural undertone of his native Hebrew was harsh in his own ears, and his Bombay lilt was comical; his grammatical errors and unidiomatic phraseology were ludicrous. To the supremely self-assured Englishman he must not just sound, but look like too, a music-hall comedian with a jutting proboscis. Did he only imagine that Rutherford Alcock's classically straight nose wrinkled in disdain or, worse, amusement?

'It does your heart credit, Mr Haleevie, your dedication to Aisek Lee,' the Consul continued. 'But do consider my position. If I intervened on behalf of every Chinaman who had a tenuous claim to my protection, I'd be infernally busy, wouldn't I? A hundred million Chinamen would line up outside my door, all demanding that I champion them against the Mandarins. There would not be enough men in all England to read their petitions . . . not to speak of the troops to enforce my jurisdiction.'

'Look here, Your Excellency, Doctor Alcock . . .'

'I don't use the medical title now, Mr Haleevie, as you should know.' Though gentle, the reproof stung. 'I haven't practised in decades.'

'I'm sorry, Consul. Forgive me . . . my fault. I couldn't know all the fine differences of titles.'

'You're a British-protected person, Mr Haleevie and, therefore, entitled to demand my intervention on behalf of yourself and your family,' Alcock relented. 'Your daughter, being Bombay-born, is a British subject. But what of yourself? Should we not see about naturalisation? You're qualified, and it's high time.'

'You honour me too much, Your Excellency, and I would see about that . . . soon enough.' Saul was not diverted by the Consul's imperative goodwill. 'Yet now I'm talking about poor Aisek Lee.'

'If you must,' Alcock sighed. 'Though I fear we've been over all that ground before . . . many times.'

'Look now, Your Excellency, the French, you know, give protection to all their religions . . .'

'Their religions, Mr Haleevie? Oh, you mean their co-religionists, do you?'

'Yes, that's right. The French Consul, if any priest comes to him, he covers with his protection a Catholic, also Chinese Catholics.'

'Yes, I grant you that, though I wonder if he should. The French have some queer ways. My esteemed colleague M. de Montigny did not hesitate to start a small war. But I digress. What's all that to do with your friend Lee? Or you, for that matter?'

'Now, Consul, I am a kind of priest, you know. Jews have no priests, not like Christian priests, but scholars who are expert in our Law. We call them rebs. And I am a reb, a clergyman you may call it, though I work also as a trader.'

'That's all terribly interesting. Someday you must tell me all about the customs of the Chosen People. But I *am* busy, and it's nothing to do with this matter.'

'Your Excellency, I, Rabbi Saul Haleevie, make a formal application to you, the Honourable Dr Rutherford Alcock, Her Britannic Majesty's Consul.' Saul painfully repeated out the much rehearsed sentence. 'I make formal application for protection for my religions . . . my co-religionist . . . Mr Aisek Lee.'

'Now look here, Mr Haleevie, I admire your ingenuity, as well as your devotion. But nothing . . . nothing in the treaty or law . . . obliges or empowers me to act as protector of *any* religion, no matter what the Frenchies do. Do you want me to start a war for Aisek Lee? What do you think I can do? I'd be relieved so fast . . . Believe me, I am sorry.'

Embarrassed by his impotence, Rutherford Alcock picked up a wax model of a hand and forearm from his mahogany desk. He swivelled in his chair to gaze at the juncture of Soochow Creek with the Hwangpoo River and continued the strained interview with his back half-turned.

The Consul's big hands stroked the model with wary affection, but, Saul saw, his grip was awkward. The entire foreign community knew that rheumatic fever had left Rutherford Alcock with chorea, ending the career

54

that had won him the chair of military surgery at King's College and a consultancy at Westminster Hospital, where he had studied medicine. He could no longer operate, and he could hardly support himself by moulding anatomical models in wax, a skill he had learned in Paris in his youth. To rescue him from that tragic impasse, he had been offered appointment in the consular service. Further recalling the tragic death of Rutherford Alcock's wife only eleven months earlier, Saul was marginally less resentful of the Consul's rejection of the last argument he could find for British intervention on Aisek's behalf.

'I'm glad to have this opportunity to discuss other matters, Mr Haleevie,' Alcock said. 'Your silks were finally released last week, I understand.'

'Yes, your Excellency, though why, I don't. . .'

'I'm not quite blind to British interests, you know. With the Customs in our hands for administration, I could finally shake the silk free. I even stretched a point. I made sure you got the lot, including that belonging – between us, of course – to your partner. That I could do.'

'I am grateful, Consul, very grateful. With that money, I have more for Aisek's defence and . . .'

'I know you're looking after him well. You've behaved most commendably. From what I hear . . . unofficially . . . he'll need all the help you can give. And you've claimed his land in the settlement as your partnership's, haven't you? You know, I did drop a word. Lee's sons will be well provided for. Mark my word, that land will be immensely valuable some day quite soon.'

'I believe also, Consul.'

'There is another matter. Not so pleasant, I fear. I'm firing a shot across your bow, Mr Haleevie, no more just yet. This trading with the Taipings, it won't do, you know. I'm telling you unofficially . . . for the moment.'

'But everyone does,' Saul protested. 'And myself only in a small way.'

'I know that too. Just don't want to see it go further. It's too dangerous. Besides, the Taipings can't win, which is even more important. I can understand why some missionaries are wild for the Taipings. Co-religionists, they call them, as you'd say. But you Hebrews don't even acknowledge the true Messiah. How can you accept a second Messiah, as that fellow, the Heavenly King, calls himself?'

'It's not religion, Your Excellency, but . . .'

'But profits, of course. Quite. And, in the ordinary course, commendable. You're here to trade, and I'm here to help you. But don't overdo it. Just a friendly warning at this stage, you understand. You really must not continue . . .'

A fresh-faced clerk in frock-coat and wing-collar slipped into the room after knocking perfunctorily and handed his superior a document. Rutherford Alcock slit the seal and read deliberately.

'What have we here?' he exclaimed. 'Well, Mr Haleevie, it's come at last, the formal indictment you wanted. Trial of Aisek Lee in one week, it says. The charge is . . . damn me . . . matricide! That's a capital offence, of course, under British law as well as Chinese law. And an abomination under Chinese law, killing a parent. But how can they? I'm baffled. Matricide!'

CHAPTER TEN

Aisek Lee was superficially little altered by his ordeal. Saul Haleevie, who was just six feet tall, saw his friend clearly over the heads of the lictors who kept the witnesses at a distance from the tribunal. He thanked God that constant pressure and copious bribes had spared Aisek the barbaric treatment that so often either killed prisoners or inflicted severe injuries before the creaking machinery of Chinese justice brought them to trial. His partner seemed to have suffered little from his confinement of almost nine months when he knelt bareheaded before the Prefect of Huating in the ashen dawn of the sixth of March, 1855.

Rather than prison rags, the defendant wore his second-best long-gown of blue silk padded with raw-silk. His head was newly shaved; his oiled queue was freshly braided; and his goatee was neatly trimmed. Since the barbarians were interested in his case, the good name of the Ching Dynasty required that the accused appear to have been no more harmed by his protracted imprisonment than he would by an equally protracted journey.

By further special favour, a small pillow cushioned Aisek's knees from the cold flagstones. Chains might yet replace that pillow, since the Criminal Code of the Great Pure Dynasty authorised that 'discomfort' to ensure that the accused spoke the truth. The size of the links and the duration of the torture were, however, precisely delimited for the sake of humanity. Schooled to public impassivity, Aisek's features revealed no more than polite interest in the proceedings that would determine his fate – and, despite himself, mild surprise at the comfort granted him.

Whatever wounds might be concealed by the long-gown, his face was not only unscarred, but fuller than it had been when he was arrested. Saul's bribes had ensured that he was well fed during those months of inactivity. His plumpness, the sign of good health in Chinese eyes, further demonstrated his jailers' benevolence. Saul, however, feared that his partner's face was actually unhealthily swollen.

If Aisek moved stiffly, sinking to his knees with evident pain, a man of forty-one could hardly expect to be supple after prolonged confinement. If his domed head was shaken by tremors and his puffy face was graven by deep lines, the cause was not the treatment he had received. Those infirmities, common among defendants, obviously arose from his apprehension, his awe of the court, and his awareness of his guilt. A prisoner facing a capital charge should, after all, be repentant. He should not come before his judge beaming with self-confidence or making little jokes – whatever his normal temperament.

Head bowed, Aisek Lee knelt before his judge as dawn flooded the courtyard of the magistrate's *yamen* with pearly light. He had glimpsed the beige turban surmounting Saul's lean height when the lictors led him before the tribunal. He assumed that other witnesses had been summoned by the court, though the throng concealed his concubine Maylu, his sons, Aaron and David, and two of his former servants.

Fifteen other defendants surrounded Aisek. Most wore sixty-pound cangues, wooden collars whose dimensions were also prescribed by the Criminal Code. Their heads lolled disembodied on the planks as if already decapitated. Aisek shivered at that portent and studied the enthroned Mandarin who was his judge.

The grave charge – and the foreigners' interest – had moved Intendant Samqua to assign the case to the Chief Magistrate of Huating Prefecture, one of Shanghai's three major administrative divisions. The middle-aged Mandarin wore the wild goose of the fourth grade on the breast of his robe, for he was an official of long and exemplary service. He chafed at his subordination to the arriviste Samqua, who had purchased – rather than earned – his eminence. He had already decided to ignore the Intendant's oblique instructions. Not only honour, but pride required him to render impartial justice. He would not be swayed by Samqua's apparent inclination towards leniency. Nor would he be swayed by the substantial gifts of the anonymous donors who contended that the accused deserved the severest punishment.

Like virtually all his colleagues, he had to accept such gifts if he were to keep his household in comfort, assure his children's future, and provide for his old age. But he would, he promised himself, render an even-handed judgment.

A frown drew the Mandarin's thick eyebrows together, and his lean face was set severely after his decades as a buffer between Chinese subjects and Manchu overlords. However, his full lips quirked upward, and Aisek discerned kindliness in his deep-set eyes. The Prefect of Huating's reputation for mercifulness was, perhaps, another reason Samqua had designated him to hear the case.

The Judge's regalia evoked awe, as it was intended to. Seated on a dais behind a table draped with red silk, he was flanked by four lictors bearing

57

the black-and-scarlet striped bamboo staves that proclaimed his punitive powers. The overhanging eaves of his *yamen* ensured that he, alone in the courtyard, was sheltered from the morning mist, while smoke from a charcoal brazier that warmed him alone seeped through the drapery. Confronted by counsel for neither prosecution nor defence, hampered by neither advisers nor jurors, he was as isolated as his master, the Hsien Feng Emperor.

'You, prisoner, are Li Ai-shih, merchant of this town?' The judge followed the fixed procedure. 'Now forty-one years of age, arrested on the night of June the 21st last year while returning from meeting the leaders of the Small Swords, the pestilential secret society that seeks to overthrow the lawful rule of the Sacred Dynasty, the legitimate heir of the Great Ming Dynasty?'

'*Shih-di . . .*' Aisek Lee volunteered no explanation since the charge was not treason. 'I am, Your Honour.'

'You are, however, *not* here arraigned for that misdeed.' The Prefect confirmed Aisek's decision. 'It pleases His Imperial Majesty to be lenient to those who were misled while the rebels usurped his authority over a minuscule portion of his domains. The law does not concern itself with trifles, and the Small Swords were no more than a swarm of mosquitoes. Nor did your deeds assist to the rebellion.

'You *are* arraigned for matricide, a most heinous crime, an abomination to all decent men and to Heaven itself. You *are* arraigned for an unnatural act of indescribable wickedness. Aside from raising a hand against the Sacred Person of the Emperor, there is no deed more vile and reprehensible than causing the death of a parent. The penalty prescribed by the Criminal Code of the Great Pure Dynasty is decapitation after torture and . . .'

'But, Your Honour, I could not . . . did not. I wasn't even there . . .' Aisek blurted his justification, though he had been warned it was foolhardy to interrupt the judge.

'The accused will be silent.' The Prefect's expression of stringent benevolence did not alter. 'Later, you will be allowed to answer questions in full. For the moment, you will reply in simple affirmatives or negatives.'

Aisek was relieved at escaping with a reprimand; another judge might have ordered the lictors to beat him and place chains beneath his knees.

'Do you, Li Ai-shih, acknowledge that on the night of February the 12th of the past year your mother, Li Chao Wen-ai, being in the sixty-seventh year of her age, did hang herself from a beam in the residence she shared with you? Do you dispute the contention that her anxiety over your actions caused her to adopt that ultimate means of protesting against your actions?'

'No . . . Yes . . .' Aisek stuttered. 'I don't . . . Your Honour.'

'You may speak more fully.'

'I thank you profoundly, Your Honour.' Aisek marvelled again at the judge's tolerance. 'I cannot confirm the facts, since I was not present. As for my revered mother's reasons, it is not for me to say.'

'I note your contentions. As far as I can see, the facts are not in question. Their interpretation is, however, open.' The Prefect's brusque dismissal of the facts threw Aisek into despair, but his hopes rebounded since the magistrate had obviously not already prejudged the case. 'I shall none the less call witnesses to establish the gross facts as the Code requires. I shall also explore your mother's motivation. The crux of this case is the *reason* for her self-destruction, *not* the fact thereof.'

Raising his eyes as he sipped his tea, the judge saw two prisoners whispering to each other. He cocked an eyebrow, and a lictor laid his bamboo stave across their shoulders. Lenient the Prefect of Huating might be, but not indulgent.

'Several interesting points of law are embedded in this case,' he mused in a louder tone. 'I look forward to their explication, which will test my poor knowledge and my feeble power of ratiocination. Fortunately, the precise formulations of the Criminal Code are an unerring guide through the mazes of the human heart.'

For the first time, Aaron Lee heard the bench clearly, and he whispered a translation to Saul Haleevie. The Jewish merchant was, of course, not permitted to express his admiration for the learning, the impartiality, and the perspicacity the judge celebrated in himself. Besides, he saw little to admire. The judge did not weigh facts and arguments presented by lawyers, but sat in judgment on evidence he presented to himself. The prisoner was denied any advocate, whether a counsel learned in the law or merely a sympathetic champion.

No wonder foreigners adamantly refused to submit themselves to Chinese law. The accused was allowed to speak for himself only at the judge's pleasure, and none of his peers sat as jurors. One fallible human being was judge, jury, and counsel for both prosecution and defence. Whatever safeguards the complex Criminal Code provided, all came down to the questionable impartiality and the impossible omniscience of that single Mandarin – rather than the cumulative wisdom of the ages examined by the interaction of many minds.

The entire Manchu Dynasty, Saul reflected, rested upon the same assumptions. Individual Mandarins possessing perfect wisdom presumably administered the Great Empire moved only by disinterested concern for the common weal. In practice, he knew too well, most Mandarins were neither wise nor incorruptible, but were swayed by vanity and greed.

'In rendering judgment, I must, above all, consider the stability of the Sacred Dynasty and the well-being of the family of man, that is, the hundreds of millions of Chinese.' The Prefect spoke loudly so that the racing brush of the clerk seated behind the partition wall could record every word in flowing grass script for future generations. 'The good order and the prosperity of *Tien-hsia*, all that lies under Heaven, depends upon *hsiao*, filial piety. If men do not render perfect obedience to their parents, how will they render unquestioning loyalty to the Emperor, who is the father of us all? If the five relationships between inferiors and superiors are not observed, how can the world be at peace? The quintessential relationship is that between child and parent. Yet we are dealing not with mere disobedience, heinous as this is. We are concerned with wilful, persistent, unrepentant acts that drove a parent to suicide. The charge is, therefore, matricide, and matricide is an abomination.'

The charge was irrefutable, Aisek realised, and self-revulsion overcame him. His round head shook, and his heart fluttered in his throat. Bowed by the realisation that he was vilely guilty, his entire body trembled in self-condemnation.

'*Yu tao-li* . . .' he muttered in despair. 'The logic is clear. I have sinned!'

Listening to Aaron's rapid translation, Saul, too, acknowledged the Prefect's logic. But it was logic stood on its head, for the Chinese had no word for logic in their rich language. *Tao-li*, the closest, did not mean logic, but 'in accordance with the *tao*,' the indefinable 'way' of the cosmos. The Chinese mind was divorced from *logos*, the Greek conviction that an ordered universe was comprehensible to human intelligence.

'I shall, I am confident, not require the services of the *hsieh-chai* in this case.'

The Prefect thus ventured a ponderous judicial jest. The *hsieh-chai*, a mythical unicorn, had served the legendary Kao Yao, the Minister of Justice who formulated the first Criminal Code for the legendary Emperor Shun millennia earlier. When even his acuity was baffled, Kao Yao had appealed to the infallible *hsieh-chai* to butt the guilty and ignore the innocent.

'That magical beast was necessary when the law was in its infancy. But today we possess the Criminal Code of the Great Pure Dynasty, as well as the wisdom of the Sages recorded over millennia. However, the court will now descend to the practical issues. Produce Wang Maylu, concubine of the accused.'

Teetering on her bound feet, Maylu fastidiously drew aside the skirts of her grey tunic as she passed among the prisoners in cangues. When she knelt, the Prefect formally established her identity. Satisfied that the thirty-one-year-old woman with the candid expression was the lawful concubine of Aisek Lee, he began his substantive examination. Having proved that Aisek's mother had hanged herself on the night of February 12th, 1854, he probed her motivation.

'The Lady said . . . said she could no longer endure to live in abject poverty.' Maylu's tremulo was barely audible. 'Yes . . . an hour or so before . . . before she . . .'

'And before that,' the judge asked, 'had she spoken often of poverty, her fears of poverty?'

'Yes, Your Honour, but it was *not* true,' the concubine asserted. 'My man . . . he was a dutiful son, always respectful and loving to his mother. And he worked very hard . . . night and day . . . to make the family prosperous. He gave his mother every luxury. He worked to ensure that his sons could pass the Civil Service Examinations and serve His Imperial Majesty. We were not poor. We were prosperous.'

'But the mother *believed* the family was poverty-stricken, did she not? She often spoke of poverty? Fear of poverty drove her to suicide, did it not?'

'I cannot say, Your Honour,' Maylu parried feebly. 'I cannot say what was in her mind just before she . . . she hanged herself. Who can?'

'Why,' the judge insisted, 'did she believe the Lee family was falling . . . had fallen . . . into poverty? Was it to do with her son's business dealings? Was it to do with his partnership with the foreigner?'

'I cannot say why she . . .' Maylu quailed under the Prefect's admonitory glare. 'Yes, Your Honour, she said the dealings with Ha-lee-vee had impoverished the family. But it was *not* true, Your Honour. It was only the mistaken idea of an old woman not . . . not quite right in her mind. We . . . the family . . . were growing more prosperous by the silk trade and other dealings in partnership with Ha-lee-vee. She didn't know what was really happening . . . what was real and what she imagined. She was sick in her mind.'

'Your loyalty does you credit, virtuous lady. But the facts, as you state them, are irrefutable. First, the mother of the merchant Lee committed suicide because of her fear of poverty. Second, her fear arose directly from the actions of the accused. Did she plead with him to alter his ways . . . to give up the association with the barbarian Ha-lee-vee?'

'Yes, Your Honour, she did. But it was nothing to do with what was really happening . . .'

'And did the accused alter his ways in response to his mother's pleading?'

'No, Your Honour, he didn't. He could not.'

'And did the poor mother plead with the accused for a long time, more than a year?'

'Yes, Your Honour, but . . .'

'May I speak, Your Honour?' Aisek asked in a strangled whisper. 'Just a word?'

Insistent as water falling on rock, the judge's questions had worn away all Aisek's remaining hope. Tormented by having failed his mother, he was crushed by the enormity of his crime – and he felt compelled to purge his conscience by confession.

'You may, accused,' the judge consented.

'I see . . . I understand now . . .' Aisek stammered. 'I have behaved vilely, even abominably. Yet . . . I . . . I could not act otherwise once I began. I could not withdraw from my business arrangements. If I had, it would . . . I'd have faced bankruptcy. No matter what my mother said, I had to continue in order to preserve the family, to maintain our property.'

'Continue doing business with this Ha-lee-vee?'

'Yes, Your Honour.'

'Your plea is noted,' the Prefect observed noncommittally. 'I shall now hear the testimony of Ha-lee-vee.'

Saul was allowed to stand because he had come voluntarily before the court, which could not summon a foreigner. His examination required no more than ten minutes, including translation by an interpreter who spoke fluent, but broken English. The judge established that Saul had been the defendant's partner in various commercial activities for five years. Saul acknowledged that Aisek had often spoken of his mother's opposition to their association, but pointed out that his partner had constantly reassured the old lady that their enterprises were making the Lee family rich, rather than impoverishing it. Furthermore, Aisek had never had any reason to believe his mother's delusion would move her to extreme action.

The Prefect of Huating listened politely, permitting the foreigner a latitude of expression he would have tolerated from no Chinese witness. He had been told the case could have political repercussions, and he had been cautioned to be circumspect with the barbarian. He saw no impropriety in following that advice, though no extraneous considerations would affect his verdict.

'Was there,' the Prefect asked gently, 'danger of serious reverses?'

'There is always such danger,' Saul replied. 'The Lord God does not smooth the path before the feet of men all their days. In His wisdom, for His own reasons, He tries the spirits and the will of mortals.'

'Did your partnership ever experience such reverses?' The judge suppressed his indignation at the barbarian's invoking primitive superstition. 'Did you ever fear that your partnership might fail . . . go bankrupt?'

'Of course, Your Honour, there were times when it seemed possible. As I have said, the Lord God . . .'

'I see!' the judge forestalled another outburst of superstition. 'Then the fears of the mother of the accused were not wholly imaginary, were they? Impoverishment could have . . .'

'True, Your Honour.' Saul's interruption strained the judge's tolerance. 'But, as I have said, it did not occur. The firm was doing well.'

'Thank you for your assistance, Ha-lee-vee.' The Prefect dismissed Saul with relief. 'I shall weigh your words.'

The witness turned to go, but the judge had one further question.

62

'Were your shipments of silk from Soochow last year held up and threatened with confiscation by the Imperial Customs? Did you then fear major disruption, perhaps bankruptcy?'

'They were,' Saul replied. 'But that was after Mrs Lee committed suicide.'

'The time has no direct bearing in this case, since motivation is all important,' the judge observed. 'You have testified that the reverses feared by the mother of the defendant did in reality occur. You may go now.'

After enduring the barbarian's unwitting insolence, the Prefect of Huating believed he had established the pertinent facts of the case. Yet the mother's state of mind was its crux. To pursue her elusive motivation through the labyrinthine recollections of others were arduous, but essential. He, therefore, called two further witnesses, the old lady's personal maidservant and the major-domo of the household.

Only two years younger than her mistress, the old amah testified through tears that the deceased had for several years bewailed the ruin her son's dealings with barbarians were bringing upon the family. In all other respects, the faithful servant declared mendaciously, Mrs Lee had been perfectly normal.

The judge listened sympathetically, interrupting only once or twice. He heard the testimony of the major-domo just as patiently, leaning forward to squiggle a note when that senior servant recalled his mistress's dishevelment, her wearing tattered clothing fit only for the grandmother of a struggling farming family, and her eating only dry rice garnished with salted vegetables, the food of the poor. The note read: 'Self-deprivation: evidence of disturbed mind *unrelated* to son's activities?'

Nineteen-year-old Aaron Lee was the last to testify, the only witness who would be considered to speak for the defence in a European court. Aaron, who had asked to be heard, was a scholar qualified to take the first Civil Service Examination. He therefore merited greater consideration than the lay witnesses and was, like Saul, privileged to stand, rather than kneel. Aaron Lee's lean features dominated by his arched nose, were fixed in grave respect as he strove for his father's life – and his sincerity impressed the judge.

'What have you to say of your grandmother's behaviour, young man?' the judge asked. 'When did she begin to act strangely?'

'Many years before my father entered into partnership with Ha-lee-vee,' Aaron replied. 'Even when I was a small boy, she would sometimes burst into unnatural gaiety, often followed by the deepest melancholy.'

'You contend, then, that your grandmother's disturbed state of mind preceded your father's business ventures with the barbarian? You are, I see, already learned in the law.'

'Thank you, Your Honour. Yes, I do so contend. I would submit that no direct connection is demonstrable between my father's business affairs and my honoured grandmother's lamentable self-destruction. I would suggest that my father's success in business actually delayed my grandmother's suicide. *If* we had not been prosperous, *if* hardship had reinforced her delusions, she would have taken extreme action much earlier. Rather than occasioning my grandmother's suicide, I submit most respectfully, my father's dealings with Ha-lee-vee prevented it's occurring earlier.

'Moreover, my father continually reassured my grandmother by showing her how prosperous the family actually was. My father should be commended for persisting in his enterprises even over my grandmother's objections. That was a truly filial action. My esteemed father behaved with perfect filial piety in extremely testing circumstances.'

'What historical basis exists for that interesting contention, young scholar?' The Prefect was impressed by Aaron's argument. 'I assume that you have a precedent.'

'I would refer to the matter of the Master Confucius and the Duke of She. Since Your Excellency is profoundly versed in the ramifications of that precedent, I shall be brief. Against the Duke's contention, the Sage judged that the highest form of filial piety was a son's *not* shielding his father, who had stolen a sheep, since that act injured the greater family, all who live Under Heaven.'

'And that analogy signifies?'

'Filial piety, I submit, Your Honour, is by the Master Sage's own judgment not a simple matter. In this case, my father would have injured the family – and his mother – if he had withdrawn from the partnership as she demanded.'

'Well argued, young scholar,' the judge commended Aaron. 'I shall consider your point. Now, accused, have you anything to say before I ponder my verdict?'

Although crushed by recognition of his sin, Aisek was heartened by his son's pleading. Yet his conviction of guilt remained fixed, since he felt the clever Aaron was just playing with words. None the less, his son's brilliance filled him with pride. The repute that penetrating argument must win for Aaron would assist his official career. Whatever his father's fate, the family would benefit thereby.

'Your Honour, I profoundly repent having contributed to my mother's great unhappiness and her self-destruction – however indirectly and unintentionally,' he declared humbly. 'I have grieved for many months, and I shall grieve all my life over my failure to preserve her into great old age. I see now how deeply I have sinned. I would only explain . . . not defend myself . . . but explain that I sincerely believed I could not act otherwise to provide best for my mother . . . and the entire family. I cast myself upon Your Honour's mercy. Do with me what you will. To live with my grief is the severest punishment I can conceive.'

Saul gasped when David translated his partner's statement. Even

Aaron's spirited argument must fail, he felt, because Aisek's admission of guilt must result in conviction. Aaron was silently attentive, but David beamed.

'He's said it just right,' he whispered. 'Humble, contrite, raising the interests of the entire family. I think he's got a chance. I really do.'

The Prefect of Huating bent over the documents on the red cloth. Occasionally referring to his notes, he jotted down the main points of his summation. He called upon his clerk several times to check the verbatim record, and he flipped again through the preliminary files. The abtruse legal points were, however, fixed in his memory.

'This is a most instructive case, replete with significance that extends far . beyond the particular circumstances.' After twenty minutes, the Prefect finally spoke with the solemnity befitting the grave charge. 'As I have already noted, the stability of the Sacred Dynasty, as well as the security of all who live Under Heaven, rests upon the bedrock of *hsiao*, filial piety. The harmonious lives of all degrees of mankind, the Sages have repeatedly stressed, requires the strictest observance of the hierarchy of relationships. A parent is a parent, and a child is a child. They must behave as such . . . or society will crumble.'

Aaron's complex intellect was so entranced by the play of argument he almost forgot that the Prefect was pronouncing his father's fate. David grimaced behind his hand, weary of the rote wisdom the judge piously mouthed.

'Fortunately, the facts are clear, . . . and the verdict is inescapable.' The Prefect resumed after leisurely sipping his tea. 'One fundamental issue remains. Filial piety is the basis of our lives, but what, after all, is filial piety? Is it the intent or the deed . . . or both? Does the intent transcend the deed in this case, as provided under certain passages of the Criminal Code? Are we concerned primarily with what the accused intended to do or with the effect of his actions? Whatever the effect of his actions, I am satisfied that his intent was honourable, even pious.'

David laughed into Saul's ear and summarised those remarks. All, he whispered confidently, would be well. Aaron was silent.

'However, my verdict must accord with precedents and law. Two earlier cases are particularly pertinent, as are sections 1504 and 1506 of the Criminal Code'. David translated the summing up for Saul: 'In the twenty-fifth year of Chia Ching of the Ming, the year 1562, one Li Ching-wen of Shansi Province rented out his land to finance development of a coal mine. Horrified at that alienation of the family's sacred patrimony and fearing destitution, his mother committed suicide. In the ninth year of the Tao Kwang Emperor of the present Dynasty, 1830, one Wei Hsing-chou of Kwangtung Province, protecting his mother from attack, wounded the assailant with a knife. Fearing disgrace when the case came to court, his mother committed suicide. Both accused were found guilty. Those instruc-

65

tive precedents are, however, not conclusive, since this case is dominated by the question of intent.

'Fortunately, we possess a circular issued by the Ministry of Justice in Chien Lung, year 26, 1762, with the Emperor's express approval. The directive clarifies the punishments for children's conduct that causes parental suicide. The circular distinguishes between: first, essentially peripheral misdeeds that result in a parent's suicide and, second, persistence in gravely immoral and illegal acts with the same effect. The penalty for the first is exile, for the second beheading.'

Kneeling on his pillow, Aisek neither hoped nor despaired. He was chiefly aware of the aching of his calves after more than two hours in that cramped posture. Besides, he could not follow the legal technicalities.

'But what have we here?' the judge continued. 'Accused, your actions caused your mother's suicide, *whatever* their intent. That you have yourself acknowledged, and your honesty counts in your favour. Moreover, the weight of the witnesses' testimony is irrefutable. On the other hand, you wished her nothing but good. Yet you knew she was melancholy and confused. Knowing she suffered delusions, you persisted in the actions that strengthened those delusions. You are, in that sense, *more* culpable.

'I congratulate you upon your son. He has not only displayed exemplary filial piety, but penetrating understanding of the Classics and familiarity with the law remarkable in one who is only a candidate for the Civil Service Examinations. He has also argued tellingly that your mother would have taken her own life regardless of your actions. And he has strikingly demonstrated that her delusions commenced before your partnership with the barbarian Ha-lee-vee.'

Aaron permitted himself a wintry smile. He also permitted himself to hope for a favourable verdict as he preened in the spectators' admiring glances. The Prefect poured a fresh cup and sipped the straw-coloured tea before referring to his notes again.

'The burden of proof, however, rests upon the accused. Knowing his mother's disturbed state of mind he took insufficient action to placate her. Rather than soothing her, his behaviour exacerbated her malady . . . if malady it was. Moreover, her fears were not groundless, as Ha-lee-vee's testimony has shown. Bankruptcy was an actual danger, not a figment of her imagination. Since financial ruin *could* have occurred, the fact that it did not is not significant. The fear that drove the mother of the accused to suicide was based upon reality.

'The son of the accused has argued that the suicide would have occurred regardless of the actions of the accused. That contention is interesting, but it is speculative. I must deal with reality, not with something that might or might not have happened had the accused behaved differently.'

66

Aaron's hopes for acquittal were shattered. The question was now which punishment the judge would inflict, exile or execution as prescribed by the circular the Ministry of Justice had issued four reigns earlier.

'The confiscation of the accused's property stands.' Having prolonged the tension, the Prefect spoke briskly. 'It is ironic that his mother's deed has created the reality she feared. Committing suicide because of imagined impoverishment, she has impoverished the family. I regret the effect upon the sons of the accused, who are guiltless. I particularly regret the effect upon the brilliant elder son, who would make an exemplary Mandarin. Yet I cannot rule otherwise, whatever my personal compassion.

'It is, further, indisputable that the accused persisted in his actions though he *could* have known their consequences. He persisted for several years despite his mother's repeated expostulations. I am therefore compelled to rule that the latter provision of the circular of the Ministry of Justice applies. Having wilfully persisted in immoral acts, you Li Ai-shih, are sentenced to be decapitated . . .'

Numbed by guilt, Aisek accepted the retribution without emotion. Concerned chiefly for his destitute sons, he did not hear the judge's final words.

'The sentence will, in any event, be carried out after the normal appellate process. However, your behaviour displayed mitigating elements. You Li Ai-shih are therefore *provisionally* sentenced to execution after the Autumn Assizes.'

Shaking with incredulous indignation as David translated the verdict, Saul half-heard Aaron whisper: 'It goes to Peking, then. It's bad, very bad, though all hope's not lost. But I fear . . .'

CHAPTER ELEVEN

April 15, 1855   *Shanghai*

Twilight lingered, loath to cede the city to the night, and a violet glow lit the plane-trees lining Szechwan Road as Sarah Haleevie strolled homeward. She perspired freely under her cotton kaftan in the lifeless air, and her split-leather slippers chafed her narrow feet. Broad leaves drooped from the tree's moss-stippled boughs, and looped-up curtains hung half-sodden in the damp heat. Glimpsed through the alleys between the riverfront compounds, the Hwangpoo gleamed glassy flat. It was typhoon weather, the unearthly stillness that normally heralded torrential rains driven by vicious winds. Though mid-April was too early for a typhoon to sweep out of the East China Sea, a storm undoubtedly threatened Shanghai.

Sarah was edgy, and her skin prickled, though she had no reason for anxiety. She had spent the afternoon chatting with her friend Rebecca, the spirited wife of the pompous currency-dealer Judah Benjamin. Their meetings usually left her bubbling with remembered laughter. But her normally spritely walk was leaden; her slender body drooped; and her oval face was pale. She nodded listlessly to the bearers lying beside the firm's sedan-chair and turned through the gateposts with the brass plates reading: S. KHARTOON AND SONS and HALEEVIE AND LEE. Glancing unhappily at that reminder of her husband's ill-starred Chinese associate, she stirred the air before her glowing face with a fan of old-rose silk and fingered the damp tendrils of hair that trailed down her neck.

The door swung open before she touched the brass knocker, and the lean houseboy offered her his customary greeting. His precisely measured bow was halfway between the profound obeisance that saluted the master of the house and his slight inclination to the children. Amused by that tacit distinction between the master and his lady, Sarah was glad to be home. This once, however, the vestibule was not a cool grotto amid the stifling Shanghai heat, but a dank cave.

Sarah's uneasiness lightened when she heard Fronah's heels tapping the floorboards above. When the heels tripped down the oiled-teak staircase, she was happy at her wayward daughter's eagerness to welcome her. Mother and daughter had enjoyed several weeks of unwonted harmony, their mutual irritation submerged in their mutual love. Sarah smiled fondly, anticipating Fronah's breathless account of her experiences in the home of her teacher, Margaret MacGregor. Fronah could always make her laugh, and the Europeans' ways were comical.

Patent-leather pumps adorned with pink-silk roses frivolously peeped beneath a swaying skirt of green grosgrain. Sarah smiled again at her daughter's wearing that heavy stuff for a family supper on the hottest day of the year. Though reconciled to Fronah's studying with the Christian woman and resigned to her wearing European clothing, Sarah was often exasperated by her daughter's consistently bad taste. She prepared to admire the girl's latest extravaganza and, perhaps, gently point out that it was not quite appropriate.

Fronah's oval face was imperfectly veiled by a film of powder, an embellishment her parents disliked but did not forbid. Her lips were vivid, and Sarah knew she had been rubbing them with moist red paper. Pendant garnets dangled on her forehead from the gilt band around her hair, and her chignon flaunted an aigrette feather. Sarah's mouth compressed in annoyance. Even her hoyden daughter should realise such an elaborate hair-do was ridiculous for a family supper.

68

When Fronah pirouetted, her dinner-dress billowed and her petticoats frothed around her ankles. Her green bodice tapered to a eighteen-inch waist clasped by a gold-and-brown-silk sash secured by a gold rosette. The décolleté, set off by cap-sleeves of Valenciennes lace, displayed three strands of coral beads. The long under-sleeves, cuffed with guipure lace, were slashed to show their white silk lining. Her looped back overdress of grosgrain lined with white was caught on her hips with gold rosettes.

'That's quite a ball-dresss, my dear,' Sarah remarked tartly. 'But a bit warm for tonight, isn't it?'

'It's not a ball-dress, Mamma.' Fronah surveyed her mother's démodé kaftan. 'It's only a dinner-dress.'

'You're going out to dinner – again?'

'Just to Jardines for a quiet dinner. Only a few guests. I'm invited because of Margaret MacGregor. The Jardine people are mostly Scottish, like her. And she'll be my chaperone. So it's all fine, you see.'

'I should be grateful, I suppose. But what would you wear for a *formal* dinner? Anyway, I've told you, I don't like your being so much with the Gentiles. What will you eat? I suspect . . .'

'Mama, I don't. You know I couldn't, simply couldn't.' Fronah shuddered histrionically at the thought of pork or shellfish. 'I just tell them I don't like meat. I tell them I have a light appetite and a delicate digestion.'

'Delicate digestion! Why you could eat stones. Light appetite! You should look at the housekeeping bills.'

'They believe me, Mama. Young ladies are supposed to eat like birds. So I have only eggs and vegetables, perhaps a little fish. They understand.'

'I don't care whether *they* understand. The pans and pots, they're used for swineflesh and shrimp . . . milk and meat mixed together. How can you keep kosher?'

'Oh, Mama, not again, please. Papa says it's all right as long as I'm careful. No meat, only vegetables and eggs or fish.'

'Fronah, you're breaking the laws. And being with Gentiles all the time. How can you?'

'Who else can I be with? Mama, please don't be so provincial. This is Shanghai, not Baghdad. The nineteenth century, not the fifteenth. How can I have any kind of life if . . .'

'What kind of life is it, engaged to Aaron?' Sarah attacked on another front. 'When will that nonsense end?'

'Don't worry, Mama. I have no intention of marrying Aaron. He's too solemn and stiff.'

'Marry? Marry a Chinaman, even if your father says he's Jewish! Why, Fronah, I never thought . . .'

69

'Nor I, Mama, nor anyone. It's just for show, and nobody knows, except the Mandarins. It'll just blow over.' Fronah could not resist another barb. 'Besides, I'd rather marry David than Aaron. Perhaps I'll marry David. He's much jollier.'

'Fronah, don't joke! Don't even joke about it. God would make you sorry. How can you even think! A Chinaman!'

'I'm sorry, Mama. I was only teasing. David's like a brother . . . a funny Chinese brother. I do love him, but not that way, Mama.'

'I should hope not!' Sarah sniffed. 'But, you mustn't go so often to these Americans and English. You know you can't marry one. Anyway, they're not interested in you that way, unless they want your father's money. You're only a plaything to them.'

'Oh, Mama, don't be silly. Of course I know. And I'm very careful. I won't . . .'

'I can't understand why you bother,' Sarah broke in. 'I know there aren't many Jewish boys in Shanghai, but young Joseph Benjamin, he's very fond of you. You should be thinking of him, not these louts you meet at . . .'

'Mama, I won't think of Joey. He's a ninny. Anyway, I'm not thinking of marrying *anyone* for years. I'm only sixteen and a half. In the modern world there's no reason for a girl to marry at seventeen.'

'Why do you want to be with those . . . those people?'

'Just to learn, Mama, and enjoy myself a little. It's a big world, and times are changing. We're not in a ghetto in Seville or Baghdad or Bombay. If I'm in Shanghai, I've got to learn how other people live. Some day, I'll see Europe, too.'

'Just be careful, Fronah. No nonsense, mind you. Be very careful.'

Taking the warning as assent, Fronah whirled out of the hall into the dusk, which had deepened from violet to indigo. Despite the threat of the storm, Szechwan Road was alive with hawkers, carts, and horse-traps as she stepped into the waiting sedan-chair.

*

While Sarah lay submerged, her bath was twice refreshed with hot water poured from wooden buckets. Since the amah feared she would catch a chill, she subdued her modesty to the necessities of life in China. Frequent baths were essential in the muggy climate, and the pipes for running water were not yet installed. Besides, there was the difficulty with the tank to store the water, which must be delivered by carts before it ran through the pipes. She did not understand the masculine mystery Saul spun around that tank, but knew it presented major technical problems.

Her delta covered with a wash-cloth, Sarah contemplated her slim body with slightly wicked approval and ignored the amah's chatter. Although

70

she was almost thirty-six, her hips were firm and her slender legs unmarred by broken veins, the nearly universal wound-stripes of motherhood in the mid-nineteenth century. She touched the scar, now white and flat, left by Fronah's Caesarean and reflected that a slim figure and smooth legs were meagre compensation for her inability to bear more children.

Saul was stoically resigned to having no son, though he had formerly railed against the Ruler of the Universe for that affront as if God were an erring elder brother. Her husband's intensely personal relationship with the Almighty was prototypically Jewish. Yet Saul swore with equal passion that he preferred her slender contours to the 'fat cows' who were the ideal – and the wives – of his friends.

Quite extraordinarily, their physical relationship was still fiery after nineteen years. Sarah fervently thanked the Almighty – and implored Him not to withdraw that blessing. At forty, her husband was almost as ardent as he had been as a twenty-one-year-old bridegroom. The young scholar had insisted, not wholly in jest, that he must lie with her at least once every night to purge his body and clear his mind for his studies. He had since then demonstrated most convincingly that his passion was not rooted in his brain, but in his heart – and their joined bodies.

Her thoughts turned inevitably to Fronah, the sole fruit of that passion and the chief source of her present worries. How could she possibly believe Fronah's assurances that her teacher Margaret MacGregor was a strict chaperone? Dr MacGregor she knew and liked – as much as she could like any Gentile. She neither knew Mrs MacGregor nor comprehended her moral standards. What kind of married woman would drink, joke, and dance with strange men?

Sarah feared Fronah was yielding to the lure of alien ways. She should really be married soon, the sooner the better. But how could she be a good Jewish wife if her head were turned by the Gentiles' free ways? Decent seclusion became a respectable Jewish matron, just as a decent distance from all infidels became all Jews – preserving their faith, their morality, and their customs.

Saul was too indulgent and too modern, tolerantly allowing Fronah to mingle with the Gentiles. She was also worried about Saul. Flexibility was, of course, necessary, since Jews had always survived in alien lands by adapting themselves. However, flexibility was one thing, corruption by alien values quite another.

At least one Haleevie, Sarah decided, must defend the traditional values and practices that made the Jews unique. Admonishing herself against false pride, she none the less concluded that she must accept that responsibility. After all, the family, which was the kernel of Judaism, was preserved by humble women, not by rabbis splitting doctrinal hairs. The law recognised the female's predominant role: a child of a Jewish mother was always a Jew, while the child of a Jewish father and a Gentile woman

71

was not. As a wife and mother, it was her duty to speak out, regardless of Saul's certain anger.

She could wait for the best time to speak out, but she could not wait too long.

CHAPTER TWELVE

April 21, 1855   *Peking*

Aaron Lee braced his arms protectively when the crush thrust the burly hawker with the evil squint against him. He imprudently reached under his felt overcoat to touch the bulge beneath his padded long-gown. Rough in its manners and villainous in its appearance, the throng jostled him pitilessly. Remembering the warnings of Shanghailanders to beware the rascals of the Imperial Capital, he stroked the bulge to reassure himself that his money-pouch was still there.

The raw cold rasped in his throat at high noon in mid-April 1855, though the natives rejoiced in their pallid spring. When he left Shanghai three weeks earlier, the azaleas were already glorious. In this forbidding city on the edge of Central Asia forsythia bloomed sparsely, while the air was grey with soot and gritty with ochre dust borne from the steppes.

The young scholar was forlorn amid the alien crowd within the compound of the Temple of Heaven on the southern edge of the Chinese City. To the north lay the Tartar City, where the Manchu overlords of the Great Ching Dynasty kept their ministries and their dwellings apart from their Chinese subjects. The sandal-shaped gold and silver *taels* in his money-pouch, each an ounce and a third in weight, were his only emotional or material security. Saul Haleevie had entrusted him with that small hoard when he said good-bye on the coaster laden with rice, silk, tea, and porcelain, the tribute the abundant and industrious south paid the meagre and indolent north. Aaron was happy to sail on a ship flying the Red Ensign of Great Britain, for the Shanghai seamen and even the British officers were reassuringly familiar.

Although the Imperial Court despised foreigners, it was forced to ship those cargoes in foreign vessels. The Grand Canal, through which the wealth of the south had flowed northward on enormous tribute-junks for half a millennium, was virtually closed by rebellions – and by floods that inundated tens of thousands of square miles as the Yellow River shifted its course.

Aaron had felt himself thrust naked into the unknown when he landed at Taku, the port of Tientsin. The ninety-mile journey from Tientsin to Peking made the nineteen-year-old aspirant Mandarin feel himself an alien within his own country. Travelling in an open litter jouncing on poles slung between two cantankerous mules, he had seen an arid landscape utterly different from his green homeland watered by life-giving streams. His travelling companions, whom he had joined for protection against bandits, were as dour as the haughty camels mincing through the Great Wall laden with furs and medicinal herbs from Manchuria.

Fearful of venturing into the strange city, he stood irresolute among the milling northerners, whom he could not quite acknowledge as his countrymen. He belonged to modern cosmopolitan Shanghai, which was enlivened by the foreigners. He now acknowledged their contribution, though he had often railed at the barbarians' arrogant – and irresistible – intrusion for polluting Chinese civilisation. He certainly did not belong to the bleak north, whose dull people took their pleasures so glumly. The holiday throng was celebrating the Dragon Boat Festival, but even the youngsters clustered round the vendors of paper-and-feather toys or watching puppet shows on portable stages showed little of the vitality of their southern contemporaries.

Moving aimlessly with the crowd, Aaron turned away from the three concentric white-marble terraces of the South Altar among its evergreens. On the round marble slab at the centre of the highest terrace, China's most sacred site, the Emperor kneeled to worship Heaven and his Imperial Ancestors at the winter solstice. That central slab was surrounded by nine concentric circles of marble slabs set in multiples of nine, the farthest auspiciously numbering nine times nine. Aaron smiled scornfully at that numerological flummery and lifted his eyes to the shrine that crowned the Northern Altar: the Hall of Eternity, popularly called the Temple of Heaven.

Awe dispelled his sour self-absorption, and exhilaration overcame his homesickness. At the summit of terraces fenced by marble balustrades stood the most beautiful structure he had ever seen. Surmounted by a golden globe, the three-tiered tile-roof of the circular temple glowed sapphire against the haze, while screens of blue-glass rods shimmered on golden chains before the carved-stone windows. Since China was *Chung-kuo*, the hub of All Under Heaven, the Hall of Eternity was the centre of the world. Aaron knew he would never forget this exalted moment.

'*Ni chia-huor* . . .' A bony elbow prodded him, and a harsh voice demanded: 'Move, fellow! You don't own the place.'

His rapture dissipated, he again touched the bulge of his money-pouch. He recalled bitterly that the Emperor who now prostrated himself in mock humility before Heaven was not Chinese, but a crude barbarian. When the Yung Lo Emperor of the Ming Dynasty built the Hall of Eternity, perfect harmony had prevailed throughout the Great Empire. But not even proximate harmony existed anywhere today, nor even fragile peace. The ideal to which he had just re-dedicated himself, the great family of the

Chinese people, did not really exist. A congeries of divergent peoples was oppressed by Manchurian savages in silk robes.

Compared to the cruel barbarism of the Manchus the evil done by the outlanders they called oceanic barbarians was trivial. It was not the outlanders who had wantonly condemned his father to death, but the perverse law of the effete Manchu princeling who reigned under the ironic name Hsien Feng, Universal Abundance. Neither universality nor prosperity prevailed amid deprivation, rapacity, and brutality cloaked by mock-Confucian moralising.

Aaron pushed through the throng that endured such government with oxlike docility. Nurtured by the fertile south, he stood a head taller than the holiday-makers with the flat, unsmiling faces. His body was lean and his face narrow, its fine-cut features burnt golden by the southern sun. He must appear a son of privilege to the stocky creatures of the bleak northern plain. Though city-dwellers, they looked like surly peasants with pores engrained by yellow earth.

Were they, he wondered, also Chinese? What did it mean, being Chinese? How could he and these brutes belong to the same land, much less the same race?

'Ai-kuo!' his fervently nationalistic friends urged. 'Love the country.' Ai-kuo? Yes, he supposed he did love his country, but his love was no longer undiscriminating. Ai-kuo did not mean that he must – or could – love the repulsive people of Peking. Ai-kuo certainly did not mean that he could love the Manchu interlopers who brutalised and exploited all Chinese.

If only Confucian virtue truly prevailed in China, all would be well. However, vestiges of the moral and legal system that had formerly made the country harmonious and prosperous did persist. The grotesque verdict passed upon his father might still be commuted, and he had come to Peking to pursue that purpose. But how could the natural and man-made calamities that afflicted his country ever cease while a degenerate alien occupied the Dragon Throne? Perhaps the Mandate of Heaven, the divine sanction that bestowed power on a dynasty, had already been withdrawn from the Ching. Perhaps only a *Chinese* emperor reigning over a *Chinese* dynasty could redeem the nation.

Aaron recoiled from his own thoughts. Musing on the possibility that the Sacred Dynasty could be replaced – much less thinking of supplanting the Manchus – was *lèse majesté*. Such high treason was punished by tortures so prolonged and so excruciating their victims pleaded for decapitation.

Aaron shuddered at his own temerity. Hastening out of the park of the Temple of Heaven, he turned north on the Imperial Way, the boulevard running due north that bisected the Northern Capital. Before him stood the Chien Men, the massively ramparted Fore Gate, which guarded the Manchus' Tartar City from their Chinese subjects. Narrow streets called *hutungs* led off the Imperial Way into mazes palisaded by blank walls. Some were barely wide enough for two men walking abreast, since the old quarters of Peking had not been built for wheeled vehicles. Except on the boulevards, most men walked, while a few were carried in sedan-chairs. Peking was secretive, its cramped thoroughfares sinister compared with the broad streets of the foreign settlement and the open shops of the South City.

Aaron turned right at a signboard advertising BENEFICENT YANG, PAWN-BROKER. Loath to ask directions of the natives with their shuttered faces, he followed the crude map drawn by the secretary of the Shanghai Money-shop Guild, which was tucked in his money-pouch between his *taels* and his letters of introduction. His memory trained by his rote education, he could see the brush-strokes on the thin rice-paper as clearly as if they were before his eyes. Yes, there it was, the textile shop with the signboard announcing that it used only the 'long yard' measure of Peking. He turned left.

Saul Haleevie had chosen the elder Lee brother to plead his father's cause. Although such intervention was not sanctioned by the Criminal Code, custom and mercy inclined senior judges to hear such pleas. And who could speak better for a man unjustly condemned than his own son? Aaron dreaded the coming months, when his father's life would depend upon the impression he made on the most learned – and most censorious – Mandarins in the Empire. Perhaps perversely, he was also stirred by the challenge, which would test his knowledge of the complex legal process.

His younger brother had remained behind to visit their father in prison. Besides, David was frivolous, while Saule Haleevie spoke only a little Shanghainese and no Mandarin. The merchant could not have pleaded for Aisek Lee even if the Ching Dynasty allowed barbarians to enter the Capital. The responsibility had, therefore, fallen to Aaron.

Yet he had, it appeared, begun by losing his way. If he did not reach his objective, his journey would be vain – and he would be stranded in an alien city.

Aaron stepped into a doorway to escape the eyes he felt watching through shuttered windows and fumbled under his long-gown for the sketch-map. Perhaps, this time, his memory had played him false.

His elbow brushed against a brass plaque in the shadows, and he stooped to peer at it. The discreet ideograms did not read: KIANGSU PROVINCIAL ASSOCIATION. The new sign said: KIANGSU SHANGHAI ASSOCIATION. Aaron was overjoyed at finding his goal, whose new designation acknowledged the importance of his native city. The signboard he expected over the door had probably been removed to placate Peking's xenophobia, since Shanghai was both the stronghold of the oceanic barbarians and the source of the new ideas that threatened the rockbound Manchu Dynasty. His hand trembling with relief, he grasped the bronze knocker.

'*Shei-yah?*' A voice called. 'Who's here?'

'A countryman called Lee.' Aaron felt tears prickle his eyelids. 'A Lee from Shanghai.'

The door creaked open. Eyes squinted suspiciously upwards in the distortedly large head of the dwarf porter. But the door swung wide, and a smile revealed blackened teeth when Aaron exclaimed in Shanghainese: 'Please let me in. I've come a long way. And I'm cold and hungry.'

The sweet fragrance of ginger and Shanghai vinegar suffused the vestibule, and Aaron heard the buzz of conversation in his own language. Even Shanghai flowers welcomed him. Dwarf azaleas in green-and-gold jardinières glowed beneath a landscape of the verdant Yangtze Delta.

*

'You can't treat them like civilised people,' the manager of the Capital Branch of the Shanghai Moneyshop Guild advised Aaron over dinner. 'Always remember that they're northern savages. The Manchus, of course, but even the Chinese. They're not like you and me.'

Exiles, even voluntary exiles like the plump banker, Aaron knew, often spoke disparagingly of their involuntary hosts. His equanimity restored by the familiar surroundings, Aaron regretted his hasty condemnation of the Northern Capital. He listened with half an ear, engrossed by the delicious food of Shanghai. When he crunched the sweet *tang-li yü*, crisp-fried lampreys, the crackling blurred his host's voice. The braised terrapin was tender but chewy, and his tongue searched for morsels trapped between his teeth. He beamed when the waiter offered sauteed eel in bubbling oil specked with white pepper.

The banker smiled indulgently. He had often seen home-sickness assuaged by the genius of the chef the Kiangsu Shanghai Association paid so lavishly. As the Association's chairman himself acknowledged, the chef was far more important than any chairman.

'Remember they're not like you and me, these northern savages,' the banker repeated. 'They're not just greedy, but unbelievably avaricious and lazy. Don't want to work for their money. Above all, they're devious, crooked as a ram's horn.'

'It sounds as if nobody can do much with them.'

'You can work on their laziness and their avarice, young fellow,' the banker counselled. 'And their deviousness. *Never* approach anything directly, but use silver for bait. Trickle it out in crumbs to draw the little birds. When the fat buzzards see what's going on and come close . . . then bring out your gold to catch them.'

'I'm afraid I don't quite see, sir.'

Aaron spoke candidly, since the banker was a friend, a fellow Shanghailander who wished him well.

76

'It won't be easy. But the barbarian Ha-lee-vee has provided ample funds . . .'

'Our own, of course,' Aaron interposed.

'Of course, your own . . . your honoured father's. Just don't worry about funds, though you'll need lots, but draw on me. And consult me before paying out large . . . ah . . . gifts. Your father put some good business my way in the old days. Think of me as an uncle.'

'I'm deeply grateful, sir.'

'Don't be grateful yet. Just be clever. Any Shanghailander, even a night-soil coolie, is twice as smart as these thick-headed northern savages. Now, I've arranged an appointment the day after tomorrow.'

'An appointment? Who?'

'Master Way, deputy chief clerk for the Ministry of Justice. Those clerks, they're not Mandarins, but they're twice as powerful. A few *taels* . . . silver, mind you . . . will buy his good will and his counsel. Time enough later for gold to buy friends.'

'I'm deeply grateful, sir, for your wisdom.'

'And don't trust anyone! Always remember these northerners are strange. No, strange isn't the word. They're weird. By Heaven, I'll be overjoyed when I go back home.'

CHAPTER THIRTEEN

April 22, 1855   *Shanghai*

Sarah Haleevie had learned restraint from her husband. Since her father had indulged her as she now deplored Saul's indulging Fronah, the lesson was painful, but she had finally learned from her husband's example to control her impulsiveness. In his youth, Saul Haleevie had fought a prolonged battle to curb his violent temper. If she lapsed from time to time, so did he.

She waited a week after concluding that it was her duty to remonstrate with Saul about Fronah's future – and their own. The appropriate moment appeared on April the 22nd, when Saul, having sent Aaron to Peking to plead Aisek's case, put that concern aside for the moment. Besides, the business difficulties that worried him appeared to be resolving themselves. Contemplating the profits from the spring tea shipment, he had almost been buoyant at lunch. By early evening, she calculated, he would be glowing with the satisfaction of a full day's work well done.

Had she known that the mail had just arrived from Bombay, she might have postponed the confrontation.

After dressing with care, Sarah slipped out the side door and took the path to the godown with the counting-house above it. Climbing the staircase to the second storey, Sarah was momentarily abashed at her own temerity. How dared she instruct her learned husband? But sometimes women had to speak out against men's excessive subtlety, which could be the devil's snare. Armoured in righteousness, she swept past clerks startled by her invading their male preserve and opened the door of Saul's office.

'Oh, it's you, my dear.' He looked up from the creased Hebrew document on his desk. 'I'll be with you in a moment. Just let me finish this letter from old man Khartoon. But what are you doing here? Is something wrong?'

Sarah settled herself in the black-leather visitor's chair, which gleamed darkly in the lamplight. Seeing her husband's face drawn, she was tempted to remind him that he should not be working so late every night. She had known for weeks that business was troubling him, though he had spoken only a few words about his problems. She almost felt herself a traitress, but she would not be diverted from her resolution by his worries.

'Saul, there's nothing *specially* wrong,' she replied. 'But there *is* something wrong. I must talk to you about it.'

'It?' he asked irritably. 'What's this mysterious it?'

'Fronah and other things. But mostly Fronah, my dear.'

'If it's Fronah again, it can wait, can't it?' Saul smiled. 'After all, it's been Fronah for sixteen years . . . especially the last year or two. A few minutes more won't matter, will they?'

'I suppose not, but only a *few* minutes. I really must talk with you. That's why I came to your office, though you . . .'

'Perfectly all right, my dear. Actually I'm glad to see you. This matter of Aisek and, now, the old man . . . old Khartoon . . .' Saul automatically smoothed the letter. 'But what's this about Fronah?'

At moments like this, Sarah Haleevie silently praised the Almighty, Who had given her Saul for a husband. They were truly one – one flesh and one spirit. Her fear of his temper and her own imperative purpose were both tempered by his glad welcome and his concern for her problems.

'No, my dear,' she said. 'First tell me what's troubling you. The letter from old Solomon Khartoon?'

'I suppose so. That and Aisek. The judge ordered execution *provisionally* after the Autumn Assizes. So there's some hope. I'm wondering what more I can do. Perhaps more bribes to Samqua, though . . .'

'What of Reb Solomon's letter?' Bored by the interminable predicament of Aisek Lee, Sarah recalled her husband to their own affairs.

'You remember, my dear, I said old Solomon wouldn't hear about Aisek's arrest or our partnership until everything was settled . . . as long as profits kept rising, he couldn't object.'

'I remember, Saul. And . . .'

'He's a tyrant, Sarah, a little brass despot like a miniature idol of Baal.' Saul's resentment erupted. 'He doesn't like the partnership, though it doesn't hurt him. He really wants me to prostrate myself before him like a Moslem towards Mecca. He hates my having any independence.'

'What can he do? Has he threatened?'

'Threats, yes. But there's little he can *do*. Our contract stipulates I can trade on my own. Replace me? Hardly likely. He couldn't find anyone else who . . . and, besides, that would make me independent. But the trouble is . . . you remember I said he wouldn't care as long as profits rose.'

'And, Saul?'

'Profits aren't rising. They're falling, if anything.'

'But how? I thought things were going well now. You've already shipped more tea and silk than any year before. How can profits be down?'

'This damned disruption of trade . . . the Taipings and, even, the Small Swords. The Chinese just aren't buying Khartoon's cotton goods. The import trade's down by half.'

'But he still makes his profits on exports, doesn't he?'

'Of course. Tea, silks, porcelains, that new line I started . . . shared with him . . . fans, leather-trunks, carpets, and furniture. Demand's never been higher. All Europe's mad for Chinese things. He's making a fortune out of Shanghai. And he only opened here on a speculation . . . because I pressed him.'

'What's the trouble, then?' At that moment, Sarah found the sacred rituals of business tedious. 'What's wrong?'

'The trouble, my dear, is it's costing him too much. He's paying out too much silver. And silver is dear. The Chinese, they don't want necessities like piece goods now. They demand payment in silver, though, of course, opium's never been more robust . . .'

'I know you don't like dealing in opium, but you say you must.'

'I must, indeed, Sarah. I'd have to even if the other goods were snapped up. I can't just give up that market. Besides, the Chinese, they're going to legalise the opium trade. They now want the taxes on opium they used to despise. Otherwise, how could they pay their armies? No, I don't like it, but . . .'

'Saul, what's really bothering you?'

'The old man's damned impertinence. How dare I, he asks, how dare I take a Chinese partner? Just as he feared I'm mixed up in a law case . . . treason and murder, which of course it's not. He's threatening to cut my percentage.'

'Can he, Saul?'

79

'I suppose he can. Our agreement stipulates that my share of the proceeds rises and falls along with the profits. Of course, it all depends on his book-keeping. But, if he sends less silver, I'm in trouble. If I can't compete for exports . . .'

'We do have other interests, don't we?' Eager to reassure him, Sarah no longer concealed her extensive knowledge of his affairs. 'The land you've bought, the buildings in the settlement and the South City, the godowns, they're all worth more every day, aren't they?'

'Of course, but only I see that now. I couldn't sell if I wanted to. I need silver, liquid assets. The only other answer's more opium, so I'll have to . . .'

'It's not that bad, opium. Judah Benjamin says it's only a mild stimulant, good for the Chinese, like a glass of wine for us, if they don't overdo it.'

'That *could* be true, Sarah, even though Judah says so. But the Chinese *will* overdo it. Besides, violence and crime grow out of the opium trade . . . smuggling and piracy. The Europeans, there are many blackguards among them. And for Chinese, particularly poor Chinese, opium is a curse. You know, they . . .'

'You're not the Almighty, Saul. You can't change the world overnight. If opium's necessary, you . . . we . . . have to sell it. Why let the Europeans and the Americans . . .'

'I suppose you're right, my dear. We must do the best we can. If only old Solomon . . . but it'll work out. I'll work it out. Now, what of Fronah? What brings you here looking so beautiful and so sad?'

'All her gadding about, she's always with the Gentiles. She won't listen when I warn her. And she says . . . claims . . . you approve.'

It was normally a joy, Saul reflected, to be married so long to a woman one loved so deeply. It was also upon occasion a problem. If he often anticipated her thoughts, she had the same insight into his. She had just revealed how intimately she knew his business affairs, which should not really concern a lady. Did she, Saul wondered, also know his altered view of their situation in Shanghai and their future? Her present concern was for Fronah, but, he feared, Sarah was also dismayed by what she must consider his own straying from the strict standards of their upbringing.

Ruddy in the lamplight, his long fingers twisted the cover of the round tin beside the onyx tray holding his pens. He extracted a stubby Burma cheroot and held it to his ear. Rolling the brown cylinder between his fingertips, he listened appreciatively to its crackling. He struck a wooden Lucifer and allowed the sulphur fumes to dissipate before lighting the cheroot. The grey-blue smoke coiled about his full beard and drifted upward to veil his eyes.

The ostentatiously casual gesture would hardly deceive Sarah. Since he normally smoked only a single cheroot after dinner, she would knew he, too, was perturbed about Fronah. But the delay allowed him to ponder his reply. He was reluctant to explore all the ramifications of her fears regarding Fronah. At that moment, he regretted fleeing Baghdad to escape the Caliph's vendetta against the Jews. Had he remained, he could probably have weathered the persecution and become a scholar of the law like his father. If he had not been forced into commerce, their present perplexities would never have arisen.

'It's not so terrible, Sarah,' he temporised. 'She's only going out to dinner occasionally, and Dr MacGregor's wife will . . .'

'Saul, don't put me off.' Sarah snapped, knowing that he feared her infrequent outburst. 'I'm not a child. You know very well why I'm so worried. It's bad enough there're so few Jewish boys here. When I think of that fat, conceited Joey Benjamin. But you also know she's making herself into an imitation Gentile.'

'My dear, there are lots of fine young men in Bombay and, even, Baghdad. Of course, she's still young, so we've got time to look. Many boys would jump at the chance to come out here. Then, all we have to do is choose . . .'

'Saul, that's the trouble. If she goes on this way, she won't accept anyone . . . no matter who we choose. She wants to be free, she says, whatever that means. It's medieval to force a bridegroom on a girl, she says. She actually thinks she can choose for herself. Sometimes, I think she wants one of those Gentile oafs. Anyway, she's not that young. Remember, I wasn't quite seventeen when we . . .'

'I remember, my dear. How could I forget? To me the perfect age for a bride, but I had the perfect bride. Still, it doesn't mean that Fronah must . . .'

'The younger the better, Saul!' Sarah fiercely defended her resolution against his flattery. 'You mustn't put me off with soft words, though you were the perfect bridegroom. And you are . . . *almost* . . . the perfect husband.'

'Thank you, my love.' Saul, too, was warmed by their verbal love-making. 'Remember, though, we can push her only so far. She won't, I fear, marry younger than eighteen or nineteen.'

'That's why we must insist, Saul. If we wait till she's eighteen, only the Almighty knows who she'll want. She must stop gadding about with Gentiles. I suspect she doesn't keep kosher. She'll be neither Jewish nor Gentile if she goes on . . . just a crazy mixture!'

'I'll speak to her, my dear,' he promised. 'Also, I'll write to Bombay and Baghdad for apprentices.'

'But quickly, Saul.'

'Sarah, we live in Shanghai, not Baghdad,' he continued thoughtfully. 'We can't shut out the world we live in. Otherwise, we won't survive. We can't live only among our own. And Fronah must speak English well. She must understand the ways of the Gentiles, particularly the Europeans and Americans, as well as the Chinese.'

81

'Saul, what's happening to us? What's to become of us?' Sarah impetuously expressed her deepest fears. 'We're changing too fast, and I'm afraid. You're changing, especially you. I wish we'd never come to Shanghai. How can we lead decent, pious lives in this crazy place? We're not a community, not a proper Jewish community. All around us there're Gentiles and heathen. We're losing everything that's important.'

'Not everything, my dear, surely. We must build our own community. More young men will be coming, and, soon, more young women, too. Soon we'll build a proper synagogue. And there are our Chinese kinfolk, the Kaifeng Jews. Aaron and David are very important to us, Chinese who know themselves Jews.'

'It's not the same, my dear.'

'What is ever the same, Sarah?' Saul smiled. 'Every life is always changing, for Jews especially. That's how we've survived . . . by changing, by adapting.'

'But not *too* much, Saul. We must take care.'

'Certainly not too much, Sarah. And we will take care. But, now, if you'll leave me for an hour or so, I'll get through my urgent work. Then we'll have a glass of wine and relax. Believe me, I'll work it out.'

Saul did not return to his papers when Sarah left, but meditatively smoked his cheroot. He started when the embers burnt his knuckles and, smiling ruefully, took another cheroot from the tin. Gazing unseeing into the blue mist that filled the room, he pondered the imponderable future.

CHAPTER FOURTEEN

April 23, 1855   *Peking*

Aaron Lee strolled down the broad Chungwen Men Chieh, the Boulevard of the Gate of Exalted Letters, which the natives called Hata Men, the popular name for that gate of the Tartar City. Remembering his dismay when he thought he had lost his way to the Kiangsu Shanghai Association, he had allowed much time to find the restaurant where he was to meet the deputy chief clerk of the Ministry of Justice. Although he could not anticipate what that worthy would say, he wanted to think about his tactics. However, he must not brood about his father's predicament, since his distress would be reflected on his features. Only experience could give him the impenetrable bargaining-face his father wore in negotiations.

Despite the banker's assumption, Saul had gently warned him that the funds available for his father's defence were not unlimited. If the deputy chief clerk read from his features the desperation that gnawed like a rat at his liver the price would rise. The Mandarins would draw out the proceedings, playing on his anxiety to enrich themselves as the Intendant Samqua had done in Shanghai. Having studied the appellate process, he knew that its stages were meticulously prescribed. None the less, the process could encounter strange obstacles to benefit the Mandarins who controlled it. As he strolled up the Boulevard of Exalted Letters, Aaron deliberately turned his mind to another matter.

Heavily casual, Saul Haleevie had suggested: 'Do write occasionally giving your impressions of Peking, particularly the political situation . . . the mood of the people . . . just general impressions, you understand.'

Aaron understood almost too well. Saul had not told him why, beyond his own commercial advantage, he wanted that information. Since Aaron did not really *know* his reports would be passed to the British Consul, he could in conscience comply with Saul's request. It would have been churlish, almost unfilial, to refuse.

He knew, of course, why foreigners were eager for news of the Capital forbidden to them. For two years, the Europeans and Americans had been pressing the Imperial Court for the promised review of the Treaty of 1842, which ended the Opium War. The five Treaty Ports in which they were permitted to live did not offer sufficient scope for their ambitions. They wanted not only to win more favourable terms of trade, but to open all China to foreign trade and foreign residence. They also wanted the Court to accept legations in Peking, to 'comply with the usages of all civilised nations', which meant the foreign powers. They were naturally anxious to learn what impression their mounting pressure was making upon Peking.

Relentless Western logic insisted that the Taiping menace must force the Manchus to grant their requests. Aaron understood why the reactionary Court feared a few score unarmed Western diplomats in Peking as much as a million Taiping soldiers. But his own logic, perhaps tainted by Western influence, led him to the same conclusion as the foreigners. Having once used force to impose their will, the great powers would not hesitate to use force a second time. Aaron was convinced they would attack again if their wishes were thwarted. The Court was foolhardy to risk that conflict by refusing even to talk with the powers when the Taiping threat was again acute.

True, the danger to Peking itself had receded. The daring northward thrust of a few Taiping columns had come closest to the Capital in 1853, when they took towns only fifty miles away. Poorly equipped and badly supplied, the Taipings were gradually being forced southward. Only at the beginning of this March of 1855 had Manchu cavalry driven the Holy Soldiers from a garrison-city one hundred and fifty miles south of Peking, and rebel remnants still held a town just two hundred miles to the south.

83

Although the heads of their officers must soon hang on the walls of Peking beside the rotting heads of earlier rebel captives, the Taiping threat was still grave.

Further south, the long-haired rebels were resurgent. Despite able leadership, the government forces were virtually besieged in Nanchang, which commanded the chief north-south routes of the Empire. The entire middle-Yangtze Valley was again under Taiping control, as was most of the deep south. While the rebels inched relentlessly towards Shanghai, the Imperial generals were as demoralised as their soldiers and their Emperor.

Walking along one of Peking's chief thoroughfares, Aaron Lee searched in vain for signs that its people were either disturbed or elated by the threat to the Dynasty. In his native Shanghai, he would have felt a galvanic stir in the air. In the Imperial Capital, the sweeping events that could transform all men's lives might have been occurring on the moon, troubling only the rabbit-in-the-moon. Yet a year earlier hundreds of thousands had fled a capital they considered doomed to fall to the flying columns of the Taipings.

True, the northerners were a dull lot, and his nerves were not yet tuned to their moods. He was none the less surprised by the listless plodding of coolies, hawkers, and serving-women in the winding *hutung* he followed towards the restaurant. He could as yet report only one impression. The capital of the world's largest empire was a dull, provincial city peopled by a dull, backward race.

Aaron turned an acute corner into the Crooked Sickle *hutung*. Lively for Peking, the alley would have appeared virtually deserted in the quietest section of Shanghai. A single hawker was crying his wares to sealed oiled-paper windows. The carrying-pole that normally supported two tattered baskets of wizened apples was propped against his crude balance-scale, and his bronzed chest was bare under the tattered jacket slung over his shoulders.

'*Ping-kuoehr*,' he shouted in his thick-tongued dialect. 'Apples . . . the best spring apples.'

The hawker drew only incurious glances from two man-servants slumped on minute stools as patient – and as animated – as chronic invalids. One waited his turn while the other submitted his grimy feet to the ministrations of an itinerant chiropodist. The wicked little scalpel twinkled in the pale sun as it grated across the bulbous corn protruding from a hooked toe.

Aaron grinned. So much for the hectic life of the Imperial Capital.

The Crooked Sickle *hutung* broadened minutely, and an imposing police-post recalled the grandeur it had possessed when it was a major thoroughfare. The virtually eternal memory of Peking set time at naught – time future as well as time past. He had been told of the disastrous fire that destroyed this district some two centuries ago as if it had raged a week ago.

The district had been rebuilt helter-skelter after the conflagration that was the pyre of the hopes of the rebel-emperor called One-Eyed Li. After reigning six weeks, One-Eyed Li set Peking to the torch before he was driven into the back-corridors of history by the Manchu conquerers, who established the Ching Dynasty. Building marble palaces for themselves, the Manchus relegated their poor Chinese subjects to warrens that would disgust a self-respecting rabbit.

Aaron read the signboard between the dust-streaked windows of a single-storey building. Fortunately, he was in no need of the services of MASTER PHYSICIAN TSAO, SPECIALIST IN BONE SETTING. Gold ideograms on the black plaque hanging across the adjoining loft advertised the restaurant he sought: LAO CHIAO WANG . . . THE OLD DUMPLING KING. Although the noon sun warmed the alley, the diamond-latticed windows were shut. Steam escaping through rents in their oiled-paper filled the Crooked Sickle *hutung* with the fragrance of sesame, garlic, and pepper. The same family, Aaron knew, had run the eating-shop for five centuries.

Feeling very young to deal with the powerful deputy chief clerk, Aaron eased the door open and stepped into a haze of steam and smoke. His streaming eyes could identify only the outlines of men and tables. When his sight cleared, he saw three cast-iron vats bubbling over wood fires in brick stoves. Wooden trays stacked on a counter held rows of puckered crescent moons shaped of white dough. Dumplings floated in the boiling water of the nearest vat, and others steamed in circular bamboo containers over the second. Strings of crescent moons crackled brown in the oil of the hemispherical pot on the third stove.

Two chefs presided over the sacramental flames with the liveliest movements he had yet seen in the Northern Capital. Garlanded with steam like priests of some esoteric cult, they wore white-cotton coats stained with soya sauce and scrolled with the scarlet ideograms: *Old Dumpling King* . Their silent welcome was the first heartfelt smiles he had seen in the Northern Capital, whose people normally wore such glum faces.

The narrow pine tables had been polished golden by repeated swabbing in the oil-impregnated atmosphere, as had the high stools on which coolies, hawkers, artisans, and poor scholars chatted. The thin man in the grey satin long-gown did not look up as Aaron approached, but continued to pick at the small dishes on the square ebony table under the rickety staircase to the loft. Passing over the boiled peanuts and the pickled radish strips, his ivory chopsticks took up a miniature tentacle of dried squid with purple suckers like tiny rosebuds. Brown lips unmoving, he waved Aaron to an empty armchair with a heavy knuckled hand – and three jade rings flashed in the sooty air.

'*Ni lai-lar! Hauerh!*' The functionary drawled in the northern burr. 'You've come! Good!'

'*Shih-di* . . .' Aaron replied as laconically to the man who might be his father's salvation. 'Yes.'

The functionary glittered, almost inhumanly still within his lustrous satin carapace. His features, polished to a ruddy gloss by northern winters, were as uncommunicative as an obsidian statue's. A black pearl glowed on his left hand, which lay nerveless on the ebony tabletop, and a string of amethysts interspersed with white-jade shimmered on his chest. His narrow slate eyes were lit by an occasional phosphorescent glimmer like an ancient well.

Aaron's hopes plummetted, and he clenched his trembling hands within his long sleeves.For what could he hope from this unblinking lizard of a man, glittering without and arid within? What could he expect of a soul dusty with the dross of a thousand clandestine transactions? Only that the long sharp tongue would flick greedily from the tight mouth to snatch every morsel within reach.

'Sit down, young Lee, sit down.' The bureaucrat spoke in a melodious baritone. 'And do stop staring. I won't eat you . . . I won't devour your substance.'

'Yes, Sir . . . Cer . . . certainly . . .'

Anxiety made Aaron stammer, and his stammering made him even more nervous. He despaired of showing an impassive bargaining face to the man who could be either his advocate or his enemy.

'We northerners normally eat *chiao – tzu* . . . dumplings . . . at the New Year. But, of course, we also eat them all year round.' The hypnotic voice had calmed many nervous petitioners. 'We also favour *tsung-tze* . . . sticky rice in lotus leaves . . . for the Dragon Boat Festival like you southerners. But the dumplings are appropriate. Like you, we settle our debts when the Dragon Boats race . . . just as we do at the New Year.'

So soon, Aaron wondered, to business? Even a crude northerner should feel it unseemly to signal so soon and so broadly that silver must change hands. But the musical voice went on soothingly.

'You won't find new-fangled delicacies at the Old Dumpling King. No simmered bear's paws or dried duck's tongues . . . certainly no humming birds seethed in honey. Just good, old-fashioned food. Dumplings steamed or boiled to your taste or fried crunchy gold. They'll also produce vegetarian dumplings for Buddhists or mutton for Moslems. But no innovations, except a filling of prawns from Tientsin. They're delicious, even if they're new.'

'I see, sir.' Relaxing marginally, Aaron feared Master Way was soothing him as a chicken is given rice-wine to make its flesh tender before its head is chopped off. 'I know little of northern food.'

'I assumed so, young Lee. Anyway, I've ordered.'

Aaron was reassured. The reptilian Master Way had not departed so far from normal courtesy as to omit the comforting small talk about food that should precede any negotiation. Perhaps, they could, after all, together snatch his father from death.

'I thank Your Excellency profoundly,' he said.

'By no means Excellency, young Lee. I'm not a minister . . . not even a Mandarin because of my lack of merit. Just a servant of the servants of His Imperial Majesty. And, I hope, a faithful intermediary for those who . . . like yourself . . . come to me in perplexity and distress.'

A boy of ten, his straw-sandalled feet tripping on the skirts of his grimy white coat, placed a platter on the table. Bits of shrimp shone pale pink through the translucent envelopes of the steamed-dough crescents. Aaron's chopsticks tonged one slippery dumpling and dipped it tentatively into the sauce. The *chiao-tze* were quite palatable, though coarse in comparison to the refined purse-dumplings of Shanghai. Surprisingly, he was, after all, hungry. He consumed most of the dumplings while Master Way discoursed expansively on the customs of Peking – and watched him with sly amusement.

'You eat well, young Lee,' the official remarked when the waiter served a tureen of thick soup. 'I hope your appetite for the complexities of the law is also strong. I always explain to my . . . ah . . . clients before discussing their individual problems. It's imperative that you understand the numerous safeguards the Criminal Code provides for the protection of the convicted. Justice is equally concerned to protect the innocent as to punish the guilty . . . and to weigh any mitigating circumstances. But can you comprehend the law's subtlety? That's the question.'

'I'm studying for the Bachelor's degree,' Aaron reminded his host. 'I know a little.'

'It'll be a pleasure to deal with a young scholar, instead of my usual ignorant dolts,' Master Way smiled. 'Now attend carefully . . .'

The Great Ching Criminal Code, the functionary explained, provided for automatic review of all death sentences. The Code was in this gravest matter, as in all matters, scrupulously fair in intent and in practice. To give every condemned criminal every possible chance for life, Senior Mandarins learned in the law examined all the facts while constantly referring to statutes, precedents, and special circulars. After a case had been reviewed by the hierarchy of courts, the final verdict was pronounced by the Emperor himself.

'So you now know the magnaminity of the law . . . how it offers much hope to a man in your father's position. The lengthy process also provides interesting . . . and occasionally, I must admit, lucrative . . . employment for hundreds of Mandarins.' Master Way baited his snare with bureaucratic humour. 'For humble underlings like myself, too. Most important, the process often . . . quite often . . . ends with commutation of execution to a lesser punishment. Upon occasion, to a full pardon, though that's unusual, most unusual. But you can certainly hope for commutation.'

87

Suspicious of the deputy chief clerk's excessive amiability, Aaron was relieved by his information that only one in ten among those condemned to death by provincial courts was actually executed. Some died in imprisonment that was, Master Way acknowledged, regrettably not always wholly benevolent. They must, therefore, move swiftly to preserve the life of Aisek Lee. Aaron wondered whether a man convicted of an 'abomination', filial impiety that had caused a parent's death, could hope for a sympathetic hearing.

'That circumstance is no bar,' the deputy chief clerk assured him. 'Certainly not when mitigating circumstances exist, as the Prefect of Huating observed. The family character of the offence, the fact that the crime arose within a filial relationship, is actually an advantage, as you'll see.'

Aaron leaned forward intently. The actual practices of the law, as expounded by Master Way, who was part of the living machinery, were remarkably different from the impression he had formed from his study of antique commentaries in preparation for the Civil Service Examination. For the first time since sentence was passed on his father, the weight of despair lifted from his spirits. For the first time, he believed his father's life might be spared. He drew a deep breath to slow the beating of his heart, for his exultation made it difficult to attend to the clerk's continuing explanation.

Somewhat inconsequentially, he realised how irrelevant his studies were to the manner the Empire was actually governed. He had not, he realised, read a single text that was less than three hundred years old.

'The prisoner is not normally examined again,' Master Way said. 'Normally, no new evidence is called. If the examiners find striking deficiencies, the process is referred back to the original court. But that need not concern us. The evidence here is full, particularly your own brilliant, though erroneous, submission.'

Aaron was pleased by that casual praise – and chastened by its immediate withdrawal. He acknowledged the compliment with a slight bow and ignored the reprimand.

'The barbarians from across the oceans, I have heard with astonishment, allow strange men called lawyers to speak for defendants,' the functionary resumed. 'Our only lawyers are, of course, the Mandarins themselves. The High Judges are so painstakingly just and so well schooled in the minutiae of the law that special pleaders would be an impertinence. Worse, an impediment, muddying the waters of impartial justice with prejudiced argument. However, opportunities exist to . . . shall we say . . . *help* the courts find the exact truth and the precisely relevant statutes. There I can be of assistance. Immodestly I must say I can be of great assistance.'

'What can I do?' Aaron's caution was submerged by Master Way's didactic eloquence. 'What do you need from me?'

'Another moment, young Lee, and we'll come to that. You know, I assume, that, speaking broadly, no capital sentence is carried out until the autumn?'

Aaron nodded. Respect for the spirits of the land prevented executions until nature herself had lapsed into the temporary death of autumn.

The deputy chief clerk explained how the Reigning Dynasty millennia later still observed that ancient prohibition – and ensured that no life was taken lightly. All appeals were first reviewed by the Assembly of the Lower Judiciary, which was drawn from the Ministry of Justice, the Court of Revision, and the guardians of the Censorate, the independent Bureau of Investigation, which was always watchful for official error. The Assembly of the Higher Judiciary, made up of Senior Mandarins from the same bodies, then re-examined every case.

'Your father's case must come before the Lower Judiciary before mid-July if the provisional postponement of sentence till after the Autumn Assizes is to be reaffirmed. We must work fast. But, given adequate support, I foresee no insuperable difficulties.'

'And then? If we succeed, what then?'

'The Autumn Assizes in mid-September. When sentences are delivered. Then, in mid-October, the Emperor's vermilion brush hooks the names of those to be executed, usually only a few. We Chinese are not bloodthirsty, whatever the barbarians say. They are far more cruel from what I've heard . . .'

'And if the Emperor does not hook my father's name,' Aaron interrupted, 'he escapes death?'

'Not quite, young Lee. Your father must escape the vermilion hook again the following year. But, as I hinted earlier, the family character of this crime means he must escape the hook only twice, not ten times like other criminals.'

'Then His Imperial Majesty is the key? And who can even dream . . .'

'There are ways, my young friend, ways to touch the Emperor's heart. Naturally, they are costly. But we can talk of cost later.'

Master Way pointedly laid his chopsticks down and set his empty tea-cup beside them. Aaron rose and took his leave of his host, voluble praising the food and courteously expressing his hope of repaying the hospitality.

'Young Lee, it's been a pleasure to talk with a promising young scholar,' the functionary replied. 'A great pleasure. Of course, we shall soon meet again.'

Aaron's mind was in turmoil when he stepped into the afternoon shadows of the Crooked Sickle *hutung*. Since the bureaucrat's optimism was infectious, his hopes had risen high. But optimism was Master Way's stock in trade. Yet the meticulous legal safeguards he had described gave reason for guarded hope.

Could the deputy chief clerk ulfil his implicit promises? Could he influence the Higher Judiciary? Above all, could he, somehow, reach the Emperor? Those were the chief questions.

No, not quite. The chief question was simple: Would the money-pouch he had carelessly forgotten on the ebony table cover 'first expenses'? One hundred silver *taels* would support an artisan's family in comfort for three years. But was it enough to initiate the arduous process of winning his father a reprieve?

Well, Aaron reflected, if it were not, he would know soon enough.

CHAPTER FIFTEEN

July 4, 1855   *Shanghai*

The Filipino band had been gleaned from the crews of merchant ships on the indisputable premises that all the short, tough men from the Spanish Philippine Islands were natural musicians. On their second public appearance, the Filipinos were justifying the confidence of Whitney Griswold, senior partner of Russell and Company, the chief American trading firm on the China Coast. Whatever their musical deficiencies, their appearance awakened pride in the host and envy in his guests on the 79th anniversary of the American Declaration of Independence. Whitney Griswold had dressed his bandsmen in an approximation of the dress uniform of the United States Marines. Fortunately, the blue tunics and white trousers with scarlet stripes were cotton. At the height of the brutal Shanghai summer, woollen tunics with choker collars might otherwise have induced apoplexy as the Filipinos blew into their gleaming instruments.

The commodore of the US Navy squadron anchored off the Bund was mildly offended by the desecration of the uniform. Too well bred to protest aloud, he had pointedly withdrawn to his flagship, *USS Susquehanna,* when the dancing began. He had not, however, ordered his officers to leave. Set off by gilt epaulettes and gold braid, their royal-blue mess-jackets stood out in elegant splendour among the motley civilians under the octagonal Chinese lanterns hanging from the ceiling. Released from the restraint of the commodore's presence, the high spirited junior officers made the most of the rare opportunity to flirt with white women.

Their prospects were, however, not splendid, for the company in the senior partner's house in Russells' compound overlooking the Hwangpoo was small by Shanghai standards. No more than fifty had sat down to dinner, forty-odd men and eight women, while only thirty men and six women were dancing after some older guests had left. Among those who took their leave shortly after the commodore – and drew the sting from his departure – was Margaret MacGregor, Fronah Haleevie's chaperone. Dr William MacGregor had an early surgery.

The rising breeze teased the scarlet tassels of the lanterns, while the riding lights of the ships in the stream rocked when wavelets slapped their sides. Through the French windows to the covered veranda the far bank of the Hwangpoo was a purple streak intermittently lit by heat lightning.

The Filipinos were playing a waltz, the new craze from Vienna, and Sarah Haleevie's direst fears were confirmed as the band glissaded into 'Die Schoenbrunner'. Parners did not embrace, but gentlemen and ladies touched each other at arm's length. Sarah would have found the spectacle not merely abhorrent, but horrifying, a recrudescence of Sodom and Gomorrah on the Shanghai Bund.

For Sarah's daughter the evening was magical. Fronah's senses were enflamed by the mingled perfumes; her adolescent fantasies were not merely fulfilled, but transcended by the sparkling lights and the brilliant company. She twirled across the shining mahogany floor, a sprite in a billowing orange ball-gown.

She hardly felt her partner's hand on her waist. The American lieutenant was no more individual to her than a resplendent mannequin in a wax museum, though she was not unaware of his compact body in shimmering blue and shining gold. She was delightedly aware that the dark-blue eyes fixed on hers and the sable-black head bent towards hers were arousing paroxysms of jealousy in young Iain Matthews of Jardines, who had, as usual, claimed most of her dances. Otherwise, Lieutenant Gabriel Hyde was just another soft-spoken and courteous American. At, she guessed, the age of twenty-three, he was another old man whose attention flattered and, she admitted, frightened her a little. Knowing she would never see him again, Fronah listened with half an ear to his banter.

'I watched you during dinner,' he was saying. 'How could any man not watch you? You're a delight to the eyes.'

'Thank you, Lieutenant.' She flaunted her new familiarity with foreign ways. 'You must be Irish with that silver tongue.'

'Not at all, I assure you. But, pardon me, I'm fascinated by your . . . oh . . . odd tastes. You took no oysters or shrimp. None of the duck or roast beef, but only fish and *oeufs à la Russe*. I know young ladies eat like birds because they're so tight-laced they . . .'

'Please, Lieutenant, don't be indelicate,' Fronah protested conventionally, though his palm rested on the whalebone that compressed her waist under the orange satin. 'Or I must ask you to escort me to my chair.'

'Sorry if I offended you, Ma'am.' Gabriel Hyde did not sound contrite. 'But, I was saying, you partook handsomely of the fish and eggs. I like a young lady with a healthy appetite, but I don't understand yours.'

'An affliction, Lieutenant. A delicate digestion, having lived long in the Orient. But you're being indelicate again.'

'And I beg your pardon again. I won't be indelicate a third time, I promise you.'

They waltzed in silence for almost a minute before Gabriel Hyde's curiosity impelled him to fresh indiscretion.

'Haleevie . . . Miss Fronah Haleevie. Now that's an interesting name, an unusual name. I wonder . . . Pardon my interest Ma'am, where does it come from?'

'Europe I suppose,' she replied airily. 'Where does any name come from? It's not a matter of much consequence to me.'

'And you say you've lived long in the Orient, a long time for such a young lady.' He remained unabashed and inquisitive. 'And your family, too? In India, as well as China, perhaps. I detect a delightful trace of a lilt in your voice.'

'For a time, Lieutenant,' Fronah parried again. 'Just a short time.'

She was determined that the stranger would not learn what all Shanghailanders knew: that she was actually alien to this congenial company. Since she had not yet learned how alluring the exotic could be, she was determined not to appear different. Failing to snub him, Fronah, who was learning fast, resorted to an age-old feminine device.

'Now, Lieutenant,' she said, 'we've talked enough about me, and I'm not interesting at all . . . Let's talk about you. Tell me about yourself.'

'There's little enough to tell,' he countered. 'School, then Bowdoin College . . . Oh, yes, poor but honest parents . . . devotion to duty . . . and molasses slow advancement through the officer ranks of the US Navy. A banal and dreary career, Miss Haleevie.'

'Molasses slow, Lieutenant? What does that mean?'

'I suppose you people call it treacle, don't you? That black, sticky sugar syrup, it flows with maddening slowness. We Americans say slow as molasses in winter. That's what promotion's like in the US Navy if you haven't been to the trade school.'

'The trade school, Lieutenant?' Suspecting that he was teasing her, Fronah retreated into naîveté. 'Another quaint American term?'

'I'm sorry, Miss Haleevie. I do apologise.' He smiled unrepentantly. 'Annapolis, the Naval Academy, like your Dartmouth.'

'I see, Lieutenant.' She stressed the British pronunciation, *left*enant. 'And you didn't attend this trade school?'

'No, thank God. A naval career's stultifying enough without having your mind set in Portland cement first. But, as you'd say, we've talked enough about me. Frankly, I'm fascinated by your name. Can you . . . won't you . . . tell me more? It sounds as if it might be . . .'

The perspiring Filipinos droned the final notes of 'Die Schoenbrunner' with dolorous gaiety that was more Spanish than Viennese, and the

92

partners separated with bows and curtseys. Delighted that Gabriel Hyde had thought her English, Fronah was equally delighted when the close of the waltz brought his inquisition to a close. He was undeniably attractive, she decided, but too curious and too rude. Too *Yankee*, in fact, far too sure of his own charm and too *damned*, she savoured the forbidden word, nosey.

'Thank you, Lieutenant,' she said. 'It was delightful.'

'Even more delightful for me.' Gabriel Hyde no longer bantered. 'Perhaps we can do it again. *Susquehanna will* be in port another week. I hope we can meet again. Could we . . .'

'I don't think so, Lieutenant Hyde.' She snubbed him without regret. 'My parents would never permit. It wouldn't be proper.'

Turning from the American, Fronah swayed towards Iain Matthews, who was seething on a spindly gilt chair with a yellow velvet cushion the same colour as his fashionably ear-length hair. She had conscientiously smiled, nodded, and fluttered her eyelashes in response to the Lieutenant's unpleasant conversation, the contrast between her words and her gestures confusing Gabriel Hyde mightily. That display was not intended for him, but for Iain Matthews. The young Englishman must not be too sure of her, Fronah felt. Besides, it was a lark to goad him to jealous rage and, afterwards, not placate him, but force him to admit how childishly he was behaving. He was most attractive when most contrite – and most malleable when most bewildered.

The muscular nineteen-year-old was, of course, a regular Sunday communicant at the Anglican church, but his deepest devotion was rendered to rugby, cricket, and brandy. His crinkled blond hair normally framed an expression of vapid superiority. His short nose, growing directly from his forehead, was pointed; his washed-out blue eyes were cunning; and his small mouth was arrogantly curved. His messmates called him Reynard, and he did look like a fox. None the less, the unfledged youth was Fronah's ideal of an English gentleman, who was also as handsome as Adonis.

'See, Iain, I've come back, just as I promised,' she smiled. 'You *were* silly, weren't you? I can dance with other gentlemen. You don't own me, do you?'

The Filipinos hurled themselves into a reel in response to the demands of the many Scots present. Twirling round Iain's extended hand and curvetting with down-pointed toes to Caledonian whoops, Fronah forgot her irritation with the American lieutenant. Her heart pounded in exhilaration, and she laughed into Iain's flushed face each time they drew near. When the reel ended with all the dancers joining hands in a whirling circle, both were panting – and his resentment was forgotten.

Equally exhausted, the Filipinos left the dais, and a red-headed giant wearing a Stewart kilt sat down at the Bechstein grand. He demanded an

93

eight-ounce beaker of whisky and waited until a circle of sycophants had formed before crashing his russet-furred hands down on the keyboard. The giant gave tongue in breathy Gaelic, and his claque shouted the chorus: 'Rabin Tamsan's Smiddy Oh!'

'Oh, my God,' Iain Matthews exclaimed. 'Another dotty Scotch song. Outside'll be quieter.'

The fitful moonlight on the columns of the veranda created shadowed havens. The rising wind cooled their flushed faces and fluttered Fronah's skirts. The riding-lights of the men-of-war see-sawed on the Hwangpoo, while sampans scurried for shelter alongside the Bund. The clouds around the moon glowed unearthly yellow, and salt-spray tanged the air.

Iain led Fronah to a wicker settee hidden in a pool of shadow. She sat primly a foot away from him, fluttering her mother's rose-silk fan.

'Whew, I needed this,' he exhaled. 'They're hot work those Scottish dances. This is better. The breeze and the quiet.'

'It's still hot, Iain, stifling. I do wish the typhoon would come.'

'You could be sorry you said that, Fronah. Look here, can't you come a little closer? I don't bite, you know.'

'But you do . . . do other things,' she giggled. 'Well, all right, just a little closer. But you must promise . . .'

'Don't be so coy. You know I wouldn't hurt you for the world. I just wanted to ask if you can come riding on Saturday? Just the two of us, and the groom, of course.'

'I shouldn't, Iain, really I shouldn't. My mother . . .'

'Oh, your mother! She's right out of the middle ages. You're grown up, Fronah, grown up and beautiful. You've got to see your mother . . . your father, too . . . as people, not some kind of saints. They're only human. They've got faults just like you and me. You've got to be independent . . . think for yourself, not just listen to their old-fashioned ideas.'

'But, Iain, I'm not even supposed to go out so much. They'd die if they knew Margaret MacGregor had left . . . knew I was alone with you.'

'Don't be a child. You know they also . . . well just like any man and woman. You've got to realise they're just people.'

'I suppose so, Iain,' she replied hesitantly. 'You certainly help me to see them as people. No, they're not all wise. And they do have some strange ideas. But I *am* becoming more independent, no? It's hard, you know.'

'Oh God, Fronah, I'm sorry. Didn't mean to badger you. Of course you're getting more independent all the time. And that's the right thing to do.'

He paused and stared at the moon with ostentatious appreciation. His red-knuckled hands twisted nervously around each other. Demurely gazing at her fan, Fronah let the awkward silence grow. He mustn't realise she was just as nervous as himself.

'Come here and put your head on my shoulder,' he finally blurted. 'We'll just relax and look at the clouds and forget about your old people and my taipan.'

His arm twined around her waist. Fronah flinched, as she did each time he pulled her close, but squashed her silly fears. She would show him that she was truly independent, truly a young lady of the nineteenth century. There was nothing to fear. He was an English gentleman, and she was armoured by her many-layered costume. When his arm tightened around her waist and his hand stroked her shoulder, she leaned towards him. She regretted having tormented him earlier, and she was resolved to make amends – within limits, of course.

She smelt whisky as his lips searched for hers. The odour was repugnant but exciting, and the strong fingers gripping her shoulder sent a thrill down her spine. She shivered and twisted closer, feeling fragile and protected in his arms.

'Oh, darling,' he breathed into her ear. 'This is wonderful. You smell so sweet . . .'

Iain had taught Fronah much since their first encounter two months earlier. She was an eager pupil once she overcame her shyness. She had come into his arms five times, each time learning new delights. If she found certain caresses exhilarating, she reasoned, so must he.

Fronah opened her lips, and the tip of her tongue darted into his mouth. His fingertips caressed the swell of her bosom, then traced the cleft between her breasts. When his hand crept lower, searching for her erect nipple, she stiffened. But the sensation was delicious, at once exciting and languorous. Leaning against his firm chest, she traced the curl of his ear with her tongue.

Fronah sighed deeply, his breath incandescent on her breast. But she struggled when he tried to force her hand down upon himself and she drew away after dropping a light kiss on his cheek. She knew just how far she would go, even if her restraint was medieval. And she would go riding with him on Saturday.

She must, however, get home before the storm broke. The sedan-chair would carry her safely to the house on Szechwan Road, where her parents waited for her inspired recounting of the brilliant conversation of Margaret MacGregor, whose side, they would be pleased to hear, she had not left all evening.

CHAPTER SIXTEEN

July 15, 1855   *Peking*

The small windows of the loft above the Old Dumpling King were open to the arid heat of mid-July in the Crooked Sickle *hutung*. A faint breeze fluttered the heaped flour-bags and swirled the steam rising through the gaping floorboards from the cauldrons below. Alone at a small table, Master Way sipped his tea and wiped his face with a damp wash-cloth. Though the breeze was laden with ochre dust and black particles of mule dung, he preferred that familiar discomfort to the stale heat that would otherwise overwhelm the loft. He irritably flapped the wash-cloth to drive off buzzing flies as large as dates.

The deputy chief clerk of the Ministry of Justice had expected tardiness of the visitor for whom he had left off his jewellery and worn a drab gown of second quality cotton. But he had already been waiting for an hour and a half, and he was not accustomed to being kept waiting. Sighing with annoyance, he turned the pages of the scandalous novel called *The Secret Lives of the Mandarins*.

The narrative held his attention for some twenty minutes. He chuckled at telling shafts of wit and marvelled at the pseudonymous author's insight into the foibles of the scholar-officials who ruled the Empire. Trade was slack at the Old Dumpling King between the noon-time rush and the early evening, when patrons would stream into the eating-shop that was the clubhouse of the poor. Master Way cocked his head when shouts from the cooks welcomed arrivals, but the timbre of those greetings was wrong. He resignedly opened the novel again and was caught up by the misadventures of the old magistrate in his favourite passage. Despite his concentration, his head jerked upright when the cooks hailed a third arrival.

Hwan-ying, Shao-yeh . . .' they chorused. 'Welcome, Young Lord. We are honored by the custom of the gallant warrior.'

That greeting he had been waiting for. He closed the book, composed his spare features in mild deference, and listened for footfalls on the staircase. He waited a further fifteen minutes with mounting impatience fraying his respectful expression.

The slender Manchu nobleman who had been greeted so fulsomely was in no hurry to join the Chinese bureaucrat. The fellow, after all, had been waiting only two hours. The Manchu chatted with the cooks, graciously discussing the choice of dumplings and gravely agreeing that it was risky to eat shrimp, which might not have been properly iced on their journey from Tientsin. He sat for ten minutes at the ebony table, sipping jasmine tea,

96

cracking dried melon seeds between his front teeth, and spitting the husks on to the packed-earth floor. Finally, he signalled the boy-waiter to keep his food and sauntered towards the door to the backyard, where the privy was set against the rear wall for easy access by the scoops of the night-soil coolies.

Master Way heard boots climbing the outside staircase and rearranged his features so that the Manchu would see a humble Chinese deferentially awaiting his pleasure. As he turned down the page to mark his place, the door creaked open. The nobleman's straight nose crinkled in distaste, and he glanced with casual arrogance at the clerk, who rose and bowed.

'You managed to get here all right, did you?' the Manchu asked.

'Always at your disposal, Sir Jung Lu.' The functionary's voice was obsequiously low. 'I am thrice honoured by Your Lordship's presence.'

The Manchu Baronet dusted the pine stool with an orange kerchief before gathering the skirts of his blue-and-purple gown and seating himself. Cocked carelessly on his high forehead, his red-crowned hat with the upturned black-brim bore no insignia of rank.

That much concession, Master Way reflected bitterly, the nineteen-year-old Manchu had made to discretion. Otherwise, he bore himself not like the second holder of the lowest hereditary title, which he was, but like a prince of the Blood Imperial. Yet the Chinese sensed another being behind the fresh cheeks and the smooth brow that framed large eyes set straight beneath eyebrows cocked in perpetual astonishment at the antics of lesser men. Despite his cultivated hauteur, the youth's open features were marked by characteristic Manchu naîveté – and, perhaps, nervousness.

'I've left my tea, and the waiter's keeping my food,' the Baronet Jung Lu directed. 'So make it quick.'

'I assure you, sir, I'll take not an instant longer than necessary. The matter is hardly involved, though the stakes are high and . . .'

'You've brought the gold, haven't you, Master . . . ah . . . Master Way, isn't it?'

'Yes, Sir Jung Lu. But, naturally, on behalf of my client, I must satisfy myself that you have . . . ah . . . access. I have no doubts, of course, but on behalf of my client, you understand.'

'You *do* know who I am, don't you?' The petty nobleman's eyebrows rose even higher. 'That I'm completely trusted by a certain lady? You know that Yehenala . . . the Virtuous Concubine . . . and I grew up together on Pewter *hutung*?'

'Certainly, sir, but I must be sure. We're not playing dice for coppers, you know.'

'Otherwise, why would I be here? You have brought the gold, haven't you? It'll be an expensive business . . . very dear. So many intermediaries, you know, the stinking eunuchs. But how else could you manage it? And, remember, the lady is as far above me as I am above you. Her name must remain unsmirched.'

'Wu-yi-di . . .' the functionary replied. 'Beyond question, discretion is paramount . . . in all my dealings. Naturally, I've brought the gold, the first portion.'

'A portion? I'm not here to waste time haggling . . .'

'There's no question of haggling, Your Lordship. Only that my client, who's from Shanghai, could not convey the full sum immediately. But I assure you . . .'

'Assurances aren't gold. Let me see the yellow colour and then . . .'

'It's not customary until . . .'

'Show me!' the Manchu demanded.

Reluctantly but reverently, Master Way placed a cloth-wrapped bundle on the splintered pine table. He had carried it himself. Wearing his normal splendid gown and jewellery, he could not have borne a demeaning burden. But the minor merchant his dress declared him to be would not entrust to a porter the few curios he hoped to sell to a demanding client.

Master Way had expected Manchu arrogance, but not such peremptoriness. Having no choice, he undid the flowered-cotton kerchief and spread the cream-silk lining.

Jung Lu gasped in awe as the afternoon sun scintillated on the seventy-five *taels* and a yellow glow lit the cramped attic. He sat motionless for some thirty seconds while he calculated his own share. After a minute, his hand, adorned with an archer's thumb-ring of white jade, lifted one slipper-shaped ingot. Raising the gold *tael* to his eye, he read the seal embossed upon its soft surface.

'The Kai Lung Money Shop certifies, you'll see,' Master Way pointed out. 'There's no question as to . . .'

'None, I'm sure, Master Way. Who would dare deceive *her*? And for this, I must ask also . . .'

'For this service, you may ask a little more, young sir.' Master Way now dominated the negotiation; it was always the same when they actually saw the gold. 'For performance . . . after *he* refrains . . . another seventy-five *taels*, lovely golden *taels* enough to . . .'

'I know what gold will buy. But what, exactly, is the task? I want no complaints afterwards . . . and no insinuations.'

'Therefore, half now and the rest later, young sir. And be assured there will be no insinuations . . . for my sake, too.'

Master Way was reassured by the nobleman's sudden timorousness. Though similar gifts passed every day, the intermediaries lived in terror of exposure. Their mutual fear was the guarantee of fair dealing. The gift once accepted, donor and recipient were inextricably bound by the strongest possible common interest: preserving their lives.

Master Way knew that such transactions – he did not like the harsh word bribery – were tolerated. But this transaction was particularly hazardous, and Jung Lu's fears were justified. If it were even suspected that a virile

Manchu nobleman was passing gold to an Imperial concubine to buy the Emperor's clemency, he and the eunuch go-betweens would lose their heads. The lady would be degraded and sent out of the Forbidden City. She might even suffer strangulation if the Son of Heaven felt his honour impugned.

The well-known companionship that had bound the Baronet Jung Lu and the Lady Yehenala before she entered the Forbidden City would assuredly kindle the basest suspicion if any word of the transaction leaked. Master Way believed that suspicion would be justified. Even the avaricious petty nobleman would not take such an enormous risk if it were not for his devotion to the Lady Yehenala. That devotion should assure his discretion as much as the threat to his own head.

The deputy chief clerk of the Ministry of Justice was satisfied that Jung Lu would handle the matter with delicacy – the greatest delicacy the callow Manchu could exercise. Still, one could not choose one's intermediaries in a transaction that touched the highest level. Fortunately, the risk was minimized by Jung Lu's justified fears, and the risk was justified by the reward.

'The giver, this young Shanghainese Lee, of course does not know the channel,' Master Way continued. 'He doesn't even dream . . .'

'I should hope not.' Jung Lu reluctantly replaced the ingot, but his fingertips caressed its gleaming surface. 'And for this you wish . . .'

'Only that His Majesty's vermilion brush does not hook my client's name . . . no more. All else is arranged.'

'You're sure? If I . . . we . . . make the effort, I want no discontented supplicant complaining of failure. I'm doing this because she wishes it, but she must not be implicated . . . not in the slightest. You are sure, absolutely sure?'

'Mitigating circumstances exist. With my . . . ah . . . guidance, there's no question the Higher Judiciary will confirm the sentence for *after* the Autumn Assizes. Then, of course, it's up to you.'

'I cannot guarantee, you know, only try.' The Manchu introduced a new issue. 'And you swear this matter . . . fundamentally . . . does not involve the accursed long haired rebels, the Taipings? You swear it, Master Way? If it turns out otherwise, I'll slice your neck myself . . . with my own sword.'

'Your Lordship, there may be whispers. But they are false. Only a few stupid words with the Small Swords, no more. Nothing to do with the Taipings, I swear it . . . on my head.'

'Your head it'll be if . . . I will not traffic with the Long Hairs, the filthy rebels. My father, you know, sacrificed . . .'

'The gallant General's virtuous death is famous. All Peking knows he gave his life to halt the Taipings. I would never be so foolish . . .'

'You don't appear a fool, whatever else.' Jung Lu knew the transaction would bring him closer to the unattainable Yehenala. 'All right then, I agree.'

'And the gold, sir? Will you now . . .'

'Perhaps you are a fool, Master Way. I certainly won't touch it now. Tonight, at the hour of the horse, you will bring it to my villa. You will come alone and deliver it only to me. Only to me, mind you.'

'As you wish, Your Lordship. Tonight at your villa at the hour of the horse.'

CHAPTER SEVENTEEN

August 8, 1855

Peking
The Forbidden City

'We are weary, Nala, very weary.' The Hsien Feng Emperor sighed. 'Weary of women and their oily ways . . . their pretty intrigues and their dirty smells. Yet no one cares how We feel. So much is demanded of Us by so many million subjects. However, an heir at last . . . an Heir is Our duty to Our Sacred Ancestors . . .'

Crouched at the foot of the wide nuptial bed, still entangled in the great peony-flowered shawl the eunuchs had wrapped around her nakedness, Yehenala, the Virtuous Concubine, stiffened with resentment. For several months, the Emperor had not summoned her, but had bestowed his favours on other concubines. More often, Court gossip reported, he had assumed the costume and the identity of a junior prince to debauch himself in the Flower Quarter with warp-footed Chinese courtesans and mincing catamites. She had rejoiced when the Chief Eunuch told her his Imperial Majesty had selected from the silken casket the ivory plaque that bore her title in cursive Chinese ideograms and square Manchu script. She had spent an hour in a scented bath, as well as hours painting her face and perfuming her body. Now this sour greeting from the man who had upon many occasions chatted with her so intimately she had almost forgotten that he was the Lord of All Under Heaven.

'Your Majesty's cares are heavy.'

She consoled herself that he was only a man to be cajoled blatantly and guided discreetly. Actually not much of a man in the nuptial bed.

'*Kua* . . .' As always when dispirited, he used the self-pitying term reserved for the Emperor, who was always fatherless. 'This Orphan *must* produce an heir.'

'Your Majesty,' Yehenala soothed, 'is the father of us all.'

'One princess of Our getting . . . just one small female child from all these women.' He slumped against the scarlet bolster. 'These chattering, useless, barren women. Heaven knows We've tried. But they . . . their wombs are dry, I know it.'

'My Lord is potent . . . powerful and thrilling,' she murmured, still crouching at the foot of the bed so that her touch would not contaminate his sacred person until he signalled that he wanted her.

'The Court Astronomers have been busy with their horoscopes and their wands. They say this night your fate and Ours cross. Tonight, from our coupling perhaps, an heir . . .'

'I am honoured, Majesty, inestimably honoured that, for this instant, this slave's destiny and My Lord's join.'

Despite much practice, Yehenala strained to sustain the extravagant speech prescribed by Court Etiquette without falling into parody that could sound ludicrous even to his insensitive ears. 'I am no more than a she-turtle in the mud, a mud-turtle gazing upward at a brilliant comet . . . My Lord's flashing course across the heavens.'

'It will be well.' The Emperor slipped off his green-silk bed-gown and extended his long-nailed hand. 'This Orphan will get an heir upon you this night, We know it.'

Yehenala crept on her hands and knees towards the head of the great nuptial bed, slithering over the mauve-satin coverlet embroidered with five-clawed Imperial Dragons. Her small breasts swayed in the pink light seeping through the half-drawn scarlet and gold bed curtains that hung between enormous vermilion pillars. She provocatively moved even more slowly than Court Etiquette required of a concubine approaching her master. The Emperor's breath quickened infinitesimally, but his small penis lay quiescent on his plump thigh like a sallow worm.

She had learned, Yehenala reflected with the greater part of her mind, which was unengaged, that this man enjoyed a woman's self-abnegation far more than either the preliminary acts of love or the coupling itself. Glancing bitterly at the orange-lacquer screen with the great gilt double-joy ideogram that symbolized conjugal love, she deliberately exaggerated the awkward waggling of her hips imposed by her humiliating posture. He would be amused and slightly contemptuous. His delight in her ludicrous movements would fan his ardour. No man, not even a deified princeling who was hardly a man, could feel threatened by a woman crawling towards him with her soft buttocks raised vulnerably.

Lifting her eyes surreptitiously, she saw that the Emperor was smiling in amusement. His pendulous lps curled minutely, revealing his small eye-teeth, and she knew that he was becoming aroused. Yet she discerned a hint of tenderness in the narrow eyes that normally glinted with petty rage or dulled with self-pity. His eyes were luminous – and not with passion

101

alone. He was almost sated with passion, this prince who had just passed his twenty-fourth birthday.

Yes, he did feel affection for her, and she treasured the small signs. The Son of Heaven rarely permitted himself to give way to affection for a subject. But his lips now smiled without derision; his blunt nose crinkled; and the minusculely pocked skin over his flat cheekbones wrinkled with tenderness. Although his body was untouched by the *tien-hua ping*, the heavenly flower disease that had marked his face, it was, she saw again with sadness, almost as soft as a eunuch's. His arms and legs were flabby. His abdomen was grossly padded with fat so that, even reclining, his belly hung flaccid, half concealing his shrunken, virtually hairless private parts.

'I am coming to you,' Yehenala whispered huskily. 'I am coming.'

Her nipples brushed the manicured nails of his small feet, and her hands crept up his plump legs. Her fingernails tantalizingly stroked his thighs, alternately darting towards and drawing away from the penis that stirred feebly. Crawling slowly along his supine length, she bent her head towards his thighs.

As her lips closed, Yehenala marvelled at her own excitement and at the rush of affection that warmed her. Giving herself to the task she knew would be prolonged, she knew her own emotion surpassed the grateful awe any well-brought up Manchu lady must feel at such communion with the Son of Heaven. She was actually moved by affection for the self-indulgent body she thus served with so little response.

Was there, Yehenala wondered, truly a spark of love? Of course there was. Beside, it was her duty to serve him and to love him.

Revulsion, too, she felt at his lordly posture, like a Buddha accepting the adoration of a worshipper, rather than a man with a woman. He hardly stirred in any part of him.

Yet she must serve him, as must any Manchu lady selected for the supreme honour. Not only for herself, though the penalty would be severe if she failed to please him and terrible if she displeased him. Not even primarily for herself, but for the imperilled Ching Dynasty, which desperately required an heir. And, further, her duty to her family and her ancestors.

Her duty to herself, as well, to bear an heir to the Dragon Throne. If she conceived a man-child, she would be the paramount lady of the Great Empire. Not the amiable and weak Empress, but she, Nala of the Yehe Clan, which had from the beginning of the Dynasty been at odds with the Ruling House. Not only the adoration of the court ladies and the twittering flattery of the eunuchs would reward her, but wealth beyond even her imagining – and transcendant power as well. She would never again demean herself before any man or any woman, since the Emperor himself must treat the mother of his heir with consideration. Even at moments like this he would show consideration, rather than the recumbent condescension that now humbled her.

She knew exactly how she would use that power to crush the rebels, banish the oceanic barbarians, and make the Dynasty all powerful again. Her devoted attention to state papers had already given her the knowledge to carry out those great tasks. The power she would wield as the mother of the heir was great. The power she might later wield as the mother of the Emperor would be immense, virtually illimitable.

This Emperor, who finally stirred under the caresses of her breasts, her hands, and her mouth, how long, she wondered, would he live? He was not robust, and his debauchery enfeebled him. To be the mother of the Emperor, that was certainly the purpose for which Heaven had fashioned her. Why else was she endowed with intelligence, knowledge, and resolution surpassing any other woman – or any man – she knew?

The virile intensity of her visions somehow communicated itself to the Emperor. She felt a hard thrust against her breasts. His breathing grew rapid, and he moaned. Abruptly, he seized her arms and rolled her over, penetrating her in the same motion. His moans mounted to shrill cries.

Yehenala's hips moved with his erratic rhythm, and she enfolded him with her entire body. Clasping him with her arms and her legs, she feigned rapture. He must not believe only warp-footed Chinese harlots, those play-acting whores, could take great pleasure from a man and thus give him overwhelming pleasure.

Yehenala's detachment was suddenly consumed by her own fire. She felt herself rise weightless, then slide down a silken slope of perfumed grass. She was swept away, borne upwards and outwards in a whirlwind of encircling light. She screamed, and her nails raked his back.

'Nala . . . Lanrh . . . my Orchid,' the young Emperor whispered when she lay with her head on his shoulder, their bodies still joined by glistening perspiration.

'Majesty, it was good?' she whispered. 'This slave has pleased Your Majesty!'

'Good? No, splendid . . . much to Our surprise.'

'This slave is exhalted by your praise.'

Yehenala bridled her resentment. His characteristic rudeness was unintended, it would never occur to him that he could wound her. The entire Forbidden City lived as if reciting parts on a stage, for rigid Court Ritual made actors of them all. She was required to mouth speeches of extravagant humility, while his role, as constraining as her own, elevated him above normal human feeling.

He was, she sensed, truly grateful – in his own way. This time he had not sat up abruptly and thrust her away as if her nearness might befoul him once her body had served its base purpose. She knew he was truly inspired by affection for her – for the moment at least.

To lie quietly entwined with the Emperor like any ordinary woman with any ordinary man once passion was spent was even more joyous than to rouse his ardour or even to receive his seed. At this moment, they were one soul and one flesh. A free-spirited Manchu lady lay beside her man in equal communion as their ancestors had when male and female were equally esteemed because each contributed equally to the survival of the nomadic clan. Such equality no mean-spirited Chinese woman could know with any man, for those simpering females always remained inferiors. No Chinese female could, of course, ever aspire to such communion with the Son of Heaven. Sacred Dynastic Law permitted only ladies of pure Manchu blood to enter the Forbidden City and bear Imperial Princes.

Perhaps the Lord of Ten Thousand Years sensed the love that exalted her. Perhaps his blood responded to the unfeigned raptures that overwhelmed her for the first time with him. Conceived in their overflowing joy, a boy-child would assuredly grow in her womb.

The Lord of Ten Thousand Years. It was strange, that Chinese title derived from the ringing salutation, '*Wan Sui!* . . . Live Ten Thousand Years!', which hailed only the Emperor. At Court no one might speak of the possible death of an emperor, but might say only: 'When ten thousand years have passed.' At this moment, she hoped that time would be long postponed. But there would be a future, even after ten thousand years had passed, and that future must belong to her.

'This time, Nala. From Our great pleasure an heir must spring.' Having surprised her with his tenderness, the Emperor astonished her with a jest: 'This time, after all, will be recorded and certified with the Great Seal . . . unlike some other times We and you . . . This time, We are certain, an heir . . . or next time. The omens require Us to lie with you often this week. An heir, by Heaven, an heir . . .'

'I pray so, Majesty. I shall offer a magnificent gift to the Goddess of Mercy from the little I possess.'

'Do so, Nala. Even a woman's prayers can sometimes . . .'

The Emperor did not rise to the lure, nor had she expected him to. However amiable he might be for the moment, he was rarely generous and never impulsively generous. But gold she must have, gold to buy the offerings of jade, silk, and emeralds that would move Kwan Yin, the Goddess of Mercy, to give a boy-child to her devotee Yehenala. Gold she must have, also, for her mother and her sister. And much gold to cement the goodwill of the court eunuchs, who fluttered through the Forbidden City like greedy magpies, making and breaking reputations with their ceaseless gossip.

Sometimes, it seemed, not the Emperor, but the court eunuchs really ruled the Forbidden City, which ruled the Great Empire. She herself liked those mincing, light-minded creatures, and she got on well with them. But, finally, it always came down to gold to ensure that their cordiality did not turn to spite, which could destroy even an empress, much less a nineteen-year-old concubine of the lowest grade. Above all, she needed gold to win promotion.

This week she actually possessed gold beyond her immediate needs. Her Senior Eunuch had ten days earlier brought her fifty *taels* to sweeten a discreet request from her old playmate, the Baronet Jung Lu. She had smiled at the fond message from the dashing officer, and she had, of course, not asked how many *taels* he and her Senior Eunuch had kept for themselves. Although she had, naturally, promised nothing, this was, perhaps, the moment to try for the favour Jung Lu desired – and to acquire more of the gold she needed badly.

'We have not gone to war, My Lord.' She stroked his chest and began circuitously. 'But the barbarians, they grow more presumptuous and more aggressive every day.'

'So soon to affairs of state, Nala?' The Emperor's smile reassured her that he intended a pleasantry, not a reprimand. 'Yes, it must be that We summoned you for your sage advice, too. So much wisdom in such a small woman's head. We have missed your counsel. Our Ministers only confuse Us with twisted subtlety and mock profundity.'

'Your Majesty is far more subtle and profound than all the Senior Mandarins rolled together.'

'Rolled together? Sometimes We wish We could roll them all together . . . roll them all together over a cliff, so We'd have a little peace.'

'What a beautiful sight, all the pompous do-nothings tumbling over a cliff.' She laughed, and her small teeth gleamed in the rosy light. 'The Chinese cowards weeping . . . the Manchus too stupid to know what was happening. Very comic. What has happened to Your Majesty's courageous Manchu counsellors? They're like foolish women . . . almost as effete as the Chinese Mandarins.'

'You must not speak so of Our faithful Manchu retainers. They try hard, but the Chinese . . . the Chinese with their contrived complications . . . always find reasons for doing nothing.'

'This slave is deeply contrite, Majesty, at transgressing . . . at forgetting her lowly place in her indignation.' Yehenala abased herself before the Emperor's febrile anger could flare and singe her. 'Does Your Majesty refer to the plan to carry the war to the barbarians?'

'Plan for war? Yes, We suppose so. The Empire is not strong enough to confront the barbarians, Our Ministers say. Bide Our time, they advise.'

'I remember well Your Majesty's resolution. Only a little more than a year ago in the Pavilion of Auspicious Twilight in the Garden of Crystal Rivulets when Your Majesty brilliantly . . .'

'It's only a matter of time, Nala. Then, We shall crush the barbarians . . . destroy their filthy machines and their poisonous trade. Lust for gold can corrupt even the proud Manchu spirit.'

'Truly, Majesty.' Yehenala hid her face against his shoulder to conceal the ravages her abandon had made in her make-up. 'But something must be done now.'

'What do you suggest, since you're so wise?' With the afterglow of passion fading, the Emperor was becoming testy. 'What do *you* suggest?'

'Your Majesty in his transcendent power . . .' Her voice was muffled by his flabby flesh. 'Your Majesty can act despite the bumbling Mandarins.'

'What do you have in mind, Nala?' She stroked his chest again, and the Emperor smiled playfully. 'You're plotting something. I sense it.'

'Only a little thing, Majesty, a little thing spun in a small woman's head.' Yehenala played to his skittish mood. 'But it could be effective . . . in a small way.'

'And that is?'

'Majesty, Shanghai is the centre of the barbarians' assault.' She spoke with care, knowing how ephemeral his good humour could be. 'A strange thing happened in Shanghai. Your Majesty's wisdom will know how to turn it to the Empire's advantage.'

'Yes, what is it? Stop havering like a Minister and tell me.'

'I am honoured by Your Majesty's patience. I thought . . . a way to fool the barbarians . . . deceive them by benevolence. Lulled, they won't press so hard. Meanwhile, Your Majesty's resolution will prepare the bold stroke that will . . .'

'Nala, what happened in Shanghai?'

'A Chinese merchant is to be beheaded for filial impiety. They say he caused his mother's suicide.'

'What's remarkable about that? It could happen any day.'

'Majesty, there are two unusual points. The man's guilt is disputable. The magistrate conceded that. Also, he's close to the barbarians . . . actually a barbarian's business-partner.'

'If his guilt's disputable, the Appellate Courts will see to it. We should not . . . will not . . . interfere. Why in Heaven's name interest Ourselves in a subject, probably disloyal, who serves the barbarians for profit? We have no time for trifles.'

'This slave fears she tries Your Majesty's patience . . . and trembles. Just . . . I thought . . . a way to throw dust in the barbarians' eyes. May I speak further?'

Yehenala knew her petition had failed. Nonetheless, she hastily described the trial of Aisek Lee. She was committed to stating the case, since she would arouse the Emperor's suspicion if she desisted. But she would not try his volatile temper by pressing the issue.

'So, this Lee was arrested after meeting with the Small Swords,' the Emperor mused. 'Not only an accomplice of the barbarians, but the rebels, too.'

'In fairness, Majesty, Lee did *not* serve the rebels in any way.' Although

106

anxious to remedy her strategic error, Yehenala was too canny to withdraw immediately – and confirm his suspicion regarding her motives. 'That charge is not made . . .'

She sketched a circle on his hairless chest. Her three-inch fingernails rasped as they flexed, and the Emperor giggled.

'This slave is deeply ashamed, Majesty.' Yehenala began her tactical retreat. 'She has erred grievously. Lee is certainly a traitor as well as a running-dog of the barbarians. He undoubtedly drove his mother to suicide. I crawl before Your Majesty and plead forgiveness for a stupid woman's foolish fancies. This slave . . .'

'You do change fast, Nala, but you are not stupid. We are puzzled as to why . . .'

'Think no more of it, Majesty,' she pleaded. 'Instead, perhaps . . . your glorious vigour is reviving. Majesty, only forgive, though this slave has erred unforgivably.'

'We are not so sure, Nala,' the Emperor mused. 'There's merit in your stratagem. You know We are advised to placate the barbarians. A gesture, say a pardon for this Lee, could disarm them . . . divert them from pressing to live in the interior. Perhaps even divert their demand to send ambassadors to the Capital. Some of Our advisors even say We should encourage Our people to trade with the barbarians . . . on Our terms, not theirs.'

'With humblest respect for your Ministers, Majesty, that is nonsense.'

Savaged by the trap she had set for herself, Yehenala momentarily wondered which side to champion. She must, she decided, only speak from conviction and she must certainly not alter her position again. No longer was only the life of this obscure merchant Lee at stake, but her own position.

'How strange, Nala. Now you respect Our Ministers.' The Emperor enjoyed her confusion. 'You are changeable today, even for a woman.'

'Majesty, I erred. Now, with Your Majesty's guidance, I see how damnably foolish I was,' she said. 'Your Majesty should not placate the barbarians. Not encourage trade or give them life of a traitor and murderer. Ambassadors in Peking? Never! The Empire must drive out the barbarians.'

'Nala, some Ministers feel We should do the opposite . . . for the moment.' The Emperor had lost interest in Aisek Lee, but not in the vital matter of managing the barbarians. 'Some say the Empire can learn from them. Learn to make and use their rifles, their cannon and their armoured steamships.'

'What has the Empire to learn from the barbarians?' Although Yehenala knew this intrigue had taken her beyond her depth, her tenacity and the gambler's recklessness that belied her shrewdness drove her to one last effort. 'Your Majesty means to lull the barbarians by a pardon?'

'By other means, Nala, by other means. We have decided that this case

107

is closed, though We are pleased that you brought it to Our notice. Few would dare do so for fear of . . . They think Us capricious and rigid, We know. We are touched by your loyalty in daring to speak out, however wrong-headedly.'

'This slave is profoundly grateful for Your Majesty's forbearance. I only meant well . . . But I know I was wrong.'

'Not so wrong, Nala, not so wrong. But this is not the way to throw dust in the barbarians' eyes. Lee's crimes make Our head spin with anger. We shall not interfere, but We pray the Higher Judges sentence him to immediate execution . . . no nonsense about *after* the Assizes.'

'Your Majesty forgives this slave's mistake?' She still feared he was toying with her. 'My stupidity does not make Your Majesty consider me a useless woman?'

'The contrary, Nala, the contrary.' The Emperor was delighted with his own sagacity. 'Your loyalty and courage make Us value you more highly.'

'I abase myself at Your Majesty's feet in gratitude.'

Yehenala felt she had received the reprieve she sought in vain for Aisek Lee. Her tongue flicked in the Emperor's ear, and her nails stroked his thigh.

'That's not Our feet, Nala,' the Emperor laughed in high good humour. 'And you've not heard all We have to say.'

'There is more, Majesty?' Fear gripped her throat.

'There is more. To reward your devotion and your courage, We have decided to advance you two grades. You are now *Ping*, concubine of the third grade.'

The Hsien Feng Emperor half-heard her exultant cry, for he was absorbed in admiration of his own cleverness. By promoting this concubine, he had calmed her mind so that she would conceive. He had also awakened the *nan chi*, the ambitious male spirit latent in her. She would certainly bear a man-child, an heir to the Dragon Throne.

*

August 9, 1855 *Peking*

The next afternoon, the Baronet Jung Lu listened to the report of Yehenala's Senior Eunuch with slight disappointment and keen amusement. He exulted when the eunuch told him Yehenala's promotion would soon be promulgated. A friend at court, indeed, she was.

A pity about this fellow Lee, but he was, after all, only a Chinese merchant. Besides, there was no reason why they could not winkle at least another seventy-five *taels* out of the son. Heaven was bountiful. And who knew better than himself how to enjoy Heaven's bounty?

CHAPTER EIGHTEEN

Though man-made, the topography of Peking now seemed as perfect to Aaron Lee as if it had been decreed by Heaven or by Saul Haleevie's God. Quite curiously, that Almighty Ruler of the Universe concerned Himself little with China, except for the few of His Chosen People He had settled so far from His normal earthly domain. Aaron did not concern himself with the discrepancy between the One True God's concentration on lesser lands and his countrymen's conviction that China was All Under Heaven. It was enough to recognize the earthly beauty and the spiritual perfection of Peking. Thus, it seemed, had it ever been, though he knew the city had not taken its present form until the Yung Lo Emperor of the Ming Dynasty chose to make it the centre of the Great Empire four and a half centuries earlier and called it the Northern Capital, while relegating Nanking, the Southern Capital, to second rank.

Aaron's perception of the city had altered during the nerve-racking months between his arrival and this misty morning of September 17, 1855. He no longer saw a welter of squalid houses on mean lanes, but an enormous park on a grid of broad boulevards set with monumental structures. Modelled on Changan, the capital of the Tang Dynasty, the meticulously planned city was almost mathematically symmetrical. Its regular perfection was accentuated by green plazas and emphasised by the irregular contours of man-made lakes.

The Northern Capital was actually three concentric cities, the outermost within a four-mile square bounded by moats and massive walls. In that city's northern quarter lay the Imperial City, a moated and walled enclosure a half mile square. At the heart of the Imperial City stood the walls of the Forbidden City, where the Emperor lived among a thousand palace women and many thousand court eunuchs. All the many palaces and all the chief gates faced south, so that the Son of Heaven always looked upon his people from the north, the supreme point of the compass. All public buildings in Peking looked south, as did numerous temples behind lacquered arches like those that spanned the tree-lined boulevards. To the south of those three great enclosures in the position of inferiority lay the Chinese City, supporting them like the base of a column.

That morning, when the drizzle gleamed crystal on the gold and green roof-tiles of the Imperial City to the north, Aaron walked in the Tartar City, the administrative centre of the Great Empire. It was bisected by the Boulevard of a Thousand Paces, the northern extension of the Imperial

Way along which he had entered Peking that April day that now seemed so long ago. After passing through the curved curtain wall of the Chien Men, the towered Fore Gate, he saw brooding distantly over its plaza, the Tienan Men, the Gate of Heavenly Peace. The ox-blood immensity of its seven storeys beneath three tiers of gold-tiled roofs was the main entrance to the Imperial City. He was, of course, not making for the Emperor's outer sanctum, which was open only to men on state business.

Pausing to orient himself, Aaron wiped sweat and rain from his narrow face with a primrose kerchief. Since the deputy chief clerk of the Ministry of Justice had warned him the Autumn Assizes were open to all, he had started early in order to find a place where he could hear the judges clearly. The proceeding that would decide the fate of his father – and many others – was also a public spectacle.

Behind the double rows of plane trees on either side of the Boulevard of a Thousand Paces rose matt red walls like twin cliffs. On his right behind the eastern wall lay the five principal executive Ministries. Behind the western wall reared the Emperor's instruments of retribution: the Ministry of Justice, more accurately, Aaron reflected, rendered in English as the Ministry for Punishment; the Court of Revision, which initiated the appellate process; and the Board for Investigations, which foreign Sinologues called the Censorate because its Mandarins watched for their colleagues' misdeeds.

Those punitive agencies imposed the fear that ensured that the Emperor's subjects would render him perfect filial piety and total obedience. They were set apart from the executive Ministries because *feng-shui*, the science of the winds and the waters, which the foreigners called geomancy, associated the element metal with the direction west. Metal was hard like the soldier's pike and brutal like the headsman's sword. The way west was a cruel road.

Aaron turned west through a portal in the red wall. He wiped his face again and thought of taking off the oiled-cloth cloak that protected his cotton long-gown. But the drizzle was growing heavier, and even a cotton gown was now to be treasured. Saul Haleevie had already poured out so much of his own gold – as well as the Lee family's salvaged gold – that the well of treasure required to wash Aisek Lee clean of guilt could soon run dry.

Sometimes detached and reptilian, sometimes unctuous and hopeful, Master Way was always asking: 'What are a few more *taels* against your father's life?'

After paying out a hundred and fifty gold *taels* and almost a thousand silver *taels*, Aaron had received no assurance that his father would escape the executioner's sword – not even from Master Way, whose word was hardly the most solid coinage of the realm.

'Who can depend on Manchus? Underneath, they're still barbarians.'

110

The functionary appealed to the solidarity – and the superiority – of the oppressed Chinese race. 'They're immoral . . . simply won't stay bought. But many of the Higher Judges are Chinese. They've accepted your gifts, and they are men of their word.'

Aaron entered the open gate amid a stream of the Emperor's subjects come to witness the Emperor's justice. Under green oiled-paper umbrellas, their black-and-scarlet-striped staffs crooked casually in their elbows, lictors ostentatiously disregarded the families anxious to hear the Higher Judges' verdicts. The public Autumn Assizes, as if the Great Empire were no more than a country village, were archaic – and sacrosanct because archaic. All were welcome, even idlers who gloated when kinsmen wept at confirmation of execution – and grumbled when the judges were lenient.

Its ox-blood walls gleaming dark in the mist, the Ministry of Justice loomed balefully. The Assizes were, however, convened in the open, recalling ages long past, when priest-kings dispensed justice under sacred trees. Attended by lictors and clerks, the High Judges were just seating themselves at tables covered with red cloth.

Aaron pushed to the forefront of the chattering semi-circle around those tables. He was startled by the spectators' jocose air – and chilled by the High Judges' sombre manner. He had expected the highest officials of the Ching Dynasty to proclaim their eminence by the splendour of their robes, as did provincial Mandarins. But all wore severe *pu-fas*, dark surcoats like those the nomadic Manchus had worn on horseback, because that egalitarian garment was prescribed for Court functions. The robes beneath the *pu-fas* were, however, embroidered with multi-coloured wave patterns, and their protruding cuffs were hoof-shaped to honour the Dynasty's equestrian origins.

The Mandarins' ranks were displayed in squares on the breasts of their surcoats. The silver crane of the first grade and the golden pheasant of the second predominated among a few peacocks of the third and even an occasional egret of the sixth. Knowing the Emperor wore five-clawed dragons within great circles, Aaron was startled to see four men wearing the Imperial dragon insignia. They were, he realised, Imperial Princes, their dragons enclosed within squares. He was puzzled by many *pi-hsieh* insigniae like the mythical unicorn that had infallibly pointed out the guilty for Kao Yao, the legendary first Minister of Justice. He grimaced, recalling the ponderous jest about the unicorn that his father's first judge had made.

'Ah, young Lee, you're here, are you?' Master Way appeared beside him as silently as a lizard sliding out of a crack in a rock. 'Why are you looking bewildered?'

'All those unicorn insigniae?' Aaron asked. 'I thought only dukes wore unicorns. But there can't be so many dukes.'

'By no means, my young friend. The unicorn also distinguishes Senior Censors. They're above all other Mandarins in their function.'

'I see.'

'The unicorn, of course, because they smell out guilt.' Flicking a rain-drop from his lustrous blue-silk gown, Master Way was implacably didactic. 'You do understand. The best verdict would be "deferred execution"? Which means never. Also good would be the two lesser degrees of commutation: "worthy of compassion" and "to remain at home to care for parents or carry on the sacrifices to the ancestors". No headsman's sword for that lot, either. At worst, exile or prison. We need only fear the fourth category: "deserving of capital punishment". But your father's case is already classified: execution *provisionally* after the Assizes". At worst, the Judges will affirm the provisional classification and it'll go to the Son of Heaven.'

'We can't expect a verdict of innocent, can we?' Fatuous hope inspired the question.

'Certainly not,' Master Way laughed. 'That never . . . almost never . . . happens. Perhaps two or three times in a reign. But all sentences go to His Imperial Majesty for confirmation. You know, I've been busy there.'

'Have you . . . Is there any definite word from . . .'

'Why should I deceive you, young Lee? One could hardly expect. But intimations, yes. I've had intimations . . .'

There was no point in asking: 'Intimations of what?' The clerk was too slippery to give a direct answer to any question, let alone that vital question. Besides, who could possibly know the mind of the Son of Heaven?

Aaron pointedly turned away, then regretted yielding to his revulsion from the self-important bureaucrat. Master Way was still essential to his father's survival. But a clumsy apology might be worse than none. Instead of speaking, he gazed at the Higher Judges, who were conferring before announcing their verdicts.

'It'll be a while yet,' Master Way instructed him. 'They've got dozens to get through before your father's name comes up.'

Aaron Lee's thoughts wandered while he watched the archaic spectacle. The law-givers of the Great Empire, the arbiters of the single largest part of mankind, were sinister in their black garments. An air of unreality hung over the solemn ritual, an atmosphere of theatrical excess.

The obsessive concern for justice demonstrated by the labyrinthine appellate process was, of course, admirable. But an element of mummery was exposed by Master Way's revelation that only one in ten criminals was executed and almost none was found innocent. The Confucian system could itself never acknowledge that it might err. Nor could its Senior Mandarins reveal grave errors, though they might adjust decisions taken at lower levels.

What man, Aaron wondered, was infallible? Was the Emperor? He was revolted by the ponderous pyramid of the Confucian state with these

Mandarins at its apex. His father, who was a decent, unassuming, and loyal subject, stood convicted of a farcical crime under an archaic statute. Once entangled in the law, he could escape only through this equally archaic ceremony.

The Manchus, knowing themselves interlopers, were naturally more orthodox than any Chinese dynasty. They pursued Confucian practices to the verge of absurdity. Their play-acting was meant to affirm the Manchu Emperor's possession of the Mandate of Heaven, but perhaps revealed fundamental flaws in the legitimacy of his power.

Perhaps Confucian morality, which governed all men's actions, was itself flawed and no longer served the people. Perhaps the Taipings were right. Perhaps the ethical, administrative, and legal structures of the Empire required radical alteration to suit modern conditions. The Taipings' alternative was nonsense, but their analysis might be valid.

While Aaron's mind speculated, his lean body was rigid with tension as he waited. At last, the presiding judge came to the Lees, and Aaron heard verdicts on three men with his fists so tightly clenched his fingers ached.

'Li Ai-shih of Kiangsu, merchant, convicted in the Provincial Court of filial impiety in that he did cause the suicide of his aged mother,' the corpulent Senior Mandarin droned before refreshing himself with a sip of tea. 'Sent forward with the notation: "*Provisionally* sentenced to decapitation after the Autumn Assizes."

The rain quickened, and a grove of green umbrellas sprouted over the spectators. The crackling as the umbrellas opened masked the judge's voice, and Aaron leaned forward to hear better.

'. . . has certain interesting features and has occasioned much discussion.' The judge observed, and Aaron hoped. 'The reviewing judges felt the mitigating circumstances merited the most thorough review and are agreed that it was not the intent of the convicted to cause his mother's suicide. That is clear.

'I could expatiate on the matter at some length. However, time presses, and others wait for justice. Yet, I must, in fairness, cite two precedents.'

For four minutes the Mandarin drew analogies between the case of the merchant Li Ai-shih in the third year of the reign of the Hsien Feng Emperor and the case of a certain carpenter Wu Chien-hsin in the fifty-fifth year of the Kang Hsi Emperor. For three additional minutes he discussed parallels to the crime of one Chang of Hunan, given name lost in the mists of time, since his transgression had occurred in the twelfth year of the reign of the Hung Wu Emperor of the Ming Dynasty, almost four centuries earlier.

'Accordingly, the judges felt that a measure of mercy might be called for,' the judge declared. 'We have considered the mitigating circumstances very carefully . . .'

Aaron was elated. Whether the merits of the case or Master Way's

113

intrigues had carried the verdict, he would never know. He smiled triumphantly at that virtuous official, who stood smugly behind the seated judge.

'. . . realised when greater wisdom pointed out to the court,' the judge was summing up, 'that the case, whatever its merits, concerned an abomination. Matricide, however hedged with mitigating circumstances, remains an abomination.'

The blood pounding in Aaron's ears drowned the judge's monotone. Seconds later, he heard again: 'Accordingly, the word *provisional* is stricken from the lower court's judgement. The verdict is: "Deserving capital punishment."'

Shock stunned Aaron. Bile rose in his throat, and he retched. He leaned forward, a yellow stream erupting from his mouth. He felt himself falling.

'You're all right, aren't you, young Lee?' The unctuous tones of Master Way were distant.

Aaron lay on the ground, his head pillowed on the clerk's knee. He shook his head, and his vision cleared. Of course! The tension had been too much for him. He had fainted before the verdict was pronounced. He tried to stand in order to hear the judge clearly, but Master Way's hands held him down.

'Of course, it must still be confirmed by His Imperial Majesty,' the deputy chief clerk was saying. 'All is not lost. I'll ask no great number of *taels* . . . Only that little which is absolutely essential. Remember there is still hope, much hope. Remember only one in ten is executed. Remember His Majesty's clemency is . . .'

Aaron looked up at the cold eyes and shook his head wearily. He made the hardest decision of his life in the next instant. He would not pour out more gold, since it would do no good. His father would not wish further vain expenditure, which would make the family paupers, reducing his brother and himself to penniless vagabonds.

Aaron was not resigned, but enraged. They had mulcted him mercilessly, the officials of the Northern Capital, playing with him like vicious cats with a stupid moth. He was grief-stricken and furious, but he could do no more.

He could only return to tell his father all hope was gone. The least he could do, the most he could do, was tell his father himself. He must bring the dreaded news before the ponderous machinery of mock justice reported the verdict to Shanghai.

He alone must tell his father in mercy, though it would be excruciating for himself. Aisek Lee would hear his sentence of death from the lips of his eldest son.

114

CHAPTER NINETEEN

Saul Haleevie touched the tan fabric distastefully. Though raw-silk, the pongee felt coarse to his fingertips. The beige cotton nankeen was considered supple, but crumpled stiffly. And those were the light stuffs for wear during the interminable Shanghai summer, which in late September gave no sign of loosening its damp grip. The flannels and worsteds of the winter suits hanging like decapitated apparitions along his office wall would be more uncomfortable.

He had finally made up his mind two weeks earlier, and he would not alter his decision. The hardest part would be explaining to Sarah, particularly after the climactic conversation last June that revealed her insecurity. She had during the intervening months frequently referred to her fear that they were in danger of losing their essential Jewish identity because they were adapting too rapidly to the alien ways of the foreign settlement.

Saul stroked the shimmering silk of his white robe with regret. He gazed fondly at the broad sash embroidered with gold thread and sadly folded the long turban with the intricate tassels. He would, of course, wear those garments, his father's farewell presents in Baghdad, in the synagogue on the Sabbath and the Holy Days. But, on all other days, he would wear the garb of the Europeans and Americans who were his competitors.

He smiled wryly. Perhaps he should tell Sarah he had only at the last moment decided against assuming Chinese dress – like some Christian missionaries. As if a man with round eyes and a big nose were less conspicuous because he wore a long-gown and in some cases grew a queue. Recovering from that fright, she might be reconciled to his appearance in bifurcated European trousers, more like a radish than a man, as the Chinese said. However she felt, the European suits were not only undignified, but constraining after the loose robes he had worn all his life – and his forefathers for millennia. That clothing was, however, not conspicuous in the foreign settlement, and there was much to be said for being inconspicuous.

He might also have to force himself to find another Chinese associate – a comprador, however, not a partner. No one could replace Aisek, and he waited anxiously for Aaron's report from Peking on the verdict of the Autumn Assizes. He still hoped his lavish bribes would buy Aisek's life, but he had to be practical. No European could do business in Shanghai without a Chinese intermediary.

115

Sighing deeply, Saul folded his robe and turban on the great rosewood chest he had rescued from Aisek's house before the bailiffs arrived. When he opened the lid, a pungent aroma billowed through the office. With customary Chinese ingenuity, the unknown carpenter had a century earlier lined the chest with camphor-wood to ward off moths. As he laid the garments in the chest, Saul felt he was interring the better part of his past. He closed the lid decisively.

He would, of course, never desert his Jewish heritage, but it was necessary to adapt. His beard, which was not conspicuous in a hirsute age, he would, in any event, have retained all his life as the law required. He would always cover his head in deference to the Almighty, even if only with a small skullcap. Unlike his daughter Fronah, Saul had no desire to obscure his origins. However, Shanghai was his future, while Baghdad was his past. He must, therefore, shape himself to his milieu without violating the tenets of his religion. He could no more repudiate his burdensome but glorious heritage than he could cut off his right hand.

That ancient heritage had won Saul respect among the Chinese, who were obsessed with tradition. Though their records were sparse until the sixth century of the Christian era, ha-Levis had been settled in Baghdad since the Babylonian captivity 2,500 years ago. Some had followed the Patriarch Abraham when the Emperor Cyrus allowed the Jews to depart, but his branch had remained. A few centuries in Spain before their return to Baghdad were only an instant in their history. The ha-Levis had prospered as merchants, while remaining scholars. He had himself been trained as a teacher of the law who was to be supported in his holy studies by his ancestors' wealth.

Saul was shattered when the Caliph's persecution forced him to make his life elsewhere. He venerated Baghdad, which none the less now seemed as remote as Eden. Bombay he hardly regretted, though it had been the first refuge for Sarah and himself, but he bitterly regretted being forced to give up scholarship for commerce. Shanghai was no more than a convenient place to make a living when he casually came to China twelve years earlier. He had suspected that he would not return to Baghdad or Bombay when he sent for Sarah and the infant Fronah two years later. He now knew that China had entered into his soul.

Guiltily aware that he had smoked six cheroots, Saul realised that the fug in his office overpowered the pungent scent of tea-leaves seeping from the lead-lined chests in the godown below. He opened the window and gazed at the angry face of the Hwangpoo across the rooftops. Muddy waves pranced on the river, while the lights of anchored ships rocked madly. Spray obscured the pagoda thrusting into the flickering moonlight on the far bank. The typhoon now approaching must this time, it appeared, strike the city.

The typhoon was coming on fast. It would clear the oppressive atmosphere, leaving a legacy of glorious weather for a few days. It would also kill or maim hundreds, wrecking frail Chinese dwellings and even some solid European structures. In China a blessing for some was invariably a disaster for others.

Saul closed the window and lit another cheroot. The rain hammering on the glass was an obbligato to his thoughts.

His personal tastes had also altered. Even more than the lamb curries, the cracked wheat with mint, and the yoghurt of Iraq and India, he now enjoyed delicate Chinese vegetable dishes, particularly the ingenious *su-tsai* of the vegetarian Buddhists. Those perfect replicas of sausages were made from pressed soya-bean curd. Sarah, too, was fond of chicken, duck, and goose prepared in a hundred different Chinese ways – after ritual kosher slaughter. Terrapin and lobster were like eel and oysters, of course, forbidden to them. That deprivation he could bear easily, though he was occasionally curious as to their taste.

Sarah had originally refused to eat food prepared by their servants. She feared they would use the same pots for milk and meat, perhaps even unclean swineflesh. She had finally yielded, knowing she must give a little to Shanghai customs if she were to be happy in Shanghai. No foreigner could live in the Treaty Port without a multitude of servants. Having taught the cooks the complex rules of *kashruth*, she presently contented herself with frequently inspecting the kitchens. Since the adaptable Chinese now believed firmly that observing the dietary laws was essential to the foreign recipes, she never caught them contaminating the utensils – or failing to prepare their own food in their own separate kitchen.

His changing taste in food was but part of his own transformation, though food was important to Saul, whose ascetic appearance concealed his sensual nature. He had also discovered an affinity for the plastic arts, which the austere Jewish tradition held in distaste. He did not himself paint, but he was moved by Chinese paintings, whether misty and suggestive or precise and literal. Abstract arabesques and Persian minia-tures now appeared childish beside sophisticated Chinese art. Stacked among the silk-covered boxes containing his treasured scrolls were others shaped to hold cobalt blue and white vases of the Ming Dynasty and willow-green celadon bowls of the Sung. Many coloured jardinières and golden brush-washers made during the present Dynasty were in daily use throughout the house. Sarah complained that they were dust-catchers and, more pointedly, that those ornaments defiled the dwelling of a pious reb, but he had several times surprised her stroking the glowing porce-lains.

He would, Saul resolved, remain essentially unchanged, but he would also enjoy the varied delights of his new home. He could, of course, never become Chinese, nor did he wish to. Despite his new attire, he would never be an integral member of the foreign settlement. Set apart

117

by his religious practices, above all by the dietary laws, he would always be an outsider to the Europeans and Americans of Shanghai.

Besides, that community was by no means as attractive to him as it was to his daughter. The foreigners, were, with a few exceptions, a dull lot. Most demonstrated mental agility only in their extraordinary conviction that Saul Haleevie and the Chinese were aliens in Shanghai, but not themselves. Yet this arrogant assumption was not wholly fallacious, for the foreigners had created their own unique world in the city on the mudflats.

Most foreigners also contended that the Chinese had compelled them to use armed might to hew out the Treaty Ports. What else could one do with a nation so pig-headed it otherwise refused to enter into equal commercial and diplomatic relations with other nations? The Jesuits, wrong-headed though they were otherwise, had actually striven to bring China and Europe together in harmony in the seventeenth century. Introducing modern science and initially winning many influential converts, including a Grand Chancellor, they had finally been rejected by the Manchu Dynasty long after it conquered the Empire in 1644. Embassies from many European nations had in the interim been received with perfect courtesy and total incomprehension. Only sixty years ago, the Chien Lung Emperor had sent packing an Embassy under the Earl Macartney. Dynastic Law, Chien Lung's Rescript declared, prohibited residence in his Northern Capital by the ambassadors of other nations, which were all manifestly inferior to China. What need had China, the Rescript asked rhetorically, to obtain foreign manufactures by trade, since it possessed all wealth, all inventions, and all wisdom within its own extensive borders?

The Chinese had, of course, traded, since they were no less avaricious than other peoples. But the restrictions they imposed finally convinced the foreigners that they wished to make peaceful and profitable commerce impossible. War had broken out in 1839 because of those Chinese restrictions, above all the Chinese refusal to permit free import of opium. The drug was, however, almost a side-issue, no more than the immediate cause of conflict that had long been inevitable.

Victorious in that small war, the foreign powers had wrung many concessions from the Chinese, chiefly the opening of five Treaty Ports to foreign trade and foreign residence. They were not, however, satisfied, since the remaining Chinese restrictions – like the refusal to accept permanent embassies in Peking – were manifestly unreasonable. The humiliated Manchus meanwhile brooded on revenge, which would restore their Chinese subjects' respect for their prowess. Though rebellions were not caused by the foreigners' military superiority, the Taiping Revolt was certainly stimulated by demonstrated Manchu weakness. Many conflicts still smouldered behind the ramshackle facade of Sino-European amity.

Saul checked his errant thoughts, though analysing Sino-European relations was no mere intellectual exercise. The past would determine the future, and he must see its shape clearly if he were to prosper. However, at the moment, more pressing matters than historical reflection demanded his attention.

Saul ground out his seventh cheroot, disgusted by their acrid stench and their stale smoke. He emptied his brimming ashtray and placed the lacquered waste-paper container outside the door. The wind was wailing through the corridors.

Thoughtlessly, he opened the window to air his office, and the gale flung it against the outside wall. He could not hear broken glass tinkle to the ground above the wind's roar and the rain's hammering. A curtain of water concealed the Hwangpoo only fifty yards away. He could not see the riding lights of the ships tearing at their anchors. Groping for the latches, he pulled the storm-shutters closed.

The weather, he remembered as he dried his hands and face, had been different when he returned to Shanghai from his last trip to Bombay two years earlier. He had felt he was coming home to the raw, brawling community in the sunlight. As his ship turned the bend into the coffee-silted Hwangpoo from the mud-dark Yangtze, he had for the first time realised that China might be his home for the rest of his life. He had not then considered the implications for Sarah and Fronah, but he must think of them now, particularly Fronah.

Sarah had been obsessed by their daughter's behaviour for the past few months. Fronah was undeniably difficult, particularly her infatuation with Gentile ways. But she was not yet the appalling problem her mother believed her. Young girls were always skittish. Sarah herself had been almost as wilful at the same age, though fathers in the closed society of Jewish Baghdad exercised far stricter control than he could in the heterogeneous foreign settlement.

Still, better Fronah gifted and high-spirited than Fronah bovine and docile. He could not prevent her trying her wings. He must trust to the moral values he and Sarah had inculcated to prevent Fronah's making irreparable mistakes. He was confident that she would desert neither her parents nor her faith to chase after the will o' the wisp glamour of the Gentiles. But there was no harm – indeed, much good – in curbing her gently. He had already told her that she must spend less time with her new friends and that he would no longer lavish expensive dresses on her. In those respects, Sarah was absolutely right.

Sarah was also right in insisting that they find Fronah a bridegroom. He did not wish to see his daughter married within the next year, but married she must be by the time she was nineteen. Although there were, unfortunately, no suitable young men in Shanghai or Hong Kong, the Gubbis and the Kadoories of Bombay had long intermarried with the Haleevies. Marking three young men of those families as prospective suitors, he had already invited them to Shanghai as apprentices. Assisted

119

by discreet pressure, propinquity and their common heritage should do the rest.

Saul restlessly cracked the shutters ajar, but the wind did not try to snatch them from his hands. The rain was lighter, and he glimpsed red and yellow riding-lights rocking on the Hwangpoo. So much for the typhoon, which looked as if it were bypassing Shanghai, though it might be gathering its force to strike again.

So much, too, for Fronah – for the moment. Aisek Lee was as great a worry. He was very fond of his partner, and he urgently needed a Chinese associate. Chinese law, which had capriciously condemned Aisek, might free him as capriciously. But the appeal might be rejected by the Autumn Assizes and by the debauched Hsien Feng Emperor. He was, moreover, bound by honour as well as affection to provide for Aaron and David. Aisek would probably not have been convicted of the fantastic crime of 'matricide by inciting to suicide' if he had not been associated with a barbarian. Besides, the young Chinese Jews could prove as useful to him as he could to them.

Bereft of his protection, Aaron and David would be destitute and homeless. The law had condemned them as surely as their father for his offence against the canon of filial piety. Since the continuing well-being of the family was the chief desire of all Chinese, Aisek would be tormented by his sons' bleak prospects. Worst of all, no line of descendants, respected because they were prosperous and influential, would pay homage to his memory. If the verdict were upheld, the boys' lives would be blighted – unless he, Saul Haleevie, intervened.

The best he could do for Aisek, Saul concluded, was also the best he could do for the boys. With his partner's consent, he would adopt Aaron and David, thus allaying Aisek's fears for their future. A Chinese practice of great antiquity and respectability, adoption would also relieve the boys of the opprobrium of a natural father who was an 'abominable' criminal. They would undoubtedly honour Aisek's memory, though formally enjoined from doing so. Adoption was not a perfect solution, but he could best assist the boys by entering into a formal relationship recognised by both British and Chinese law.

Sarah would undoubtedly protest, but she would finally accept the boys willingly. He would give Aaron and David proper religious training, but he would not press them to live as orthodox Jews. Doing so could make them outcasts in their own country, though the Chinese were normally tolerant of all religions. He would encourage them to broaden their study of English and 'Western learning,' as the Chinese called it. They must, further, continue their rigorous tuition in the Confucian Classics so that they could take the Civil Service Examinations and become Mandarins.

The Almighty, diligently reminded, would undoubtedly reward his philanthropy. If either Aaron or David chose instead to assume Aisek's partnership, the firm of Haleevie and Lee would be immeasurably strengthened. Whoever did so would share almost equally with Fronah and her future husband, since he would be the indispensable link to the Chinese community. If either should become an official instead, it would do Saul Haleevie no harm to have a Chinese son who was a powerful Mandarin.

Saul was drawn again to the window. The shutters opened easily, for the wind had subsided. He could see many lights rocking gently on the Hwangpoo. Errant moonbeams lit the face of the river as the clouds opened. The typhoon had thrown its fury against unfortunates elsewhere, hardly brushing the charmed city of Shanghai.

CHAPTER TWENTY

Peking
October 21, 1855   *The Forbidden City*

Cold and pure, dawn over the Forbidden City pierced the eyeballs of the Senior Mandarins with pain. The white-marble balustrades of the Hall of Earnest Diligence glistened cruel and hard, as if they would slice any hand that touched them. Twenty-four Mandarins kneeled before a dais as if frozen within an immense crystal cube.

The Senior Mandarins of the Great Pure Dynasty were assembled before the Dragon Throne to witness the Emperor's verdict of mercy – or punishment – for criminals already judged by his courts. Despite their padded robes, the Grand Chancellors, Ministers, and Senior Censors shivered in the unheated chamber. Over their surcoats they wore the coarse white garments of mourning prescribed for the proceedings that would send scores to the execution ground.

The young Hsien Feng Emperor was sallow in the pitiless light reflected from his own white robe. But a secret smile quirked his flaccid lips, and his narrow eyes shone with furtive joy.

Composing his expression into solemnity, the Emperor glanced at the lists of the condemned laid on the white-covered table by a kneeling minister. But delight hovered irrepressibly in his downcast eyes. Yehenala, the Virtuous Concubine, had the previous afternoon been examined by the Palace Physicians, who could, of course, not touch her, but only inquire as to her symptoms. The Emperor *knew* she would bear a man-child, the heir the Sacred Dynasty desperately required. The future of the realm was assured, since all the threats to his reign would be dissipated when Nala

121

gave him a boy. In the spring when the heir was born, the Ching Dynasty would be reborn.

The Emperor's plump fingers lifted an ivory brush with the sable bristles and dipped it into the vermilion pool in the jet inkstone. Delicately, almost playfully, he twirled the bristles into a point and shook off the excess ink. The brush would descend, apparently at random, to check the names of those who were to die.

Most presented no problem, and most would live. He had listlessly approved the arrangement of the columns of ideograms, agreeing without questions to lenience or severity. No case evoked his particular interest.

Yet one he remembered. What was the fellow's name? Yes, of course, Lee, Lee Ai-shih, a merchant of Shanghai, condemned for matricide. The wretch was mixed up with the barbarians and the rebels. Yehenala, he recalled, had suggested he placate the barbarians by reprieving this Lee. But the crime was heinous and the circumstances horrifying. He had, instead, intervened directly, indicating his displeasure to the Higher Judges, who were planning to reduce the sentence. He had thus assured that the criminal would be classified as 'deserving capital punishment'. Death this Lee certainly deserved for his abominable crime, not to speak of conspiring with rebels and barbarians.

The vermilion bristles hovered, desultorily checking one name in every twenty. The Emperor barely glanced at the list, since the black ideograms were arranged so that he already knew exactly where to flick his brush. But he saw the name of Lee Ai-shih, the vicious criminal. Lee the Lover of Truth, the name meant. Lover of truth, indeed! The ivory handle descended to check that name boldly.

The brush halted a millimeter above the paper, then withdrew. The tip hovered above the ideograms Lee Ai-shih, dripping a vermilion fleck on the name below, which had been scheduled for reprieve. Why waste his time on a man who had killed his mother as surely as if he'd drawn the noose tight himself? The brush descended decisively.

The white-clad Mandarins stared in astonishment. The Emperor was sitting as if paralyzed, his brush poised above the list. In the former reigns of conscientious sovereigns, the rendering of the Emperor's mercy had occasionally been interrupted by last minute reflections. But in this reign never. For four years, the present Son of Heaven had been content to check those names his counsellors advised, anxious to complete the boring ritual.

It would do no harm, the Emperor pondered, to spare one criminal for state purposes. Throwing dust in the eyes of the interlopers from across the oceans would be a secret delight. Besides, it would please Nala, and it was essential to please Nala at this moment. If she were content and gratified, she would undoubtedly bear a boy. He was already certain the child would be a boy, but there was every reason to reinforce the propitious omens.

Nonsense, the Emperor decided, total nonsense. Why spare a man whose death would positively benefit the Dynasty by demonstrating that stringent punishment invariably followed a severe infraction of the Criminal Code? The omens could look after themselves.

The vermilion bristles circled the three ideograms Li Ai-shih. Not merely a check-mark, but a circle. The brush went on briskly to check the next name selected for execution.

'We have circled one name, that of Lee Ai-shih.' The Emperor looked up at his Senior Mandarins sheepishly. 'For reasons of state, we have circled that name. This Lee's sentence is immediately commuted to exile. Do not list him again next year. This is Our final decision.'

Nala would be pleased. In fact, she would be delighted, and she would also be much richer. The Emperor reflected complacently that he knew more about the underhanded dealings among his concubines than they would ever realise.

BOOK II

April 1, 1856 – November 7, 1856

THE HEAVENLY KINGDOM

CHAPTER TWENTY-ONE

April 1, 1856   *Chenkiang, the Citadel of the River*

Even this far inland, more than two hundred miles from the open sea, the night breeze on the Long River was hauntingly tanged with salt. Gabriel Hyde sniffed the phantom scent of the ocean and buttoned the blue-serge jacket he wore over the nankeen trousers and shirt that were now his working uniform. Moonlight darting through the broken clouds above the river lit his tensely muscled body as he leaned with arms crossed on the taffrail of the Imperial Gunboat *Mencius*. His gaze shifted from the dark fortress-city of Chenkiang, fitfully illuminated by the lanterns of the Taiping sentinels on the walls.

The cuffs of his jacket were marked only by darker strips and loose threads where the gold stripes of a lieutenant in the United States Navy had gleamed a few months earlier. He ruefully touched his shoulder, where the epaulette had shone, and felt only a minute pit where the brass button had been snipped off. Similar pits on his choker-collar recalled the gilt anchor he had proudly stroked when he was first commissioned. In unconscious dismissal, his hand swept down the row of plain black buttons that now closed his jacket.

At least, he reflected, he no longer had to badger a messboy to keep that brass gleaming. At least his equivocal position granted him a certain freedom from formality. He wore the lynx of a Military Mandarin of the sixth grade on a sky-blue tunic as was required of him when reporting to his superiors in the Imperial Water Force, but his own half-piratical Chinese seamen would have laughed at such display on active service. Besides, his loose nankeen garments did not hamper his movements, and he enjoyed the feel of the rough planking under his bare feet despite the chill. It was cold on the water towards midnight, although a flush of heat had suffused the afternoon of the last day of March 1856.

Since *Mencius* might engage the enemy that night, Gabriel Hyde was dressed for battle. His crew slept at their action-stations, the gunners shifting restlessly beside the quick-firing Forest guns mounted on the paddle-wheeler's poop and forecastle. *Mencius's* makeshift conversion from a coaster to a warship had been completed by the antiquated muzzle-loaders that poked through the eight gunports cut in her bulwarks. Gabriel Hyde feared those primitive weapons served by half-trained gun-crews as

127

much as the junks of the Taiping Water Force, which might sweep down upon *Mencius* and the flotilla of Imperial warjunks. Those cannon could tear loose if a gunner failed to secure a shackle pin or the bolts holding the restraining tackle were ripped from the thin planking by the guns' recoil. Half a ton of bronze rolling wildly across the decks to smash the matchwood bulwarks could maim and kill quite as fearsomely as the Holy Soldiers of the Heavenly King.

He had for the past month driven and cajoled his motley crew, but the gunboat was hardly a paragon of smartness. No bosun's pipes had shrilled when he boarded *Mencius*, the ungainly, slab-sided, river-going tub that was his first command.

His predicament was largely his own fault, due, to put it bluntly, to his big mouth. He regretted his sarcastic remarks in the wardroom. He winced when he remembered playing the dashing worldly-wise sea-rover for that outrageously attractive girl, who was also outrageously conceited, at Russell's Fourth of July dance. He'd been a young fool then, cocksure at twenty-three. Almost a year older – and years older in experience – he would never indulge in such bravado again.

Still, she was enough to turn any man's head. What was she called? Lewis? Levy? No, Haleevie. Fronah Haleevie, a tantalizing name and a tantalizing girl. He'd find her the next time *Mencius* put into Shanghai.

But she had nothing to do with the pickle he'd landed himself in – or his abrupt transformation from a lieutenant, USN to a lieutenant commander, Imperial Chinese Water Force. 'Detached for administrative convenience,' his senior officers had ruled, unwilling to cite the true cause. Perhaps he had gone too far, but he could not take the commander's slur on his family lying down. At any rate, he had duly applied for extended leave after the secret hearing. The Navy was probably no more certain than he was of his present status.

That smoke-screen helped preserve his reputation, but did not put bread in his mouth. Despite the odium of mercenary service, he'd been very glad to join the Manchu Emperor's raggle-taggle river-squadron. Hardly a swan-like frigate with gleaming brightwork and holystoned decks, *Mencius* was the pride of that squadron. Since no Chinese officer alive could handle that ugly duckling with her reciprocating engine and her quick-firing Forest guns, the Mandarins had commissioned a foreigner.

He had been offered other employment that afternoon. The terms were astonishingly generous, though the prospects were not exactly glowing. But to what could he look forward in the Imperial Water Force? And the new offer was truly munificent.

A match flared on the foredeck, where the sailors were playing in an endless game of cards, and Gabriel Hyde left the taffrail to shout a sharp command. 'Dowse that light!' he already knew too well in Chinese, as he did 'Step lively!' and 'Aim before firing!' Surprisingly skilled seamen, his patchy crew was about as disciplined as Shanghai pye-dogs. Still, they would fight like real seadogs with good leadership.

He could not push his sailors too hard. Like himself, they served primarily for pay, and even less than himself were they bound to strict discipline by their *pro forma* oaths. Besides, the twenty silver *taels* paid an able bodied seaman each year must command less loyalty than his own 3,000 *taels*, which, he smugly calculated, came to £1,000 sterling or a princely $5,000.

The offer made that afternoon by the Taiping General called the Four-Eyed Dog beggared that sum: 7,500 *taels*, $12,500 a year. when President Franklin Pierce himself received no more than $25,000. Gabriel Hyde couldn't believe his services were worth that much to anyone nor that the cocky Taiping general could make good his promise. Finally, he was by no means certain he could organise and command a flotilla of gunboats for the Taipings. Self-confidence was one thing, vainglory another.

He had felt he was stepping into a fantasy when he slipped ashore in a sampan, his blue eyes and straight-bridged nose concealed by a boatman's conical straw-hat. Conducted around the besieging Imperial troops by side-paths, he had been received in the former Imperial prefect's *yamen* by General Wu Ju-hsiao, who had taken Chenkiang three years earlier and since then held off constant government assaults on that eastern outpost of Tienking, the Heavenly Capital, as the Taiping occupiers called Nanking. Chenkiang's name also proclaimed its strategic importance. It meant the Citadel of the River.

The Taiping General, servant of a cult Hyde considered on a par with devil worship, was surprisingly fluent in pidgin English, the *lingua franca*, the business language, of the China Coast. Chinese pronounced business pidgin just like pigeon. The rebel General had, he boasted, done 'big pidgin' as a merchant in Canton before joining the Taipings. His nickname, the Four-Eyed Dog, apparently delighted him.

The stocky general's puckered features resembled a mastiff's: the nose small with prominent nostrils, the wide mouth bristling with discoloured teeth, and the low forehead permanently wrinkled. Beneath his alert eyes shone livid spots, so that he appeared to possess four bright eyes.

'Have got four piecee eye,' the General chuckled complacently. 'Can look see two times bettern mens have got only two piecee.'

The Four-Eyed Dog had discussed the military situation as if they were allies, rather than enemies. A major action, he hinted, was impending, a great battle that would crush the Imps.

'Number three year of Heavenly Kingdom begin start.' The General, Hyde knew, meant early 1853, for the Taiping calendar began in 1850. 'Holy Soldiers follow longside me and drive out Imps from Chenkiang, where we now sit so fat like Mandarins and so safe like gods.'

His complacency was hardly justified, for a ring of Imperial troops was closing around the fortress-city. But the American was accustomed to outrageous Chinese exaggeration and listened with outward respect to the Four-Eyed Dog's monologue, which alternated between braggadocio and lamentation. In 1853, the General recalled, Taiping strategists had launched a march on Shanghai to join the Small Swords. When the task force was recalled to defend the Heavenly Capital against renewed Imperialist attacks, the opportunity was lost. A Manchu general finally retook the South City from the Small Swords in early 1855, and his troops then moved upriver into the Taiping domain.

'Imps only takee South City because have got help from Frenchmens,' the Four-Eyed Dog swore. 'Cursed idolators! Damned Froggymen pay idols joss! Make jin-jin jossee allee same pagan Chineemens.'

Chinese troop movements were interminably slow and the Manchu advance soon stalled. After driving off the Imperialists threatening their Heavenly Capital at Nanking, tens of thousands of Holy Soldiers were now advancing under clouds of yellow and scarlet banners. Astonishingly, their chief weapons were spears and swords, supplemented by handmade muskets, blunderbusses, and horse-pistols, while their cannon were hollowed tree-trunks strengthened with metal hoops. None the less, the Taipings were rolling up the Imperialist threat to the outlying cities that guarded the Heavenly Capital.

With the Great Kingdom of Heavenly Peace resurgent, the Imperialists had to bring their protracted siege of the Citadel of the River to a triumphant close within the next few weeks or fall back. Chenkiang, the gate to the middle Yangtze Valley, was in grave danger. Yet the Four-Eyed Dog was extraordinarily confident.

For half an hour he extolled the unique virtue and justice of Taiping rule, impressing Gabriel Hyde despite his prejudice. The General then casually made his proposal. If the American would join the Holy Cause, he would hold the rank of commodore and command all the Taipings' steam-powered gunboats – all, that was, he could manage to purchase. In addition to a munificent salary, he could enjoy a harem of scores of devoted female Holy Soldiers.

'So many beautiful womens,' the Four-Eyed Dog rhapsodised. 'Allee same like Heavenly King and Heavenly Princes, you catchee many, many womens.'

The young man from puritanical New England couldn't quite see himself as the lord of an Oriental seraglio. But he had heard graphic tales of the ardour of Chinese women. A harem of passionate Oriental beauties! They would gasp in Salem when he returned to tell that tale.

The American had not made up his mind, for the Four-Eyed Dog had urged: 'Takee much time think . . . No wanchee hurry . . . no wanchee Lieutenant be rash.' But the ten gold *taels* he had accepted as a pledge of the Taiping's sincerity were hidden under his *China Coast Pilot* beside his sextant and chronometer in his double-locked sea-chest.

'Small piecee lyesee,' the General had said expansively. 'Good frien' allee time pay good frien' kumshaw . . . only present, savee?'

After living for months amid genial graft, Gabriel had not rebuffed the valuable gift, which was not really a bribe. Every officer of the Imperial Water Force gladly accepted kumshaw from his subordinates and anxiously bribed his superiors. Besides, he could not close the door by offending the Four-Eyed Dog.

The crucial issue was clear. *Could* the Taipings win? That question perplexed the merchants of the foreign settlement, whose self-preservation and self-enrichment both depended upon cool assessment of the rebel dynasty's prospects. The consuls pondered the same question in the sacred light of national interest. If the Taipings conquered China, Gabriel Hyde's rank and his wealth would raise him far above the displeasure of the US Navy. Salem did not ask awkward questions of her sons returning from abroad with fortunes to spend. Besides, the Taipings' fanatical rectitude was appealing to an officer enmired in the morass of corruption called the Imperial Water Force.

The bell-tower of Chenkiang proclaimed the double-hour of the sheep, one a.m. on April 1, 1856. The brazen clamour rolled down the shore, where the watch-fires of the besieging army were a curtain of flame against the night. As clouds covered the moon, the tolling resounded across the Yangtze, where the battle-lanterns of the warjunks illuminated long, scalloped pennants undulating in the breeze. Those lanterns blazed, the warjunks' captains said, to placate their crews' superstition by driving away demons – and, Gabriel suspected, to proclaim the warjunks' presence to the Taiping flotilla, so that both sides could avoid a clash. Torches flared as the guard changed on the walls of Chenkiang, and loud male chanting rose to the sky: '*Tsan-mei*! All praise to the Heavenly Father!'

Shivering in involuntary awe as the echoes of the bronze bells and the chanted prayer reverberated over the water, Gabriel Hyde heard the murmur of bare feet across teak decks as the watch changed aboard *Mencius*. The quartermaster had obeyed his order not to sound the ship's bell, though his crew, like all Chinese infatuated by noise-making devices, delighted in striking the hours. Cymbals clashed and gongs boomed on the warjunks in response to the enemy's clamour.

When the echoes died, an oar slapped the wavelets. Gabriel stiffened in watchfulness and cocked his head. Blind in the darkness surrounding *Mencius*, his eyes were dazzled by the lanterns of the warjunks. He listened intently for almost a minute, but relaxed when the sound was not repeated.

Three minutes later, the oar slapped the water closer to *Mencius*, anchored on the fringe of the flotilla. Craning into the darkness, Gabriel saw a white splash among the dainty white caps. It was, he concluded with relief, only a fish leaping.

Despite the Four-Eyed Dog's broad hints, the night was quiet on the Long River. He would have gone below to his cabin if he had commanded an American naval vessel with alert lookouts, but he could not trust the vigilance of his half-trained crew. He could not even allow himself a cat-nap on the quarterdeck.

Resigned to sleeplessness, the American reached into his pocket for a cheroot. His hand was arrested by an emphatic slap on the water. That was no fish, those splashes drawing closer to his ship. He whispered to the bosun, who padded towards the foredeck, casually kicking the gun-crews awake as he passed. A match flared, and an acetylene searchlight lanced the night. The blue-white beam probed the darkness for almost ten minutes. As Gabriel Hyde opened his mouth to order the searchlight dowsed, yellow radiance flared above the waves. The beam impaled a small sampan in which a fisherman wielding a trident crouched over the lantern that lured his prey to the surface.

The sailors laughed, and one shouted: 'Be careful, little brother, that the fish don't get your balls!'

The fisherman waved casually and resumed his scrutiny of the water. His spear darted, and he triumphantly displayed the wriggling carp transfixed by the tines.

A lone fisherman in a cockleshell amid the formidable flotilla appeared strange to Gabriel, but his crew was neither surprised nor alarmed. While fleets and armies clashed, other men stolidly reaped the waters and the land. Farmers ploughed hillside plots while cavalrymen sabred each other in the valleys, and cargo junks plodded around the baleful thunder of naval cannon. The people stoically ignored the gory quarrels of Manchu rulers and power-mad Chinese.

The sampan drifted downstream, the fisherman silhouetted against the lantern peering into the ruffled river. Gradually, almost imperceptibly, the yellow radiance veered towards the southern bank, fading into the distance and finally vanishing. The nineteen-year-old fisherman rose and stretched before sculling the sampan to the river bank below the Imperial camp. When the prow grounded, he jumped ashore and strode along the same hidden paths Gabriel Hyde had taken into the Citadel of the River earlier in the day.

'Chen Cheng-hsiang . . .' he told the first Taiping picket he encountered. 'Lieutenant General Chen with urgent intelligence for the Four-Eyed Dog.'

*

When the bell-tower of Chenkiang tolled the double-hour of the monkey at three in the morning, Gabriel Hyde yielded to his bosun's urging and climbed into the hammock slung between the taffrail and the mizzen mast. The sun would rise at 5.47, and no further danger threatened that night. The Four-Eyed Dog's hints were apparently intended to throw him off balance. Besides, no Chinaman, not even a General of Holy Soldiers, could resist bragging like a small boy. A few hours' sleep would fortify him against the inevitable alarms of the coming day, when the captains of the Imperial Water Force would again confer anxiously on strategy – as they had every day for two weeks without reaching agreement.

His seaman's instinct awoke Gabriel a minute before the battlements of Chenkiang erupted with flame and smoke. The Holy Soldiers were firing their few iron cannon and their long-barrelled flintlocks into the Imperial camp outside the city-walls. The bombardment roared for half an hour, sharper explosions signalling the self-destruction of iron-hooped wooden cannon. The hail of musket balls and nails, scrap iron and potsherds fired by the crude guns scythed down all troops within their limited reach. Those weapons were even more lethal to their crews, often blowing up after a few shots. This morning only Holy Soldiers died, for their enemies were out of range.

The rising sun fringed the gun-smoke clouds with pink. The helmets of the Imperial troops glinted as they ate their breakfasts, occasionally pointing scornfully with their chopsticks at their stupid foes. Laughing at his own response to the empty threat, the Manchu major commanding a battery of three Krupp cannon returned the fire. The shells, Gabriel saw through his binoculars, threw up gouts of red brick-dust when they struck the fifty-foot-thick city wall. Doing no real damage, their impact only increased the innumerable pockmarks on the face of Chenkiang.

The Taiping volleys halted abruptly. As the smoke blew away, a tide of yellow banners flowed out of the gates of the Citadel. Gabriel was astonished. It was madness to sally from the fortress against the long-range Imperial cannon. Gleefully, the Manchu major depressed the barrels of his Krupp guns and hurled shells into the rebel mass. Each time a yellow flag toppled, a Taiping officer died, for even sub-lieutenants flew their personal banners. The insane assault was disintegrating as the Imperialists' iron muzzle-loaders also came into play.

Sweeping the battle-front, Gabriel's binoculars spied a wave of yellow banners lapping at the Manchu left flank. The Imperial artillery did not respond, for all the guns were trained on the assault from the city. The wave swelled into a torrent, and the Manchu left flank began to crumble. Advancing over the bodies of their fellows, the Holy Soldiers from the fortress engaged the Manchu centre while a third assault broke their enemies' right flank. Within the Citadel the Four-Eyed Dog had obviously received orders to co-ordinate his diversionary manoeuvre with the relief forces' flanking attacks.

The American wondered momentarily about the lone fisherman in the night before the rattle of musketry on the river diverted him. A fleet of junks flying yellow and scarlet banners was probing the Imperial flotilla. Gabriel ignored the signal pennants whipping on the flagship to make his own decision. The warjunks could deal handily with the water-borne attack. *Mencius* could most effectively utilize her superior speed and her heavier armament in support of the hard-pressed infantry.

Her paddle wheels churning the muddy water into brown froth, the gunboat slewed past the milling warjunks. Smoke billowed from the stovepipe funnel, and soot drizzled on the teak decks. As the gunboat gathered speed, the stays securing the rickety smoke-stack vibrated like violin strings.

Gabriel Hyde's black hair ruffled in the breeze stirred by the gunboat's passage. A half-smile revealed his white teeth, and an incongruous dimple twinkled in his right cheek. Laugh wrinkles creased his forehead, and his straight nose crinkled.

'Fire port broadside!' he shouted. 'Forward and fantail guns fire at will!'

The gunboat heeled sharply to starboard and skidded across the water when the four muzzle-loaders roared. Half-blinded by the smoke, the helmsman wrestled with the big teak wheel as the chocolate-froth wake corkscrewed. The breach-loading guns on the prow and stern barked a constant obbligato. Their shells arched high before *Mencius* shook off the water that had poured over the starboard gunwales and returned to an even keel.

The helmsman put the wheel over, and the gunboat slewed back on a reciprocal course. When the starboard battery bore on the Taiping infantry, Gabriel chopped his hand down. Shrapnel flailed the rebel ranks, and officers' yellow banners fell like daffodils beneath a sickle.

Mencius steamed alongshore for half an hour, wheeling repeatedly to loose her alternate broadsides while the quick firing breech-loaders yapped like eager terriers. Gabriel's blue eyes glowed in the mask of a face stained black by powder fumes, and his lips curved in a lupine grin. Although the Holy Soldiers returned the gunboat's fire with their clumsy flintlocks, the slow-flying balls whined harmlessly amid the rigging.

Gabriel Hyde was revolted by the slaughter his guns wrought, and copper bile rose in his throat. His binoculars clearly revealed the lanes his muzzle-loaders' round shot cut through the ranks of the Taiping infantry-men. The breech-loaders' explosive shells threw up fountains of crimson flesh. This was not a battle, but a massacre.

None the less, *Mencius*'s guns could not drive the powerful Taiping force from the wide battle-front. Since Manchus and Taipings were intermingled, further salvoes would kill as many Imperial troops as Holy Soldiers. Gabriel signalled his crew to cease fire before turning his binoculars to assure himself that most of the Taiping Water Force had withdrawn after diverting the warjunks from the battle on the shore. *Mencius* could only stand off and observe the battles on the land and the water.

The gunboat remained at her post throughout the day, though the warjunks fled downriver. The occasional Taiping vessel that approached *Mencius* turned and ran when the quick-firing guns barked. Gabriel Hyde watched the Imperial troops disintegrate under the three-pronged assault. The Four-Eyed Dog must be grinning in delight at his enemies' rout.

An hour before dusk, the American turned the gunboat's prow towards Shanghai. Exhilarated by their victory, the Taipings were swarming over the Imperialists' remaining outposts. When the Holy Soldiers' yellow and crimson banners blossomed across on both banks of the Long River, Gabriel Hyde felt he was sailing through broad fields of daffodils.

CHAPTER TWENTY-TWO

April 3, 1856   *Shanghai*

Sarah Haleevie was once again startled by her daughter's behaviour. She was also gratified, a feeling Fronah aroused less frequently. She nodded approval of the beige kaftan the girl wore in place of a furbelowed European dress over a tight corset that indecently accentuated the bosom. Fronah's tawny hair was not tortured into an elaborate European coiffure, but hung loose under a green-cotton scarf. Her modesty in dress and demeanour gladdened her mother's heart.

The concubine Maylu leaned on the girl's arm as they left the house on Szechwan Road for a Friday afternoon's shopping in the South City. Fronah's latest – and, Sarah thanked God, innocuous – passion was collecting Chinese fans. For decorum's sake, the girl's personal amah walked respectfully three steps behind the ladies. Her daughter's behaviour, Sarah reflected, had been exemplary for the past several weeks. Perhaps too exemplary? She reproached herself for that unworthy thought. Why must she assume the girl was acting deceitfully when there was not the slightest reason for suspicion?

Fronah had even smiled beguilingly at young Samuel Moses, who should have been in the counting house dealing with last minute rush before the Sabbath. She was not concerned with that breach of her husband's discipline, but with the growing intimacy between her daughter and the twenty-year-old apprentice Saul had brought from Bombay four months

135

earlier. Samuel pleased Sarah, for he was obviously attracted to her wilful daughter. Instinct told her the youth's affection was sincere. The Moseses were rich enough so that young Samuel had no need to seek a wealthy bride. But, naturally, a sensible young man's heart would range more freely where the money was.

Delighted by Samuel's interest, Sarah wondered when the children would speak of their mutual affection. They were, naturally, shy, although at seventeen Fronah should already be betrothed. Parents could, of course, arrange a marriage, as her own marriage to Saul had been arranged. But it was better if spontaneous affection sprang up between the bride and groom beforehand. That was the modern way, and they were living in the modern age – as Fronah constantly reminded her.

For the first month or so, the girl's attitude towards the slender youth had puzzled Sarah. She had wondered whether her daughter was put off by his swarthiness and the Baghdad robe he still wore, a coarser, high-buttoned version of the garment Saul had abandoned. But Fronah had flirted modestly with Samuel for the past few weeks, and they often walked together after the day's work. Sarah was doubly pleased: her daughter was behaving with maidenly reserve, while the slow growth of mutual affection promised a long, happy marriage.

Aaron and David Lee were not pleased by Samuel's intrusion, although Fronah's mock engagement to Aaron had, thank God, lapsed of its own accord. Sarah frankly acknowledged that she did not understand the ramifications of the legal processes by which she and Saul had adopted the boys before their father was taken to Kansu Province, some 2,000 miles away, to labour in the Imperial Jade Mines in perpetual exile.

After the formal adoption Saul had laughed at her worries over the betrothal of convenience. Aaron and Fronah could now never marry, he told her, because they were brother and sister, not that there had ever been any real danger. He had not told her that Chinese families often adopted prospective bridegrooms for only daughters just as Jewish merchants took apprentices with the same consumation in mind. Of course, she had never really believed Fronah wanted to marry the Chinaman, any more than the girl would want to marry one of the young Gentiles she had so frequently met before Saul curtailed her social life.

Fronah had even taken that restriction with good grace. She was apparently content to attend an occasional dance or dinner under the eye of her teacher Margaret MacGregor, who, Sarah had decided after two meetings, was a good woman. Realising that her parents were acting for her own good, Fronah had not protested. Despite her natural restlessness, she was a dutiful daughter. Sarah thanked the Lord God for His blessings, though much credit was, of course, due to her husband's wisdom.

'Fronah,' she called impulsively, 'just a minute!'

The slim girl in beige and the Soochow woman in the narrow azure gown slit to reveal black-satin trousers waited beside the gatepost with the brass plates reading in English and ideograms: HALEEVIE AND LEE: *Merchants*.

'*Here, my dear.*' Sarah counted out *five silver Maria Theresa dollars. 'In case you find a very* pretty fan. Enjoy yourselves.'

Fronah kissed her mother's soft cheek. Her eyes misted as she inhaled the fragrance of attar of roses, which had breathed loving security all her life. Smiling reminiscently, she led Maylu into Szechwan Road, eager for the pleasures the afternoon would bring.

'You won't be late for evening prayers, will you, Fronah?' Sarah called. 'Mr Henriques is coming to dinner, the English gentleman who brought a letter of introduction from your Uncle Solomon. Your father wants him to enjoy a real family Friday night. He's very religious, Solomon says.'

Whatever curiosity Fronah might have felt was quelled by her mother's recalling their guest's devoutness. His name sounded terribly grand and terribly English: Lionel Howard Stanley Henriques. But he was probably just another stuffy, middle-aged Jew with a long beard.

*

As they strolled along the lane of the fan-makers, Maylu chattered apprehensively about the Taiping victories that were sweeping the Yangtze Valley after the relief of Chenkiang. Despite her hatred for the Manchus, whom she, like the rebels, called Imps, the concubine was frightened by the tide of Holy Soldiers surging towards Shanghai.

'They don't rape and loot, everyone says,' Maylu said. 'But how can you believe that? Soldiers are soldiers.'

'They won't dare touch the foreign settlement,' Fronah consoled her absently. 'Sometimes I think you *want* to be raped, you talk so much about it.'

They did not stop at the fan-makers, though Fronah glanced avidly at the jewel-like displays. Darting into a side-alley so narrow they had to edge sideways around the bales stacked on the cobbles, they stooped under strings of translucent drying fish, which were like flat bleached leaves showing their fragile spines and ribs. How different, Fronah mused vagrantly, their salty stench was from her mother's attar of roses. The South City was a Chinese world far removed from her parents' cosy Jewish enclave within the smug foreign settlement. She smothered a pang of guilt. It was ridiculous to feel disloyal because she was not always wholly candid with her parents and she feigned attraction towards that swarthy youth, Samuel Moses. She quite simply was equally at home in those different worlds.

Maylu turned into a doorway beneath the discreet sign: *Old Mother Wang, Midwife*. Fronah climbed apprehensively behind the concubine, who clung to the splintered handrail the midwife had installed so that

137

patients with feet bound into 'golden lilies' could clamber up the steep stairs. The amah trotted easily up the staircase to the third floor, her youthful vitality unhampered by bound feet. The poor farmers who were her parents could not afford to bestow the erotic and social advantage of that disfigurement on their daughters, since the girls' labour in the fields – or the small sums they could earn as servants – was essential to the family's survival.

The women nodded to Old Mother Wang, who sat in the dark anteroom among the accoutrements of her trade: the low hoop of a birthing-stool, the long examination couch, the newly washed bandages, and the earthenware jars containing medicinal plants or animal's organs. While the concubine and the amah sipped tea with the midwife, Fronah slipped into the bedroom cubicle to transform her appearance.

A quarter of an hour later, Maylu emerged into the alley. Two maidservants wearing short tunics and wide trousers decorously followed her through the lane of the silversmiths to the square surrounding the scarlet teahouse. Fronah's tawny hair was tucked under a black scarf, the stiff fabric drawn forward to shadow her face. With her eyes cast down her features were invisible to passers-by, and she mimicked the young amah's splayed gait. Having settled the concubine in the tea-house, the maidservants, released from the slow pace imposed by Maylu's golden lilies, scampered through the lanes towards the South Gate of the Chinese city. Leaving Fronah, the amah reminded her to return on time, and the girl darted past the guards towards the Tonkadoo, the Roman Catholic Cathedral.

Under the eye of a barefoot Chinese groom, three ponies bent their short necks to crop the coarse grass on the lawn surrounding the Cathedral, gleaming English hunting saddles incongruous on their shaggy backs. Iain Matthews sprawled on the lawn in the shadow of the spire, meditatively chewing a stalk of grass. The frown that clouded his vulpine features cleared, and he rose to his feet with insolent grace. He had been wondering whether she would appear, for she had been skittish lately. His watery blue eyes glowed in triumph, and his small mouth pursed in self-satisfaction. Caricaturing a profound bow, he offered her a slender packet wrapped in silver-and-mauve paper.

'Your new fan, Milady,' he smirked. 'Hope Mama'll approve your choice.'

'I'm sure it's lovely, Iain, and not too gaudy, though. Do keep it for me till we get back.'

'Of course, my dear. You'll like it, I promise.'

Iain cupped his hands to help Fronah mount before vaulting with ostentatious ease into his own saddle.

'Mafoo,' he told the groom, 'you no come longside. Stay this place waitee us come back.'

138

'No, Iain, he's to come with us.' Fronah stifled a giggle at his clumsy pidgin. 'You promised. Otherwise I won't . . .'

'What are you worried about? Afraid I'll eat you?'

'No, Iain, not that, but something else. Remember, you promised.'

'All right, Fronah, if you insist.'

The girl took the lead, riding exuberantly along the path through the green-tufted paddy fields. April was wonderful, Fronah exulted, a glorious respite between winter's chill damp and the humid heat of summer. The swallows hunting beetles amid the rice-sprouts wheeled and swooped with pure joy.

'*Mafoo*, no forgetee my words.' Iain Matthews drew his finger across his throat before cantering after Fronah. 'Suppose forgetee, Master cuttee neck.'

'Me savee, Master.' The groom knew his family could not survive without his monthly salary of three silver dollars. '*Mafoo* behave proper, Master.'

'Suppose *Mafoo* behave proper, he catchee two string cash.'

Iain Matthews was delighted with his preparations for the afternoon. Fronah's Chinese costume shielded her from scandal – and protected him, as well. During one ride only the groom's alertness had prevented their discovery by a rowdy paper-chase over the green shoots of flooded fields. Though the Haleevies were isolated, the incessant gossip would have reached her father's ears. Fronah would have been locked up, and he would, at the least, have taken a wigging from his taipan.

With Fronah disguised, any foreigners they met would just think it odd that young Matthew's Chinese popsy could ride. The griffins, the young bloods of the foreign settlement, were prohibited from marrying until they were twenty-five and had served in Shanghai for five years. Besides, unattached European ladies were not only rare, but virtually forbidden. The griffins might, however, divert themselves with native women – as long as they avoided the public gaze.

European women *were* different, though Iain's messmates, making a fetish of their deprivation, insisted, 'Yellow meat's tastier than white.' He'd had more experience, and he knew it wasn't so. Besides, he needed a change, he told himself with deliberate cynicism, reluctant to acknowledge the tenderness the tawny-haired girl awakened in himself.

When Iain joined her, Fronah's glance lingered on the sun glowing through his yellow hair and lighting his face. The perspiration gleaming on his bare forearms excited her oddly, and her smile taunted him. It did not matter that they had little to say to each other, for their silence was companionable. It was lovely to be appreciated, and it was glorious to canter through the afternoon sunbeams free of her mother's nagging and her father's silent disapproval.

When a cloud drifted before the sun, shadows darkened the path – and

Fronah's mood altered minutely. Iain was, she had to admit, occasionally tedious. She admired the refined English words that now sprang spontaneously to her mind. Tedious was just the word, though he was, of course, only occasionally a little tedious. Besides, he was often thrilling.

It was her parents' fault that she kept seeing him on the sly. No, she amended, not on the sly, but clandestinely. In reality, discreetly was the best word. If her parents had not disapproved so blatantly, she might have dropped him months ago. If her father had not insisted that she refuse most invitations to dances and dinners, she would have no reason to continue seeing Iain, even discreetly. As it was, she was only proving her independence.

But she would not drop him till someone else came along. Yet how could she possibly meet anyone else when Margaret MacGregor, goaded to vigilance by her mother, watched her like a hawk?

If her parents weren't so unreasonable, it would all have been over months ago. Why should she blame herself for behaving as would any high-spirited young woman? If she did not assert her independence, she would never mature. She had to make her own mistakes or she would never learn. Since her parents forced her to act slyly, the guilt she felt was really their fault.

'Come on, Iain!' Fronah cried with forced exuberance to dispel her depression. 'I'll race you to the trees over there.'

'What forfeit?'

'No forfeit,' she replied severely. 'Just the joy of racing.'

'Hold up, Fronah.' He clutched her reins. 'The *mafoo*'s in trouble. Looks as if his pony's gone lame. We'll have to wait for . . .'

'Forget the *mafoo*, Iain!' She slapped the pony's neck. 'I'm racing you, not the *mafoo*. You're not afraid of losing?'

The pony's hoofs threw up clumps of grass from the narrow path between the fields. Since Iain's bigger mount could still overtake them, she shrilly urged her pony on. The path widened as it approached the grove, and raindrops stung Fronah's face. Leaning forward in his saddle, Iain swept past her into the dense canopy formed by the plane-trees. Though the rain rattled on the leaves like gravel, they were snugly sheltered.

Laughing in exhilaration, Fronah slid from her saddle. Iain dropped from his pony to help her. He stiffened in excitement when he felt her breasts and thighs, unfettered under her flimsy tunic and trousers, press against him. The rain that confined them to the grove could not have been more opportune, while the *mafoo*, nursing his opportunely lamed pony, would not reappear that afternoon.

'I did win, you know.' He pouted when she slipped out of his embrace. 'To the victor the spoils. Give us a proper kiss.'

'I said no forfeit,' she reminded him primly. 'Winning's reward enough.'

140

Fronah leaned forward, bending from the waist so that only their faces touched, and brushed her lips against his.

'Now, Iain,' she chided. 'You promised . . . and it's only afternoon.'

'What's that to do with it? I hardly ever see you any more . . . not properly . . . with Maggie MacGregor watching like a gorgon.'

'It just isn't right in the afternoon. Anyway, we came for a ride, not for . . .'

'Ride in this downpour? All right, hands off, if you say so. But have some brandy to keep you warm.'

Young ladies did not drink brandy from gentlemen's hunting flasks. Perhaps with ginger-beer and a slice of lemon in a long glass, but neat brandy was a man's drink. Still, it was cool in the shaded grove.

'Just a sip, Iain,' she agreed. 'Just to keep warm.'

The brandy was sweet in her mouth, unlike the harsh whisky she had tried just once when he dared her. It trickled smoothly down her throat, and delicious warmth tingled outward to her limbs. Perhaps it wasn't quite ladylike, but why should gentlemen always have the best of things? A little more, just another sip, would do no harm. Surely a tot of brandy was better than catching cold.

'Looks as if we'll be here a while,' Iain said. 'Might as well settle down. And do take off that ridiculous scarf.'

He unbuckled the blanket rolled behind his saddle and spread it over the layers of old leaves that carpeted the grove. Fronah hesitated. Joining him on the blanket was daring, even reckless, but he was insistent. Yet there was really nothing to worry about. No one could possibly discover them, and Iain was always the perfect gentleman. A quick word or a hurt look invariably stopped him from becoming too ardent.

'You'll be good, won't you, Iain?' she reminded. 'Remember, I'm not one of your Chinese popsies.'

Feeling vulnerable in the thin Chinese clothing, Fronah clasped her arms around her knees. She would be careful, though Iain was really no more dangerous than a friendly puppy, a golden puppy with floppy ears. His chuckle mocked her posture of maidenly modesty. She deliberately leaned back on her elbows, though her breasts thrust against the flimsy cotton jacket.

'Don't worry, my dear.' His words were minutely slurred. 'I won't attack you. A little more brandy?'

Fronah smiled her acceptance. She only sipped, while he gulped, his Adam's apple bobbing. The more he took, the more easily she could keep him within bounds. Drink made him clumsy and, often, sheepish.

Relaxed and confident, Fronah did not draw away when his mouth came down on hers and his arms slipped around her. For the first time, they lay stretched beside each other as if on a bed. His caressing hand was gentle on her shoulders. The brandy was surely making him drowsy, as it was herself.

141

She did not protest when his hands cupped her breasts over her jacket, nor when he fumbled at the buttons. That much she had already permitted him – and enjoyed. She would, of course, permit him no more.

Fronah gasped when Iain opened the jacket and inched up her gauzy chemise to free her breasts. She thrust him away feebly, but relaxed again when he whispered to her. His tongue flicking in her ear sent a galvanic shock through her body, and she pushed him away firmly.

'Just want to look at you . . . and touch you a little,' he slurred. 'No harm in that. By God, you're beautiful. So beautiful.'

She blushed, the blood rising from her bare bosom to dye her throat and face. Suddenly aware of the glaring daylight, she clutched the jacket around her. He murmured soothingly as he gently unclasped her hands and pushed the jacket off her shoulders. Unthinking, she lifted her arms to let him slip off the sleeves.

'It is nice, Iain, very nice,' she sighed. 'But no more. Remember, you promised.'

He looked up at her and smiled lazily. His lips brushed her breast, and his tongue circled her nipple. She shivered in delight, though she knew she should call a halt. But the new sensation at once thrilled and lulled her. Besides, he was always a perfect gentleman. Even far from any other people, she could control him. Her arms tightened of their own accord, pressing his face to her breast.

Fronah smiled dreamily when his hands slipped to her hips and strayed lower to cup her buttocks. Iain looked up adoringly at her slack features. Her hand trailed of its own volition down his bare chest.

Fronah stiffened. This was wrong, she realised, completely wrong. Knowing she must resist, she pushed her palms against his chest. But the gesture was feeble, her arms somehow powerless, and he only chuckled in his throat. She felt a fierce pulsing between her thighs, a rush of moisture. Then it seemed only natural when his hand slipped under her loose waistband to caress her stomach. She arched her back to help him slip off the trousers.

She was naked, she saw with detached surprise. She was naked, and Iain's hands were roving eagerly over her body. She should, she felt vaguely, make him stop. But she could not. Her resistance was overwhelmed by her body's demands. Half aware, she opened her legs in response to the urgent pressure of his hand between her thighs. It was delicious, absolutely delicious – and it was only natural.

*

'Not rape, Maylu! You couldn't call it rape!' Fronah protested, her fears fanned by the concubine's horror. 'It was my fault, too. Really, he couldn't help himself. And he was *so* sorry afterwards.'

'Afterwards, Little Lady, afterwards!' the concubine replied bitterly. 'Afterwards, some are sorry . . . and some don't care, but say they're sorry anyway. Afterwards is too late!'

'But, Maylu, I couldn't stop him . . . Somehow, I just couldn't,' Fronah stammered. 'And you always talk about . . . about you know . . . as if it didn't really matter.'

'My sin, Little Lady, my stupidity!' The concubine's voice shrilled towards hysteria. 'I'm a stupid slave. I should never have helped you meet him. What to say to your mother?'

The concubine had fretted when the girl returned an hour late. She was sceptical when Fronah blamed her tardiness on the rain and a lame pony. The girl was pale; her manner was abstracted; and she clasped her hands to keep them from trembling.

Maylu had wandered into Old Mother Wang's bedroom cubicle where Fronah normally washed away the horse-smell before resuming her normal clothing. When her eyes were caught by the smears of blood on Fronah's thighs, Maylu reached the inevitable conclusion. The girl could not deny the concubine's suspicion, though she had looked for sympathy and comfort, not paroxysms of grief and wild accusations.

'You should never have let it go so far. But it's my fault. I'm evil. I should commit suicide to wipe out my sin. I would if I had the courage. I will . . .'

'Then everyone would guess.' Knowing the Chinese, Fronah did not take the threat lightly. 'And what would Uncle Aisek say? Please, Maylu, no!'

'You're right. This slave cannot even suicide to erase her sin.' Maylu's shrill tone subsided. 'I must look after you, Little Lady. Remember, if something . . . something happens, Old Mother Wang has medicines.'

'Something? What something? Oh, you mean if . . .' Fronah had not even thought of pregnancy. 'But it doesn't *always*. Does it, Maylu?'

'No, not always, Little Lady. But it's good to remember Old Mother Wang. And your mother must *never* know.' Maylu moved away from frenzy towards calculation. 'We'll tell her we're late because I twisted my ankle. Do you have the fan or must we buy one?'

'Maylu, is it always . . . you know . . . always so . . .?'

'No, my dear, not so swift and so unpleasant. He was clumsy, your foreign devil. And it *was* your first time. The first time's always unpleasant.'

'It wasn't *so* unpleasant, Maylu.' Fronah sought refuge from shock in detachment. 'It wasn't enjoyable, of course. Certainly not ecstasy! It was only a little disappointing.'

'He's spoiled you,' Maylu moaned in renewed self-condemnation. 'You're a spoiled virgin, though no one must know. And he's spoiled you for pleasure, too.'

'It wasn't *that* bad, Maylu!' Fronah consoled her consoler. 'It was fine, lovely until he . . . he . . . until then.'

'Never! You must never again!'

'Maylu, there *must* be more to it. After all, so many people . . . so many women, you've told me, they love to . . . But how can I face my mother? One look and she'll know.'

'It's not so easy to see, Little Lady.' The concubine was again practical. 'Remember you fell trying to help me when I stumbled. We were accosted by . . . no, that won't do. She'd never let us out of the house again. Not that I'll ever help you meet *him* again. You fell and hit your head. Simpler is better.'

*

Sarah Haleevie glanced up distractedly from the candles she was lighting when she heard the front door open. A shawl draped her hair, where the tawny highlights of her youth were fading. Striving to concentrate on the ritual, she could not put her worry about Fronah out of her mind. The girl should have been home an hour ago to join her in Friday evening prayers, reserved for women by male-dominated Judaism. Their heads piously covered, Saul and their Chinese sons, Aaron and David, watched from their chairs at the dining-room table. Their guest Lionel Henriques, a most improbable-looking Jew, murmured devoutly. A black skullcap was perched incongruously on his blond head.

After the opening door broke Sarah's concentration, she hurried through the prayer. Perfunctorily blessing the candles, she turned to her impromptu congregation.

'Dinner will be ready in a moment,' she said with forced cheerfulness. 'And I think I heard them come in.'

Fronah and Maylu, who had been waiting for the rite to end, entered the dining-room with exaggerated decorum. Sarah felt something was amiss, but knew it couldn't be serious. They had, after all, spent the afternoon innocently shopping. But Maylu leaned heavily on Fronah's arm, and her daughter's face was pinched.

'What's wrong, my dear?' She did not wish to embarrass their guest. 'Why are you so late? Are you ill?'

'It's nothing really, Mama,' the girl replied listlessly. 'Maylu tripped and twisted her ankle. When I tried to catch her, I fell and hit my head on a stone.'

'Are you all right, now?' Sarah's flicker of suspicion died. 'Does it hurt badly?'

'It's all right now, Mama. I was just dazed. There's no blood, not even a bump.'

The lean houseboy silently set a blue-and-white tureen on the mahogany table. He was nonplussed when he saw the chopped chicken liver still untouched and the crisp rolls still unbroken. Normally they would have finished the first course by this time. Normally the menu would have been quite different. But, the servant knew, his mistress had consulted with her friend Clara Weinstein to plan a meal that would please their English guest's taste better than their own more highly seasoned dishes. Normally, too, they were as punctual as clocks, and the houseboy prided himself on producing each course at the precise moment they finished its predecessor.

An awkward pause followed the houseboy's intrusion. Embarrassment drew all eyes to the tureen. Flecked with yellow droplets, the clear chicken soup steamed invitingly. Fluffy dumplings floated just beneath the surface like white clouds reflected in a golden sea.

'My word, Mrs Haleevie,' Lionel Henriques said heartily. 'I haven't seen such perfect chicken soup since I left London. It's like being home again.'

The Englishman's light-blue eyes unobtrusively assessed the girl. She was, he concluded judiciously, a beauty, quite virginal, though perhaps a little overblown. She was fetching in the kaftan that flirted discreetly with the curves beneath but avoided crass display. Her eyes were shadowed after her mishap, and their lids appeared bruised. She was hurt and vulnerable, altogether most attractive.

Fronah shyly acknowledged her father's introduction. Mr Lionel Howard Stanley Henriques of Samuelson and Company, Merchant Bankers. The name had a grand ring, and the man carried it well. He was slim and tall; his skin was fair; his nose was aristocratically arched; he wore a gold signet-ring with an incised coat of arms on the little finger of his left hand; and his grey frock-coat was cut with restrained elegance. His nonchalant manner seemed to declare that, since he had already seen everything, nothing could ever surprise him or shake his composure.

'As I said, Mr Haleevie, I'm here to keep an eye on Derwents,' the guest resumed. 'Since they have substantial obligations to Samuelsons, it was felt my presence in Shanghai would be helpful.'

'You'll be here long?' Saul asked.

'Oh, indefinitely, Mr Haleevie, indefinitely.' Henriques spoke in a pleasant tenor. 'Of course, Derwents are fundamentally sound. We . . . Samuelsons . . . merely thought I might be of assistance, you see. So I'll be in China for quite a while, perhaps a year or two.'

Saul genially nodded his understanding. Something about this Henriques jarred upon him. Perhaps the man was just a shade too English for a good Jew. Perhaps, though, he himself was being foolish. His brother Solomon's private letter in Hebrew, which recommended Henriques glowingly, had arrived on the same ship as the letter of introduction in English and its bearer. He must, Saul chided himself, learn to suppress his instinctive reaction against men like this Anglicised Jew. Although Sarah felt he was himself veering from the straight Mosaic road, he could not let her

145

prejudices divert him from the great success upon which he was determined.

Fronah gratefully let the men's talk drone past her. She was relieved that her mother had accepted her story so easily. She was so relieved she could almost forget the dull ache inside her. Mr Henriques's presence was, of course, a God-given distraction. Except for his advanced age, he was also a most attractive man. Some day, when Iain was more mature, he would look as elegant as Mr Henriques, she reflected spontaneously, and he would speak with the same imperturbable confidence.

Iain! The name intruded violently into her thoughts. My God, Iain! He had acted like a beast, a wild beast. Even if she had been a little weak, his behaviour was inexcusable, truly evil. She would not, Fronah resolved, think about Iain now.

CHAPTER TWENTY-THREE

April 18, 1856   *Shanghai*

'You've been impossible for weeks now.' Sarah's tone was elaborately casual. 'What's wrong, my dear?'

'Impossible?' Fronah fenced. 'What do you mean, Mama, impossible? I'm just the same as always.'

Fronah had been withdrawn and irritable for more than two weeks, staring into the distance and snapping when addressed. Even her confidante Maylu was alternately ignored and stabbed by her sharp tongue. After flirting with Samuel Moses, Fronah now refused to grant him a single word. Offered ten dollars to add to her fan collection, she had declared that she was totally bored by both fans and the South City. To Sarah's astonishment, she had brusquely refused an invitation to dine at Derwent and Company, though her father and his new associate, Lionel Henriques, urged her to accept.

Sarah had asked Fronah to help her that late April morning, hoping the cosy atmosphere would draw her daughter out. Since she had been barely tall enough to crane over the counter-tops, Fronah had loved the kitchen. She had particularly delighted in the bustle of prepared *kreplach*, the large meat-filled dumplings for which Saul had acquired a taste from Carl and Clara Weinstein, the only German-Jewish family in the Shanghai community. If Sarah allowed the cook to prepare them, he complained that they had a Chinese flavour. *Kreplach* should not, he protested, taste of ginger, anise, and soya sauce.

146

Glad of the excuse to use her own kitchen, Sarah had early initiated Fronah into the mysteries of preparing the dumplings and they normally joked and gossiped, their laughter punctuated by the slapping of dough on the flour-dusted marble slab and the soft soughing of the rolling-pin. Today Fronah made little pretence of helping. She had barely got her hands white before seating herself on a tall stool to stare moodily through the basement window at the feet of the coolies carrying bales into the godown.

'Is the view that fascinating?' Sarah tried again. '*What* is bothering you, dear? You've been out of sorts ever since you bumped your head. Maybe Dr MacGregor should have a look.'

'Don't keep on at me, please. I'm just bored. Haven't you ever been bored?'

'Not often, my dear. But we'll do that. Dr MacGregor must give you a good going over.'

'He looked at my head when I had my lesson with Margaret.' Fronah lied evenly, afraid the physician's eye would discover her secret. 'There's nothing wrong.'

'It's not your time of the month, is it? Maybe that's why you're cranky. You're not having troubles, are you?'

'Mama, I said I was fine. But it does feel as if it's coming on. I think I will go and lie down.'

Sarah stared in frustration as her daughter's grey morning-dress retreated through the kitchen-door. Fronah had always been secretive when she was troubled. Sarah sighed and vigorously kneaded the unoffending dough.

Fronah did not lie down, though the light filtered soothingly through the violet-sprigged curtains of her bedroom. Instead, she emphatically swept aside the jumble of Chinese writing-brushes and paper-bound books on her leather-topped escritoire. Drawing a sheet of note-paper from a cubbyhole, she dipped a steel-nibbed pen into the crystal inkwell and began to write:

Dearest Iain.

No, that wouldn't do. She drew out a fresh sheet and printed the date and the hour in the upper right-hand corner. *My dear Iain*, she wrote and cocked her head to admire the blue letters on the cream paper. But that was too formal. Chewing on the pen, Fronah blankly regarded the blank sheet.

She loved him, she knew, and she had forgiven him. He couldn't help himself, for she *had* been provocative, almost shameless. It was all the brandy's fault, not his or even hers.

She *did* love him – with all her heart. And he loved her, too. She knew beyond doubt that he loved her deeply.

But what could account for his silence since that day in the grove? Perhaps, as some novels warned, he'd had his way with her and no longer respected her. But that couldn't be. Not Iain, not her Iain.

Perhaps he was ashamed to face her. Why otherwise could he, at the very least, not send her a note or contrive a chance meeting? They could not, of course, go riding again, but would have to find another way to cover their tracks, since Maylu flatly refused to conspire at their secret meeting. Any future shopping excursion to the South City would be just shopping. For the moment, Maylu wouldn't even go shopping because, the concubine said, she feared the girl would slip away. Fronah could only send Iain secret notes with her amah, who was bound to secrecy by generous tips.

Perhaps he was afraid, as well as ashamed. She'd written six times and had not had a single word in reply. Though she still hoped a messenger would slip a note into her hand, she no longer lingered by the gate or strolled along Szechwan Road. She feared he would never reply, although she had assured him that no one would ever know what they had done – and had repeatedly told him how much she longed to see him. Miserable at his neglect, she was growing angry at Iain.

Still, one more note would do no harm – and might just move him to reply. A sincere message, she decided, the more straightforward the better. Her pen-nib scratched decisively on the third sheet of note-paper. *Darling Iain*, she wrote, *I must see you. It doesn't matter that you haven't answered my letters. I understand and . . .*

*

His small mouth set, Iain Matthews took the envelope from the amah. He thrust it into his pocket, and glanced around furtively to reassure himself that no one had seen the amah come to the wharf where he was checking a consignment of tea-chests. He would read the note in his bedroom when his messmates were out. That much he owed Fronah.

He also longed to see her again. Somehow, the air was brighter when she was near, as if the day itself responded to her sparkle. The last few weeks had been dreary without Fronah.

His messmates were ragging him unmercifully about her notes, knowing from his earlier broad hints exactly who wrote them – and why. Unfortunately, their taunts made good sense, damned good sense. Iain Matthews was not only frustrated and confused by his own feelings. He was, also, badly frightened.

'Look here, Foxy,' Duncan Finlayson, Jardines' senior cadet, had volunteered. 'You've landed yourself in a beastly mess. Better stick to Chinese doxies from now on.'

It was, Finlayson had explained, damnably dangerous to fool about with a Jewess. 'Worse than Sicilians for revenge, the Yids are,' he'd said. For all Iain knew, a gang with long beards and long knives would jump out of the shadows one night when he was innocently strolling along the Bund. 'They'll cut your throat, of course. Probably carry away a cup of your blood to make *matzahs*. But first they'll hack off your bollocks.'

Naturally he was frightened. She'd told him how jealous her father was –

wanting her not to go to parties. The old Jew with the reddish beard would stop at nothing. Look how ruthless he was in business.

'And, she's got those Chink brothers,' Finlayson had added. 'The Chinks are worse. They'd make you eat your bollocks before they chopped off your head. Slice you up a little for fun first. You've heard of the death of a thousand cuts. It happens, Foxy! And you're a prime candidate.'

Iain was almost as terrified that Jardines' taipan would learn of his affair with Fronah. The firm might have been hand-in-glove with Chinese pirates smuggling opium, and it might still shave Custom's dues. There was, after all, nothing wrong with opium or with diddling the Chinks. But scandal was another matter.

Griffins weren't allowed to have anything to do with white women – for very good reasons. They couldn't marry till they had proved themselves, and the taipan's wife had approved their brides. Anyway, dalliance with European ladies always seemed to come out. Since the small foreign settlement could be riven by the consequent dissension, any griffin involved in a scandal was immediately sent home. And how would he explain that to the strait-laced parson, his father, who had made so many sacrifices to give his son a flying start towards making his fortune?

'It's not worth the risk, old son,' Finlayson had concluded vehemently. 'Even if she's only a Yid, there'd be a hell of a stink. And you'd get the chop. Or maybe you'd like to marry her? Marry a Yid?'

Iain pretended horror at the thought, and Finlayson chortled: 'Can you imagine getting permission from the taipan? And, if you did, your bairns would be born without foreskins, but with long beards. Drop it quick, Foxy. Maybe it'll teach her to keep her legs together. Above all, pray she keeps her lips together!'

Recalling that advice, Iain concluded that Fronah was simply not worth the risk. He felt forlorn without her, but there it was. Still he couldn't resist reading her latest letter. Just her writing on the perfumed paper was enough to get a chap excited. Besides, he acknowledged reluctantly, he was eager to see what she had to say. Despite his forced cynicism, he also wanted to hear her tell him how much she cared for him. Slinking into the corner of the go-down, he opened the letter – and her scent enveloped him.

Darling Iain,

I *must* see you. It doesn't matter that you haven't answered my notes. I understand and, one day, we'll laugh about this together. Some day soon, as soon as possible. Then we'll be together always.

We could meet for a moment, but no more now. I'm sure you understand.

I know you may be worried. But, believe me, dearest, no one will ever know about *us*. I'll never tell about that day in the grove. It will be our secret, darling.

I *must, must* see you. I love you *very* much, and I known you love me. Don't listen to what anyone else says. Only listen to your own heart.

Your own adoring,
Fronah

He glanced ruefully at his distended white cotton trousers. Her letters did get a chap up. But she couldn't have been clearer, and he didn't dare see her alone. There'd be no more jolly rogering for them for a long time. He wanted to answer her letters, just as he wanted to see her. But, he regretfully concluded, the risk was too great.

All those hints! *Forever*, she wrote, *always*. Did she really think they could even consider marrying? It was a great shame, but he'd be an idiot even to think of marrying a Jewess. He couldn't ruin his life that way, no matter how he sometimes felt.

Iain thrust Fronah's note into his pocket and walked stiffly towards the wharf. He'd burn it as soon as he was sure he was not observed – as he had sadly burned her previous notes.

*

February 22, 1856   *Shanghai*

Lee Dawei, sometimes called David Haleevie, sat over his books in the makeshift schoolroom above the godown. From time to time he turned over a double-folded page printed with vertical columns of ideograms, though his thoughts were far away from the teachings of Lord Shang Yang, the political philosopher who had inspired Chin Shih Hwang-ti. the first Emperor of China. He mechanically lit the oil-lamps as the afternoon trailed into twilight, but his eyes looked into the past, recalling the six months since his father had departed into exile in the wild north-west. When he thought of the monstrous sentence, his head throbbed. Some day, he would rescue his father from exile. Some day, too, he would avenge himself upon the callous Mandarins who had condemned his innocent father to death.

Aisek Lee had sought to make his family prosperous so that his revered grandmother could live out her days in serenity. It was not his father's fault that the venerable lady had taken her life because her mind was deranged. Quite the contrary! Yet the ponderous machinery of justice of the Confucian state had condemned his father to death for violating the canon of filial piety and only at the last minute reprieved him for a living death thousands of miles away from his beloved sons and his native place.

Perhaps, David Lee pondered, there was something fundamentally wrong with a system that painstakingly rendered such absolute injustice. The judicial machinery urgently required overhauling, but perhaps that

150

was not enough. Much worse, it was impossible, since the judicial machinery was inextricably embedded in the immovable bedrock of the Confucian state. Perhaps the Mandarinate itself, the prime mover of the Manchu Dynasty, was itself obsolete.

The Taipings, the Long Haired Rebels, were, of course, fanciful in believing they could supplant the millennia-old Confucian system with their own Utopian structure. Still, David mused, it would be instructive to see what those rebels had built in Nanking, which they called the Heavenly Capital. They had reportedly done away with the blatant injustice that his father had suffered. Perhaps the best revenge would not be reforming the Confucian system, but helping the Taipings to destroy it root and branch.

David shook his head in frustration. Since he could hardly see the Heavenly Kingdom of Great Peace for himself, it was pointless to waste energy in dreams of testing that alternative to the Manchus.

In his distress, the eighteen-year-old realised he had, perhaps, paid too little attention to his adoptive sister Fronah. Yet he was puzzled and hurt by the distance that had opened between them. The girl he had loved since they were small children treated him like a stranger, as if she forgot both the escapades and the affection that had brightened their childhood. He had always considered her his sister – even before Saul Haleevie formally adopted him. It stung when she withheld the affection – and the obedience – a younger sister owed her elder brother. She spoke to him pleasantly enough, but they might have been no more than acquaintances.

Moreover, her mock betrothal to Aaron still rankled. Neither brother had ever believed that betrothal was only a pretence for Fronah's visiting Aisek, though neither was quite sure what else Saul's clever contrivance implied. David's logic, as well as his emotions, were distorted by the conflicting pressures of two disparate cultures. No more than Europeans, of course, did Chinese marry their sisters, but an adopted brother was a different matter. An adopted brother was *expected* to marry a sister who was an only child. How else carry on the family name and ensure that the ancestors would be venerated by future generations?

Unaware, David turned over two pages at once. His brother did not care for Fronah as profoundly as he himself did. Yet Aaron had been her prospective bridegroom – even if a sham betrothal. David knew a younger brother should not be betrothed when the elder was still unpledged. Acknowledging that Saul Haleevie had chosen the best possible way, he was none the less bitterly resentful.

David did not notice that the smoking lamp-wicks needed trimming. He was deeply grateful to Saul Haleevie, and he owed the merchant profound respect for championing his actual father. They were also linked by their common religion, for David considered himself both Jewish and Chinese, at once Mosaic in belief and Confucian in manners.

Saul had behaved with perfect benevolence, a virtue equally prized by

151

Jews and Chinese. But he was a foreigner, and David did not like being dependent upon a foreigner. That reservation was, he knew, both unworthy and unfilial. Though he had reproached himself for his baseness, he could not suppress the feeling.

'Oh, David!' Fronah's voice broke into his reflections. 'Isn't Aaron here?'

'You're looking for Aaron?' he asked abruptly. 'You startled me. I didn't hear the door open.'

'*Tang-jan, Erh-ko* . . .' For the first time in months, she spoke the Officials' Language he preferred. 'Naturally, Second Brother. You were studying too hard. But I wasn't looking for Aaron.'

'For me, then? That's hard to believe. You haven't seemed anxious to see me lately.'

'I know I've neglected you, Second Brother, shamelessly,' she continued in the Officials' Language. 'I haven't been quite myself. My heart's been troubled. But to whom else would I turn when I need comfort?'

'*Kau-su wo, Mei-mei* . . .' David's round face glowed with pleasure at Fronah's appeal. 'Tell me about it, Little Sister. What's troubling you?'

'I want to go away for a while. And I want you to come with me. You're the only person in the whole world I want to be with.'

'What? . . . What did you say?' he asked in his astonishment. 'Go away? Where? How?'

'I don't know exactly, but I thought you might have an idea.'

Fronah smiled at his agitation, which touched her. She remembered her old fondness for the devil-may-care scamp, and she regretted having neglected him for so long.

'You thought *I* might. The idea never . . . well, hardly . . . entered my head till you put it there. It has some merit, I must admit. Why do *you* want to go away?'

'I hate all men except you, David. And I'm fed up with my parents.'

'You're going too fast for me. What's all this about hating men?'

Intent upon her grievances, Fronah did not see that he was gently laughing at her. Forced to be secretive with her old-fashioned parents, her open nature required an intelligent confidant. But Maylu was too flighty and, apart from the concubine, David was closest to her. She did not appreciate his rising anger as she told him about her clandestine meetings with Iain Matthews, about the afternoon in the grove of plane-trees, and, finally, about the griffin's cutting her off without a word. All she saw was the dark top of her brother's head as he stared down at his desk.

'. . . it's all my parents' fault, you see,' she concluded. 'If they weren't so strict, I'd never have gone with Iain. *They* pushed me into it. You do understand, don't you, Second Brother?'

'I see many things, Little Sister,' David spoke slowly. 'I see you've been a fool. And that son of a turtle-bitch, I'll see to him. He'll regret it all his life . . . if he lives.'

'You mustn't, Second Brother.' Fronah was oblivious to his jealousy. 'I still love him, and he couldn't help it. You mustn't hurt him. Still, he *could* send me a note. And I'm afraid everyone'll learn about . . . about Iain and me. When they do, how can I hold my head up at a party? I must get away.'

'Of course you realise,' David said grimly, 'that he's brought disgrace on the family?'

'You mustn't tell the parents, Second Brother. If Papa knew . . .'

'I won't tell . . . if only to spare our father. But, later, I'll deal with the foreign devil.'

'I'll never let you. Right now I just want to go away. They'll all be sorry: Iain and the parents. You'll help, won't you, David dear? You and I . . . we've always helped each other. You'll come, won't you?'

'It *sounds* mad at first,' David mused. 'But is it really? I can't live on Father's charity forever. And I could do without Aaron's company for a while. You know we swore revenge on the Intendant Samqua for my former father's arrest. But Aaron won't even talk about it. He's as stubborn as dead bones.'

'How can you revenge yourself on Samqua? What could you do?'

'I'm not sure, but I've got an idea . . . a vague idea.' David's irrepressible humour impelled him to laughter. 'For that matter, where can you . . . we . . . go? It's impossible to go anywhere with the Taipings rampaging . . .'

'That's just what I thought, Second Brothers. It would be fascinating, you'll admit.'

'I'll admit what, Little Sister? What would be fascinating?'

'Why, to go and see the Taipings, as you suggested. It's perfectly easy. You could . . .'

'Only a seventeen-year-old girl could think of such nonsense . . . Yet, thinking about it, it's not really . . . No, it would never work.'

'Is it nonsense really?' Fronah marshalled the arguments she had rehearsed. 'We both want to go away . . . Why not to the Taipings? You hate the Imperialists, and I know you want to see what the Taipings are up to.'

'What makes you think they would take us in?' David was wavering, moved by his affection for Fronah and his own wild streak. 'Why should they?'

'I've also thought about that . . .'

'Obviously, Little Sister!' he grinned.

'. . . and there are many reasons. The Heavenly King is eager for Western knowledge, and we both have some. He needs educated men, and you're *practically* a Bachelor of Arts. So he'd welcome us both.'

'Practically a Bachelor is not the same as a Bachelor. And I'd never become a Bachelor if I went to the rebels. So . . .'

'That's not true, Second Brother. If we don't like it, we can always come

153

back. The Imperialists are eager for information about the Taipings. Why you'd be a hero.'

'I don't know about that,' David said dubiously. 'But, I'll grant you, it's not as mad as I thought at first.'

Knowing his sister's stubbornness, he was half-convinced. Rejected and resentful, she would slip away even without his help. Since he could not tell their parents, it was his duty as Fronah's older brother to go with her and protect her. Besides, her scheme intrigued him. Perhaps the Taipings were the key to his own revenge.

'You could arrange it easily,' she insisted. 'You know just who to talk to.'

'I'm not sure of that either,' he resisted feebly. 'But I'll give it some thought.'

CHAPTER TWENTY-FOUR

April 28, 1856   *Peking*

The Baronet Jung Lu was roused by the beat of drums, the clash of cymbals, and the shrilling of pipes in the *hutung* outside his villa just before the double-hour of the cock on April 28, 1856. At five in the morning, the boulevards, streets, and lanes of the Imperial Capital were swarming with revellers. He stretched his cramped limbs under the green-silk quilt and disconsolately listened to the joyous din.

Amid the rattle of firecrackers and the booming of gongs the Manchu nobleman heard repeated hisses as sky-rockets arched above the low buildings of Peking. It would, he knew with sour certainty, be another perfect day. The sun would be bright in a cloudless sky, and the wind would be a southerly zephyr. The carolling of whistles on the legs of the doves released in jubilation was already penetrating. The sky-rockets were exploding over those rainbow-dyed flocks, spraying gold-and-crimson radiance across the heavens. In the parks and the *hutungs* the revellers were waving paper lanterns in time to the rhythmic chanting that thrummed on his ear-drums. Their slurred cadence showed they were already half-drunk at sunrise.

'*Ai, lai cha . . .*' the Baronet shouted. 'Hey, bring tea and soured milk.'

When the major-domo bowed and scuttled out, the Baronet gingerly leaned against the bolster. Even his fingers ached as he rubbed his forehead, and his eyes stung.

154

The petty nobleman had heard the news from the Forbidden City early the previous evening and had sat down to drink himself into oblivion. Quite alone, he had dourly tossed down Heaven alone knew how many cups of rice-wine before calling for *bai-garh,* the potent sorghum spirits. He remembered little thereafter, not even the servants' putting him to bed. He only remembered that his mood had grown more sombre with each drink until he was overwhelmed by depression.

After gulping the cool milk, the Baronet wiped his face with a steaming towel and poured tea from a cylindrical pot. He did not, he realised, feel as miserable as he should. For some unfathomable reason, he was quite chipper. He shouted for rice-wine, and sipping the warm amber drink, examined his emotions and his prospects.

He had, naturally, hated hearing the news. But was it truly worse than the first devastating knowledge that Yehenala had entered the Forbidden City? Or, for that matter, more wounding than the report of her pregnancy? Why should he have raged last night when she had been beyond his reach for five years?

Would he, he castigated himself, have been happier if the child had been deformed or still-born? Would he have been happier if it had been a girl? Would he have been happier if Yehenala had died in childbirth? Manifestly not! Her misfortune would have been his misfortune – and her destruction would have destroyed him.

They why should her jubilation not be his jubilation and her triumph his triumph? Although the day-old infant had, naturally, not yet been designated Heir Apparent or, even, Heir Presumptive, he was the only legitimate son of the Hsien Feng Emperor. Nala was the mother of the boy who would, unless Heaven intervened, some day ascend to the Dragon Throne. Her power had expanded manyfold the moment the midwives saw that the infant was male. When he was designated Heir Presumptive, she would be second in power only to the Emperor.

The Son of Heaven had every possible reason to make that announcement immediately. An heir would prove to the Chinese people that the Great Pure Dynasty would continue to rule despite its present difficulties. Though not required by Dynastic Law to designate his first-born son his heir, the Emperor would prove himself an even bigger fool than he was if he did not.

When the Hsien Feng Emperor acted, torrents of good fortune would overflow – and the mother of the heir would be deluged with gifts. A goodly portion, better offered discreetly, would pass through his own hands. A presumptive Dowager Empress could also arrange a deserving officer's promotion with a flick of her finger, and he was eager for promotion.

He had, the Baronet Jung Lu concluded, every reason to rejoice – and no more reason to grieve than he had known every waking moment from the past five years. He would that morning make a generous offering of thanksgiving to Kuan Ti, the God of War, his own patron spirit. Suddenly

155

moved by frenetic gaiety, he sent for a barber to shave his face and his crown.

Afterwards, he bathed and chose clean undergarments, though he had washed his body and changed his clothes only a week earlier. He must not brood at home, lest the rumour-mongers speculate on his seclusion, but his mood was volatile, alternating between exaltation and depression. It was, therefore, better not to seek the company of his peers. He put on his robe of ceremony bordered with green and white wave patterns and strode into the *hutung* to join the revellers.

He would breakfast at a street-stall, where his splendid presence would excite awe. It might be eccentric for a Manchu nobleman to mingle with the Chinese rabble on a day of Dynastic rejoicing. But an heir was also the Emperor's gift to his people. It was their day, as much as the Court's day. Reflecting that the insecurity that oppressed both rulers and subjects had lifted, the Baronet stepped through the circular gate into the throng in the *hutung*.

'*Hsiaorh lung lai-la . . .*' A coolie with an enormous carbuncle scarlet on his forehead waved an earthenware flask of *bai-garh*. 'The small dragon has come! A small dragon for the Dragon Throne!'

Of course! This was the Year of the Dragon, supreme among the twelve animals of the zodiac, which gave their names to the years. To be born in the year of the Dragon, to be a dragon, meant to be endowed with great talents and great prospects. It was gloriously propitious for the infant who was to be the eighth of his line to mount the Dragon Throne.

As Jung Lu pushed through the throng, his spirits rose higher. For once, he was not oppressed by the commoners' stench of garlic and sweat. Even the yellow dust raised by hundreds of shuffling feet was a radiant cloud. The nobleman gave himself without reserve to the joy of the crowd and to his own anticipations.

All Peking bubbled with gaiety. Rainbow lanterns dangling beside gates glowed like the lights of a fairy kingdom. Scarlet bunting fluttered from eaves, and golden streamers gyrated on poles above the throng. Cymbals clashed two inches from Jung Lu's nose, while firecrackers rattled above booming drums and the undulating horns.

'*Hsiaorh lung lai-la . . .*' The Baronet shouted at a fat merchant. 'The small dragon's arrived. Rejoice! It's a great day!'

The infant should have been *his* son, he paused and reflected, *not* the son of that weakling on the Dragon Throne. Why was he rejoicing? Only a fool would rejoice at this ultimate humiliation. He snatched a flask of *bai-garh* from a waving hand, gulped the raw spirits, and dropped the flask. Why, a watching coolie wondered, should the young Manchu Lord's face be twisted in a demon-scowl on such a glorious morning?

*

156

The bed-chamber of the Virtuous Concubine was that morning not only the centre of the Forbidden City, but the focus of the hopes of all loyal subjects of the Great Pure Dynasty. The lanes leading to Yehenala's dwelling were alive with twittering women and lisping eunuchs like flocks of tropical birds in their brilliant robes. The morning sun caressed the gifts they bore: glittering gold and silver; shining jades and pearls; glowing rubies and sapphires; bright lacquer-ware and shimmering porcelains. No expenditure was too great to woo the favour of the twenty-year-old concubine who was now supreme in the Imperial Court. Her goodwill could not only shield them from the Emperor's febrile rages, but could enrich them manyfold. Heedless of dignity, the great ladies of China jostled and reviled each other like streetwalkers in their anxiety to be among the first to lay their tribute at Yehenala's feet.

The Empress Niuhura's gilt-and-scarlet palanquin was tossed by that throng before court ladies and eunuchs reluctantly gave way. She, who had failed to give her Lord a son, was also eager to present the lavish gifts carried by files of eunuchs in green and yellow brocade. The placid Empress was almost Chinese in her docile virtue, while the fiery Yehenala was a throwback to the head-strong women of the nomadic Manchu tribes. Niuhura still enjoyed formal precedure, but she knew she was no longer pre-eminent.

Bobbing on the tide of females, the Empress's palanquin approached Yehenala's modest dwelling. The eunuch bearers were lowering it to the ground when a torrent of acclamations rolled over them.

'*Huang-shang wan sui! Wan wan sui!*' Court ladies and eunuchs chanted the salutation reserved for the Son of Heaven. 'Ten thousand years! May Your Majesty live ten thousand times ten thousand years!'

The scented, silken sea opened before an enormous golden palanquin, whose curtains swayed with the jaunty trot of the twelve eunuchs in dragon-scrolled robes under its gilt carrying-poles. The Emperor had not mustered the armed eunuchs who guarded his sacred person and his glittering regalia on state occasions. Time enough when he offered sacrifices of thanksgiving to Heaven and ritually informed his ministers of the birth of his son.

He was none the less splendidly attired for the felicitous occasion. His plump, self-indulgent features were lit by jubilation under his conical summer crown covered with golden tassels. His sparse eyebrows were cocked high in delight, and his slack lips were drawn back to reveal his stained teeth. His brocaded robe glowed golden when the sun touched the five Imperial dragon-heads embroidered among the twelve symbols of his spiritual and temporal authority. At this moment of triumph, the twenty-five-year-old Son of Heaven radiated the authority he too often failed to demonstrate.

He alighted nimbly from the palanquin and, waving jauntily, ascended

157

the narrow marble steps. The bright-hued sea froze into unmoving waves as court ladies and eunuchs kneeled to touch their foreheads to the ground. Entering the open doors, the Emperor strode through rooms heaped with presents.

'*Dai-lai huang-tze* . . .' he commanded. 'Bring the prince to me.'

Only the infant's head was visible above the Imperial-yellow swaddling-clothes. The Emperor carefully examined the pale face marked by red striations, but the infant did not respond when he gingerly extended his forefinger. The crumpled baby features contracted in fear, and the small mouth wailed. The nursemaid, herself the daughter of a marquis, was torn between responsibility for her charge and deference to her sovereign. She bobbed an awkward bow and clucked soothingly to the infant.

'He has my eyebrows,' the Emperor declared complacently. 'A good portent, such fine thick eyebrows. He's a strong baby, isn't he?'

'Very strong, Majesty, and very beautiful. Also highly talented. The signs are written on his face.'

'No need for soothsayers' tricks,' the Emperor smiled. 'No need to read his fate on his face. With *his* ancestors . . . his *father* . . . he must be strong and talented.'

'And his mother so beautiful, Majesty.' The marquis's daughter played to her sovereign's vanity. 'The Virtuous Concubine is the beauty of the Forbidden City.'

'Yes, that too,' he agreed grudgingly. 'The Virtuous Concubine's quite beautiful.'

The Emperor had momentarily forgotten the woman whose womb had nurtured the infant that was his personal triumph. He recalled the title given Yehenala when she entered the palace. *Yi*, literally virtuous and chaste, further implied that she was an exemplar among women. Still, he reflected, they could have done worse. They could have called her modest and dutiful, qualities she emphatically did *not* possess.

Yehenala's bed-chamber overlooked a small garden, where orange azaleas and scarlet rhododendrons framed dwarf pines gnarled by time and the cunning of generations of eunuch gardeners. The scent of the white-flowers of wild ginger was astringent amid the musky perfumes of the women who scurried out when the Son of Heaven entered. The room stank of women, he noted. No wonder no man other than the father could visit a mother for a month after her confinement for fear of pollution. The rank, feral female odor was unclean.

Yehenala lay in a nest of aquamarine-velvet cushions, the silver-embroidered pleats of her old-rose bed-gown soft above the amethyst coverlet. Her features were drawn, the perfect oval of her face dinted by hollows beneath her cheekbones. Her blue-black hair lacked its normal sheen, though it was as intricately coiffed, for her hairdresser had just finished. White powder coated her translucent skin, and her eyes, outlined by kohl, sparkled with belladonna under sapphire-painted lids. Her mouth gleamed scarlet like a peony moist with dew.

Decorum, as well as vanity, required Yehenala to adorn herself to receive her lord, who normally sent eunuchs to fetch her. An emerald-jade dragon set with pearls transfixed her hair, and a white-jade plaque shimmered on her necklace of tourmaline and amethysts. Her fingernails were protected by three-inch gilt sheaths enamelled with indigo orchids, while rubies within green-jade hoops dangled from her ear lobes. That display was diminished by the treasure-hoard heaped on her rosewood sidetable.

'You are well, Nala?' the Emperor asked awkwardly. 'Truly well, I mean.'

'This slave is well, Majesty, and drunk with happiness.'

'Then all is well in the Empire,' he declared magisterially. 'All is indeed well.'

His awkwardness touched Yehenala deeply. She knew he spoke from the heart, though it was difficult for him to express his love for her. He had all his life been trained to curb his tongue and bridle his emotions lest he impair his dignity. It was difficult for the Supreme Monarch to tell her of his devotion even when they were alone. It was impossible for him under the eyes of a dozen ladies-in-waiting, eunuchs, and maidservants. No man, certainly not the inhibited Emperor could speak from the heart when so many ears listened. Every word they uttered would be repeated through-out the Forbidden City within hours and would be the gossip of the *hutungs* tomorrow.

'We, too, are drunk with happiness,' he declared. 'And the infant? It is in good health?'

'They tell me, Majesty, the prince is strong and healthy. My ladies say they've never seen a more robust baby.'

'Splendid, Nala, splendid. This is the happiest day of Our life. An heir at last! The happiest day of Our life, even though . . .'

'Even though, Majesty? Is something wrong? What can possibly cloud . . .'

'Just the same old thing, Nala. Our armies fighting the Long Hairs have suffered further defeats. We are, unfortunately, accustomed to such news.'

'Further defeats, Majesty? How frightful! In my joy, I'd forgotten the rebels. What can be done?'

'When you're fully recovered, Nala, after the celebrations, let us talk about the Long Hairs. We more and more think you're right and Our counsellors are wrong. A strong hand is needed.'

'Your slave is honoured by Your Majesty's confidence. But for now . . .'

Yehenala glanced around the room, and the Emperor, instinctively conspiratorial, grasped her meaning immediately. The hands of the eunuchs and maidservants sorting the presents did not move, and the

159

needles of the ladies-in-waiting hovered motionless over their embroidery frames while they listened avidly.

'The happiest day of Our life,' the Emperor repeated. 'And We wish you to be happy, too.'

'Happy, Majesty? Your slave is ecstatic. To bear a son is joy enough for any woman. To bear a son to the Lord of Ten Thousand Years is the greatest joy Your Majesty's slave can imagine.'

'And nothing could make you happier?' He smiled archly. 'Nothing?'

'Nothing, Majesty. My joy is complete.'

'Well, then, We see no need to tell you . . .'

'Of course not, Majesty,' Nala laughed, he pretending amusement at his heavy, tantalising banter. 'Your Majesty is, always, the best judge.'

'Since this is so, We *shall* tell you. This evening We shall promulgate your promotion. As of this moment, you are no longer *Yi Ping*, but *Yi Fei*.'

'I am overwhelmed, Majesty.' Yehenala reached out her hands, though she could not embrace him before the underlings. 'I am overwhelmed by Your Majesty's magnanimity.'

It was good news, very good news. It was also the least he could do. Advancement from *Ping*, concubine of the third rank, to *Fei*, the second rank, was only fitting for the mother of the Emperor's only son. He could, of course, having given her the first rank, but her rise had been rapid, only five years from the fifth rank to the second. So many were jealous of her behind their carmine smiles and their perfumed congratulations, it was, perhaps, better that he had not fanned their envy by skipping her a grade. At any rate, she was now a secondary wife, who could not be discarded at his whim.

'I thank Your Majesty profoundly,' she repeated. 'Your Majesty's slave prostrates herself at Your Majesty's feet.'

'As is no more than fitting, Nala.' The Emperor glanced at her attendants, but none smiled at his humour.

'No more than fitting, Majesty,' she laughed, reflecting that it was sometimes sad to be so far above ordinary mortals they dared not smile at your jests.

'We have also considered the infant's name.' The Emperor flicked his hand in dismissal and was silent until all her attendants had left the bed-chamber. 'The prince will be called Tsai Chün.'

Yehenala gasped in jubilation. The name bestowed on the prince, her son, was far more important than her being raised in rank. It meant, quite simply, that he would in his turn be emperor.

It was inevitable that he be called Tsai. The first word of the name of each successive generation of the Imperial Family had been determined a century earlier by the great Chien Lung Emperor, in a classical couplet. Her son could not have been called anything but Tsai, meaning to promulgate.

But Chün, which meant purely majestic, was an inestimable honour for the infant prince – and for his mother. That title affirmed that the boy stood first in line for the Dragon Throne. Since he was the Emperor's only son, it was likely that he would succeed his father. But the Emperor might yet father other sons, and Dynastic Law did not require him to designate his first-born the Crown Prince. The Hsien Feng Emperor would probably not do so for some time. No emperor was eager to anoint his successor. None wished to think over much about his own inevitable death 'when ten thousand years had passed', and none wished to create a cabal of ambitious eunuchs and officials around an anointed heir.

The Emperor had gone as far as he could – or should – by implicitly affirming the infant Heir Presumptive. Formal designation as Heir Apparent, entirely at the Emperor's pleasure, might be awarded later. Of course, her son might not succeed. He might not even survive the first perilous month of life.

Yehenala thrust away that sombre thought. It was equally possible that the Emperor would father no other sons or, if he did, that she would be their mother. Only a week earlier her favourite soothsayer had, at once, dismayed and delighted her. The eunuch had predicted that she would bear a prince who would mount the Dragon Throne before another cycle of twelve years had passed. Tears welling, she prayed to Kwan Yin, the Goddess of Mercy, to keep the Emperor vigorous.

But, her implacable intelligence told her, she would exult in the position of mother of a child-emperor. No woman could exercise greater power than a mother-regent. If the Hsien Feng Emperor should ascend the Heavenly Dragon, she, Nala of the Yehe, would be supreme in the Great Empire.

CHAPTER TWENTY-FIVE

May 17, 1856   *The Yangtze near Pachiaochen*

The old *Low Dah* grunted in satisfaction as his eyes swept the heavens. Knowing the moon would be only a sliver of light, he had chosen this night to run the gauntlet of Imperial warjunks patrolling the Long River between Pachiaochen and Taiping-held Chenkiang, a stretch as familiar as the cabin of his own black junk. The scattered islands eighty miles above Shanghai were a blessing for smugglers and pirates, while the constant skirmishing between the Imps and the Taipings impelled peaceful villagers to keep their houses dark. But no man could have known that a veil of clouds would draw closed at midnight, so that not even steely starlight imperilled his vessel.

The owner-master gave thanks to Tien Mu Hou, the Mother Empress of Heaven, the patron goddess of all who hazarded their lives on the waters. He had known he enjoyed her esteem since the lunatic voyage from Soochow more than two years earlier had brought the mad foreigner and the Chinese who was almost as mad safely to Shanghai. The Goddess was again demonstrating her special favour, he reflected complacently. Two bags of silver Maria Theresa dollars lay in the wooden chest in his cabin beneath the scarlet shrine where incense sticks smoldered before her carved image. He had been paid twice for this voyage: once by the barbarian Ha-lee-vee, whose contraband he carried; and again by the young scholar who was so desperate to reach Nanking, the old Southern Capital. He must remember to call that metropolis Tienking, the Heavenly Capital, as it was now.

The rudder, as large as a temple-door, responded to his light touch on the tiller, and water gurgled through the diamond-shaped holes cut in the teak to reduce its weight. The junk pointed towards the shore, where the downstream current ran less strongly. The loom of the banks would prevent its being silhouetted by even the faintest light, while the shallows frightened the deep-hulled Imperial warjunks.

'*Hwen-dan* . . .' he said softly. 'You addled eggs, you dogs' droppings! Scull harder. They're real, those big warjunks out there. Their guns are real, too. Scull harder if you want to live. And, for Tien Hou's sake, smear some grease on the oar-locks. They're squealing like sows under the butcher's knife. You're less use than a eunuch's prick. You scull like old whores rotten with pox. You're as . . .'

His lips closed, imprisoning even richer epithets behind the palisade of his blackened teeth. Though his sons, who were his crew, were as competent as one could expect of boys in their twenties and thirties, it always helped to encourage them with obscenity-spiced exhortations. He did not fear that his hoarse whisper would carry across the river. But that girl who had come aboard with the young scholar, there was no need to offend her ears.

She was probably a tart making the foolhardy voyage because of a promise of many silver dollars, for she spoke down-to-earth colloquial Shanghainese like his own daughters. None the less, she might be a lady, the young fellow's wife or concubine – though that was unlikely. The scholar was obviously a bit mad or he wouldn't sail on a smuggling junk, but even so he would not imperil a lady of his own family. Besides, she strode confidently on unbound feet, and no scholar would take a wife or concubine from a family that couldn't give its daughters golden lilies. There was something very odd about the girl in the simple tunic and trousers. Though she carried herself as proudly as an empress, she hid her face.

Still, it wasn't his affair what idiocies the gentry got up to. His business was to con his junk to the Heavenly Capital and deliver his cargo of gunpowder, lead, rifles, and printer's type. Why the Taipings wanted type so urgently only Tien Mu Hou knew. But that wasn't his affair either.

His own affairs were worry enough for one night. Even since the disaster at Chenkiang, when their besieging armies were routed, the Imps had patrolled the vital stretches of the Long River as if their lives depended on it. Fear of losing their heads could inspire the captains of warjunks to remarkable vigilance, and they all knew that smugglers loved to slip through the back channel around Yangchung Island. The shallow water, which now offered security, could become a trap.

Following the sharp northward curve of the bank, the junk entered the channel. The *Low Dah* momentarily regretted the blackness where the lamps of the Liu Family Village would normally serve as a landmark. Despite the shallow draught that made her agile in the narrow waters, his craft could also run upon a sandbank. The total darkness now threatened the junk as well as hiding her from Imperial patrols. Fortunately, every variation on the silhouetted banks – every temple and pagoda, every cluster of houses, every weir, landing-stage and tree – was etched upon his memory.

The old *Low Dah* drew a deep breath and stood erect. Shifting his hold on the tiller, he let his arms hang free for a moment to unknot his tense shoulder muscles. He did not relax his scrutiny of the night.

He saw no alien presence, though the clouds were shifting and starlight glinted on the water. He heard only the occasional leaping of fish and the hum of men and animals in the villages on the shore. No Imperial warjunk could be lurking on the river.

The *Low Dah* stiffened in terror when he saw a steel-blue effluorescence glowing under the lip of the promontory. He whispered aloud, imploring the Empress of Heaven to protect his vessel. Only once before had he ever seen such an unearthly light: At Kua Tao, Orphan's Island, where the spirits of the dead congregated beneath the monastery on the cliffs that fell vertically to the Long River. The blue glimmer could not be man-made, and no star ever dipped so low. As he prayed, the ghost-fire flared again. The *Lao Dah* promised Tien Mu Hou a great feast of lacquered ducks and suckling pigs to bring him safely out of the clutches of the demons. He licked his lips, remembering that the Goddess fed only on the aroma of such offerings. As the ghost-fire sputtered out, he ordered his sons to hoist the matting-sails. Demons could fly over the water, but he would be a fool not to try to escape.

For three minutes the river was lit only by starlight, and the junk drew towards a crag that might deflect the demons' flight. The *Low Dah* sternly

163

reminded Tien Mu Hou that he had never broken a pledge to her. The silence was broken only by a metallic clatter under the promontory where the ghost-fire had flared. Once again, the Goddess had drawn her invisible cloak around her favourite.

A sapphire spear lanced the darkness. The *Low Dah* ordered his sons to aim the gingal, which was an enormous blunderbuss. The beam skittered over the wavelets like a blind man's stick scraping across cobble-stones. In the back glow, the *Low Dah* saw a boxy shape bristling with tall spines breathing red sparks. A malignant water-dragon was searching for his vessel with its incandescent blue eye.

The terrified crew sculled frantically for the rock that reared out of the water. Drawn by the phosphorescent bow-wave, the light inched closer to the junk. After veering to light the water-grass clinging to the fissures of the granite crag, the sapphire lance impaled the junk.

The *Low Dah* felt like a fighting cricket caged under a glaring lamp. Every pore and every wrinkle of his weathered face, every stay, plank, and rope of his vessel was drenched with unearthly light. The dragon-eye had fixed his junk. In an instant, dragon-fire would consume them, leaving not a fingernail or a hair, not a splinter of wood or a scrap of metal.

The *Low Dah* cursed his fate and his sons. But the malignant water-dragons were creatures of another age, born long before the black-haired race populated China. He had almost forgotten the gingal. Since they were normally aloof from men and their ancient brains were sluggish, the great dragons had no knowledge of modern inventions. No man-made weapon could wound the water-dragon, but the gingal might terrify it.

'Fire!' he screamed. 'Fire.'

Orange flame belched from the blunderbuss, and the junk slewed crabwise, pitching under the recoil. Chains and potshards mixed with broken bottles and iron bolts whistled over the water towards the fire-breathing shape. The dragon-eye blinked, then glared remorselessly again. The *Low Dah*'s shoulders drooped dispiritedly as his sons sculled the junk behind the crag. The dragon-eye blinked again, flared bright, and vanished. The *Low Dah*'s hoarse, exulting cry echoed across the water.

On board the gunboat *Mencius*, Gabriel Hyde did not break stride as the shrapnel whistled past. Running barefoot to the foredeck, he pushed aside the bosun, who was tinkering with the temperamental acetylene searchlight. First not enough lime pellets, then not enough water to dissolve the pellets into gas. And now what?

The tube that carried the gas to the burner was blocked, for the Chinese would never clean anything properly. Swearing to himself, the American twisted a wire through the tube. He assured himself that it was clear by blowing through it, struck a match, touched the flame to the burner, and replaced the lens. The steel-blue beam again lanced over the water to impale the junk.

The *Low Dah*'s head sank to his chest in defeat. Even the barbarian gun could not frighten the ancient beast, perhaps because it was too stupid to be afraid. Whatever the reason, he was beyond even the succour of the Mother Empress of Heaven. He waited for the dragon's fiery breath to consume him.

David Lee rose from the slimy deck boards. Glancing behind him to make sure Fronah was safe in the cabin, he grasped the *Low Dah*'s arms.

'Don't give up,' he urged. 'We can still get away.'

'The dragon can't be frightened away,' the *Low Dah* replied. 'What more can I do against a demon?'

'It's not a demon, you fool, only a foreign-devil invention, that light. Keep the junk moving.'

The quick-firing gun on *Mencius*'s foredeck coughed three times. As the echoes died, the *Low Dah* heard a voice shouting in an outlandish language. He saw the angular vessel hurtling down upon them, and his voice cracked with fear.

'Worse, far worse!' he moaned. 'The barbarians are devils in human form.'

'What do you know?' David demanded. 'Get the boat moving!'

'It's no use. In Shanghai the barbarians sometimes behave like human beings. On the Long River, they're all pirates, demon pirates. I've had friends attacked by foreign devils . . . Throats cut, cargoes stolen, and junks scuttled.'

'I know about barbarian pirates.' David also knew the savage punishments inflicted on scholars for trafficking with the Taipings. 'But that light isn't a pirate. It can only be an Imperial gunboat with a foreign captain. For Tien Mu Hou's sake, scull to the shore.'

'It's all over with us, Young Lord,' the *Low Dah* sighed. 'We can't escape the living foreign demons. Worse than the worst Chinese ghosts, they are.'

David gazed at the dark bank fifty yards away. Despite the current in the back channel, he could swim that distance. The Imperial Edict was unequivocal. Any scholar, even only an aspirant Mandarin, caught collaborating with the Taipings would be tortured and summarily decapitated. He saw that the gunboat was lowering a boat. He began unbuttoning his jacket so that it would not impede his struggle with the Long River.

His fingers paused, then slipped the buttons back into their holes. Fronah could never make that swim, and he could not leave her to face the gunboat's crew alone. If the captain were a foreigner, he might treat her well. But who could be certain? He, too, knew that foreigners in the Imperial service were the most callous rascals on the China Coast.

'Go on, David!' Fronah urged. 'You've got to get away.'

'For every smuggler captured, a hundred get through.' David grinned ruefully. 'Why did we have to be the hundredth?'

'Never mind, David. Just go!'

'I can't, Fronah, I can't. It's too late.'

The boat was bearing down on the junk. When Fronah slipped her hand into David's, he grasped it convulsively. It was, he realised inconsequentially, very small and very cold. Hand in hand, they waited for the sailors to board the junk.

Gabriel Hyde swung himself onto the smuggling vessel. Normally, his bosun would command the boarding party. But he had wanted to see the vessel for himself. Rocking on the balls of his feet, he watched his sailors prod the junk's crew on to the fantail.

Hardly a great haul: nine men, one a boy of no more than twelve from his size. Whatever else they lacked, the smugglers had courage. Defying the Long River and the Imperial warjunks in this cockleshell was no pastime for the faint-hearted.

'Have catchee smugglers, Cap'n,' the cockswain chortled, emerging from the hold. 'Have look-see bottomside plenty powder and guns.'

'We'll take the junk in tow,' Hyde decided. 'But first get these people on to *Mencius*.'

Silhouetted by the searchlight, the smugglers clambered from the junk into the boat. Apathy had succeeded the *Low Dah*'s terror. Why, he wondered, had the Goddess deserted him when he lavishly honoured every pledge he made her? And what would become of the hoard of silver in the chest under Tien Mu Hou's shrine?

As the boat pulled away with the first six prisoners, Gabriel Hyde glanced at the remaining three.

'That's no boy,' he exclaimed. 'Not with that scarf and that shape. What is she? The master's wife?'

'No savee, Capt'n,' the cockswain grinned. 'Maybe damned smuggler's whore. We makee jig-jig tonight. Bettern Flower Boat.'

'Not on my ship,' Hyde admonished automatically.

'She's a European lady, Captain.' David's voice quavered. 'You must see that she's treated respectfully.'

'I'll be damned,' Hyde exclaimed. 'A Chinaman speaking perfect . . . well, almost perfect . . . English. Who are you, my lad? A European lady, you say? This is a night of wonders!'

'You've caught me fairly, Captain. Whatever becomes of me, I deserve it. But the young lady . . .'

'A Chinaman who speaks English,' Hyde marvelled. 'And a European lady who doesn't. Can't she speak for herself?'

Fronah's hands trembled as she unknotted her scarf to face the foreign captain, even more fearful because of his American accent. Only vicious foreigners entered the Imperial Water Force, and the Americans were notoriously the most vicious. Though she was frantic with worry for David, she realised that she, too, was in grave danger. No Chinese captain would dare molest a foreign woman. But who could tell what an American might dare?

'Why, Miss Haleevie,' Hyde exclaimed. 'If it isn't my old dancing partner, the mysterious Miss Fronah Haleevie.'

'You know me?' she asked unnecessarily. 'I'm afraid . . .'

'That's not very flattering, Ma'am.' Gabriel Hyde yawned to conceal his laughter. 'Forgetting me so soon. But I remember you well. Fourth of July at Russells' with the Filipino band.'

'I do recall, Lieutenant . . . ah . . . Lieutenant . . .'

'Hyde, Ma'am, Gabriel Hyde, formerly lieutenant, US Navy.' With light malice he mimicked her pronunciation, *left*enant. 'Now lieutenant commander in His Imperial Manchu Majesty's Water Force. At your service, Ma'am.'

'Lieutenant Hyde? Yes I do recall, now. You must pardon me, but I am . . .'

'This is no place for a chat, Miss Haleevie. Let's go aboard *Mencius* and sort this out.'

'My father will pay well if . . . if you can forget where you found us . . . and you let us go.'

'I don't bargain with young ladies, Miss Haleevie. On the other hand, I'm not out to catch boys and girls, only smugglers. And you're the most unlikely smugglers I've ever seen.'

*

'Well, what are we to do about you and . . . ah . . . young David here?'

Gabriel Hyde spoke from the eminence of his four years' seniority to the Chinese youth. They were seated in cane chairs in the captain's cabin on *Mencius*, sipping jasmine tea from handleless blue and white cups. Outwardly as self-possessed as if entertaining the American in her own parlour, Fronah had formally introduced her brother David – and Hyde had gravely shaken the young man's hand.

'Do? she said lightly. 'Why it's quite simple, Commander. When we get to Shanghai, just let us slip off your ship.'

'That's a reasonable suggestion, Ma'am, most reasonable. After I've cut the smugglers' throats, I see no reason why . . .'

'Cut their throats,' Fronah gasped. 'You can't mean it. How could you . . .'

'They *are* criminals, you know, smugglers caught red-handed. Worse, they're traitors. It would be a mercy to spare them the headsman's sword.'

'You can't, Commander!' Fronah protested. 'You just can't.'

'Of course I can. I'll just pass the word to my bosun. He'll positively enjoy it!'

167

'Why, Commander? David asked. 'Why cut their throats?'

'Plain as the nose on your face, young David. It's your lives or theirs, not to speak of the young lady's reputation.'

'I don't see . . .' Fronah began.

'Fronah, he means they'll talk otherwise,' David explained glumly. 'And if the Mandarins learn I was caught on a smuggling junk, I'm dead, too. If the Shanghai ladies gossip about your running away with me . . .'

'Right, the first time, young David.' Gabriel Hyde was saturnine. 'Go to the head of the class.'

Fronah knew the American was enjoying their predicament. The mouth that could be so amiable smiled cruelly, and the dark blue eyes were hard.

'Look, Commander, I can see the risk for you, too,' David said. 'But our father'll pay you well. Just drop us off quietly and then deliver your prisoners. Five hundred . . . no, let's say a thousand . . . dollars are surely worth the risk.'

'Let them go,' Fronah pleaded. 'Don't kill them. How could we live with the memory? Your killing them to save us.'

'Even if you're game for the risk, there's my crew. They'd understand my cutting a few throats, but they'd never understand letting prisoners go.'

'Have you searched the junk, Commander?' David asked. 'Did your men find a thousand silver *taels* and several hundred Maria Theresa dollars?'

'Many thanks, David,' Hyde replied. 'If you hadn't told me, my rascals would've gotten away with it. And that might just be . . .'

'Might be what, Lieutenant?' Fronah prompted.

'It might just be the answer,' Hyde mused. 'Suppose I let them keep their loot, but let them know I know. Then sink the junk and let the prisoners go. Nobody'd talk then, not my cut-throats or your smugglers.'

'A perfect solution, Commander.' Fronah smiled beguilingly. 'You're very clever.'

'What about yourself, Commander?' David asked.

'You've hit the nail on the head, young David. *What* about myself indeed?'

'There's this.' David offered the moneybelt containing his small hoard of silver. 'Will this help?'

'Not really, David,' Gabriel Hyde drawled. 'I don't take candy from babies.'

'What *do* you want, Commander?' Fronah hastily moderated her peremptory tone: 'How can we possibly reward you?'

'I guess I'll just have to satisfy myself with the prize money. Let me see. The junk was, unfortunately, holed and sank, but not before we unloaded the contraband. That'll bring me a penny or two, and for the rest . . .'

'For the rest, Commander?' Fronah asked as his silence prolonged itself.

'For the rest, Miss Haleevie, you can satisfy my curiosity. Where *does* your name come from?'

Astonished by his strange demand, Fronah told Gabriel Hyde of the Haleevies' long journey from Spain to Shanghai by way of Baghdad and Bombay. In hope of dazzling the enigmatic American, she exaggerated her father's wealth.

'Jewish, just as I suspected,' Hyde remarked with grim satisfaction. 'Well, that's cleared up, then.'

'And that's all, Commander?' she asked. 'All you want?'

'Just put in a good word for me with your father and your wealthy friends. Who knows, I might need a wealthy friend some day.'

Fronah sighed in relief, forgetting the terrible scene David and she would face with her parents. Some day, she might know why Gabriel Hyde had toyed with them. For the moment, she only knew that they had escaped lightly – and that she owed the American immense gratitude for sparing David's life and her reputation. Some day, he would demand payment. Despite his magnanimity, he was a mercenary.

CHAPTER TWENTY-SIX

May 28, 856

Peking
The Forbidden City

'The poor chickens,' Yehenala laughed. 'I pity the poor chickens.'

The abstracted Emperor gazed past her into the garden, where bronze chrysanthemums bloomed in lime-green jardinières among the dwarfed pines. It was already half past the double-hour of the snake, ten in the morning by the ingenious Western clocks which he, like his predecessors, avidly collected. He must soon leave for the Hall of Supreme Harmony to welcome Imperial Princes, Grand Chancellors, Ministers, and Senior Mandarins to the banquet celebrating the first month of life of the Prince Tsai Chün. Jaded after Yehenala's banquet for several hundred court ladies the previous night, he had horrified his entourage by coming on foot to her mansion. However, the palanquin despatched by the scandalised Chief Eunuch waited outside.

'Why are you talking about chickens? They're stupid birds.'

'I still pity them, Majesty. All those red eggs . . . hundreds of thousands of red eggs. Tens of thousands of chicken families destroyed. The chicken ancestors must be weeping in poultry heaven. No descendants to offer sacrifices for the happiness of their spirits.'

'But it's customary, Nala. Fathers always hand out red-dyed eggs a month after a birth. And We . . . We of course . . . must distribute red

169

eggs to the entire Capital. Anyway, fowls don't sacrifice to the spirits of their ancestors.'

'I deeply regret having intruded my levity into Your Majesty's profound concerns.'

'Oh, you were joking,' he smiled. 'We see. Very funny.'

Secure in her new status, Yehenala was not disturbed. None the less, she reminded herself, she must avoid either subtlety or irony with the Emperor, who had become more pompous since the birth of the prince. The prestige of even the Lord of Ten Thousand Years had been exalted because he had finally fathered a son in the twenty-sixth year of his life.

He looked truly majestic. His Robe of Ceremony was pale yellow to shimmer in the artificial light at the audience he had granted the chief men of the Great Empire at dawn. Writhing dragons were embroidered in brilliant gold thread to stand out. She herself wore a simple blue-silk gown since she was not required to endure another ceremonial banquet to celebrate the close of her month of enforced seclusion and the Prince Tsai Chün's attainment of full human status. Her son's spirit was now securely united with his flesh after hovering for thirty days in limbo. *Man Yueh*, the passage of the Full Month, gave reasonable assurance that the infant would survive – as so many did not.

'I was joking, Majesty, since we are alone for a moment.' Despite her recent resolution, she slipped into self-parody; in the hope of amusing him. 'Your slave beseeches her Lord to smile. Can Your Majesty not cast off his cares on this auspicious day?'

'It's hard, Nala, hard,' he sighed. 'Have you seen the latest Memorials from the Army South of the Yangtze? We sent you copies.'

'I am concerned, Your Majesty, much concerned. But no one can correct in a few days the errors of many years. Today, Your Majesty should be happy.'

'We shall try, Nala. We shall try to forget how badly served We are.'

'The commander of the Army South of the Yangtze is brave and loyal. Besides, he's a good strategist. Your Majesty possesses at least one Manchu commander of talent.'

'The Army of the South was routed a week ago, Nala. We received the Memorial yesterday. The Army disintegrated when its headquarters were overrun. So much for *that* commander of talent.'

'In her concern for the prince, your slave failed to read that Memorial, Majesty.' Yehenala was puzzled. 'But the commander had besieged Nanking for three years, always drawing closer. How could the Army of the South disintegrate in a single day?'

'It all began with the relief of Chenkiang two months ago. The rebel lout they call the Four-Eyed Dog destroyed the loyal armies ringing the Citadel of the River. Incidentally, Our commander there has been killed. A cannon-ball squashed him. What can We do when the oceanic barbarians sell cannon to the Long Hairs?'

'He was no great loss, Majesty, even if he was a Manchu,' Yehenala consoled him. 'He was just a civilian playing at commanding troops. No more a general than I am.'

'You could do better, Nala!' The Emperor smiled at the thought of the small concubine bestriding a war horse. 'Even a woman could do better than Our generals.'

'Your slave does not merit such praise, Majesty. But how did the defeat of the siege of the Citadel lead to this . . . this latest catastrophe?'

'Simple, Nala, much *too* simple. When the rebels attacked other key cities, Our commander despatched most of his forces to help those cities. He believed his remaining troops could hold the Great Headquarters Camp. And then disaster. The Long Hairs concentrated their forces and overran the Great Camp. The commander has fled, and his troops are dispersed. We now have *no* effective force south of the Long River.'

'What's to be done, Your Majesty?'

'This Orphan has beseeched Heaven for guidance, but has been vouchsafed no reply. The Taipings are celebrating like lunatics. Their greatest victory in the five years since they rose in rebellion, cut off their queues, and let their hair grow long. A catastrophe . . . worse for Us, even, than the fall of Nanking. This Orphan asks you: *What* is to be done?'

'Your slave has given much attention to all Memorials except that last one, Majesty.' Yehenala spoke cautiously; when he called himself Orphan. the Son of Heaven was volatile – and dangerous. 'Your slave believes there is good reason for hope.'

'Do not humour Us,' the Emperor snapped. '*Nothing* can be done until we find men of true talent.'

'The Army North of the Yangtze is intact, is it not?'

'That's true, Nala. Things could be worse.'

'They could, Majesty, when one recalls that the Army of the North is brilliantly led. General Tseng Kuo-fan, Governor Tseng, is truly a man of talent.'

'Your words aren't totally empty, Nala,' the Emperor conceded. 'You would, We assume, advise Us to give Governor Tseng command of the Army of the South? If he can find those remnants, of course!'

'Majesty, your slave would suggest that you place Governor Tseng in command of *all* the troops fighting the Long Hairs.' She ignored his outburst. 'The Army of the South *and* the Army of the North. Your Majesty's forces would thus be unified and, then . . .'

'A remarkable thought, Nala. Brilliant!' The volatile Emperor was enthusiastic, then cautious. 'Yet, is it wise to give such great power into the hands of one man? A Chinese, at that. However, We'll think on the matter.'

171

'Majesty, please condescend to search for other men of talent, as well. They need not hold sweeping authority, as Your Majesty has so wisely pointed out. But fresh talent is essential.'

'Do you have anyone else in mind?' the Emperor asked suspiciously. 'You're remarkably well informed, Nala.'

'Your slave is only a woman, an idle, useless woman,' she replied carefully. 'I have lately been idle, remaining in seclusion. But I have not entirely wasted my month of enclosure. I've read the Memorials from the field with great care. As far as my limited ability permits, I have grasped the details as well as the general situation.'

'What else do you recommend, Nala?' He was mollified by her strenuous self-abasement. 'I'm sure that's not all.'

'Very little more Majesty. But it has struck me that one of Governor Tseng's subordinates is himself very able. The Mandarin Li Hung-chang passed high in the Doctoral examination when he was only twenty-one. He is now thirty-three and a most capable field commander. Your Majesty might care to watch him.'

'Another Chinese, Nala? If We did not know better, We would suspect you of plotting to turn the Empire over to the Chinese.'

The Emperor laughed at his own jest, and Yehenala joined him in relief. He had cut a little too close to the bone. Both Governor Tseng Kuo-fan and the Mandarin Li Hung-chang were, of course, highly competent. She had satisfied herself as to their competence after accepting the handsome presents Li Hung-chang offered upon her elevation to concubine of the third rank the preceding year. Governor Tseng's offerings had not been as lavish, no more than prudent presents to a lady who was rising rapidly in the favour of the Son of Heaven. But the Baronet Jung Lu had assured her that Governor Tseng would soon be wealthy – and appropriately grateful for her patronage.

Both would be discreetly informed that she had spoken for them when they were next promoted. The Forbidden City was not the world, and, some day, she might need allies who wielded military power. A pity they were Chinese, but she, like the Empire itself, required the services of men of talent regardless of race. It would be foolhardy, she decided reluctantly, to press for Jung Lu's advancement now. However, quite soon.

'Well, Nala, We shall grant one request on this auspicious day.' The Emperor was again amiable. 'The Mandarin Li Hung-chang, We'll make him a prefect. As for Governor Tseng's appointment as commander-in-chief against the Taipings . . . We'll consider it. But, now, We must leave for the great banquet.'

Yehenala rose and bowed. When she began to kneel, the Emperor's hand under her elbow restrained her.

'No need for such obeisances when We're alone with you,' he said gently.

She fondly watched the Dragon Robe pass through the doorway.

Hearing the murmurs as her eunuchs and her ladies-in-waiting prostrated themselves, she reflected that she had fought her own battles ever since coming into the Forbidden City as a minor concubine. She had won her own victories, and she was now in possession of the battlefield. She was also in possession of the Emperor's affection, and she would serve him as best she could while prudently providing for her son, her family, and herself. Her own interests and the Emperor's interests, as well as the interests of the Great Empire, were for the moment identical. She hoped that they would always remain so.

*

Glowing under the immense octagonal lanterns suspended from the gilt-and-scarlet beams of the Hall of Supreme Harmony, the lonely golden figure of the Hsien Feng Emperor descended cautiously from the throne dais. He had taken off his conical hat, and his cheeks were flushed with the drink he had consumed since the banquet began five hours earlier at one o'clock, the double-hour of the sheep. He was not drunk, the Emperor reassured himself, just a little tipsy. Firmly planting one foot before lifting the other, he shuffled down the four steps that separated the dais from the hall where the grandees of the Manchu Empire were still dining. His guests were all male, while he had been the only male at Yehenala's banquet for the court ladies.

The grandees toyed with the dishes that flowed from the Imperial Kitchens, where stout eunuch cooks swore at mischievous eunuch scullery boys. As the rectangular tables were cleared for the 236th course amid the clatter of utensils, the rulers of China joked and laughed, shouting boisterously at the finger-matching game. Having failed to best his quicker – or less inebriated – opponent in predicting the sum of his extended fingers, the loser happily downed another cup of spirits.

Some men displaying the silver crane of a Mandarin of the First Grade on their black surcoats had already surrendered to the liquors. Sliding from their lacquer stools, they lay peacefully on the floor till the eunuchs carried them to their sedan-chairs. The clamour within the Hall of Supreme Harmony, which rang with vinous goodwill this day, was punctuated by the explosions on the walls of the Imperial City. Rockets whistled into the clouds; prolonged salvoes of fire-crackers rattled; grenades erupted; Catherine wheels whirled in torrents of sparks; and brushes of flame painted evanescent pictures of dragons and phoenixes against the darkening sky. The din did not awaken the wrinkled Minister of Finance, who sat miraculously upright, his elbows propped on the table. Even his conical hat with its ruby button of rank and its peacock plumes of distinction remained square on his long head. Gentle belches occasionally interrupting his snores, he slept on.

173

The jaded diners had, the waiters saw, left the crackling skin of suckling pigs and roast ducks virtually untouched. Many left-over delicacies would supplement the portions the cooks had put aside for the staff. A hundred pairs of eunuchs entered bearing enormous double-skinned platters filled with boiling water to keep warm great yellow fish steamed with shrimp and conch. When one waiter slipped on a discarded bone, the domed lid of a silver serving-platter, gold-chased with mythical sea denizens, clanged on the floor.

The befuddled Emperor did not reproach his servants when the unfortunate waiter's partner overbalanced and fell. The Emperor grinned when the double-platter crashed on the flagstones and the boiling water scalded the prostrate waiters. He laughed when the enormous fish skidded across the floor to glare reprovingly at the pompous Minister of Justice. It was a pity, the Emperor mused blearily, that this was not an old-fashioned Manchu banquet where the hounds gorged themselves on morsels flung to the floor.

Still, it was the next best thing. A staid Imperial Banquet of the first class, the menu prescribed to the last grain of rice by Dynastic Law, was normally stultified by Court Etiquette. Even the streams of liquors were normally consumed so solemnly they made men sodden rather than jolly. Today gaiety was stoked by draughts of fermented mare's milk called koumiss; by rice-wine and grape-wine; by brandies of plums, peaches, and cherries; by spirits distilled from millet, sorghum, and wheat. Today's was not only a state feast, but a family feast, and the Mandarins who governed China on behalf of the Lord of Ten Thousand Years roistered in good fellowship. The new father, who was also the father of the nation, felt he was entertaining hundreds of unruly but good-humoured sons.

The Emperor halted at each table to hold out his porcelain thimble-cup to the Imperial Wine Steward. When the amber rice-wine brimmed, he raised his cup in salutation. Burbling congratulations, the Mandarins joined their sovereign in a toast to the Prince Tsai Chün.

'Ten thousand years!' they cried with unconscious irony. 'May Your Majesty live ten thousand times ten thousand years!'

The Emperor took no notice of the *pièce de résistance*, camel's hump braised with wild garlic. He was already replete, though he had taken no more than the obligatory bite of each dish. His distended paunch rumbled beneath his stained robe, and he felt queasy. Besides, he found the camel hump tough, stringy, and invariably overdone.

As the Mandarins picked at that dish of kings, the Emperor continued his peregrination. Court Etiquette required him to toast all his guests. Balanced with precarious dignity, he shuffled towards a table of four men wearing the five-clawed dragon of Imperial Princes on their surcoats. The Manchus broke off their argument as the Emperor approached. They rose leisurely, bowed, and lifted their cups.

174

'Give me koumiss!' the Emperor commanded the Imperial Wine Steward. 'A true Manchu drink for a true Manchu prince! Koumiss for Manchu warriors.'

The Steward filled deep bowls with the frothy white fluid. Kneeling on one knee he offered each Imperial Prince a bowl before genuflecting to the Emperor. The Princes raised their cups, and the Emperor responded. Heads thrown back, they drained their bowls and tossed them to the Wine Steward.

'Brother, is't you?' The Emperor blinked at the nearest Prince. 'S'you, isn' it?'

'Your slave ventures to celebrate the birth of his nephew, Majesty,' the Prince replied, 'and Your Slave begs for forgiveness.'

'S'all right . . . s'all right, Little Brother.' The Emperor waved his arms expansively. 'Come'n drink 'nother cup with Us.'

The Emperor genially clutched the arm of the Prince, whose square face was almost as drink flushed as his own. Together, they stumbled out of earshot of the three remaining Princes, who stared in amazement.

Twenty-one-year-old Prince Kung, the sixth son of the previous Tao Kwang Emperor, had a year earlier been relieved of all his offices by his half-brother, the Hsien Feng Emperor, who was the fourth son of the Tao Kwang Emperor. The ostensible reason was Prince Kung's failure to observe the full ceremonies of mourning for his mother, the Dowager Empress, who had reared the Hsien Feng Emperor after his own mother's death. The true reason for the breach between the half-brothers, who had been closer than most full brothers, was bitter disagreement on strategy against the Taipings, compounded by rivalry over a Chinese flower girl.

All the Princes and Mandarins lowered their eyes to their cups. By the Emperor's own decree, his half-brother should have been excluded from the banquet. If the Son of Heaven was now pleased to greet him and drink with him, it behove lesser men to behave as if they did not see Prince Kung, who was, officially, not present.

'Well, Little Brother, how goes't?' the Emperor slurred. 'Ver' glad t' see you.'

'I pray that Your Majesty will relent and relieve this slave of the burden of the just punishment Your Majesty imposed.' Prince Kung, a shade more sober, enunciated with painful clarity. 'Though that punishment is less than I deserve.'

'We . . . We'll . . . think about it, Little Brother. Meanwhile, no talk about that Chinese tart. Got something . . . something else . . . talk about.'

'Your Majesty commands?'

'Nala, my Small Orchid, she's come up with an idea. What do you think about one commander for all the armies fighting the Taipings? 'S not bad idea, is't?'

175

'The idea has merit, Majesty,' Prince Kung replied magisterially. 'Yet such great power in one subject's hands? Who would the man be, Majesty?'

'The Governor, you know, Governor Tseng Kuo-fan, she thinks.'

'A *Chinese*, Your Majesty? A *Chinese* commanding the combined armies? The Virtuous Concubine is a lady of much wisdom.' Prince Kung was circumspect, having already ingratiated himself by presenting Yehenala with two dozen solid gold serving-dishes. 'Your slave would not presume to question her advice. But I wonder . . .'

'So do We, Brother, so d' We. That's . . . at's why We asked.'

'Majesty, perhaps better to postpone that decision? The Sacred Dynasty has need of men of talent, but Governor Tseng is a Civil Mandarin. The Dynasty requires a commander, preferably a Manchu, who understands modern weapons. I do not believe Governor Tseng has such knowledge.'

'Saying no, Brother, are you?' the Emperor probed. 'Don't wan' Us do it? 'S that it?'

'Your Majesty's slave counsels serious consideration, not immediate rejection. The matter should be . . .'

'We understan',' the Emperor interrupted. ''S ver' . . . ver' clear. Don't wan' Chinese take-over from inside, do We?'

'Not when Chinese rebels are fighting to establish a Chinese dynasty. The Great Pure Dynasty will soar high with Your Majesty's wise guidance now that an heir is born. Heaven smiles upon Your Majesty!'

'You want the job?' the Emperor asked brusquely.

'I am unworthy, Majesty. My talent is small, and I lack knowledge of modern weapons.'

''S right, you do.' The Emperor's speech grew more slurred in his perplexity. 'But who has it? 'S a big problem, y' see.'

'Your slave does not oppose the appointment, but advises profound consideration.'

'We know what 'at means, Little Brother,' the Emperor chuckled. 'Any . . . anyway 's worth thinking 'bout. We'll just think 'bout it.'

The Hall of Supreme Harmony reverberated as twenty giant sky-rockets exploded above the Forbidden City, and an enormous orchid flamed purple and white against the clouds. In the big square south of the Gate of Heavenly Peace, the common people gazed in awe at the gigantic flower in the sky. An heir was vouchsafed to the Emperor, and the symbol of the mother of the heir was emblazoned across the face of Heaven.

'What're we celebrating?' A stout merchant condescendingly addressed a grimy beggar as an equal. 'What're we celebrating? The first month of the heir to the Dragon Throne? Or the elevation of his mother?'

176

CHAPTER TWENTY-SEVEN

Saul Haleevie slipped off the stiff leather oxfords and wiggled his long toes in relief. Replete after lunch, he drowsily admired the round rose-bed bisected by the gravel path from the gate of the compound to the veranda of the house on Szechwan Road. Gauzy wings whirring to support their bulbous bodies, yellow-striped bumblebees buzzed among the concentric circles of full-blown orange, white and red flowers. How could such minute wings, Saul wondered idly, possibly lift such ponderous insects? For that matter, how could any creature fly, even the graceful herons with their compact bodies, long necks, and broad wings?

A droning sound from a second-storey window reminded him that his adopted sons, Aaron and David, were assiduously studying the Chinese Classics in anticipation of the First Civil Service Examination in the autumn. Perhaps the cumulative wisdom of more than two millennia of Chinese sages offered answers to questions that had vexed mankind since Adam and Eve were expelled from the Garden of Eden. But he doubted it. Chinese sages preferred to search ancient books rather than look directly at the works of God. Even less than the assured scientists of nineteenth-century Europe, however, could they penetrate the secret purposes of the Almighty. Besides, the Chinese detested innovation. Incessantly quarrel-some, they couldn't even equip their armies with modern firearms. If a Chinese David had proposed to slay a barbarian Goliath with a slingshot, he would have been derided because there was no precedent for that weapon.

Rather than seek enlightenment in the petrified Confucian Classics or chase the will o' the wisp new science, Saul concluded comfortably, he would rely upon the traditional wisdom subtly expounded in the *Talmud*. It was tempting to speculate on how birds flew. It was also blasphemous. He preferred to forego the intellectual challenge – and avoid sacrilege.

Besides, more mundane matters pressed upon him. The Taipings were resurgent throughout the Yangtze Valley, which produced most of China's exports and consumed the bulk of her imports. Yet the Imperialists appeared united by new resolution after the birth of the Prince Tsai Chün two months earlier. How could one weigh the profits of trading with an insurgent régime against the Imperial Government's certain retribution should it suppress the insurgency? *If*, of course, the Imperialists finally suppressed the rebellion; *if* the Taipings did not finally overthrow the Manchus. By dealing with both sides, he supposed. By making himself indispensable to both Taipings and Manchus while increasing his holdings in the autonomous foreign settlement. That was not the perfect answer, but it was the best available answer.

Stretching comfortably in the cane longchair, Saul luxuriated in the light breeze which was hardly impeded by his loose cotton shirt and trousers. He peeled off his black-cotton socks so the breeze could play on his toes.

'Saul,' his wife asked from her adjacent chair, 'what *are* you thinking of, taking off your socks where anyone can see you? You have a position to keep up.'

'Some position, my dear!' When Saul bent over to grope under his chair, his voice echoed hollow from the stone veranda. 'None of my customers or suppliers is interested in my socks. They're only interested in the quality of my goods and the colour of my money.'

He triumphantly flourished the split-leather Baghdad slippers with the upturned toes he had prudently told the houseboy to leave under his chair. His smile would have been a grin on features less austerely lean and less impressively bearded.

'The old ways are best, after all, aren't they, Saul?'

Sarah flapped her fretwork fan, the Chinese device she now found indispensable in the summer, and the fragrance of attar of roses mingled with sweet female perspiration. Aroused by her scent, Saul fondly studied the delicate features framed by her tawny hair. His eyes moved from the curve of her bosom to the sweep of her hips and legs under the cornflower-blue linen kaftan.

'It's too hot . . . much too hot for that.' Noting his gaze, Sarah smiled. 'But the old ways *are* best, aren't they?'

'It all depends whether I'm sitting on the veranda or calling on bankers. Baghdad slippers for one. Respectable European shoes for the other.'

'For women, the old ways are far better,' she insisted. 'Especially for young women . . . for foolish virgins.'

'Perhaps, my dear. Though how one forces even a wise virgin to keep the old ways, I don't know. Well, today even Fronah can't get herself into a scrape at a picnic.'

'Saul, what *are* we to do with her?' Sarah interrupted. 'She can't go on this way.'

'I'm very much aware of that, my love. I've spent hours worrying about Fronah since that American sailor brought her and David home.'

'And . . .' Sarah prompted, 'what have you decided in your wisdom.'

'Simply that I could bear the loss of the junk's cargo,' he evaded. 'After all, the profits of dealing with the Taipings are so high. But I couldn't bear the loss of a daughter.'

'Do you think I could, Saul? She's a trial, God knows, and she makes me very angry. But I do love the minx. I couldn't bear losing her.' Sarah paused, abashed by her own vehemence, then resumed in a subdued tone. 'Sometimes, you know, the only way to keep a daughter is to lose her.'

'You mean, I assume . . .'

'. . . that it's high time she married, past time. Otherwise, I know it, she'll do something stupid . . . and ruin herself. It's Shanghai . . . this hothouse where the women flaunt themselves indecently. Just look at Fronah's dresses! All the men think about is . . . is . . . womanising. Thank God, she hasn't . . .'

'I do,' Saul replied fervently. 'I thank God every day for that. But marriage is another matter. She's still very young, Sarah. Anyway, who's she to marry? She hardly looks at young Sam Moses.'

'I simply don't know, Saul, but there must be someone.'

'Presumably, there is . . . somewhere. But not, as far as I can see, in Shanghai. Remember what the *Talmud* says: *Parents blessed with a good son-in-law gain a son, but parents with a bad son-in-law lose a daughter.*'

'Please don't quote the *Talmud*. It doesn't help.'

'What does help, Sarah?' His voice rose, and he leaned towards her. 'First a flirtation with some Gentile oaf, I'm almost certain. Thank God, we watched her so carefully she couldn't . . . Then she runs off and only the grace of God kept her alive. *Your* favourite David, a fine rascal he is taking my daughter on a smuggling junk. I should throw him out. If I hadn't promised Aisek, I would. But, I ask you, what can help Fronah?'

'Don't lecture me, Saul. I'm not the one who's giving you all the worries, but your precious baby. Why don't you lecture her?'

'I have, Sarah, I have. Why just last night I told her that her secretiveness wasn't independence, but foolishness. I told her we only wanted to help her . . . not dominate her.'

'What did she say?'

'What do you think?' Saul shrugged. 'What she always says. She did listen to us, and she loved us. She even cried a little. Then she blew her nose and smiled and said she was sorry, *really* sorry she caused us so much worry. And she promised to be better.'

'Did she admit she's headstrong and foolish? Will she, at least, talk with us . . . tell us the truth, sometimes? What does she really want?'

Sarah leaned across the gap between their chairs and touched his arm with her fingertips. Saul shivered and took her hand. After nineteen years of marriage he should not still be in thrall to her body and her spirit. At thirty-nine, she was old in most men's eyes, but to him at the peak of her attraction. Her dark eyes against her fair skin captivated him. She was the only woman who pierced him with desire. She was also the only human being to whom he could talk without restraint.

'Saul,' she persisted, 'I'm so worried about Fronah. We've got to guide her . . . even if she hates it. Thank God you stopped her gadding about so much. I shudder when I think what could happen at those balls . . . outside on the veranda or in the bushes.'

'How can you talk that way, Sarah?' He was outraged. 'Your own daughter! I hope . . . I know . . . we've taught her moral values. Not *all* our own values, perhaps, but enough. She's a religious girl, Sarah. She'd never.'

'Girls do, you know. Even religious girls. It's the way they're made, though men . . . especially fathers . . . like to think . . .'

'This isn't getting us anywhere, Sarah. What are you worried about now beside her wildness? What's bothering you?'

'This American sailor, this Hyde, does he have to be around so much? I don't like the way she looks at him.'

'She doesn't like him, Sarah. She thinks he's flip and arrogant.'

'Saul, that means she wants him to pay more attention to her. You simply don't understand girls. Why does he have to be around so much?'

'Not all that much. Besides, I'm grateful to him. He could have made a scandal. With those two aboard, Fronah and David, who would have believed it wasn't my cargo? But he brought them home quietly. You're right about one thing, though. I don't understand girls . . . or women, either.'

'No, you don't, and you never will,' Sarah laughed. 'But what else is there about this Hyde? It's not just gratitude, I'm sure.'

'He could also be very useful,' Saul confessed. 'He does command a patrol boat, you know.'

'You think he'd turn his back on smugglers sometimes? How else could he be useful? I don't like the way he looks at her either.'

'I'm not quite sure, but I know he could be very useful. Anyway, I'll try to keep them apart to please you. But I still think you're seeing things, my dear.'

'We'll see, Saul. She likes young Gentiles too much. Sometimes I suspect he's not the only one. There could be others.'

'Not any more. We'd know.'

'*How* would we know, my dear? We *must* find her a husband very soon.'

'Sammy Moses might as well be a stick of wood for all the notice she now takes of him. I suppose I could get another apprentice out . . . maybe more than one. But, right now, there's no one else she could marry.'

'No one at all? Saul, did you ever think of Mr Henriques, Lionel Henriques?'

'No, and I won't think of him now.' Saul guffawed. 'To start with, he's so much older.'

'Only fifteen years, not so much for a man. And she's fascinated by him.'

'Only because he stands for the things she wants – and, maybe, his glamour, the blond hair and the aristocratic airs. He stands for Europe and sophisticated society . . . everything that isn't Shanghai.'

'He *is* Jewish, Saul.'

'You've said you want her to have what we have . . . not settle for second best. Is she going to find magic with Lionel Henriques?'

'Perhaps not. But who can tell? Only God himself. Lionel Henriques is here now. And she *is* interested. Saul, we must do something. There's very little time. She's ripe . . . for marriage or for trouble.'

'All right, I agree we must do something. But I'm not convinced Lionel Henriques is . . .'

'Who else is there, Saul?' she asked reasonably. 'He may not be perfect, but he *is* here.'

*

The croquet mallet smacked smartly, and the orange-striped ball streaked across the coarse grass of the embankment. Fronah shook her head in ostentatious annoyance when the ball struck a large stone and cannoned towards the Hwangpoo. Her white kidskin shoes flashed scarlet-satin bows beneath her scarlet-sprigged skirt as she followed towards the river's edge.

Whatever the luck of the game, she knew she was fetching in her white dimity frock caught with a scarlet sash. Though she was a novice at croquet, the men at Jardines' picnic were eager to partner her. She was not only slim, but vivacious in the sunlight. The older women were buttressed with heavy corsets, but she needed only wispy summer-stays of lace and slivers of whalebone. Even her teacher Margaret MacGregor was lumpy. Fronah darted an irritated glance at the Scotswoman, who sat on a folding-chair in the shade of the plane trees, her red pompadour close to Gabriel Hyde's dark head.

Whatever did Gabriel find to talk to her about, she wondered. Margaret was at least seven years older than he. She was already thirty, practically middle-aged.

'I'm sorry, very sorry. I apologise.' Iain Matthews spoke to her slim back. 'I've said it fifty times. What more can I say?'

'Don't go on so, Iain,' she replied without looking at him. 'It really doesn't matter.'

'It does matter . . . and you know it.' He plucked at the green-and-blue scarf that served as his belt. 'You know you're only annoyed because you . . . because you still care about me.'

'That's news to me.' Fronah stooped to study the lie of her ball. 'What makes you think I ever cared? What have you got to say that's so important?'

'I didn't write . . . didn't answer your notes. I admit it. For God's sake, you told me you couldn't see me for a long while, said it wasn't safe to write.'

'Safe for who? You or me?' She turned to face him, an angry flush staining the olive skin over her cheekbones. 'Tell me that! Tell me why you

181

waited until we bumped into each other today. You know I didn't hear a single word from you after . . . after . . .'

'So you do care about me,' he said triumphantly. 'Otherwise why did it matter not hearing? Admit it. You do care?'

'Not particularly. I was amazed, and I still am. No gentleman would behave like that. No gentleman would leave a lady without a word for months after . . . after . . .'

'After . . . after that,' he grinned. 'It was wonderful, wasn't it? I still remember you and . . . But, I promise you, I didn't write only because I was thinking of you.'

Practiced in prevarication, Fronah knew a lie when she heard one. She knew Iain was lying, though she could still not understand why he had heartlessly deserted her after that afternoon in the grove. Since the foreign settlement was so small, it was inevitable that they should meet again – and they had met on her first excursion into society after her father lifted the ban imposed for her escapade with David. She had looked forward to seeing Iain, and his penitent air touched her heart. Seeing again his light-blue eyes and shining blond hair, she knew she still loved him. But she would not relent until she had punished him for his neglect.

'What do you want, Iain?' Her full lips were set, her amber eyes cold. 'Exactly what do you want of me?'

'Say you'll see me again. Say we can go riding again . . . see each other alone.'

'I'm afraid that's impossible. My parents would never . . . And I know better than to be alone with you. But we'll meet . . . the way we're meeting now.'

'That's not good enough for me, Fronah. Anyway, why are you making such a fuss? All the ladies of the settlement have their . . . ah . . . friends. Why can't we be friends again?'

'That's all you want, Iain, isn't it? To be *friends*, as you call it. You've never . . . ever . . . even suggested we might . . .'

Fronah bit her lip and looked down at the croquet-ball. Genuinely puzzled, Iain waited for her to continue.

'Suggested what, Fronah?' he finally asked. 'I don't follow.'

'You never . . . never . . . suggested we might . . . might be more than friends.' She stammered, then blurted. 'People do marry, you know.'

'Marry!' He was astonished. 'You know I can't marry for years. I never thought you . . .'

'No, Iain, you never thought, did you?' Fronah was in command again. 'Anyway, it's all too late now.'

'You're right, I should've thought about . . . more about you.' He placated her. 'I see it now, and I'm sorry. But it never crossed my mind. What would your father and mother say? You Jews don't . . . excuse me, Hebrews . . . you don't marry Christians.'

182

'You can say Jews, Iain. Jews is quite all right.' She was wounded by his callousness and by his reminding her that she would always be an outsider amid the easy kinship of the foreign settlement. 'So you thought you were safe?'

'Fronah, you knew I couldn't marry for years, so I never thought . . .'

'Iain, let's just forget it, shall we? Let's forget anything ever happened between us.'

Fronah gripped her mallet behind her back. Forcing a smile, she glanced negligently at the plane trees, where Margaret MacGregor and Gabriel Hyde were still engrossed in conversation.

'I'll never forget you, and I know you can't forget me. We could talk about . . . about marrying one day. You know I can't now, but . . .'

Iain stopped abruptly. Why did she keep glancing at the picnickers seated under the plane trees, sipping hock poured from long green bottles into crystal beakers by houseboys in white jackets? A picnic at Shanghai was no rustic improvisation, but a banquet held outdoors. Following her glance, he saw Gabriel Hyde bow over Margaret MacGregor's out-stretched hand and stroll towards the croquet-players.

'I've been watching you, Fronah,' Iain said ominously. 'Why do you keep looking at that Hyde fellow?'

'He's a friend,' she replied stiltedly. 'I hope I may look at a friend if I wish. Or does that displease you?'

'It certainly does,' he exploded. 'He's a conceited ass . . . a cashiered officer . . . a mercenary. Even the *Americans* wouldn't keep him on. I don't want you to see him.'

'It would be hard not to,' she laughed. 'He's often at our house. Some business with my father.'

'Fronah, before he comes this way, promise me one thing for old times' sake,' Iain said urgently. 'Promise we'll see each other again and really talk.'

'If you insist, Iain, all right. I'll think of some way and let you know. But only for old times' sake. Don't deceive yourself that it means anything more.'

Despite Fronah's feigned hostility and Iain's feigned contrition, both were pleased by their encounter. She was delighted that he still longed for her. He complacently assured himself that he was already half-way to his goal. She could have avoided the Jardines picnic, where she was certain to meet a Jardines cadet. Besides, she could have dropped a few words and walked away, knowing he couldn't make a spectacle of himself by pursuing her.

As Gabriel Hyde approached, Fronah smiled and let her eyelashes fall langurously. She'd brought Iain to heel again, which was good for him. And she knew again with passionate certainly that she loved him. Iain's pale eyes glittered, and he licked his pudgy lips. They'd meet again very soon, he was sure, and she'd not only be willing, but eager. Besides, he did care for her, though even the thought of marriage was impossible.

Gabriel Hyde was trim in starched, choker-collared summer whites, though the peaked cap under his arm displayed a curled Imperial dragon where the American eagle had formerly screamed. The three gold stripes of a commander gleamed on his black shoulder-boards, though the lynx of his Chinese rank had supplanted the five-pointed star of a line officer of the US Navy. Fronah knew the few foreign officers in the Chinese service designed their own uniforms. Gabriel Hyde's was modest beside the cascades of gold-lace, the festoons of silver aiguillettes and the rainbows of medal ribbons that adorned his fellow officers.

'Afternoon, Lieutenant,' Iain Matthews drawled offensively. 'I *am* sorry, I should've said Commander. Or are you an admiral by now, Hyde? These *Chinese* ranks are so hard to keep in mind.'

'No trouble for me at all, young Matthews.' Hyde smiled coldly. 'Afternoon, Miss Fronah. Keeping well, I see. You're radiant today.'

'Thank you, Commander,' Fronah dimpled. 'And you're very handsome in your whites.'

'Very dashing in your sailor suit,' Iain Matthews sneered. 'I feel so safe knowing you're defending us from the terrible rebels.'

'Glad to hear you feel safe, young Matthews,' Hyde replied. 'Now, Miss Fronah, I think the children's hour is over. Won't you take a turn by the river with me?'

Her chin high in triumph, Fronah touched Gabriel Hyde's white sleeve with her fingertips. The American suppressed a smile at the extravagantly ladylike gesture. Gabriel Hyde, she reflected, was again the useful foil he'd been at the Fourth of July Ball. He had not only ticked off Iain, but fanned the griffin's jealousy. Of course, Gabriel Hyde was no more than a foil.

*

Darkness fell swiftly on the foreign settlement while Fronah and David chatted in the purple twilight. After supper, the industrious Aaron had returned to his books, and his low chanting invoked the abrupt transition to indigo night. The stars were distant, the moon obscured by clouds, but fireflies shone pale-green among the shrubbery. Oil lamps flickered through the open windows, and a red ember glowed on the veranda each time Saul drew on his cheroot.

'Father's let me go out, too.' David's expression was veiled by the darkness. 'Not much punishment for our misbehaviour. My other father, he'd have beaten me. Filial obedience, he'd say, must be enforced.'

'He was filial,' Fronah replied, 'and look what happened.'

'You're right. It didn't do him much good. But I haven't forgotten. Some day, I'll . . .'

184

'Don't think about it,' Fronah counselled. 'One day he'll come back to us. Meanwhile, Papa isn't bad. In the end, he lets me do what I want.'

'So I've noticed,' David said drily. 'By the way, who was at the picnic today?'

'They really wanted you to come, David. You've got to get over the idea that just because you're Chinese . . .'

'Fronah, I won't go where I'm not welcome. Who did you say you saw?'

'Well, Doctor Willie and Maggie MacGregor, Jardines' taipan, Iain Matthews, Gabriel Hyde, and a lot of other people.'

'You spoke with that . . . that Iain again, did you?' David demanded. 'You said you'd never.'

'Of course I did.' She was startled by his vehemence. 'What else could I do in public?'

'And you'll see him again, will you?'

'Well, I may.' She saw no need to deceive her confidant. 'But, I promise you, I'll be very careful. No more . . . no more . . . nonsense.'

'Of course not, Fronah. You're too smart for that.'

'I do learn from my mistakes, no matter what Papa says, don't I, David?'

'Of course you do, Fronah. No matter what Father says.'

David was silent, thinking about his real father in exile thousands of miles away. What would Aisek Lee say about his adoptive sister's escapades? Young women, he'd always maintained, had to be kept on a short rein to keep them from disgracing the family. Fronah should certainly be kept on a very short rein. What, David wondered, could be done about that foreign devil?

'Fronah!' Saul called from the veranda. 'Come here, please.'

Tautly defensive, Fronah settled on a cushion at her father's feet. He meant well, though he was hopelessly old-fashioned. Still, he was, as David pointed out, also indulgent. She must, she warned herself, not fight with him again.

'Fronah,' Saul asked softly, 'what do you really want?'

'Want? What do you mean, Papa?'

'Try not to fence with me, my dear.' Exasperation seeped into his voice. 'Don't put me off.'

'One day, Papa, I guess, I want to marry and have children. But I'd also like to . . . I suppose . . . to be something. I want to do something on my own.'

'You do want a husband and children, then?' He ignored her childish ambitions. 'Do you think you're going about it the right way?'

'The right way? Really, Papa, I'm not fencing. I don't understand what you mean.'

'We've talked about your running away, Fronah. I won't start on that again. Maybe you've actually learned something from your narrow escape. But you don't want anyone your mother and I think good for you, do you?'

'You mean Sammy Moses? No, I certainly don't want Sammy. I'd rather die childless than . . . oh, Papa, I don't want to marry *anyone* now.'

'Not one of those young Gentiles you flirt with? No one, Fronah?'

'No, Papa, no one.'

'But you were keen on one of them, weren't you, Fronah?'

'Yes, Papa, I was.' Since he seemed to know about Iain, Fronah felt it wise to be candid. 'I did see Iain Matthews once or twice alone.'

'Iain Matthews?'

'You know, Papa. He's with Jardines.'

'I've heard of him . . . heard he's considered rather unpromising,' Saul said with pitiless satisfaction. 'Now, Fronah, what about this Matthews?'

'Now nothing, Papa,' she laughed. 'I swear to you that nothing . . . nothing whatsoever . . . happened. You know what I mean, don't you?'

'I understand, Fronah. I never thought that it did . . . that it could. It's all over now, is it?'

'Sometimes I still think about him, Papa. I can't get over it so quickly. But I'll never see him again . . . never.'

'There's no one else?' Saul was pleased by her candour and her resolution. 'No other Gentile? Nobody at all?'

'No, Papa. I told you I really don't want to marry anyone now. Not for a long time. I'd like to do something on my own. But when I do marry, then someone like . . .'

'Like who, Fronah?' he prompted. 'Like who?'

'Oh, someone like Mr Henriques,' she laughed. 'Only not so old. Mr Henriques is clever and kind . . . an English gentleman. But, of course, he's too old for me.'

'He's not that old, Fronah. You know . . .'

'Papa, that's silly. I've promised I'll behave better from now on. But that's just silly. Mr Henriques! Why he's *so* old. He's certainly not for me.'

CHAPTER TWENTY-EIGHT

July 17, 1856   *Shanghai*

David, who was transferring entries from dockets into the shipping ledger at his small desk in the corner of Saul Haleevie's office, nodded a friendly greeting to Gabriel Hyde. The young Chinese smiled and wondered why the American chuckled as he accepted a cheroot from Saul.

He liked Hyde, though he sometimes resented the officer's quizzically paternal manner towards Fronah. At least the American wasn't out to seduce his sister, David told himself and returned to the ledger. He did not know whether he wanted to go into business or to pursue the official career to which his elder brother Aaron was dedicated. But he would work hard at his commercial tasks because his industriousness pleased his adoptive father. Whatever his choice, David knew, Saul would encourage him and help him.

Though the door was wedged open and the window was latched against the outside wall, no breeze relieved the oppressive morning of July 17, 1856. The fringed punkah hanging from the ceiling only roiled the humid air like a spoon stirring pea-soup when the coolie outside remembered to pull the cord. It was a burdensome summer, inordinately hot and much troubled as the Taipings tightened their grip on the rich Yangtze Valley. Along the five hundred-mile stretch from Wuchang to Chenkiang, the Citadel of the River fifty miles from Shanghai, the yellow banners of the Heavenly King fluttered unchallenged.

The complacent foreign community had finally awakened to its own peril when the commander of the shattered Imperial 1st Army of the South died of fever and despair in bivouac a week earlier. That death capped a series of Manchu disasters: the decisive defeat of the Water Force of Governor Tseng Kuo-fan in Kiangsu Province, south of the Long River, and the rout of Imperial infantry in Hupei Province to the north. After the elation that followed the birth of Yehenala's son, the Dynasty would have despaired if it were not inpenetrably shielded against reality by arrogance. The Heavenly Kingdom of Great Peace had by July of 1856 attained the widest extent and the greatest power since it raised the standard of revolt in the remote south-east six years earlier.

At home, Fronah had again cajoled David's father's concubine into deceiving her parents. Maylu sat, sternly disapproving, in an adjoining room of the tenement in the South City where the couple met, the door always open so that she could see them. But Iain, Fronah confided, was becoming surly, demanding that she see him 'really alone'. David feared the certain result when she finally yielded, as he knew she would. He had finally decided that his responsibility as an elder brother required him to protect Fronah from her own folly – and to preserve the family honour.

Lulled by the heat and the heavy odours of tea and camphor seeping from the go-down below, David did not listen to the conversation between his adoptive father and the naval officer. His attention, however, was aroused when Saul spoke briskly.

'So, Commander, you're agreeable,' the merchant beamed. 'Only two small shipments of watches consigned to Soochow and Wuhsi. Just drop them off at Chiangyin on your regular patrol.'

The American nodded and puffed on his cheroot. Through the grey smoke swirling around Gabriel Hyde's head, David saw that his face was creased by an enormous smile.

'Nothing that isn't above board, Commander, nothing we couldn't tell the Maritime Customs and the commodore of the Water Force.' Saul knew his reputation for absolute honesty ensured that his word was accepted. 'Your usual commission. Ten percent of the value c.i.f. Shanghai. I do wish you'd let me compensate you for your earlier trouble. You know how valuable . . .'

'No payment for that, Mr Haleevie.' Lounging insouciantly in the cane armchair, Gabriel Hyde chuckled disconcertingly. 'I shouldn't have told you about the blockade dispositions that night. Too much to drink, perhaps.'

'I assure you, Commander, it wasn't contraband. Just cotton goods that had to get there quick.'

'Well, no payment for that, anyway. And I can't do that sort of thing again. I definitely . . .'

The American set both feet on the floor, his head bobbing, and his shoulders heaving. His hands clutched his stomach, and he choked on the cheroot's smoke. When Saul smiled in sympathy, David saw the American was convulsed with laughter.

'You've been grinning like a tiger since you came in, Commander,' Saul said. 'Can you let me in on the joke?'

'It is funny . . . very funny.' Another spasm of laughter choked Hyde. 'But . . . but . . . you may not think so.'

'Try me, Commander.' Saul offered. 'I'm not so solemn.'

'One of those . . . those young sprigs at Jardines. Young lad called Iain Matthews. Do you know him, sir?'

'I've heard of him.' Saul was guarded. 'I believe he has a reputation as a . . . what do you say . . . cad, isn't it?'

'I wouldn't, sir. Not my kind of word, though the Limeys might. To me he's just a juvenile . . . an adolescent lecher. Well, a very funny thing happened to Iain Matthews last night.'

David set his features impassively, while Saul checked a disquieting suspicion.

'They found him on the Bund early this morning,' Gabriel Hyde continued. 'Trussed so tight he couldn't move a finger . . . could hardly bat an eyelash.'

'That's not so funny.'

'I assure you it was. He was stripped, absolutely bare-ass . . . ah . . . not a stitch on him. Only a dunce cap on his head. And his face was painted bright red.'

'A peculiar sense of humour, these young English have. Some prank of the griffins, was it?'

'Anything but.' Hyde shook his head emphatically. 'A sign in Chinese

188

and English was pinned to his chest. *That* wasn't funny. Must've hurt like the devil.'

'And this sign?' Saul was losing interest. 'What did it say?'

'Just this: *All red-haired devils play with our Chinese women thus be punished*! There he lay, buck-naked and shivering in the heat. Some Chinese father's had a grand revenge.'

David permitted himself a small smile. He had not been certain the carpenter was speaking the truth when he swore he could carry a proposal to remnants of the Small Sword Secret Society. He'd now have to pay the additional ten *taels* promised on fulfilment of their contract. But he'd gladly pay ten times as much to humiliate the barbarian.

'That's not all, Mr Haleevie, not at all . . .' Gabriel Hyde hesitated. 'But I don't want to offend you.'

'Try me, Commander, so I can get back to work.'

'Well, you'll pardon the language, but his penis and testicles . . . were painted red, too. A little sign was tied around . . . around it. The message said: *Next time, blood is real. Next time him eunuch*. His mates laughed so hard they couldn't untie him for minutes.'

'As you said, somebody's had his revenge.' Saul was relieved that the culprits were patently Chinese. 'And I suppose it *is* funny, though unpleasant.'

'There'll be a great to-do now.' Hyde chortled again. 'Pardon me, but I can't help laughing.'

Lionel Henriques wafted through the open door on a wave of indignation. His beautifully cut double-breasted nankeen jacket hung open, the high lapels skewed around his butterfly collar and maroon cravat. His pale-blue eyes glittered as he passed his slender hand through his blond hair.

'Haleevie, my dear fellow, have you heard of the outrage?' he demanded. 'What next, I ask you?'

Henriques nodded to the American officer. David he ignored.

'This young chap Matthews, have you heard?' he resumed. 'It's an outrage. The quack thinks he has concussion, perhaps a fractured skull.'

David Lee felt a twinge of guilt. His instructions had been clear: the rascal was to be shamed, but not injured. That decision was not influenced by compassion. The humiliation would be all the more galling, he'd reasoned coolly, if Matthews were unhurt. He wanted to make the griffin a laughing stock, not a martyr. His smile faded.

'It was not well done,' Saul pondered. 'Whatever these Chinese had against this Matthews, they should have gone to law. Or left him to his conscience. Vengeance is *mine*, saith the Lord!'

'A fat lot of good that would've done them.' Gabriel glanced sharply at David. 'Chinese law can't touch him . . . and English law won't. Anyway, what makes you think he *has* a conscience?'

189

'We live among barbarians,' Lionel Henriques muttered. 'You haven't heard the rest. When they turned him over, his . . . ah . . . bottom and thighs were seamed with cuts. And another sign was stuck into . . . ah . . . between his buttocks. *Next time, the jewels*! it said. Absolutely barbaric.'

'Somebody's pretty annoyed at that young fellow,' Gabriel Hyde laughed.

David was puzzled, since the American was normally humane. If anything, he was too concerned with the well-being of others, almost quixotic. David savoured the word he had learned only the preceding week. Gabriel Hyde had demonstrated that weakness by refusing any reward for returning the runaways captured on the smuggling junk.

Why, David wondered, should the American feel such enormous delight at Iain Matthews's humiliation? Had he guessed the identity of the lady on whose behalf it had been carried out? Did he feel more for Fronah than fondness mingled with amusement? But his attitude towards her had always been avuncular – another treasured new word. David smiled thinly and filed the question in the back of his mind.

'Well, gentlemen, I must be going,' the American said. 'My rascals'll sell the engine out of *Mencius* if I leave them alone too long.'

'Commander, can you drop by next week?' Saul invited. 'I may have something to offer you. It's only a thought just yet. But it could be interesting.'

'I'll do that, Mr Haleevie. Goodbye for now.'

Gabriel Hyde nodded to Lionel Henriques and waved cheerfully at the young Chinese in the corner. What, David wondered, did his knowing smile imply?

'There's also a matter I'd like to talk over with you, Mr Henriques.' Saul was again briskly businesslike. 'I promise I won't keep you too long.'

'Do call me Lionel,' the Englishman suggested. 'And, if I may, Saul. We are, after all, brethren in this iniquitous place.'

'Tell me, then, Lionel. Your responsibilities to Samuelson and Company, your duties at Derwents, do they keep you very busy?'

'No, Saul, I'm not much occupied. Mine's a watching brief.'

Saul nodded. He had wondered why Lionel Henriques was virtually the only man in bustling Shanghai who seemed to have almost unlimited time at his disposal.

'Much leisure for curio-hunting,' Henriques went on. 'Have you, by the way, seen the Ming saucers Old Curiosity Soo is offering? Chia Ching period he claims, and I believe he's right. Blue and green lotus pattern.'

'I've heard, Lionel, and I look forward to seeing them.' Saul resented his own passion for Chinese ceramics distracting him from business. 'But I'd like to explore an idea with you now.'

David sat tensed in his corner. Foreign parents, he knew, did not employ professional go-betweens to propose marriage as Chinese did to prevent either party's being shamed by rejection. He also knew that his adoptive father regretted the disregard of that old Chinese – and Jewish – custom. Saul Haleevie was, he told himself, too civilised to offer his daughter's hand in the presence of a third person. Yet it appeared that he was on the point of 'exploring' the prospect of a marriage between Fronah and the Englishman while his adopted son sat by.

'I've often thought of setting up entirely on my own, you know, Lionel,' Saul began tentatively. 'The Khartoons are the best employers a man could have. And I already do a pretty fair trade on my own account. But, you understand, for a man of spirit, it can sometimes . . .'

'Saul, no one ever thinks of you as an employee,' Henriques interposed tactfully. 'They call you the taipan of Haleevies, not the manager of Khartoons.'

'Still, it's galling when I see a good opportunity and can't take advantage,' Saul continued meditatively. 'Besides, a man who's independent can do the best for his family. Someday, Fronah will be very comfortable . . . a wealthy young lady.'

David tried to think of something pleasant like Iain Matthew's humiliation, so that his smiling face would conceal his dismay. His adoptive father was actually offering Fronah's hand to the languid Englishman before a witness while disregarding the preliminaries essential to that – or any other – transaction. He was shocked by Saul's lack of finesse.

'I'm sure she will, Saul,' Henriques replied neutrally.

'And that's where you come in . . . or might come in.'

David closed his eyes and wished he could cover his ears. Though forced to listen to the demeaning negotiation, he did not have to watch Saul barter away his daughter so barbarously and so unskillfully.

'. . . need someone to work with me,' Saul continued. 'When I strike out on my own, I'll have some need for additional capital as well. From what my brother Solomon wrote, you're just the man for . . .'

David did not hear the rest of the sentence while castigating himself for his lack of faith. His adoptive father *was* as civilised and as subtle as he'd thought. The merchant was *not* offering Fronah's hand, but proposing a commercial arrangement. Whether he ever discussed marriage would depend on the Englishman's response – and his subsequent performance.

Saul Haleevie was very canny. He was not only making his proposal before a witness who could, if the need ever arose, testify to the terms. He was also drawing his adopted son deeper into his business affairs, while showing that unworthy son that a partner could be found outside the family circle if necessary. Though David's admiration for Saul's sagacity was confirmed, he felt the broad hint regarding Fronah would better have been left unsaid.

'Tell me, Saul, what do you have in mind?' the Englishman asked. 'How can I serve you?'

191

'You understand, Lionel, I'm merely trying out ideas.'

'Try me, Saul.' Lionel Henriques was irritated by the merchant's Levantine circuitousness. 'I've lots of time, as I said.'

'Well, Lionel, I was thinking. The Taiping troubles aren't good for business. But they could also be a big opportunity. If I could be sure of enough silver, there are some wonderful buys in the Taiping areas and . . .'

'Samuelsons won't play, Saul.' Henriques interposed defensively. 'It's not even worth asking. Otherwise, I could commit quite substantial sums on my own say so. But the bank is too heavily subscribed to Derwents to venture further sums on the China Coast at this time. Later . . .'

'That's not what I had in mind, Lionel. I don't want to borrow in London, not even from Samuelsons. There's loose silver in Hong Kong and Canton, too. With trade disrupted, they don't seem to know what to do with their silver. But *I* do. Also, I need a representative not directly connected with me . . . a man with an irreproachable reputation among the Gentiles, and . . .'

'I'm your man, Saul.' The Englishman did not hesitate, and David again deplored foreigners' undignified haste in business. 'What precisely do you have in mind?'

'It's not all that urgent, of course,' Saul equivocated. 'Take some time to think it over.'

'I assure you, my dear chap, I'm quite prepared to undertake your commission,' Henriques pressed. 'And without any talk of the consideration. I know I can depend on your fairness.'

'Fairness, Lionel my friend, looks different depending on where you sit. When the time comes, we've got to understand each other right down to the ground. But I won't rush you into . . .'

'You're not rushing me, I'm quite certain that . . .'

'No, Lionel, better take a few weeks. But, if it works out, I'd be forever in your debt.'

'I don't see the need to delay.' Henriques laughed. 'However, as you wish. Now, tell me, Saul, is this incident with Iain Matthews the beginning of a wave of lawlessness?'

David nodded approval for his adoptive father's tactics. Saul Haleevie was so subtle he might almost be Chinese. He had thrown out lures to both the American and the Englishman without committing himself to either.

What complex scheme, David wondered, was his father spinning? He was delighted that Saul had followed the old Chinese maxim: *The intelligent fisherman does not jerk the line, but lets the lure dance in the current until the pike eagerly hooks itself.* Not one, but two fish were darting around the lure.

*

192

The evening meal was sacrosanct in the Haleevie household, for Saul insisted that his daughter Fronah and his sons Aaron and David join their parents in the sombre dining-room of the house of Szechwan Road. But he was tolerant of his Chinese sons' wish to eat Chinese food at lunchtime, and he did not require them to obey the laws of *kashruth*. Fronah was often permitted to join her adopted brothers for lunch in the new conservatory. Sarah shook her head in disapproval, since she could not believe her daughter would eat only fish, vegetables, or eggs. Besides, the cooking pans, the serving platters, and the fragile rice bowls were contaminated by the pork and the shellfish indispensable to the Shanghai cuisine.

Sarah did not agree with her husband that their daughter must be allowed some latitude if she were to live comfortably in the cosmopolitan Treaty Port. Even the tolerant Saul would have been shocked to learn that Fronah loved to eat shrimp dumplings and braised crab on her excursions with Maylu into the South City. Urged by the concubine, Fronah had twice nibbled crisp morsels of roast pork. The first time, she had vomited; the second time, she had only felt queasy. But revulsion – and guilt – ensured that she would not taste the flesh of swine for some time to come.

After a light lunch with her parents on the sultry afternoon of July 17, 1856, Fromah pushed aside the feathery ferns trailing across the doorway of the conservatory to demand a bite of her brothers' bream steamed with scallions and ginger. Tendrils of damp hair curled about her high forehead, and her rounded cheeks were flushed. She plied her scarlet-silk fan so vigorously the gilt ribs creaked. She had reverted to a cotton kaftan over only a flimsy linen shift, but the pervasive damp heat drained her energy. Fish, Maylu said, was a cooling food.

The brothers leaned back in their cane chairs as Fronah entered. She wondered what secrets they had been discussing in rapid Shanghainese with their heads close together. The earnest Aaron rarely confided in her. At twenty, he considered himself mature, and Chinese gentlemen did not discuss serious matters with women. The scapegrace David never kept anything from her. Despite his brother's admonitions, she could always winkle out his innermost thoughts. Today both looked sheepish, and neither spoke – neither Aaron in his gentleman's cotton long-gown nor David in his raffish open jacket and baggy workman's trousers.

'I want some fish.' She settled in a vacant chair. 'What were you whispering about?'

'*Mei shen-mo* . . .' David assured her. 'Nothing of importance, Fronah. Believe me.'

'I don't believe you,' she replied equably, attacking the fish with her chopsticks. 'But it's too hot to argue. You'll tell me after a while, I'm sure.'

Sprays of brown and yellow slipper orchids curled around David's round face, while his lean brother sat in a bower of giant purple cattleyas. The conservatory had been built to accommodate Sarah Haleevie's new passion for orchids and the flamboyant orange bird-of-paradise flowers that seemed to flit amid the greenery.

'All right, Little Sister, though it may disturb you.' Surprisingly, Aaron broke the long silence. 'There's been an outrage. Someone you know well. Actually Iain . . . Iain Matthews.'

Fronah's chopsticks clattered on to the serving platter. When her left hand dropped to her side, her fan furled its scarlet panels.

'What's happened to Iain?' she demanded. 'Tell me what's happened. Is he hurt?'

'Not badly, Fronah,' David replied soothingly. 'Doctor Willie MacGregor thinks he may have a slight concussion, but not likely. And besides . . .'

'It's not fit for her ears,' Aaron interjected. 'You can't tell her the whole story.'

Since Saul's delicacy had obviously kept him from mentioning the incident to the ladies, the brothers were reluctant to discuss the lurid event. They hesitated, stuttered, and back-pedalled. David stared into his teacup, feeling truly guilty for the first time. But she demanded every detail of Iain Matthews's humiliation.

'I must go to him.' Fronah's cheeks were chalk-pale. 'I'm going to him right now.'

'Fronah, you can't,' David expostulated. 'Think of the scandal. Besides, Father doesn't know about . . .'

'Thank God I told Papa. He knows I was seeing Iain, that's all. Don't you two say another word.'

She paused among the ferns in the doorway, and David hoped she was regretting her impulsiveness. Instead, she asked accusingly: 'David, you didn't . . . didn't have anything to do with this terrible business, did you? I know your tricks.'

'Of course not, Fronah,' he lied uneasily.

'That's just as well,' she said flatly. 'Otherwise, I'd never speak to you again. And I'd report you to the magistrates.'

The ferns trembled in the doorway after her departure. Saul would, David knew, be angry at her rushing off and he had only recently forgiven them for their escapade with the smugglers. Besides, she was inviting a public scandal.

No Chinese lady would behave like Fronah. How could she retain either respect or affection for a man who had been so basely exposed to public ridicule? No matter how much she might have thought she loved that luckless scamp, no Chinese lady would expose herself in turn to ridicule.

David shook his head in perplexity. He would never understand how foreigners behaved, despite his love for Fronah and his Western education. Regretting his sister's unhappiness, he was distressed by his stratagem's failure. Instead of rejecting Iain Matthews, Fronah had rushed to the lout's bedside.

David did not regret the twenty silver *taels* the assault had cost. Revenge was worth more than that, and the family's honour was redeemed. But he would never understand foreigners, not even his own sister.

CHAPTER TWENTY-NINE

August 1, 1856   *Shanghai*

The atmosphere in the house on Szechwan Road had been strained for two weeks. Saul Haleevie knew it was no fault of Sarah or himself, for their rapport had not altered. Intense as always, it had, as always, been troubled by quarrels over trifles and exalted by moments of profound emotional and physical communion. Nor, after their first shocked anger, had they protested at Fronah's visits to that unfortunate lad from Jardines. But the children, as he still called them, had been irritable and withdrawn since the disgraceful – and, Saul conceded, comical – attack on Iain Matthews.

Fronah's distress was understandable, though dramatised. She was, after all, a good friend of the lad. What stronger tie might once have joined them he preferred not to inquire. She had assured him again: 'All *that* was over long ago!' Whatever *that* meant.

Though Matthews had suffered neither a fracture nor concussion and his superficial cuts had healed, Fronah visited him every afternoon. Her impulsive kindness reflected greater credit on her heart than her head, but Saul could not condemn her. He was, however, distressed by the offensive rumours aroused by her behaviour. Shanghai would always gossip – with or without cause.

The boys' unease was harder to understand. Aaron, who should have been past such adolescent play-acting, had been portentously silent since the attack on young Matthews, stalking through the house like the guardian of some occult mystery. David appeared depressed by Fronah's suffering when he was not whispering conspiratorially with his brother. But when he thought himself unobserved, he grinned with elation.

Saul did not like mysteries within the family. Aaron's secretiveness was disturbing, while David's gloating was annoying. Above all, Fronah's behaviour appalled him. She carried herself like a tragedy queen, her face often tear-stained. When she could not avoid David, she shot suspicious glances at him. Profound sighs emphasised her protracted silences. Eyes clouded and shoulders bowed, she drifted through the house as if in mourning.

Saul looked out his office window. There she sat on the garden bench, gazing into the distance as if awaiting the end of the world. His heart went out to her, and he wondered how he could console her. Perhaps she might lighten her own heart by confiding in him. But he feared she would only stare down at him from the cold heights of her grief, or, worse, sob incoherently.

Fronah brooded, unmoved by either the first breath of autumnal coolness or the fragrance of the concentric circles of orange, white and red roses. Unaware that Gabriel Hyde, who had just come through the gate, was watching her with a half-smile, Fronah immersed herself in the exquisite pain of her memories. Equally oblivious to the cries of the street-hawkers and to Maylu's chattering from the second-storey window, she endured her anguish like a mother unpacking the meagre belongings of a son slain on a distant battlefield.

It seemed an eternity ago, the afternoon two weeks earlier when she had hurried to Jardines' compound. She had found Iain lying on his stomach in an airy room where furled mosquito-nets hung over the unoccupied beds of his mess-mates like tethered clouds. Instinct alone had impelled her to leave the door open to the stares of the houseboys suddenly drawn by urgent tasks. Only the same instinct for self-preservation had kept her from flinging herself down weeping beside Iain.

'Oh, it's you,' he'd said wearily. 'What are you doing here?'

'I've been frantic . . . wild with worry . . . since I heard,' she replied. 'Oh, Iain, how are you? Are you all right?'

'What do you think? How right *could* I be?'

He was, somehow, smaller and pathetically vulnerable. His face was pallid, and the bloom had vanished from his blond hair, which seemed filmed with dust. His features seemed to have shrunk around his long, prehensile nose. She could now see why his fair-weather friends called him Foxy, his fellow cadets who had deserted him because they feared contamination by his disgrace.

She blinked hard to dispel a mist of unshed tears, but his face was still slack and blurred. When he grasped her hand, she realised that he was afraid. She soothed him with meaningless words like a frightened child. His spirit momentarily seemed to revive, and he laughed ruefully. But the bright male assertiveness had also deserted him.

'What happened, Iain?' she asked tremulously. 'What have they done to you, my dear?'

'If *you* don't know, who does?' he answered faintly. 'It's all *your* doing.'

'What do you mean?' She grasped his hand harder. 'What can you possibly mean?'

'Come off it, Fronah!' Despite his harsh words, his tone was plaintive. 'You know damned well what I mean.'

'I don't . . . not at all. How could I?'

Fronah restrained the anger that stirred in spite of herself. For the first time, she forced herself to contain her own feelings for another's sake. Poor thing, he couldn't know what he was saying in his pain.

'For Christ's sake, Fronah, don't try to bamboozle me. You concocted it . . . you or your Chink brothers. Maybe your Jew father with the long beard. You've ruined me.'

'Iain, you're not . . . not hurt badly?' She ignored his ranting. 'Not that . . . that way?'

'Nor any other way. I'll heal all right. But I'm ruined anyway. And it's all *your* fault.'

'What do you mean? How could you know . . . even if it was true?'

'How could I know?' he sneered. 'They told me they wanted me to know why I was . . . punished, they said. For the little foreign girl, they said. I hope you're happy.'

'Iain, don't be silly.' She forced a laugh. 'You know you don't understand Chinese.'

'Did you ever hear of pidgin?'

'Besides, weren't there . . . others?' She withdrew her hand. 'There must have been . . . been . . . Chinese girls. You used to boast.'

'Others? Of course there were. Lots . . . even when I was swearing you were the only one for me. But Chinese, not foreign girls.'

She had endured his accusations every afternoon for the next six days, occasionally wondering if she did not, perhaps, merit that upbraiding. Her father, she was certain, had nothing to do with the assault. But her brothers? Despite their Western gloss, Aaron and David, like any Chinese gentlemen, might have felt compelled to defend the family honour – even by means no European gentleman would consider. Above all, she loved Iain, and she would not desert him.

Fronah returned every day until Iain rose shakily from his bed. She did not, however, return alone. Maylu rode behind her in a Haleevie sedan-chair and sat on the veranda near the open door. Her father had initially agreed with her mother that she must not visit the griffin, even if they had to lock her up. But he had quickly relented, stipulating only that the concubine must chaperone Fronah and that they use the sedan-chairs with the firm's name scrolled on their black sides in silver ideograms.

Since he would not – or could not – forbid his daughter to visit the stricken youth, Saul had decided to draw the gossips' teeth by demonstrating his approval. The community considered him righteous, indeed strait-laced, and no respectable father would permit his daughter such visits if he had the slightest reason to suspect her relationship with the young rake. Besides, no upright father would consent if he – or his family – had had a hand in the retribution that befell the rake.

Sarah herself accompanied Fronah to the clipper *Orion* when Iain Matthews embarked for Hong Kong on the thirteenth day after his

197

humiliation. Sickened by the need to appear civil to the young Gentile, she had almost rebelled. Finally accepting Saul's wise decision, she had even smiled distantly at Iain Matthews as Fronah said her farewells. Saul had charged his daughter not to weep in public. To her own surprise, she had not wept even when Iain lamented his fate with tears in his eyes.

'What'll I say to my pater?' he demanded. 'After all his sacrifices, I'm coming home in disgrace. He'll . . . he'll half kill me. I'll never amount to anything.'

'Now, Iain, you know it'll be all right.' Having forgiven his vile reproaches, Fronah truly believed her own consolation. 'With your ability . . . your charm . . . you're sure to be a success whatever you do. Just forget this episode. You'll make a great career at home, I know it.'

'Don't treat me like a child,' he snapped. 'And I will forget you . . . just as fast as I can. It's all your fault. If it weren't for you, I'd never . . . You led me on. You're no more than . . . you're practically a tart.'

Fronah smiled for the other passengers and their well-wishers. It would not be much longer. Only a little while longer would she have to endure this parting from the man she had once loved so deeply, the man she still loved in spite of his poisonous last words. The wind was whipping the sails loosely furled on *Orion's* yards. On the main mast, the Blue Peter fluttered, the blue pennant with the white box, which signalled that the vessel would soon sail. When the whistle hooted three times to warn passengers' friends to disembark, relief overwhelmed her.

'Goodbye, Iain.' She could no longer smile even for appearance's sake. 'I wish you all the good fortune in the world.'

'It's all your fault . . . yours.' He vehemently repeated his accusation. 'I was wrong. You're not a tart. You're a rotten whore . . . a dirty Jew whore.'

Fronah descended the gangplank to their sampan, one hand grasping the rope hand-rail, the other holding down her whipping skirts. She halted to wave to Iain, despite her anger and her revulsion. She waved and smiled again. She smiled still when she sat in the sampan, smiled till her face felt as if it were frozen.

Every foreigner on *Orion* was watching her with unconcealed curiosity, probably every Chinese too. All Shanghai knew why Iain Matthews was leaving in disgrace. Jardines' taipan had dismissed him briefly, though not brutally. Every griffin knew the house could forgive most transgressions – but not scandal. No, there was no hope of transfer to Hong Kong. There was, candidly, no future for Iain Matthews with Jardines or, the taipan felt it only fair to warn, anywhere on the China Coast. No wonder every foreigner stared, hoping she would break down and confirm their prurient speculation.

Nonetheless, Fronah reflected, she had to see him off – and not just to give the lie to the gossips. Since not one of his fair-weather friends would risk bidding the black sheep farewell, she could not have let him stand alone on the ship's deck. Having climbed the gangplank, she had to put the best possible face on their parting. Moreover, she had to behave as if she were only a friend – as if she had never loved him.

She had succeeded. Her father had praised her behaviour and observed that the petty scandal would now blow over. She was, she acknowledged bitterly, glad he had gone quickly, since he had to go. Besides their parting had destroyed whatever vestigial affection that had survived his earlier accusations. Angry and disgusted, she realised she had never really loved the youth whose last words to her were: 'rotten whore . . . dirty Jew whore.'

She had, Fronah consoled herself, truly begun to mature because of the ghastly experience. She would in the future not dismiss her parents' counsel. She would listen carefully, though she would, of course, finally make her own decisions. Her mother and her father had warned her against the young bloods of the settlement from the moment they allowed her to mingle in Christian society. Those lechers regarded a Jewish girl as fair prey. She would never forgive David for interfering, but, she had to admit, his revenge on Iain had its comic side.

Perhaps, as her father suggested, an older man might be better for her, providing, of course, that he was Jewish. She would be eighteen in just six months time. Only one older man in Shanghai could interest her, and only one could possibly be interested in her. Lionel Howard Stanley Henriques was a true English gentleman, unlike 'that counter-jumping lout,' as Margaret MacGregor called Iain Matthews. He was highly cultured, and his home was in sophisticated Europe far from money-grabbing Shanghai.

But could she be truly happy in a distant country she had never seen? Most English people didn't know chopsticks from knitting needles, much less Confucious from Buddha. They might well find her fascinating because she was a freak. She longed to be respected in her own right, respected for her own accomplishments, not just her husband's position.

Still, it would be a remarkable accomplishment for a Jewish girl from provincial Shanghai to preside over her own circle in a white house on Belgrave Square, the centre of sophistication. How, her thoughts veered, would Lionel Henriques be, as Maylu would undoubtedly ask, *that* way, between the sheets? Fronah blushed. She was, Margaret MacGregor said, always crossing her bridges before they were built. Papa had not even spoken to Mr Henriques yet. He probably had a financée in England, the daughter of a baronet or even a baron.

Another name bobbed to the surface of her mind. Gabriel Hyde might be a more exciting lover than Lionel Henriques, for he was masterful and vital, even if, as he would say, somewhat homespun. She blushed again and admonished herself to curb her wayward thoughts. Never before that instant had she considered the American anything but an amusing companion and a foil to pink Iain's jealousy. Anyway, Gabriel had never shown the slightest interest in her. He was more drawn to Margaret MacGregor. Above all, he was not Jewish, and she would be a fool indeed if she had not learned to stay away from Christian men.

'What's up, sweetie? You're as quiet as patience on a monument. Daydreaming or brooding?'

The crisp American voice recalled Fronah to the world around her, and she saw the naval officer idly twirling a full-blown orange rose from her father's most treasured bush. Fronah smelled the fragrance of roses on the autumnal breeze. She heard the noodle-hawker's high-pitched whistle and the strolling knife-sharpener's clanking scissors in the street outside the compound. She waved to Maylu, who was hanging out of the second-storey window laughing at her surprise.

'I heard you put on a wonderful act the other day.' Gabriel was casually jocular. 'Worthy of a great actress like Julia Dean. I'm told.'

'Act? What do you mean, Gabriel?'

'Don't pretend, Fronah,' he replied. 'It's only old Uncle Gabe.'

He was parodying himself, playing the hayseed to take her out of herself. She could not say how much Gabriel knew – or surmised – of her relations with Iain Matthews. She wondered whether he suspected that her vengeful Chinese brothers had contrived Iain's downfall. Still, she wasn't certain of the boys' complicity. She was confident that Gabriel didn't know of her shame, but only thought her flighty.

'I just mean it was very brave of you to see that scamp Matthews off,' he continued. 'I'd have been there myself only I was upriver. He got a raw deal, no matter what he did. I reckon he did plenty. But those mealy-mouthed hypocrites at Jardines. Turfing him out for getting caught when every griffin carries on the same way with Chinese . . . ah . . . ladies. You did wonderfully.'

'You're very kind, Commander.' She dimpled, then abruptly dropped her arch manner. 'I just felt some one had to see the poor boy off. Though, of course, whatever he did to . . . to make the Chinese act that way . . . that was . . . was' . . .'

'Not quite the thing to do, though the punishment may've been a little beyond what he deserved. But, pardon me, that's no fit subject for a young lady's ears.'

'I'm not as unworldly . . . as sheltered as you think, Gabriel. But it's good to see you.'

'I just dropped by to chat with your father and see how the young lady was doing.' He was less breezy. 'Still, you might be interested in some of the remarkable things I've been learning about Shanghai.'

'Shanghai's always remarkable.'

'Even though dry history doesn't interest young ladies. I've been looking at the old charts. You know this city was nothing . . . only a swamp a thousand years ago. The whole thing's man-made. And we have the nerve to look down on the Chinese . . . think they're children when it comes to dams and dredging. Why, they make the Dutch look like children.'

'You're so right.' Fronah was totally serious. 'The boys' tutor showed us a history of the Prefecture about three hundred years ago under the Ming Dynasty's Wan Li Emperor. Water-control was *the* major responsibility for the government. Otherwise, there'd be no commerce. Not only that, but there'd be no irrigation for the rice-fields.'

'You're quite the scholar, Miss Fronah, aren't you?' He regretted the gibe immediately. 'But, forgive me, of course you are. Tell me now . . .'

Gabriel Hyde was startled by Fronah's knowledge and surprised by her enthusiasm for a subject that would reduce most girls of her age to glazed boredom. David had spoken of her Chinese studies, but he had not realised that Fronah's intellectual curiosity was as great as her brother's. He had become fond of David, who was not only friendly, but candid and quick-witted. Still, he had thought a devoted brother was exaggerating his sister's accomplishments.

Fronah was, Gabriel reflected, hardly as flighty as he'd thought. There was solid worth beneath her frivolous manner, itself not unattractive. A young lady with her fine appearance and active mind was remarkable. Why not come right out and say it – to himself, at least? Not just a fine appearance, a milk-and-water description. She was very pretty, extraordinarily pretty, almost beautiful. Dammit, she *was* beautiful when she left off her airs and feeling lit her face.

But he mustn't think about Fronah that way. She was much too young for him to think of her as a woman. She was emphatically not the sort of girl for a quick roll in the hay. Besides, that wasn't really his own style. She was essentially serious beneath her levity. He'd have to be serious with her if the day ever came.

He, too, was essentially serious beneath his jocose manner. How could he be anything but serious? His father was not just a small town lawyer, but a New England puritan who had taught him that the life of the mind was the highest pursuit of a civilised man. Another reason for making haste very slowly. The Hydes of Salem did not marry young, though the farmers and craftsmen might. If the day ever came, there would be difficulties with her parents. But he'd face that problem when the time came – if it ever came. Meanwhile, he enjoyed talking with her as he'd enjoyed few talks since he was stranded on the China Coast.

*

Saul Haleevie was unaccountably restless as he examined the samples of duck feathers. It was, he told himself, becoming too easy. Perhaps he needed new challenges. Duck feathers were all very well in their place,

201

presumably, either on ducks or on European beds. But duck feathers could hardly capture the imagination of a scholar who knew by heart most of the *Talmud* and half the *Dialogues* of Plato.

He had dealt, competently and automatically, with the samples sent by his agent in Wuhsi. The first lot he had rejected summarily as brittle and dry. The second, he had concluded after a moment's thought, would be worth considering under other circumstances, but not when the third lot was perfect. Fluffy and bulky, they would plumply stuff pillows and featherbeds. There was no need to bother with the second-rate when the first-rate was abundant and cheap. For some unfathomable reason, the Chinese did not use that ideal material in their own quilts or coats, preferring more expensive raw-silk fibres.

If the Taiping offensive neither overran Wuhsi nor halted bulk shipments, that decision would at the year's end result in a gratifying profit on his books. That increase in wealth would make his family more secure and, at God's pleasure, happier, too. But selecting grades of duck-feathers hardly challenged a man who had once been the most promising student of the law between Madrid and Bombay.

Saul lit a cheroot and leaned back in his chair to contemplate the ceiling through the tendrils of smoke. Not only his faith, but his innate curiosity would prevent his ever being overcome by inert boredom, accidie, which Christian theologians counted among the mortal sins. The Lord God, who gave man free will, punished withdrawal from the world of His creation as severely as he punished turning away from Himself to worship false gods. Saul none the less feared that his intellect would grow flabby with too little stimulus.

China had been an utterly new world when he had landed in Shanghai fifteen years earlier. Immediately fascinated, he had learned much about that world since that time. But opportunities to learn more were receding: he was now virtually confined to Shanghai by the demands of business and, lately, by concern for his daughter. He could no longer make the dangerous and stimulating trips into the interior. More than two years had passed since he journeyed in disguise with poor Aisek Lee to Soochow to find a new silk for the markets of Europe. It seemed an age.

Less than two hundred miles away, the Taiping stronghold at Nanking, now called the Heavenly Capital, could offer exciting new intellectual challenges – as well as business opportunities. The rebels were shaping a new society under the Heavenly King, who claimed to be the younger brother of Jesus Christ. That was patent idiocy, a second false Messiah claiming kinship with the first false Messiah, who was actually no more than an innovative moral philosopher. But beyond that moonstruck theology, the Taiping experiment was fascinating – if one could call a regime that ruled almost half China an experiment.

The Holy Soldiers, it was reported, did not rob the common people.

Such restraint was remarkable for any army – and, if true, virtually miraculous for a Chinese army. All property was reportedly held in common in the Heavenly Capital – an assertion Saul viewed almost as sceptically as the claim that Taiping armies did not loot. Female soldiers like the legendary Amazons fought for the Heavenly King, while men and women lived apart. How, he wondered, did they produce little Taipings? Or was that function performed only by the hundreds of concubines who reportedly filled the harems of the Taiping Emperor and his subordinate kings? Above all, he wondered, could a theocracy actually thrive in the modern world, a state that regulated every aspect of its life according to the expressed will of its God?

Saul rose from his chair and began to pace the small office. Walking always helped him think.

The Heavenly Kingdom of Great Peace controlled the extraordinary productive Yangtze Basin, which was also the greatest potential market in the world. A journey of exploration into the Taiping realm was not only an intellectual challenge, but a practical necessity, for the future of the firm of Haleevie and Lee. He had to know whether the Taipings actually possessed the potential to destroy the Manchus and bring all China under their rule. If he did not understand their heterodox movement, he could not judge which way China was moving. If his plans for the future were not based on reliable information, his small firm could go under or, at best, fail to seize its opportunities.

Yet he could not leave the foreign settlement for the necessary length of time, since his affairs required his presence. Besides, he could not take his eye off his troublesome daughter. Why, after all, was he determined to expand the business, except to provide for Fronah and her future husband?

Saul halted in his pacing only to tap the ashes off his cheroot in a polychrome saucer. He reasoned more clearly when he was moving about, just as his studious forefathers had exercised their undervalued bodies while disputing the subtleties of the Law. After finishing his second cheroot, he rebelled against the fug filling the room and leaned out of the window that overlooked the front garden.

The tableau he saw might have appeared idyllic to another eye. The white figure of the American naval officer was bent attentively towards Fronah, who was demure in a tight-waisted dress of pink cotton, her pleated skirt a many-petalled flower on the stone bench.

Saul was briefly charmed by the scene. But it had not altered for more than an hour as the young man and the girl chatted animatedly. Paternal instinct alerted him. Instead of feeling pleased that an absorbing conversation had broken Fronah's brooding, he was alarmed by the intimacy of the two youthful figures.

Fronah was, naturally, susceptible to Gabriel Hyde's charm after young Matthews' ignominious removal, but she must not become involved with

203

another Gentile. The more attractive Gabriel Hyde's dark handsomeness and easy good hunour were to her now, the worse it could be for her later.

The decision Saul had been pondering was determined by his fear. Forgetting his dignity, he leaned out the window and called to the American. Gabriel Hyde waved and, after bidding an extremely protracted farewell to Fronah, sauntered around the house towards the entrance to the godown.

'Commander, I've been thinking about the idea I mentioned the other day,' Saul began without the normal pleasantries after Hyde had accepted a cheroot. 'Or may I say Gabriel?'

'My pleasure,' Hyde replied negligently.

'Gabriel, then. I have got a proposition to put to you. How would you like to visit the Heavenly Capital?'

'Well, it's a new idea all right,' the American drawled. 'It certainly has the charm of novelty.'

'No, Gabriel, I'm very serious. Please hear my words out.'

'Pardon me, Mr Haleevie. I thought you were joking. It sounds crazy, but I'm all ears.'

'I've been thinking, Gabriel,' Saul began slowly. 'A clever young fellow like yourself is just what I need. And, of course, I'll make it worth your while. This is what I have in mind.'

Disdaining subterfuge, the merchant reviewed his recent chain of reasoning for the American. A long stay in the Heavenly Kingdom would, he stressed, be necessary to evalute the Taipings' political, military, and commercial potential. In addition to expenses, Gabriel Hyde would receive a commission of ten percent on all transactions his efforts generated, as well as a fee of £200, say US$1,000, for his report. The Taipings, Saul believed, would welcome the American. They wished to attract foreign officers into their service – and they were also avid for trade.

'That's fine, Mr Haleevie, just dandy,' Gabriel replied. 'But you seem to have overlooked two little points. I don't wear this uniform just for show. Remember, I'm an officer in the Imperial Water force. Somehow, it strikes me, the commodore wouldn't be wild about my consorting with the enemy. It's not done, you know.'

'Ah, Gabriel, it is. The Imps won't turn down the chance to learn about the Taiping Water Force, not to speak of general military strength. Also, I can drop a word or two . . . a few *taels* here and there. And you're not tongue-tied yourself.'

'You want me to spy? I don't see that . . . No, I don't like that.'

'Not a spy, Gabriel. How a spy if both sides know exactly who you are? Rather a diplomatic observer.'

'Well, it would make a change. Going up and down the Yangtze like a ferry captain gets boring. Anyway, I'm damned curious to see how the Taipings operate. Let me think about it.'

'And your second point, Gabriel?'

'I almost forgot. You know, my pidgin Chinese is good enough to give orders on *Mencius*. I'm working on the language, mind you. But my Chinese won't take me very far in Taiping country.'

'Give me credit, Gabriel. I'm not planning to send you deaf and dumb to the Heavenly Capital. I'll be giving you a Chinese tongue and Chinese ears.'

'Surgery's really progressed by leaps and bounds lately, Mr Haleevie, has it?' Gabriel laughed. 'Who's to perform that miracle, Dr Willie MacGregor?'

'I am, Gabriel, temporarily. David will go with you. Aaron might be better, I admit. He's more sensible. But he has his examination in a few months. And for . . . ah . . . certain reasons, it might be a good idea for David to . . . ah . . . not be seen in Shanghai for a while. You and he get on well, don't you?'

'Yes, sir. He a good boy, lively and quick, too. I'd like to take David.'

'Then it's settled?' Saul offered his hand to seal the agreement. 'We're agreed? When can you leave?'

'Not quite settled, Sir. I need to mull it over. If I do take you up, I'm due leave. Say the day after tomorrow.'

'Unless I hear otherwise by tonight, I'll count on it, then. Now, if you'll allow me, I want to make an arrangement or two.'

From the window, Saul watched the officer's white back dwindle along the gravel path through the circles of roses. Though Fronah had vanished into the house, Gabriel Hyde gazed for a time at the stone bench.

The merchant congratulated himself. He would rather go himself, but he could not, However, Gabriel and David would together do almost as well as himself. Equally important, the American would be out of Shanghai for a long time. With Hyde out of the way, he could pursue his plans unhampered by Fronah's volatile emotions. His other scheme needed a month or so to mature.

CHAPTER THIRTY

September 6, 1856   *Shanghai*

Saul Haleevie felt a twinge of anxiety for his son David and Gabriel Hyde. He had not heard from them since the old *Low Dah*, his favourite smuggling captain, returned to report that their warm welcome in the

Heavenly Capital of the Great Kingdom of Heavenly Peace. However, foreigners constantly travelled to the insurgent realm and there was no reason why he should – or could – have received news so soon after their stealthy departure at twilight on August 3, 1856.

He recalled that the *Low Dah* had wanted to sail at noon to show off his new junk, which was ten feet longer and two knots faster than the vessel that lay at the bottom of the Yangtze. But the smuggler and his sometime captor could hardly sweep down the Hwangpoo to the Long River in the glare of the midday sun with banners flying.

Saul's lean features wrinkled in a scowl when he thought of his apprentice Sammy Moses. Though a nonentity, the lad had been honourable when he declared forthrightly that he proposed to seek the hand of Miriam and Moses Elias's daughter Rebecca. Of course Fronah wanted nothing to do with the apprentice. Still, it rankled when *his* daughter was spurned by a greasy mediocrity.

Sammy was only trimming his sails to the prevailing wind in the Jewish community. The exclusive Moseses, Weinsteins, and Benjamins were horrified by Fronah's friendship with young Iain Matthews. How could a chaste Jewish girl be seen with a Gentile who was a notorious rake? None the less, she was contaminated, and no respectable Jewish boy would pay her court.

Besides, Fronah's fundamental discontent would endure and corrode her life unless he acted firmly. Sarah sometimes complained that he took too much upon his shoulders – and too much into his hands. He did not enjoy manipulating others, but Fronah *was* his responsibility.

Saul's mind was made up. Sammy Moses's effrontery had erased his reservations. He closed the office-door resolutely behind him and went in search of his wife.

*

Fronah's contralto mingled with Aaron's baritone and the old tutor's reedy tenor from the adjoining schoolroom. After her conversation in the garden with Gabriel Hyde twelve days earlier, Fronah had returned to her neglected Chinese studies. Saul was pleased by her again questioning him about commerce and Chinese politics, though another father might have felt such interest unseemly for a female. However, he deplored her new interest in military, particularly naval, affairs. Its inspiration was obvious.

It was, as Sarah said, past time for her to be bethrothed, and her marriage must not be long delayed. After a decent interval, so that the gossips could not say she had to marry, Fronah and Lionel must stand under the wedding canopy. She would forget both her childish infatuations and her unrealistic ambitions once she became a wife and, if God pleased, a mother.

He found Sarah in the conservatory, her dark eyebrows drawn together in concentration. On the round marble table stood a shallow brass bowl from Seoul, which tinkled to summon the servants when struck with a small wooden mallet. A single white rose floated in the clear water, its purity reflected in the gleaming bottom. Sprays of red roses soared around a sprig of yellow azalea blossoms in a bell-mouthed *famille noir* vase of the Yung Cheng reign.

Lifting her eyes from the celadon vase in her hands, Sarah smiled defensively and offered her husband her lips. Saul kissed her and smiled at the casual caress that expiated her guilt. She knew very well that he did not like her to cut twigs from the azaleas or to put flowers in the brass bowl. She also knew that the pale-green vase with the narrow neck should be left untouched on the display-shelf. Dating from the Koryu period in Korea, some six hundred years ago, it was virtually unique in Shanghai.

'I was just wondering which orchids I could bear to sacrifice, the cymbidium or the cattleya,' she parried. 'Your vase needs one perfect spray.'

'Then don't make any sacrifices,' he suggested. 'Not your orchids or my vase.'

'Saul, is something wrong?' She put the vase down. 'Why did you leave the office in the middle of the morning?'

'No, dear, nothing's wrong. Quite the reverse. I've decided you're right . . . absolutely right.'

'I'm always right, Saul. Except . . .'

'. . . except when you're wrong,' he completed their familiar joke. 'But this time you're really right. Fronah must be married . . . very soon. Otherwise, with this Gentile and that Gentile, who knows? At least I got Gabriel Hyde out of the way.'

'And not too soon. But, Saul, don't worry about it quite so much. She'll be all right in the long run. Young girls are like that.'

'But you agree, don't you?'

'How could I *not* agree. I've only been telling you for a year or more. Of course she must be married as soon as possible.'

'And you still feel this . . . this Henriques?'

'Yes, Saul, I do. I know you've got reservations, but only angels are perfect. She is attracted, and he's very acceptable. You know I warned she'd never find a Jewish man she could like. And I'm sure he'll make a good husband.'

'All right, then. Why don't you have a word with Fronah?'

'I'm to have a word with Fronah? You know she thinks I'm an old frump. What did she call me the other day? Yes, a back number? *You* have a word with her.'

'You win, my dear. We'll *both* have a word with her at lunch.'

Grateful that Aaron had not wished to interrupt his studies to join them,

Sarah raised the matter as the luncheon dishes were cleared away and they sat over glasses of lemon tea at the mahogany table. Saul realised with relief that he could be silent while his women talked about what was, after all, women's business. Chastened by her experience with Iain Matthews and grateful for her parents' tolerance, Fronah was receptive. She was so acquiescent that her mother glowed with satisfaction. Her father was unaccountably disturbed by her lack of spirit.

'Only a betrothal, you understand, Fronah,' he interposed. 'Of course, a betrothal usually means a wedding. But if . . . if you felt unhappy . . . why it would only be a betrothal.'

'That won't happen, Papa, I promise you. I've been thinking hard since we talked. Maybe I don't love Mr Henriques. I don't know . . . can't know. But I *do* like him very much and I *do* admire him. I *really* do.'

'A betrothal's a betrothal, Saul,' Sarah chided. 'She mustn't start with the idea of getting out. The child says she's sure. Stop putting doubts into her head.'

'And you'll go with him wherever he goes like Ruth with Naomi. You understand, Fronah, don't you? This isn't playing. It's the rest of your life.'

'Certainly, Papa,' Fronah felt it would not be politic to mention her dream of a grand house on Belgrave Square. 'I'm not a child any more, I promise you.'

'Of course, your father will offer Mr Henriques a partnership. One day, the business and the property, it'll all be yours and his. So there's no need even to think of leaving Shanghai. I know how you'd hate to leave.'

'Of course, Mama,' Fronah agreed. 'Who would ever want to leave Shanghai?'

Actually, Fronah's fondest hope was to sail for England. The Gentile milieu of the Treaty Port no longer glittered as it had when it first offered her a tentative welcome. Her thrice weekly lessons with Margaret Mac-Gregor had not only taught her to dress with flair and to speak with proper English understatement. The romantic Scotswoman had also inflamed her imagination with second-hand tales of the glamour of London society. Self-exiled in Shanghai by her faith, Margaret muddled the reality of industrial Britain with the realm of chivalry depicted in the Waverley Novels of Sir Walter Scott, which she loved reading with her pupil. Yet, the Scotswoman's judgment of people was shrewd – and she was justly proud of the transformation she had wrought in the Jewish girl, like Pygmalion creating Galatea. She had, she felt, given the breath of life to a charming and intelligent young woman. She was only half-aware that she had also fired Fronah with aspirations that were virtually impossible of realization.

*

Saul Haleevie was unaccountably disturbed by the speed with which his plans unfolded when Lionel Henriques kept his appointment that afternoon. But, he told himself, he was only uneasy because he was accustomed to bearing down opposition and to overcoming difficulties. There was no challenge when his wishes were unopposed, indeed enthusiastically taken up.

After expressing delighted surprise that a man of Saul Haleevie's standing should honour him by suggesting marriage with his only daughter, Lionel Henriques insisted upon revealing his financial position 'as one man of business to another'. Embarrassed at probing the affairs of a gentleman who was as secure financially as he was socially, Saul protested ritually that the revelations were unnecessary. So great was Lionel Henriques' charm and so transparent his candour, the canny merchant almost believed his own protestations.

'So, you see, Saul, I'll have £1,500 a year when my Aunt Selma goes. Poor dear, she's eighty-two and won't be with us long, I fear. My mother is, thank God, hale, though she's almost seventy-five. Unless God ordains otherwise, she'll light my days for years to come. But I would be less than candid if I did not tell you that she enjoys an income of £5,000 from my late father and another £2,500 from her father, all to come to me as the eldest on her passing. Then there's my connection with Samuelsons. I can assure you Fronah will never know want.'

'I never doubted that, Lionel.' Saul was understanably gratified and unaccountably piqued. 'Nor am I a pauper. I can't give precise figures like you, but Fronah will have at least half of everything I own. I must provide for Aaron and David, you know. Of course, if you came into partnership, there'd be a bigger share for Fronah and yourself.'

'Are you offering me a partnership, Saul?' The prospect allayed Lionel Henriques's indignation at his future father-in-law's proposing to give a portion of his substance to two Chinamen. 'I'm honoured that you consider me worthy of a partnership.'

'What else, Lionel? After you're married, a good working relationship. Then, after a year or so, a partnership.'

It would do him very well, Lionel Henriques concluded. Far better, actually, than he'd dared hope. The old boy, who was only nine years older than himself, was a great money-spinner, a shrewd Hebrew trader in the old mould his own family seemed to have mislaid. Since Haleevies would undoubtedly need a representative in London some day, he could bide his time happily.

The girl herself was by no means unattractive, still delightfully young and pliable. She was, of course, somewhat wilful, but there was little harm in her high-spirits. It would be a pleasure to curb her and a joy to polish her rough edges. He could hardly have done better, Lionel Henriques concluded.

'When do you plan the betrothal party, Saul?' he asked.

'You'll be leaving for Hong Kong in a week.' Saul's native prudence reasserted itself. 'Let's say as soon as you return.'

'That suits me down to the ground, Saul. Now, about my mission to the money men of Hong Kong? I've been thinking, and I feel . . .'

Saul was startled by Henriques's abrupt transition to business. He had not even suggested that he talk to Fronah. However, Lionel's practical approach demonstrated that he would make a reliable husband. He was no impulsive youth but a mature man of substance and good sense. None the less, Saul was relieved by his prospective son-in-law's words when they had agreed on their tactics in Hong Kong.

'Now, Saul, may I pay my court to Miss Fronah?' Lionel Henriques asked. 'Business is all very well in its place, but I'm longing to see her.'

CHAPTER THIRTY-ONE

September 16, 1856   *Shanghai*

It was absolutely true, Fronah realised, the boast ostensibly made in jest. Because females were so few in the foreign settlement, a presentable lady could enjoy a dance, a musical soirée, or a dinner party six nights of the week if she pleased. She did not even have to be attractive as long as her manners and her dress were acceptable. In the ten days since Lionel Henriques asked permission to pay his court they had attended seven such gatherings. All were delightful, and all, it seemed, revolved around herself. Even the small Jewish community, which had virtually snubbed her two weeks earlier, was giving a dinner the following Sunday.

Her parents would join them at that festive table for the first time. They could, of course, not dine at the Gentiles' non-kosher tables. Besides, it did not occur to the Christians to ask the leader of the Hebrew community. If it did, they resisted the temptation because they knew he would feel uncomfortable in their homes.

Lionel Henriques was, however, almost one of them. Though he might be Jewish and a bit finicky in observing the dietary laws, those lapses were forgivable. He was indisputably British, and he was cloaked in the prestige of a powerful banking house. Founded upon trade, the foreign settlement was naturally concerned with money above all else. Which great merchant knew when he might not need an additional line of credit? Besides, Henriques was a good fellow, a first-class shot and a fine horseman, even if he was a little mannered. You'd hardly think, they said, that he was a Hebrew.

The same self-serving tolerance now embraced Fronah Haleevie. Though she was not yet formally betrothed to Lionel Henriques, all Shanghai knew they had reached an understanding. For the first time, the Europeans welcomed her as one of themselves, rather than an exotic creature who lent colour to a dull evening like an emerald cockatoo chattering in strange accents. That girl had been left to the griffins, with whom, gossips whispered, she had been a shade too free before the understanding with Henriques drew her back from the brink just in time. The intended bride of Samuelsons' man, however, merited the hearty gallantries of the elder merchants who dominated the settlement. Even their wives could not object to such avuncular attentions to a young lady who was virtually betrothed.

Fronah was, naturally, not the guest of honour at Derwents' dinner-dance on September 16, 1856, but she was the centre of attraction. Beakers of claret and goblets of champagne were lifted to her, and ladies as well as gentlemen beamed on the prospective bride. She was delighted to have finally attained the acceptance whose vain pursuit had, she now realised, led to the unfortunate episode with Iain Matthews. That childish infatuation seemed to have occurred aeons ago, almost in another life.

The candles on the mahogany table, whose Foochow-lacquer finish was burnished to a mirror sheen, cast a glow upon the company. Lionel Henriques was, Fronah judged dispassionately, quite the most impressive in his severely tailored tail-suit. The broad black-silk lapels spread like the wings of a midnight-blue butterfly beside his snowy stock and his looped bow tie. He needed neither a showy uniform nor trumpery medals to lend distinction to his patrician features framed by his wavy silver-gilt hair. His manner was perfection: relaxed and attentive to the conversation, but slightly aloof. He was far above the stolid men of commerce, but he was too well bred to flaunt his superiority.

Fronah smiled when his light-blue gaze rested proudly on her for an instant. Her amber eyes sparkling over the rim of her champagne-goblet, her lips pursed in a kissing movement only he could see. She almost laughed with joy when he smiled in return. He then shook his head in infinitesimal warning to restrain her impulsiveness. Displaying one's emotions was not, he had previously advised, good form – never in public and better not in private.

She still had so much to learn, but he would teach her. He was possessive and protective, eager that she should be a credit to herself – and to him. Lionel was no raw and eager youth. He had kissed her on the lips only once for a fleeting but delicious instant. Unlike grubby Iain Matthews, a true gentleman did not paw a lady. Profound respect prevented his forcing himself on her. Besides, there would be time for that when they were

211

married. With Lionel *that* would be an exquisite delight, not a rough, sweaty tumble. She shuddered in horror at the memory – and smiled in derision at the foolish fears she had felt immediately after promising herself to Lionel.

Never had she looked better, she knew. The pink roses in her hair, which was looped softly above her nape, complemented the coral-pink taffeta of her skirt, which fell in three scalloped flounces beneath her short overskirt of Brussels lace. Appearing to reveal much without revealing too much, the basque of the same coral-pink grosgrain, which left her powdered shoulders bare, discreetly concealed the cleft of her breasts behind a cluster of three pink roses. For once, her mother had protested neither at the extravagance of the gown, which was her reward for obedience, nor at the cost of the string of pale-green Peking jade-beads set between chased gold links to set if off.

Fronah was for a moment disconsolate when she remembered that Lionel must leave for Hong Kong in a week's time. But, as he said, the joy of their reunion would make even separation an exquisite pleasure. It was odd that her other admirers had all left Shanghai. Iain Matthews first. She'd made a fool of herself over that young ruffian. She was delighted that he was gone, though a little sorry he wasn't there to see her triumph. Of course, Gabriel Hyde wasn't really an admirer, just someone to laugh with. And David? Why, David was her brother, and she naturally missed him.

Yet none really mattered except Lionel, and he would soon return. When he did, her father had promised a gala party to seal their formal betrothal.

Perhaps she was too eager for future joys. Her mother said it was foolish to rush your life. But the foretaste of the future she already enjoyed was intoxicating. Perhaps she did not love Lionel utterly – not yet. But she knew she would grow to love him deeply – as a woman loved, not a silly young girl.

CHAPTER THIRTY-TWO

October 6, 1856   *Nanking*

The rainbow beam pierced the narrow embrasure and played on the rough-hewn stones. Looking up from the leather-bound journal, Gabriel Hyde blinked. The brilliant light was painful after the guttering candles to which he had become accustomed during his month-long confinement in the tower of the massive South Gate of Tienking, the Heavenly Capital of the Kingdom of Great Peace. He laid his goose-quill down on the green inkstone and rubbed his smarting eyes with his knuckles.

After studying literature at Bowdoin College, he had not plied a pen with such concentration for years. Besides, the goose-quill constantly split and splattered the black ink on the glossy paper. His hosts, for he could not really think of the Taipings as jailers, were eager to supply everything he required. But they would not give him leave to walk through their capital –or leave it. Nor could they provide a modern steel-nib to lighten the labour of composition. Compiling the journal and writing out a fair copy were his chief diversion, aside from exchanging lessons in the English language and Western history for the Chinese language and Oriental history with his fellow internee, David Lee.

The American rose and stretched. Although their hosts allowed them to stroll on the ramparts twice a day, his cramped muscles ached for more vigorous exercise. Although he knew they were confined for their own safety, as well as the convenience of the embattled Heavenly King, he resented the inactivity inposed upon him. The high-spirited David, normally even more energetic than himself, accepted their predicament with Chinese resignation. He was stretched on the thin quilt covering the hard pallet like a black tomcat in repose. Only the slight movement of his lips as he whispered prolonged passages from the Confucian Classics revealed that he was not totally relaxed.

Gabriel had grown even fonder of the Chinese youth in their enforced intimacy. But he was annoyed by David's meticulously enumerated gratitude for confinement because: first, it gave him the leisure to review his studies; second, it kept them both from injury – or worse; third, it proved their lack of complicity with the Taipings; and fourth, it allowed them to record their experiences in the Heavenly Capital for Saul Haleevie. The Chinese, Gabriel had become convinced, were not really fatalistic but, rather, adept at finding minuscule pearls of consolation in the roughest oyster. If his companion was a fair example, they were also indefatigable compilers of lists. To the three primary virtues, the five fundamental relationships, and the twelve celestial signs, David had now appended the four self-consolations.

Gabriel prowled across the square flagstones to the embrasure and leaned his elbows on the rough stone sill. He craned through the narrow aperture shaped to shelter crossbowmen when the Founding Emperor of the Ming Dynasty had raised the twenty-mile wall to make Nanking, his new Southern Capital, impregnable. That wall was erected almost three hundred years before the Ming re-discovered firearms at the beginning of the seventeenth century. By then it was too late, David had taught him, for the green-bronze cannon cast by Jesuit missionaries to save the Ming from the Manchu invaders. The extraordinary events that had occurred in the

Heavenly Capital during the month just past might, however, save the Manchu Dynasty from extinction, though its position was almost as precarious as the Ming's had been in the seventeenth century.

Gabriel watched the afternoon sun glint on the Chinhuai River flowing beneath the cliffs on which the sixty-foot walls reared. The brilliant rays that had broken his concentration were reflected from the ten-tiered Porcelain Pagoda on the slope of Purple Mountain to the east of the city. Clad with brilliant glaze tiles, that tower had been erected, David said, by the second Ming emperor in the grounds of the Buddhist monastery called *Pao En*, Benevolence Rewarded. At a distance its lustre appeared undimmed, but he had seen while they were still free to move about that the tiles were streaked with soot. When they had occupied Nanking three years earlier, the Holy Soldiers had put the Porcelain Pagoda to the torch, since their passionate inconoclasm sought to destroy all vestiges of 'Buddhist superstition'. Either their fervour had flagged or folk-superstition had prevailed when the timber-framed shrine failed to collapse. The pagoda still rose above the violet hill like an admonitory forefinger.

Gabriel grinned. He was becoming as superstitious as the Chinese, who saw supernatural intervention in almost every occurrence. Even in the Holy Capital of an aspiring new dynasty that declared itself Christian, the old superstitions were almost as powerful as the new doctrines. The Porcelain Pagoda would not now be destroyed because it had been preserved by Heaven – and the spire would admonish the revolutionaries to remain true to the glorious traditions of China.

Resuming his chair and his goose-quill, Gabriel reflected that China always remained China. He laughed at his own sententiousness, replaced the quill on the inkstone and turned to the beginning of the journal. Since it helped David polish his English, Gabriel read aloud before copying into a second journal for Saul Haleevie the introduction he had just written:

> The high hopes with which we came to Tienking, the Heavenly Capital, have been dashed. We are in reality prisoners, though we are guests in name and our warders bear us no ill-will. Quite the contrary, they do all in their power to make us comfortable. Unfortunately, their capacity to do so is severely limited. I must also regretfully advise that the great expectations for trade with the Heavenly Kingdom we originally discerned dwindle each day as the prospects of that Kingdom grow progressively more sombre.
>
> You will, perhaps, already have received news of the terrible disturbances in this presumably God-fearing capital before you read this account or hear of our experiences from our own lips. It is, therefore, not superfluous to assure you that we have every hope of returning unharmed to Shanghai, though I cannot say when.

214

However, since this journal should come into your hands before we return, I have written this brief introduction to assure you of our safety. What follows is the account David and I set down day by day before and during the calamitous occurrences we have lately witnesed.

'I suppose that's what you'd call a fine literary style?' David grinned. 'And you foreigners complain that we Chinese don't write the way we talk.'

'It wouldn't be fitting, Davy,' The American explained. 'The style must fit the tragic events. Who knows? Some day others may read our tale.'

'Just as well, then, you're not telling them why I wanted to see the Long Hairs, Gabriel.'

'A confidence is a confidence. But I hope you'll give up that notion. Anyway, I reckon these Holy Soldiers'll never be able to help you revenge your father. Not if they go on the way they're going.'

'You may be right. It's no joy, being here. Though it's damned interesting.'

'*Too* damned interesting. Wrestling a crocodile's also interesting, but hardly great recreation.'

'Toppling the Manchus isn't exactly a recreation. But let me have the journal. All that optimism, it's damned funny.'

13th August 1856, a glorious summer day. [David read aloud and admired the swirls of Gabriel's Spencerian script, though it was primitive beside the simplest Chinese calligraphy.] We were welcomed to the Heavenly Capital like honoured guests whose arrival has long been eagerly awaited. Introduction by General Wu Ju-hsiao, who is called the Four-Eyed Dog for his courage and his curious physiognomy, we were given an audience this afternoon by the Tung Wang, the King of the East, who is the Commander-in-Chief of the Taiping Armies. A lean man with a glittering ambitious eye and the dark skin of a southerner, the East King condescended to step down from the dais where his throne stands to receive us. He appears as anxious to recruit my services as was the Four-Eyed Dog at Chenkiang, the Citadel of the River, last spring. David's welcome was, of course, assured, since the Taipings profess an almost reverential regard for scholars, who are few among them. None the less, it is, perhaps, advantageous that David has not yet essayed the First Civil Service Examination, since the supreme Taiping monarch, the Heavenly King, himself repeatedly failed to secure entry to the Mandarinate through that portal. That failure is, of course, *never* discussed in the Holy City. Farmers and workmen fill their ranks, while converted Buddhist or Taoist monks, soothsayers, and other mystics too numerous to cite, as well as failed Mandarins, are

215

among their leaders. In any event, the letter from the Four-Eyed Dog, which we secured on our passage upriver, was an Open Sesame to Taipingdom.

The East King exercises virtually all temporal power, both civil and military, the two being so intertwined as to be identical in Taipingdom. The Heavenly King, the monarch of this theocratic realm, does not call himself Emperor, though he claims divinity, because the title Heavenly Emperor is reserved for the Lord God. The Heavenly King is rarely seen, having withdrawn to devote himself to theological, literary, and philosophical pursuits. The East King is, therefore, the effective ruler of tens of millions and the commander of standing armies that number more than a million.

Like all the Taiping princes, he is jealous of the prerogatives and the trappings of his exalted rank. He wore a long yellow robe embroidered with dragons as does the Manchu Emperor. A coronet of gold wires set with rubies rested on his pepper-and-salt hair, which bristled on a head untouched by the barber's razor that makes the Manchus and their loyal subjects half-bald. Plaited into a braid intertwined with a scarlet ribbon, his long hair was coiled around his head, the tail falling over his left shoulder.

'He acted just like an emperor, the East King.' David looked up from the journal. 'How can there be two emperors?'

'All these Taiping Kings are mighty proud for men fighting to make everyone equal,' Gabriel remarked. 'All the pomp and panoply.'

'That's the Chinese way, Gabriel. They say they have to live in splendour so the people will respect them. Then they get to like the splendour.'

'I can see why. They do themselves proud, don't they? For men who swear they want to change all the old ways, they cling to all the old privileges like barnacles.'

'I never thought of it that way before, but you're right. Since the Han, every new dynasty's tried to out-shine the one before. The Taipings are no exception, even if they did take aboard some Western ideas.'

'Well, read on, Davy. Though what you can possibly learn from *my* remarks on a Chinese city, I don't . . .'

'I can understand a little better how the Occidental mind works,' Dave laughed. 'Anyway, it's good for Chinese to see how we look through other people's eyes.'

26th August, 1856: In the streets, we were most struck by the *absence* of certain phenomena. Most astonishingly, we saw not a single mendicant, not one wretched beggar imploring alms. Both the tho-

216

roughfares and the byways of the Holy City are also distinguished from Shanghai and the cities under the rule of the Manchus by a curious stillness. Men wearing tight-fitting red, green, or blue jackets over wide petticoat-trousers of black stuff go briskly but silently about their errands, which are chiefly quasi-military. All are armed with daggers and many with clumsy pistols thrust into their scarlet sashes. All are under stringent discipline, and all, it appears, live in constant fear of the Draconian punishments their monarch inflicts for any violation of their numerous ordinances.

Not a single man so much as glanced at the numerous women who walked freely but decorously among them clad in similar colours, their tunics falling to their ankles for modesty's sake. The multitude of women, all unfettered by foot-bandages, abroad in the Holy City is a constant astonishment. Mostly they go in small detachments under the orders of female corporals and sergeants. Those females exceed by many times the maidservants and the women of the lower orders seen in the streets of the foreign settlement, where, of course, Chinese ladies do not go abroad. Males and females must be fully equal in both rights and duties, the Heavenly King has decreed, because they are created equal by Almighty God.

Not only are men and women considered equal, but all human beings except, of course, those who have risen by their outstanding talent. Yet superior position not only bestows great privilege, but also heavy responsibility to assure the wellbeing of the commonalty. In Taipingdom, the vision of 'communism' promulgated by Mr Karl Marx, special correspondent for the *New York Tribune* in London, appears to have become reality. Not only are all men and women, except the anointed rulers, equal in rights and duties, but all, in theory at least, hold all goods in common.

The East King, himself a former charcoal burner, is responsible for the innovations that make the Taiping realm not merely unique in China at this time, but, I believe, unique among all civilizations throughout human history. His design for the life of the commonalty is fiercely puritanical, passionate for abstinence and self-denial in the service of the Lord. That passion accords ill with the 'divine revelation' which inspired his ruling that all the Taiping Kings, like the Taiping Emperor, must take multitudes of wives and concubines, whose numbers rival the seraglio of the Grand Turk of the Ottomans or the venerable Solomon himself. To the common people he is, however, a stern father, who enforces separation of husbands and wives except on the infrequent days appointed for indulgence.

217

The majority of those strictures must none the less arouse approbation in any liberal-minded man who has seen the extraordinary laxness and corruption of Chinese society under the Great Pure Dynasty. Like the spectacle of the streets, it is most convenient to enumerate the abuses that do *not* exist in Taipingdom.

The use of opium has been extirpated, whether taken in pellets or smoked. Neither may the submissive subjects of the Heavenly King avail themselves of the consolations of tobacco or spirits in any form, even the mildest of rice-wine being stringently prohibited. Footbinding to produce 'golden lilies' has also disappeared, largely I suspect (prompted by David, my guide among the mysteries of things Chinese) because the Taipings originated among the lower orders of the south who infrequently bind their women's feet – and further, because females could not perform the arduous tasks assigned by this puritanical 'communism' if they were hampered by maimed feet. Also strictly proscribed are gambling and slavery, both unfortunately common elsewhere. Ancestor worship and idolatry are, of course, prohibited. Polygamy, too, has been outlawed, except for the rulers. In practice, the normal cohabitation of monogamy has been virtually outlawed for the commoners.

This arduous manner of life is reckoned to stimulate great ardour for the 'emancipation' of all China. On the day when the Heavenly Kingdom comes into his entire Kingdom, the strictures will presumably no longer be necessary to sustain the disciplined ardour of a people in arms. The savage penalties for transgressions are at least equally effective in maintaining that servile discipline. The punishment for offences ranging from petty theft through insubordination and rape to murder is the same: death.

David broke off to remark: 'It's always been that way, Gabriel.'
'What's always been that way?'
'Harsh punishment. No one can rule China by lenience. Benevolence, virtue, and universal love don't work . . . no matter what Confucius taught.'
'Well, Davy, the Manchus aren't doing that well. And they're pretty harsh, aren't they? Though, I grant you, they don't cut off heads with quite the same careless abandon as the Taipings. Harsh punishment isn't the answer, is it?'
'At least, *not* for filial impiety!' David agreed bitterly and resumed his reading.

28th August, 1856: We have just returned from witnessing how the holy 'communism' functions. Above all, it works. Certainly, the people of Taipingdom are both more orderly and less deprived than those under Manchu rule.

The statute called *The Disposition of Land under the Heavenly System* is virtually a written constitution, a furbelow the Manchus dispense with. That tremendous step forward is, if I may say so without undue pride, largely inspired by the American missionaries whom the Heavenly King first met in Canton and with whom he has maintained close relations since his transmogrification into an earthly divinity. The Taiping Constitution prescribes not only regulations for land tenure, which are the bedrock of the political economy of the agrarian state. It also prescribes the forms of both military and civil administration and defines the judicial and educational systems.

All the children of God are entitled by their birth-right to share equitably in His blessings. All must, therefore, be provided with the essentials of a life of dignity: acres to cultivate, adequate food, sufficient clothing, and the means to purchase those things they can neither make nor grow themselves. The land is, therefore, apportioned according to the number of persons in each farm family and the quality of the soil, that is, its fertility and water supply. Thus, every individual is in principle in possession of equal capacity to produce the fruit of the earth, but *not* the land itself, which remains the communal property of all. Thus, the similarity to the 'communism' of the ingenious Mr Karl Marx. In reality, the land, like all else, is actually in the possession of the rulers.

No more than any man possesses his own land does he possess any other private property aside from his clothing and the few personal articles a Chinese requires for the meagre comfort to which he is inured. All other property and all agricultural produce surplus to the individual's needs must be surrendered to the communal storehouses, which are the treasuries of Taipingdom.

The controllers of that wealth and the first arbiters of the fate of all the Heavenly King's subjects are the Master-Sergeants who preside over the basic social unit, which on the land consists of twenty-five families. Each such unit possesses its own church and its own communal storehouse, the twin pillars of everyone's existence. The Master-Sergeant is at once mayor, schoolmaster, pastor, treasurer, and magistrate, presiding equally over litigation and education, as well as marriages and funerals, and every Sunday shepherding his flock to the *Li-pai Tang*, the Hall of Worship, where men and women sit apart.

219

Every farmer and his wife, as well as every one of his sons and daughters above the age of 14, is also a Holy Soldier. The same Master-Sergeant commands them in battle through the corporals appointed over each five soldiers. The hierarchy rises through captains, brigade commanders, and division commanders to the general of an army of 13,156 soldiers. The military organization is, naturally, not a perfect replica of the civilian organization nor, of course, does each army in time of war, which is virtually constant, comprise precisely the allotted number of men. However, legions made up entirely of females are as fierce in battle as their menfolk and even more strenuously devoted to the Holy Doctrines. The Heavenly King draws his bodyguard from the hundred thousand Amazons commanded by his sister, as do many subordinate Kings. However, eunuchs are unknown, even in the extensive seraglios of the various Kings.

Some institutions, like the Females' Camp, may appear unduly harsh, as may normal families' being permitted to live together only on the land, where they are essential for cultivation. All women not working the land or serving as soldiers are segregated in the vast Females' Camp under stern female officers, who ensure their industrious application to tasks ranging from sewing uniforms to hammering out swords, spears, and daggers. They are prohibited on pain of death from meeting any man in private. But such as have previously had husbands may speak with them once a week through an open doorway – at a distance of at least five paces.

That strict segregation, which appears to a non-Chinese to rub against the very grain of human nature, is extended to other groups. The Taipings maintain special establishments for youths, for maidens, and for the aged, who cannot, of course, live with their non-existent families. They are kept in austere sufficiency, for which they exchange their labour. The young people are also given tuition in the arts of reading, writing, and reckoning, as well as the Holy Doctrine.

The principle of absolute equality of the sexes touches the very heart of Taiping civilization, ruling even education and their Mandarinate. Most remarkably, women may take the Civil Service Examinations, whose substance is not the Confucian Classics, but the Holy Bible, Christian tracts, and the administrative proclamations of the Heavenly Kingdom. For that reason, the traditional literati, my young friend David notably vehement among them, deprecate the Taiping Examinations as rather less than rigorous. Besides, David tells me with withering scorn, *anyone* may essay those Examinations – even fortune-tellers and conjurers.

'Give them a thousand years,' David said, 'and the Taiping Examinations might come up to snuff.'

'I'm glad you approve of at least one entry in the journal. But I'm afraid they won't have a thousand years.'

'Not very likely, is it?'

Taipingdom [David read on] is rigorously *ordered*. No one exercises discretion over his own actions; there is no *freedom* as that term is understood in our Judaeo-Christian culture. All live under stringent military discipline, both men and women, even the normally unruly boatmen and fishermen who make up the powerful Taiping Water Force. All the Holy Soldiers wear red turbans and identical regimentals, the various colours of their tunics denoting different units. In common with all military forces, variations in cut, fabric, and insigniae declare different ranks. It is, nonetheless, coldly depressing to reside in a city inhabited *only* by those uniform beings.

Moreover, every subject of the Heavenly King carries at all times a small plaque that details his personal characteristics, as well as his assigned place in the ranks. These 'tags' are strictly checked by the guards before their holders are permitted to enter or leave the Holy City. They are therefore scorned as 'tag soldiers' by the Manchus.

Daily life is none the less enlivened by constant religious observances and festivals, which are celebrated with great fervour. Theirs is a new kind of Christianity, a totally comprehensive Christianity, perhaps never elsewhere seen except in monasteries and convents. Even the seasons and moments of joy are rigidly prescribed. The Taipings exult in order. However, for the first time in more than two millennia in China, a radically new system – a corpus of faith, morals, etiquette, political economy, and administration – does *not* proceed from the teachings of the Sage Confucius.

Can the Heavenly King succeed in fundamentally altering the immemorial character of the China race? I cannot now answer that quintessential question confidently. However, I believe so.

Beneath severity, however, the new spirit of the commonalty makes Taipingdom a happier realm than the Manchu domains, where ordinances of almost equal rigour go largely unenforced. The subjects of the Heavenly King toil hard, but they toil with dignity, inspired by confident hope for the future. The Taiping kingdom is an epochal turning-point for the Chinese, a tremendous watershed in the long

221

history of their race. For the first time, the people have been offered security and equality.

The Taiping realm for the first time also promises fruitful cooperation between Chinese and foreigners for their mutual benefit.

We are still discussing with receptive officials prospects for specific commodities, terms of trade, and the like. However, we can already assert with confidence . . .

David leafed through several pages, snorting at a passage describing the Taipings' hopes for 'amicable and mutually profitable commercial relations with our brothers in Christ after the inevitable emancipation of Shanghai'. Further comment was clearly superfluous. They were voices from another era, those confident predictions of 'the imminent and certain victory of the Holy Armies'.

30th August, 1856, a soft and hazy evening [David read aloud]. The South Gate is the chief portal of the Holy City as in all Chinese capitals, since an Emperor always looks upon his domains from the north, the position of supremacy. The Holy Gate of the True God, as the Taipings call that portal, was built by the Founding Emperor of the Ming Dynasty in the late fourteenth century to proclaim and to guard the splendour of his new capital. No city in Europe can boast a fortification so immense. It is actually not one but four separate structures, each some forty yards in depth and more than twenty yards in height, standing one behind the other on the cliffs overlooking the swift flowing Chinhuai River. Garrisoned by more than three thousand men, the Holy Gate is primarily an impregnable fortress, rather than a means of ingress and egress.

The Taipings have for more than three years hurled back repeated Imperialist attacks against the Heavenly Capital. They have strengthened the fortifications by erecting outside the city-walls great entrenchments studded with pointed bamboo stakes behind high earthen banks. Except for the sparsity of artillery, only two nondescript cannon being mounted on each of the nine gates, the fortress-city would be impregnable.

Not only the disciplined strength of the Holy City, but its orderly splendour testify to the benevolent firmness of the Heavenly King's rule. The streets are dusty at this time of the year, but both the broad boulevards and the narrow lanes are scrupulously cleansed – as they are in no city under the rule of the Manchus, who do not enforce elementary hygiene on their alien subjects. The main square

222

behind the Holy Gate is swept clean daily and garnished with fresh banners.

Yet we have discovered disturbing undercurrents beneath the surface splendour, power and amity of the capital of Taipingdom. The East King, who is our host, is plotting further to enlarge his already enormous powers. He is the principal soothsayer of the realm and his claim to receive visions from the Heavenly Emperor, that is, God, is not disputed by the Heavenly King, whose authority is founded upon his own visions. However, two suns cannot shine in one sky, as the Chinese say. The East King, who is already the Vice Emperor, is determined to be the *only* heavenly orb.

He already holds virtually Imperial state, being invariably saluted: 'Live Nine Thousand Years!' Only a thousand years separate him from the Heavenly King, who receives the acclamation reserved for an emperor: '*Wan Sui*! Live Ten Thousand Years!' Yet the East King now demands that he also be hailed as the Lord of Ten Thousand Years.

Submitting to the East King's demonic visions, the Heavenly King has allowed other kings, including his own elder brother, to be flogged. He once even professed himself willing to yield his own sacred person to caning for his transgressions, winning remission of that sentence only after repeated pleas.

However, the East King's demand for the Imperial accolade finally awakened the Taiping Emperor from the torpid indifference to affairs of state that apparently arises from his intense concentration on spiritual affairs – and, perhaps, on his Brobdingnagian harem. The Heavenly King has, further, acted circumspectly since becoming aware that the soothsayer was determined to displace him. Having obeyed the summons of the East King, who was, by some Chinese conundrum, at the moment both his temporal subordinate and his spiritual superior, he stood in the soothsayer's palace in the Park of Respectfulness, where we ourselves then lodged. The Heavenly King meekly promised that the East King would be accorded the accolade 'Ten thousand years!' on his birthday, which falls on September 23rd, some three weeks hence. The soothsayer's formal enthronement would bestow upon him status equal to his sovereign's – in reality, of course, dominance.

Delighted by his easy victory, the East King allowed the Taiping Emperor to return to the Great Brilliant Palace, where further disquieting news awaited him. A repentant henchman of the would-be usurper reported that an assassin had already been chosen to slay the Heavenly King if he should at the final moment refuse to enthrone the East King.

This latter intelligence we had from a senior official, who represented himself as concerned for our safety in the event of disturbances. The same official further informed us that the Taiping Emperor had already summoned in secret the 'tigers' the East King sent far from the mountain. He alluded to the folk-tale of the canny prince who took possession of a valuable hill by luring away to better hunting grounds the tigers who infested it. The 'tigers' are the three greatest Taiping military generals, all of whom support the Heavenly King because they have all suffered from the East King's ruthless ambition. Two of these holy tigers have already returned to the Heavenly Capital.

'You got it almost right . . . for an outsider,' David observed. 'But you left out so much no Chinese could make head or tail of your account. You forgot that . . .'
'Even Saul Haleevie hasn't got Chinese patience. It *is* written for him, remember.'

2nd September, 1856, a dark and ominous evening [David read again]. So much blood had flowed in the past twenty-four hours that I am at a loss where to begin this account of the fratricide in the Holy City. David and I have escaped by an undoubted miracle, though the East King's palace has been transformed into a slaughterhouse. Of the entire household of the Taiping Prime Minister, only four men and not a single woman emerged alive from the massacre: ourselves, the senior official I dare not name, and the second son of the would-be usurper. We hid in a dusty space under the throne, watching through the folds of the draperies covering the dais. The official hurried us into that sanctuary only five minutes before the attack he knew was imminent.

'*Sha Chiu-chien sui! Sha! Sha!*' I shall never forget the shrill screams that signalled the assault on the walls of the Park of Hopefulness. 'Kill the Lord of Nine Thousand Years! Kill! Kill!' the Heavenly King's soldiers chanted like demons. Each imprecation ended with the words: '*Tsan-mei! Tsan-mei!*' meaning 'Praise! Praise!', the Taipings' equivalent of the joyous 'Alleluia' or the reverent 'Amen' that close Christian prayers elsewhere. The torrent of sound rolled ever closer to the reception-chamber in which we lay. When the shouting momentarily subsided, we heard the wooden

224

walls splinter under the pikes and axes of the soldiers loyal to the Heavenly King. We also heard the terrified screams of the East King's female attendants.

The Holy Soldiers were initially obedient to the orders of the West King and the Prince of Yen, the 'tigers' who had returned to the Holy City to defend their sovereign. The Heavenly King had charged them to kill only the usurper and his three closest confederates. The loyal troops did not, therefore, slay either the armed bodyguard or the dependents of the East King, but brushed those followers aside in their rush to the reception chamber, where the usurper stood defiant before his gilt-and-scarlet throne.

Through the drapery of the dais, I saw only the hem of his golden robe and his green-cloth shoes, embroidered in the Taiping fashion with purple asters. Those blossoms alternately shone and darkened in the wavering light of the great ceiling-lanterns as the East King advanced to face his enemies. Cautiously parting the drapery, I saw the tide of Holy Soldiers pour into the reception-chamber around islands of ponderous ebony furniture. Their faces were twisted with hatred beneath their scarlet turbans, and they swung their swords and halberds wildly. Still the East King stood unmoving in the centre of the reception-chamber, his lean back erect beneath a robe embroidered with stylized unicorns and lions. The wide black trousers and orange tunics of his bodyguard curved like the horns of a water-buffalo on either side of him.

The vengeful tide halted five paces from the East King, restrained by awe for the prince second in spiritual and temporal authority only to the Taiping Emperor. The East King checked his restive bodyguard with an imperative gesture of his lean hand and asked mildly why the intruders dared enter his palace.

Doubt clouded the faces of the assailants, and they glanced irresolutely at each other. Fear of the soothsayer's supernatural powers prevailing over bloodlust, they turned towards the exit. The wavering ranks opened before two men wearing the long yellow robes of Taiping nobles. The West King and the Prince of Yen confronted the usurper, the jewels of rank pendant from the cowls covering their heads glittering sombrely in the capricious light of the candles in the ceiling-lanterns. When the East King squared his shoulders to remonstrate with the leaders of the assailants, the golden folds on the back of his robe undulated. The three great princes of the Heavenly Kingdom confronted each other for a few seconds.

A snarl distorted the pudgy features of the West King, the third in the hierarchy. He darted forward, snatching a dagger from his sash, and buried the blade in the usurper's stomach. Scarlet blood stained the golden robe. He wrenched the dagger upward, half disembowelling the usurper, who uttered no sound. The West King freed the dagger and allowed the corpse to crumple to the flagstones.

An appalled hush which seemed to last forever, but could actually have endured no more than twenty seconds, followed the first killing of one Holy Prince by another. Rousing themselves from their shock, the dead man's bodyguards hurled themselves at his assassins. Their charge broke upon the intruders' spears, and, within seconds, the mêlée became general.

I despised myself for cowering under the dais while women's shrieks ended with throaty gurgles. The official and David held me fast after drawing together the draperies. In the darkness, our ears alone informed us that the slaughter continued until the early hours of the morning. Shrieks and pleas for mercy echoed under the dais. From the streets outside we heard not only screaming and clashing blades, but the flat reports of firearms. The entire Holy City was caught up in a frenzy of killing and destruction.

When the official finally judged it safe, we emerged into a blood-stained dawn. The sky was streaked with crimson, while the silent courtyard of the palace was heaped with still forms, their colourful garments sodden with blood. We picked our way through the corpses to the front gate, where a brisk, though bloodless struggle was in progress.

Seeing our arms empty, the antagonists let us pass. As men laden with loot emerged from the yellow-and-scarlet portals, others snatched baubles, furniture, and embroidered robes from their bloody hands. Only determined men united by common greed could emerge with their booty intact from the fearful scrabbling among the mute corpses.

Walking from the devastated palace to the Holy Gate of the True God, we saw hundreds of dead sprawled in the dusty streets. Women were almost as numerous as men among the still forms at which the ubiquitous pariah dogs sniffed warily. Equal in the rights and duties of life, males and females had been equally in peril and were wholly equal in death.

226

We are now safely ensconced by courtesy of our protector, the senior official, in a tower-room of the South Gate. We shall see what develops, since we are free to walk about the city, though our friend advises great caution. I cannot, however, imagine what further atrocities can yet be perpetrated. With the death of the usurper, the East King, at the hands of those ferocious 'tigers', the West King and the Prince of Yen, the *coup d'état* appears crushed. Since the Taiping Emperor is secure on his throne, true peace should now return to the Heavenly Kingdom of Great Peace. David, however, derides my optimism. Once Chinese begin killing each other, he warns, they will not stop until a strong hand reimposes order.

David closed the journal and smiled wryly at his companion.
'Please don't say it, Davy,' Gabriel muttered. 'You were right, and I was dead wrong. But, considering what we knew that night, no one could expect . . .'
'All right, Gabriel, I didn't *know* there'd be more killing. I only remembered what's happened every other time an emperor's soldiers turned on each other. You've heard enough, I suppose.'
'Let's have the last bit. Might as well hear the whole sad story. By the way, it's pronounced *yew*surper, not *oos*surper.'
'Dammit, Gabriel, I've had enough. Read it yourself, if you're so eager.'

4th September, 1856, a deceptively gentle· twilight [Gabriel stubbornly read aloud]. The previous entry in this journal appalled the narrator. As he makes this entry, he is revolted equally by the suave duplicity and the raw brutality of the Heavenly Kingdom of Great Peace. We were summoned just before dawn, along with large numbers of the populace of the Holy City, to an astonishing spectacle. Having witnessed the deeds of the loyal supporters of the Taiping Emperor, I still find it virtually impossible to believe they actually occurred.

The West King and the Prince of Yen grossly exceeded their orders, slaughtering thousands despite resistance that destroyed at least a thousand of their own followers. The conspiracy, they contended, was so deep-rooted that the Taiping monarch would be secure only when all adherents of the slain usurper were also slain. The two 'tigers' cited the maxim: 'Weeds simply cannot be cut, but must be pulled up by the roots!' Throughout the sanguinary second day of September 1856, they despatched their soldiers into every quarter of the city to massacre all men and women suspected of collusion with the East King. When that day closed, the Heavenly Capital had been scythed by mass carnage.

227

The Taiping Emperor ordered their criminal insubordination punished. A decree of September 3rd condemned both the West King and the Prince of Yen to the bastinado, that is, whipping on their naked soles. The Taiping monarch summoned more than five thousand spectators to his Great Brilliant Palace to witness his even-handed justice, among them many adherents of the slain usurper. With our protector, the senior official, David and I were seated close to the Throne within the steel thicket of the Heavenly King's bodyguard at the far end of the courtyard.

The two princes I had first seen through the draperies presented themselves for punishment. The pudgy West King and the younger Prince of Yen bowed contritely to their sovereign and submissively lay down on low benches, their feet bared to the springy canes of the executioners. They writhed each time those switches struck and moaned piteously. The princes who had preserved their sovereign from assassination were thus not only tortured, but grossly humiliated.

Thousands in the halls flanking the courtyard relished that degradation. They chatted, laughed, and called out to the executioners to strike harder until the Taiping monarch's bodyguard locked the doors of the halls. The two princes sprang nimbly to their feet, showing no sign of injury, and their soldiers charged into the unarmed spectators in the halls. Though I have seen much killing in China, I find it almost impossible to describe the terror of the helpless men and women as sabres, battle-axes, and spears cut them down. I shall always remember a gleaming sword's hewing the wrists a slender woman raised in supplication. The stench of blood and excrement was nauseating. The shrieks of the dying mingled with the throbbing of my own blood in my ears.

The Heavenly King, the supreme ruler of the insurgent empire, had meekly concurred in the 'tigers'' plan to exterminate all the dissidents. He sat stolidly on his throne, his square features expressionless as the slaughter proceeded. Though David insists the Taiping Emperor visibly suffered while his followers slew each other, I discerned no more than the mild interest of a spectator at a cricket fight.

We were taken back to the tower-room of the Gate of the True God, where we have since been confined. That imprisonment is, our friend the senior official says, solely for our own protection. I must believe him, since he has candidly told us of the subsequent scenes of the dark drama that still continues on this 4th day of October.

228

The surviving followers of the would-be usurper, the East King, barricaded themselves in a few blocks of the Holy City. Led by able officers, they stoutly resisted the unremitting assaults of the troops of the West King and the Prince of Yen. Further tens of thousands were slain in the fratricidal strife that raged for two weeks. All died with affirmations of loyalty to the Heavenly King and reverence for the One True God on their lips.

In mid-September hopes of ending the strife rose with the return of the Assistant King, the third of the 'tigers sent away from the mountain'. Arriving with a small bodyguard withdrawn from his siege of Wuchang, five hundred miles away, he remonstrated with the two fierce tigers. Further slaughter, he warned, would result in the disintegration of the Heavenly Kingdom, since the Imps would seize the opportunity presented by internal strife to attack the Heavenly Capital in force.

The West King coldly replied that the new arrival spoke like a supporter of the usurper. Realizing that his head was also in peril, the Assistant King withdrew with apologies for his presumption and slipped out of the Holy City after having stayed only a few hours.

On his return journey to Wuchang a messenger from the Taiping monarch overtook him. The Assistant King learned with grief that his fears had been justified. During the night after his departure, a strong force under the two 'fierce tigers' surrounded his palace. When the assailants found their prey flown, they revenged themselves on his family and followers. After slaughtering his young wife and his son, they killed his concubines and every male or female guard of his palace. The bereaved prince swore a blood oath to return with a great force and 'sweep away all the devil-doers who surround the sovereign'.

There matters stand. The fate of the Heavenly Kingdom of Great Peace is sealed, for the so-called Christian realm is beyond question doomed.

If I commanded two battalions of US Marines and a battery of artillery, I could take the Holy City. I cannot imagine that the Imperialists will not strike and crush the rebellion that has convulsed the Empire for half a decade. Hopes for the birth of a new order in China have been brutally dispelled by the fratricidal lunacy of the Taipings. Wherever salvation may come to a nation groaning under corrupt and oppressive Manchu rule, it will not come from the Taipings.

'So much for my hopes of revenging my father through the Taipings,' David interjected glumly. 'The only hope now it to change the Dynasty from within. It can still be reformed, though not overthrown.'

David and I are still confined 'for our own protection' as the strife rises and ebbs [Gabriel continued to read aloud without replying]. It would be extremely hazardous to attempt to return to Shanghai just yet. However, our friend, the senior official, has promised to convey this copy of our journal to Saul Haleevie.

When we shall ourselves win through to freedom we cannot say. We are, however, determined to leave behind the agonies of Taipingdom as soon as we possibly can. If necessary, we shall escape from our lax warders and make our way secretly to Shanghai. Whatever our previous castigation of foreign overlordship, the foreign settlement is a haven of peace, justice, and reason in a nation afflicted by cruel and virulent excesses, which are virtually indistinguishable from mass lunacy.

CHAPTER THIRTY-THREE

November 7, 1856   *Shanghai*

Saul Haleevie was jubilant in a dove-grey frock-coat, a silver-brocade cravat pierced by a pearl stick-pin spreading between his charcoal grey lapels. His normal reserve abandoned, he greeted each guest expansively. He had reluctantly rejected his wife's suggestion that he wear the white silk robe and the embroidered turban he kept for the synagogue, since this was not the occasion to parade his distinctiveness from the foreign community.

He was none the less distinctive in all but dress. He might have been a medieval Jewish patrician welcoming his guests to a villa in Andalusia or a Biblical patriarch receiving them in a marquee in the desert. That exotic impression was heightened by the *shamiana*, the striped canvas marquee that covered the front garden of the house on Szechwan Road. Beneath that canopy, charcoal-braziers of beaten brass glowed among the roses against the chill of the early November afternoon.

Standing beside her husband, Sarah Haleevie appeared totally self-possessed in a gold-embroidered kaftan of beige satin clasped by a cloth-of-gold cummerbund. An amethyst and diamond necklace gleamed around her throat, and diamond pendants hung from her earlobes. She was, Saul reflected proudly, hardly the conventional mother of the bride-to-be. She was far too attractive and too vital for a matron. Though she appeared serene, she was also nervous.

'Are we doing the right thing, Saul?' she had asked half an hour earlier. 'Are you sure she's not too young? What do we really know about Mr Henriques?'

'There's no doubt about it,' Saul had reassured her, since their decision was irrevocable in his view. 'Lionel'll be a good provider . . . a good husband and a good father. He's proved his mettle. I couldn't have brought off the Hong Kong silver loan better myself. Perhaps not as well. It takes not only a Jewish brain, but British self-confidence to deal with that Hong Kong crowd.'

Sarah was, however, not concerned with Lionel Henriques's financial acumen, for Saul had pronounced him sound commercially. She was concerned with Fronah's happiness, and she confessed to apprehension. Would the girl settle down once married? Could she be happy with the man who was her parents' choice, rather than her own?

Saul had laughed at his wife's infection by their daughter's advanced ideas. Since when, he'd asked, did foolish virgins choose their own husbands? Had Fronah, who was notoriously reckless, suddenly been blessed with wisdom greater than her parents? Just look at her, he advised. She was not merely happy, but radiant. Once betrothed, she would begin to settle down. Once married, responsibility would curb her flightiness. In any event, he had pointed out reasonably, the mother of the bride-to-be was always nervous.

Sarah had dabbed at her eyes and smiled. She now stood beside him to welcome the taipans and the consuls who had never previously called at the house on Szechwan Road. Her glance noted with approval that the houseboys were pouring champagne generously while the amahs deftly passed the titbits Shanghailanders called small chow. The curry-puffs, sausages, and meatballs were, of course, all *kosher*. Those staples were abundantly augmented with *kreplach* prepared from Mrs Weinstein's recipe; with *pirogin*, small pastry horns crammed with spiced liver; and with lamb kebabs.

An enormous phoenix carved of ice cradled fifty pounds of Beluga caviar under its glistening breast. Illuminated within by a candle, by some Chinese magic the sculpture did not melt. Though they could not serve the spiny lobsters, the giant shrimp, or the Ningpo oysters that normally graced such gala receptions, the Haleevies would not be outdone in either hospitality or ostentation.

That abundance celebrated Fronah's maturity – as demonstrated by her betrothal. The House of Haleevie and Lee had also come of age – as attested by the glittering guest-list. Every senior merchant and consul was present, as well as the foreign commissioners of the Chinese Maritime

231

Customs and the senior military officers of the Treaty Port. The Intendant of Shanghai was resplendent in orange, while the particoloured robes of his chief subordinates shimmered around him.

The Chinese stood apart, bemused by the barbarian rite at which women in draped and flounced frocks chatted shamelessly with strange men. Sleek in silk long-gowns topped with blue jackets, Saul's most valued customers joked with the invaluable compradors. Those pidgin-speaking Chinese were the essential link between the two disparate communities that dwelt uneasily together beside the muddy Hwangpoo River for mutual profit.

Saul was not disturbed by the separation of the two races or his co-religionists' tendency to cluster apart. Miriam Elias was chatting with Rebecca Benjamin, while their husbands conversed with Karl Weinstein. The Jews' clothing also set them apart. Only three men wore suits, the rest Baghdad robes. Except for Mrs Weinstein's plum satin creation, the ladies were all in kaftans.

The only link among the three communities was his adopted son. Aaron chatted briefly with all the guests, not to attempt the impossible by drawing them together, but simply to demonstrate their hosts' pleasure at their presence. David should be performing the same duty, Saul recalled censoriously, then grimaced wryly. Where, he wondered, was David now?

'If only David could be here,' Sarah said softly. 'David and that nice American.'

'You didn't always think that American was nice, Sarah.' Saul was sometimes still startled by her instinctive perception of his thoughts.

'Well he is. That worry's all over now with Fronah betrothed. I only hope Gabriel's looking after David wherever they are. You must have some idea, Saul?'

'I know you think I'm very clever, but I'm not that clever. I don't know, just as I didn't know they were going into any danger in Nanking. You saw the journal my old *Low Dah*, the champion smuggler, brought. You know as much as I do.'

'Saul, that was weeks ago. And the Taipings are still killing each other. If we *only* knew!'

'We'll only know, my dear, when they come through the gate. But that Taiping fellow, the one Gabriel calls the senior official, he'll look after them.'

'I've prayed, Saul. At least, Fronah looks happy, just as you said, radiant.'

Fronah hung on Lionel Henriques's arm among the chief men of the settlement. Her oval face was framed by a frill of mauve silk, which circled her neck and dipped to a vee over her bosom. The reception gown, as the tailor proudly called it, having culled the grandiloquent name, as well as the pattern from *The Lady's Gazette of Fashion*, was as elaborate as any *robe de soir*: the skirt of white silk pleated horizontally was revealed by a mauve overdress looped open in front and falling in a brief train. Dutifully admiring that creation, Saul had remarked that he would be delighted when her husband had to pay for her clothes.

Fronah was pensive when that jest pierced her excitement. Once married, a cold voice told her, she would no longer be subject to the will – or enjoy the protection – of her occasionally stern, but normally indulgent parents. Though she could, naturally, still appeal to their generosity, she would have to bend to Lionel's wishes. She would still be dependent. But not *too* dependent, she vehemently promised herself.

Those misgivings forgotten, Fronah looked up adoringly at Lionel Henriques. Content to clasp his arm in feminine self-effacement she did not join the men's discussion of the topic of the hour: the clashes between the British and the stubborn Imperial Viceroy in Canton, the southern port where foreigners' freedom was still severely restricted despite the Treaties. It had already come to fighting in Canton, British gunboats against Chinese spears and muskets. Since those clashes could provoke a new war against the Manchus, the leaders of the foreign settlement were eager for first-hand reports. Since Lionel Henriques had disembarked from Hong Kong five days earlier and had been in Canton when the incident erupted, they pressed him for his news and his views.

Fronah was equally concerned, but the golden haze that suffused the afternoon diverted her skittish thoughts. Lionel's assured authority distinguished him even among the most distinguished men of Shanghai. His slender height was set off by the fawn morning-coat he wore over a shawl-collared waistcoat. The ruffles protruding from his turned-back coat-cuffs sparkled white, as did his stiff shirtfront, and his high stock encircled by a voluminous yellow bowtie. The sunlight shining through the *shamiana* was a golden patina on his blond hair, his arched nose, and his firm mouth.

'I assure you, sir, the disturbances will soon be under control,' Lionel declared confidently to the American consul. 'I sensed that from the beginning.'

'You actually saw it begin, did you, Mr Henriques?'

'By chance, sir. October 8th, it was, a Wednesday. We were taking breakfast on Jardines' terrace when we saw a commotion on the river. Two Chinese craft drew down on the lorcha *Arrow*, each carrying a fat Mandarin sitting under a big umbrella and perhaps thirty Chinese soldiers.'

'Lorcha?' asked a Royal Navy commander who was new to China. 'What kind of vessel might that be?'

'It's an old Portuguese term, Commander.' Lionel gladly shared his superior knowledge. 'A hybrid with Chinese sails and a European hull, something between a proper ship and a junk. Lorchas go where bigger ships can't. But they carry more cargo than junks, and they're faster. The *Arrow* is British, Hong Kong-registered, though she's owned by a China-man with some outlandish name like Pong or Fong.'

233

'What actually happened, Mr Henriques?' The American consul was anxious to supplement fragmentary official reports. 'We're all dying to hear.'

'The Chinese ran down the Blue Peter – and the Union Jack, though it's hard to credit. Her captain was ashore, a young chap called Thomas Kennedy from Belfast. When he reached the *Arrow* he found the Mandarins in occupation and his Chinese crew already bound hand and foot in the Mandarins' boats. One crewman, by the way, was trussed like a pig. An older Chinaman, he was.'

'And then?' the consul prompted.

'Kennedy palavered with the Mandarins, but they couldn't understand a word of English. So he hoisted the Union Jack and went off to call young Harry Parkes, Her Majesty's Acting Consul . . .'

Fronah's attention strayed. Instead of listening to the tale she had already heard several times, she admired the long line of Lionel's close-shaven jaw. Her fiancé's eagerness to talk about his brush with history was not only endearing, but reassuring. She had feared he might be a shade too self-possessed, too cool and too aloof, perhaps blasé. His enthusiam set the seal of perfection on the man she was to marry.

The *Arrow* affair was, Fronah knew, complex. Since the vessel was registered in Hong Kong, she was not subject to the Mandarins' jurisdiction. Yet they had high-handedly ignored her extra-territorial status and seized her crew. It did not matter if the older Chinese crewman were, as they charged, a notorious pirate. Although the lorcha's certificate of registration had expired ten days earlier, the Viceroy in Canton could not have been aware of that legal nicety. Besides, a vessel whose certificate lapsed while she was on a voyage could fly the Union Jack and claim British protection until she returned to renew her registration. The Viceroy had deliberately flouted British rights and insulted Britain's flag. Those were no light matters under either international law or the Treaties that governed relations between the Chinese Empire and the foreign powers.

Although the dignitaries clustered around Lionel were demanding minute details, the rest of the tale was more straightforward. Acting Consul Harry Parkes had required that the Viceroy not only release the captured crewmen, but apologise. At first recalcitrant, the Viceroy had rendered up the entire crew when Parkes ordered an Imperial warjunk seized in retaliation, and the *Arrow* had returned to Hong Kong. But the Viceroy would not apologise.

He could not apologise, Fronah knew, for an apology would acknowledge that he had erred. Because he acted directly for the Emperor, no Senior Mandarin could make such a confession. An apology would not only humiliate the Son of Heaven, but would imperil the Viceroy's career – and, perhaps, his head.

Apparently just as stubborn, the British could not overlook the insult to

234

their flag. Not only pride moved them, but the conviction that all trade would be imperilled if they did. Should a major article be flouted with impunity, their Treaty would be meaningless. Should the hard-won Treaty no longer apply in its entirety, the Manchus would retreat into surly isolation – and dam the stream of commerce.

Failing to receive the impossible apology, Rear Admiral Sir Michael Seymour ordered his gunboats to bombard Canton on October 23rd. His purpose was to humble the Chinese, rather than to inflict great destruction.

The Viceroy was profoundly humiliated when his forces proved powerless to halt the bombardment, which continued for five days. At precise ten-minute intervals, shells fell on the Viceroy's *yamen*, except on October 26th, which was a Sunday and, therefore, declared a day of rest for the British crews. His humiliation deepened by that contemptuous respite, the Viceroy ordered his frail gunboats to attack Admiral Seymour's flotilla on 28th. His humiliation was abysmal when that attack was easily repelled. In retaliation, the British not only seized the forts protecting Canton, but marched on the Viceroy's *yamen*, which they looted.

There matters stood for the moment. Tempers were high on both sides, and indignation could move either to further provocation. Fronah's adoptive brother Aaron was talking of war against Britain. That sober young man, who had no reason to love the Manchus, though he loved his country, was a reliable barometer of moderate Chinese sentiment.

'. . . so you see, gentlemen, I'm confident it'll all blow over,' Lionel was saying. 'Just a whiff of grapeshot, that's all the Chinese need. Only way to deal with them.'

'Lionel,' Fronah said impulsively, 'perhaps the Chinese don't see it that way.'

The dignitaries were startled by her interjection. Lionel Henriques flushed, and his eyes narrowed. Fronah feared an angry retort.

'It *is* rather complicated, my dear,' he said tolerantly instead. 'I'm afraid I don't quite see what you mean.'

'The Viceroy can't apologize,' she persisted. 'If he does, he humiliates the Emperor. Why it could mean . . . it could mean anything. He'd be thrown out of office, and all his possessions would be confiscated. He could even be beheaded.'

'Surely the Chinese aren't that savage, Miss Haleevie?' the Royal Navy commander asked.

'They are, Commander,' she said. 'They do terrible things to each other. The Viceroy can't apologise. I'm afraid the Chinese won't give in. Even in Shanghai, they're talking about war.'

'My dear, it won't come to that, you know.' Lionel patted her hand. 'I . . . we all . . . respect your knowledge of the Chinese . . . and your sympathy for them. But the whiff of grapeshot's done it. I assure you it won't come to war.'

235

Fronah flushed and did not reply. He was somewhat condescending, but it was forward of her to advance strong opinions that conflicted with his first-hand knowledge. They would, naturally, discuss the matter when they were alone, as her parents did when they disagreed.

The conversation was silenced by an imperative tinkling. Standing on a chair, Saul Haleevie lifted a goblet of champagne to toast the betrothed couple.

'You Excellencies, Gallant Officers, Ladies and Gentlemen,' he began his much rehearsed speech. 'We are met today to wish good fortune and happiness to . . .'

Fronah clasped Lionel's arm and pressed closer to him. They would have to rub off each other's rough edges, as her mother had warned, but in private, never in public. She would never again contradict him in public, not even implicitly. Their disagreement was, after all, a trifle beside their mutual love.

Sunlight streamed through the panels of the *shamiana*, and motes of dust danced in the radiance. Lit by the golden glow, Fronah and Lionel raised their glasses to acknowledge their guests' good wishes.

BOOK III

August 24, 1860 – September 1, 1864

THE COLLAPSE

CHAPTER THIRTY-FOUR

Gabriel Hyde stiffened in surprise when his pony trotted into the square before the red-brick church banded with granite, which dominated Zikawei, the Roman Catholic village south of the French Concession. The late afternoon scene was astonishingly commonplace. He had expected to see the devastation the Holy Soldiers normally left behind them nowadays, for their puritanical discipline had deteriorated in the four years since the fratricidal slaughter of late 1856. The Loyal King, who was the Taiping Commander-in-Chief, had that morning withdrawn from Zikawei after six days in occupation. Instead of maimed corpses, burning houses, and a gutted house of worship, the American saw humdrum tranquility.

The long shadow of the church spire imprinted a great black cross on the cobblestones. The Lord of Heaven, as Chinese Catholics called their God, had, it appeared, set His mark indelibly on this small corner of the Manchu Empire. Like glossy crows in their black cassocks, six European Jesuits strolled around the square serenely reading their breviaries. Through the open windows of the schoolhouse treble voices chorused rote responses to a catechist's baritone interrogation. Already released from their studies, other children lazily kicked shuttlecocks beneath the stone arch erected to commemorate Candida Soo. That first great lady of Chinese Catholicism had endowed the school in her ancestral village at the close of the Ming Dynasty. Like that arch, the plaque on the tumulus covering the remains of her grandfather, the Grand Chancellor Dr Paul Hsü, whose labours had planted the Catholic Faith in China, was untouched by the Holy Soldiers' usual destructive wrath against that 'idolatrous and superstitious creed'.

Bumble-bees droned among the scarlet blossoms of the oleanders standing like green-uniformed sentinels before the church. Sparrows chirruped amid the cawing of the starlings in the pink-spiked chestnut trees, and billows of yellow butterflies floated above frilled jasmine flowers. From the fields the peremptory lowing of water-buffaloes summoned the herd-boys to lead them home at the close of the day.

As the cool dusk succeeded the heat of the late August afternoon in the year 1860, the Catholic village drowsed in unbroken peace. Resurgent after their prolonged fratricidal strife, the invaders had spared the centre of the creed they hated as much as Buddhism and Confucianism. Zikawei was untouched by the fury of the most sanguinary conflict in the history of mankind, which had cost more than twenty million lives in the past decade.

Gabriel Hyde turned in his saddle to speak to his confidant David Lee. But David trotted towards the red double-doors of the church, the rhinoceros of a Military Mandarin of the Ninth Grade lowering on his blue jacket.

'Look at that, Gabriel.' His quirt tapped the parchment nailed to the door. 'Just look at that.'

'I could look all day and be none the wiser,' Gabriel laughed. 'What does it say?'

'For a moment I forgot you were illiterate. A proclamation signed by the Chung Wang, the Loyal King himself: *Any soldier who molests any foreigner or damages any foreign property in the slightest, any Holy Soldier who desecrates any church of any foreign creed, even the idols of the false creed of the Lord of Heaven, will suffer immediate decapitation. No appeal will be entertained. Heed this or die!*'

After six tumultuous years, China had virtually lost all capacity to surprise the American officer. But he was astonished by the Taipings' withdrawing before their assault on Shanghai had fairly begun – and by their leaving unscathed the stronghold of the Catholics. He was inured to atrocities. But he was shocked by chivalry, astounded when either Taipings or Manchus behaved decently.

Since David and he had, nearly four years earlier, fled the suicidal convulsions of the Heavenly Kingdom of Great Peace, its resurgence was also astounding. Just before they escaped from the Gate of the One True God in January 1857, the Assistant King has returned to the Heavenly Capital with an overwhelming force. After crushing the revolt against the Heavenly King and imposing a funereal peace with the sword, the Assistant King had himself broken with his sovereign and marched west to establish a virtually independent realm in distant Szechwan. Once again, the ferocious theocracy appeared doomed by the intransigence of its adherents, the loss of its most capable leaders, and the apathy of its sovereign, whose interest was engaged only by his visions and his seraglio.

Even the effete Hsien Feng Emperor in Peking moved more vigorously than the peasant-scholar who had almost overthrown the Great Pure Dynasty. The Manchu's sloth was enlivened by the energy of his half-brother, Prince Kung, and by the prodding of his favourite concubine, Yehenala, the mother of his only son. Encouraged by that formidable pair, the Emperor had restored much of the vigour of his armies. His most telling measure was appointing a single commander for the forces fighting the Taipings. The Imperial Court had recently given Generalissimo Tseng Kuo-fan far greater power than any Chinese had previously wielded under the Manchu Dynasty. As Viceroy of two rich provinces in Central China, the Imperial Commissioner for Suppressing the Rebellion was the most powerful commoner in the Great Empire.

240

The doom of the Taipings appeared sealed by his appointment. But the Taipings struck while the Viceroy methodically tested the levers of his new power and regrouped his forces.

An obscure rebel general called Li Hsiu-cheng had been gathering his own forces virtually unnoticed. A minor brigadier at the relief of Chenkiang, the Citadel of the River, in 1856, Li Hsiu-cheng's cool competence during the subsequent internal strife won him the title Chung Wang, Loyal King – and the command of all Taiping armies. From the convulsions of the Heavenly Kingdom emerged a twenty-six-year-old Generalissimo who was not only fearless in battle, but a brilliant strategist. He was also a gallant foe, who hated the atrocities that marred the rebel cause. A horde of religious fanatics, medieval in their ferocity, had cast up a paladin of medieval chivalry.

Under the Loyal King's leadership, the Holy Soldiers again destroyed the Imperialists' Great Headquarters Camp south of the Long River and routed the Manchu armies that again threatened the Heavenly Capital. The Taipings then swept over all Kiangsu Province except the foreign enclave of Shanghai. The Loyal King now maintained his headquarters in the Mountainview Tower in Soochow, the city of silks. He was confident he would soon destroy the Manchu Dynasty and establish the Heavenly Empire – as was divinely ordained.

The Loyal King was also determined to correct past errors of strategy, above all the Taipings' failure to exploit the Small Swords' occupation of the South City in the early 1850s. As long as the rebels were cut off from direct access to the technology and the trade of the foreign settlement, they could not overthrow the Manchus. After making his base secure, the Loyal King had therefore led his legions south-east towards Shanghai in the summer of 1860. He confidently expected the foreigners, who were his 'brothers in Christ', to welcome him.

The Taiping Commander-in-Chief, Gabriel Hyde reflected, must be utterly bewildered by the outlanders' response to his pacific advance. Not only the Catholic French, but the presumably friendly Protestant British aggressively defended Shanghai. The Loyal King had just withdrawn rather than hurl more than fifty thousand Holy Soldiers at a thousand or so stubborn foreign troops. No hot-headed swashbuckler, the Loyal King realised that the victory he could so easily win by force would in the long run be a defeat.

He required a victory by consent, and he required the foreigners' willing co-operation. But those prizes were denied him. After havering for years, while some official envoys and many missionaries encouraged the Taipings' expectations of foreign support, the first major intervention of regular European troops in China's civil war had decisively benefited the Imperialists.

Though Gabriel Hyde wore the tiger of a captain in the Imperial Water Force, his personal sympathies were in flux. Having once despaired of the barbaric Taipings, he again wondered whether their triumph might not be possible – and desirable. Even David Lee, seconded to military service after qualifying for the Mandarinate by his brilliant performance in the first Civil Service Examination, sometimes wondered wistfully whether the Taipings could yet crush the decadent Manchus. His elder brother Aaron, bitter after twice failing the Examination, was vehement against the Imps and threatened to join the Taipings. But that was just talk, Gabriel was reflecting when a Jesuit broke into his reverie.

'The rebels, they were vicious in Shanghai, *non*?' the French priest with the beaked nose asked. 'The Lord God moved them to spare Zikawei. But they looted and killed in Shanghai, *non*?'

'Not at all, Father,' Gabriel replied. 'They hardly touched the city.'

'My son, there are columns of smoke over Shanghai, and we heard much shooting. The cursed rebels must have rampaged through the foreign settlement till our brave soldiers drove them off.'

'That, Father, was the brave defenders, not the rebels,' Gabriel answered bitterly. 'But what's happened here? We're ordered to report on the situation in Zikawei, though our escort lost itself on the way.'

'There's little to tell, my son. Only six days ago, the rebels marched in. Our little garrison of thirty French riflemen naturally hurried to join the defence of Shanghai itself. And then nothing till this morning when the Loyal King withdrew quietly. But what of Shanghai?'

'It wasn't as simple as it sounds, but we've learned the Taiping Prime Minister was so confident he came along to discuss an alliance with the consuls. The Loyal King obviously never expected to use force, even beheaded one his men for violating his pledge not to harm foreigners. The poor fellow's unit clashed with a patrol and killed four foreigners in the Manchu service.'

'The same theme here. *We come in peace*, the rebels said. But in Shanghai?'

'The Loyal King believed he'd been promised a free hand and in turn, promised the consuls he'd protect all foreign nationals. He directed them to fly yellow flags over their property so it wouldn't be damaged. In the only clash his troops drove off that Imperial patrol. As they pursued it towards the city-gate, British soldiers opened fire.

'The Loyal King, I gather, was astonished . . . not only by that resistance, but by seeing foreign flags instead of the yellow flags he expected. He took no action for an hour or two while his troops milled about awaiting that expected truce. The English and the Sikhs killed several hundred Holy Soldiers. It was like shooting fish in a barrel.'

'And the fires . . . the fighting inside the city?'

'All our own work, Father. The French, if you'll pardon my saying so, started pillaging, then the British joined in. Finally the Loyal King led his full force towards the British settlement, this time certain they'd be welcomed. They were welcomed warmly by rifles and field-pieces, while the warships on the Hwangpoo lobbed shells. We heard the Loyal King was hit in the cheek before he withdrew to Zikawei.'

'He *was* wounded, my son. He looked pale and weak when he rode out this morning. A fine soldierly man, even if a heretic, he's tall and fair, and his nose is well-shaped. Except for his eyes, you'd think him an Italian or Spanish cavalier. The children liked him, and he seemed fond of them.'

'So the invasion's finished,' Gabriel commented. 'It wasn't much.'

'The British and French are now committed to the Imperial cause? The rebels can expect no more sympathy from civilized men?'

'I guess you're right, Father, if we're civilized.'

'This so-called Loyal King did behave impeccably, and he was very fond of the children. I shall pray for his soul.'

'Yes, Father. And now, if you'll excuse us, my friend and I have to return to make our report.'

*

The ponies' hooves scuffed along the dirt road, throwing up pink dust in the twilight. As the sun dipped below the horizon, darkness crept over the paddy-fields. Beneath the clouds that screened the moon, lanterns guttered in scattered villages. Worried about Taiping stragglers, Gabriel slapped his pony's flank.

'What's your hurry, Gabriel?' David asked.

'Got to get back.' The American was laconic. 'Besides, we could meet some Holy Soldiers.'

'More danger from *your* people,' David pointed out. 'The way they're acting.'

'It's funny, Davy.' Gabriel allowed his pony to resume its weary shuffle. 'For years, the people of Shanghai have lived in fear. The city's crammed with refugees from the terrible Taipings, and the foreign settlement's been quaking for months. So the demons in human form finally arrive . . . and what happens?'

David was silent, having made his point, and Gabriel resumed savagely: 'The city's duly looted . . . as everyone feared. But not by the Taipings. They turn out to be damned near angels in human form. Not the Taipings, but the gallant European soldiers.'

'This battle will be remembered, Gabriel. All Chinese will remember it: a glorious failure for the Taipings and a shameful victory for the barbarians. And . . . some day . . . But we can't report that the Taipings behaved like angels in Zikawei. That won't go down well.'

'It'll damned well have to, even if it doesn't please our masters. You know, Davy, I'm tired of this play acting.'

'Count your gold, Gabriel. That'll make you feel better.'

'Only in China, Davy. Only in China could a junior naval officer make a young fortune in trade with his superiors' happy assent.'

'They get their share, after all. That's the way it works. Even my appointment as a Mandarin, it was my father Saul's influence and bribes that did it.'

'I wish Saul could do something for your brother. Otherwise Aaron'll run wild and ruin himself. He's so bitter about failing . . .'

'My father will do it. He'll see that Aaron's all right.'

'Saul's not God, you know, Davy. I respect him, but he's not God.'

'What do you mean?'

'Just look at Fronah. That wasn't the smartest more, marrying her off to Henriques.'

'She needs time to settle down, Gabriel. They've only been married two years. The maxim says a new wife, like a new saddle, takes three years to break in.'

'I've had enough Chinese maxims for one day.'

They rode on for fifteen minutes, the usually voluble Gabriel unspeaking and the usually irrepressible David preserving a hurt silence. When the flames to the north glowed ruddy on their faces, Gabriel spoke again.

'Two years from betrothal to marriage was sensible. But Fronah should've stalled longer.'

'My mother Sarah was frantic, and my father Saul finally did as she wished. You weren't around for the family quarrels. Believe me, Fronah couldn't have stalled a minute longer.'

'Anyone can see it, Davy. She's *not* happy. And Henriques is a cold fish if I ever saw one.'

'Maybe she's not, Gabriel. But she hasn't said a word to anyone, not to me . . . not even to Maylu.'

'She wouldn't, would she? But the bloom's gone off her. She used to sparkle, but she doesn't anymore. An occasional flash, but that's all.'

'Oh, the fire's still there. Why only last week . . .'

'I guess so . . . but it's smouldering, not leaping.'

'What do you make of Henriques, Gabriel?'

'He's a mystery to me, always cool and polite. But talking to him's like shouting through a sheet of glass.'

'Well, there's nothing we can do.' David shrugged off his concern. 'It's too late . . . much too late.'

The flames of Shanghai laced the low lying clouds with crimson. Silhouetted by the glow, the American and the Chinese rode towards the French concession. Their black shadows brushed the still corpses of hundreds of Holy Soldiers.

CHAPTER THIRTY-FIVE

'We could, of course,' Lionel Henriques drawled, looking up from his book. 'We could sail for England tomorrow.'

'Then why not, Lionel?' Fronah wanted to put down her book and kneel beside his chair, but feared offending him by such mawkishness. 'Why can't we go just for a while . . . just a year or so?'

'It wouldn't be right, Fronah. It's just not done.'

'But, my dear, just to please me?' she cajoled. 'You miss London, I know. Why not go, for Heaven's sake?'

'I'm sorry, Fronah. Please don't distress yourself. We've left all that Oriental emotionalism behind us, you and I. We're living in a nineteenth-century British settlement, not a medieval ghetto. I am sorry, but you do understand.'

'I don't, Lionel, really I don't. I do know you're not terribly busy here. And you just said we *could* go.'

'No, I'm afraid you *don't* understand.' He smiled patiently. 'Actually a gentleman needn't busy himself like a barrow-boy . . . or a merchant. I'm not in trade, you know. Still, I can't just up sticks.'

Fronah was momentarily furious. After two years of marriage, she had thought herself inured to his occasional slights at their common Jewish heritage, as well as his occasional oblique, perhaps unconscious, denigration of her father. Although perhaps superior to Saul Haleevie in his self-assurance and the respect he commanded in the Gentile community, her husband had no right to disparage a man who had accomplished so much without the advantages to which he himself was born. Besides, the Haleevies had been scholar-rabbis in Spain when his ancestors were ragged pedlars trudging between the hawthorn hedges of English country lanes.

'Lionel, I'm also troubled about the gifts we keep taking from Papa,' she said evenly. 'He's *too* generous . . . And we shouldn't really.'

'I've told you, Fronah.' He was still patient. 'It's only a loan to tide us over a temporary embarrassment . . . just remittances delayed. Your father understands perfectly.'

For a moment, Fronah wondered bleakly why she had ever hoped that marriage would bring her independence. Her freedom was more circumscribed than it had ever been by her indulgent father or even her sometimes acerbic mother. Besides, their occasional frank anger was more natural than Lionel's cool reasonableness. Like the hot-blooded Chinese, he prided himself on restraining his emotions. But she feared he had suppressed all feeling as ignoble. Still, when she probed his carapace, he

245

would reveal profound affection for herself – and her own affection for the complex man she had married would rise again.

Fronah continued to probe, because Shanghai had become hateful to her. She felt imprisoned by its complacent insularity and by the Taiping threat, which made excursions hazardous.

The fires that had raged in the native quarters since the Loyal King's withdrawal ten days earlier were finally burning themselves out. The lingering stench recalled the conflagration that had swept the South City in 1855, when the Chinese rebels burned the people's houses to cover their retreat. The rapacious European troops had put hundreds of buildings to the torch for their amusement, though the fires consumed the valuables they hunted.

Lionel himself had joined the troops on the wall to pour bullets into the milling ranks of Holy Soldiers, who had been ordered not to return the fire. Having once believed the settlement an island of good sense and good will amid a sea of Manchu folly and cruelty, Fronah now hated the foreigners' brutality, as did the Chinese.

'Lionel, please try to understand how I feel.' Fronah pleaded, knowing her husband was not insensitive. 'I beg you to try.'

'I'm trying, my dear, though it's hard,' he replied. 'What's bothering you? Why are you so set on leaving? Do tell me.'

'I suppose I'm bored. Remember, dear, I've really never seen any other place, and I want to . . . desperately. When you talk about London, you're very casual. But to me London is a fairyland.'

'Hardly that, my dear. London's a city much like any other. But, I promise you, just as soon as I can in honour . . . just as soon as possible . . . we will go.'

Lionel Henriques hated fencing with his wife, and he disliked dissembling with her. However, he simply could not return to England just yet. It would be inconvenient, devilish inconvenient – impossible, in fact.

'Very soon, I hope,' she exclaimed. 'Oh, Lionel, I'm bored . . . so bored.'

'Honestly, I don't see why. Not with your historical studies and . . . and all this.'

The sweep of his hand embraced the drawing-room and the adjoining morning-room of the villa that had been Saul Haleevie's wedding-present. Completed only seven months earlier because the merchant demanded the finest craftsmanship, heedless of expenditure that had made his wife blanch, it was the most elegant house in the foreign settlement. The Chinese called it *Lo Wo*, the Nest of Joy, because it was so exquisitely proportioned and so auspiciously situated.

Fronah had for a year and a half been happily occupied in ensuring that *her* house would be perfect. She had fended off her mother's pleas for thrift, and she had resisted Maylu's predilection for gaudy opulence. Lionel and she had moved into the Nest of Joy on her twenty-first birthday,

February 3rd, 1860, and until late July she had been absorbed in her role as its mistress. Then, so abruptly she surprised herself, she began murmuring in discontent.

Lionel Henriques knew better than to take much notice of female vapours. The ladies didn't think but only felt. Hysteria, Dr William MacGregor said, pointing out unnecessarily that the Greeks had coined the term some two and a half millennia ago. Hysteria from *hystera*, the womb, explained not only female frenzies, which bedevilled sensible men, but female fancies, which confounded all logic.

Perhaps that was the explanation. Perhaps Fronah was pregnant. A son would not only carry on the Henriques line, but would ensure his father-in-law's eternal gratitude. Giving Saul Haleevie a grandson would make him wholly secure.

Lionel dismissed that pleasant speculation. Naturally, he did not impose himself upon her so frequently as to know the rhythm of her menses. But he had a few days earlier learned that she was not carrying a child.

'Perhaps it's only a passing fancy, this notion of yours about England,' he reiterated complacently. 'Probably you'll soon get over it.'

Lionel pretended not to hear Fronah's exasperated gasp. His thoughts turned to the two sinuous Wei Dynasty statuettes he had seen yesterday at Old Curiosity Soo's shop. The dancing-girls, pale green and faded rose, would beautifully frame the turquoise swan with the graceful neck that stood on the white marble mantelpiece. But he still owed for that relatively modern piece, and the dancing-girls were expensive. He could not stretch his credit further.

He thought resentfully of Saul Haleevie, who seemed to dominate his life. The merchant had built the Nest of Joy as much to display his wealth as to indulge his loving daughter and reward his dutiful son-in-law. Besides, the plot lay between his own compound on Szechwan Road and Derwents' compound on the river. The merchant had gained a window on the Bund, the centre of commerce, finance, and fashion, which was to Shanghai all that Park Lane, Bond Street, Pall Mall, and Threadneedle Street were to London.

Although Fronah loved the Nest of Joy's bijou charm, her husband felt it too small, only a grace-and-favour cottage in the shadow of Saul Haleevie's mansion. Besides, he found the villa's exotic splendour disquieting. Although he had imposed some restraint on the Oriental fantasies of his wife and her father, the tented ceiling of the morning-room recalled a pavilion in a desert. The velvet drapes and furniture were reassuringly substantial despite their barbarically glowing colours. But there was a superabundance of heavy Chinese satins, gold-embroidered Indian tissue-silks, and particoloured Persian rugs.

Granted, it was all quite modern. Water ran to the marble bathrooms through pipes set in the walls, hot water, as well, from the boiler the coolie quite remarkably had not yet forgotten to stoke. A web of iron tubes had

247

been installed against the day Shanghai was provided with illuminating gas. However, the French windows opening from the morning-room to the gleaming terrace of Yünnan marble made him feel exposed, and the entire effect was garish.

Lionel started as the door opened without warning. The stout number-one houseboy glided into the drawing-room, belatedly announced by the rattle of china as the number-two houseboy wheeled in the silver-mounted tea-wagon. Chinese servants were eerie, either shuffling about in cloth slippers or making a horrendous clatter. He longed for a bluff, heavy-footed English butler instead of these slinking Asiatics.

None the less, he smiled jovially as the houseboys arranged the paraphernalia of high tea: the silver teapots, creamers, and sugar-bowls surrounded by delicate blue and white china. The second houseboy smiled in return, but number one's plump features were set as he offered cucumber and watercress sandwiches, poundcake, and scones accompanied by strawberry jam and clotted cream. Lionel smiled again and rubbed his hands together. This was proper food, not the airy Chinese delicacies his wife craved.

'Allee piece chiles belong you allee numbah one fine, Boy?' he asked expansively. 'Cow chile belong you fine? She very good look at.'

'Mis'ible cow chile fine, Mastah.' The number-one boy grinned nervously. 'More better Mastah no worry 'bout mis'ble cow chile. Maybe cow chile go 'way look-see old Auntie.'

'Good! Good!' Lionel beamed, as he took a scone. '*Ding gua-gua!* All very fine.'

Fronah wondered why Lao King was playing the fool with her husband. The houseboy was normally dignified, and his pidgin was not normally the travesty he spoke to Lionel. Did a hint of insolence, she wondered, shadow his demeanour? Was he mocking his master? Did she sense a rebuke in his response? Or was it fear? She told herself she must talk to Lao King.

'Lionel,' Fronah said when the door closed behind the servants, 'it's no good just saying I shouldn't be bored.'

'How so, Fronah?' He twisted the gold signet-ring on his little finger.

Fronah's throat tightened. Though casual, Lionel was imposing in a shantung shirt and tight-fitting nankeen trousers secured under his patent-leather half-boots by elastic straps. Neither his patrician appearance nor his cool manner had altered perceptibly in the four years since their betrothal. After each of their misunderstandings, which seemed more frequent lately, he left her convinced it was her fault alone.

'I don't know why I feel so empty,' she persisted. 'But I'm sure a trip would help. I do so want to see London before I'm too old to enjoy it.'

'I've promised we'll go just as soon as we can. But I can't commit a breach of trust.'

She pressed her lips together in annoyance. Her eyes glinted with unshed tears. She blinked her eyelashes to flick them off, and her lips pouted. The childlike gesture accentuated the minute fullness around her mouth. The effect, Lionel felt, was remarkably sensual.

'Perhaps it's your debt to Papa. Is that why you feel you can't leave, my dear? I'm sure he'd understand . . . And no, *he* hasn't told me. But you do leave papers around. Several thousand dollars already . . . isn't it?'

'You're right, of course, Fronah,' he admitted. 'I am temporarily embarrassed, though it's a bagatelle. But I really can't go off when . . .'

His full indebtedness to her father was not several thousand Shanghai dollars, but almost ten thousand pounds sterling. Saul said tolerantly that he regarded the sum as an advance against future earnings from their joint business ventures. But those ventures were not promising. Fronah *must* produce a grandchild for Saul Haleevie very soon, Lionel concluded, though he would settle his debt to his father-in-law just as soon as he could.

He had believed his marriage would solve his financial problems. Despite the merchant's open-handedness, it was not working out as he had planned. He could not deny that bleak reality, and he was already far too dependent on his father-in-law. Worse, he was ultimately dependent on his wife. Though Fronah behaved as if theirs was a normal marital relationship with both her property and her person legally at his sole disposal, she could always appeal to her father, who had cannily placed only a nominal sum in her name on their marriage. He must not provoke her so that anger succeeded her present febrile resentment. He would also have to simulate greater ardour – not only to placate her, but to get that invaluable infant. Besides, her distress troubled him, though it was difficult to reach over the walls that enclosed his emotions to comfort her.

'Of course you're worried, my dear.' Fronah rubbed her eyes with her knuckles, again the childlike gesture excited him. 'But aren't you being *too* honourable. I just feel I must . . .'

'Of course you do, my dear. Don't worry yourself. I won't be long away, and afterwards we'll talk about a journey to London.'

'Oh, Lionel, you are good to me.' Withheld in anger, her tears flowed in contrition, and she touched his arm gratefully. 'You are a dear, and I'm so spoiled. It's so nice that we'll . . . afterwards . . . *Afterwards* . . . *not long away*? What *do* you mean?'

'I'd planned to tell you, when it was all fixed, but I suppose I'd better do it now,' he said carefully. 'You know Lord Elgin and the Expeditionary Force are close to Peking. I'll be leaving within a few days to join the expedition as an observer. It's an excellent opportunity to assess prospects for trade in the north after their victory. Besides, a little time apart will be good for both of us.'

The more Lionel turned the new idea over in his mind, the more he liked it. Saul Haleevie prided himself on his alertness to political developments, which, he asserted, were the shifting sands upon which the foundations of commerce unfortunately rested. His father-in-law would certainly agree that he should go north – and the journey would give him a breathing spell from domesticity.

'Perhaps you're right, Lionel.' Fronah was still contrite for having misjudged him. 'I'm very grateful. You're always thinking of what's best for us.'

Was there a hint of mockery in her reply? No, there could not be, for she was smiling artlessly.

'Will there be more killing in the north?' She looked at him narrowly. 'More slaughter?'

'Slaughter? Hardly, my dear. Naturally, John Chinaman must be taught his place. But slaughter? Hardly. No more than there was here the other day.'

'No *more*, Lionel?' She curbed her indignation. 'There was so much killing here.'

'It won't be as bad, I promise you. After all, Lord Elgin is an honourable gentleman . . . a highly civilized nobleman.'

Serenity had been restored to his household, Lionel Henriques realised gratefully. They sat in comfortable silence, turning over the pages of their books, until it was time to dress for Jardines' masquerade ball. Fronah was looking forward to the gaiety, the two orchestras, the champagne, and the guests frolicking in costumes ranging from Roman senators to Watteau shepherdesses.

*

Lionel was as jolly as his temperament permitted when they climbed the staircase to their bedroom at two in the morning. Fronah was muzzy after two bottles of champagne, but still bubbling. She hummed 'Drink to Me Only with Thine Eyes' as she stepped out of her panniered skirts in the dressing-room. When he joined her in the rosewood bed under the blue-satin coverlet, which matched the watered silk on the walls, she smiled with remembered pleasure.

Yet she was sad when he turned down the oil-lamp on the rosewood bedtable, distressed by the prospect of his leaving. She knew she would miss him badly. He did put up with her moods so patiently, the poor dear.

Lionel kissed Fronah and drew her close. She was surprised by the haste with which he lifted the skirt of her white lawn nightdress. He was not often so ardent. His infrequent lovemaking was always gentle and considerate. He did not press her with the terrible urgency she had read about – and experienced just once.

CHAPTER THIRTY-SIX

The Park of Radiant Perfection
The Summer Palaces near Peking

'Majesty, it would not be well done.' Yehenala pleaded. 'Your Majesty ought not . . .'

The Virtuous Concubine of the Second Grade paused prudently when the Hsien Feng Emperor's small eyes rolled threateningly in their fleshy sockets. She was momentarily taken aback by her own temerity. The Son of Heaven notoriously allowed the mother of the Heir Presumptive great latitude, not only because her unique contribution to the Dynasty set her above all other women, but because he valued her forthright counsel. Yet even she might not tell him flatly that he could not pursue the rash course upon which he had decided. Not even she might say: 'Your Majesty ought not . . . *must* not flee before the barbarian invaders.'

Thanking Heaven that she had checked her tongue before uttering the fatal imperative, Yehenala glanced out the latticed window of the reception-chamber at the clock tower. The squat red-brick structure was capped by a three-tiered tile-roof in the traditional Chinese manner, but the round clock under the second tier, like the miniature spires studding the roof, revealed the hand of the alien architect. The insolently misshapen tower designed for the great Chien Lung Emperor by an Italian priest of the *Yehsu Hui*, the Society of Jesus, seemed to Yehenala to have portended the desperate peril the Great Pure Dynasty faced on the evening of September 21, 1860.

Muttering a Manchu oath, she cursed the day the first barbarian priests had come across the seas into the Great Empire with their holy books, their science, and their green-bronze cannon. They had been the vanguard, but their strategy and the strategy of the other barbarians who followed them was always the same – always monstrous. They began with ingratiating words and ingenious mechanical gifts. Afterwards, they presented humble entreaties to trade. Then, they made demands, muted at first, but later imperious. Finally, came the soldiers in scarlet coats like monkeys – with their long rifles and their barking cannons.

Warships with bellying white sails had first assaulted Canton in the eighteenth year of the Tao Kwang Emperor, when she was only seven, and she was now twenty-five. They had again bombarded Canton only four years ago and carried off to India that fool, the Viceroy who, as the popular jingle mocked: 'would not make war and would not make peace; would not mount a defence and would not flee; would not surrender and would not die.' During the past three years, the barbarians had dared to strike towards Peking itself, demanding that their so-called ambassadors must actually reside in the Northern Capital.

She smiled, recalling that the barbarians with the flag of three crosses had been decisively defeated fifteen months earlier when the Son of Heaven, emboldened by her encouragement, sent an overwhelming array against them. But the barbarians were now approaching the outskirts of the Northern Capital in force, and several barbarian prisoners lay a hundred yards from the clock-tower. She smiled again, recalling that one of the prisoners seized when they came under a flag of truce was Harry Parkes, whose insolence regarding the matter of the lorcha *Arrow* had led to the present crisis.

Her smile faded. This time, she feared, the barbarians with the flag of crosses could neither be lured away nor driven away. They were, moreover, supported by other barbarians under a flag of broad red, white and blue stripes. Above all, the cowardice of the father of her child was shameful before Heaven and mankind. She would herself be pulled down by her enemies if her four-year-old son did not some day ascend the Dragon Throne. If she could not sway the Lord of Ten Thousand Years in this final hour, his pusillanimity would imperil her son's future.

'Your slave, Majesty, abjectly regrets her intemperate tone.' Yehenala regained her composure. 'Your slave pleads with Your Majesty to reconsider. Your Majesty's troops are fighting with inspired valour. Think, Majesty, of the effect upon their spirits if you withdraw the radiance of the Imperial Countenance.'

'You really believe We can still win, Nala?' The Emperor asked dubiously. 'The barbarians seem to sweep all before them. If only We had not been misled by false counsellors . . . if only We had hurled them into the sea when we could.'

'It is *not* too late, Majesty,' she insisted. 'The Sage said: *Those who flee a horde of demons often fall and break their legs, but those who face them often see the demons dissolve into mist.* The barbarian demons appear fierce, but are really no more than mist.'

'Well, Nala, We shall see.' The Son of Heaven was cheered by that spurious counsel from the Master Confucius. 'But We could not bear their spying, Nala. You understand, it is not Our life for which we fear, but our Imperial dignity. Allowing the barbarians to spy on Us would be intolerable. The one demand above others We cannot grant is allowing the barbarians to establish embassies in the Capital . . .'

'Of course, Majesty. Permanent embassies are contrary to the usages of the Sacred Dynasty.'

'Worse, Nala, far worse. They would erect tall towers, as they have in Shanghai. From their towers overlooking the Forbidden City they would spy on Us . . . on Our Court . . . through their far-seeing glasses.'

'All the more reason to face them, Majesty, and destroy them.' Even the seasoned Yehenala was astonished by his frivolousness. 'If Your Majesty

252

leaves the Capital, the barbarians will enter and settle and build their towers.'

Sometimes she wondered if his wits were addled, as the street-balladeers blasphemously hinted. At this supreme crisis of the Ching Dynasty, the Son of Heaven was concerned above all that the barbarians might catch a glimpse of his palanquin before the Hall of Supreme Harmony. She had seen those strange devices with glass lenses for making distant things appear near, and she had heard that the barbarians used them on the battlefield or to watch horses race each other. She wondered if it was true, as she had also heard, that the magical science of the barbarians had also devised lenses that could look through the panels of palanquins and the walls of palaces. That would be indecent, since those lenses could, presumably, also pierce clothing. Anything could be true of the obscene barbarians, but she did not really think so.

'When such desecration threatens,' she added, 'it is essential that Your Majesty remain to inspire his people.'

'You don't really care about Our person, do you, Nala?' he asked with disconcerting shrewdness. 'You only think of Us as the Son of Heaven who must sacrifice all . . . Our life if necessary . . . for Our people. Admit it, Nala.'

'Your Majesty has had many proofs of this slave's devotion . . . not only to the Son of Heaven but to Your Majesty's person.' She wondered whether his habitual suspicion might not in this case be correct. 'Your slave lives only to serve Your Majesty. But should such words be spoken . . . now and here?'

Yehenala glanced around meaningfully. In the lingering summer twilight only a few candles were lit, their flames pale against green and gold walls painted with spreading white chrysanthemums and full blown scarlet peonies. However, the Emperor's inquisitive entourage could see that he and the mother of the Heir Apparent were locked in disagreement. The reception chamber was heaped with red-leather chests, ebony jewel-caskets, and lacquered coffers, as well as straw valises and cloth-wrapped bundles. The eunuchs' eyes were decorously cast down, but their ears were alert as they carried their burdens to the rows of carts, sedan-chairs, and wagons waiting outside the palace. The court ladies were for once silent, but their eyes darted spitefully at their most successful rival. Seated on ebony chairs, the Emperor and Yehenala were an island in the fast-flowing tide. He was dressed in a pongee summer-robe slit front and back for riding, while she wore a plain turquoise gown with only a few jewels.

'Perhaps not, Nala, perhaps it isn't wise to speak too freely,' he replied wearily. 'Though sometimes We . . . even We . . . must say what is in Our heart. We seek safety not because We fear the barbarians, but because We must preserve Ourself for the sake of the Sacred Dynasty and the people. It would be an enormity for Us to fall into the barbarians' hands. An Imperial hostage, what more could they want?'

253

'Your slave understands, Majesty. She knows Your Majesty's tiger-like courage . . . and profound compassion for the common people. Your slave only begs Your Majesty to face the barbarian demons and dissolve them into mist.'

'We have already told Our ministers We are not fleeing, but placing Ourself at the head of Our troops in the field.'

'Then, Majesty, why this great bustle of packing? Why are the post-stations to Jehol ordered to make ready provisions and fresh horses? Majesty, talk of leading the army deceives no one. Least of all the Lord of Ten Thousand Years himself.'

'You dare!' he exploded. 'You dare question Our word?'

'Not I, Majesty, not this slave, but Your Majesty's Generals and Ministers. Majesty, condescend to recall the Memorial received this morning after Your Majesty's intentions were revealed to the Ministers. I have a copy here . . .'

'You would, Nala, you would have a copy. Our ancestor the Kang Hsi Emperor was absolutely correct when he decreed that women and eunuchs must never be permitted to interfere in affairs of state. But read it, if you must.'

The Hsien Feng Emperor's pallid features set in afflicted patience as his favourite concubine read aloud his Mandarins' tortuous response to his planned flight. They had not directly refuted the pretext that he was going to the old Summer Palace at Jehol in Manchuria to hunt. They had refrained from commenting on his claim that his reputation would not suffer because the barbarians would believe the pretence that Dynastic Law obliged the Emperor to mount a ceremonial hunt each autumn in memory of the great chases that had bound the nomadic Manchu tribes together. His respectful counsellors had, however, objected to his suggestion that the people be told he was planning to take personal command of the troops opposing the barbarians.

'At a time of public distress, the man of heroic character is prepared to die at his post.' Yehenala read the censorious Memorial aloud. 'Moreover, both high and low must practise perfect sincerity and truthfulness. Your Majesty's Ministers have today respectfully read the Rescript declaring that Your Majesty's hunting expedition is to be presented as preparation for taking the field in person. They have noted Your Majesty's declaration that, if the enemy is engaged near Tungchow to the south-east, Your Majesty will proceed with a powerful army to the north of Peking.

'Your Majesty's Ministers are struck with wonder at Your Majesty's courage and Your Majesty's strategy. However, the Ministers fear the common people, who are slow-witted and suspicious, will place another interpretation upon Your Majesty's manoeuvres. If the barbarians appear to the south-east of the Capital, the people will say that Your Majesty, having abandoned a hunting expedition to take the field in person, should

254

proceed to that field of battle. If Your Majesty takes up a position to the north, they will say it is really a hunting expedition.'

'Precisely what We wish the barbarians to think,' the Emperor exclaimed with satisfaction. 'You see how dull witted Our ministers are . . . too stupid to appreciate Our brilliant stratagem.'

'Majesty, there *is* another Memorial.' She had kept that harsh document for a last resort. 'Your Majesty's slave fears it is not tactfully phrased. Your Majesty's Senior Censor askes bluntly: *Will Your Majesty cast away the inheritance of Your ancestors like a broken shoe? What will a thousand generations to come say of that deed?*'

'*Kua* . . .' The self-pitying term warned of her danger. 'This Orphan is surrounded by Ministers who care as little for Our life as they do for a broken shoe . . . and concubines, also. You do not do well to taunt Us, *Yi Kuei*.'

Yehenala was chilled by his using her title, *Yi Kuei*, Virtuous Concubine, rather than calling her familiarly Nala or Lan, Orchid, the Chinese name he gasped in passion. She was, she knew, testing the limits of his toleration, though she had spoken the words of the fearless Censor rather than her own. Only fear of being left alone amid his numerous entourage, she sensed, kept him from ordering her to leave the reception-chamber – or kept her from more severe retribution. She was, however, determined to shame him into behaving like a true Manchu Emperor. Only she could shatter the shell of his self-deception and make him act like a man.

'This Orphan is not well served. Our counsellors' advice had always been disastrous.'

A flush mottled his pendulous cheeks, and his small eyes stared pathetically.

'You remember when the barbarians began pressing for ratification of the Treaty of Tientsin two years ago?' he asked plaintively. 'It does not matter, Our envoy said. Majesty, please grant their wishes: ministers resident in Peking; new Treaty Ports inland; free travel in the interior; even an indemnity for that wretched lorcha, the *Arrow*. The peace treaties are only pieces of paper, Our clever counsellor said. Just sign them and the enemy warships will withdraw. Later, Your Majesty can charge the ministers with disobedience and mismanagement. Your Majesty can then repudiate the treaties, and all will be as it was before.'

'This slave, Majesty, did not share that opinion,' Yehenala reminded him. 'Your slave supported Your Majesty's secret plan to exempt the barbarians from all customs dues in exchange for withdrawing their demands. Since the barbarians are interested *only* in money, your slave reasoned, they will prefer the profits of free trade to the expense of military operations.'

'It did *not* work out, Nala.'

'Your Majesty's wise plan was never implemented. Besides . . .'

'Nala, all that is past,' he sighed. 'The treaties were signed, and now We

255

eat the bitter fruit. Twenty thousand barbarians are marching on Peking. They demand . . . demand of Us . . . that the treaties be ratified in The Forbidden City itself. We cannot do so. We must go hunting in Jehol.'

'Majesty, if the Imperial Presence is withdrawn, there can be no hope of holding the Capital.' The weary Yehenala persisted. 'If Your Majesty will only consent to remain . . . only another few days until . . .'

'So be it, Nala.' His abrupt alteration startled her. 'We shall give Our armies two more days to prove they can defend Our Sacred Dynasty . . . and Our Sacred Person.'

Yehenala was elated by her victory. Ironically, the main body of the barbarians was marching on Peking while a few defended Shanghai from the Taipings. The Manchu dispositions were the reverse. A small force screened the Northern Capital against the barbarians, while the main force defended remaining Imperial positions in the Yangtze Valley and, incidentally, the Treaty Port, from the Taipings. The might of the Empire, all troops not engaged against the Long Haired Rebels, must now concentrate to defend the Northern Capital. It was not too late.

She was exhausted by her struggle against the mindless obstinacy of the weak Emperor. Arguing with him was like grooming her *shih-tzu kou*, the lion-dogs the Dalai Lama sent her from Lhasa. The beasts squirmed so that she had to exercise great care not to pull out clumps of their fur, scratch their tender skin, or break their delicate bones. Their soft fur curled back into snarls as the comb passed, and they snapped at her hands with their needle teeth.

The slightest disagreement with the Emperor demanded almost inhuman restraint. If she bruised his fragile self-esteem, he would turn and rend her. Almost inhuman patience too. She had to repeat her arguments over and over again because he constantly reverted to his original position or raised irrelevant issues.

Light-headed with exhaustion, Yehenala leaned her forehead against the latticed window. Night had fallen, and the clock-tower was a black triangle against the star-bright sky, its red-brick base splashed with crimson by pitch torches. The yellow rays shining through the open doors of the palace lit the streams of eunuchs flowing around the waiting vehicles.

Yehenala closed her eyes against that disorder, so unlike the normal preparation for an Imperial Progress. Hearing a gabble behind her, she turned to see a eunuch kneeling before the Emperor.

'Majesty . . . Majesty . . . catastrophe!' The terrified man babbled. 'A disaster . . . only a few miles away . . . almost at the gates of the Capital.'

'Now, fellow, pull yourself together.' Surprisingly composed, the Emperor steadied the messenger. 'We still sit here, don't We? Get a grip on yourself and give Us your news.'

'Majesty, at Palichiao . . . hardly nine miles from Peking,' the eunuch reported incoherently. 'A great force of barbarians . . . cross-flag and three-colour flag barbarians together. First salvoes of cannon, then the three-colour barbarians stormed our batteries with knives on the ends of their rifles. Our troops at Tungchow are isolated. The last stretch of the Grand Canal is taken. Peking is naked to the enemy. Majesty, the barbarians are advancing like the wind.'

Yehenala promised herself she would have the eunuch roundly thrashed for alarmism. Slightly cheered by that thought, she awaited the Emperor's inevitable decision.

'We thank you for your promptness in reporting,' he said calmly. 'Go now and convey Our orders to Our Chief Eunuch. We depart before dawn on Our hunting expedition.'

Striding past the kneeling messenger, Yehenala swung her hand and knocked him to the floor. Frantic at the collapse of her hopes, she spoke impulsively to the Son of Heaven.

'You *cannot*. You *must* not leave now.' Not only the prohibited imperative spilled from her lips, but the familiar 'you' never addressed to the Son of Heaven. 'It cannot be as bad as this stupid servant says. At least, wait for a proper report. You *must* not flee.'

'*Yi Kuei* . . .' He replied with frigid formality. 'Virtuous Concubine, female slaves do not say *must* to Us. Nor do they say *you*. Our mind is made up. We depart before dawn.'

'Majesty, I implore you . . .'

'Cease plaguing Us, woman. We leave before sunrise.'

'Without me, then. One Manchu of the Imperial Family will remain at the post of danger. Your Majesty journeys without this slave.'

'So be it!' The Emperor rose and smiled with cold rage. 'Of course, Our younger brother Prince Kung remains. He will, perhaps, be glad of your counsel. Leave Us. Go now and say farewell to the child.'

'The child, Majesty?'

'Prince Tsai Chün, naturally, travels with his father. We are leaving *solely* to keep the barbarians from seizing this Imperial hostage. Did you think We would leave them another almost as valuable?'

'Your slave will accompany Your Majesty, if she is permitted.' Yehenala bowed in submission. 'Your slave profoundly regrets her effrontery, Majesty.'

'It is too late for regrets, *Yi Kuei*. Your insolence has passed all bounds. Our lenience has been tried too far. Do not expect Us ever again to speak with you familiarly. Now, woman, leave Us.'

CHAPTER THIRTY-SEVEN

'Revolting, Sir, utterly depraved!' The Colonel's long face was scarlet with indignation. 'They are a race lost to all sense of decency.'

Lionel Henriques lifted his panama hat and patted his damp forehead with a silk handkerchief. He fastidiously edged his rough-haired pony a pace further from the choleric officer, whose heavy red-barathea tunic was already soaked across his shoulders at eight in the morning. Lieutenant Colonel Garnet Wolseley, quartermaster of the British Expeditionary Force, stank of sweat, though he had sluiced himself with cold water before they rode out of camp. Cleanliness was impossible for troops bivouacked for almost three weeks beside the Grand Canal waiting for the siege artillery train that had finally arrived the preceding night.

Escorted by a detachment of Sikh cavalry, Henriques and Wolseley were making a wide circle around Peking across the ochre North China plain. Shorn millet was a brown stubble on the fields beside the dirt road which rose gently as it led them north-west. Behind them, the Northern Capital's grey-tiled roofs were frozen waves within granite walls. Before them, the golden roofs and the sparkling waterways of the Summer Palaces shone against the seamed backdrop of the Fragrant Hills. The russet leaves of the maples cloaking the valleys beneath the snow-dusted summits stirred in the north wind blowing out of Manchuria across the mountains girdled by the Great Wall of China. Somewhere on the plains north of the Great Wall the bedraggled cavalcade of the Hsien Feng Emperor of the Great Pure Dynasty was still struggling towards the old Summer Palace at Jehol.

Lionel gasped when he saw the majestic panorama of castles, palaces, temples, and pavilions glowing from horizon to horizon like an immense fairyland. He had not believed the Summer Palaces so vast, though he had been told the Imperial pleasure grounds, almost a century and a half in the building, included more than two hundred edifices spread over almost a hundred square miles.

What forces, he wondered, had broken the truly Imperial resolution of the Manchus, which had built that gigantic monument? An army of 11,000 British and Indian soldiers, supported by 7,000 Frenchmen and Annamese had created blind panic in the capital of an Empire that fielded more than two million soldiers. Though he had never doubted that a determined European assault would prevail, he was astonished by the flabbiness of the defences. Aside from occasional harassment, the elite troops guarding the Northern Capital seemed to have been blotted up by the arid plain.

'I assure you, Sir, lust and sensuality are graphically represented in

258

hideous nakedness . . . in their most disgusting aspects.' Colonel Wolseley was still vehement. 'The lama temples, Sir. Religion they may call it, but it is no more than pornography . . . the vilest pornography. The images of their deities are revolting. They exhibit extraordinary perversions of sensuality: women, men, and children all entangled. Also ponies, dogs and monkeys. And the priests who exhibit those beastly carvings positively gloat over the abominations. Those spectacles must be loathsome to any but bestial souls. Lust is deified.'

'A matter of some anthropological interest, I should imagine, Colonel. Will you view them again?'

'Only to ensure the accuracy of my report to the Royal Geographical Society, sir. But I should be glad of the company of an impartial gentleman to testify to my accuracy. Otherwise, no decent-minded man would credit the depths of depravity.'

Was this blond Hebrew, the Colonel wondered, truly a gentleman? One would hardly call the brilliant, but flashy Benjamin Disraeli, lately Chancellor of the Exchequer, a gentleman, though he had been baptized in the Church of England as an infant. Though this Henriques made no show of his Jewishness, he was patently not a Christian gentleman. However, his association with Samuelson and Company had over-ridden all objections to his attachment to the Expeditionary Force as a gentleman observer. Lord Elgin, the Ambassador Plenipotentiary, was pleased to indulge a connection of the great merchant bankers. A Lieutenant Colonel who still had his way to make in the world could do no less. Like the hereditary nobleman, he, too, might some day be glad of Samuelsons' goodwill.

*

Their ponies' iron-shod hooves rang cheerily on the stone-slab pavement of the road from the village called Haitien to the Summer Palaces. Though the slopes of the Fragrant Hills were already dappled with shadows, the Italianate marble palaces of the Park of Eternal Spring gleamed amid emerald groves, while the Tower of Buddha's Fragrance soared brilliant over the Mount of Myriad Longevity above Kunming Lake in the Garden of Crystal Rivulets. The road ended at a towering gate. The closed vermilion doors were protected against cavalry by a hedge of spikes and against demons by a wall on which porcelain dragons disported under a coping of Imperial-yellow tiles. For arcane reasons half-lost in the mists of Chinese mythology, spirits could move only in straight lines. Malignant devils could not skirt the spirit-wall to enter the Yüan Ming Yüan, the Park of Radiant Perfection, the central glory of the Summer Palaces.

The stone wall that actually guarded the Emperor's seclusion extended westward towards the Fragrant Hills beneath the overhanging boughs of giant cedars and spruces, its moat spanned by arched stone bridges. They rode west past ponds carpeted with white lotuses and pink water-lilies, which rippled with the flow of the stream. All the waterways were man-made, as were the hills within the Yüan Ming Yüan. Prodigious labour had created the fantasy realm to which the Emperors of the Great Pure Dynasty retreated from worldly care. Yet the reigning monarch had abandoned the best beloved corner of his empire to the European invaders.

The road curved to the right and soared on an many-arched stone causeway over an artificial lake. The tricolour of France fluttered above a vermilion-pillared temple behind the yellow, blue and scarlet Imperial pennants still drooping from slender flagpoles. No sentry challenged them, for the French outpost was deserted.

The British rode though the silent afternoon towards the western gate of the Park of Radiant Perfection. No human sentinel stood before the gate, which was guarded only by two stylized bronze lions, their domed heads covered with tight-curled manes. The female shielded a cub with an upraised forepaw, and the male clutched an orb that symbolized dominion over *Tien hsia*, All Under Heaven.

Gilt tracery shimmered on the open vermilion doors, which revealed beams painted with a sapphire and emerald frieze so bright it might have been painted a few hours earlier. Around the wooden birds carved on those beams wire nets were stretched to prevent feathered birds fouling their beauty. Built high to allow easy ingress only to pedestrians and palanquins, the sill of the gate was sharp-edged and mirror-bright. The cracked thresholds of the ramshackle town-gates of the Yangtze Delta were as different from that immaculate stone-work as this Imperial magnificence was from those shabby towns.

A princely share of the wealth of China, Lionel realised, had flowed into the Yüan Ming Yüan for more than two centuries to create and maintain this impeccable fantasy. His heart-beat quickened when he envisioned the treasures he would find within. The greatest porcelains of two millennia had, he knew, been gathered into the Summer Palaces by the acquisitive Imperial House.

The ponies stepped gingerly across the high sills into the passageway. A French corporal in a royal-blue frock-coat piped with red popped out of the guard-room, jerky as a clockwork soldier. His fringed epaulettes quivered as he brought his long rifle to the salute.

Through the open door of the guard-room Lionel Henriques saw the survivors of those few guardians of the Imperial retreat who had remained faithful to their trust. Forty wretched eunuchs, who had been broken by a single French volley the preceding day, huddled on the flagstones. All were manacled, and many were wounded. Their gaudy robes were torn, and their plump faces sagged in mortal dejection. If the barbarians did not slaughter them, they would be certainly decapitated for failing to hold the Yüan Ming Yüan.

The low building shining at the far end of the long courtyard moved

Lionel so profoundly that he failed to hear the querulous trilling of a French bugle. The emerald-tiled roof of the Hall of Audience of the Park of Radiant Perfection floated on slender crimson pillars above marble flagstones in the golden twilight. Mesmerized by this other worldly beauty, Lionel checked his pony.

'What's this?' Colonel Wolseley's voice was harsh with shock. 'What the devil are the Frogs playing at?'

A ragged formation of eight infantrymen stood behind the bugler, who wore a Mandarin's round fur hat surmounted by a ruby button and clutched a silver candelabra. The soldiers' frock-coats were unbuttoned, and they staggered as they aligned themselves. Despite the bugle's entreaties, only those nine among the hundreds of French milling before the Hall of Audience fell into rank.

The courtyard was brilliant with silk robes draped over grimy uniforms. Spiky beards wet with wine bobbed above the dainty pink-and-violet gowns of young court ladies, while Mandarins' hats with upturned brims had replaced red-piped *kepis*. Every soldier cradled his own treasure: gilt statuettes, gleaming porcelain vases and ebony jewel-cases. His sword abandoned, a fresh-faced lieutenant plunged his hands into a split red-leather chest. As fast as he stuffed gold coins into the breast of his tunic the yellow stream cascaded onto the flagstones. Some privates sprawled in drunken sleep while others clumsily searched their pockets.

Bolts of silk unfurled across the courtyard in a splintered rainbow. Some soldiers pranced with small golden images from the household temples. Others minced in robes embroidered with Imperial dragons, while happily shredding scrolls. The officers, more discriminating, stuffed their pockets with pearls and jades. A sergeant wept with joy over a bag of uncut emeralds, but laughed when a two-foot ox-blood jardinière slipped from a wine-fuddled private's grasp to splinter on the flagstones.

'By God, it's an orgy of looting,' Wolseley exclaimed. 'You'd think even the Frenchies could control their men better. But troops will loot, sir, troops will loot.'

Sliding off his pony, he tossed the reins to a Sikh. The guards posted before the crimson pillars of the Hall of Audience were reasonably sober and reasonably presentable, except for the gem-finialed Mandarins' hats all wore. The corporal saluted the British officer and stepped aside to allow him to enter, but a French sergeant followed suspiciously. Outside, the guards struggled with soldiers shouting in rage.

'Understand the lingo, do you, Henriques?' Wolseley asked. 'Never could get my tongue around it. What're they saying?'

'They're just complaining, Wolseley. Why should we be allowed to hunt for more treasures? It's unfair to let the British in while keeping honest Frenchmen out. It's an insult to the honour of France.'

'Soldiers will loot, Henriques. Why not let 'em loot? Spoils to the victors, you know. They'll fight harder next time if they hope for booty.'

261

'By God, look at that!' Lionel was deaf to the Colonel's wisdom. 'Just look at that!'

The horizontal rays of the setting sun coruscated on a floor of thousands of white marble lozenges, flooding the Hall of Audience with a pearly radiance. The detailed painting of the Summer Palaces on the near wall glowed in three-dimensional reality in that intense luminescence. Upon either side of the rosewood throne at the far end stood black-lacquer screens gleaming with rubies and emeralds set in blue-enamel peacock feathers. State scrolls were heaped among ormolu clocks before the carved peonies and chrysanthemums climbing upon the gilt trellises behind the dais.

'Interested in porcelain, you said, Henriques.' The Colonel's voice intruded upon Lionel's rapture. 'What do you say to that little lot?'

An emperor's hoard was ranged on altar tables with upcurved ends and ebony cabinets. Lavender saucers in fretwork stands were splashed with crimson roses so dark they appeared indigo. The melting glaze of pearl-grey vases also produced under the Mongol Dynasty in the thirteenth century was so soft his fingertips seemed to sink into them. He smiled at the mundane Chinese designation: mutton-fat ware.

The Englishman flitted from Imperial yellow censers of the Kang Hsi reign to lentil-green crackled celadon of the Sung Dynasty, some eight centuries earlier. He admired an enormous pair of *cloisonné* unicorns, whose rounded green-enamel flanks were inlaid with swirls of gold wire. He was reaching towards a rice-bowl of the intense pale blue called sky-after-rain when the Colonel's voice jarred upon him again.

'Can't stand here gawking all day, Henriques. Must make a recce before the Frenchies strip it clear. By God, the General will have to let our lads have a go.'

Dazzled by the splendours he had seen, which were not a thousandth part of the full splendour of the Park of Radiant Perfection, Lionel followed the officer to the door concealed by the screen behind the throne. Through that same door, the Lord of Ten Thousand Years had entered his Hall of Audience before seating himself on his rosewood throne to receive his Senior Mandarins.

A maze of paths wound among grassy mounds displaying almost every plant that grew in the Great Empire from the tropical lowlands of the south to the frozen tundra of the north. Crossing tinkling streams on hump-backed bridges, Lionel glimpsed the fir-screened roofs of the villas of Imperial concubines. Descending rustic stone-steps, he saw tall, blanched boulders from Lake Tai near Soochow, which the currents had carved into monstrous shapes.

Pondering the love of the grotesque that so oddly complemented the exquisite Chinese taste in ceramics, he was startled when the path opened upon a circular pond covered with pink lotus flowers two feet in diameter. The structure beside the pond was so like the Hall of Audience he

momentarily thought they had retraced their steps, but its pillared verandah was patrolled by an impeccably uniformed platoon. A French lieutenant, whose personal authority had kept his men from joining the general
looting, explained that they were entering the Emperor's personal apartments.

A broad bed was set in an alcove separated from the largest room by
lavender curtains. On the yellow-satin coverlet lay a small green hat
embroidered with a symmetrical *shou* – longevity – ideogram which Lionel
knew from its recurrence on porcelains. Examining the long pipe chased
with silver and the embroidered tobacco-pouch abandoned on a side-table,
he knew that a harassed young man had found in these apartments
sanctuary from the perplexities of politics. He realised that the monarch
who appeared the incarnation of evil was a bewildered human being.

Lionel felt the fugitive monarch's presence even more poignantly when
he saw on the waterways winding behind the private apartments a flotilla of
miniature junks, each mounting a minute bronze cannon. It was,
somehow, pathetic that the young Manchu who was adored as the Son of
Heaven should have been forced to seek diversion by watching eunuchs
fight mock sea-battles in those Lilliputian vessels.

'What have we here?' Wolseley stooped to peer under a dwarf rho-
dodendron. 'Oh, you would, would you, you little devil?'

Deep growls defied him. But he reached beneath the shrub and brought
out a small dog whose face was hidden by the same red-gold pelt that
cloaked its body. He cradled the animal in his arms, his long features
glowing with the proprietorial affection a dog aroused in the heart of every
English gentleman except the most depraved.

'He's a lion, you know, a lion-dog,' Wolseley expounded. 'A Tibetan
breed treasured by the ladies of the court. Handsome little beast, ain't
it?'

'What'll you do with it?' Lionel was amused by the Colonel's concern.
'You can hardly take it campaigning.'

'Wouldn't dream of it, Henriques. He's too delicate, a ladies' dog, after
all. Perhaps he belonged to the Empress . . . But here's a thought. Lord
Elgin might like to present it to Her Majesty the Queen.'

'You could call him Loot,' Lionel suggested sarcastically.

'No, not that. Too bald. But Lootie, that's a fine name. Lootie he is.'

Lionel wondered whether the lion-dog might actually belong to the
Empress or an Imperial concubine, perhaps a young concubine just
budding into womanhood. He knew the name of only one concubine, who
was no pubescent flower, but the Emperor's evil genius. Yehenala,
incongruously called the Virtuous Concubine, was notorious for her
bellicosity. A mastiff was more her style. Yehenala, he reflected, would
hardly shower her fierce affections on the small lion-dog.

*

James Bruce, 8th Earl of Elgin and 12th Earl of Kincardine, was weary of journeying to China to resolve problems other statesmen found intractable. He had, however, responded loyally to the Prime Minister's request that he return again to the Far East as Ambassador Plenipotentiary, though at forty-nine he would have preferred to remain on his estates in Scotland.

His younger brother had failed to bring the Chinese to terms. The Honourable Frederick Bruce had been belligerent when diplomacy was required, and he had shrunk from force when only force could prevail. To redeem the family honour the Earl had set out on a four-month voyage to China, unhappily protracted by a shipwreck off Ceylon.

Finally seated in the Hall of Audience of the Yüan Ming Yüan, the white-haired nobleman reviewed the impasse with the Mandarins, who were alternately as subtle as chess masters and as brutal as Huns. He had, unfortunately, pledged not to sack Peking itself. Resigned to that inconvenient restriction, he discussed their situation with his brother-in-law, Lieutenant General Sir Hope Grant, the General Officer Commanding, who had made his name in the Indian Mutiny three years ago.

Lord Elgin had a few minutes earlier acquiesced with the same mild resignation to the suggestion of his ambitious Quartermaster General, Lieutenant Colonel Wolseley, that he present the Empress's lion-dog to the Queen-Empress Victoria. Although its plucky spirit touched him, he forgot the beast as soon as his orderly led it away. Only with difficulty was he to recall the incident when Her Majesty thanked him for the 'darling dog' at Balmoral two years later.

The General Officer Commanding had just presented His Excellency the Ambassador Plenipotentiary with advice that soured their previous victories. The Earl found all generals irritating, and Sir Hope Grant, the Hero of Delhi, the husband of Lord Elgin's favourite sister, was no exception. Generals being what they were, it was a miracle that any campaign was ever won. Like all of them, his brother-in-law combined rash impetuosity with excessive caution. He and the French General de Montauban insisted that their troops could not be exposed to the harsh Peking winter. No later than the first week of November the army must return to Tientsin, where it could, if necessary, embark on its 150 transports for the more hospitable south. They could not be responsible for the consequences, the Generals respectfully submitted, if their advice were rejected.

Since the Manchus showed no sign of yielding, that counsel left the problem in Lord Elgin's lap – as usual. Instructed to secure ratification of the Treaty of Tientsin in the Forbidden City, he was determined to do so. He could allow his judgment to be swayed neither by his indignation at the Manchus' having taken captive envoys negotiating under a flag of truce nor by his anger at the brutal treatment accorded those envoys and his rage at the slaughter of a half-dozen British prisoners of war. No more could he allow himself to be mollified by the envoys' subsequent release. He could not in honour leave the Manchus virtually unscathed while they still obdurately rejected his lenient terms.

Besides, the Treaty of Tientsin was his own creation. The Prime Minister would believe him as inept as his brother Frederick if he could not in 1860, backed by the most powerful European army ever landed in China, secure Imperial ratification of the Treaty to which he had compelled the Emperor's Ministers to agree in 1858, though supported by a much smaller force. Like Alexander the Great, he would have to find a Gordian solution.

Sir Hope Grant had also plagued him with a lesser problem. that touched another raw nerve of the Bruce family. Lord Elgin was proud of the arduous efforts of his father, the 7th Earl, to preserve the ancient sculptures on the Parthenon of Athens by securing the permission of the Turkish rulers to take those statues to Britain. That selfless act had been denounced as 'rapacious vandalism' by a pack of slanderers led by the poetaster Lord Byron. In 1816, a Parliamentary Commission declared the 7th Earl innocent of wrongdoing and recommended the statues' purchase by the British Museum. (The £35,000 paid fell absurdly short of the true value of the Elgin Marbles.) Despite this vindication, the Bruces were sensitive to charges of looting. His brother-in-law had pressed him to approve looting on a spectacular scale.

The Earl was, however, moved by the General's submission that they would otherwise face a major disciplinary problem. The issue, Lord Elgin agreed, was actually neither moral nor legal. The contents of the Summer Palaces were clearly the personal property of the Hsien Feng Emperor, who had expressly forfeited his rights under the rules of war. The problem was practical. Reaching the Yüan Ming Yüan first, the French had skimmed off the most valuable articles. British officers and other ranks alike were murmuring angrily that they had been cheated by their wily allies.

Sir Hope Grant allowed his soldiers to take what treasures remained, but that was not good enough. The outnumbered French were, therefore, compelled to disgorge most of the gold ingots from the Emperor's Treasury. In fairness, all British soldiers were then compelled to disgorge all their loot – except a few baubles. One such bauble was the triple-strand of black Caspian pearls Lionel Henriques had scooped from an overlooked jewel-case in Yehenala's villa. It would look well on Fronah, and a civilian like himself did not come directly under the General's orders.

*

October 10, 1860   *The Park of Radiant Perfection*

An auction of all the loot, Sir Hope Grant ruled, would ensure that every soldier received a fair portion of the loot. While the undisciplined French scoffed, a colonel and two majors sold off the Emperor's treasures.

Lionel Henriques was an eager bidder. He was also an intelligent bidder. While others competed for gaudy silks and knick-knacks set with semi-precious stones, he bought the porcelains he knew. Most officers were not interested in 'China pots', which were fragile and unwieldy. He was too discreet to bid on the one garment that did catch his eye. The Emperor's blue-satin robe bearing four Imperial five-clawed dragons and the twelve symbols of earthly power went to Lord Elgin for a few shillings. Lionel also gracefully underbid so that Colonel Garnet Wolseley could acquire a matched pair of three-coloured-glazed Tang Dynasty funerary horses for £16.

'Infantryman myself, Henriques,' Wolseley confided. 'But there's something about those beasts. Fearful price, though.'

Lionel restrained his impulse to offer double, though he knew he could sell the horses for ten times as much to Old Curiosity Soo in Shanghai. He was not as self-abnegating when the bidding jumped to £4. 10s for a foot-high blue and white flask of the Yung Lo reign of the Ming, made in 1416 and exquisitely decorated with a bird singing on a cinnamon branch. He flicked his fingers to bid an even £5.

'Sold to Mr Henriques for a fiver.' The auctioneer colonel was enjoying himself hugely. 'A fabulous price, but how can poor devils or soldiers compete against Messrs Samuelson and Co?'

The auction of the Emperor's personal treasures brought in £8,258/12s/3d to be distributed among the troops according to rank. Every private received £4, almost a third of his yearly pay, while sergeants and officers received more. That night Sapper-Captain Charles George Gordon jubilantly wrote his sister that he had received £48. Aside from some grumbling among his staff officers, who like himself were excluded from the share-out, Sir Hope Grant had quelled his troops' dissatisfaction.

Lionel Henriques was euphoric. His aesthetic passion was for the moment sated, and he believed his financial problems were solved. The porcelains he had bought were worth at least twice the £8,000 raised by the entire auction. Best of all, they had not yet cost him a penny. The General was happy to take his note on Samuelsons in London. He would decide later how much he would pay against those notes – whether, indeed, he would pay at all.

*

October 17, 1860   *The Park of Radiant Perfection*

Lionel Henriques' self-satisfaction was not unclouded. He regretted the removal from this perfect setting of the treasures accumulated by successive Manchu emperors. He felt a physical pang at the Imperial hoard's being distributed piecemeal throughout the British Isles.

What would a Manchester iron-monger make of the jade tiger acquired by his sub-lieutenant son? Would even great noblemen like the Churchills of Blenheim comprehend the eighth-century funerary charger carrying a barbarian guardian-spirit, who arrogantly flexed his muscles? They would assess the horse's points, and they might see the humour. But would they ever feel the awe that statuette evoked in the Chinese – and in himself?

Lionel might have spared his regrets. Lord Elgin had found his Gordian solution to the impasse created by the cautious Generals and the recalcitrant Manchus. The nobleman resolved all issues, practical or moral, by a single stroke. He assured ratification of the Treaty of Tientsin; he punished the slaughter of British prisoners; and he transformed the pillagers into conservators of Chinese culture.

The 8th Earl of Elgin no more considered his decision discreditable than the 7th Earl had so considered the stripping of the Parthenon. Nor was he ever to realise that he had, quite unintentionally, crippled the Manchu Empire's finances, so that its subsequent endeavours to meet the challenge of the West by modernizing its industrial base and its military forces would fail. But no one could have foreseen that extraordinary consequence of the collision between the disparate natures of James Bruce, Earl of Elgin, and Yehenala, the Virtuous Concubine, who never met in this life.

*

October 19, 1860   *The Park of Radiant Perfection*

The nobleman had formed his intention on the 17th of October as he sorrowfully watched the burial of the four Britons and three Sikhs whose captors had allowed them to die in agony. His resolution was fixed the following day, when the slain French prisoners were interred in the seventeeth-century Jesuit graveyard just outside Peking. When the stalwartly Protestant Ambassador Plenipotentiary and his senior officers acceded to their Catholic allies' wish that they sprinkle Holy Water on the raw graves, his resolution became inflexible.

As a Jew and, therefore, an outsider, Lionel Henriques was wryly amused by his countrymen's reluctance to participate in Papist rites. He was, however, horrified, when Lord Elgin announced his decision.

Men were killed in war – and women too. If they were Europeans, it was lamentable, but the soldiers had known that death might await them. If they were Chinese, hundreds of millions stood ready to replace them. But the masterpieces created through many centuries by inspired artistry were irreplaceable – and Lord Elgin had resolved to destroy those masterpieces.

Lionel remained ever afterwards convinced that Lord Elgin's chief purpose was not to compel the wavering Chinese to accept his terms, but to punish their recalcitrance and their killing of prisoners. The Chinese had opened one gate of Peking on October 13th, a few minutes before massed batteries of artillery were scheduled to bombard it at point-blank range.

267

The Northern Capital, therefore, already lay in the Allies' grasp. Cut off from reinforcement and resupply, Prince Kung, the Emperor's half-brother and deputy, would, in any event, have ratified the Treaty and agreed to pay an indemnity.

Lionel, whose opinion was not solicited, agreed that it was necessary to humble the arrogant Manchus and ensure they never again dared to flout civilized diplomatic and commercial practices. But he was absolutely horrified by the means chosen to attain that end. Curiously, the French, who had happily pillaged the Yüan Ming Yüan, were also aghast at Lord Elgin's decision. Their objections were summarily over-ruled.

The 1st Division under Major General Sir John Michel marched from its encampment near Peking to the Summer Palaces on October 18th. Like all the British generals, Sir John was smarting at Lord Elgin's voluble injunction to greater vigour. The plenipotentiary complained that he was even more sorely plagued by his senior officers' lack of energy than he had been in 1858. The 1st Division energetically fanned out through the Park of Radiant Perfection to bring 'fire and the sword to the heathen'.

Among the most energetic officers on the morning of October 19th was the sandy-haired captain of engineers called Charles George Gordon. Sapper officers were normally considered eccentrics, perhaps not quite gentlemen, and fanaticism flickered in Gordon's prominent blue eyes. He belonged to the apocalyptic sect of the Plymouth Brethren, and perused his Bible so assiduously that even the devout Earl was discomfited. Captain Gordon's brother officers felt it was not quite *pukka* to ascribe almost every action to divine inspiration.

Captain Gordon brought special skills to the terrible execution of justice, for he was adept not only in constructing fortifications, roads, and bridges, but also in destruction.

The Hall of Audience behind the West Gate was blazing fiercely minutes after the fires were lit. The dry wood, seasoned over the centuries, burned like cardboard. The immense painting of the Summer Palaces on the wall was a sheet of flame within seconds. The rosewood throne flickered briefly and was consumed. Red-hot roof tiles and flaming beams crashed on to the shimmering white marble floor, leaving it cracked and charred. Just before the Hall of Audience collapsed, it was outlined by flames like an enormous firework display. The tower of smoke was visible in every *hutung* of the Northern Capital.

The soldiers cheered and laughed as they scampered through the maze leading to the Emperor's private apartments and the villas of his concubines. The conflagration engulfed the gardens that exhibited the horticultural diversity of the Great Empire. The needles of firs and the pointed leaves of rhododendrons withered and cracked in the intense heat before vanishing in brilliant explosions. The thick bark of cedars smouldered and contracted before bursting into flame. When fiery trees toppled into the canals, the water seethed and hissed under a carpet of grey ash.

Because its chief building material was wood, the conflagration leapt across the Park of Radiant Perfection. Only the square brick base of the clock-tower remained when the beams supporting the three-tiered roof disintegrated. The Pavilion of Precious Clouds west of the Tower of Buddha's Fragrance in the Garden of Crystal Rivulets was preserved because the Chien Lung Emperor had ordered it constructed of bronze in 1750. Glowing cherry-red, the bronze pavilion stood intact amid a welter of smashed roof-tiles coated with soot. The Romanesque palaces designed by the Jesuit Castiglione for the Garden of Eternal Spring were obdurate, since they were faced and crowned with stone. But the sappers' scientifically placed charges brought them down handily, leaving only gutted facades.

Red-coated Sikhs raced through the billows of smoke, exuberantly waving golden ingots they had discovered in an outlying hall overlooked in the comprehensive looting of the preceding weeks. That trove, General Sir Hope Grant immediately resolved, would not be shared with the niggardly French. The first sappers to enter a remote pavilion stared in astonishment at two gilded coaches, which had been presented to the Chien Lung Emperor by the Earl Macartney, Britain's first envoy to reach Peking. Those European vehicles, never used during the intervening sixty-five years, must also burn to administer justice to the Manchus.

The north-west breeze whipped the flames and showered embers on the streets of Peking. The Yüan Ming Yüan was the centre of the holocaust, but there was no reason to spare the outlying parks. The troops diligently put to the torch all the two-hundred odd edifices of the Summer Palaces of the Manchu Emperors.

British officers remained characteristically cool as they inflicted their hot revenge. Lieutenant Colonel Garnet Wolseley took the opportunity, as he said, 'to inspect the countryside around the palaces while the work of demolition was going on.' Lionel Henriques trailed unhappily behind as the officers climbed the ridge of the Wan Shou Shan, the Mount of Myriad Longevity, where the bronze Pavilion of Precious Clouds glowed red. He was silent when Wolseley remarked that the view was charming, but nodded when the Colonel observed with satisfaction: 'Like a damned prolonged eclipse, ain't it, Henriques? The smoke's so thick the whole world's in shadow.'

Looking down upon the billows of smoke lanced with flame, Wolseley added: 'And those Frenchies, what hypocrites! They pillaged like Visigoths, but objected for form's sake to our administering the *coup de grâce*.' A black cloud eddied around them, briefly veiling the holocaust, as Wolseley continued equably: 'Our gallant allies left us only the bare shells of buildings to wreak our vengeance for the inhuman cruelty our unfortunate countrymen suffered.'

The stench choked Lionel, and his eyes streamed. He did not see Captain Charles Gordon appear like a genie through the smoke, apparently satisfied that the demolition could proceed efficiently without his supervision. The pious Captain was as mercurial as he was dogmatic. The near-frenzy in which he began his work had given way to melancholy. His protuberant blue eyes were dull; his sandy hair was filmed with ash; and the firm mouth beneath his bushy moustache drooped.

'Fire and the sword!' Gordon declared lugubriously. 'Fire and the sword! The vengeance of the Lord! We've destroyed all, like new Vandals. The damage must come to twenty million pounds. It can never be replaced.'

*

October 24, 1860   *Peking: The Forbidden City*

Negotiations naturally proceeded smoothly thereafter, though it took a few days to settle the details. On the 24th of October, 1860, the 8th Earl of Elgin was carried through the streets of Peking in a vermilion sedan-chair on the shoulders of twelve sturdy bearers. Four companies of infantry marched in his triumphal procession while one hundred cavalrymen pranced in the shadow of the great Meridian Gate of the Forbidden City.

Prince Kung, his youthful vigour depleted by the humiliation, appeared wizened when he rose to receive the Scottish nobleman in the Hall of Supreme Harmony. His eyes were sunken in his square face, and his wen appeared enormous against his pallid grey cheek.

Their business was soon done. The Treaty signed in Tientsin in 1858 was ratified in the Hsien Feng Emperor's paramount Hall of Audience in 1860. The additional Convention of Peking provided, among other conditions, that a first instalment of three hundred thousand *taels* was to be paid immediately against a total indemnity of eight million. When the silver was duly delivered, Lord Elgin withdrew without rancour from the citadel of the barbaric power whose cruelty had required severe chastisement.

Having already forgiven his enemies with Christian charity, the Earl felt profound satisfaction at achieving so much at so little cost. He had redeemed the Bruces' reputation for quiet competence, while diplomatic and commercial relations with the Chinese Empire now rested on a solid foundation. Peking was spared, as he had promised. Allied casualties were negligible, and Chinese casualties only a few thousand, though an accurate count was impossible. The common people, he had been assured by his Sinologues, bore the British no rancour whatsoever. They understood that their oppressive rulers had to be taught a firm lesson.

Lord Elgin was also gratified by the prudent measures he had taken to inform the Chinese populace of the true facts of the matter. Placards written in great black ideograms by the Expeditionary Force's linguists were posted throughout Peking to prevent the Manchus from retailing a fallacious version of the destruction of the Summer Palaces.

Colonel Wolseley, who had a gift for words, wrote in his journal: 'Lord

Elgin's knowledge of human nature, and of Chinese dispositions in particular, pointed out the only substantial method then within his power of taking vengeance for the crime [of killing prisoners of war] . . . The destruction of [the Emperor's] favourite residence was the strongest proof of our superior strength; it served to undeceive all Chinamen in their absurd conviction of their monarch's universal sovereignty . . . [The posters] prevented the authorities from giving a false colouring to our actions, as they would no doubt have otherwise endeavoured to spread abroad the impression of our having destroyed that place simply for the sake of plunder.'

Lionel Henriques's knowledge of human nature was enlarged by the experience, as was his comprehension of the peculiar character of the Chinese. Though he would always afterwards maintain that a bold stroke of vengeance and intimidation had been necessary, he could never condone the atrocity that had destroyed the Summer Palaces.

'The Chinese can understand everything.' He could almost hear the comment his wife might make if she had watched Lord Elgin's sedan-chair leave the Imperial City through the Gate of Heavenly Peace. 'But they would understand it far better – and be far more ready to forgive – if they thought we had done it simply for plunder.'

CHAPTER THIRTY-EIGHT

March 30, 1861   *Jehol in Manchuria*
                                                    The Imperial Hunting Park

A mood of utter desolation in a desolate place! The sinuous grass-writing flowed down the mulberry paper. *Cold amid the hot springs, my heart, too, is ice*!

Yehenala signed the couplet with bold strokes and laid her writing-brush down on the malachite inkstone. The image poignantly conveyed the despondency that oppressed not only herself, but the entire Court in exile in the disused Imperial Hunting Park at Jehol, the Place of the Hot Streams 150 miles north-east of Peking at the end of March, 1861.

The Lord of Ten Thousand Years had for months ignored Price Kung's pleas that he return to the Northern Capital, despite his half-brother's warnings that prolonging his absence could imperil the Dragon Throne. He was, the Emperor said, too ill to travel – and his constant debauchery could soon make that pretext a reality.

The Emperor sulked in rustic seclusion because he could not face the humiliation that awaited him in Peking. It would pain him to face the

Ministers who had counselled against his precipitate flight, and it would distress him to see the scorched ruins of the Summer Palaces. Above all, he dreaded receiving the European ambassadors in audience – as he must if he returned. Having won at gunpoint the right to reside in the Northern Capital in violation of Sacred Dynastic Law, the foreigners now insisted upon presenting their letters of accreditation to the Emperor himself. But they refused to perform the kowtow, the triple prostration required of all men granted the honour of looking upon the face of the Son of Heaven. They would gladly kneel, the barbarians said, as they knelt to their own kings, but they would not touch their foreheads to the ground. Not nine times as prescribed, not even once. The Hsien Feng Emperor of the Great Pure Dynasty could not allow the barbarian envoys thus to assert their savage monarchs' equality with the Supreme Ruler of All Under Heaven. At that ultimate affront, Heaven would tremble, the earth would crack, and the Dragon Throne would collapse.

Actually, Yehenala believed, the feeble spirit of the Lord of Ten Thousand Years had finally broken. The rash flight against which she had so vehemently advised, was, however pusillanimous, his last decisive act. Like the ill-omened Viceroy of Canton who had been taken captive to India, the Emperor had lapsed into apathy. He would not fight the barbarians, and he would not make his personal peace with them; he would not exercise his Imperial powers with vigour, and he would not delegate his authority to enable others to act. He did not wish to live, she sensed, but he lacked the courage to die.

Instead, the man whom she had so faithfully served with her body and her mind for a decade sought oblivion in the wine-pot, the opium-pipe, and the arms of Chinese harlots. He recoiled from his sanctified wives as if, having tacitly abdicated his Imperial power over the state, he had also resigned his rights to the Imperial Seraglio. Besides, those lawful mates were all Manchus, and their devotion was a mute reproach to his cowardice. Of course, her own reproaches had never been mute.

The Emperor turned from dissipation only to participate in the diabolistic observances of the lama temples that clung to the crags overlooking the valley of the Hot Springs. Like his nomadic ancestors, he disdained the refined practices of Chinese Buddhism to embrace the savage Tibetan-Mongolian rites – with their manifold reincarnations, their black sorcerers, their trance-dances, and their bestial pornography, which presumably tempered the celibate monks through temptation. The lamas and nuns, she had heard, actually celebrated some holy days with orgies, ritually enacting the most revolting perversions under the sway of hallucinatory drugs.

Yehenala's scroll-painting signed with her doleful couplet was dominated by those sombre monasteries. Beneath their fortified towers she had drawn the palaces of the Imperial Hunting Park built by the great Kang Hsi and Chien Lung Emperors as a manly alternative to the soft pleasures of the Summer Palaces near Peking. Like most ladies, she preferred to sketch birds and flowers, but the raw Manchurian landscape dominated her spirit as the eldritch monasteries dominated the Hunting Park.

Yehenala shivered and pulled a sable-lined cloak around her shoulders. Untenanted for four decades, the palaces of Chien Lung were no longer mock-rustically magnificent, but dilapidated piles. No rugs covered the cold stone floors, and the wind off the steppes whined through fissures in the walls. Broad strips of paint were peeling from the gilt and carmine beams, and the murals depicting ceremonial hunts were splitting beneath their grime. Coarse weeds and evergreen seedlings had rent the broad terraces, and the storms of forty winters had stained their shining marble. The snow melting on the faded Imperial-yellow roofs poured filthy rivulets through the broken tiles.

The Hsien Feng Emperor had chosen to immure himself in this bleak valley to escape the challenges of the civilization bounded by the Great Wall. Deliberately or not, he had also chosen to imperil her future and to blight the prospects of her son, the Heir Presumptive. The Emperor was apparently prepared to die amid this decrepit splendour rather than face the terrors with which his febrile imagination populated Peking. He had not only abdicated the responsibility that was as much the legacy of his forefathers as his wealth and power. He had also turned away from the men and the women who still sustained his Imperial state. In his passion for extinction, he had turned away from Yehenala herself.

The silver writing-brush slipped easily into the carved cinnabar holder among the heavily tufted brushes for broad strokes and those of a single mink-hair for cobweb lines. Yehenala's stilleto fingernails crackled as she stroked her glossy sable ceremonial winter-crown, which mutely recalled the glory that had slipped away from her during the past half-year. On the cracked marble table, the three golden phoenixes surmounting the red-tasselled dome gleamed as brightly as they had in the Forbidden City; and the hundred-odd pearls set in the gold filigree still shone softly luminescent. She wondered if she would ever again stand behind the Emperor wearing that crown.

The weakling had turned his face from her after she vehemently opposed his decision to flee and abandon the Northern Capital to the barbarians. Her blunt counsel he might have forgiven. He could not forgive her deriding the pretexts he invented to deceive the people – and himself: the sham of 'taking the field to command the troops in person'; the pretence that he was merely going hunting; and the ridiculous contention that the barbarians would respect his duty to mount a 'sacred hunt'. Any excuse except the truth: terror-stricken, he was running away like a *yamen*-clerk caught in petty theft. He might even have forgiven her if she had, after they finally reached Jehol on the day the Yüan Ming Yüan burned, not persistently urged him to return to Peking. Finally, he had banished her from his presence.

Ostracized within a Court in exile, she was shunned by the man she still

273

loved despite his spinelessness. Having vanquished hundreds of rivals to win his love, she had triumphantly sealed their love with the most splendid gift any man, even the Lord of Ten Thousand Years, could receive. She had given the man a son, and the Emperor an heir. Yet his spite now deprived her of his affection and destroyed her pride.

Shortly after they had come to Jehol he had also deprived her of the five-year-old Prince Tsai Chün, who was her son and her hope for the future. Declaring Yehenala 'unsuitable to rear the Heir Presumptive', he had given the child into the care of the wife of an Imperial Prince of the collateral line. The Virtuous Concubine was only permitted to glimpse her son during Court ceremonies. Her enemies had told the Emperor that she flirted with the officers of the Imperial Guard. As soon as the lax atmosphere in Jehol gave her the opportunity, the conspirators whispered, she had shown her true nature, which was salacious. The Emperor had believed their lies.

She almost wished she had intrigued with officers of the Guard. But she had – like a fool and unlike others she could name – been chaste in every action and every thought. She had occasionally smiled to thank a subaltern for some service, but she had only smiled – and never twice at the same man. Exalted above all other women by bearing the Heir Presumptive, she had never dreamed of allowing a commoner to defile the sacred vessel that was her body.

Hoofs clattered in the forecourt, and soldiers' voices shouted greetings. The Mother of the Heir should have been secluded from the rough soldiers, but she had been relegated to a tumbledown villa near the chief gate of the wall surrounding the Imperial Hunting Park. She was far removed from the Palace of Serenity, where the Emperor lived, and the adjoining Hall of Perfect Satisfaction, where he held his audiences. His cowardice had exiled the Imperial Court, and his spite had exiled her from that Court.

Despite the interminable journey of the unwieldy Imperial cavalcade, Jehol was no great distance from Peking for robust cavalrymen. The tumult in the forecourt signalled the arrival of a detachment from the Capital after a ride of no more than three days. The officers would be demanding news after reading with awe the black plaque hanging over the gate.

The square ideograms written by the great Kang Hsi Emperor read: *Pi-shu Shan-chuang* – The Hill Manor Shunning Heat. To call a city of palaces a secluded manor-house was not mock modesty, as the snide Chinese whispered. The simple name propitiated Heaven and the jealous gods by avoiding vainglorious boasting. The Imperial Hunting Park, Yehenala mused bitterly, should now be called: *Pi-huo Shan-chu* – The Mountain Hermitage Shunning Life. The fearless Kang Hsi and Chien Lung Emperors had been succeeded by an Emperor who was almost as afraid of living as he was of dying.

Fingernails grated on the splintered door, and the serving-maid seated in the corner of the cavernous room rose to open it. When Yehenala saw the slender figure in the green eunuch's robe standing on the verandah, she flicked her fingers to dismiss the maid. The eunuch drew the door shut before bowing and speaking softly.

'Of course, Little An,' Yehenala said delightedly. 'Of course, if he's not afraid of being contaminated. Naturally, you'll remain. And bring the wretched maid back. Two witnesses are better than one.'

Her favourite eunuch, An Hai-teh, slipped out the door. Not yet twenty years old, he was small and neat, self-effacing and attentive. He was also rapacious; in short, the perfect servant. Though she believed he returned her affection, his greed guaranteed his loyalty. If she prospered, he must prosper, too. Nor could he desert her, since he was indelibly tainted by his service to the woman the Emperor's spite had made a leper. He had already laid up substantial wealth in her service, and he constantly reassured her that their twin stars would soon rise again. She was, when all was said and done, still the Mother of the Heir Presumptive. Ten thousand years, he whispered, would pass much faster than anyone thought if the Son of Heaven continued as he was going. She no longer reproached Little An for discussing the Emperor's debauchery or for thus wishing for the Emperor's death.

The door creaked open, and the Baronet Jung Lu entered on thick-soled riding boots, his black helmet under his arm. His forehead was curiously striated. The grimy band left by his helmet's rim demarcated the pale expanse above from the sun-burnt skin below. His blue tunic was travel stained, the bear of a lieutenant colonel obscured by ochre dust. But his large eyes were eager, and he moved easily despite his burden of fatigue.

'Jung Lu, welcome!' Yehenala spoke first. 'It is kind of you to call on a neglected lady.'

'Highness!' he bowed extravagantly low. 'I cannot believe that you are neglected. You will never be neglected as long as I live.'

'I'm delighted to hear that.' She wondered if he knew that she was in disgrace. 'But you are always gallant. To how many ladies have you sworn eternal devotion?'

'I'm *never* gallant, Highness.' A smile tempered his arrogance. 'Only truthful. You know I've sworn devotion to no other lady in this world . . . *none!*'

She half-believed him. The twenty-four-year-old Baronet, her cavalier since their childhood together, was bound to her even more strongly by affection than by the profitable transactions they had so long conducted together.

She shuddered delicately, remembering for the first time in years her youthful folly in appealing to the Emperor to spare that Shanghai merchant convicted of filial impiety. What was the fellow's name? Yes, Li . . . Li Ai-shih, the only one for whom she had pleaded directly. She had never repeated that mistake, but had thereafter used her influence discreetly. An intimation of her interest had been sufficient to sway Senior Ministers' decisions.

Her efforts had, of course, been well rewarded, and Jung Lu, too, had profited greatly. They would both face decapitation if suspicion regarding their relationship arose. But her conscience was clear, for they had done nothing remotely improper since she entered the Forbidden City. She had never thereafter allowed herself to feel more than sisterly fondness for the young Baronet, and she would certainly not change now.

'You almost convince me,' Yehenala laughed. 'But was it a hard ride?'

'I wouldn't want to do it every day. But I would to see you.'

'Enough gallantry for one day.' Lowering her voice, she glanced at the eunuch and the serving-maid sitting just out of earshot. 'What news of the Capital?'

'The forsythia are budding beneath the city-walls . . . and wild flowers are springing up in the ashes of the Summer Palaces.'

'That bad?'

'Bad enough. Prices are sky-high, and the people grumble because their rice is shipped north to feed the idle Court in Jehol.'

'Let them eat wheat. Most never tasted rice till we Manchus brought prosperity. What brings you to this sad valley?'

'I must report to His Majesty.'

'Report what? New disasters?'

'Nothing unexpected, Highness. Just that the foreign envoys arrived in state five days ago and . . .'

'The barbarians in Peking? Disgusting! Why I . . .'

'. . . and to plead with the Lord of Ten Thousand Years to return,' he continued. 'Prince Kung entrusted me with a confidential message. The Emperor *must* return, he says.'

'What good will that do?'

'My pleas or the Emperor's return?'

'Jung Lu, he will *not* return. And, if he did, he'd do little good.'

'None the less Prince Kung entreats you to use all your power of persuasion with the Emperor. If he does not return, the reactionary faction will run wild, and we're not strong enough to fight the barbarians again so soon. Or the appeasers could come out on top, the fools who see no need to build up our armies. The Emperor must return . . . to placate the common people and restore stability. It is imperative, Prince Kung says, that you use all your influence.'

'I have *no* influence, Jung Lu. I've been cast aside. The Emperor would listen to the scruffiest serving-maid before me.'

'So bad, Nala? I heard rumours, but couldn't believe . . .'

Jung Lu impulsively grasped her arm. She allowed herself that comfort for a moment before patting his hand and gently placing it on the marble table-top.

'I'm no use to Prince Kung or to you . . . no use even to myself. I've ceased to exist.'

'No use to me? Nala, you'll always be greater than any empress to me . . . and far more beautiful. Nala, I'll always . . .'

She smiled mistily at his devotion, which had warmed her all her life, perhaps the only disinterested affection she had ever known. Though the Emperor spurned her, she was still beautiful in Jung Lu's eyes. Her self-confidence revived minutely, and her eyes lingered fondly on his lean features. Her smile vanished after a few seconds, and her oval face set severely.

'Don't speak foolishly . . . and don't call me Nala. It's too painful . . . too dangerous. Now go to the Emperor.'

'Highness, Prince Kung also told me to request your support in other matters. I suppose now, though . . .'

'Tell me quickly anyway. Knowledge is never wasted.'

'As you know, the Emperor gave his assent to setting up the General Office a few months ago.'

She nodded. The *Ko-kuo Shih-wu Tsung-li Yamen*, the General Office for Managing Affairs with Foreign Countries, was the fruit of Prince Kung's new enthusiasm for dealing with the barbarians. After declaring a half year earlier that all Europeans were ferocious beasts untouched by humanity, Prince Kung had recently changed his mind. He now believed the barbarians would honour the promise of peace they had made after extracting humiliating concessions at gunpoint. The Emperor had assented to the establishment of the General Office because he could not be bothered to veto it.

He had also observed that it was not only superfluous, but probably deleterious. The old *Li-fan Yüan*, the Bureau for Managing Barbarians, could do the job as well – or as badly. It had, after all, dealt quite adequately with Mongols, Vietnamese, Koreans, and Japanese for many centuries. But, if Kung wanted a General Office for Foreign Affairs because Europeans conducted diplomacy through Foreign Offices, he could have his new toy. Much good it would do him.

'For the moment, the Office brings all dealings with the barbarians under one roof,' Jung Lu said earnestly. 'But we've got to have a modern army. Prince Kung wants to start with a corps called the Peking Field Force, which is to be armed with modern rifles and artillery. I'm to be a colonel.'

'I congratulate you, Jung Lu. You were never happy behind a desk.'

'I thank Your Highness profoundly. Of course, the Field Force also requires the Emperor's assent. Prince Kung hoped you . . . but you say that's no use now.'

'None whatsoever, Jung Lu. Now go before the Emperor . . .'

He drew his hand back when she folded hers in her lap. He clapped his helmet on his head, wheeled, and strode to the doorway. But he turned to look again at her before leaving.

As the door closed, Yehenala picked up her brush. After a moment, she returned it to the cinnabar holder. Flicking her fingers to dismiss Little An, she told the serving-maid to bring her mother-of-pearl-inlaid make-up box.

She studied her oval face for a full minute in the mirrored lid, frowning at the infinitesimal line between her eyebrows. With sudden decision, she took up a damp powder-puff and began to remove her makeup. When her face was free of cosmetics, she studied herself again in the mirror. Smiling in approval, she applied a fresh coat of white powder. As she accented her cheeks with rouge, she hummed softly. The song, she realised, was 'The Warrior's Return' from her favourite Peking opera.

'And a different gown,' she told the serving-maid. 'I think the hyacinth blue with the phoenixes.'

Jung Lu would probably not return that afternoon. He might not call on her again until he departed for Peking, if then. He was, thank Heaven, too canny to take unnecessary risks. Still, there was no reason why she should not look her best. Unaccountably, she felt much better, almost cheerful.

*

The eunuch called Little An scratched on the splintered door again in the early evening after Yehenala had eaten a light supper. She saw with astonished delight that the Emperor's Chief Eunuch, resplendent in an orange robe adorned with Imperial dragons, stood behind her own smiling attendant. In exile the Emperor no longer chose his bed-partner by selecting one of hundreds of ivory slips inscribed with his ladies' names. Nor was the lady carried to his bed by eunuchs, her nakednes wrapped in a silken rug. It was as well that she had put on his favourite robe.

The Lord of Ten Thousand Years did not receive Yehenala in his bed-chamber, but in the Throne Room of the Palace of Perfect Satisfaction, which was redolent of its cedar walls. His sallow face was plump under a simple cap embroidered with the longevity ideogram, and the lines scoring his haggard cheeks had vanished. But a second look revealed that he was not growing healthier. The dropsy from which he suffered, as well as other complaints, had swollen his features. Distended with fluid, his stomach bulged under his plain robe. His eyes dull and his hands twitching, he was obviously in no mood for love-making.

'Respect! Respect!' The Emperor wheezed as she kowtowed. 'We are glad someone still renders Us respect.'

'Everyone under Heaven renders Your Majesty infinite respect,' still crouching, she replied. 'How would any human dare otherwise?'

'That's all very well, Nala. All very well for you to say it. This Orphan gets precious little respect nowadays.'

Again that self-pitying term, This Orphan. Really, he needed a nurse-maid rather than a concubine.

'Oh, get up, Nala, get up. Come and sit at my feet.'

278

Yehenala mounted the four steps to the yellow-carpeted dais where golden standards flaunting enormous peacock tails flanked the golden throne that stood before a gold-mounted marble screen. When she sat on the edge of the dais, he looked at her dully for a minute before glaring at the two eunuchs, who slipped out of the Throne Room. Despite great practice in assessing his temper, she could not tell whether his eyes were contemptuous or appealing.

'We have summoned you . . . That is, We have caused you to come to Us . . .' His tone was imperative, but his words were disconnected. 'This Orphan . . . We would amuse Ourself. Yes, amuse Ourself by listening to your counsel. Heaven knows, We hear much counsel . . . mostly not very amusing.'

'This slave awaits Your Majesty's command.' She must be very careful. 'Whatever your slave's poor ability, she will . . .'

'Of course you will, Nala, of course you will. You wouldn't dare otherwise . . .' He paused for almost a minute before resuming inconsequentially: 'We have been thinking . . . only thinking, mind you . . . The Virtuous Concubine is not always obedient. None the less We have been thinking . . . We are . . . perhaps, mind you, perhaps . . . of a mind to restore the Heir Presumptive to your care.'

'Your Slave rejoices at Your Majesty's magnanimity. She will devote . . .'

'Be silent, woman, and listen. Your counsel, We said. What do you think of Our younger brother Prince Kung?'

'A good man, Majesty, your slave ventures to believe. Not always as stalwart as he might be. But he grows in wisdom, and he is utterly loyal.'

'So We think, though We . . . However, that's another matter. It's done now. He's ceded all the territories north of the Amur River and east of the Ussuri to the Russians. Four hundred thousand square miles. That scamp of a brother of mine says he had no choice. If the Russian Ambassador hadn't promised support, he couldn't have faced down the French and the British. Their terms, Kung claims, would have been far worse.'

'Majesty, the position *was* impossible. Your Majesty's generals behaved disgracefully. If only they hadn't been so cowardly. But Prince Kung had no choice.'

'No more talk about our fleeing to preserve Our person and the Dynasty? No more reproaches, Nala? You know now We were absolutely right, don't you?'

'Your Majesty,' she breathed.

'Of course We were right. But this new matter. The Russians are offering guns and officers to train Our troops. Kung wants to form a new modern army. Wants to call it . . . what was it? The Peking Field Force, that's it. The core of new armies, he says. What do you think, Nala?'

'A brilliant idea, Majesty. All barbarians are evil and treacherous, but we must use barbarians to control barbarians. When the Armies of the

Yangtze have crushed the Long Haired Rebels, then, Your Majesty will possess powerful new forces with modern weapons. Your Majesty can then drive out all the barbarians and . . .'

'A capital idea, Nala. Just what We thought. A woman, a woman of all things, with more sense than all Our Ministers. We're really of a mind to restore the Heir to . . .'

The Chief Eunuch slipped from behind the marble screen and leaned over to whisper in his sovereign's ear. After listening intently, the Emperor waved the eunuch away and turned again to Yehenala.

'*Yi Kuei* . . .' His voice was bleak. 'Virtuous Concubine, We are informed that you received the officer Jung Lu in your chamber this afternoon. Is that true?'

'It is, Majesty.' She was only minutely alarmed. 'Jung Lu brought a message from my sister in Peking. Your Majesty may condescend to recall that we grew up together, Jung Lu, my sister, and I.'

'You admit it, then?'

'Of course, Majesty. It is true, and no harm . . . or . . . disrespect . . . was intended. My senior eunuch and a serving-maid were, naturally, present.'

'Mitigation, but not sufficient, *Yi Kuei*, not by far.' His cheeks flushed scarlet, and the veins bulged in his temples. 'We decide what is proper in Our Court. We may have prudently decided to vacate the Forbidden City for a time, but We have given no orders that permit such lewdness to . . .'

His face became deadly pale, and his voice faltered. Stunned by his rage, she waited.

'We shall *not* restore the Heir Presumptive to your care.' Neither hesitation nor digression now marred his speech. 'Instead, We may well *remove* Prince Tsai Chün from the succession. Born of such a mother, how could he . . . We shall, perhaps, choose a nephew. However, We shall not act hastily. We shall consult with Our faithful counsellors. But it is likely . . . very likely . . . that We shall find a new heir.'

He smiled in satisfaction. Despite her horror, Yehenala realised that his feeble grasp on reason was slipping. He actually smiled as if he had taken a masterly decision. Yet only a fool or, more likely, a madman could fail to see that disinheriting the Heir Presumptive at this moment of crisis would cast the Imperial clan, the Mandarinate, and the people into utter confusion. Such a decision would gravely imperil his throne, rather than consolidate his power. He smiled, and she remained silent.

'Nothing to say, *Yi Kuei*? Of course not. Even you wouldn't dare. Now go. We do not wish to look upon you again.'

As she walked through the courtyards between the two eunuchs, Yehenala was astonished at her own calmness. Transcending fear, her mind was extraordinarily clear.

Her position was really no worse, in certain ways actually better. She now knew she had no hope of regaining the favour of the man who had raved at her so irrationally. Since she could expect only hostility from the Emperor, her fate lay in her own hands. She must immediately set in motion certain actions she had already planned. He might yet not disinherited the Heir Apparent, but she must provide against his madness. She must now act to save her son and herself.

She smiled in the moonlight, and the Chief Eunuch looked at her in amazement. Little An smiled thinly. He knew what she was thinking, and he knew what they must do.

CHAPTER THIRTY-NINE

June 18, 1861   *Shanghai*

Fronah Haleevie Henriques heard the sweet trilling of the thrushes in the garden and smiled in drowsy contentment. The shrieks of the scavenger gulls fighting for scraps on the Hwangpoo sounded like the mewing kittens rather than the caterwauling toms. Even the squeals of wooden axles on the Bund drifted through the open windows of the Nest of Joy like a benison, and the cries of the street-hawkers in Szechwan Road were a choral.

The whiff of gas was making her light-headed, as William MacGregor had warned. She did not feel disoriented, though the physician had also warned she might be troubled by hallucinations. To the contrary, she luxuriated in the well-being that had supplanted both her pain and her fear. She languidly patted her abdomen, which was a rounded hillock under the linen sheet, and smiled again. Although the heat spilled trickles of perspiration between her swollen, tender breasts, she almost wished the infant would delay much longer. It would be delicious to float for days on the tide of euphoria.

The onset of pain had been sharp, and the contractions had continued for five hours before William MacGregor offered the whiff of nitrous oxide, which laymen called laughing gas. If she had calculated correctly, the child was more than two weeks overdue, but William felt that no cause for alarm. 'Quite common in a *prima gravida*,' he said learnedly. She smiled when he explained that the Latin was: 'medical jargon for a first confinement'.

The child had been growing in her womb so long he must be immense, Maylu observed, though all barbarians were large and ungainly. Like Lionel, the concubine was certain the child would be male, though Fronah and her mother Sarah were neither as certain nor as eager for a boy. The

281

prospective grandfather had no doubt whatsoever. He already insisted that the boy must be called Judah, though Lionel winced at the atavism and Fronah hovered between resentment of her father's imperiousness and amusement at his dynastic pride.

She was also surprised at the detachment from the world she had felt since her abdomen began to swell. Fortunately, the steel-and-whalebone crinolines that supported her sweeping skirts had decorously concealed her condition for almost seven months. She pointed out that advantage to her mother, who still disapproved of European modes. Moreover, the corset, whose constriction she had originally considered the penalty for her emancipation from the outlandish kaftan, was an unparalleled blessing. The maternity model dispatched by Mrs Bell's shop at 22 Charlotte Street, London, not only supported her burden, but expanded with ingenious springs as that burden expanded.

'It doesn't seem quite right.' The missionary doctor had joked. 'The daughters of Eve are spared the punishment of Eve in the enlightened 19th century. Modern medicine and engineering have banished the pain and danger of perpetuating the human race.'

Maylu volubly objected to male interference in the female business of reproduction, and her mother was dubious. None the less William Mac-Gregor's humour and wisdom had sustained her. Everyone, particularly her husband, was so attentive that her pregnancy had been anything but the protracted ordeal she had originally feared. Since Lionel returned from Peking in mid-November of last year to rejoice at her news, she had known the happiest days of her life.

Lionel was transformed by his experience in North China and, she flattered herself, by her love. Tears had started in his light-blue eyes when she told him he was soon to be a father. Again as ardent as he was during the first month of their marriage, he had struggled to control his ardour because of his concern for herself and their unborn child. William MacGregor, who was professionally inquisitive, had laughed when she told him her husband no longer shared her bed. She knew Lionel was nobly denying himself, even if the doctor insisted there was no danger whatsoever until the seventh month.

The spring of the year 1861 had been glorious, brilliant with azaleas and fragrant with honeysuckle. Although Derwents' increasing financial difficulties were troubling his employers, the Samuelson Bank, Lionel generously gave her most of his time. They made excursions into the countryside and enjoyed many dinner-parties, even more frequent now that more respectable ladies lived in the settlement. Though her father's delicacy prevented his confiding in her, she knew that he, too, was well pleased with her husband – and not only because his first grandchild would soon lie in the mahogany cradle of Foochow lacquer. Lionel told her he had settled his debt to her father by selling a few of his porcelain treasures from the Summer Palaces. Saul was also delighted by Lionel's gift: a matching pair of three-foot-high vases of the Kang Hsi reign painted with yellow dragons rising from blue billows. Her mother, who had favoured Lionel from the beginning, was now triumphant at the proof of her good judgment.

The city itself seemed perpetually *en fête*. Her elder brother Aaron was the only Shanghailander who brooded darkly on China's future and his own. Her younger brother David and Gabriel Hyde were 'having a whale of a time playing soldiers', as Lionel laughed, although the Taiping tide had receded. Newly secure from rebel attacks, the foreign community rejoiced at Lord Elgin's humbling of Manchu pride – and ensuring that trade would increase still further. Though horrified by Lionel's account of the vindictive destruction of the Summer Palaces, Fronah, too, was confident that a new era of peace and prosperity had begun when the ambassadors settled in Peking. Not only she herself, but her entire world burgeoned with new promise in mid-June of 1861.

The contractions had begun twenty minutes apart, increasing in frequency until pain transfixed her at three-minute intervals. After William MacGregor's whiff of laughing gas, her muscles relaxed and the pain receded. She felt only fuddled pleasure for almost an hour before she was again gripped by pain.

Moisture seeped between her thighs an instant later, and a gush of fluid soaked her nightdress. It was not painful, just unpleasant.

'The waters have broken,' her mother said authoritatively. 'It won't be long now.'

'Mrs Haleevie, it could be several hours,' William MacGregor remarked from a great distance. 'It's a breach, you know.'

Absorbed by the struggle beginning inside her body, Fronah shut out the intrusive voices. She would, she decided, distract herself by thinking of pleasant things. She would think of Lionel. To her surprise, that thought made matters far worse. At that moment she hated him, and, lanced by shafts of pain, she swore aloud in Shanghainese.

Maylu smiled grimly. Her countrywomen often swore at the men whose pleasure inflicted pain on them. The concubine was astonished when Fronah's tone altered. She was praising her husband, babbling of her love for him and reciting his virtues.

*

Lionel Henriques sat unspeaking with Saul Haleevie under the tented-ceiling of the morning-room. They had waited interminably, it seemed, since Fronah's pains began just past noon, almost six hours earlier. Lionel was drinking his fifth whisky and soda, while his normally abstemious father-in-law sipped brandy. Silence lay heavy between them, though not entirely because their thoughts were in the bedroom above.

'I'll do it,' Saul said abruptly, 'even if it's a girl.'

283

"Thanks so much,' the Englishman replied. 'That's a great weight off my mind.'

'Perhaps I shouldn't. But a fresh start's worth trying. A fresh start for a new life.'

'You'll see, Saul, it'll work out well. You won't be sorry, I assure you.'

'Fronah doesn't know, does she?' Saul asked suspiciously.

'Of course not, Saul. You said I wasn't to . . . And when my old mater goes, I'll make it up.'

'No need, Lionel, as I said. Above all, I don't want Fronah worried.'

Excused his debt of almost £10,000 as a present from his father-in-law to the infant striving towards life in the bedroom, Lionel should have been delighted. He had calculated correctly. Saul Haleevie was normally as stringent in demanding payment of his accounts as he was scrupulous in honouring his own obligations. Though Lionel thanked God that his father-in-law looked at a debt within the family differently, he did not feel the triumph of a successful gambler.

Saul Haleevie might cancel his debt, but Lieutenant General Sir Hope Grant would hardly be as magnanimous. The thousand-odd pounds he owed for the porcelains would have to be repaid somehow. The stern Scottish soldier must already have discovered that his promissory notes were just that: empty promises.

Samuelsons would not pay £10 on his signature, much less a thousand. His brother Rupert would not help, not even to spare the Henriques family another scandal. Rupert had made that quite clear when their mother died a year earlier. Lionel's quarterly remittance would continue as long as he did not return to England, but there would be no more lump sums, 'no further rescue operations'.

How, he wondered desperately, would he raise a thousand pounds? Certainly not from the porcelains he'd had to store in Derwents' godown in boxes labelled pig-iron. Only that deception kept Saul from realising how deeply committed he was. Only by hiding the porcelains had he prevented Fronah's learning that he had not sold them to repay her father. He would sell them all in an instant if he could. But there was simply no market. He had miscalculated disastrously there.

Old Curiosity Soo was stubborn. He could not, he said, dishonour his name by purchasing treasures looted from the Summer Palaces. Besides, he added practically, it would be as much as his head was worth if he were found out. Of course, he'd consider taking them off his old friend Henriques's hands as a favour. He'd even pay a price Lionel reckoned a hundredth of their value for goods he'd have to trickle on to the market over a number of years.

That proposition was worse than useless, since every Chinaman in Shanghai would know the seller. The old rogue had probably put the word out already. Few native collectors, however avid, would buy the Emperor's treasures. Not patriotism, Lionel suspected, but self-preservation inspired that refusal. He must either sell at Old Curiosity Soo's derisory price or not at all.

His predicament would be bad enough if the notes drawn on Samuelsons were his only problem. Sir Hope Grant's wrath would destroy his position in Shanghai and dispel whatever credibility he still retained in Saul's eyes. But a greater danger hung over him. If the old harridan in the South City carried out her threat, even Fronah would abandon him. He simply had to get hold of more money for that blackmailing crone, though he'd already poured every penny he could find into her hands. Lionel Henriques laughed sourly, and Saul Haleevie looked up from his intent contemplation of his brandy-snifter.

'Sorry, Saul,' Lionel said. 'Just thinking of the joy when it's all over. I'm desperately concerned about Fronah. Can't help it, you know.'

'It didn't sound like joy to me. I know how you felt.'

Saul would never know how he felt. The merchant was too pious to lay himself open to blackmail. The pleasure was delightful, but, by God, it was costly – and likely to be much more costly soon. Lionel bit his lip to keep from exclaiming bitterly. He'd almost forgotten the additional threat. If Saul discovered the full facts regarding the silver loan he had negotiated in Hong Kong a few years ago, it would be the end. However, he wouldn't torment himself with that remote possibility. His present troubles were heavy enough.

Lionel heard the bedroom door close, and after an interminable minute, Dr William MacGregor shuffled into the dining-room. His face was pale, and his forehead was lined with fatigue beneath his dishevelled sandy hair. He smiled with an effort.

'A boy, gentlemen,' he said. 'I congratulate you both most heartily.'

'And Fronah?' Lionel asked.

'She's fine, perfectly well. So's the baby.'

'You're not looking well, Doctor,' Saul said. 'A brandy, perhaps.'

'Looking well? No, I'm not so fine. It was the devil of a breach delivery. Had to use forceps. He's rather large, your son, Lionel. Nine pounds three ounces.'

'But he's all right, isn't he?' The grandfather was more anxious than the father. 'Judah's fine, too, isn't he?'

'Absolutely, Mr Haleevie. A perfect specimen and deuced big, as I said.'

Saul grinned with delight. He could forgive his irresponsible son-in-law a good deal more than £10,000 in return for this joy. He splashed brandy into a snifter for the doctor and lifted his own.

'*L'chaim*! . . . To life!' he said. 'To life . . . and Judah!'

285

CHAPTER FORTY

When the eunuch Little An brought the small Prince Tsai Chün to her just before dawn, Yehenala had been fully dressed for an hour. Her thick hair, glossy with scented pomade, swept in two raven-black wings off her forehead. The serving-maids had spent almost two hours applying full Court make-up over the moistened rice-powder that whitened her face. A flock of paired mandarin ducks, the symbol of connubial harmony, floated on her lavender robe, and the summer-crown that completed her formal regalia lay on the marble table. The new scarlet tassels glittered beneath wire-tracery studded with rubies and garnets around a single splendid pearl. Even her shoes were new, immaculate white kidskin sheathing their six-inch platforms.

'*Hau-chiu, Ma-ma* . . .' the five-year-old Heir Presumptive lisped. 'Such a long time, Mama. Somebody said you went away.'

'I'm here now, my treasure,' she soothed him. 'I'll always be here whenever you need me.'

'The Lady Yee is never cross, Mama.' His small body squirmed in her arms, and his agate eyes glinted with juvenile cunning. 'Not like you, Mama. She never scolds me.'

'I'm sorry, treasure. Sometimes, your Mama thinks of other things. You know I have to help His Majesty, your Papa, with important matters. You understand, don't . . .'

'I don't mind, Mama. But I wanted to see you. I told those stupid eunuchs over and over again.'

'You'll come to me whenever you want from now on. Soon, we'll be together always, I promise. And today we'll see your Papa and wish him joy on his birthday. We'll wish him a long, long life, ten thousand years of life.'

'Everyone wishes Papa ten thousand years, Mama. It's funny. Always ten thousand years.'

'Because your Papa is the Emperor . . . And everyone loves him, treasure.'

'I know that, Mama.' His plump lips curled complacently. 'And I'm the number one prince. Some day, I'll be Emperor, Lady Yee says. After ten thousand years. Mama, are you the Empress?'

'Not yet, treasure, not yet. But some day soon, very soon. Now be a good lad and let me finish getting ready.'

Yehenala set the small boy on his feet. Clumsy in miniature riding-boots with rigid soles, he almost fell when he stretched to take the stick of candied crab-apples from her hand. He was still the Heir Presumptive, the number one prince, as he said, and she congratulated herself as she watched him lick the sugar from the carb-apples. He was still the Heir Presumptive because she had marshalled all her resources to keep his spiteful father from carrying out the threat to disinherit him.

The Baronet Jung Lu had ridden for twenty-six hours without a halt, exhausting relays of horses from the Imperial Post Stations, to carry her pleas to Peking. Fearful that his own return would inflame the Imperial rage, Jung Lu entrusted Prince Kung's message to a brother officer.

The Emperor's best-loved brother sent him an intimate letter, which was profusely courteous, but uncharacteristically direct. He was, Prince Kung wrote, appalled by the rumour, which he could hardly believe true, that his wise elder brother planned to disinherit the Heir Presumptive. If his Majesty did so, the Imperial Clan would be distressed – and the Mandarinate would be horrified. Already dismayed by the Emperor's protracted absence from the Northern Capital, the people would be frantic at that apparent proof of the Sacred Dynasty's instability. The Prince-Administrator did not flatly threaten to resign if his brother acted so rashly. But he ominously regretted his inability to control the consequent disorder.

Two days later, the Baronet Jung Lu himself returned with a second private communication to the Son of Heaven. Prince Chun, the seventh Imperial brother, who was the husband of Yehenala's youngest sister, also pleaded with the Emperor to change his mind. The Imperial family, he wrote, might split if the Emperor designated a nephew, rather than his own son, Heir Presumptive. Dynastic Law, of course, empowered the monarch to choose his own successor. Any prince of the next generation could offer the obligatory sacrifices to the Imperial ancestors and to his immediate predecessor. But, Prince Chun counselled, it would be unwise to try the loyalty of either the people or the Imperial Guard, since both were devoted to the Virtuous Concubine. When the present crisis had passed, the Son of Heaven could take whatever action he pleased, guided, as always, by Heaven's inspiration. But not just now.

The Emperor had finally yielded, as he always yielded nowadays. It was less trouble to give in than to insist. Besides, he could not dismiss the urgent advice of his brothers, who selflessly renounced their own sons' chances to mount to the Dragon Throne. The Emperor yielded – and sulked. Balked of public revenge, his spite had to content itself with barring Yehenala from his presence, even at formal Court ceremonies.

The barrier was now to be breached. His brothers remonstrated with him again when they learned that he planned to exclude Yehenala from the formal celebration of his thirtieth birthday. Even her enemies, who were his counsellors in exile, believed that public rebuff would serve no purpose. Since the Emperor had not removed her son from the succession, slighting the Mother of the Heir would only win her sympathy – and strengthen her position. The Emperor had again yielded with ill grace, and Yehenala was attired for her triumphant public return to Court.

The Lady Yee, governess of the Heir Presumptive, resented being required to allow the small Prince to visit his mother. The scheming Yehenala not only aroused her feminine malice, but impeded her husband's ambitions. The junior lady-in-waiting assigned to accompany the Heir fretted in silence when he soiled his turquoise-silk robe with the sticky crab-apples. She dared not protest, though she would be chastised if the golden dragon on his chest were smeared with syrup when he joined his father to receive the courtiers' congratulations.

Yehenala was unaware of the junior lady-in-waiting's perturbation in her maternal delight at the small figure standing before the silver screen painted with black-necked swans in flight. The baby features were still unformed, but the sparse, high-cocked eyebrows were undeniably his father's. His eyes and the oval shape of his face, were, however, her legacy. The face that would some day inspire awe beneath the Imperial Crown bore the stamp of the Yehe tribe.

'You must go now, treasure.' She adjusted his cap and patted his bottom. 'Your Papa's anxious to see you.'

'Why can't I come with you, Mama?'

'You must stand on the dais beside your Papa's throne. But ladies stand below. That is proper etiquette.'

'Etiquette, always etiquette!' the Prince protested. 'But We must act properly, mustn't We?'

'Yes, treasure, always. And you mustn't say We . . . not yet.'

He put his chubby arms around her neck and rubbed his face against hers, smearing her make-up. Unconcerned, she hugged him tighter before reluctantly releasing him. As Little An opened the door, the junior lady-in-waiting was already scrubbing the crab-apple smears with the damp cloth she always carried.

Yehenala savoured her coming triumph while her maids repaired her make-up. For the first time in two months, she had embraced her son, joyous at holding him and proud of his intelligence. His brief visit was itself a significant political victory, while her palanquin would soon convey her to the Birthday Rites. Her triumphant reappearance would mean not only personal vindication, but a major political victory.

Perhaps the Emperor was really changing, she pondered, not merely yielding to the pressure exerted by his brothers and his counsellors. He had a year earlier reached thirty *sui*, the age at which, the Sage Confucius had pronounced, a man stands erect, having become fully adult. The barbarians, she knew, reckoned age from the actual date of birth, and he had lived just thirty years today. The barbarians were illogical; having lived so long in the womb, an infant was truly a year old at birth. However, the times were out of joint, and the Hsien Feng Emperor was notoriously tardy in his development. Perhaps he would today begin to act like a mature man, rather than a pampered child.

He had shown a flicker of independent judgment in his rebuke of the Court Astronomers, who prepared astrological forecasts. While her maids put away their brushes and pigments, Yehenala re-read the Imperial Rescript issued the preceding day. It was a model of good sense. Recalling that the astronomers had earlier warned that the appearance of a great comet presaged the wrath of Heaven, the Emperor remarked with asperity that they had now declared the conjunction of the planets most auspicious for his birthday.

Since We came to the Throne, he then observed with somewhat more regard to appearance than truth, *We have consistently refused to credit auspicious omens, with good reason, considering the spreading rebellions in the south and the pitiable state of Our people.* He had been unable to refrain from expressing the hope that the *present auspicious conjunction of the planets portends happier days and the speedy end of the rebellion.* The spoiled child was speaking again. But he had directed the Court Astronomers *not* to report the new omen to the Historical Chroniclers for inclusion in the annals of the reign, *so that all men may know We possess a devout and sober mind.*

Though self-serving, the Rescript showed not only sobriety, but maturity. Besides, no Emperor could govern effectively if he did not look to his own interests. Perhaps the tide of his mind was truly turning.

Yehenala rose when Little An scratched on the door. It was unseemly to feel eagerness, and it was undignified to display eagerness. But her eunuch knew how she longed to return to Court.

'I'm ready, Little An,' she said. 'The palanquin, it's here?'

'No, Highness.' His face was grim. 'I have not summoned the palanquin, Highness. Your presence is *not* requested.'

'It has already been requested. Summon the palanquin immediately.'

'It would not be wise, Highness. I have already taken it upon myself to tell the escort you are ill.'

'Ill? How dare you?'

'Highness, the Lord of Ten Thousand Years has forbidden you to appear at the Birthday Rites.'

'Forbidden?'

'Specifically, Highness, forbidden. I am stricken with grief.'

Yehenala spat Manchu obscenities. She hurled her crown to the floor and ground her high-platformed shoe on the gold filigree. The wires snapped, and the great pearl crumbled into powder. She snatched up her inkstone and drew her arm back to throw it at Litte An.

As abruptly, she replaced the inkstone and sat in her high-backed chair. Raging would not help her. She must consider the implications of the Emperor's monstrous insult. For two minutes she sat unmoving.

'He believes he can humiliate me with impunity.' Her formal tone concealed her fury. 'And he is absolutely correct!'

'Correct, Highness?'

'For the moment. You did well to tell the escort I was taken ill. Help me off with the robe. I must go to bed immediately. And see that the Imperial Guard learn that I am ill.'

'They won't believe it, Highness.'

'I do not wish them to believe it . . . only to behave as if they did. I want no demonstration. Not just yet.'

'Highness, whatever you say, this will be a scandal.'

'Of course, but the Guards must not protest yet. Tell them I command them to behave normally. There must be no provocation.'

'And that is all, Highness?'

'No, not quite. Messages must go to Peking. Prince Kung must act. The Emperor is obviously not in control of himself. His mind is unbalanced.'

'Highness!' the eunuch murmured in reply to her *lèse majesté*.

'Tell me, Little An, what are the eunuchs saying? They don't believe the Emperor's condition is improved, do they? Who actually drafted the Rescript to the Court Astronomers?'

'Highness, the Son of Heaven is not improved, but grows worse. And I hear Prince Yee drafted the Rescript.'

'The Emperor still takes deer's blood for his health?'

'Deer's blood among many other remedies, herbal and animal. But he does not improve. His mind wanders, and his body grows weaker.'

'Well, Little An, we must do everything we can to assist the Emperor.'

'Highness, you *do* mean everything we possibly can? *Everything*?'

'Little An, it is our duty to help the Emperor.' Her voice was flat, divested of all emotion. 'We must do everything we possibly can. *Everything*!'

CHAPTER FORTY-ONE

August 3, 1861   *Shanghai*

The veranda of the Nest of Joy was an islet of light as the tide of dusk crept over Shanghai on August 3rd, 1861. Furry-winged moths hurled themselves against the bulbous glass-shades shielding the hurricane-lamps, their impact a roll of drums under the shrill chorus of the locusts in the oleanders. Some dropped into the saucers beneath the lamps, while others fluttered away stunned – to renew their assault as soon as they recovered. The candles were ringed with dying moths, wings scraping on the tile-topped table. The most vigorous swooped triumphantly – to flare bright in the flames. The glass-shades were soon choked with charred bodies.

Though fascinated by the macabre aerial ballet, Fronah Henriques would have like to blow out the candles. Since her husband was immersed in his newspaper, she resigned herself to that constant reminder of mortality.

'The Buddhist monks burn themselves, too,' she mused. 'I wonder if they know what they're doing any more than these moths.'

'What's that?' Lionel Henriques looked up from the smudged print of the *North China Herald*. 'I didn't quite catch . . . .'

'Nothing really, Lionel. I was only thinking aloud.'

'That's fine.' He irritably adjusted the reading-glasses he could no longer pretend he did not need. 'You know that fellow's still skulking. Extraordinary!'

'What fellow, Lionel?'

'Sorry, my dear. The Emperor, of course. Still skulking in that place in Manchuria. I can never pronounce it.'

'Jehol, dear,' she smiled. 'Hot Springs.'

'Don't be so deuced superior, Fronah.' He replied without rancour. 'If he were a gentleman, he'd go back to Peking and get on with it. He could set the seal on the new era. Peaceful cooperation for prosperity . . . the Chinese trading happily . . . even learning to use modern arms. That's fine, as long as it doesn't go too far. They mustn't get too strong or . . .'

'You're desperately interested in Chinese affairs nowadays, aren't you, Lionel. It's quite a change.'

She shouldn't really tease him, for he was sensitive and, occasionally, humourless. He had witnessed two crucial events of the past four years: the Mandarins' seizure of the lorcha *Arrow* and the Allies' march on Peking. Because he had seen them himself, those events now loomed transcendentally important in his mind – and he discoursed on China with great facility.

'You and your father are not the only ones who can comprehend the Chinese.' An aggrieved note crept into his voice. 'Or that American Hyde. He's still learning Chinese, I hear. That's all right for diplomats and women, but an officer? I ask you!'

'Quite, Lionel,' she replied. 'Quite so.'

She would not tease him again, though his earnestness tempted her. They were quite the old married couple after four years. They rubbed along comfortably, despite her occasional annoyance at his pretentiousness and his occasional irritation at her pertness. The ardour he had so restrained before Judah's birth had, however, not revived. Still, her son was not yet seven weeks old, and Lionel was most attentive in every other respect. She should be very happy with a devoted husband and a handsome son.

'Hyde'll never learn Chinese properly,' Lionel persisted. 'It's one thing to be brought up with it like you. Otherwise, it's impossible for a civilized tongue to twist itself around the lingo. Even your . . . ah . . . brother Aaron says so. But you're not listening, Fronah.'

'I am Lionel, I assure you. You were saying that Aaron . . .'

As often as not, Lionel reflected, Fronah didn't really hear what he said because she was obsessed with the baby. He was, naturally, delighted to have a son, and the doting grandfather was not inclined to question his tangled finances. Moreover, there had been no more talk of boredom or a trip to London. As he'd hoped, motherhood has altered his wife, but the infant had indeed tied her down. And the milky smell that floated around her was almost revolting.

She was, he supposed, a fine-looking woman – if one liked the overblown type. Not his taste, but many men would find her high colour and her swelling figure attractive. When she smiled, the curve of her cheek and the glint in her brown eyes was piquant, almost gamine-like. However, her matronly serenity since the lad's birth was not at all attractive. Of course, it wouldn't be, he reminded himself slyly, would it? Yet, he supposed, she would appear slim, even too slender for most men, who slavered after over-developed females with bovine bosoms.

'Aaron was saying no European can learn Chinese properly,' Lionel resumed. 'Not speaking of you, of course.'

'Thank you, Lionel. I'm glad to be the exception.'

'Something else he said. Damned interesting . . .'

'I didn't know Aaron and you were close. He puts me off nowadays. He's so sour and sarcastic since he failed the Civil Service Examination the third time.'

'Aaron's a good chap. A splendid chap for a Chink . . . ah . . . Chinaman. He's not bitter at Europeans, only the Manchus. He says it's no wonder Lord Elgin permitted the looting of the Yüan Ming Yüan. After all, Chinese armies have to loot.'

'Have to loot? Aaron said that?'

'Yes, my dear. How else would they get paid, he says. And he recited a little jingle. Seems it goes back centuries: *If the generals don't pay up, the troops won't show up. If they can't plunder, the ranks'll come asunder.* Quite amusing, isn't it.'

'Not terribly, though I suppose Aaron's right.' She added, though she knew it would annoy him: 'The great strategist Sun Tze advised generals: *The soldiers must have their rewards, so that they see the advantage of defeating the enemy.*'

'Always my little female scholar!' he laughed. 'But you do see it. Elgin was right . . . even by your blessed Chinese standards. Though he shouldn't have burned the Summer Palaces.'

'We agree on that, Lionel. Destroying the Yüan Ming Yüan was barbaric. But so was the looting . . . and your blessed auction. We're supposed to be civilized. You can't compare a medieval rabble like the Manchus and the soldiers of the greatest civilized power in the modern world. You can't . . .'

'Fronah, you're being contentious. I think I'll take a stroll. It's a bit close tonight.'

'If you wish, my dear. But you were complaining that I wasn't interested. And then when . . .'

'There's a vast difference between interest and argumentativeness.' He twisted the signet-ring on his little finger, and the gold gleamed in the lamplight. 'Perhaps you'll learn that some day, Fronah. Ah well, not to worry. Don't wait up. I may be late.'

His lips brushed her cheek, and he threw his linen jacket over his arm. His white figure strode briskly through the shrubbery to the gate opening on the Bund. Apparently untroubled by the heat, his gait was jaunty. A minute after the gate clanged behind Lionel, a man in dark clothing closed the gate noiselessly behind himself. Fronah recognised the rotund figure of the number-one houseboy and wondered briefly why he was furtive. However, Lao King's time was his own after he had finished his duties. His stealthy departure was also his own concern.

'The master's gone out, Little Lady, hasn't he?' the concubine Maylu asked softly from the darkness. 'Did anyone go with him?'

'I though I saw Lao King.'

'That devil, too. Little Lady, I think we should call the sedan-chair. It's a nice evening for a ride.'

'I can't Maylu. Judah'll be hungry. Take your maid with you.'

'That wouldn't do, not at all. I'd like you to come with me, please. Perhaps it's important.'

'And Judah? He'll be howling.'

'Not if you don't wake him. It's all nonsense, this barbarian notion of waking babies up to feed them so they'll sleep. The baby-amah can look after him if he does wake.'

'I really shouldn't. You're sure Judah'll be all right? Well . . . if it's that important . . .'

'It is, I assure you. Or it could be.'

Fronah knew she would get no more out of the concubine, who could occasionally be as infuriatingly tight-lipped as she was normally indiscreet. Her 'important' matter was probably trivial. But the older woman had strong claims on both her affection and her loyalty. Yielding to Maylu's love of melodrama, as well as her superior knowledge of infants, Fronah followed her to the Szechwan Road gate. She would have been surprised if the double sedan-chair had not been waiting for them.

As the four chair-bearers swung south towards the French Concession, the globular lanterns on the ends of their carrying-poles swayed, casting yellow rays. Entire families lay asleep on straw-mats spread beside the roads. The men's torsos were bare in the heat, while the women wore just enough to preserve their modesty. Their possessions were heaped around them in wooden boxes and rattan valises. All Shanghai, particularly the foreign settlement, was crammed with refugees.

The slapping of the coolies' bare feet on cobblestones was succeeded by their sloughing through the dust of unpaved roads as they approached the narrow bridge over Yangkingpang Creek. Six years after the French had been granted the additional territory bounded on the north by the creek, that wedge of land remained largely undeveloped. Refugees' huts clustered in the spaces between the few buildings. When the chair-bearers' pace did not slacken, Fronah looked sharply at Maylu. The concubine's features were stubbornly uncommunicative in the moonlight.

The coolies finally halted before the gate of the South City. Maylu whispered to the corporal of the guard and listened intently to his soft answers. When she handed him a string of copper cash, the doors creaked ajar to admit the sedan-chair.

'Go slow, now,' Maylu told the coolies. 'No hurry for us.'

After winding through a maze of alleys, the chair entered a lane Fronah knew well. The fan-makers were putting up their shutters, but pedestrians clustered around itinerant barbers and restaurateurs, while eager children surrounded candy-hawkers and toy-peddlers. It was too early for sleep in the South City, too early and far too hot. Fronah started when the coolies halted at the mouth of an alley so narrow she and Maylu could not walk abreast. The drying fish strung between the housefronts brushed their hair.

Fronah finally knew their destination, if not their purpose. She motioned Maylu to precede her, for the climb to the third floor was hard for bound feet. Fronah herself was panting slightly when they reached the door marked *Old Mother Wang, Midwife*. She had not been winded when she raced up those stairs to change into Chinese costume before meeting Iain Matthews five years earlier.

Maylu pushed the door open to reveal that time had worked no alteration in Old Mother Wan's establishment. Sitting unchanged among the unchanging implements of her craft, the midwife nodded.

Fronah's mouth opened in astonishment when she saw her stout houseboy cosily sipping tea by the light of cheap tallow candles. Maylu hissed at her to be silent and eased open the door to the bedroom cubicle.

Memory afflicted Fronah. She recalled the concubine's hysteria at seeing the blood on her thighs. The memory was so vivid that she saw only that scene.

When Maylu nudged her, Fronah returned to the present. She saw her husband, lying on the wood-plank bed and drawing on a long opium-pipe. His patrician features were blurred by the fumes that trickled from his nostrils. She felt her imagination had conjured him up in the cubicle, which was illuminated only by the flicker of a miniature hurricane-lamp.

Willing him to disappear, Fronah closed her eyes. When she opened them, Lionel still lay on the bed.

Her thoughts whirled incoherently. Tragically, Lionel needed opium, but why did he come to this sordid tenement? She would have been unhappy had she known, but she would assuredly have tried to help him – and she would never have driven him to such squalor. He knew she hated opium, but why must he leave his home to smoke his pipe? And why had

Maylu, who liked an occasional pipe herself, contrived this dramatic revelation?

Lionel had not moved during the few seconds she had been standing in the doorway. She saw with surprise that he was quite naked in the heat, though he was normally modest. She saw with astonishment that he was partially aroused, though he was so infrequently ardent with herself.

Lionel carried through the motion begun as the door opened, and she realised that he was still unaware of her presence. He extended the pipe, and a small hand reached out of the darkness for the glinting bamboo tube. His hand groped towards a pale gleam in the shadows behind him.

A naked young girl with budding breasts entered the dim light. She was giggling coyly, and she was, Fronah noted automatically, not quite pubescent. Lionel's arm clasped the child's waist, and his hand played between the child's thighs. A second girl emerged to encircle his erect penis with her elfin child's fingers.

Fronah slammed the door shut. Unseeing, she dashed through the anteroom and down the narrow staircase. She ran down the alley, brushing aside startled pedestrians, until she reached the sedan-chair. The coolies stood stolidly immobile when she screamed at them to move.

Teetering on her maimed feet in the moonlight, Maylu appeared a few minutes later. The coolies trotted off at her sharp command.

Fronah turned her back and shrugged the concubine's sympathetic hand away. Her tears finally started, and she sobbed as they passed through the French territory. When the sedan-chair approached Szechwan Road, her weeping subsided, and she heard the concubine's consoling murmur. But Fronah would not deepen her humiliation by speaking in the coolies' hearing.

When they entered the garden, she demanded: 'How could you, Maylu? How could you do that to me?'

'Would you have believed me, Little Lady?' the concubine asked gently. 'If I only told you?'

'The shame, Maylu, the shame. To think that he . . . that I . . . Maylu, what can I do?'

'You must decide, Little Lady. Only you can decide. But it was my duty to show you.'

'The houseboy . . . Lao King?'

'Obviously, he arranged it for the . . . the master.'

'Why, Maylu, why?'

'Why is he . . . your husband . . . that way? I cannot say. Many men are like that, only liking children. Lao King wished to protect his own daughter. Your husband wanted Lao King's daughter.'

'It's fearful, Maylu, horrible. I'm sorry for him, but I'm not a Chinese wife. I can't tolerate . . . I can't . . . the humiliation. Spurning me for . . . for those infants. The vileness! If it were just opium . . . But how can I bear . . .'

'He can't help it, Little Lady. If he only paid Old Mother Wang, I'd never have known. He's really depraved . . . your husband . . . won't pay his debts.'

'Won't pay his debts?' she laughed hysterically. 'That's funny . . . very funny. He's depraved . . . utterly depraved. He won't pay his debts.'

'I'll give you something to make you sleep. But, first, feed little Judah. It'll make you feel better. You'll see.'

*

October 5, 1861   *Shanghai*

Lionel Henriques did not return to the Nest of Joy that night. While her household pursued its normal routine the following day, Fronah sat in the yellow-velvet chair in the morning-room and listened for his footsteps in the hall. The servants revealed that they knew of her tragedy only by their excessive desire to please, a flicker of subservience alien to independent Chinese. Mutual reticence preserved the decencies, though she knew they considered neither opium-addiction nor, even, paedophilia a gross perversion – indeed hardly unnatural. They respected her grief, though they could not comprehend it.

Curiously, Lao King, the number-one houseboy, appeared least affected. He was, as always, brusquely efficient, though his eyes slid away from her gaze. He would not apologise for the injury he had done her by pandering to the master's tastes, because he had done so to preserve his own daughter. She would have to sack him, Fronah decided, but she would find him a good job.

Though the servants neither quarrelled raucously nor cracked ribald jokes, the Nest of Joy otherwise maintained its normal efficient hum, punctuated by the clanking of the cast-iron polisher on the teak floors. But Lionel's betrayal had destroyed the purpose of the villa. The ritual of housekeeping was as pointless as a play performed to an empty theatre. What, Fronah wondered hopelessly, would she say when he did return?

Fronah slept little the next night, despite the bitter draught Maylu forced on her, and she insisted on having Judah's cradle beside her bed. She lay awake long after midnight, haunted by her worry for Lionel and her fears for the future. She only knew what she must *not* do. While not helping herself, confiding in her parents would cause them anguish. She rose from time to time, believing she heard Judah whimpering, but her son was sleeping soundly.

Could Lionel, she wondered, have done something desperate? However, he lacked the passionate disposition of men who took their own lives. Yet, she reflected bitterly, she had thought him also lacking in carnal passion.

After a few hours of troubled dreams, she awoke to a sense of

296

overwhelming deprivation. It was a minute before she remembered the reason.

That lapse cheered her slightly. The great world had not come to an end with her discovery of her husband's perversions, but continued to revolve as usual. Nor was that discovery necessarily the end of her personal world.

She would, somehow, cope. Perhaps William MacGregor could cure Lionel's depravity. Perhaps he was only emulating Chinese men's passion for unbudded virgins. Perhaps he and she would now go away, leaving the vices of Shanghai behind him. Having taken that tentative decision, she was almost cheerful as she dressed.

Fronah did not hear the tread in the hall for which she had waited. She was not aware that Lional had finally returned until she heard him asking the houseboy for a pot of coffee. He was clean-shaven and clear-eyed when he joined her in the morning-room, his white-linen suit freshly washed and pressed.

'That tastes good.' He sipped appreciatively. 'I did miss my coffee. Missed you, too, my dear.'

'I'm so sorry,' she replied in the same tone. 'A pity. I'd have sent you coffee if I'd known where . . .'

'Not at all, my dear Fronah. How could you know?'

His normal hauteur appeared unshaken. He was quite composed, perhaps faintly amused. She gazed at his lean face, searching for signs of his depravity. His features displayed neither vice nor contrition.

'Well, my dear,' he finally remarked, 'that's that, isn't it?'

'That's that? Is that all you have to say? All you can say?'

'What else is there to say? Any rate, I must get on with my packing.'

'Packing?' He had managed to put her on the defensive. 'You're going away? Why must you go?'

'Now, I hardly thought after . . . after that . . . you'd want me lounging around.'

'Lionel, you've mistaken me – and yourself. I don't want you to go. I want to help you. What can we do? I thought . . .?'

'Fronah, I'm sorry, very sorry.' His mask of insouciance slipped, and he leaned towards her imploringly. 'It was a bad day . . . a catastrophic day . . . for you when you married me.'

'Catastrophic?' she repeated tremulously. 'Lionel, we've had a wonderful four years. I'm certain I can help. Together, we can . . . .'

'You know, Fronah, I'm awed, truly awed. It does you credit . . . great credit. I thought you'd be furious, but, even so . . . .'

'I am, Lionel. I'm absolutely furious at your behaviour. And now, running away. But I still love you and I want . . .'

'. . . I can't help the way I'm made.' He ignored her interruption. 'Why do you think I'm here in Shanghai at all?'

'I have no idea. I thought about it, but I really have no idea. You've never been too candid, you know. I should hate you. Your vile . . .'

'Because of my . . . ah . . . predilections. The family wanted me out of England. They make me an allowance as long as I don't come back. If I did, there wouldn't be a penny . . .'

'I never dreamed. I thought you were a man of property. And your work for Samuelsons?'

'A smoke-screen, I'm afraid, my dear, a favour from Samuelsons to the family. I'm actually what's called a remittance man. Regular . . . though not generous . . . remittances as long as I stay out of England. The family's dead scared of scandal. Can't say I blame them.'

Fronah was stunned by his compulsive revelations. She wondered why he was determined to paint himself so black.

'If I'd only kept to the little girl brothels, it might've been all right. But I couldn't keep my hands off the gardener's daughter. A lovely little thing she was. They hushed that up. But when . . . little Pamela Snelgrove . . . she was only eleven, but she loved it as much as I did. More, in fact. She led *me* on, think of it. I *had* to leave, then.'

'Lionel, I can help you,' Fronah insisted. 'I know I can.'

'If anyone could, it would be you, my dear. But I'm afraid not. It's too strong, this . . . ah . . . predilection of mine. Besides, that's not the only . . . maybe not the chief reason I must go.'

'What else, Lionel? Dear God, what else *can* there be?'

'My debts, Fronah. Not just disgrace, but jail. When those promissory notes I drew on Samuelsons come out, they'll have me in a cell. I've only one hope.'

'One hope?' she echoed dully.

'Your . . . ah . . . brother Aaron and I've been talking. He has his reasons, too. Hates the Manchus and his own disgrace. Failing the Civil Service Examination three times. Swears he knows it's his enemies' work. He's been shopped, he says. Besides, he wants revenge for the injustice to his father and . . .'

'I know all that, Lionel. Where are you going, you and Aaron?'

'You can't stop us, Fronah. You won't. I knew you wouldn't tell old Saul about my sins. And you won't tell him now. We're going where Aaron can have his revenge and I can amass some of the ready. Then, I'll be back. Perhaps, then, I can change my . . . ah . . . curious ways. Meanwhile, we're going to the Heavenly Capital.'

'The Heavenly Capital? How ridiculous!' Her shrill laugh warned Fronah that she was on the verge of hysteria. 'With your tastes, Lionel? The Taipings will cut your head off if they catch you out.'

'I'm aware of that, my dear. But I've been doing some hard thinking since you . . . ah . . . came upon me so unexpectedly. I'm sure the Taipings'll welcome me. They're eager to employ Europeans, and they pay them well. You'll grant that, won't you?'

She nodded.

'I've also been thinking about my other troubles. I've a healthy respect

298

for my head, you know. I like it where it is . . . square on my shoulders. If anything can cure . . . though why I say cure, I don't know. If anything can control my predilections, it's knowing my head'll pay for any lapse.'

'Oh, Lionel, I *am* sorry . . . so sorry,' she exclaimed. 'I'm so very sorry. If only I could help. Why can't . . .'

'You can't. And there's no other way for me. Now I'll pack. No need of a tailcoat, I imagine.'

Hands locked together, she sat unmoving in the yellow velvet easy-chair. He paused between the yellow-velvet curtains of the doorway.

'I am sorry, Fronah,' he said without bravado. 'More sorry that I can possibly tell you. A little sorry for myself, surely, but deeply . . . profoundly . . . sorry for what I've done to you.'

CHAPTER FORTY-TWO

August 21, 1861   *Jehol in Manchuria*
                                        The Imperial Hunting Park

The scarlet hibiscus flaming beneath the weeping-willows on the shores of Fulfillment Lake did not divert Yehenala's eyes. The slender woman followed by a eunuch and a nurse-maid leading a small boy was not moved by the pale-pink water lilies cupped in green celadon leaves. Though she loved perfumes, she was oblivious to the fragrance of jasmine and wild ginger. The beauty of the sub-tropical plants flowering in late August in the valley of Hot Springs in the bleak north did not touch her. She who was normally responsive to beauty in any form.

Yehenala strode unseeing through the Pavilions of the Mist, whose starkness she considered unseemly for an Imperial Park. Their cracked roofs were supported only by faded red pillars, as if the builders had been called away before raising the walls.

Even if she had been happy in the Hill Manor Shunning Heat, she would have found its mock simplicity offensive. Aesthetes praised its fidelity to nature, but she longed for the Yüan Ming Yüan, where civilization had imposed its discipline on nature. Yet she would never see the Park of Radiant Perfection again. The Emperor's pusillanimity and his counsellors' stupidity had allowed the barbarians to destroy that masterwork of Confucian artifice.

She was herself neither afraid nor foolish. When she ruled the Great Empire, she would be revenged on the barbarians – and she would rebuild the Summer Palaces. She would make the Park of Radiant Perfection more splendid than it had been during the reign of the great Chien Lung Emperor.

With her meagre entourage, Yehenala swept towards the doors of the

299

Palace of Serenity, which was really a long single-storey box capped by grey tiles. She ignored the crossed pikes of the Imperial Guardsmen, who were ordered to keep intruders from the bedside of the failing Hsien Feng Emperor. Her lip curled contemptuously at the rustic banality of the Palace, and the sentries, taking her scorn for anger, raised their pikes in salute. No Guardsman would willingly oppose her will. All admired her courage, and all feared her rage.

When her platformed shoes clicked on the stone floor, eunuchs and courtiers stared in astonishment. Rigid-soled riding-boots laid aside, they all shuffled in cloth shoes. The normal clamour of the Court was stilled, the attendants' voices hushed.

The Emperor was sleeping after a troubled night, when he had burnt with fever and shivered with chills. No man dared disturb his repose or profane the solemnity of the hour with loud talk. Ten thousand years would soon have passed. The Hsien Feng Emperor must soon mount the Heavenly Dragon to be reunited with his Imperial Forefathers.

Grief tinged Yehenala's resolution, but she could not give way. All would have been different if the Emperor had possessed courage and intelligence. Her own life would have been wholly different, and she would not have been required to display the abrasive determination her enemies derided as unwomanly. Nor would she have been forced to hazard this last cast of the dice, which would decide not only her own fate and her son's, but the destiny of the Empire. During the next ten minutes she would either grasp decisively at supreme power or she would be disgraced, perhaps imprisoned, conceivably condemned to death. Yehenala had no time for sorrow.

Sweeping through the anteroom, she already thought of the Emperor as dead. Even his vices, she reflected, had been tawdry. If he had devoted himself to the ladies of the seraglio, the eunuchs would have brought in unbudded virgins to renew his vigour. But he had immured himself in the arms of ageing Chinese harlots, as if determined to destroy himself. Because of that perversion, he was rotted with diseases, the most virulent the plum-poison sickness contracted from some filthy Chinese whore. The little worms of syphilis now battled in his blood, driving him to spasms of rage indistinguishable from madness. After a squalid reign, the Hsien Feng Emperor was coming to a squalid end in self-imposed exile from the splendour of the Forbidden City.

The floor of the bed-chamber off the inner courtyard was covered with layers of carpets to deaden footfalls, and the bamboo blinds were lowered against the fierce sun. Princes, Ministers, and Senior Mandarins watched each other jealously, fearful that their rivals might snatch some advantage from the dying monarch. Prince Yee, the collateral Imperial Prince whose wife was the Heir's governess, sat on a stool beside the alcove filled by the Emperor's bed. Behind him stood his henchmen, a second minor Imperial Prince called Cheng.

Both were attentive to the words chopped by the knife-blade lips of the Assistant Grand Chancellor Su Shun. Though he was no more than the sixth son of the twelfth generation of descendants of a younger son of the Founding Emperor, Su Shun's ruthlessness had made him the conspirators' leader. The unholy triumvirate had almost a year ago convinced the Emperor that he must abandon the Northern Capital. The upstart glared as Yehenala entered the bed-chamber, her slight form outlined by the sunlight streaming through the open door.

Returning the glare, the Virtuous Concubine strode towards the alcove, though the eunuch Little An Hai-teh and the frightened nursemaid lagged behind with her son. Without looking back, she stretched out her hand. Little An led the small Prince Tsai Chün forward. She grasped her son's shoulder and guided him past the three men beside the Emperor's bed. Even the Assistant Grand Chancellor Su Shun did not dare stand between the Heir Presumptive and his father the Emperor.

'Majesty,' Yehenala said softly, 'Your Slave is deeply grieved by the state in which she finds . . .'

'*Kua* . . .' the Emperor quavered. 'This Orphan is ill . . . very ill. We wish only peace. We do not wish . . .'

'Your slave presents Your Majesty's son.'

The gentle pressure of his mother's hand on his shoulder impelled the small Prince to his knees, and he performed the kowtow as she had rehearsed him. Yehenala, too, prostrated herself, touching her forehead to the dusty carpet.

'*Hau*!. . .' the Emperor wheezed. 'Good! We are glad to see . . . but We require rest. We do not wish . . .'

'Majesty, this is *your* son . . . your *only* son. You must act now . . . or the Dynasty will be imperilled.' Yehenala ignored the Chancellor's outraged gasp at the familiar *you*. 'If you do not act, the Imperial Ancestors will be shamed by your unfilial neglect. Their rage will . . .'

'What do you want of Us, Nala?' he panted. 'Only leave Us to die in peace. All We ask . . .'

'In peace, but not in shame. Your Majesty *must* proclaim Prince Tsai Chün the Heir Apparent. Only make your son the Crown Prince . . . and you can die in peace. If you do not, the Dynasty will be torn apart by fratricidal strife. The rivals will destroy each other . . . and the Dynasty. Make Tsai Chün your Heir, Majesty. I implore you.'

'So be it!' The Emperor's voice was stronger. 'We proclaim Our only son Our only heir.'

'The Imperial clan and the people will bless Your Majesty's resolution. Your Majesty's memory will be revered. Your Majesty's spirit will be worshipped for its wisdom and . . .'

'*Our* resolution, Nala?' The Emperor's purple lips twisted. '*Our* resolution' You should say *your* resolution. Is that all you want?'

'Almost all, Your Majesty, except . . .' She crept on her knees to the side of the bed and took his swollen hand in hers. 'Majesty, Your Slave only wishes to say a word more. Your slave loves you . . . and blesses you. Farewell, Majesty, farewell!'

Leaning on Little An's shoulder, Yehenala withdrew from the death-chamber. She trembled, and her sight was blurred by tears. She had attained her first objective, the goal towards which she had striven since the birth of the small prince. She knew she would attain all her further goals. But, she swore, she would never again allow the struggle to tear her heart with iron claws.

*

Jehol in Manchuria
August 22, 1861   *The Imperial Hunting Park*

'Highness, ten thousand years have passed.' Little An knelt before his mistress. 'The Son of Heaven has mounted the Heavenly Dragon. His majesty was reunited with his Imperial Forefathers almost an hour ago.'

Though she had prepared herself for this moment for months, Yehenala was stricken by desolation. The sunlight faded on the marble table, and the outspread wings of the swans on the silver screen lost their lustre. Her hands were cold in the heat of summer. Less than twelve double-hours earlier, she had fearlessly faced down the cabal of courtiers. Now her shoulders bowed and her head drooped.

She must not, Yehenala warned herself, weep for her Emperor and her youth, both now irretrievably passed. Later there would be time for grief, private grief. Not even Little An might see her weep. His belief in her implacable will was vital to the struggles that lay ahead. She would triumph if all men believed her as impregnable as the Great Wall.

'I am stricken by sorrow, Little An.' Her voice was devoid of emotion. 'However, the Emperor's spirit soars on the Heavenly Dragon to the throne of the Jade Emperor, the Ruler of Heaven. His spirit now enjoys serene delight.'

'Beyond question, Highness,' her eunuch replied ritually. 'But here on earth the common people will wail for their departed father, and the skies will grow dark with sorrow. However, as Your Highness percipiently points out, His Majesty's spirit already revels in the transcendent joys of Heaven.'

'And the Imperial Farewell Decree, Little An?'

'It is done, Highness. The Prince Tsai Chün is designated Crown Prince and Heir Successor in the Farewell Decree. This slave kowtows in utter abjection before the young Lord of Ten Thousand Years.'

'Your loyalty, Little An, I shall never forget. Nor will the Emperor ever forget your services.'

'There is further news, Highness,' the eunuch ventured hesitantly. 'I

302

must further report that the Farewell Decree appoints a Council of Regency of eight members to rule until the young Emperor comes of age. Prince Yee is chief of the Council, while Prince Cheng, as well as the Assistant Grand Chancellor Su Shun are named . . .'

'I expected this, Little An. We will deal with them. I did not say the struggle was over, though the crucial victory is won. Prince Kung will . . .'

'Prince Kung is *not* named to the Council, Highness. Nor Your Highness's second brother-in-law, Prince Chun.'

'Prince Kung *not* included? His favourite brother . . . the hero who managed the barbarians . . . *not* included? That is almost beyond belief. The weak fool! Always a weakling and a dolt, even on his death-bed.'

'I am further constrained to report that the customary lauding of the virtues of the Imperial Consorts is omitted from the Farewell Decree. Neither the Empress nor Your Highness is mentioned. Not a word for either the Senior Consort or the Mother of the successor Emperor.'

Yehenala did not reply. Before she spoke she must master the fury that dyed her cheeks scarlet under the white powder. Little An had seen her rage in the past, and he would see her rage again. But a display of wild anger at this moment could shake his confidence – and she now required his total confidence desperately.

She had not yet attained such eminence than she could indulge her temper freely, and she might never attain that eminence. She glanced sourly at the plum Robe of Ceremony hanging on the mirrored cupboard. The Imperial phoenixes mocked her with their ruby eyes.

She had never doubted that both the Empress and herself would be raised to the rank of Dowager Empress. It was unthinkable that the Senior Consort of the deceased Son of Heaven should be so denied and intolerable that the mother of the successor Son of Heaven should be so humiliated. Not only she, but her son the Emperor was thus humiliated, for a reigning Emperor's mother was always revered as Dowager Empress. Her enemies' effrontery was beyond belief. Their arrogance was shameless – and foolhardy.

'The Farewell Decree was written in the former Emperor's own hand, was it not?' she asked finally. 'Or, at least, signed by himself and authenticated with his seal?'

'No, Highness, it was not.' Little An's deepset eyes glittered with malicious understanding. 'He was too weak, they said, to take up the vermilion brush. And the Great Seal could not be found.'

'How extraordinary! How extraordinary that the Great Seal of Lawfully Transmitted Authority could not be found. The Farewell Decree is, I fear, a forgery, though many men heard the former Emperor designate his successor. The former Emperor could not have failed to honour his loving consorts, could he, Little An?'

'It is inconceivable even to my dull wits that the Son of Heaven could be so lax . . . however ill.'

303

'Inconceivable to me, too, Little An. And, I dare say, inconceivable to a great many others.'

'Your instructions, Highness?'

'Prince Kung must be warned immediately that conspirators are attempting to usurp power. You must go to Prince Kung. Before you go to Peking, I have a small errand for you.'

'I await your command, Highness.'

'The Imperial Guard must, of course, not be incited to indignation. The officers are all chivalrous gentlemen. They would rise against the conspirators if they knew the insult offered to two helpless widows on the morrow of their bereavement. That would never do, would it, Little An?'

'It is impossible to keep that disgraceful act a secret, Highness.'

'So I fear, but we must do everything we can to avert violence. Little An, you must play the peacemaker. Assure the commandant that the Farewell Decree is not valid because it lacks the Great Seal. You may inform him that the corps of eunuchs considers it a forgery.'

'And further, Highness?'

'Assure the commandant that the true Farewell Decree *will* be authenticated by the Great Seal. I speak, of course, of the Decree conferring the dignity of Empress Dowager upon the former Empress and upon the former Virtuous Concubine. The great Seal will be found, I am quite sure.'

'Empress Dowager, Highness? Not Dowager Empress?'

'That is correct, Little An. Empress Dowager.'

'Not Empress Dowager Regent, Highness?'

'We must not go too fast, Little An. Later, Little An, will do very well. Though not too much later. Go now.'

*

Jehol in Manchuria
August 23, 1861   *The Imperial Hunting Park*

The following dawn was made brilliant by banks of silver-and-scarlet clouds. The rising sun was a fiery disc in the eastern sky while the moon still gleamed like a pearl in the west. That bright dawn closed a troubled night. The barracks of the Imperial Guard had seethed with indignation, and troops had surrounded the dwellings of the eight members of the new Council of Regency. Finally, the eight yielded to the logic of their position – and the morning was glorious.

The Hill Manor Shunning Heat was hung with banners, and fireworks resounded to hail a Manchu ceremony that had not been celebrated in Manchuria for centuries. The five-year-old Crown Prince was proclaimed Emperor, and his Reign Name, which would date every state document, was promulgated: Chi Hsiang, Propitious Omen. The two Empress

304

Dowagers were accorded the honours due their eminence, second in the Great Empire only to the Son of Heaven himself.

Yehenala's son was Emperor, and she would be rendered abject respect. She rejoiced and stroked the Imperial phoenixes on her robe. The placid senior Empress Dowager would undoubtedly be content with that ceremonial eminence. But Yehenala was not – could not – be so easily content. Her enemies were too numerous, too persistent, and too vicious.

Yehenala's triumph was flawed. Unless she destroyed her enemies, she could never enjoy her eminence with an untroubled mind. Though she wanted no more, she must struggle still to attain that tranquillity.

CHAPTER FORTY-THREE

September 18, 1861   *Jehol in Manchuria*
                                     The Imperial Hunting Park

'The flaw is fatal, Elder Sister, and twofold,' Yehenala explained. 'Our weakness exactly matches our enemies' weakness. If Prince Yee and Chancellor Su Shun were different, we could attain harmony, which is all you and I want. But they are rapacious. Either they perish . . . or we do.'

'Your talk frightens me, Little Sister,' the senior Empress Dowager replied. 'Why can't we just leave it to the men? It's unseemly, unwomanly, to talk about killing.'

'But seemly to die without resisting? Virtuous and womanly to go like silly sheep to the slaughter?' Yehenala snapped, but was instantly conciliatory again. 'This stalemate can't last. Think of a fat Mandarin cramming himself into a skinny beggar's coat. Before long the coat will split, won't it? You do see, Elder Sister?'

She was not overstating the peril, the junior Empress Dowager reflected. She faced myriad threats, and any one could prove fatal. Yet her most perplexing problem was the plump woman etiquette required her to call Elder Sister, though she was actually a year younger. Negotiating in secret with Princes, Ministers, and Generals was harrowing. She must win their allegiance by offering sufficient inducements, but not so much that she undermined her own position. It was nerve-racking to face down her enemies or charm them with fluttering deference. However, she enjoyed those confrontations, for the danger made her blood flow faster. Besides, she understood men and knew how to deal with them, misleading the arrogant with feigned feminine helplessness and confounding the irresolute with her decisiveness. But this pleasant woman called Niuhura was like a lion-dog puppy, too silly to frighten and too stubborn to cajole.

'I don't want to kill anyone,' Niuhura repeated.

'Do you want to die?' Brutality might penetrate where reason had failed. 'Do you want to sacrifice your life for the glory of Prince Yee and the multi-millionaire Chancellor Su Shun?'

'We are the Empress Dowagers, Little Sister.' Niuhura reverted with pathetic dignity to the single aspect of the crisis she understood. 'I'm not interested in power. Being Empress Dowager is enough for me. I want no more.'

'Nor do I, Elder Sister.' Yehenala was quite sincere. 'Except to see my son secure on the Dragon Throne and grow to manhood and rule wisely, unhampered by a Council of Regency. But there's little hope unless you and I act boldly now.'

'I'm confused, Little Sister. Can you explain again? One thing puzzles me most . . .'

'What is that?'

'You say we must be bold, but you want me to approve an Edict renouncing what little power we hold. Be bold, you say. But you want to give in. Isn't that so?'

'It appears so. It is meant to appear so, since it's the only way to lure our enemies into our trap.'

'I'm afraid I still don't understand. And I won't place my seal on the Edict till I do. I'm sorry, but I can't.'

'It is confusing, so many strands to this embroidery. But, once you understand the pattern, everything'll be clear.'

Yehenala prayed Heaven for patience. She could forgive the senior Empress Dowager's slowness. The woman was born dull – and never encouraged to sharpen her mind. Niuhura had been proclaimed Empress without the struggle for advancement that honed the dullest wits. She could not so easily forgive Niuhura's stubborness, the obstinacy of weakness beside which a Shansi mule appeared eager to please.

She must, however, break down that obstinacy. She had not exaggerated the peril that threatened them both if they appeared to oppose the usurpers' ambitions. Prince Yee and the Assistant Grand Chancellor Su Shun would prefer to see herself dead and the weak Niuhura their compliant tool. But they would cheerfully stage a fatal accident for both ladies to whom they now bowed with ill grace if they believed both stood in their way. Niuhura's petulant stubbornness could, therefore, destroy them both.

As the day faded into evening, they sat at ease in the inner courtyard of the Palace of Perfect Satisfaction, which was now their joint residence. Niuhura, the senior, occupied the east wing because east was the superior direction, while Yehenala occupied the west wing. The stream of Princes, Generals, and Mandarins with whom they had treated all that exhausting day had slowly dwindled and finally dried up. Their ladies-in-waiting and eunuchs had discreetly withdrawn beyond earshot. Yet their apparent relaxation was an illusion.

306

'Please be patient with me, Little Sister.' The senior Dowager responded to the resonance of Yehenala's desperation. 'I'm not as clever as you.'

Yehenala wanted to reply: *Neither as clever nor as womanly. You gave the former Emperor no heir. The present Emperor is my son, not yours.* Instead, she bit her lips and, once again, strove to simplify the complex intrigue for Niuhura's simple mind.

'The crux is this: they're not really Regents, whatever they may call themselves.' Yehenala found new words for the same facts. 'If they were Regents, they could dispense with us. They wouldn't care about you and me, because we'd be no threat to them. As it is . . .'

As it was, she continued automatically, the Council of Eight designated by the suspect Farewell Decree required the assent of the Empress Dowagers to validate their decisions. The Council was empowered only to 'advise and assist' the infant Emperor, not to act in his name. Perhaps because the Assistant Grand Chancellor Su Shun was so junior in the Imperial Clan that he could not serve as a Regent, perhaps because they had not dared arrogate *all* power to themselves – the eight had not designated themselves Regents. They could, therefore, not themselves use the Imperial Seal, whose imprint was required to make their decrees law. Since both the Empress Dowagers were the legal ancestors of the child-Emperor, maternal authority reserved that essential power to them.

The Council could not act without the Dowagers' sanction, while the Dowagers could not initiate policy. Compromise had apparently resolved that impasse. The Dowagers would review the Rescripts, Decrees, and Edicts prepared by the Council, withholding their consent only for the gravest reasons. The Council assumed their consent would never be withheld.

In practice that compromise meant Yehenala would confirm – or, infrequently, question – the decisions of the Council of Regency. Niuhura could barely read the elided language of state papers, much less understand their arcane complexities.

The Dowagers had agreed in return that they would neither hold open court nor give private audience to any man except members of the Council. Never imagining they could not control the women, the eight thereafter behaved as if they were the child-Emperor's sole guardians in law, fully empowered to act in his name on all matters.

'You remember, Elder Sister, when Prince Kung came to see us, don't you?' Yehenala asked rhetorically. 'It all came out then.'

'Of course I remember. What a frightful fuss it was.'

A frightful fuss? That was an extraordinary description, but, Yehenala supposed, it had appeared only another domestic drama to the senior Dowager. Furious because he – like all the former Emperor's brothers – was excluded from the Council of Regency, Prince Kung was determined to confront the conspirators. Secure in their arrogance, they forbade him to come to Jehol to attend the preliminary obsequies for his brother, the former Emperor – and ordered him to remain in the Northern Capital to 'administer affairs'. After the eunuch Little An journeyed secretly to Peking, Prince Kung arrived unannounced in Jehol in mid-September. When the Council threatened him with punishment, he produced the invitation from his sisters-in-law the eunuch had brought him.

Impotent to over-ride the Dowagers' authority in a family matter, the usurpers could only warn Prince Kung and his sisters-in-law to avoid private meetings, which 'might arouse suspicions of impropriety or conspiracy.' They ignored that feeble threat, and, after conferring with Yehenala, Prince Kung returned to Peking – ostensibly to carry out the Council's orders. He had actually agreed with Yehenala that they should take no action in Jehol. He would launch a counter-offensive as soon as he reached the Northern Capital, which was the centre of his power.

He was, Prince Kung told the Dowagers, confident of success. Not only did he command the loyalty of the Metropolitan Army, but he had secured a commitment from the British, who were still camped near Tientsin. Should the need arise, the barbarian troops would intervene to restore legitimate rule to the Empire. A new era had begun, but neither Kung nor Yehenala reflected on the irony of their requiring the support of the same army whose attack had precipitated the crisis.

'Our brother-in-law Kung's counter-attack has been *too* successful.' Yehenala led Niuhura through the maze of intrigue again. 'If he hadn't been so vigorous, it would not have come up until we returned to Peking for the former Emperor's burial. In Peking, we would have been secure. But here in Jehol we're at their mercy if we don't give in.'

'The new Edict, you mean?'

'Precisely! If he had not encouraged that Senior Censor to submit a Memorial urging us to take all power as Empress Dowagers *and* Regents, the Council would not have been alarmed. As it is . . .'

'But there is no precedent for Empress Dowagers acting as Regents. Sacred Dynastic Law prohibits . . .'

'The Sacred Law, Elder Sister, does *not* prohibit Empress Dowagers Regent. Only precedent, the lack of precedent, can be argued against us.'

'But always in the past . . . when the Shun Chih Emperor and, even, the great Kang Hsi were children . . . all the regents were Princes, never the Imperial Mothers.'

'And all those male Regents were imprisoned or executed for abusing their trust. That's hardly an inspiring example, as the usurpers know. It's time to try what we women can do.'

'But, without a precedent . . .'

'*Chiu-lien ting-cheng . . . Empress Dowagers sitting behind the bamboo screen so no man may see them and administering the government.* You know the expression. Precedents exist. In previous eras, under other dynasties, Empresses did rule.'

'So there's this new Edict, which you want me to sign.'

'Precisely. I told you it was easier than embroidery once you saw the pattern. As you know, the Senior Censor's Memorial not only exhorted us to conduct administration behind the screen, but also proposed that the both Prince Kung and Prince Chun, the former Emperor's brothers, be designated to advise the Council. The usurpers almost broke their teeth on those stones in their rice.'

'And they had to strike back, Little Sister. Otherwise, we'd hold all power . . . with our brothers-in-law, Prince Kung and Prince Chun.'

'You now understand fully, Elder Sister.' Yehenala's head ached from the prolonged catechism. 'The usurpers *had* to issue a new Decree, declaring it illegal for Empress Dowagers to rule behind the screen because there was no precedent under the Great Pure Dynasty. I've held out for two days, refused to put my Seal on that Decree. Now we *must* give in.'

'I understand everything – except that. Why give in?'

The veins in Yehenala's temples pounded, and even her obtuse Elder Sister saw the angry flush under her heavy make-up. To gain time she snapped her fingers, and a eunuch brought a fresh pot of chrysanthemum tea. She sipped slowly, striving to recover her equanimity. She could not allow her temper to erupt when she was so close to her goal.

'Because that fool of a Manchu who commands the Metropolitan Army also acted too soon,' she finally replied. 'Hoping to curry favour with us, he's placed our lives in danger. His Memorial arrived this afternoon. He supports our position completely.'

'But that's good. With military support we can . . .'

'We'd never live to enjoy his support. If we don't ratify the Decree, the usurpers will kill us. It'll be an accident, of course. But we'll be just as dead . . . and their rule will be unchallenged.'

'But if we agree, we lose all . . .'

'We *must* agree. We must formally renounce our rights so that the usurpers feel secure. The funeral cortege will then depart for Peking, and Dynastic Law requires us to precede it. Once in Peking . . .'

'You mean make them feel secure so we can lure them to Peking?'

'So we can *survive* to lure them to Peking, where we'll hold all the cards.'

'I *do* understand now, Little Sister. How clever of you. You're really clever . . . for a woman.'

'Perhaps not so stupid even for a man,' Yehenala muttered to herself. 'I've never been a man, so I can't be sure.'

'What's that, Little Sister?' Niuhura asked. 'I didn't quite hear you.'

'Nothing important, Elder Sister.' Having finally triumphed, Yehenala allowed herself to crow subtly. 'I was only thinking of the words of the greatest strategist of all time. The wise Sun-tze wrote: *The great general modifies his tactics in accordance with his enemy's character.*'

'You can recite Sun-tze from memory, Little Sister?'

'You, too, must learn, Elder Sister. He gives us answers to all our perplexities. Now that you've agreed, we've attained the position Sun-tze

309

advised: *The best fighters of ancient times first secured themselves against defeat, then waited patiently for the enemy to provide the opportunity to defeat him.'*

'I think I see, Little Sister,' Niuhura said dubiously. 'We make them over-confident – and then strike back.'

'It's really quite simple,' Yehenala replied. 'Isn't it, Elder Sister?'

CHAPTER FORTY-FOUR

October 28, 1861   *Near Kupeikou, Manchuria*

'Your Maternal Majesties!' Prince Yee's voice was laden with deference. 'I beseech Your Majesties' permission to draw closer.'

The Chief of the Council of Regency was rotund within the coarse white mourning-robe that covered the field uniform of a lieutenant general. His riding boots squelching in the liquid mud, he knelt on a stone before the improvised lean-to that sheltered the Empress Dowagers from the driving Manchurian rain on the early afternoon of October 28, 1861.

Before they left Jehol, Prince Yee had affirmed his unique supremacy by taking the title *Chien Kuo,* Lord Protector of the Nation, which had not been used for a century. He believed his authority unchallengeable, since the Dowagers were powerless after ratifying the Decree of Renunciation. However neither mockery nor pretence marred the profound obesiance he rendered Niuhura and Yehenala's *ceremonial* precedence.

'No need to kowtow, Prince Yee.' Yehenala's concern was saccharine. 'The yellow mud is sticky.'

'I humbly thank Your Majesty.'

'We thank you for protecting two helpless widows on this sad journey.' Niuhura was equally courteous. 'Without your kindness, we'd be lost.'

'The danger is almost over, Majesty. Once past the Five Dragon Mountain and through the Great Wall, all will be serene.'

'Unfortunately, Prince, We do not control the weather.' Yehenala observed. 'Heaven must be angry. I've never seen such a wild storm.'

'It's not unusual in these passes, Majesty.' Prince Yee bowed again, and his conical hat tumbled off. 'I myself believe Heaven has been weeping for the former Emperor these past two days.'

Yehenala smiled at the bedraggled figure to temper her tart remark. His queue was tied with the white ribbon of mourning, while grey stubble bristled on his crown and his cheeks, which were normally shaved every morning. No male subject of the Great Pure Dynasty could permit the touch of a barber's razor until the final obsequies for the deceased Emperor were performed in the Northern Capital. The rain-drenched and mud-splattered Lord Protector looked more like the brigands they feared than an Imperial Prince as he knelt before the rock-face of the ravine.

Yehenala bore Prince Yee no malice, any more than she did his henchman, the younger Prince Cheng. Both believed they were behaving with perfect propriety in accordance with Sacred Dynastic Law. The Princes were an obstacle in her path, but she could no more hate them than she could hate the boulders on which her litter-bearers stumbled.

She both hated and feared her mortal enemy, the Assistant Grand Chancellor Su Shun, who was the architect of the conspiracy. He was, fortunately, already a full day's march behind them, and he would arrive in Peking several days after them with the cortege conveying the former Emperor's remains. Prince Yee and Prince Cheng, too, should have accompanied the bier, but they were anxious to reach the Northern Capital to carry out their duties. Besides, they did not want to let Yehenala out of their sight.

Her sister's husband Prince Chun also rode beside the Imperial Cata-falque, an immense, gilded structure borne over the mountains with glacial stateliness on the shoulders of a hundred and twenty-four bearers. Dynastic Law providentially required the brother of the former Emperor to escort the Imperial Remains to the Forbidden City, though it forbade the child-Emperor and the Empress Dowagers to do so. Her brother-in-law could, therefore, keep watch on the evil Assistant Grand Chancellor. But, Yehenala wondered, could the vigilance of that naïve twenty-one-year-old frustrate the wily forty-six-year-old Mandarin who had made himself the richest commoner in the Empire while serving as Minister of Finance?

Not until she entered the Imperial City through the Gate of Heavenly Peace would she feel safe under Prince Kung's protection. Despite her pride in her Manchu heritage, Yehenala knew she was a creature of the warmer south, not of these bleak plains broken by precipitous mountain ranges. Once this exhausting journey was over, she promised herself, she would never again venture north of the Great Wall, which marked the edge of civilization. The splendidly restored Yüan Ming Yüan would be her refuge from the summer heat, rather than the Imperial Hunting Park in Jehol.

Their chief danger was the brigands who swarmed on the marches of the Empire. She could not dismiss the malice of the Assistant Grand Chancellor, but he could do little to harm her at present, for the Imperial Procession was guarded by Prince Yee's Household Troops. That upright – though grievously misguided – Manchu would not use violence against the child-Emperor or the Empress Dowagers, though he would have turned a blind eye to any 'accident' that befell the defiant Dowagers in Jehol.

Her son squirmed on his small stool beside her, and she stroked his head. The baby stubble on his crown was soft as new grass under her palm. His fingertips protruded cold-whitened and wind-chapped from the cuffs of his padded coats, which held his arms out like a rag-stuffed doll. Even the common barbarian soldiers wore small divided bags to warm their hands, but the descendants of the nomadic Namchu warriors scorned hand-bags as effete – even for children and women. Yehenala chafed her son's hands between her palms before tucking them firmly into his cuffs and drawing his sleeves together.

She would give ten *taels* for a pair of sleeve dogs, one to warm her hands and another for the child's. The flight from Peking had been so hurried that she had not been able to bring her own pet lion-dogs, much less their minuscule cousins which ladies, eunuchs, and old gentlemen carried in their capacious sleeves. She had wept for her six lion-dogs, above all for the arrogant golden male Semkila, and her heart still ached for him. Still, no sleeve-dog, however stunted, was small enough to fit into her son's sleeves.

'Mama, I'm cold,' the child-Emperor complained. 'When can we go home?'

'Very soon, treasure, we'll be home,' she soothed him. 'And we'll always be together. In just a few days, we'll be in Peking. Do you remember the Forbidden City?'

'A little, Mama, but not much. Will Papa be there, too? Is he waiting for us?'

'No, treasure, you are the Emperor now. Your Papa can't be there.'

'Why not? Doesn't Papa want to see me?'

She had been dreading that question for two months. It was not her Dynastic duty to tell him of his father's death, a task prescribed for the eldest male of the former Emperor's generation. Prince Kung had wished to tell him in Jehol, but she had forbidden it.

Yehenala felt only she could tell the little Emperor his father had departed forever. She alone could comfort the boy, and she alone could fill the place his sometimes affectionate but often distant father had held in his heart.

'Your Papa has mounted the Heavenly Dragon, treasure,' Yehenala said gently. 'He's gone to see the Jade Emperor, the Ruler of Heaven. You and I won't see your Papa again till we go to Heaven many years from now.'

'Why did Papa go away? Is he angry at me, Mama?'

'No, treasure, he's not angry. He didn't ask to go, but the Jade Emperor called him. Even the former Emperor of the Great Pure Dynasty had to obey, just as all men must obey you on earth because you are the Emperor now.'

'He obeyed the Jade Emperor, Mama?' The child's intelligence awakened her pride. 'Then he must be happy.'

'Very happy, though sad to leave us. But you and I will always be together, and I won't ever scold you again.'

'Then I'm happy too. But it's warmer in the palanquin. I want to go to the Forbidden City and sit on the Dragon Throne.'

The caravan resumed its march ten minutes later. Chair-bearers, soldiers, and eunuchs were all eager to find a site for the evening halt, since the rising storm would prevent their reaching Kupeikou, where simple dwellings and rude inns had been cleared to accommodate them. They finally camped just before dusk. The temporal and spiritual authority of the world's largest empire rested temporarily in a rivulet-scored ravine between steep cliffs twenty-three miles north of the Great Wall.

The coloured tents with silken linings rose in Imperial splendour against the scarred rock. Each Dowager's pavilion was divided into a reception-chamber, sleeping-chamber, and quarters for her attendants. Prince Yee and Prince Cheng also occupied their own pavilions, the Lord Protector's only slightly smaller than the Dowagers'.

The most magnificent, as large and as many chambered as a villa, was erected in the centre of the encampment, the Emperor's personal standard flying from a scarlet pole before its entrance. But the sentinels in the sodden blue and scarlet dress uniform of the Imperial Guard kept their vigil over an Imperial Travelling Palace devoid of its chief occupant. The drowsy five-year-old hailed as the Son of Heaven was put to bed in an alcove adjoining his mother's sleeping chamber.

A detachment of the Imperial Guard patrolled one segment of the loose perimeter and Prince Yee's clan troops the rest. The wind shrieking through the ravine hurled spears of rain to pierce the soldiers' oiled-canvas cloaks. They swore at the rigidity of their officers and the inflexibility of Dynastic Law, which kept them at their posts for no reason. Neither moonlight nor starlight penetrated the murky clouds. In the pitch darkness, where sentries stationed at ten-foot intervals could not see each other, no enemy could possibly mount an attack. Not even the rapacious brigands of the mountains would stir in this filthy weather.

The wailing of the wind and the drumming of the rain drowned the normal noises of the night. Within her pavilion Yehenala did not hear the creaking of trees and the cries of animals. Only the awful roar of the boulders that broke from the cliff face to thunder upon the encampment rose above the clamour of the gale. When the wind abated momentarily, as if crouching for the next assault, the silence was eerie and terrifying.

Yehenala sat on a folding chair in her bed-chamber, warming her hands over the charcoal brazier whose glow lit the orange-silk walls. She was happy to gather her thoughts in solitude before retiring to the bed invitingly spread with an old-rose counterpane. She had removed her sodden clothes, washed in the tepid water the serving-maids brought from the kitchen-tent, and slipped a quilted-silk robe over her nakedness. When the wailing wind and the drumming rain briefly gave way to silence, she whispered a prayer to Kwan Yin, the Goddess of Mercy. She was still

313

fearful, though the fury of Heaven had left the camp unscathed and she knew no human enemy could strike on such a night.

Her prayer froze on her lips, which were soft and vulnerable without their normal pigment. The clashing of swords rang in her ears, though muffled by the double tent, and a ragged volley of musket shots echoed through the ravine. Swords clattered again before the tumult of the storm drowned all other sounds.

Tensely upright, Yehenala waited for her attendants to report to her. Even at a moment like this, particularly at a moment like this, she could not impair her dignity by sending for news.

After waiting for some minutes, she rose. Her Imperial dignity required a pretence of aloof unconcern, but her too human nerves were strung tight. Forcing herself to walk slowly on the Samarkand carpet spread over the plank floor, she grasped the curtains barring the corridor to the reception-chamber. The curtain parted of itself, and she saw Little An.

'A visitor, Highness.' The agitated eunuch forgot her new title. 'A visitor demands to see you.'

'*Demands*?' she asked. 'Who dares to demand to see the Empress Dowager?'

'The Baronet Jung Lu, Colonel of the Peking Field. He's most insistent, Majesty.'

'I know who Jung Lu is, you fool. Don't keep him waiting. Show him in.'

The Baronet Jung Lu swaggered in his sodden tunic slit by a sword-stroke. As he handed his dripping cape to Little An, Yehenala saw that his normally ruddy cheeks were pale in the brazier's glow. After Little An offered a towel and withdrew, Jung Lu dropped to his knees.

'Majesty,' he said, 'I . . .'

'Get up, you idiot,' she commanded fondly. 'Come and sit beside the brazier. You look exhausted and . . . you're not hurt?'

'No, Majesty.' He sat on a second folding chair. 'Only my tunic, and it can be patched.'

'Tell me why you are here!' she commanded. 'I thought I heard shots.'

'Your Majesty did.'

'Not Majesty, Jung. Tonight call me Nala and say *you*. Call me Nala again – for the last time.'

'Nala! I've dreamed of saying Nala again. You know I've yearned to . . .'

'You are a young idiot. You must not talk so. But, if you must, tell me later about your yearning. First tell me what's happened.'

'You're quite safe now, Nala. Your sister's husband Prince Chun and I . . . with the cortege . . . we watched carefully as instructed. The troops of the Assistant Grand Chancellor, somehow their number dwindled. Prince Chun commanded me to ride after them with my own men. That's about all, Nala, my love. I've yearned so to . . .'

'Later, Jung, later!' Yehenala realised that her command was also an implicit promise, but she could withdraw that promise – if she wished. 'First finish your story.'

'Brigands . . .' he said wearily. 'Su Shun's troops were disguised as brigands to kill you. We fell on their rear as Prince Yee's clansmen were withdrawing before their attack. A little sword-play . . . a few volleys . . . and they broke.'

'The shots I heard? Yee's men have no muskets. But you're exhausted. No need . . .'

'Nala, I'll finish if I may. You're safe now. I ride with you to Peking. Since Prince Kung commanded me to protect the Emperor, no one can challenge my right – not with your assent.'

'Given gladly, Jung, gladly. I not only assent, but command you to . . . to accompany me.'

A glow suffused his lean face at that covert invitation, for she did not wish to retract her implicit promise. She was destined always to take the initiative, it seemed, earlier because of the Emperor's jaded appetites, now because of her rank. She stretched out her hand and tentatively touched his shoulder.

'Nala, by Heaven, I've dreamed . . .' His voice was hoarse. 'For years . . . a decade . . . I've dreamed . . .'

'Be quiet, idiot,' she said softly. 'Just be quiet.'

He could not make the first move. But he took her like a man. Impatient and rough, then tender and gentle, he forced the pace – and she yielded to his ardour. Later, she drowsily measured his urgency against the Emperor's quiescence, which had required her to play the man's role. For the first time, Yehenala happily surrendered her body and her will to a man – and, afterwards, she was languidly content.

'We'll be together always, won't we?' she whispered, her head resting in the crook of his arm. 'We'll never part, my darling.'

'As you wish, Nala. It's not for me to say. But, by Heaven, if they beheaded me tomorrow, my life will have been crowned. Tonight is worth . . .'

'No one'll behead you, Jung,' she laughed. 'And we will be together always.'

She brushed his cheek with her lips and embraced him fiercely. If she triumphed, they would often be together. But, she knew with a sudden chill, she would always be alone in her eminence.

CHAPTER FORTY-FIVE

The light that drenched the Northern Capital on the morning of November 1st, 1861 was as hard and as brilliant as a shower of diamonds. Polished by the storms of the preceding week, the awful clarity of the atmosphere subtly distorted the vision of men accustomed to seeing their city through a haze of ochre dust and black soot. As the Imperial Procession approached, the golden roofs of the Gate of Western Justice appeared to transfix the blue arch of the sky and to cradle the wan crescent moon in their upswept eaves. Beneath their crimson cloak of maples, the Fragrant Hills towering fifteen miles distant appeared within arm's reach.

The five-year-old Emperor, resplendently uncomfortable in a stiff Imperial-yellow tribute-silk robe embroidered with metallic gold Imperial Dragons, sat beside his mother on the yellow cushions of the foremost gilded palanquin. Imperial-yellow pennants whipping in the brisk breeze, the mile-long procession moved in an aureate glow. Mounted drummers summoned roars from the kettle-drums hanging beside their saddles, and conch shells rumbled beneath the skirling of long brass horns. The ancient Manchu instruments heralded the advent of the child-Emperor as they had heralded the six-year-old Shun Chih Emperor, the first of his line to enter Peking, exactly 217 years earlier.

Like Yehenala, the Senior Empress Dowager Niuhura avoided looking at the immense black scar that disfigured the earth where the Summer Palaces had gleamed little more than a year ago. But she saw the glance the junior Empress Dowager exchanged with the Baronet Jung Lu, who commanded their escort. As he rode beside the Imperial palanquin, his eyes dwelt on the petite figure framed by the open curtains. No man, Niuhura reflected sadly, had ever looked at her as the slim officer with the reckless mouth looked at Yehenala, his gaze alternately adoring and imploring. For an instant, Yehenala's eyes softened in response. An instant later, they flashed cold in dismissal and, perhaps, in warning.

Jung Lu's mouth hardened. He slapped his horse's neck and cantered to the head of his cavalry to return the salute of the infantrymen palisading the road. Their scarlet helmets gleamed, and the *yung* – brave – ideograms on their chests rippled as they raised their halberds.

A blue-striped marquee almost an acre in expanse had been erected before the Gate of Western Justice against the volatile weather. Propitiously, only a few benevolent white clouds drifted in the clear sky above the city, though the wind snapped the cavalcade's pennants and whipped the slender flagpoles before the marquee. Above the clashing cymbals and the booming gongs, a vast throng shouted: '*Huang-ti wan sui*! . . . Imperial Majesty, live ten thousand years!'

The child-Emperor had come home to Imperial Peking. For the first time, he was received in his Northern Capital with the acclamation reserved for the Son of Heaven: '*Huang-ti wan-wan-sui*! . . . Majesty, ten thousand times ten thousand years!'

A tall man with a square face stood before the ranks of Princes, Chancellors, Ministers, Censors, and Senior Mandarins assembled to welcome their new sovereign into his inheritance. Like all the officials, Prince Kung's robe of ceremony was covered by a sombre surcoat, which revealed only its hoof-shaped cuffs and the wave-pattern on its skirts. Later, the grandees would put on white mourning-clothes to show their grief for the former Emperor. They now wore Court Regalia to welcome the Chi Hsiang Emperor, the eighth of his line to rule the Great Empire.

Followed by five Princes, Chancellors, and Censors, Prince Kung walked slowly through the crystalline morning towards the palanquin bearing the Emperor and his mother, the junior Empress Dowager. Their heads were high, but their eyes were cast down. The Prince sank to his knees to perform the kowtow, the three-fold prostration rendered only to Heaven and to Heaven's representative on earth, the Lord of Ten Thousand Years.

The portly Prince Yee, Lord Protector of the Nation and Chief of the Council of Regency created by the Farewell Edict, had been striding with self-conscious dignity from his own palanquin towards the marquee. As Prince Kung rose before kneeling for the final prostration, the Lord Protector broke into an awkward trot in his clumsy riding boots. Determined to assert his primacy, he stood before the open doors of the Imperial Palanquin between Prince Kung and the child-Emperor.

Prince Kung reached behind him to take the yellow-silk-encased scroll of a Humble Memorial from an attendant Mandarin. Though the Lord Protector flicked his fingers in dismissal, the Emperor's uncle stepped forward unperturbed.

'Prince Yee, it is not for any man to interfere between the Son of Heaven and the least of his subjects.' Yehenala's voice was hard. 'To stand between the Son of Heaven and his Imperial uncle is a heinous crime.'

Prince Kung advanced towards the Imperial Palanquin, the silk-cased Memorial extended before him. The Lord Protector's head swivelled nervously to see the regulars of the Metropolitan Army standing all around. His own troops were blocked by the Baronet Jung Lu's cavalrymen of the Peking Field Force. The Lord Protector was, however, no more a coward than he was, by his own lights, a usurper.

'I do not seek to interfere between His Majesty and the Imperial uncle,' he asserted. 'But I hold the Empress Dowagers to their word. They swore to give audience to no man not a member of the Council of Regency.'

'Under duress,' Yehenala said. 'A promise made with a knife at our throats.'

The Lord Protector held his ground as the muscular Prince Kung advanced upon him. He heard a low command, and the regulars lowered their halberds. Only when it appeared the younger man would walk over him did Prince Yee step aside.

'Go, dotard!' Prince Kung finally commanded. 'Be thankful that I do not arrest you for usurpation . . . and your other crimes.'

Prince Kung presented the Memorial to the Emperor who playfully rolled the scroll between his palms before handing it to his mother, who negligently tucked it behind the cushions of the Imperial Palanquin. The Memorial she and Prince Kung had drafted in Jehol would play an important part in the drama, but not just yet. She smiled and placed her arm around the child's narrow shoulders as the waves of sound broke over them again: '*Huang-ti wan sui! Wan-wan sui!* . . . Imperial Majesty, live ten thousand years! Ten thousand times ten thousand years!'

After the chief men of the realm had kowtowed to her son, Yehenala took a second scroll from the small gilt and scarlet casket at her feet.

'On behalf of the Emperor, the Empress Dowagers express gratification at the welcome offered by His Majesty's *loyal* counsellors.' She emphasised the word *loyal*. 'The Empress Dowagers, further, hand down an Imperial Rescript.'

Prince Kung bowed to receive the scroll from her hands. Like one of the protracted Peking operas Yehenala loved, the drama had been drawn out for months. It was now moving rapidly towards its climax.

The first scene of the final act had just proceeded exactly as they had rehearsed it in Jehol. Prince Yee's intervention was unexpected, but it only made the scene more effective. Yehenala frowned, half-regretting the role assigned the self-anointed Lord Protector in the next scene. She smiled grimly when she recalled the role the Assistant Grand Chancellor Su Shun was destined to play.

*

He was, Prince Kung mused, the seventh son of the Tao Kwang Emperor, whose reign had ended a decade earlier, as well as the half-brother of the Hsien Feng Emperor, whose reign had ended three months ago, and the uncle of the child who was now hailed as the Chi Hsiang Emperor. The Imperial succession continued unbroken, though the new Emperor faced a wholly different world. Even his immediate predecessors had lived in a world little altered since the reign of the Founding Emperor of the Great Pure Dynasty two centuries earlier.

His own education, Prince Kung knew, had really begun the preceding year. At twenty-eight, he was just attaining comprehension of the new forces working in the Great Empire. The old ways had suited the old days, which were ended forever. The new era created by the barbarians' intrusion required Princes and Mandarins to learn new ways. Not to change fundamentally, but sufficiently to use the barbarians' weapons – and make the Great Empire once again vigorous and supreme.

The brute force of guns appeared more powerful than the word, which was the foundation of Confucian civilization. Ultimately, however, the word controlled even the most formidable weapons, as the barbarians' behaviour proved. Having compelled the Dynasty to accept the Treaties by force, the barbarians had – to the astonishment of the Mandarinate and his own surprise – withdrawn their troops from Tientsin and Canton. True to their word, they were not seeking to conquer the Empire, but only to trade on relatively equitable terms.

Despite the radical changes of the past two years, the word remained pre-eminent. Having given their word, the barbarians were keeping their word. The internal difficulties of the Empire, too, must be composed by new words that were in harmony with traditional Dynastic Law.

He read again the Edict Yehenala had handed him after accepting his Humble Memorial. Although he recognised the style of his younger brother, Prince Chun, the inspiration undoubtedly derived from Yehenala, who could not quite write the edided formal Chinese with the grace necessary to sway Grand Chancellors and Ministers. The Edict was a forceful indictment of the eight-member Council of Regency.

The names of Prince Yee, the Lord Protector, and his henchman Prince Cheng stood first, followed by the Assistant Grand Chancellor Su Shun. The charges were devastating: arrogating Imperial authority to themselves by issuing the counterfeit Farewell Edict; systematically deceiving the former Emperor for their own benefit; offering fallacious counsel regarding the barbarians, in particular advising the detention of the British envoys, which had led to the destruction of the Summer Palaces; encouraging the former Emperor's catastrophic flight to Jehol; insulting the Imperial Majesty of the Empress Dowagers; and attempting to usurp supreme power by hoodwinking the young Emperor.

The irate junior Empress Dowager had subsequently sent him an addendum written in her own hand in her own crude, vigorous style: 'The conspirator's audacity in questioning the Empress Dowagers' right to give audience to Prince Kung this morning showed a depth of wickedness almost inconceivable to normal human beings. They stand convicted by their own actions of the most heinous designs. The punishments previously contemplated for their innumerable crimes are wholly inadequate to the abominations they have committed.'

The stubble on Prince Kung's cheeks prickled, and he scratched it nervously. She was not only formidable, this young sister-in-law of his. She was implacable. One day he too might have difficulties with her imperious temper. But, he assured himself, recalling the Humble Memorial he had submitted that morning, he could cope with her. She was, after all, a woman – and no woman, however resolute, could prevail unless supported by a man.

Though clothed in far more elegant language by the Grand Chancellor, assisted by the Ministers of Finance and Justice, the Humble Memorial was even more pointed than the Edict. It forthrightly implored the Empress Mothers to take the course upon which they were already determined. The petitioners begged the Empress Dowagers to assume responsibility for state affairs until the child-Emperor came of age eleven years hence. As Empress Dowagers *Regent* they would 'listen behind the screen and administer the government'.

The future, Prince Kung reflected wryly, would be interesting – and arduous, though he was confident that he could manage the self-willed Yehenala. Meanwhile, all was proceeding as they had planned at their clandestine meetings in Jehol. He tapped a small gong with a padded mallet, and the Baronet Jung Lu entered.

'We can wait no longer, Colonel,' Prince Kung said. 'Bring the *former* Assistant Grand Chancellor Su Shun to me. His presence at the catafalque of my brother, the previous Emperor, is a profanation . . . an abomination. Bring Su Shun to me immediately. And Colonel, you need not be too gentle.'

*

November 7–8, 1861   *The Forbidden City*

The Imperial Clan Court assembled on November 7th, 1861 in the Hall of Earnest Diligence, where emperors reviewed sentences of death. The white marble balustrades, which had glistened so cruelly when the Hsien Feng Emperor reprieved Aisek Lee, were without lustre in the grey dawn. The Dragon Throne was unoccupied, for the child-Emperor still slept in his mother's palace.

Attired in full Court Regalia, Prince Kung sat at the centre of the long table set before the dais. As Chief Justice of the Imperial Clan Court, he normally presided over the eight Manchu Princes who tried their peers. Since the prisoners were charged with treason against the state as well as violation of Clan Law, the tribunal had been enlarged. The three Grand Chancellors were flanked by the six Ministers and the nine Presidents of Boards who directed the chief organs of government. Four Senior Censors wearing the unicorns of their extraordinary rank on their dark surcoats ensured the propriety of the proceedings.

Wearing short tunics of coarse white cotton, the eight conspirators kneeled before the Court. The blunt features of Prince Yee, so briefly Lord Protector of the Nation, were expressionless in his fleshy face. His dupe Prince Cheng was a bewildered and fearful youth again, all his illusory assurance vanished. The Assistant Grand Chancellor Su Shun glared defiantly, his lean body rigid.

'We shall deal with the most heinous offender first,' Prince Kung declared. '*Former* Assistant Grand Chancellor Su Shun, your towering crimes offend Heaven. Not even at the ultimate moment did your sins cease. When the troops found you in the camp beside the Imperial Catafalque, you were in bed with your youngest concubine. For that crime alone, you deserve death by slicing. You know it is forbidden for any man to lie with any woman during the period of high mourning for the departed Emperor. But to fornicate in the presence of the Emperor's spirit . . .'

'Prince Kung, how many men obey that stricture?' Su Shun's knife-blade lips chopped his words. 'If you kill me for that, you must kill half the men in the Empire.'

'Half the men in the Empire were not charged with the sacred mission of conveying the earthly remains of the former Emperor to their final resting place, Su Shun!' Prince Kung said softly. 'Half the men in the Empire did not conspire to usurp the Imperial Authority. You, you above all, plotted . . .'

'Not I alone . . . and not I above all.' The arch-conspirator's beaked nose was arrogant in his shrunken face. 'I could tell you . . .'

'No need for accusations. You may only confess. Confession will ease your spirit and . . .'

'What am I to confess?' Su Shun demanded. 'What imaginary crime?'

'Not crimes, Su Shun!' A Grand Chancellor spoke for the first time. 'Not crimes but abominations, virtually every one of the ten abominations. Usurping Imperial Authority and deceiving the Emperor, those are great abominations. Impugning the Empress Dowagers' Majesty by attempting to turn them against each other is a great abomination. Actually seating yourself on the Dragon Throne is a blasphemous abomination. The most heinous abomination is your brazen flouting of the laws of filial piety. The Emperor is the father of all, and your every act grossly insulted the Emperor. For all we know, you hastened his death . . .'

'Not I, certainly not I,' Su Shun shouted. 'Not I, but . . .'

'The accused will be silent,' Prince Kung hastily directed. 'He may not bandy words with the Court. I recommend death by slicing, the most extreme penalty prescribed by the Criminal Code. You must be made to suffer as you have made the nation suffer.'

'Not I, but . . .' Su Shun ranted, and a guard clapped a hand over his mouth.

'Remove him!' Prince Kung directed. 'We shall now deal with the other accused.'

Prince Yee, the former Lord Protector, and his dupe Prince Cheng accepted the sentence of the Imperial Clan Court with stony Manchu dignity, grateful that they were to be allowed to hang themselves, rather than suffering decapitation. Since the remaining five conspirators had been the pawns of the arch-conspirators, they were only to be dismissed from their offices and placed under a perpetual interdiction. Never again would any of the five be permitted to serve the Dynasty in any capacity. They were disgraced, and they were impoverished, all their goods confiscated. But they were to live – and the turning wheel of fate might yet restore them to power.

Prince Yee and Prince Cheng preferred to go quickly. When they were arrested, they had bidden farewell to their families in expectation of the death sentence. Two hours after the Imperial Clan Court rendered its verdict, Prince Yee helped Prince Cheng hook the silken ropes due their rank over the beams set conveniently low in the Empty Chamber of the Imperial Clan Prison. He then adjusted his own noose precisely, and, when his junior did not falter, he kicked away the low stool under his feet.

The warders came for the former Assistant Grand Chancellor Su Shun just before dawn of the following day. They hauled him, squirming and screaming, from a cell in the Forbidden City normally reserved for erring eunuchs, where he had been confined alone to prevent his spreading slanderous allegations against personages of high standing. The unspeaking warders forced his trembling limbs into the rough grey tunic and short trousers of a condemned criminal. They thrust a gag into his mouth before they trundled him on a wheelbarrow through the morning bustle of Peking. When they approached the public execution ground through a narrow *hutung*, the condemned man quivered at the reek of blood.

'By the mercy of the Court, you are *not* to endure death by slicing.' The chief warder finally spoke. 'You will not suffer hours of agony while the executioners slice the flesh from your body bit by bit. The mercy of the Court, as in response to the Empress Dowagers' request, directs that you are to be decapitated. You will, of course, not speak or . . .'

Su Shun nodded acquiescence, and the warder removed the gag. Barefoot on the half-frozen ground, the former Assistant Grand Chancellor stumbled on a round object, which skittered away. He looked down at the severed head, and bile choked his throat. He trembled and almost fell when he saw the four decapitated felons still lying on the iron-hard ground.

The condemned man saw little else except a blur of movement on the edges of the execution ground. He did not see the workmen, servants, and beggars who had congregated in a holiday spirit to watch him die. He did not see the food hawkers or hear them calling their wares. He did not see the four judicial Mandarins assigned to certify his death standing aloof from the throng, their perfumed fans held fastidiously before their noses.

A calloused hand thrust the former Assistant Grand Chancellor to his knees. Sodden with blood, the ground yielded beneath him. The executioner's apprentice grasped his queue and pulled his head forward to bare his neck to the two-handed scimitar. Su Shun again struggled desperately. Though his hands were pinioned behind his back, he shook his head and body so violently the apprentice's grasp slipped.

'I told them,' he shouted. 'I told them we should kill the bitch in Jehol. Before she killed us, I said, the murdering bitch, like the Emperor. I . . .'

The apprentice grasped the queue with both hands and jerked with all his strength. The scimitar fell, and Su Shun's head tumbled among the stones. His mouth was still stretched open in protest.

*

The gales that had stormed through the mountain passes of Manchuria and across the Great Wall two weeks earlier swept north-west to pelt the grasslands of Mongolia before veering abruptly and returning to harry Peking again on the evening of November 10th, 1861. The following morning, the sun reappeared to sanctify the new reign with its auspicious rays, but translucent arrows of rain still fell.

Crystalline streams poured from the gaping mouths of the thousand dragon-head spouts on the edges of the three jade terraces that rose seventy-five feet to the Palace of Supreme Harmony at the precise centre of the Forbidden City. Between the marble-balustraded stairways, torrents cascaded down the broad marble plaque carved with Imperial dragons and phoenixes. Sparkling iridescent in the morning light, the cascades portended the bounty of sun and water Heaven would shower on the fields of the agricultural Empire during the reign of the new Emperor.

The floor of the great hall was hidden by the multitude of Princes, Grand Chancellors, Ministers, Censors, and Senior Mandarins assembled for the enthronement. The flames of ten thousand candles gleamed on eighty-four cedar pillars embossed with gold and vermilion. The tracery of gilt beams supporting the vaulted roof framed an octagonal panel with a circular plaque, on which was carved an enormous golden Imperial Dragon. Since an immense ball of pale gold encircled by six smaller golden globes like planets hung from that plaque, the common people called the largest wooden structure in the world the Palace of Golden Bells – as the Tang and the Sung Dynasties had called their Throne Halls a millennium earlier.

The five-year-old Emperor appeared minuscule on the broad Dragon Throne, which stood on a gilded platform reached by arched scarlet and gold stairs. The small figure in the brocaded Imperial-yellow gown scrolled with metallic gold Imperial Dragons faded almost into invisibility amid the aureate glow cast by the candles on the cloth-of-gold hangings. He was minute beside the great cerulean-porcelain urns shaped like the sacred bronze vessels of the Shang Dynasty, which had ruled three and a half millennia earlier. He was dwarfed by the silver cranes that towered slender and graceful around the Dragon Throne to symbolise longevity. His splendid regalia, which should have enhanced his state, diminished the child-Emperor.

Two men stood beside the Dragon Throne: on the right, Prince Chun displayed his new dignity as adjutant general, chief equerry to the new monarch. In the place of honour on the left, Prince Kung beamed in

323

triumph. He would dominate the new reign as Senior Grand Chancellor, Minister of the Imperial Household, and Chief Justice of the Imperial Clan Court. His unique pre-eminence was attested by a title not granted since the reign of the magnificent Chien Lung Emperor a century earlier. The favourite brother of the previous Emperor was hailed as *Yi-cheng Wang*, Prince Counsellor of the Great Pure Dynasty.

A nine-panelled screen covered with fine yellow silk stood behind the Dragon Throne. Two silhouettes were visible through the gauzy fabric like famale characters in a shadow-play. On the left-hand throne sat Niuhura, the senior Empress Dowager, newly consecrated Tzu An, Maternal Tranquillity, and on the right, Yehenala, consecrated Tzu Hsi, Maternal Auspiciousness. For the first time in the annals of the Manchus, women were dominant at an Emperor's coronation. They were the child-monarch's Regents emplaced in the position previous dynasties had called *chiu-lien ting-cheng*, listening behind the screen and administering the state.

When Prince Kung glanced at those shadows, his eyes lingered on Yehenala. Perhaps, the Prince Counsellor pondered, he had yielded too much power. All major decisions, even military decisions, were to be considered by himself and the other Grand Chancellors *after* the Empress Dowagers had dealt with them. Imperial Edicts would be affirmed by the Grand Chancellors *after* they were drafted by the Empresses' secretariat. Every official proceeding to a senior provincial post would, as specified by Dynastic Law, report in audience to the child-Emperor. The Empress Dowagers would sit behind their translucent screen, Niuhura comfortably silent while Yehenala asked sharp questions and issued peremptory commands.

Even the reign name was altered, ostensibly to repudiate the usurpers, who had called the child-Emperor's reign Chi Hsiang, Propitious Omen. The ideograms Tung Chih, the new reign-name, would seal official documents and validate the currency.

The people were already saying that Tung Chih – literally Common Rule – really stood for Co-Equal Government by the two Empress Dowagers. Elided from the classical phrase *tung-kuei yu chih,* Tung Chih was actually intended to express the *common* desire of the Dynasty and the people to restore *order* and revive the grandeur of the Great Empire. Unfortunately, the people believed it asserted the Dowagers' supremacy.

Behind the screen, Yehenala smiled in undisguised triumph. She had at twenty-six attained far greater glory than the small girl in the little house on Pewter *hutung* had ever imagined. She had attained the power of which she dreamed when she was a junior concubine slavishly serving the depraved former Emperor. The docile Niuhura was no impediment to her will, and she would balance the compliant Prince Chun against the proud Prince Kung. If the Baronet Jung Lu's arrogance impelled him to foolish demands, she would naturally discipline him. But his devotion was still unblemished, and she would continue to enjoy him – discreetly.

She had also ensured her personal wealth. Some twenty million *taels* amassed in Peking by the arch-conspirator, the executed Assistant Grand Chancellor Su Shun, were already forfeit to her private purse. Her chief eunuch Little An Hai-teh was now en route to Jehol to determine the extent of the further treasure Su Shun had secreted in his new palace there. She was, however, already the richest individual in the Empire.

'*Wan sui! Wan wan sui!*' The courtiers acclaimed her son, the Tung Chih Emperor, who nodded on the golden Dragon Throne. 'Ten thousand years! Ten thousand times ten thousand years!'

Yehenala was confident that she would enjoy great longevity amid Imperial splendour. She would have much time to set the affairs of the Empire in order. She would humble the barbarians, though she would not disdain their ingenious mechanical devices. And she would crush the Long Haired Rebels. Who but she had earlier arranged the appointment as commander-in-chief of the Viceroy Tseng Kuo-fang, who was already moving decisively against the fanatical rabble?

Unparalleled peace and unprecedented prosperity would bless the Great Pure Dynasty, since many decades of unchallengeable power lay before her. He was a good boy, her treasure. Even after he came of age, he would dutifully attend to his mother's wise counsel.

CHAPTER FORTY-SIX

February 3, 1862   *Shanghai*

Saul Haleevie smiled ruefully as he trimmed his beard with nail-scissors before the small mirror on his dressing-table, though he had promised his wife he would put business worries out of his mind for their daughter's birthday party. Sarah had sworn in return that she would refrain from smothering Fronah with mournful solicitude which made the girl more unhappy, and he hoped she would keep her promise. His wife's eyes were over-bright, and the minutely crinkled skin around them was pink. She had been crying again, he saw angrily. Neither the belladonna drops nor the trace of cosmetic applied after cold compresses could completely conceal the marks of her tears.

Sarah twirled for his admiration in the silver-embroidered cream satin kaftan she considered more fitting to her forty-three years than the bright patterns she had worn for festive occasions in her youth. The swirling hem revealed cream satin shoes with silver bows tied at the instep. She had grudgingly adopted two-inch heels a year earlier because Fronah insisted she would be even more graceful if her slight stature were enhanced. Now she would never be without them.

'You're beautiful, my dear, quite beautiful,' he said. 'Anyone would think *you* were twenty-three, certainly not the mother of a twenty-three-year-old daughter or a grandmother. Remember, she's still young and strong. Her life's in front of her.'

'Don't Saul, please don't,' she replied. 'Don't be too jolly. It's enough if I don't cry.'

'It's not an absolute disaster. Now smile for me.'

'If you'll smile, too. You're as solemn as an old rabbi on Yom Kippur.'

He actually smiled spontaneously at that flash of her old spirit. They could not grieve constantly over Fronah's unhappiness. Neither could he tell Sarah that he hated her silver embroidery nor, certainly, why. She had, this once, not questioned his vague explanation that he was worried because trade was slow and old Solomon Khartoon was, as usual, demanding higher profits.

He could not tell Sarah that he hated the colour of silver because of Lionel Henriques. Her admiration for the Englishman had turned to detestation when he deserted Fronah to join the Taipings. Her detestation would turn to hatred if Saul told her the true reason for his worry. He was struggling to meet the extortionate 20 percent penalty interest the Englishman had secretly promised should the silver borrowed in Hong Kong to expand the firm's operations not be repaid in full after five years. Compared to that burden, paying their son-in-law's debts had been a featherweight. Saul did not want his wife to hate the Englishman, since he still hoped for a reconciliation.

Six months after Lionel's disappearance, he had not sent Fronah a single word. Only through Aaron's infrequent cryptic messages to David did the Haleevies know that their son-in-law and their adopted son were still alive. Amid the renewed turmoil as the Taipings resumed the offensive against the coastal provinces, the fugitives were doing well. As chief secretary to the Taiping Commander-in-Chief Li Hsiu-ching, who was called the Loyal King, Aaron drafted orders and proclamations. He also commanded a battalion of Holy Soldiers in action. When not serving with the Taiping artillery, Lionel acted as an adviser on foreign trade to the Heavenly Kingdom's Ministry of Finance. The Taipings would need all the help God could give them, Saul ruminated, with a financial adviser who was not only a thief, but a fool about money.

The merchant laid the nail-scissors down and looked hard at himself in the mirror. His russet hair was streaked with grey, and many lines had appeared on his high forehead during the past half year. Although denying himself the debilitating luxury of hatred, he despised his cavalier son-in-law.

Saul Haleevie was almost forty-seven. His fortunes should have been securely established, and he should have been anticipating the arrival of more grandchildren. He was instead struggling desperately to meet the debts the profligate Lionel had laid upon him, and he was riven by anxiety for his lonely daughter and her son.

He could, Saul reflected, forgive the profligate his irresponsibility, even his deceit in concealing the rising scale of interest. Though it would gall, he could forgive Lionel those transgressions if it would make Fronah happy. But he could not forgive himself for failing to guard against the plausible Englishman's malfeasances. Lionel was devoid of moral sense, just as some men were incapable of distinguishing certain colours.

A little earlier, Lionel might have been useful to Haleevie and Lee in the Taiping camp. His scapegrace son-in-law had, however, joined the Taipings just as he had cut off his own dealings with them. After the British and French aligned themselves with the Manchus against the Heavenly Kingdom, Saul considered the insurgent regime doomed.

'We'll be late if we don't hurry, Saul,' Sarah warned. 'Stop trimming your beard and come along. It's already a perfect patriarch's beard.'

'Some patriarch! I can't even control one imbecilic son-in-law . . . not to speak of a stubborn daughter.'

'She'll agree in time, Saul, and call the baby Judah Haleevie-Henriques. Just give her time.'

Saul and Sarah were late for the small birthday party to which Fronah had agreed in place of the gala reception they had wanted, to show that the Haleevies still held their heads high. But they were not the last to arrive. As they approached the ill-omened Nest of Joy through a garden draped by fog that February evening in 1862, they heard the clatter of a pony trap on Szechwan Road. Gabriel Hyde joined them at the door, his coat bedewed by drizzle and his face drawn. He stood long watches on the Long River with the Taipings more aggressive each day.

'Evening, Ma'am, Mr Haleevie,' the American said. 'A nasty evening. I'll try to contribute to the gaiety of this joyous occasion.'

'Do, Captain,' Sarah urged. 'Try hard. But it's not a joyous occasion, even though Fronah's still young enough to remember her birthdays. I remember, when she was a little girl, how she loved birthday parties and . . .'

'He's not interested in your memories, Sarah,' Saul chided. 'Of course, Gabriel, she's sad. It's her first birthday without her husband.'

'Well, she had birthdays before she met Mr Henriques,' Sarah observed with uncharacteristic spite. 'And, God willing, she'll have lots more. Probably better without him.'

Gabriel Hyde was pleased when Lao Woo, the undersized number-one boy who had replaced the portly Lao King, opened the door and relieved him of the need to reply. He understood Sarah's bitterness, but he was surprised by her frankness. In his exhaustion he had almost ignored the invitation delivered when *Mencius* tied up two hours earlier. But duty had kept him from seeing Fronah for two months, and he could not slight her when the settlement was buzzing about her virtual withdrawal from the social life she had loved. How badly, he wondered, was she taking the first major disappointment of her pampered existence?

He had never thought Fronah capable of deep feeling. Her emotions were vehement, shallow – and transitory. A half-year after the shock, he would have expected her to have recovered much of her ebullience. But the enduring effect must be profound if her normally discreet mother spoke so forthrightly before an outsider like himself. Saul Haleevie's indulgence had apparently made his daughter vulnerable, rather than resilient.

'Mama! Papa!' Fronah hugged her parents. 'I thought you were never coming.'

'Congratulations, darling.' Sarah proffered a scarlet parcel tied with silver ribbon. 'Many happy returns.'

'Gabriel!' Fronah smiled. 'Now I'm really happy, even if I am getting old. You've been neglecting me lately.'

'How could I, Fronah, my dear?' He played to the light mood for which she was obviously striving. 'Blame the Taipings, not me. Only duty could keep me from seeing you.'

'. . . loved I not honour more,' she quoted with gentle irony, her fingers stripping the wrapping from her parents' present. 'I can't forgive the Holy Soldiers, but I'll forgive you.'

While she peeled away the scarlet paper, Gabriel reproached himself for tactlessness sprung of fatigue. One should not speak of rope in the house of the hanged man, but his greeting had referred to the Taipings, to whom Lionel Henriques had fled. Still Fronah was as clever as he remembered her. Unlike her mother, she would not speak bitterly of her husband, but neither would she avoid any mention of the insurgents, who were the topic of the day.

'Oh, Papa, it's lovely.' Fronah impulsively raised the disc of shining *tsui-fei* jade to her lips before clasping the gold chain around her neck. 'It's beautiful, absolutely perfect.'

The pendant was beautiful, the American agreed, perfectly simple, obviously ancient, and exquisitely carved with a phoenix. Gabriel would have expected Saul to console his daughter with a showy present, perhaps a diamond necklace, which he could well afford. But Saul – or, perhaps, Sarah – had chosen a gift whose intrinsic beauty overshadowed its substantial monetary value.

The chastened American conceded that he had once again erred in his assessment of the merchant's complex character. He had apparently also erred in concluding from her mother's outspoken bitterness that Fronah was stricken by Henriques' desertion. Perhaps she was more resilient than he believed. Her shallow emotions might be as tumultuous as a mountain stream, but would not scar like a deep river. His dark-blue eyes hooded by exhaustion, he watched Fronah move among the ill-assorted guests in the drawing-room, where the turquoise watered-silk wallcovering set off two enormous Ming-yellow vases.

Her manner was, perhaps, too bright for a self-assured hostess. Her gestures, just a shade too hectic, mimicked her mother's birdlike air. He had always considered Fronah's spontaneity her greatest attraction. When she was happy, she was unabashedly joyous; when she was sad, she was envoloped by almost palpable gloom. Perhaps her forced gaiety tonight showed that she was belatedly growing up, for society required women to dissimulate more than men.

She had never been more attractive physically. Her features were finer and more sensitive, moulded by the hollows beneath her cheekbones, which made her eyes appear larger. Her wrists and hands were thinner, and her gold wedding-band flashed on an almost excessively slender finger. She was fined down like a high-strung filly, her entire body much thinner as far as he could tell beneath her enveloping dress with its high neckline.

Her dress contrasted oddly with Fronah's manner. Though she darted like a cockatoo swinging its gold-plumed head, she was attired like a grey wren. The subtleties of feminine clothing were beyond Gabriel Hyde, but he felt Fronah's dress was comparatively unadorned. It displayed only a few bands of lace on the wide skirt and the demure bodice, while its restrained colours hinted of mourning. The silk was dove-grey, albeit with a silvery sheen, and the braid trimming the neckline was, like the broad sash, violet moiré. Only her shimmering new pendant and her amethyst bracelet relieved the faintly funereal effect.

Gabriel did not know that she had worn the high-necked dress so that she would not be tempted to flaunt the black Caspian pearls her husband had appropriated from the villa of the former concubine Yehenala in the Yüan Ming Yüan. But he sensed that her costume revealed her mood more accurately than did her febrile manner.

'You remember Sammy Moses, don't you, Gabriel?' Fronah asked. 'Papa's old apprentice, you'll recall. His wife, Rebecca, you haven't met, I believe. Nor her parents, Mr and Mrs Benjamin.'

Gabriel acknowledged the introductions with weary courtesy. Malcolm Wheatley, the sixty-one-year-old taipan of Derwents, was floridly genial, though his French wife Nicole, who was thirty years younger, assayed the American speculatively. Derwents was tottering on the brink of bankruptcy, largely because of Lionel Henriques's speculations and his baseless assurances that Samuelsons would rescue the firm. Malcolm Wheatley apparently believed that Saul was anxious to make amends – and hoped that the immense wealth attributed to the non-existent 'Hebrew Combine' would shore up his falling house.

The American nodded to Moses Elias, Saul's chief clerk, and to his wife Miriam, Sarah's confidante. He bowed to Whitney Griswold of Russell and Company. Dr William MacGregor cocked a quizzical eyebrow when his red-haired wife Margaret greeted the American with open delight, but looked remarkably unconcerned. They agreed to meet for a round of whist as soon as Gabriel's duties allowed.

The men's talk inevitably dwelt on the renewed Taiping threat, and, for once, the women listened intently. Some three hundred thousand Holy Soldiers under the Loyal King himself were closing around the Treaty Port, despite the promised commitment to the campaign against the Taipings of the British and French forces withdrawn from Tientsin and Canton. Wheatley and Griswold confidently predicted that the insurgents would be routed if they challenged the European armies and praised the Ever Victorious Army, the Manchu-paid force of Chinese and Filipinos led by foreign adventurers. The Army's commander, Gabriel's townsman from Salem, Frederick Townsend Ward, had been miraculously transmuted from a renegade into the saviour of Shanghai. Though the American heard a note of apprehension beneath the taipans' loud certainties, he was pleased to be welcomed as another guardian of their lives and treasure. A few months earlier the same men had condescended to him as a mercenary serving the barbarous Manchus.

Gabriel did not, however, share their confidence in the outcome of the next battle for Shanghai, for the Loyal King had learned from his repulse by the foreign soldiers whom he had expected to welcome him eighteen months earlier. The Taiping Commander-in-Chief had recently issued a proclamation in which David Lee saw his brother's hand. Anticipating *no* assistance from the foreigners, the Loyal King asserted his implacable intention of liberating the Treaty Port from the Manchu Imps. He urged the foreigners to remain neutral; the Ching Dynasty's Chinese troops he counselled to submit, rather than die for the alien oppressors; and the common people he advised to await their liberation quietly – and without apprehension.

The Chinese populace, swollen by a hundred thousand new refugees, had little choice but to remain quiet – and apprehensive. If the Holy Soldiers took the city, they would, presumably, be allowed to live in peace . . . *if* they submitted to the Taipings' militarised theocracy, that extraordinary realisation of Mr Karl Marx's ideal 'communism' Gabriel had seen in the Heavenly Capital. If the Manchus won, civilians could expect to suffer the customary slaughter, rapine, pillaging, and arson at the hands of the undisciplined Imperial soldiery – unless the foreigners elected to defend not only their own settlement but also the South City against the bloodthirsty victors.

The American rubbed his forehead wearily, but his face brightened when he saw David Lee, the quail of a Mandarin of the Eighth Grade bright on the breast of his orange robe. The Haleevies' adopted son, serving as a deputy magistrate in Huating Prefecture, broke away from the two rotund Chinese merchants in blue damask jackets over long-gowns whom he had been shepherding through the alien throng like a powerful sheepdog.

330

'Gabriel!' he said buoyantly. 'I've been looking for you.'

They impulsively clapped each other's shoulders, though that display of affection was alien to both their cultures. Gabriel smiled at the enthusiastic rush of David's words. Most foreigners were surprised by the young Mandarin's 'un-Chinese' ebullience – and astonished by his idiomatic English with its slight New England accent. Even now, after their shared captivity and campaigning, the American was himself occasionally startled by David's abrupt oscillation between Chinese and Western behaviour.

'I'm glad you turned up, Gabriel, very glad. The family needs support, and your stock's high right now . . .' The sentiments were Chinese or, perhaps, universal; their expression was wholly Western. 'Your uniform's a big asset now. All the taipans are scared to death, so they love the uniform. Even a junior Mandarin's very welcome. Shows we all stand shoulder to shoulder.'

'I'll pretend to be a tower of strength, Davy.'

'It'll work out. You'll see.' The ever optimistic David was suddenly grave. 'But I'm worried about Fronah. Have a talk with her, but be gentle and patient. Go easy with her.'

'Was I every anything else? But the crown prince has arrived.'

Maylu teetered through the company carrying Fronah's son. The ladies cooed over Judah, and even the preoccupied gentlemen smiled. The fine hair on his long head was fair, and his large blue eyes were curious. Although his features were delicate, the infant was enormous for his age, and although the Valenciennes-lace robe he wore was a frail wisp against the green satin of Maylu's long tunic, he was assertively masculine at eight months.

Fronah took Judah in her arms for a moment, then surrendered him to his beaming grandmother. While Sarah clucked over her most treasured possession, the boy's mother returned – with relief, Gabriel sensed – to her conversation with Whitney Griswold, the taipan of Russell and Company.

'A fine boy, Fronah.' The American interrupted, and Whitney Griswold turned to Malcolm Wheatley. 'He'll be a big man.'

'So everyone says.' She seemed detached. 'Everyone says he's a fine boy. I know he is . . . And I'm proud of him. I *do* love Judah.'

'Of course you do. Who'd doubt it?'

'But I don't quite feel he belongs to me. His father . . . but not just that. What with Mama and Maylu and the amahs constantly fussing over him, there's precious little I can do for him. He doesn't really need me.'

'He will, Fronah, certainly later. David and I . . . if Lionel doesn't . . . we'll do everything we can to help. But he'll need you most of all.'

'I know you will, but who knows what'll happen in the meantime?' She paused, then made up her mind. 'Can we talk now? I've hung a new scroll in the morning-room I think you'll like. A boatman by Ma Yüan.'

Cast again in the role of Fronah's confidant, Gabriel remembered his promise to David. He listened attentively to her light chatter as she led him to the unoccupied morning-room.

'Dinner'll be served in half an hour,' she added inconsequentially. 'I'm afraid it's kosher for my parents and the others. You don't mind, do you?'

'Not at all. I've always liked kosher food. Certainly not if it means Mrs Weinstein's *kreplach* and your mother's lamb with prunes and almonds.'

'You really do like those things, don't you, Gabriel?' she laughed, though her figure was sombre against the yellow-velvet curtains of the French windows to the terrace. 'Too greasy for me, I'm afraid. Anyway, I don't have much of an appetite nowadays.'

'You are thinner. But it's becoming . . . very becoming.'

'What does that matter?' Fronah gesticulated so broadly that champagne slopped over the rim of her goblet, and he wondered how much she had already drunk. 'I don't care how I look. It isn't important.'

'It's not the end of the world, Fronah. We've all had bitter disappointments. But the earth doesn't stand still. Things change, sometimes with astonishing speed. You'll see. Even Lionel . . .'

'Don't humour me, Gabriel, please!' She was petulant. 'Anyway, it's not Lionel . . . Well, not only Lionel, not mainly Lionel. It all seems pointless. I feel so depressed. My life's over . . . and nothing accomplished. Lionel? Really Lionel, his running away, only brought things to a head. For a long time I've felt . . .'

'Yes, Fronah? How've you felt?'

'You know, Papa wants me to change Judah's name . . . Call him Haleevie-Henriques.' The abrupt *non sequitur* puzzled Gabriel. 'I suppose I'll give in after a while. But I won't give up Lionel.'

'I see,' he said neutrally.

'There's something about Lionel I can't tell anyone . . . not even you, Gabriel. Maylu knows and I think David does too. But I can't tell you and certainly not Mama and Papa. It's not the sort of thing a lady can talk about. It's funny. Papa suspects I was too independent . . . that, maybe, Lionel ran away not only because of his debts, but because I kept fighting his wishes. Really, I could never get Lionel to do anything . . . anything at all . . . I wanted. But Papa thinks I'm spoiled.'

Gabriel did not reply. Despite his promise to David, it was not his part to plumb her troubled mind in order to discover for what peccadilloes she blamed her husband. Neither was it his part to agree that she was indeed spoiled. Uncomfortable in his unsought role as her confidant, he wondered how he could ever have been drawn to Fronah.

'Anyway, no one will ever know,' she continued. 'David's shut her mouth. The old harridan's terrified of talking. As long as that . . . that thing . . . doesn't come out, let Papa think I'm bad . . . spoiled. Let him think Lionel ran away because of me and his debts. I don't care.'

'You don't care about much, do you, Fronah?' In his fatigue Gabriel could not conceal his exasperation with her disjointed conversation. 'You keep saying you don't care.'

'I can't trust anyone,' she continued as if he had not spoken. 'I always thought Papa was so wise. But he pushed me into marriage. And now Mama and he blame me.'

'No one blames you, Fronah. Everyone's very sympathetic.'

'It's always the woman's fault. I couldn't keep an English gentleman, people say. I was too wild . . . too wilful. I know it.'

'Shouldn't you be telling Willie MacGregor, not me?'

'You think I'm mad, don't you? People do, I know. Papa thinks I'm getting strange, even though he knows . . . Uncle Solomon wrote him Lionel was sent to Shanghai to keep him away from England. But even Uncle Solomon doesn't know why. Anyway, I just don't feel like eating. What difference does it make?'

'It could make a lot of difference.' He spoke carefully, though he was so exhausted he sank into a yellow-velvet easy chair. 'You've got a long life ahead of you.'

'Have I? I wonder. What difference does it make? I tried so hard, Gabriel. I wanted to learn and to understand the Europeans and Chinese. You have no idea how hard I had to try. Not being Jewish, you couldn't know.'

'No, Fronah,' he replied gently. 'I couldn't possibly.'

'Now, I'm back where I started. An ignorant girl who'll never accomplish anything . . . only older. No one wants to have anything to do with me . . . not the Jews or the Gentiles. They're all beginning to hate me.'

'That's not true, Fronah, not at all. They all . . .'

'And you, too. You're laughing at me inside. I know it. You're only pretending to be sympathetic. I don't want your pity. Just don't laugh at me.'

'I'm not . . . and I don't understand why . . .' He could not bear her irrational accusations much longer. 'Do try to be reasonable, Fronah. You're not making sense.'

'Oh, why don't you leave me alone!' she snapped. 'Why I ever thought you could understand, I don't know . . . Just leave me alone!'

'I'll do that, Fronah,' he said shortly. 'I'll leave you alone.'

Gabriel Hyde left the morning-room before her anger turned to tears. Distressed and bewildered, he reproached himself for losing his patience. David would be furious if he learned of the conversation. But what more could anyone say or do? Fronah was incorrigible. She would never grow up. How long, he wondered, must he in courtesy wait before recalling an urgent matter that demanded he return to his ship?

CHAPTER FORTY-SEVEN

Unearthly serenity cloaked the Long River, and an imperial – almost divine – radiance gilded the shoals, extending from the wooded hills above the steep eastern bank to the low foreshore faintly seen in the west. The setting sun appeared inextricably entangled in the foliage screening the shallow cleft of Ma-an Shan, Saddle Mountain. Filtered by wispy clouds, the sun's rays clothed the flotilla with a golden patina. An intense yellow film, so thick it seemed to cling to the men's skin, covered the firs clustered around the miniature temple perched on the eastern cliff. All the visible world gleamed as if sheathed with gold-leaf by industrious Titans.

The other-worldly tranquillity was not only illusory, Gabriel Hyde reflected, but transitory. A powerful army, modern by Chinese standards, was sailing in European steamships from the Imperialist-held upper Yangtze Valley towards Shanghai to mount a new offensive against the Taipings. The Tung Chih Emperor's most effective military unit must, however, first run the gauntlet of the rebel-controlled middle Yangtze Valley. Tonight would be the last moments of peace the soldiers would know and could well be the last night some would ever see, but they appeared eager for action – unlike most of the Emperor's forces.

'We three Lis are at peace this evening, Captain,' the tall Mandarin who commanded the army remarked in the Officials' Language. 'Myself, my clansman, young David – and the spirit of the poet Li Po.'

Watching the golden foam spray from the paddle-wheels, Gabriel Hyde remained respectfully silent. No answer to David Lee's rapid translation was required or desired, he felt. The most impressive Chinese official the American had ever met was virtually communing with himself in the cane longchair on the steamer's fantail. He was truly at peace – and wholly at ease. He had laid aside his circular official hat with the upturned brim, though Mandarins rarely appeared bare-headed in public. But the ruby button of the First Grade gleamed imperiously in the golden aura that surrounded him.

Although the naval officer had met the commander of the Army of Huai only the day before when they sailed from Anking, he already felt that the man called Li Hung-chang was the epitome of the Confucian scholar-official, Plato's ideal philosopher-king miraculously come to life in distant China. His retinue addressed him as Governor, anticipating his appointment to rule Kiangsu Province – from Shanghai until the Taipings were defeated and from Soochow thereafter. But the American thought of him simply as *the* Mandarin. Governor Li Hung-chang was throughout their acquaintance to remain *the* Mandarin to Gabriel Hyde. He was supple yet principled, intelligent yet humble, proud yet compassionate. In short, he possessed all the attributes of the 'princely gentleman' the Sage Confucius had millennia earlier charged to rule the common people benevolently and firmly.

'You may know, Captain, the poet Li Po was an inspired fool . . . an incompetent genius,' the Mandarin continued leisurely. 'Most officials write verse. I still do myself, though my efforts are poor. Perhaps I wrote better in my youth. But poor old Li Po could never hold on to an appointment. He was too often drunk. At the end . . .'

Gabriel nodded, fearful of breaking the enchanted mood with a jarring word. Only in China, he reflected, could this extraordinary conversation take place. Only in China would the commander of an army sailing through a hostile countryside pause to recollect with the same warm affection with which he might speak of an intimate friend the lyric poet who had died eleven centuries earlier. He could not imagine an American general's remembering Chaucer.

An American general? His mood darkened. When his own country was tearing itself apart in a civil war, he wondered why he was enmeshed in the fratricidal quarrels of an alien people twelve thousand miles away. But the Mandarin was speaking again.

'So they built that little temple on that small cliff overhanging the Long River. So many dynasties later, the common people still honour the memory of my great kinsman. But I was telling you how Li Po died . . . is said to have died.

'He was drunk again, drunk with poetry and drunk with the wine, he drank to dull the anguish of exile. He was drinking wine and composing verse while floating in a small boat, and the full moon was reflected in the still water.

'Li Po had never seen anything more lovely. He leaned from his sampan. Not to embrace the moon as the common people say, not to grasp the moon. He wanted to immerse himself in the water-moon's splendour. Being drunk, he overbalanced and toppled into the water. Being drunk, he drowned. But, I believe, he died happy . . . immersed in beauty.'

'A poignant tale, Your Excellency,' Gabriel finally said. 'In America . . . in Europe . . . we've had our drunken poets. Many have died young, and some have drowned. But none, I think, so happily. And we do not build temples to the spirits of our poets.'

'You do not?' the Mandarin asked. 'How extraordinary!'

'Not at all, Your Excellency, though it almost seems extraordinary to me after living a while in China. You see . . .'

'I've never had a chance to discuss poets with a barbar . . . a foreigner,' the Mandarin broke in. 'But I must not indulge myself this evening. I summoned you from your gunboat because my young clansman David tells me your insight and your knowledge can be of value to me.'

335

'*Kuo chiang* . . . I am unworthy.' Gabriel responded with the rote self-deprecation of Confucian courtesy, and David Lee smiled in approval. 'Your Excellency's expectations are beyond my merits.'

'Perhaps, Captain, perhaps they are,' the Mandarin replied with sharp-edged humour. 'But you must let me be the judge of that. I'll need to cooperate with the bar . . . the foreigners, that is . . . when I arrive in Shanghai. I'll also need to use steam gunboats against the rebels. You can enlarge my limited understanding of both. Also, David tells me you are well acquainted with the foreigner Ward. His Ever Victorious Army will come under my command.'

'*Wo-men shih tung-hsiang* . . .' Gabriel again ventured his imperfect Chinese, though David had warned that every subordinate who spoke with the Mandarin was being tested. 'We are fellow townsmen, Excellency. That bond is strong in America, though not as strong as in China. Ward is a brilliant adventurer.'

'An adventurer? What, then, are you, Captain?'

'A professional, Your Excellency, a professional naval officer, who presently serves China. I came to . . .'

'Very interesting, but another time. Tell me about Ward now.'

His Chinese commodores had asked Gabriel similar questions, not only regarding Frederick Townsend Ward, but regarding foreign ways and naval tactics. The Mandarin's inquiries were more subtle, more searching, and more pointed, but were essentially familiar. Traversing well trodden ground, Gabriel responded automatically. His own interest was engaged by the questioner, rather than the questions.

In a nation where most men were short and many were disfigured, Li Hung-chang commanded respect by his physical presence. He overtopped Gabriel Hyde's five feet eleven inches by three inches; his shoulders were broad, and his forehead wide above his marked features. The ferocity of his thick black moustache did not conceal the humourous quirk of his mouth, while the minute indentations under his cheekbones gave him an air of benevolence. He was wholly relaxed in utilitarian blue campaign tunic and trousers. None the less his innate authority commanded obedience, and his inherent vigour was apparent in the powerful fingers that grasped his hat.

Just past his thirty-seventh birthday, the Mandarin Li Hung-chang would have been young for his responsibilities in Europe or America. In the Manchu Empire he was a prodigy. Empress Dowagers and Prince Counsellors might come young to power, but they preferred senior officials seasoned by age. Of course, he was the protégé of the Empress Dowager Yehenala. He would, however, not have advanced so rapidly after she sponsored his first major promotion unless his ability and his performance had been absolutely outstanding. Quick-tempered and self-willed, he had broken with the Viceroy Tseng Kuo-fan over strategy against the Taipings. After the Viceroy Tseng Kuo-fan's capture of Anking in September 1861 had broken the rebel grip on the upper Yangtze Valley and virtually ensured Yehenala's triumph, he had again summoned his former subordinate. The Mandarin Li Hung-chang was truly that rare being, the indispensable man.

In his native Anhwei Province, the Mandarin had created a modern army, far superior to both the degenerate Manchu Bannermen and the decrepit Chinese regulars, by recruiting salt smugglers, roving bandits, and the adventurous sons of the local gentry to defend their homes against the Taipings. His army was loyal, above all, to himself, secondarily to the Viceroy, and distantly to the Imperial Court. Though the victories of Yehenala's Chinese protégés had sustained her, Manchu instinct warned her that they were creating provincial armies and provincial power-bases that could rival the Northern Capital.

The threat was still remote, and Yehenala was, above all, determined to crush the Taipings. Like her collaborator Prince Kung she considered the God-intoxicated rebels a mortal threat to the Ching Dynasty, far more dangerous than even the arrogant barbarians. She was also fascinated by modern weapons, in part because the Baronet Jung Lu rhapsodised over their potential. Unlike the former Emperor, Yehenala was quite ready to alter age-old Dynastic practices to ensure the Dynasty's triumphant survival.

Though her nature made it impossible for her to refrain from interfering, she not only tolerated, but encouraged the mobilisation of effective regional armies. Sluggish communications gave the Viceroy and the Mandarin great freedom of action, as did the self-confident Court's reversion to the traditional practice of allowing officials in the field much autonomy. Both regularly availed themselves of the traditional privilege of demurring from Peking's less realistic instructions by respectfully submitting alternative suggestions. Meanwhile, albeit less respectfully and less conventionally, they pursued their own policies. By the time Edicts responded to their Memorials, the situation on the ground was often so altered that Peking's commands were irrelevant.

Such effusively respectful and tortuously insubordinate behaviour had resulted in the scene Gabriel saw as the poet Li Po's temple dwindled in the golden dusk. A dozen paddle-steamers churned north-east towards the great bend of the Long River dominated by Nanking, the old Southern Capital, which the Taiping occupiers called Tienking, the Heavenly Capital. The steamers carried some 4,000 troops of the Mandarin's Army of Huai, the ancient – and still the popular – name for Anhwei Province. A third of the soldiers carried muskets or flint-lock pistols, while ten platoons, two to each of the five battalions, were armed with small mortars called *pi-shan pau*, mountain-smashing-cannon. The force was sailing towards Shanghai, though the Court had ordered them to march overland to Chenkiang, the Citadel of the River.

Having to fight their way past the Taiping stronghold at Nanking, the troops would run the gauntlet of the lower Yangtze, which was dominated by the Holy Soldiers. *Mencius* and two other gunboats, as well as a flotilla of warjunks already left behind by the swift steamers, had therefore been detailed to escort the troopships. Feints by British and French soldiers might divert the Taipings, as might sallies by the British gunboats.

Gabriel had little confidence in the plan. He wondered again why he was risking his life in the Manchu Empire when his own country needed every trained naval officer. Besides, he was fed up with Chinese intrigue.

Though the Court would tolerate creative insubordination, it would not acknowledge that Shanghai was the key to crushing the rebellion. Yehenala had, therefore, repeatedly directed the Viceroy to dispatch the Mandarin Li Hung-chang and his Army of Huai to Chenkiang, the Citadel of the River, to consolidate the Dynasty's only remaining base on the lower Yangtze and to challenge the Loyal King's stronghold at Soochow. Influential Mandarins from Shanghai, however, pointed out that their native city was the Empire's richest source of revenue, and wars were fought with treasure as well as weapons. Besides, guns and steamers, obtainable only from the foreigners at Shanghai, would enable the new regional armies to finally crush the Taipings.

Yehenala was not convinced. The Viceroy filed her latest Decree, which would have ensured the destruction of the Army of Huai by despatching it overland to Chenkiang. But he had no vessels to transport that army to Shanghai, and the governor of Kiangsu Province was unco-operative, employing the same delaying tactics against his superior, the Viceroy, that the Viceroy used against the Court. The Taipings did not frighten him half as much as the threat to his perquisites posed by the Mandarin Li Hung-chang.

Having reached Shanghai, the Army of Huai would defend the lives and property of the foreigners. But European shippings firms were not in business for their health – or, it appeared, for their security. Since profits were their right, the foreign ship-owners demanded 200,000 *taels* to charter steamers for the Army of Huai. Approximately £70,000 (or US $325,000) was an immense sum, and the Viceroy's war-chest was empty. Chivvied by Saul Haleevie, some foreign merchants finally agreed to meet that cost in conjunction with Chinese merchants chivvied by David Lee. Once the flotilla passed Nanking unscathed on its passage upriver, the Army of Huai was committed to sailing for Shanghai.

Gabriel Hyde did not believe the troop convoy would reach the Treaty Port unscathed. Since the Taipings' intelligence network was highly effective, they undoubtedly knew the convoy's destination, as well as its purpose. The rebels would hardly allow a formidable new enemy force to establish itself unopposed in their rear.

The Mandarin Li Hung-chang broke into the American's thoughts and his technical discussion of the breech-loading cannon.

'I can't take in any more now,' he said. 'We'll talk again later. When, by the way, do we reach Nanking?'

338

'At this rate, sir, shortly after dawn tomorrow morning.'
'In that case, perhaps you'd better return to your ship.'

*

The lookouts saw the mountains standing sentinel behind Nanking just before dawn. The grey crags were both menacing and enigmatic, since no one in the Imperial convoy knew what action the Taipings planned. The spires of pagodas on the ridges gleamed as their tiles caught the rising sun, and Gabriel felt a thrill of fear. He recalled the uniformed host, an entire people in arms, who garrisoned the city where David and he had been captives six years earlier. A horde of fanatics lay hidden behind the cliff-like walls of the Holy Capital, and a powerful fleet lurked in the river flowing beneath those walls.

A cannon echoed across the Yangtze where it veered eastward around the great fortress of the Heavenly Kingdom. A grey puff drifted above the river gate, and broad yellow banners rose on the slender flagpoles rimming the battlements. The north wind that shredded the smoke of the sunrise gun and whipped the banners meant the Taiping Water Force would have to beat out of its anchorage against the wind to attack the convoy.

Gabriel barked at the bosun to hurry the men at their breakfast. The sailors dropped their bowls and trotted to action stations when they saw the pennants of the Taiping infantry clustering on the foreshore beneath the walls.

Across the muddy face of the Long River rolled the melancholy war-music of the Holy Soldiers: horns wailing and cymbals brassy above the roar of oxhide drums. Narrow galleys with crude cannon mounted on their prows poured out of the mouth of the Chinhuai River, their sweeps flashing in the watery dawn-light.

Gabriel shouted orders, and *Mencius* churned towards the enemy flotilla. He glanced over his shoulder to assure himself that her sister gunboats were following and saw that the big steamers were drawing together for mutual defence. Since foreign captains under a resolute Chinese commander were taking co-ordinated action, the Army of Huai might escape the ambush only slightly mauled.

A curtain of orange flame and black smoke rippled along the battlements of the Heavenly Capital, and, an instant later, Gabriel heard the thunder of a hundred cannon. The salvo fell short, raising a wall of white spray a hundred and fifty yards from *Mencius*. The next salvo thundered a half-minute later. Not only the Imperialists, but the insurgents, too, employed European officers to command their artillery. Gabriel conned *Mencius* through the water-spouts, keeping a weather-eye on the oncoming galleys.

The first shot from the Forest gun on the foredeck arched over the lead galleys to splash in the open water between the first and second squadrons.

339

The second shot skipped between the two foremost galleys. Both vessels slewed around in a tangle of snapped sweeps and drifted broadside down on the second squadron.

Cannon barked from the prows of twenty galleys. The shots threw up widely dispersed water-spouts, since the rebel gunners were firing from pitching platforms into the rising wind. The galleys would have to close with the more agile Imperial gunboats if the weight of their numbers were to tell. They would have to close and board.

'Hard astarboard,' Gabriel commanded when fire and smoke rippled along the battlements again. 'Now, port. Port, I say.'

Mencius dodged between the great spouts raised by the salvoes of the shore-guns. Gabriel was blinded by the solid spray. He heard a crash amidships, and his vessel trembled. A solid shot was embedded in the gunboat's planking behind the deckhouse. *Mencius* shook herself like a drenched retriever and ploughed doggedly through the roiled water, twisting and swivelling as the big teak steering-wheel moved.

Behind him Gabriel heard the high-pitched yapping of the light cannon on the steamers and the popping of muskets. When *Mencius* emerged from the smoke-bank of her own broadside, he saw that the convoy was half-obscured by powder-smoke. A swarm of galleys was bearing down on the steamers from the north shore. Their sweeps shining wetly in the sunrise, their small purple sails were distended by the following wind. Behind the galleys, Taiping warjunks cut through the swells of the Long River, white water curling from their heavy prows. The Taiping squadrons concealed behind the cape on the north bank were borne down on the unprotected convoy by the north wind.

Mencius wheeled, her paddle-wheels hurling coffee-dark spume, and raced towards the lightly armed troopships. Gabriel leaned forward as if his weight could move the gunboat faster. The convoy would be overwhelmed unless the gunboats could cut the rebel squadrons off from the steamers. *Mencius* had not covered half the intervening distance when he saw with despair that the foremost Taiping war-vessels were only a hundred yards from the vulnerable merchantmen and closing fast. He watched, fascinated and impotent, as they drew upon their prey.

Gabriel's mouth dropped open in astonishment. A minute later, he smiled with incredulous relief.

The convoy was sailing through the rebel flotilla. The frail hulls of galleys and war-junks were brushed aside and shattered by the steamers' powerful bows, and Taiping sailors were struggling in the choppy waves. As vast and as impregnable as floating castles, the paddle-steamers churned through the wreckage.

He might, the American realised, be watching the turning point in the civil war that had engulfed two-thirds of the Manchu Empire, engaged millions of troops, slaughtered tens of millions of civilians, and almost toppled the Great Pure Dynasty after more than two centuries of despotic rule. Not just the speed of steam engines and the shells of quick-firing guns had effortlessly broken the mass attack by traditional Chinese war-vessels. The size of the steamers made them virtually invulnerable to the swarm of lighter craft. The ships of the Imperial convoy had passed through the Taiping ambush almost unscathed, and the Army of Huai would soon scour the countryside from its base at Shanghai.

The first major Western intervention in the Chinese civil war, which had begun with the commitment of French and British regulars in January, was proving decisive.

Gabriel Hyde spoke softly to the coxswain at the teak steering-wheel. In response to her captain's command, *Mencius* pointed her prow downriver, leaving the Heavenly Capital behind her bluff stern.

CHAPTER FORTY-EIGHT

May 12, 1862   *Soochow*

The Loyal King brooded over his battle-maps under the arched wooden ceiling as the afternoon clouds drifted across the distant hills, veiling the granite outcrops that scarred their green faces. It had pleased him to build the simple two-storey pavilion in the mock-modestly named Garden of the Humble Administrator after he took Soochow, the city of silk and pleasure, in mid-1860. It had also pleased him to call his retreat Mountain-view Tower and to join it to his staff's offices with a path that writhed like a rampant dragon under a black-tiled roof. He now regretted yielding to his officers' insistence that the residence of a king, even if austere, must impress his subjects with his majesty. If he had been planning Mountain-view Tower today, he would not have allowed the builders to arch its roofs and stud their black tiles with spikes so that the pavilion appeared to be the head of an Imperial dragon with gaping jaws.

He nodded, and his long hair brushed his neck. The Commander-in-Chief of the armies of the Heavenly Kingdom of Great Peace realised that he was falling asleep. He pushed his war maps away and looked through the bank of windows at the man-made pond, where weeping willows drooped over grey boulders. His dispositions for the envelopment of Shanghai were already fixed. Directed by the failed Mandarin Lee Ailun, whom the foreigners called Aaron, his secretariat had yesterday drafted the final orders. He could do no more until the troops marched at dawn.

A frown clouded the high brow of the thirty-eight-year-old rebel Generalissimo, and doubt flickered in his candid eyes. His chief failing as a

341

strategist, he recognised, was his excessive straightforwardness. It was meet to fight God's battles in accordance with God's command to be truthful and unafraid. This once, however, he had chosen to throw a dust-storm of deceit between his enemies and himself.

The tall Englishman with the yellow hair was vital in the offensive against the enemy's minds. He was obviously better born and better educated than most of the foreign adventurers drawn into the service of the Heavenly Kingdom by hope of gain or to escape punishment for prior crimes. Also far more clever than those rascals, the Englishman was the prime mover of the campaign to break their foreign enemies' will.

Although he hated aristocrats, having spent his life fighting their oppression, the Commander-in-Chief found this English aristocrat congenial. Most important, he was beyond doubt a fervent convert to the doctrines of the Heavenly King, the younger brother of Jesus Christ. The failed Mandarin Lee Ailun, the Englishman's brother-in-law, was a sceptic, inspired not by faith but by passion for revenge upon the Manchus.

The Generalissimo assured himself that he was absolutely confident. Still, it would be useful to review the mind-warping campaign with the Englishman and his brother-in-law. He tapped a gong and instructed his orderly to summon them. While he waited, he watched the shadows creep across the pond, his hand, delicate for a soldier of his prowess, nervously stroking the polished window-sill. Honest with all men, above all with himself, the Loyal King knew he was staking the future of the Heavenly Kingdom on the assault against Shanghai. Could his armies this time take the Treaty Port or would they exhaust themselves against the Army of Huai and the foreign troops? But he would take Shanghai because he *must* take Shanghai.

He turned to greet his subordinates, both already dressed for the field in the green-fringed yellow tunics of field-grade officers over black trousers tucked into leather half-boots. The Englishman's complexion, browned by the sun, contrasted with his fair hair. The failed Mandarin Lee's long face was scholarly pale, but his arched nose bespoke resolution.

'I regret interrupting your leisure,' the Loyal King apologised. 'But it is necessary.'

'Another general would have berated us for not being on hand immediately,' Aaron Lee answered.

Lionel Henriques nodded agreement when Aaron translated the exchange for him. The cold Englishman, Aaron saw, felt the same fondness for their general he himself did. Lionel could not truly appreciate the extraordinary consideration the Loyal King extended to his officers, but instinct awakened affection for their remarkable Commander-in-Chief.

'The rumours are afoot, Lee?' the Loyal King asked. 'Is the enemy taking the bait?'

'It's early to tell, Sir,' Aaron replied. 'But my brother-in-law believes the measures are already effective.'

342

'The foreign settlement must be in a panic,' Lionel interposed. 'They're probably quaking in their boots.'

'Can we be certain they believe a frontal assault will fall on Shanghai?'

'From what I've heard,' Aaron said, 'they're pulling back their forces to defend the city.'

'And leaving the countryside open to us? Then the strategy of the flags is working on the foreign garrisons.'

'I believe so, Sir,' Lionel replied. 'The foreign officers are always nervous isolated in a hostile countryside. And they don't really trust their Chinese soldiers. If they believe they're facing overwhelmingly superior forces, they'll surely draw back.'

'Are they doing so?'

'I can't be certain, but there are signs. I propose that we triple the number of flying columns showing their flags. Particularly around the foreign-garrisoned towns.'

'They *must* believe my forces are so strong they'll be crushed by weight alone,' the Generalissimo mused. 'All right. Triple the flag columns.'

'Yes, Sir.' Aaron made a note. 'Further instructions, Sir?'

'Not until we move out. Do you have any further suggestions?'

As fervently as the Loyal King, Lionel longed for a Taiping victory, which would change his life. If the Holy Soldiers took Shanghai, he would no longer be an outcast, but a senior officer of the conquerers. His father-in-law, whom he despised as a parvenu but respected as a shrewd trader, would acknowledge that he had been wise to join the Taipings. Moreover, his new faith exhorted him to care for Fronah and their son Judah. How better to reclaim his family – and his father-in-law's goodwill – than by protecting the Haleevies amid the disorder following a Taiping victory? Besides, his influence would ensure great profits in trade with the Heavenly Kingdom.

'More gold, Sir, for the foreign officers,' Lionel finally suggested. 'I know a dozen men who'll come over if we meet their price.'

'Are you certain?' the Loyal King asked. 'Our stock of gold is small.'

'Use it now, sir,' Lionel urged. 'The foreigners must believe we possess not only overwhelming force, but overwhelming wealth. Power and riches are the only gods they worship.'

'You don't think highly of your countrymen, do you?' the Generalissimo said. 'I remember how they deceived me, promising to open the gates, then massacring my poor soldiers. Well, I'll consider it.'

*

To Lionel Henriques Soochow was the most appealing city in China. Not primarily for its baronial private parks like the fifteen-acre Garden of the Humble Administrator, where the Loyal King had his headquarters, but for its extraordinary *ambiance*.

With its mansions and shops, the foreign settlement of Shanghai was a dreary simulacrum of a provincial European town, while the Chinese-inhabited South City was inexpressibly squalid. Though he lamented the destruction of the Summer Palaces, he had not found the Imperial splendour for which Peking was renowned. For all its martial fierceness, Nanking, the Heavenly Capital, was dirty and dusty.

Soochow was, however, quintessentially beautiful and quintessentially Chinese. Its canals recalled Venice, and it also resembled Kyoto, the ancient capital of Japan. But Soochow was unique.

Lionel stood on an arched stone bridge near the Garden of the Humble Administrator, his hand resting on the miniature stone lion that capped its balustrade. Gondola-like sampans glided along the canal, pausing at the landing-stages between the wooden houses with overhanging balconies. The cascades of purple wisteria intertwined with creamy clematis on the unpainted eaves were reflected in the still water. The elusive fragrance of Soochow was wholly different from the stench of Shanghai or Nanking. He could be happy here, Lionel knew. A lifetime would not suffice to penetrate the mysteries that lay behind shuttered doors and latticed-paper windows.

'You've found something here, haven't you, Lionel?' Aaron asked presciently. 'I've never seen you so much at peace.'

The Englishman dropped a pebble into the canal and watched the gentle ripples widen

He was reluctant to discuss his emotions, though Aaron was not only his companion and his interpreter, but his sole remaining link to Fronah. His feelings about his wife had not altered materially, though he now felt acute guilt for deserting her – unavoidable as his flight had been. She was, he supposed, a satisfactory wife and a worthy woman, and he would not be true to the Taiping faith he had embraced if he did not return to her.

Fortunately, that faith kept him from self-destructive pursuit of budding virgins. Faith and the summary decapitation that would follow discovery. The same fear prevented his smoking opium, which could be found in the Heavenly Kingdom, albeit with difficulty. The concentric circles of ripples were vanishing on the canal, when he turned to Aaron.

'Yes, serenity,' he finally said. 'I have found something I've been looking for all my life.'

'A pity we can't stay in Soochow.'

'We'll be back, after we take Shanghai. A summer-house in Soochow. Think of it.'

'A bit muggy in summer, my friend. And, what makes you so sure we'll take Shanghai?'

'It's inevitable, Aaron, the will of the Lord. Besides, the Loyal King is absolutely determined. And he's undoubtedly the best general in China. It's certain we'll take Shanghai.'

'I'm only certain the fighting will continue and many men will die. But you really believe, don't you, Lionel? You really believe in the Heavenly King's revelations. I'd have thought you the last man to . . .'

'I do, Aaron. They've given me peace . . . and a purpose.'

'And your . . . your peccadilloes. You say you regret them, but don't you ever feel . . .'

'Let's walk towards the Forest of Lions.' The Englishman evaded the question. 'I'd like to see it again.'

He was silent as they crossed two arched bridges and approached the towers adorned with porcelain lions among a grove of evergreens. Infantry units under yellow pennants were marching on the cobblestones to their assembly points. Men and women in civilian clothing also strolled the narrow lanes, for the Loyal King had not imposed on his personal domain the ascetic rigour of the Heavenly Capital. The hand of Taiping puritanism lay lightly on the most beautiful city of the Yangtze Delta.

'That fire there, the smoke,' Lionel finally said. 'I wonder what it is.'

'Probably burning rubbish before we march,' Aaron replied. 'But I asked you . . .'

'It's not easy to discuss, Aaron. I think I've conquered my base desires. But I must still struggle against temptation.'

'Worse if you give way,' Aaron said brutally. 'Anyway, the Taipings keep you busy.'

'You like that, don't you? I'd swear you were born to command Holy Soldiers, even if you don't really believe.'

'Belief in revenge is enough for me. I've had a taste of revenge, but I'm not sated yet, not nearly.'

The lane opened into a small square before the arched gate of the Forest of Lions. Holy Soldiers wearing yellow tunics with scalloped borders of red or green or blue to mark their units fed the bonfire blazing in its centre with Confucian books and wine jars, erotic paintings and opium pipes.

A squad of female Holy Soldiers marched out of the gate of the Forest of Lions. A hard-faced woman in her early twenties led them, but many were younger, some no more than twelve or thirteen. Most carried small opium lamps, while several cradled jars of opium, which were covered with dust and streaked with cobwebs.

'Must've discovered a cache when they were cleaning up,' Aaron remarked. 'Probably more still hidden in corners all over Soochow.'

Lionel did not answer. His gaze was fixed on the girls and their burdens. His eyes glittered, and his tongue licked his upper lip.

345

CHAPTER FORTY-NINE

'Insubordination, Kung!' Yehenala raged. 'Barefaced insubordination! It's intolerable!'

Respectfully and prudently silent, Prince Kung lifted his fan to conceal the smile he could not suppress. He had learned that this woman, whom he had thought would be his docile tool, was headstrong and self-willed. Her wishes, even her whims, were not lacy feminine caprice, but steely masculine resolve. She was in reality what he had assumed she would be only in semblance: a *regnant* Empress Dowager.

The Prince Counsellor had also learned to read her moods, and he knew his Imperial Mistress was not deeply angry. It was simply that she had not yet learned the wisdom of turning a blind eye to refractory subordinates – as long as they were successful. However, she was only raging to prove to him – and to herself – that she wielded supreme power.

'They think they can flout our commands with impunity, those insolent Chinese. We raised them high, both the Viceroy Tseng Kuo-fan and the Mandarin Li Hung-chang. We can dismiss them in an instant if We wish. It is Our will to . . .'

'I shall, of course, carry out orders, Majesty.' Prince Kung interjected. 'But their tactics have not been wholly ineffective.'

Prince Kung leaned forward in his chair and snapped his fan closed to emphasise his point. As Prince Counsellor, the highest official in the Empire, the Emperor's uncle was excused the kowtow, as were the seven Grand Chancellors and Senior Censors. Only Prince Kung might sit before the Empress Dowager in the reception-chamber of her apartments in the Western Palaces of the Forbidden City. He would, however, not exceed his statutory privileges, for she was as jealous of her prerogatives as she was of her power.

The kidskin-covered platforms of Yehenala's satin shoes rested on a high footstool set before the yellow-cushioned throne. She was so petite she would have appeared insignificant without those Manchu demi-stilts. The footstool kept her feet from dangling ludicrously, while the raised dais of the throne ensured that her eyes were level with the subordinates who stood before her.

Yehenala actually looked down on the seated Prince Counsellor, who preferred not to meet her imperious gaze. His eyes strayed to the black lacquer plaque inscribed with silver ideograms she had hung above the throne. *Te Hsia Liu Kung*, it read: Virtue Suffuses the Six Palaces.

The six palaces in the north-west quarter of the Forbidden City were Yehenala's personal domain, where she ruled directly over the ladies and the eunuchs of her court. Her motto obliquely affirmed the untrammelled authority which she was discovering she could *not* assert over the entire Empire.

'Yes, their tactics have been successful . . . so far.' Her oval face flushed beneath its coating of white powder. 'We concede that. But they cannot be allowed to run wild. Since we cannot oversee every battalion and every regiment Ourself, we must allow these Chinese Mandarins much latitude. But, never forget, they could be a threat to Us . . . to the Sacred Dynasty itself . . . if they are not disciplined.'

'The danger of allowing excessive concentration of power in the provinces is always in the forefront of my mind,' Prince Kung replied carefully. 'But, at the moment, the Long Haired Rebels are a far greater danger. We should, I submit, weigh one danger against the other . . . temper our indignation with . . .'

'Naturally, Kung. But they've gone too far. Seven times We ordered the Mandarin Li Hung-chang to move his Army of Huai to Chenkiang on the lower Yangtze, but . . .'

She reached towards the green-glazed porcelain cylinder on the side table. Despite its three-inch nails sheathed in gold-wire enamelled with tiny orchids, her small hand deftly extracted the Memorial she sought from the scrolls bristling in the vase. She began to read, and the Prince Counsellor marvelled at the spectacle.

She was utterly feminine, meltingly feminine in her gestures and her vanity. Even for this informal audience, her slight figure was attired in stiff orange and silver tribute silk embroidered with violet chrysanthemums and hung with pearls. Jade pendants dangled from the stiff wings of her jet-black headdress, which appeared to be an extension of her own glossy hair. Though she still lamented the loss of her black Caspian pearls, she wore a magnificent emerald necklace. The rubies, garnets, and sapphires that encrusted her slender fingers complemented the softer hues that tinted her lips and enhanced the brightness of her eyes. She looked like a frivolous princess who was devoted only to her own pleasure and her own adornment. But she read with masculine authority and almost a Senior Mandarin's command of the dense bureaucratic phraseology.

'Kung, just listen to this. A Memorial presented some two months ago by the Viceroy Tseng from Anking. If these Memorials didn't take so long to reach Us, matters wouldn't be in such a tangle. However, the Viceroy memorialised: *In your humble servant's opinion, Chenkiang on the lower Yangtze is well sited strategically as an offensive base. However, Shanghai is the best place to raise revenue. Since the two cities are equally important, neither must be neglected. Above all, neither must be lost. When foreign vessels could not be obtained to carry Your Majesty's troops, the Mandarin Li Hung-chang's force prepared to advance overland to*

Chenkiang. Truly that plan was born of extreme desperation! Now was it, Kung?'

'Majesty, officers in the field must judge the situation better at first hand. That is why Your Majesty employs them. Perhaps I was hasty in pressing for an advance through rebel territory.'

'Yes, Kung, that may have been rash.' She was placated by his assuming the blame for her stubbornness. 'In fairness, perhaps We agreed without sufficient reflection. Still, it was Our command. And it was flagrantly disobeyed.'

'As I recall, the Viceroy Tseng explained his decision fully.'

'The steamboats, Kung. Once he got hold of those barbarian vessels, he ordered the Mandarin Li Hung-chang to proceed straight to Shanghai. At least the barbarians and the Shanghai gentry paid the extortionate cost of their charter.'

'We must conserve the Dynasty's resources,' he replied sententiously. 'I was well content with that outcome. Still, I am aware of the sentiments that aroused Your Majesty's just anger.'

'Of course, Kung. The Viceroy promised: *After the Army of Huai has deployed to Shanghai, the Mandarin Li Hung-chang will himself journey to Chenkiang. Having surveyed the strategic and tactical situation, he will Memorialise with his opinion on the best dispositions to defend both strongpoints.* Will memorialise, indeed!'

'Has the Mandarin Li not done so, Majesty? I have not seen his recent Memorial, his first directly to the Throne, I believe. But I am told it was received by the Secretariat two days ago and immediately transmitted to the Empress Dowagers.'

'This once, the Memorial arrived promptly. By sea, I believe. But the fools in the Secretariat sent it first to Niuhura, following strict precedence. That dear, sweet woman said she intended to send it along to me immediately as usual. But she was diverted by some nonsense about an ailing lady-in-waiting. She forgot all about the Memorial, I suspect. It only came to light this morning. In future, let the Secretariat make a copy for Niuhura to play with, but send the original to me without delay.'

'I'll see to that, Majesty. But the Mandarin Li's Memorial? He's certainly made his reconnaissance of Chenkiang by now. What does he recommend?'

'That's the point. He hasn't. He's sitting happily in Shanghai, and he shows no inclination whatsoever to move.' Yehenala selected the Memorial from the sheaf in the green-porcelain cylinder. 'Here it is, his demur: *The military situation in Shanghai is far more grave than your humble servant had anticipated. Moreover, administrative and fiscal affairs are so complex and so disorganised that Your humble servant is almost overwhelmed by pressing matters. Furthermore, the barbarians here are both apprehensive and importunate. It would, in your servant's opinion, be unwise to alarm them by the precipitate departure of the army for whose*

348

transportation to Shanghai they paid so generously. Paid themselves generously, of course, chartered their own ships. And this Mandarin Li ends: *For all these reasons, it is difficult for your humble servant to fix a date for his tour of inspection of Chenkiang.'*

'The long and the short of it is that he has no intention of going. Is that how Your Majesty reads his words?'

'What other meaning could We abstract from those thickets of persiflage? He as good as says he's determined to ignore Our command, just as the Viceroy flouted Our command that the Army of Huai march to Chenkiang. They're obsessed with Shanghai . . . probably taking foreign gold in return for protecting Shanghai. But Chenkiang . . . Chenkiang . . . is the key to the Long River. We are cursed with insubordinate servants.'

'Still, Majesty, it hasn't worked out badly so far, has it? Better an intact Army of Huai in Shanghai, where it can draw on that city's rich revenues, than the same army advancing with great losses . . . and at great cost . . . through territory the rebels occupy. Besides, Your Majesty's Ever Victorious Army has been released by the presence of the Army of Huai. The barbarian Ward has won a string of small, but useful victories.'

'Yes, Our own costs should be sharply reduced by the Shanghai revenues.'

'As Your Majesty so wisely points out. Besides, it would not do to alarm the barbarians at this time. At the *Tsung-li Yamen*, the General Office for Foreign Affairs, we find them more co-operative every day, the British particularly. Their support made it certain Your Majesty would crush the usurpers, and now their forces have checked the Long Hairs.'

'And what of this insubordinate Mandarin Li Hung-chang, Kung? We must take action.'

'The revenues of Shanghai amount to more than two hundred thousand taels a month,' the Prince Counsellor replied tangentially. 'The Dynasty required a diligent and honest Mandarin to husband those funds . . . and relieve the drain on the Ministry of Finance.'

'His younger brother, a junior Mandarin, is already called the Bottomless Purse because of his rapacity.'

'But not the Mandarin Li Hung-chang, Majesty. He is upright, I understand.'

'As upright as can be expected. He must, after all, live. No one objects to a Mandarin's looking after himself up to a point.'

'He awaits confirmation of his recommended appointment as Governor of Kiangsu Province, does he not?'

'He does.'

'Then, Majesty, if I may venture a suggestion, let him wait. Reprimand him in a private communication. And let him wait for his formal appointment.'

'But not too long, We think. We do not wish him to become malcontent. Nor do We wish his ability to serve the Dynasty weakened by public display of Our lack of confidence.'

'A perfect solution, Majesty. May I express my admiration of your statecraft?'

The interview, Prince Kung felt, had been taxing, but satisfactory. Capable men were inclined to act on their own, regardless of the Court's Edicts. Such behaviour was annoying, but tolerable. Better to tolerate a degree of intelligent, well intentioned insubordination than to nurture a Mandarinate of sycophantic bumblers.

Yet, he wondered, who had actually dominated the audience? Had he discreetly guided Yehenala or had she manipulated him like a master puppeteer skilfully controlling the bamboo rods attached to a mannikin's limbs and head?

CHAPTER FIFTY

June 2, 1862   *Shanghai*

'*Pieh li-kai wo, Hsiao Lee* . . .' The Mandarin Li Hung-chang glanced around the main hall of the Imperial Customs House. 'Don't go too far from me, Young Lee. I need my English tongue.'

Like his superior, David Lee wore a light summer robe of blue silk. The atmosphere in the hall on the evening in early June was too close for the heavy ceremonial robes the Mandarins would otherwise have worn to overawe the impressionable barbarians who were their hosts. Both, however, displayed their insignia on their chests: a silver crane of the First Grade for the acting-Governor and a drake of the Seventh Grade for Saul Haleevie's adopted son. Even above his recent promotion, David valued his chief's affectionate form of address.

'*Hsiao Lee* . . . Young Lee,' the Mandarin Li Hung-chang had said. An Englishman might say 'old man' when he finally accepted you as a friend. Hierarchical even in their terms of endearments, Chinese called each other 'Young Lee' or 'Old Wang' according to their respective ages. His round face shining with pleasure at the compliment, David concluded comfortably that the Chinese way was more logical.

It was an immense honour for a novice official of twenty-four to be invited to join the Mandarin's *mu-fu*, his private secretariat. To be called 'Young Lee' after hardly three months' acquaintance was an inestimable accolade.

Despite his profound respect and growing affection for the Mandarin, David Lee smiled at Li Hung-chang's obvious discomfiture. The man who casually defied the vengeful Yehenala in his Memorials and coolly faced the Taiping fanatics on the battlefield was uneasy facing a large number of foreigners for the first time. Despite his regard for the outlanders' technical, military, and commercial skills, appreciation virtually unique among Senior Mandarins, he was nonplussed by the outlanders' hospitality.

The Mandarin was particularly put out by the presence of some thirty ladies. They wore fantastically ruffled, frilled, sprigged, braided, and draped dresses, whose trailing skirts, almost twenty feet around, swept the black-and-white diamond pattern of the floor. Years of familiarity had not reconciled David himself to the foreigners' lack of respect for their wives and daughters. How could they make a public spectacle of ladies who should have been decorously secluded in their own quarters in the family mansion?

David's pleasure in his chief's confidence was further marred by his concern for his sister Fronah, who hovered on the edge of the throng. She was pale, thin, and obviously distraught. Despite her reluctance, their father had insisted that she attend the reception for the man to whom the foreign community looked for safety from the Taiping scourge.

The Mandarin Li Hung-chang reflected that he had better ways to spend his time than listening to the gabble of outlandish languages from pallid mouths in pink-grey faces enthicketed by beards. He had, of course, not expected to enjoy the barbarians' gross diversions, but he had not thought he would be acutely uncomfortable. The tuneless music wrung from brass horns and tin drums by the sweating military band hurt his eardrums. Chinese melodies were pure and lilting. Yet the foreigners actually appeared to enjoy the rhythmic din which sounded like pigs squealing in a cannonade.

As he had feared, the food was not merely inedible, but disgusting. Slabs of half-cooked beef stood among sugar-pink haunches of ham, macabre whole lambs, and obscenely feathered pheasants. The abbatoir stench would have been sickening untainted by the reek of cigars and the revolting odour of people who consumed not only raw spirits and cheese, but spread their bread with yellow grease made from cow's milk. No wonder the women doused themselves with perfumes. They would otherwise be unapproachable by any man whose olfactory sense functioned normally. He had been assured that the barbarian ladies were no more promiscuous than Chinese ladies, despite their brazen display of nearly naked bosoms. He would never dream of testing the virtue of these twittering, shameless females.

However, not only courtesy, but policy required his presence. The foreigners had paid to bring his army to Shanghai, and they wished to honour him by forcing him to attend this barbaric rite. In their arrogance, the foreigners might have demanded that the previous Emperor receive ambassadors who refused to kowtow like cultivated gentlemen. But he could not spurn their exhausting hospitality because they had no manners.

351

A gentleman did not embarrass others gratuitously, not even barbarians. Besides, he needed their cash and their guns as much as they needed his protection.

The Mandarin uttered platitudes, trusting David Lee to improvise plausible replies to the barbarians' chatter. David had explained that barbarian etiquette restricted conversation to trivialities and absurdities at a reception. Yet Chinese gentlemen understood that the purpose of such gatherings was to create a congenial atmosphere in which official and commercial business could be discharged pleasantly.

The barbarians' manners were peculiar – to say the least. They and the Shanghai gentry had laughed at his troops' utilitarian uniforms. They apparently believed gaudy uniforms made men good fighters, though the first clashes with the rebels should have altered their ideas. Obviously, the barbarians were impressed only by power, display, and wealth. Even their officials spoke with feeling only about profits.

What would their attitude be, the Mandarin wondered, if the Taipings were not implacably opposed to the opium trade and the Dynasty had not reluctantly legalised it four years earlier? If the reverse were the case, the profit-mad outlanders might have turned against the Sacred Dynasty. Young David Lee had explained that the interlopers could not balance their books if they did not peddle the drug. Balancing books, whatever that meant, was manifestly a rite as essential to the barbarians' welfare as the sacrifices the Emperor offered each spring at the Altar of Heaven were to the harmony of the Empire.

Since Heaven behaved capriciously, he must content himself with the world as it was. Since the outlanders' need to balance their books made them his allies, he would gladly fight the Long Haired Rebels by their side. He was thankful that Heaven chose to mitigate the greatest peril the Ching Dynasty had ever faced by thus luring the outlanders into the fray.

Some two hundred barbarians were milling in the hall under the pseudo-Chinese roofs of the Customs House. The Mandarin looked longingly through the open doors, where the Hwangpoo gleamed deceptively cool. His gaze encountered the dapper Frederick Townsend Ward, who commanded the Ever Victorious Army. His pointed black beard waggling, the adventurer was chatting with a colonel of the Army of Huai. The American's father-in-law, the squint-eyed profiteer Yang Fang, whom the outlanders called Takee, was interpreting. That uncultured opportunist, who supplied and paid the Ever Victorious Army on behalf of the provincial government, was prospering even more blatantly after marrying his ill-favoured daughter to Ward. Takee's affairs would require further examination, for preliminary inquiries had already found a nauseating stench of corruption.

The Mandarin saw with pleasure the great globes of peonies shining crimson in emerald pots before banks of orange and pink azaleas, which he always associated with Shanghai. The American officer who commanded the gunboat *Mencius* stood chatting with a young woman among dark firs in brown jardinières scrolled with yellow dragons.

Gabriel Hyde normally found Fronah stimulating, though her listlessness had disturbed him at their last meeting. He now found her acutely depressing. Saul and Sarah were regrettably mistaken in believing that the reception would bring her out of herself. Despite her former love of such gatherings, she was listless. Her light-brown eyes stared enormous in cheeks from which the flesh had melted so that the bones stood out starkly. Her hands were frail claws, which seemed hardly capable of holding her grey tissue-silk shawl embroidered with silver arabesques.

'You've been avoiding me, Fronah, haven't you?' Vestigial affection inspired Gabriel to the effort of talking with her. 'I've come by several times since I got back from Anking. And every blessed time Maylu or that poisonous new houseboy said the same thing: *Missy not feeling well today. More better you come back 'nother time.*'

'I haven't been at my best, Gabriel,' she said weakly.

'Are you avoiding me?'

'Not you, Gabriel. It's just that . . . that I'm tired all the time.'

'What does Willie Macgregor say?'

'He can find nothing amiss. He says I must get out more. But, Gabriel, I can't force myself to . . .'

'Don't you eat, Fronah? You look worse than the refugees. You're almost emaciated.'

'I do eat, Gabriel, believe me. I force myself to eat. But I can't keep it down. I keep getting sick.'

'What does Willie say about that?'

'No physical cause, he says. It must be in my mind. Anorexy, he calls it. That's why I'm so thin. You see, it's not really my fault.'

'That's nonsense, Fronah,' he said hotly. 'How can your mind make you sick?'

'Just looking at all this food makes me nauseous. Sometimes I wonder how long it can go on.'

Gabriel was exasperated despite himself, and he wondered why he bothered. Perhaps because he hated remembering that this inert – almost torpid – creature had, only a few years ago, been a vibrant girl grasping at life with eager hands – as exciting as a thoroughbred filly or a sleek racing sloop. But she was turning into a withered crone, deliberately making herself a feeble invalid. David had told him with distress that she only swallowed a few spoonfuls of rice-gruel when Maylu forced her to. Afterwards, the concubine sometimes caught her taking emetics to make herself vomit.

'Fronah, just look around you.' His tone did not reveal his exasperation. 'Not at these fat cats here. But look at the refugees streaming into the city. They're *really* hungry and weary . . . some badly injured.'

'Please don't bully me, Gabriel.' Tears trembled on her long lashes. 'Besides, what've the refugees to do with me?'

353

'Forget about yourself for a moment, Fronah! I'd almost swear you're enjoying your misery. Forget about yourself and think of other people.'

'Willie says the same thing, only more gently. He wants me to help in his hospital . . . help the injured and the sick. I've always wanted to do something useful, but I'm so tired.'

'Then stop worrying about yourself. Eat properly and try to help others, Fronah.'

'It's no use, Gabriel!' Tears stained her pale cheeks. 'Sometimes, I think it would be better . . . better if I just let myself die. No one cares . . .'

'It's sinful, Fronah, talking that way.' He was no longer exasperated, but angry. 'I care. Your parents, David, Maylu, so many care . . .'

'I do try.' She looked up at him dully. 'But I know it won't . . .'

'You'll have to excuse me, Fronah,' he broke in. 'I see I'm wanted. But remember what I said and, for God's sake, try to . . .'

The unspoken and not unwelcome summons came from David Lee. The junior Mandarin again lifted his chin imperatively as the American pushed through the throng.

The interruption was most welcome to the Mandarin Li Hung-chang. He had been on the verge of an unseemly public quarrel with Takee, Frederick Townsend Ward's father-in-law, and Takee's henchman, the Customs Intendant Wu Hsü when the orderly whispered in David's ear. The Mandarin could hardly ignore the profiteer's challenge. Taking advantage of the congenial setting, Takee and the Customs Intendant had impertinently suggested that he share the enormous profits of their illicit enterprises by assisting them.

The henchmen were not only milking the customs dues, but discounting contribution tickets. Those emergency certificates, sold to defray the cost of the civil war, entitled purchasers to nominal official appointments. Takee and the Customs Intendant were buying certificates for a tenth their face value and selling at half face value. Their profits were enormous, but the revenue the government received was derisory.

The Mandarin Li Hung-chang was pleased to escape that confrontation for the moment. He was not yet so well established in Shanghai that he could clash with the local bureaucracy. The administrative structure he was building with his own tried men would require at least another six months for completion.

'Military necessity, gentlemen,' he said brusquely. 'You must excuse me.'

That curt explanation was no pretext, Gabriel learned when he spoke to David.

'The Long Hairs are moving up in force,' his friend said. 'Our outposts report the Loyal King is finally mounting his all-out attack. A hundred thousand men are marching on Shanghai. The Mandarin plans to take them on himself. He believes this could be the climatic battle.'

CHAPTER FIFTY-ONE

Each of the opposing generals issued his final orders for the decisive battle in a state of fury. Both raged against their superiors and their allies as dawn crept over the Yangtze Delta on the 19th of June, and the armies that had skirmished for weeks moved towards a confrontation. Vapour spires were already rising, though the sun had not yet risen to bake the sodden land laced with water courses. The muggy atmosphere inflamed the temper of the generals and sapped the resolution of the troops.

The Loyal King was eager to launch his attack before the rising sun dazzled his soldiers' eyes. His attention was, however, diverted by the stream of messages demanding that he return to relieve the Heavenly Capital of the implacable pressure exerted by the armies of the Viceroy Tseng Kuo-fan. He was, moreover, fearful that Soochow, which he had been forced to leave virtually undefended, would fall to enemy columns outflanking his 60,000-strong assault force. Like Lionel Henriques, the Taiping Commander-in-Chief had found in the twenty-three-century-old city of silks the serenity he had been seeking for almost all his thirty-eight years.

Even the Loyal King's relentless honesty flinched from acknowledging that Soochow was his personal refuge as well as his personal domain. He ascribed his disquiet equally to the Heavenly King's interference and to the venality of his seven hundred-odd foreign mercenaries.

Without those foreigners, his field-pieces would be ineffective. Yet he had stripped all other Taiping armies of cannon to mass artillery for the climactic attack on Shanghai. If golden bullets induced the foreign officers fighting for the Imps to withdraw or desert, as the blond Englishman had predicted, how could he depend upon his own rascals? Dormant patriotism, as well as natural affection for their countrymen, could be awakened by promises of reward or amnesty. Without the stiffening of mercenaries many of his newly mustered units would crumble.

The Mandarin Li Hung-chang was distracted by repeated thunders from the Northern Capital, which sometimes appeared even farther removed from the realities of the modern age than it was from the battlefields of the south. He had swallowed the Empress Dowager's private reprimand with a smile, but it lay heavy on his stomach. He had humbly acknowledged Yehenala's drumfire of reminders that Chenkiang, rather than Shanghai, was the key to the lower Yangtze Valley – and had ignored her commands to shift his forces to that stronghold. Though he knew he would pay for his temerity, he would not abandon the industry, trade, and revenues of the Treaty Port to the Long Haired Rebels.

Yehenala would not forgive his insubordination, even if he were successful – even less, perhaps, if he were too successful. As the protégé of a favourite concubine, he had advanced rapidly. As the whipping boy of the same lady, now Empress Dowager Regent, he could suffer demotion and exile. Though she had already shown herself as quick to degrade as to promote, he could not act otherwise, even in self-protection. If he shifted his forces to Chenkiang, he might ultimately pay with his head for the even greater disasters that must follow the certain loss of Shanghai.

His foreign allies were also distressing the Mandarin. The Treaty Port was the key to the Yangtze Valley because of the foreigners' economic and military power – and the foreigners were the key to Shanghai. Yet not only the coming battle, but the campaign, perhaps the war, could be lost by the lack of their stiffening. British troops and the foreign-officered Ever Victorious Army had initially put up a brave show, but it was only a show.

During the past three weeks the foreigners, overawed by the Taipings' overwhelming strength, had withdrawn from a half-dozen fortress towns. They had been deceived by a hoary stratagem: a flag-campaign had made the rebels appear far more numerous than they were. Had some foreign officers also succumbed to golden bullets? They were a venal lot, even more easily bribed than his corrupt countrymen.

As dawn silvered Soochow Creek, the Mandarin Li Hung-chang stood at bay. The sun rose and kindled the scarlet and the yellow flags of twelve columns of Holy Soldiers converging from the west. At that moment, the Loyal King launched his assault.

Aaron Lee commanded the veteran battalion protecting the two Taiping batteries facing Chapei on the northern edge of the American settlement. Those batteries were commanded by Lionel Henriques through the mouth of a former yamen clerk from Canton, who had perfected his pidgin and his opportunism as a go-between for foreign merchants and Mandarins.

Before dawn, twenty-eight-year-old Major Aaron Lee had burned incense to Kuan Ti, the God of War, in a ramshackle village-temple. His patrician scepticism had yielded to a prudent wish to propitiate Heaven, which might actually direct events on earth. Lionel Henriques, a decade older, had then joined Aaron in intoning 'Shmai Yisroel! . . . Hear, oh Israel!', the Hebrew prayer praising the One True God, before reciting the Taiping version of the Lord's Prayer. His supple spirit saw no inconsistency in such twofold worship.

David Lee shifted uneasily from foot to foot among the staff officers clustered around the Mandarin Li Hung-chung. He was facing his first major battle at twenty-four, but his natural ebullience sustained him. Though many officers could get down no more than a spoon of rice-gruel, David had swallowed three bowls of congee. His rumbling stomach told him that he might have been unwise, and he broke wind noisily.

356

David's uneasiness arose not only from natural fear, but the demeanour of his commander, whom he held in reverence verging upon awe. The Mandarin had visited his displeasure with his allies upon his liaison officer to the foreigners. Distrusting both the regular British commanders and the mercenary leaders of the Ever Victorious Army, the Mandarin charged David to convey orders in terms no self-respecting officer could accept. His vicious temper was not allayed by his knowledge that David's translation would draw the sting from his words. The young man with the gift of tongues at that moment embodied the perversity of his allies for the Mandarin: He did not call David 'Young Lee,' but '*Ni, chia-huo* . . .You, fellow.'

Gabriel Hyde was still considering the Mandarin's invitation to become his English Secretary. The thirty-two-year-old American had been detached from *Mencius,* since the British squadron would bottle up the Taiping Water Force in the Long River. With four Royal Navy officers, all equally uneasy on land, he had been detailed as a liaison officer to the British infantry, which the Mandarin could not command, but only advise, and the Ever Victorious Army, which the Mandarin could command – if its fractious officers would obey. David Lee found Gabriel sharing hard tack and dried beef with the British officers around a camp-fire that was a flicker in the sullen dawn. David's round face was set in a grimace so lugubrious it was comical.

'The General presents his compliments, Gabriel . . .'

'Let's have it, youngster, What's the bad news?'

'He's not happy with the colonel commanding our batteries on the Chapei front. He's also worried about the foreign gunners. He knows they're insubordinate, and he's afraid they'll run away.'

'What's it to do with me?'

'You're to take command. He thinks your Chinese is adequate. *Barely* adequate, he says.'

'Thank him for the compliment, but tell him its crazy to give me that assignment at the eleventh hour.'

'I wouldn't argue, Gabriel. He's in no mood to listen. And if I go back with . . .'

'All right. But I'll need a piece of paper.'

David unrolled a parchment scroll. The black ideograms were ratified by the Mandarin Li Hung-chang's signature and by two vermilion impressions: his personal seal and the four-inch square seal of the Army of Huai.

'If you people were stranded on a tropical island,' Gabriel laughed, 'you'd need a document authorising you to gather firewood.'

'Of course, Otherwise, there'd be no discipline.' David did not smile at his own feeble joke. 'Good luck!'

'The same to you, youngster.' Gabriel swung onto his horse. 'Remember, duck when you see the flash. It's too late when you hear the report. I'll see you after the party.'

*

357

The yellow and the scarlet banners began moving forward in the false dawn before the sun could blind the Holy Soldiers attacking from the west. The great battle-flags of divisonal commanders were widely dispersed, as were the progressively smaller flags of the commanders of the regiments, battalions, and companies. Having learned caution from previous encounters, the Loyal King had not ordered the massed charge that normally terrified the Imps, but could today expose his men to the foreigners' deadly rapid fire. Instead, the Holy Soldiers utilised the little cover the flat terrain offered, firing their crude small arms behind dikes and houses, while their cannon probed the enemy's breastworks. After five minutes, the banners were furled one by one. The Loyal King knew they would not demoralise his new enemy, but mark choice targets for that enemy.

The Imperial forces and their allies waited on a curved four-mile front. Sharpshooters fired when the yellow tunics flashed or cannon hurled ranging shots. Chinese and Manchu spearmen waited tensely, while British infantrymen nervously fixed bayonets in fortifications as strong as improvisation could make them. Their weapons were far superior, while the boggy land criss-crossed by dikes and streams hampered the attack, Nonetheless, the enemy's tactics were shrewd, and his opening barrage was surprisingly well aimed. Besides, the soldiers knew the Loyal King, who was by far the best Taiping general, had concentrated his crack units for the climactic battle – and the rebels outnumbered them almost three to one.

Gabriel Hyde longed for his own quarter-deck and his own disciplined crew. Never happy fighting on land, he was doubly unhappy as the rising sun transformed the paddy-fields into bright mirrors. The Chinese colonel he had relieved hovered resentfully in the background, while the four British mercenary gunners were almost as loath to take orders from a Yank as from a Chink. Besides, he felt trapped.

The Mandarin had sited the batteries a mile north of Soochow Creek, so that the artillerymen could not run away. If they abandoned their guns, the Creek was too far away to provide refuge – even if they could cross it. Though the breastwork sheltering the cannon were substantial, Gabriel had no confidence in the two companies of Imperial Braves protecting the precious guns.

The Taiping artillery was, moreover, firing with dismaying effectiveness. A shell exploded on the lip of the breastwork to shower the revetment with shrapnel. Rising from the sodden ground, Gabriel saw that two Chinese gunners had fallen. Through his telescope he watched his counter-battery fire and marvelled at the skill of the enemy gunners. Normally, Taiping artillery was as ineptly handled as it was crudely cast. But the man giving the orders a mile and a half away obviously understood his trade.

The duel of the big guns continued for almost an hour. A direct hit hurled one of Gabriel's guns from its carriage and crushed three gunners in a spray of crimson flesh. After tying his handkerchief around his arm, he forgot the fragment that had pinked his bicep. Yellow flashes in the silver paddy-fields showed that the Holy Soldiers were moving up relentlessly, sheltering briefly behind the low dikes before dashing forward again.

'*Hsia san-tien* . . .' he shouted. 'Three points lower. Batteries . . . fire!'

The iron balls smashed into the earthen dike, throwing up fountains of mud. Half splashed harmlessly in the shallow paddies, and Gabriel longed again for his well trained crew. The dike quivered and slipped, then stubbornly settled again. Abandoning its protection the first wave of Holy Soldiers waded through the paddy-field, while the second wave fired its blunderbusses behind the dike.

'Open sights!' Gabriel shouted. 'Fire at will. Fire shrapnel over open sights.'

The four surly British gunners, Gabriel saw with astonishment, were standing fast. Determined that the Yank would not see them run, they swore at their Chinese mates in tones all men understood – and obeyed. The harsh tempo of the guns quickened, and shrapnel shredded the wave of yellow tunics. The charge faltered when wide gaps opened in the line and yellow heaps splotched the muddy water like clumps of broken daffodils.

Straining to see through the smoke, Gabriel allowed himself to hope he could throw back this first assault. But afterwards? How could he repel a second charge with his infantrymen fading away? He turned to order a runner to the regimental command post to plead for infantry reinforcements.

A torrent of yellow tunics was pouring over the sides of the revetment. By God, he was outflanked. He was drawing his revolver when a halberd crashed down on his head.

Aaron Lee dispassionately watched his corporal raise the halberd's spear-tipped head to impale the fallen officer. An instant later, almost an instant too late, he knocked the halberd aside with his sword. The man was a foreigner, who was better kept alive – to ransom or to suborn. He grimaced in astonishment when he recognised the features beneath the grime and blood.

*

The American stirred some time later. The blow, which might have crushed his skull, had glanced off his temple because he was turning his head. He winced and almost fainted when his hand touched the wound. Blood trickled from the clot on his temple. His eyelids closed again, and he saw a whirl of colour before a grey haze descended.

'Leave him alone.' A tantalisingly familiar voice spoke in English. 'There's nothing we can do for him now.'

Trembling on the verge of consciousness, Gabriel heard his guns firing again. He saw when he opened his eyes gingerly that they were pointed

359

towards Shanghai. Then he slipped again into blackness haunted by yellow demons brandishing spears.

He shuddered when a torrent of water poured over his head. His eyes opened slowly, and he shook his head. The red lightning of pain lanced his temples.

'Wake up, Gabriel!' The voice was insistent. 'Wake up, man!'

Focusing his eyes with great effort, the American looked up. The lean face of Lionel Henriques swam amid grey circles. He closed his eyes wearily.

'Can you hear me, Gabriel?' the Englishman demanded. 'You must listen.'

'Hello, Lionel.' The American forced his eyes open and smiled muzzily. 'Funny place to meet . . .'

'Listen to me, Gabriel! Listen now!' Lionel insisted. 'We're pulling back and . . .'

'Pulling back . . . back where?' Gabriel said. 'Pulling what?'

'You must listen, Gabriel This is our high-water mark. We're withdrawing and leaving you. Play dead and you'll be all right till your people come up.'

'Thanks, Lionel. That's . . . that's decent of you, I'm sure.'

'Stop playing the fool, man. Tell me you're listening.'

'I'm listening, Lionel.' Gabriel forced himself to concentrate despite his pain. 'What's . . . what's so important?'

'Tell her . . . tell Fronah I love her. And I'll come back to her.'

Gabriel Hyde let his eyes close again. In the comfortable darkness he felt warm and secure.

CHAPTER FIFTY-TWO

June 23, 1862   *Shanghai*

David Lee wore his conical straw-hat crowned with the gold finial of a Mandarin of the Seventh Grade for the courtesy call. But he had left off his official robe for a light tunic of tan pongee. High summer stifled the Yangtze Delta like a vast, sodden fleece on June 23rd, 1862, four days after the battle of Soochow Creek. The young Mandarin casually fanned himself with his official hat, and its scarlet tassels whipped.

The cubicle with the examination-couch behind a screen was heavy with the cloying reek of chloroform and the powdery tang of iodoform. But those medicinal odours could not overcome the pervasive stench of gangrene. Although the big doors and the small windows of the godown Saul Haleevie had loaned Dr William MacGregor for his emergency hospital were all open, no breeze could cleanse the charnel-house atmosphere.

More than two hundred wounded Imperial Braves and Holy Soldiers suffered on straw-mats spread on the floor of the warehouse. They were attended by two foreign doctors, twenty Chinese orderlies, and six foreign volunteer nurses, all ladies. The heroic example of Miss Florence Nightingale in the Crimea had made it respectable for ladies to minister to the sick. Her example could, unfortunately, neither make them skilful in their ministrations nor inure them to the nauseating stench of rotting flesh, compounded by the fetid odour of unwashed bodies and the amoniacal reek of slopping chamber-pots.

'The Old Man ordered me to inspect the hospital,' David laughed deprecatingly. 'What do I know about hospitals?'

'Still it's a damned good idea.' Gabriel Hyde answered. 'You know this is the first time *any* Chinese official, much less a Governor-to-be, has shown the slightest interest. For years, the foreign settlement, mostly Willie MacGregor, has been looking after Chinese patients . . .'

'Supported by fat contributions from Chinese merchants,' David interjected. 'My father Aisek used to give more than a thousand *taels* a year, together with my present father Saul, of course.'

'Be that as it may, Davy, no senior official's ever cared enough even to ask – much less send a dignitary of your standing to inspect a hospital.'

'Dignitary of my standing? He could hardly find anyone more junior, could he? But you're right, Gabriel. The Old Man's different. He doesn't hate foreigners. In some ways, he even admires them.'

'That's a nice change, Davy. I had a different impression the other day.'

'Oh well, he was upset. Harassed by the Court and worried about the foreign forces. I suppose you know he's been confirmed as Governor of Kiangsu. Only acting for the moment, but permanent status soon. We've heard by the back door.'

'Congratulate him from me . . . if he's still speaking to me. Of course, after the victory, even Peking couldn't do anything else. How could the Empress Dowager not . . .'

'The Old Man also told me to pass his compliments to you and find out if you're feeling better.'

'As you see, Davy.' The American shrugged and winced when his left arm shifted in its black sling. His head was enveloped by a turban-like bandage, and his face was chalk-pale. 'We'll see what Willie MacGregor has to say. You know, I thought your boss would never speak to me again.'

'On the contrary. He's very pleased with you. He says nobody else could've held the battery so long. If you hadn't, our entire line would've collapsed.'

'You're right, Davy. He *is* different. Most generals, foreign or Chinese, would've had me shot for losing the guns.'

361

'He's a great man, Gabriel. His mind's always ranging. He says it doesn't matter now that the British regulars are withdrawing from action because Shanghai's safe. If a foreigner could do what you did, he says, the Ever Victorious Army'll be enough to support his own troops.'

'I'm not sure Shanghai's all that safe. An awful lot of Taipings are out there.'

'The campaign's just begun, he says, but he plans to make it the final campaign. The tide turned when the rebels pulled back from Shanghai.'

'Well, maybe the Loyal King's crossed his Rubicon . . . the wrong way. We'll see.'

'There's another thing, Gabriel. I'm supposed to do it formally: The Mandarin Li Hung-chang presents his compliments to Captain Gabriel Hyde and hopes the gallant officer is mending fast. The acting Governor further reiterates his invitation to Captain Hyde to serve as his English and Military Secretary.'

'It's tempting, youngster. I'd really like to. But I can't do it.'

'I hate to carry back a flat "No". Think about it, will you? I'll tell him you're considering.'

'As you wish, but the answer'll still be "No thanks!"' The American shook his head and winced again. 'You see . . .'

The warped door groaned open, and Dr William MacGregor entered his examining-room. His sandy hair was dishevelled, and grey semi-circles emphasised his bloodshot blue eyes.

'The Mandarin David Lee himself,' he said with mock formality. 'We'll go round the wards in a minute, David. First I want a look at our friend's hard head. Sorry I had to ask you to come to me, Gabriel, but I couldn't get away.'

'That's all right, Willie. Just don't scalp me when you take off the bandage.'

'Are you still vomiting?' the doctor asked. 'Any dizzy spells?'

'I didn't lose my dinner last night. Breakfast stayed down, too. I'm still a little shaky, but not nearly as bad.'

'That's good, Gabriel. That's fine. Now let's have a look at your eyes.'

'My thick skull's what's wrong, Willie, not my eyes.'

'I'll make a note to instruct you in navigation, young Gabriel,' William MacGregor smiled.

'Damn it, Willie, that hurt, really hurt.' Gabriel protested when the doctor's fingers touched the wound in his temple. 'I hope you're amusing yourself.'

'Greatly, I'm sure. Well, young man, you'll be all right. A slight fracture, perhaps, but you'll heal. And do thank God for your thick skull.'

'Is it really thicker than most? They say the Hydes are hard-headed, stubborn as mules.'

'Just normal, Gabriel, though I'll vouch for your stubbornness. You were lucky. If he'd hit you square, your head wouldn've been crushed like an egg.'

'When do you want to see me again?'

'Always delighted to see you, Gabriel. But not professionally unless vomiting recurs. Naturally, if the dizzy spells get worse, trot around. Otherwise, I've got better things to do. Some of those poor Chinamen out there are badly hurt. And terrified I'm planning to kill them off so I can grind their assorted organs up for medicines.'

'You don't need to *try* to kill your patients, do you, Willie? I thought it was a gift.'

'That'll be all, Captain.' MacGregor tied the new bandage. 'If you're feeling so frisky, take a turn around the wards with David and me. It may even make you think of taking up another profession. God, you military men!'

'I'm sorry, Willie. That was a little heavy-handed.'

Gabriel contritely followed William MacGregor and David Lee into the cavernous warehouse. He smiled when the young Chinese squared his shoulders, shortened his normal lope to a dignified pace, and set his good-humoured features in grave benevolence. The lordly manner of a Mandarin in public would soon be natural to him. The American's mood altered abruptly as he walked between the rows of patients.

Despite the light breeze blowing through the open doors, the stench was appalling. Half-inured to the reek of medicines and the sweat stench of corruption, he choked on the fetid odour of rotting rice, which always surrounded indigent Chinese.

Drenched with sweat, the wounded lay rigid on their straw-mats. Red fluid seeped persistently through bandages encrusted with black clots, and yellow pus stained the swaddling of amputated legs. The fear in the dark eyes was most appalling. Though the haggard faces strove for impassivity, he saw that most were terrified.

How would he feel, Gabriel wondered, if he were one of these hapless soldiers? Flesh lacerated by weapons that spat lightning and thunder, they lay helpless in a terrifyingly alien world. As if he woke to find himself tended by Eskimos whose medicine, language, and customs were utterly strange. Except, of course, the Chinese *knew* the barbarians were diabolical.

'They can't understand why we bother with them,' William MacGregor remarked. 'Don't expect to get out alive.'

'No Chinese ever expects to get out of hospital alive,' David observed with uncharacteristic tartness. 'Particularly a barbarian hospital.'

'Well, if they expect to die,' the doctor said cheerily, 'a lot are going to be disappointed.'

'Nothing against you,' David added. 'All hospitals are bad. Except for patients' families, no Chinese ever enters a hospital voluntarily.'

Yet a Chinese woman was bending over a youth with a bandage covering his eyes. Her head inclined solicitously, she spooned minced meat into his mouth.

'You see what I mean? David anticipated the question. 'A mother or sister come to look after that boy.'

When the woman glanced up, Gabriel saw it was Maylu, Aisek Lee's concubine and David's first surrogate mother. She smiled and spoke in rapid Shanghainese.

'I was half wrong,' David confessed. 'She says Fronah dragged her here to help.'

'Fronah?' Gabriel exclaimed. 'Last time I saw Fronah she could hardly drag *herself* anywhere.'

'She's helping in the loft, Maylu says.'

'If you'll excuse me, I've got a message for her. I've been wanting to see her since the battle.'

The American was appalled by his first glimpse of Fronah leaning against the window frame at the end of the loft lined with straw-mats. She was much thinner than she had been when they parted at the reception for the Mandarin Li Hung-chang. She was emaciated, her skin almost translucent, and her plain linen kaftan hung in folds. Her breasts were no longer proudly assertive, but flaccid and shrunken under the cream fabric. Lit by the afternoon sunlight glimmering through the grimy window-panes, her face was distracted. Within a curtain of loose dark hair, her taut, grey skin showed the contours of the bones beneath.

'Oh, Gabriel, it's you.' She dropped a bandage into a waste-bin. 'Willie MacGregor said you might come by. How are you, my dear?'

'Worried about you.' She had never called him dear before, but her solicitude apparently embraced all the wounded. 'But all the better for seeing you.'

'Don't be flip, Gabriel, please. I've been terribly concerned about you. William MacGregor said you were too ill for visitors. Then I kept expecting to see you here. And these poor fellows needed me. How are you, *really*?'

'Much better, Fronah, really. Willie says I'll be fine.'

'That sling and the bandage on your head?'

'Willie'd say let *him* practise medicine. Anyway, they're just window-dressing. Make me look a hero. I'm really a fraud, practically all healed.'

'I'm so happy, *really* happy.' Her smile was moonlight through a frosted pane. 'It's wonderful to see you, my dear.'

Her fingertips touched his forearm, and a spark leapt between them. He shifted his sling and laid his hand over hers. When she gently withdrew hers after almost a minute, he was stricken by intense deprivation. She had seemed an amusing child, precocious and pert, before she became a dull married woman. Why, then, the sense of overwhelming loss when she withdrew her hand? And why such joy at her anxiety for himself? It would be brutal to break the mood. But he must pass on his message – and relieve her greater anxiety.

'I saw Lionel. He was looking tired, but well.'

'Lionel?' she spoke as if the name were strange to her. 'Oh, yes, Lionel. Where did you see him?'

'During the fighting. Out of the blue. Looking well, as I said. Before retreating with the Taipings, he gave me a message of you.'

'A message?' Bemused by their encounter, she appeared almost indifferent to his news. 'What was it?'

'He said . . . he said . . .' It was hard to carry a message from her husband to a wife whose light touch had sent an electric shock through him. 'What I mean . . .'

'Yes, Gabriel?' she asked evenly. 'What did he say?'

'He said he loved you.' The words tumbled out. 'Loved you very much . . . and he'd be coming back to you.'

'What else did he say? Did he ask about Judah? *When* is he coming back?'

'There wasn't much time, Fronah,' the American explained conscientiously. 'He could only say a few words but he's coming back to you.'

'Well, you've delivered your message. I only wish it was more of a message.'

'It doesn't sound much, but it was. He loves you, and he's coming back to you. What more could he say in a minute? But I'm not here to plead his case.'

'Then why are you here, my dear?'

'To let Willie MacGregor look at my wound. And to see you . . . to find out how you really are. You weren't top-notch when I saw you last.'

'That nonsense is over, Gabriel, I hope. I've been asleep . . . having nightmares . . . for almost a year. But I'm waking up now.'

'And you're eating properly?'

'I'm trying, really trying. I promise you I'll be all right. Two weeks ago, I couldn't have forced myself to come here. But these poor men need help . . . and they're so much worse off than I. My nonsense is over, I hope. Can you tell me any more about my . . . about Lionel?'

Gabriel Hyde strove to draw a verbal picture of the grimy figure of the Englishman who was Fronah's husband, and the Chinese, who was her adopted brother, amid the smoke of the battlefield. He could not tell from her expression whether he was succeeding. He could not sense what she was thinking or feeling.

His own emotions were chaotic. Suddenly loath to pass on her husband's message, he had been cheered by her initial indifference. He was now dismayed by her apparent intense concern for Lionel Henriques. But she would be very strange if she were not concerned about the husband she had not seen for almost a year. Besides, the renewed affection he felt for Fronah was still avuncular, only a little stronger. The spark that had leapt between them was meaningless. It could mean nothing, since they were both under strain and both very tired.

'Another thing, Fronah,' Gabriel added. 'I also came to say goodbye. I'm leaving Shanghai next week.'

365

'Back to duty when you're not well? That's barbaric. I suppose you can't say when you'll be back, but we'll . . .'

'I'm sorry. I haven't made myself clear. I'm leaving Shanghai for good . . . leaving China. I'm going back to the States.'

'Gabriel!' Her face no longer translucent, but bloodless, she repeated: 'Gabriel!'

'I have to, Fronah. I'm recalled to duty by the US Navy. With the Civil War, they need every officer they can . . .'

'God knows, I'd stay if I could, Fronah. I think I . . .' But since they could make no promises to each other, it was better to close the miraculous interlude. 'But I'm ordered home, and I can't refuse. Besides, Fronah, it's too late.'

'Too late?' she faltered. 'Too late? Everything seems too early or too late. Oh, my dear, I . . .'

Fronah turned towards the sunlight shining through the dusty window-panes. Her fingertips touched her eyes, and her head drooped. A moment later, she turned and looked at him again.

'Goodbye, Gabriel,' she said. 'Goodbye, my dear.'

She brushed past him and ran towards the rickety staircase. Gabriel watched the pathetically thin figure in the cream-linen kaftan vanish down the dark stairwell. He turned to gaze through the grimy window at the Hwangpoo. Alive with junks and sampans, cradling clippers and men-of-war, the river gleamed sombrely in the late afternoon sun,

CHAPTER FIFTY-THREE

July 6, 1862   *The Foreign Settlement*

Friday evening had for thousands of years been a moment out of time to the people of Israel, a joyous interval between the mundane cares of the week and the austere devotions of the Sabbath. It was good to toil and bring forth the bounty of the earth as the Creator ordained. His people were exalted by their duty to praise Him, abstaining from both labour and diversion on the seventh day as He Himself had done. The eve of the Sabbath had, however, been set aside immemorially for His people to savour the fruits of their toil after simple rites of thankfulness.

The heavy fragrance of roasting lamb and cinnamoned *choln*, a compote of sweet potatoes and prunes, floated through the dining-room of Saul Haleevie's house on Szechwan Road the evening of Friday, July 6th, 1862. None among the small company felt it incongruous to celebrate with such rich food in alien Shanghai when the thermometer hovered around ninety and the air was sodden. Their ancestors had partaken of similar feasts in sun-blasted deserts, where the heat was as great and the aridity was as wearing as the present humidity.

The Ruler of the Universe dispersed His people throughout the world of His creation. Cast out of Israel, they were as much at home in the delta of the Yangtze as in the mountains of Andalusia, the valley of the Euphrates, or the plains of the Ukraine. A Jew was always in exile, never truly at home anywhere, and therefore, at home everywhere. That apparent paradox hardly challenged the subtle Talmudic mind.

The empty chairs at the oblong mahogany table reminded the depleted Haleevie family of Lionel Henriques and Aaron Lee on the early July evening. At least they now knew that both had been alive and uninjured two weeks earlier. They also knew that Lionel had sworn to return, a promise Saul viewed with little enthusiasm. He should, he supposed, be pleased that the Englishman was determined to rejoin his daughter. Yet he felt little confidence that Fronah would be content if her husband did return.

The pretence that they were a united and happy family was wearing thin. Saul and David had watched with their accustomed grave attention while Sarah and Fronah blessed the candles. They had taken their normal pleasure in the women's graceful movements in flowing kaftans and colourful head-shawls. They had, as usual, remarked appreciatively on the food, and Sarah had accepted their compliments with her usual grace. They had chatted about both domestic affairs and the great events unfolding around them. But the daughter of the house was a brooding spectre at the feast of thanksgiving.

Fronah hardly spoke and no longer pretended to eat. The febrile revival of her former vivacity a few weeks earlier had been brief. She was even more wasted than she had been before that fleeting animation impelled her to assist William MacGregor. Relapsing into distraught silence when Gabriel Hyde bade farewell to Saul Haleevie a week earlier, she had rarely spoken thereafter – and she had not taken enough to sustain a mocking-bird.

'You must take something, Fronah.' Sarah's universal panacea was, this once, appropriate. 'Just a little cake, perhaps. You can't go on this way.'

'Oh, Mother, what's the use of pretending?' Fronah's voice was flat. 'I can't . . . I simply can't.'

'You'll starve,' Sarah warned.

'I just don't care, Mama. Even if I did, it wouldn't do any good.' Fronah drained her wine-glass. 'I'd just . . . just throw it up, anyway. Sometimes, I take pills to . . .'

'That's wicked, Fronah, sinful,' Saul erupted. 'You're spitting in God's face. The Almight commands us to savour His bounty and be joyful. You're not only hurting yourself and causing us grief. You're defying God's will.'

Saul paused in consternation. William MacGregor had warned against losing his temper with his daughter. She was, the doctor said, suffering from 'pathological depression and morbid anorexy'. Railing at her would make her worse.

'You should really wear your pretty European clothes sometimes, Fronah,' her mother interposed hastily. 'I'd like to see you in those big skirts again.'

'You know you hate them, Mama. Anyway they'd just hang on me. I'm only skin and bones now.'

'Then why don't you do something about it?' Saul exploded. 'It's entirely up to you. Also, why don't you go out to parties any more? When I didn't want you to . . . but now when I'd be happy . . .'

'Everyone asks why they don't see you around anymore,' David told her. 'They do miss you, Fronah, believe me.'

'It's nice of you to lie, David. But they don't. I know no one wants to see me.'

She had tried! God knew she had tried. She had offered to work in the hospital because it was her duty and had then been surprised by the satisfaction she felt bringing comfort to the wounded. She had, as she told Gabriel Hyde, begun to come alive again.

She had been astonished by her rush of love for Gabriel, and his spontaneous response had filled her with joy. For a moment the sun had shone bright on them. When he told her he was leaving China, clouds had covered the sun – and she knew they would never again lift.

She was perhaps foolish, but she was not stupid. She knew that Lionel's desertion had thrown her into grey depression. Gabriel's desertion had shattered her spirit as it began to revive. Twice abandoned, why should she make the effort her parents demanded?

Fronah,' her father said softly, 'you can only find it inside yourself.'

Find what, Papa?'

'Whatever you're looking for. It's not just Lionel, is it? And you never felt anything for Gabriel, did you?'

'No, Papa, not for Gabriel,' she lied listlessly. 'And Lionel? I don't know. But the humiliation!'

Saul nodded knowingly – and enraged her.

'Anyway, you made me . . . you and Mama . . . you made me marry him,' Fronah flared. 'I hope you're happy now.'

'Child, how could we be happy when you're so unhappy?' Sarah remonstrated. 'We thought we were doing the best thing . . . and you agreed. Remember nobody forced you. But maybe we were wrong.'

'We *were* wrong, Sarah,' Saul conceded. 'Very wrong to press her so hard.'

'That's obvious, Papa,' Fronah laughed bitterly. 'And what do you think I should do now?'

'Your father and I will support whatever you decide.' Sarah suggested firmly. 'Separate from Lionel and make a new life for yourself. Even divorce him.'

'Mama, we're already separated, aren't we? But divorce? You know it's practically impossible . . . for a wife. How can I make a new life? It's not just Lionel . . . not just the men, you know.'

For the first time in years, Fronah expressed her deepest emotions, surprising even herself. Since Sarah was finally breaking through the wall of her secretiveness, her father and her brother remained silent while the women talked.

'If not the men, what is it then?' Sarak asked. 'Can't you tell me?'

'I'll try, Mama. I feel so . . . so useless. I *am* useless! No good to myself . . . to you . . . or anyone else! I used to believe I would do something great. Maybe it sounds silly, but something noble . . . something *really* important. What can I do here? In Shanghai, everything's business or frivolity. What can I do?'

'Judah's important, my dear, Your son's important.'

'I know he is, but he doesn't need me. You and Maylu, the baby-amahs, you all look after him very well. Anyway, that's not what I mean.'

'Being a mother's not important, you think?' Sarah probed.

'There's no need for me. Even you'll admit that. Anyway, I want more. I must accomplish something *really* important, not just dandle my baby.'

'Children *are* important, aren't they, Fronah?' David broke his silence. 'You agree, don't you?'

'Of course, David,' she agreed irritably. 'Don't be so obvious. Without children, there'd be no future.'

'Then why don't you work for the future?' David persisted. 'Their future . . . and your own?'

'What nonsense are you talking, David?' she asked defensively. 'You're being sly and Chinese . . . sly and Jewish.'

'Perhaps I am. But my idea's quite simple. In Huating Prefecture alone there must be a thousand abandoned children, and they need . . .'

'They need everything, David, I know that. But I can't give it to them. Not even Papa can give them everything they need, no matter how much money he . . .'

'No one can given them *everything* they need. Obviously you can't help them all. But there is something you can give . . . even if only to some of the older ones.'

'That's ridiculous, David!' she countered. 'What can I give them?'

'A chance in life,' David persisted. 'You can start with basic lessons . . . reading and writing.'

'Me, Davy? I'm too tired. Besides, hundreds are better qualified.'

'They won't help . . . or can't. If you start, perhaps others will help. Someone must start.'

'I can find accommodation for a few dozen,' Saul interjected. 'Also feed and clothe them.'

'It's not possible, not really,' Fronah mused. 'Perhaps . . . but . . . *No*, it would never work. Let the Chinese do it. Let them educate their own children.'

'That's the point, Little Sister,' David explained. 'The Chinese won't. These kids aren't anyone's children. They've got no families. You know the Chinese won't look after anyone but their . . . our . . . own. And, Little Sister, it *is* important.'

'It's important, I'll grant you that,' Fronah conceded. 'Very important. But it's not for me.'

'No one else can . . . or will,' David persisted. 'If you don't try, the poor kids . . . '

'It's too much, of course.' Faint interest coloured Fronah's voice. 'And it would need careful planning. It wouldn't do to start too big.'

'Of course not, Fronah, as long as you make a start,' David insisted, and Saul blessed the day he had adopted the youth. 'Father'll help. And my boss is interested. Just give it a try.'

'Maybe . . . probably it'll be too much for me,' Fronah said slowly. 'I suppose I could try. Anyway, I'll think about it. But don't expect . . .'

CHAPTER FIFTY-FOUR

October 6, 1862   *Peking*

The autumn breeze teased wavelets from the Pei Hai, the North Lake beside the Forbidden City. When the flotilla of ten flat-bottomed barges yawed gently, the eunuch oarsmen fluttered their sweeps to steady the awkward craft. Bunting fluttered on the garish deckhouses, and Imperial pennants streamed against a sky filmed with ochre dust.

A smile curled the carmined lips of the female deity seated on the marble-inlaid throne in the prow of the leading barge. Delight in the illusory danger created by the wind momentarily dispelled the histrionic majesty that stamped Yehenala's delicate features. Looking straight ahead, she spoke to the senior eunuch standing behind her throne.

'Fire the cannon!' she commanded.

'Majesty, the wind rises,' the eunuch cautioned.

'Do not argue with Us. Aim close to the courier boat.'

A miniature brass gun, not quite two feet long, coughed asthmatically on the stern of the Imperial Barge, and a miniature ball, no larger than a hen's egg, shot from the gleaming muzzle. Yehenala laughed as the ball ploughed the water a yard from the gaudy courier-sampan. She laughed louder when spray drenched its passengers and the triangular banner bearing the single ideogram *Ling* – Obey – which declared that it carried Imperial despatches.

The junior Empress Dowager, still not twenty-eight years old, was amusing herself extravagantly. She happily bore the weight of her archaic scarlet and blue robes of stiff tribute-silk encrusted with gold and silver. She gladly endured the burden of her antique head-dress, a dome of gold wires entwined with peacock feathers and set with gems. She was attired as Tien Mu Hou, the Mother Empress of Heaven, the goddess of seafarers, while her entourage was dressed as attendant deities. Though she could not rebuild the gutted Summer Palaces while the Taiping Rebellion still ravaged the Empire, she would not be denied all entertainment. She loved plays and operas enacted by professional actors who were gelded so that they could perform in the Forbidden City. Even more she loved to don gorgeous costumes and stage her own dramas with herself the chief performer.

Her Chief Eunuch An Te-hai was normally at her side to direct those spectacles, but she had today reluctantly relinquished his presence to make the maritime pageant more authentic. Little An stood in the prow of the second barge, resplendent in a vermilion robe voluminously cut in the style of the Ming Dynasty. He clutched a telescope with disdain for the anachronism, and the square of rank on his chest displayed the silver unicorn of a duke. He was playing the great eunuch Admiral Cheng Ho, who had been created Duke of the Three Treasures in recognition of the seven great voyages his fleets made to India and Africa in the fifteenth century. Other captains and their crews wore the costumes of different ages – from the simple armour of the Han Dynasty to the gauzy panels of Buddhist saints.

Yehenala chuckled, recalling her gratifying conversation with Little An before they embarked on the North Lake. Aside from the cares of state, which she cannily refused to admit she found exhilarating, her chief concern was her personal finances. Though she practiced stringent frugality, more gold, somehow, flowed out of her purse than into it. For the moment at least, her constant need was allayed. The eunuch had just reported the complete success of their latest scheme to supplement her income.

Always resourceful, Little An had two weeks earlier written friendly notes to twenty contractors who supplied the Forbidden City with articles ranging from rice and gold-leaf to paints and meat. Saluting the recipients as his Elder Brothers, those intimate meassages assured the contractors of the Chief Eunuch's fraternal affection – and the warm regard the Empress Dowager felt for their worthy selves.

May I venture to inform you that your unworthy younger brother is deeply embarrassed by the temporary emptiness of his purse? Little An had closed. *Could you find it in your heart to relieve my embarrassment by a short-term loan of ten thousand* taels?

Yehenala had been pleased, though not surprised, at the immediate response from eighteen of the addressees. More than half were so eager to alleviate their younger brother's embarrassment that their contributions arrived the same day. Another seven sent their tribute within the week. Two contractors were, however, dilatory, and Little An was drafting them courteous reminders. But the two outstanding loans had arrived early that morning – with abject apologies for, in one case, a temporary shortage of funds and, in the other, absence from the Capital.

Yehenala remembered her Chief Eunuch's consternation when it appeared that all his Elder Brothers might not pay up – and smiled. She smiled even more broadly at having been relieved of financial pressure for at least a month. Her smile faded when she recalled the two dilatory donors. She would remember their tardiness when they had long forgotten – as they must prudently forget – extending the short-term loans. She would remember, and they would suffer.

She spoke again without turning her head, and the eunuch standing behind her repeated her command. The eunuch oarsmen leaned on their sweeps, and water foamed along the sides of the barge. The despatch-boat was drawing rapidly toward the Imperial Barge. It would be amusing to let the boat chase the barge for a while, though she would resist the temptation to fire the miniature cannon again.

Yehenala teased the despatch-boat for almost ten minutes, her barge turning and wheeling at her command. The flotilla followed the writhing wake in close formation. She laughed when the anguish supplanted respect on the faces of the oarsmen in the boat, but relented and allowed her own oarsmen to rest on their sweeps.

Her Master of Cuisine stepped gingerly from the despatch-boat on to the gilded gangway of the Imperial Barge. Flustered by the chase, the portly eunuch breathed heavily as he bowed before her. He was dressed as Tsao Chen, the Kitchen God. His corpulence was appropriate to that role, and the make-up artists of the Palace Bureau of Theatrical Affairs had pasted a drooping moustache and a goatee on his beardless face under his many-petalled head-dress. Water splashed the deck-planking from his green-and-orange robe with pendant sleeves and from the broad sash hanging over his paunch.

'Don't come too close!' Yehenala accepted the scroll he presented. 'Don't drip on me!'

She ran her eye down the menu for the evening meal. Since the Court was celebrating no special occasion, it was not elaborate. Although the proposed dishes were well balanced for flavour and texture, she struck out thirty dishes and added ten. As a matter of principle, it would not do to be lax. The eunuchs might believe they, rather than she, made the decisions if she routinely granted approval.

'We wish a simple meal tonight,' she observed. 'No more than eighty courses.'

When the Master of Cuisine had withdrawn, an even more splendid figure boarded the Imperial Barge. His supple height and muscular grace ideally suited to his role, he swaggered in an ancient domed helmet and a cuirass of large armour-plates interlaced like dragon-scales. Yehenala had expected the Baronet Jung Lu to appear as the God of War, who was his personal patron as well as the patron of the Dynasty. She had not expected the new Brigadier of the Peking Field Force to appear so early in the day. Touched by his pride in his men and his time-consuming devotion to training them with modern weapons, she often allowed him, alone among her Court, to attend her when he could, rather than when she required.

'Jung Lu, We are pleased to see you.' She greeted him. 'You're early. Something vital to report?'

'Not vital, Majesty,' he replied. 'But of some importance. Since my troops are on field manoeuvres, I presumed to come early. I beg your Majesty's indulgence.'

Even from him, who held a unique place in her affections, this public deference was required. When they were alone, he showed her no such respect – and she surrendered her body and her spirit to his domination.

They did not meet in private as frequently as his ardour demanded nor as frequently as she would have liked. Not only decorum but prudence required extreme discretion. She was still in the first year of her regency, and her power was by no means unshakeably established. Her many enemies would delight in discrediting her, and they had many informers in the corps of eunuchs. She could, unfortunately, no more execute every suspected spy than she could execute all her enemies. As she explained to her hot-headed lover, she could, at this early stage, only execute her most virulent enemies – knowing their fate would deter those who were less resolute.

'What is this matter, Jung Lu?' Yehenala asked, for he might in public speak only in reply to her questions. 'Is it bad news?'

'The men of the Ever Victorious Army have braided the white ribbons of mourning into their queues, Majesty. Their barbarian general, Ward, was killed in battle two weeks ago.'

'Who commands the Ever Victorious Army now?'

'Another barbarian, another American. His name's hard to pronounce. Something like Bu-erh-ge-way. However, Majesty, one barbarian is much like another. They're useful like chopsticks, but, like chopsticks, they're hard to tell apart.'

'Some chopsticks are made of bamboo, Jung Lu, others of ivory or silver. Ward was difficult, but a faithful servant of the Dynasty. Though he refused to grow a queue, We shall honour him with a Commemorative Rescript and posthumous promotion.'

'Your Majesty is, as always, benevolent almost to excess.'

'How will Ward's death affect the situation?' she asked. 'Will the Ever Victorious Army still fight well?'

'One hopes, but who can tell? Soon, Majesty, we can dispense with barbarian officers. Only the barbarian weapons make them formidable. Neither their courage nor their tactics are outstanding, only their formidable weapons. The Peking Field Force is already becoming skilled with barbarian weapons under Manchu and Chinese officers.'

'We must have more barbarian weapons, Jung Lu. Not only muskets and cannon, but gunboats. For a time, it may be necessary to tolerate barbarian officers. Better that We crush the Long Hairs without too much barbarian help. The campaign goes well?'

'Your Majesty's forces are going over to the offensive. But the rebels hold many provinces with vast numbers of fanatics. I fear the struggle will be long and hard.'

'Prince Kung says the same,' she observed. 'But victory is inevitable, is it not?'

'With barbarian arms, Majesty, victory is inevitable.'

'Well, We shall get more barbarian arms.' She nodded emphatically. 'But let's talk of more pleasant things. As I recall, you prefer crystallised lotus stalks to red-date cakes, don't you, Jung Lu.'

Yehenala took the lid from the octagonal orange box at her side. Frowning in concentration, she selected three translucent filigree circlets from the compartmented interior. Jung Lu bowed to acknowledge the honour of receiving the sweetmeats from her fingers.

'Tonight?' he whispered when their heads were close together. 'Tonight, Nala?'

She pondered for twenty seconds, her forehead creased in mock concentration to tantalise him. It would be possible, since Little An had prepared a new secret way into her palace.

'Yes!' she whispered. 'Tonight, Jung!'

CHAPTER FIFTY-FIVE

November 18, 1862   *Shanghai*

The squad of Foreign Settlement Constabulary nervously fingered the frogs of their semi-foreign-style tunics and stamped their thick-leather boots importantly. Their corporal casually twirled his wooden truncheon, but his bravado failed to conceal his uneasiness. He was deeply worried by both the volatile temper of the white-skinned devil who was his inspector and the uncertain temper of the crowd. Each minute ten newcomers joined the throng of refugees, which had already spilled out of narrow Yuehtung

Road into Broadway. He would be severely reprimanded if he did not keep the boulevard along the Hwangpoo River clear for pony-traps, man-drawn wagons, and bullock-drays.

Formerly the chief thoroughfare of the American community, Broadway remained the major artery of the territory north of Soochow Creek which the Americans had two months earlier joined to the British territory south of the creek to form a unified Foreign Settlement. A single municipal government with uniform laws, flexible enough to adapt to Chinese practices, was necessary for the rapidly expanding Treaty Port. A unified police force was also necessary to control the hundreds of thousands of refugees from the Taipings who found asylum in the Settlement. The French had jealously retained autonomy in their concession between Yangjingbang Creek and the South City when the Anglo-Saxons finally rose above their mutual rivalry. The French retained the right to co-operate – or to interfere – when it pleased them.

Differences among the barbarians did not interest the corporal, who was concerned only to keep his spotless record and his expensive uniform unstained. The Settlement Constabulary were proud of their royal-blue tunics with choker collars and silver-metal insigniae, which were so new the tailors' creases had not yet yielded to their wives' coal-irons. Their peaked caps with white covers still creaked stiffly on the queues neatly coiled beneath them. The caps were particularly costly, and some would be damaged if the ragged mob became violent.

The corporal pondered his next move. If he were still serving under the green banner of the Chinese Armies of the Manchu Dynasty, he would not have hesitated. He would either have charged the throng or sauntered away. But that white-skinned devil of an inspector had been most explicit. The task of the police was to preserve the public peace. Ths constables were neither to provoke clashes nor to ignore disturbances in the hope that the miscreants would injure only each other.

The corporal sighed in exasperation. Sometimes, the barbarians' thinking was virtually impossible to comprehend. Still, he had enrolled in the Constabulary to fill his family's stomachs, and he would not break their rice-bowls by disregarding orders.

Yet he remained irresolute. He could not fathom the mood of the crowd, made up of tattered countryfolk and equally tattered artisans from provincial towns. All were obviously refugees, *nan-min*, 'people who faced hardship,' and all were accompanied by children. Stooped grandmothers with hobbled feet clutched infants to their meagre bosoms. Wiry fathers and wind-burnt mothers led toddlers with green mucus streaming from their nostrils, while cocky boys and shy girls carried sobbing babies. As they pushed towards the head of the disorderly queue, scuffles flared and died like sparks. Although their unsanctioned assembly was unquestionably a threat to the peace, the refugees' temper was not belligerent.

Pugnacious only in defending their places in the queue, they were both

375

eager and reluctant, at once hopeful and fearful. Some grinned ingratiatingly while tears drenched their weather-beaten cheeks; other faces were as grim as the dark, drizzle-swept afternoon in mid-November. Some looked as if they had just seen the first ray of spring sunshine after a grey winter. Others stared desolately into their neighbours' faces, seeking consolation in the eyes of strangers as miserable as themselves in this alien world.

Perplexed by his orders and puzzled by the throng's behaviour, the corporal behaved as he never would under the green banner of the Great Pure Dynasty. Ordering his men to stand fast, he strolled towards the crowd, himself almost as astonished as the refugees that a man in uniform should approach them in peace. The throng and the policeman stared at each other across a barrier no less impassable for being invisible. The corporal occupied a secure position in life, sustained by the status and the wages his foreign sponsors bestowed. The refugees were flotsam of the great rebellion, exercising no more control over their fate than the shattered timbers of a foundered ship.

For a full minute, the refugees stared in blank-faced fear at the corporal, who smiled placatingly. After a few minutes, the refugees ignored his menacing uniform and resumed their agitated talk.

'I know it's hard to believe, but barbarians are capable of any folly,' observed a man who had from the cut and fabric of his tattered coat been a well-to-do craftsman before the tide of Holy Soldiers swept him from his home. 'And there's no alternative. What can *we* do for them now?'

'It's true, I tell you!' An old farmer with his year-old grandson cradled in his calloused hands was vehement. 'They're crazy, but what choice've we got? We've got to give up the kids!'

'But everyone knows the barbarians do horrible things,' the craftsman's wife objected. 'The white-skinned devils want to make them little barbarians. They soak Chinese kids in water and mumble barbarian spells over them. Afterwards, they're not Chinese anymore. Those kids are barbarians.'

'Better a live barbarian than a dead Chinese,' her husband replied grimly. 'Besides, that's nonsense. The Emperor would never let them.'

'What is it, old fellow?' the corporal asked. 'What *are* you talking about?'

'The word went round our camp this morning, sir,' the grizzled farmer answered. 'They say a barbarian lady is taking in needy kids. Gives them food and clothes. Even teaches them a few ideograms and some passages from the Classics.'

'Don't get your hopes up.' The corporal paraded his superior knowledge. 'They do crazy things, the barbarian devils. But *that's* not on. A barbarian lady teaching ideograms and the classics! Now, I ask you!'

It would not be wise, the policeman felt, to tell the wretches who were so anxious to rid themselves of their children that the rumours might be true.

He had even heard of the Jesus disciples' *buying* children to bring up in their macabre religion, which worshipped a man dying in agony on a wooden cross. But his job was to keep the peace. If he encouraged their hopes, they would fight to reach the head of the queue. What could one expect of men so desperate they wished to give their sons away, leaving no one to perform the ancestral rites that would ensure the tranquillity of their spirits in the afterworld? Common humanity tempted him to warn the refugees that the barbarians would steal their children, but the truth would make them violent.

The policemen felt a pang of conscience. When he put on the barbarian uniform he had not sworn to deceive his own people for the sake of the white-skinned devils. But his chief duty was to his own family. If a riot erupted, he could find himself disgraced, impoverished – and, perhaps, struggling to give away his own sons.

Raucous shouts rolled into Broadway from the narrow mouth of Yuehtung Road. The corporal expected the din to die down like the previous scuffles. But the tumult rose louder, and he heard the thud of blows. When women screamed, he waved his arms imperatively and trotted towards the intersection. His men followed, slashing a path through the combatants with ebony truncheons.

Restraint was no longer advisable. If they were to preserve themselves from the refugees' fate, the constables had to reach the centre of the disturbance. As the throng opened before the flailing truncheons, the corporal forced his way towards the head of the queue. He must find out for himself what was happening, not depend on the gossip of these wretched people.

*

Within the refurbished tenement of Yuehtung Road, the wax fragrance of furniture-polish contended with the sour smell of boiling diapers. Coals burning in bronze braziers cast their light on the drawn curtains that cut Fronah Haleevie off from the misery in the streets that ashen autumn afternoon. Unaware of the rumbling outside as the refugees pushed towards her door, she proudly showed her brother David the school-desks installed against the day her thirty-five orphans began their studies.

The concubine Maylu had insisted on climbing to the third floor on her bound feet. She considered herself as much responsible as Fronah for the children's home created in the tenement that was Saul Haleevies' contribution to his daughter's happiness – and his propitiatory offering to the God who had made him wealthy amid such great poverty. Maylu considered herself wholly responsible for the halting progress Fronah had made towards health since reluctantly accepting David's challenge three months earlier.

The girl was definitely improved, the concubine reflected. Her hands were no longer like chicken claws. Her cheeks had not regained their glow, but were no longer the colour and texture of soiled parchment. She even smiled occasionally, though it was more than a year since the concubine had heard her laugh.

When reminded that she must eat, Fronah would dutifully swallow a few mouthfuls. Yet the child, as Maylu still thought of the twenty-five-year-old matron, took no pleasure in food. The concubine sighed, recalling how Fronah and she had giggled together as they gorged on forbidden shrimp dumplings and golden crisp roast pork.

Maylu would not be content until Fronah was again as buoyant as the sparkling thirteen-year-old she had met after the suicide of old Mistress Lee, Aisek's mother. The concubine expelled the memory of that death and her man's exile from her mind. She would today concern herself only with Fronah and the surprise she had arranged for Fronah.

David's plan to awaken Fronah from her morbid preoccupation with herself by engaging her interest in the children's home had been brilliant – as far as it went. But it had not gone far enough. Instead of retreating into herself, Fronah had retreated into the artificial world Maylu and she had created. Not her illness but the children's home was now her refuge from reality. She was playing lady bountiful as she had many years ago played families, though flesh-and-blood orphans had replaced her cloth-and-plaster dolls.

It was, unfortunately all too easy. Her father had not only furnished the tenement lavishly, but had hired ten Chinese women to staff it. Her charges were too few, too young, and too docile under the amahs' eyes to make strenuous demands on Fronah herself. Still shielded by her father's bounty from the pressures that affected most human beings, she was slipping back into the twilight of her own mind. Pallid self-satisfaction with a minor accomplishment, rather than torpid self-pity, was now her dominant mood,

What Fronah really needed, like every woman including herself, was a man to worry about, Maylu concluded. Sadly, the black-haired sailor had gone off to fight in America just when the girl's interest was stirring. The concubine had always been wary of Lionel Henriques, not least because of his inhuman yellow hair. She now despised him. She had always been fond of Gabriel Hyde, and she had wept when he bade her goodbye. Fronah, dry-eyed, had pretended not to be disturbed by his departure.

Maylu could not conjure up an acceptable barbarian suitor, but neither could she allow Fronah to relapse into torpor. She had, therefore, the previous day dropped a few words to the refugees who pleaded with her to take their children into the home. The foreign lady, she told them, had decided she would no longer restrict her beneficence to thirty-odd orphans, but would accept perhaps a hundred needy children tomorrow.

Still, Maylu congratulated herself, she was by no means a fool, even if Fronah sometimes reproached her for flightiness. She had wisely invited

378

David to visit them today. The authority of a Mandarin of the Seventh Grade would ensure that the refugees behaved with decorum. If the throng got out of hand, Daivd would simply summon a detachment of Imperial Braves. She knew neither that a Mandarin of the Great Pure Dynasty had no authority in the Foreign Settlement nor that Manchu troops might enter only on invitation, which would not be forthcoming.

David made a show of interest in the school-room. He exclaimed at the scrolls exhorting youth to treasure knowledge, and he examined the writing-brushes, inksticks, and inkstones laid out for infants who would not touch them for years. Pleased by Fronah's interest, he was appalled by her lack of realism.

She had taken up his challenge. Her condition had, at least, not deteriorated, though he could see only minimal improvement. But what did this pretty dolls' house have to do with refugee camps stalked by hunger and disease? He had not planned that Fronah should immure herself in a fantasy realm peopled by eager servants and well-brushed infants.

The young Mandarin was not only dismayed, but bored. He twitched a curtain open and saw leaden mist pressing against the window-panes.

Glancing down, he was surprised by the crowd overflowing the road. All the streets of the Foreign Settlement were nowadays thronged with thousands of refugees, some listlessly seeking employment, some merely wandering, rather than remain in their fetid hovels. But the hundreds of men and women jamming Yuehtung Road were not moving. They looked up at him and muttered menacingly. David opened the casement window curiously.

'Gracious Lord,' an alert father shouted. 'Take my son. Save my son, Your Honour!'

'Take our children!' The crowd began to chant. 'Gracious Lord, save our children!'

'What the devil,' David exclaimed, 'is this nonsense?'

Fronah craned out the window beside him, while Maylu shrugged with ostentatious innocence and said: 'Stupid, ignorant common people. They must be mad.'

When the refugees saw that the benevolent barbarian lady actually existed, they were suddenly still. An instant later, an enormous sigh drifted upward. The crowd pressed against the barred doors, the foremost pounding on the heavy teak panels. Since even the benevolence of a barbarian lunatic must have its limits, the first to plead with her would win admission for their sons or daughters to this children's paradise.

David watched unmoving for almost half a minute. He was afraid for Fronah and Maylu, afraid even for himself. He had conquered fear on the battlefield, but the pleas of parents eager to save their children by giving them away terrified him. These people were beyond hope for themselves – in this world or the next. Why else surrender the offspring who were their passports to immortality? Broken only by thudding of fists on the door-panels and the wailing of babies, the refugees' silence was more menacing than the din of battle.

'David, what can we do?' Fronah appealed. 'They'll break the door down.'

'I'm afraid they will, Fronah,' he answered. 'But I don't see how we can stop them.'

'We've got to talk with them, David. The poor things are pitiful, so anxious. I must explain there's nothing I can do for so many.'

'How *can* you talk to them?' he demanded. 'Would they listen to you . . . to me . . . to anyone? There's a trap-door to the roof, isn't there? We must get your orphans out. Ourselves, too.'

'David, I can't just run away. Somehow, they've got the idea I can help them. I must explain why I can't.'

Despite his fear, the young Mandarin glanced sharply at his sister. He had not heard such determination or such urgency in her voice since her swine of a husband deserted her. But the door was creaking under the assault.

'Later, Fronah!' He grasped her arm. 'First get the babies out. Then ourselves.'

'Not later, David, but now!' Fronah insisted. 'I'm going down.'

She shook off his hand and turned to the narrow staircase. It was blocked by amahs carrying their charges.

Tempered by the precarious life of a city constantly under threat, Fronah's staff had not waited for instructions. They were determined to escape to the roofs of the adjoining buildings. As David helped the amahs towards the trap-door, he praised them for not abandoning the orphans.

Fronah felt herself superfluous. Enraged at David's callousness, she seethed at her own helplessness. She returned to the window and heard harsh grinding as the door-panels began to yield to the refugees' battering.

If it were not turned away, the mob would soon break in and sack the children's home. If they destroyed that sanctuary, her privileged orphans – and she, too – would suffer a great loss. She realised that she cared desperately for the home and the helpless children. She was not, as she had thought, dead to all feeling.

'The dam's burst, Fronah.' When David spoke to her rigid back, she thought for an instant he meant the dike that had pent her emotions. 'We're beginning to break the Taipings, but refugees are pouring into the Settlement. The flood had to touch us soon or later.'

'It has, David, it has!' Her intensity startled him. 'The babies . . . my babies . . . they're all safe now? Maylu's with them? Then I *must* go down and talk with these poor people. I must!'

'It's damned dangerous. Who knows what they'll do? I can't let you, Fronah.'

'I'll go alone, then. Unless you stop me by force.'

380

'I couldn't do that.' David grinned. 'All right, I'll go with you. I'm not wearing my bird. But I've got my gold-button hat, and the staircase is narrow. I think I can hold them.'

'I'm sorry to ask you, David. But you do see, don't you? I can't just run away. Somehow, they think I can help them. I must, at least, talk with them.'

'And say what?'

'I haven't the faintest idea.' The spontaneous smile he had thought vanished forever lit her face. 'But I'll think of something.'

'Then, my beloved Little Sister, if you'll be good enough to follow me, we'll face the raging mob.'

The front door splintered, its panels grating, rasping, and finally groaning like men in agony. When they reached the first-floor landing, Fronah heard a crash as the mob stormed into the house. Pushing her behind him, David descended to the ground floor to confront a hard-faced farm woman and her husband, who was disfigured by a purple scar curving from his eye to his jaw. The mob was already pawing at the plush chairs and the mahogany tables. Neither the farmer nor his wife turned when a vase splintered on the floor. Clutching three small children, the couple moved towards the stairwell. Behind them, the tumult of destruction mounted.

'Good people!' David shouted. 'Hear me! Let me speak!'

Though his words were unintelligible, his voice attracted their notice. The farmer advanced menacingly. He paused when he saw the gold-button on the Mandarin's official hat, then advanced again, his thick lips gaping in a scream.

Despite the crash of breaking furniture, David heard the familiar obscenities. Simple men under strain were not notable for imagination. The profanity he had learned from the servants as a boy assailed him – and he remembered to be afraid. Gesturing again for silence, he wondered why the farmer should curse *him*.

'Shit-faced running dog of the Manchus!' the farmer shouted into the hush. 'Out of my way. We'll burn this pesthouse, you son of a turtle-bitch.'

The scarred man thrust his son at his wife and advanced on David with hands clawed. Letting the child find his own feet, the woman grasped her husband's shoulder.

'First talk to the barbarian lady,' she directed. 'First talk, fool!'

'You dog-turd,' the farmer screamed at David. 'We'll burn this pesthouse if we can't speak to the barbarian whore!'

'She'll talk to you,' David shouted. 'She'll talk when you stop breaking up her house.'

'Don't tell us what to do, shit-head.' The farmer's scar writhed. 'A Mandarin are you? A scabby dog who can't look after the people. A fat pig who hides behind the barbarians.'

'Fronah, get out of here!' David spoke over his shoulder. 'Get up the stairs and out. Nobody can reason with them.'

Thought she knew he was right, Fronah stubbornly stood her ground. She

381

was weary of running away, ashamed of fleeing from responsibility. Her thoughtless benevolence had incited this danger, and she would not leave her brother to face it alone. Behind her Maylu screamed imprecations, and she was sorry that loyalty had compelled the concubine to return.

Pushed forward by the crowd, the farmer stood a few inches from the young Mandarin. David looked into pig-small eyes reddened by anger. He recoiled from the stench of rotten teeth and glanced warily at the broken nails of the menacingly raised hand. Courageously standing fast, Fronah and Maylu had cut off his retreat.

The young Mandarin chopped his hand down on his opponent's collar bone. The farmer staggered, but did not fall. Screaming, he lurched forward again. As David grappled with the assailant, he wondered fleetingly what masters of the martial arts did when cunning blows failed. Their locked bodies would temporarily block the narrow staircase, protecting the women. But the mob's numbers must soon overwhelm him.

Teeth closed on his ear, and his rigid fingers stabbed at his opponent's eyes. The scarred man recoiled, then hurtled forward with his head held low. As David side-stepped his charge, the farmer's hands closed on his left arm. He saw a flash of white light, and he felt agonising pain in his shoulder. In desperation, he drove his fist into the farmer's stomach.

The assailant staggered back, and David tasted triumph. But the pain stabbing his shoulder made him reel. He knew he could resist only a few seconds longer.

The farmer stood irresolute, and the refugees' shouts were suddenly muted. From the staircase, the young Mandarin saw a royal-blue wedge driving into the room. A police corporal brought his truncheon down on the farmer's head. The man dropped to the debris-littered floor, blood oozing from his cracked crown.

'Your Honour!' The corporal saluted. 'I'll have this rubbish removed.'

'Thanks, old fellow,' David replied weakly. 'Glad you turned up.'

'Gaol for this lot,' the corporal continued. 'Pity the barbarians are so soft-hearted they won't get the caning they deserve.'

'Let them stay!' Fronah exclaimed. 'They must not go to gaol.'

The policeman looked around in perplexity. He believed he had seen the tawny-haired barbarian lady speak, but she couldn't be talking perfect Shanghainese. Yet the Chinese lady beside her had not opened her mouth. A refugee woman must be playing tricks on him. He looked around the battered room, suspicion warring with incredulity on his features.

'The lady says no, old fellow,' David smiled. 'If she won't press charges, you'd be wasting your time taking them in. However, I'd appreciate your staying around for a while to keep order.'

'Surely, Your Honour,' the policeman replied. 'But it's bad policy.'

'I'll speak with any six of you you wish in a few minutes.' Fronah raised her voice over the refugees' frightened murmurs. 'Just give me time to clear up and find some food for you.'

The constable prodded the refugees out of the tenement. Knowing their unpredictable barbarian superiors, they were only mildly surprised by Fronah's eccentricity. The astonished refugees thanked Heaven that the reports they had heard were correct. Instead of ordering them flogged for their vandalism, the lady was going to feed them. All barbarians were obviously mad.

David winced as pain gripped his shoulder. But he shrugged off Fronah's concern, fascinated by her vigour. She rattled off instructions to the amahs, who were sheepishly returning with their infants. Galvanised by the decisiveness of their normally apathetic mistress, they scurried to clear the debris and bring in a table on which to serve their own evening meal to the refugees. Watching with delight, David did not interfere.

The scarred farmer and his hard-faced wife led an impromptu delegation of six refugees into the room fifteen minutes later. A wispy old man, perhaps a village teacher by his manner, bowed and offered abject apologies. Since it would have been discourteous to interrupt, Fronah heard him out before replying: 'There is nothing to apologise for, Gentlemen and Ladies. You were naturally a little agitated. It's my fault for not receiving you properly.'

The six were astounded by her forbearance, but, above all, by being addressed as 'Gentlemen and Ladies'. They forgot both their surprise and their shame when the amahs brought them food. They were soon making small talk with the barbarian lady, who understood that eating came before business, however urgent.

'You will pardon my speaking before you've finished.' Fronah was still chewing a steamed bun stuffed with honey-roasted pork. 'I should be honoured if you would confide in me why you came here. What tale brought you to my door?'

'They said . . .' the farmer's wife began. 'They said that . . . that is that . . .'

'Be quiet, woman, and let the teacher speak,' the scarred man instructed. 'He's educated, you know.'

The old teacher spoke haltingly of the rumours that had swept the refugees' shanty town that morning. Of course he now realised they were nonsense. How could the gracious lady undertake to care for so many children? But, if the gracious lady pleased, there were a few particularly deserving orphans.

'Not all, I regret to say,' Fronah answered. 'I am ashamed that I cannot offer a home to all the children. But not just a few either. If you'll come back in four days, a hundred, certainly, perhaps more. Will you, Master Teacher, bring me a list of names, original homes, and ages . . . as well as the parents' circumstances. It would also be helpful if . . .'

'Fronah, do you know what you're saying?' David interrupted in English. 'How can you promise? You can't possibly take so many?'

'Yes, David,' she answered equably. 'That is, yes and no. I do know what I'm promising. But I don't know how I'll cope.'

383

'Then, shouldn't you talk a little smaller? It's quite impossible!'

'I can't allow it to be impossible. Somehow, I'll manage.'

She bowed and renewed her promise: 'Four days from now I'll see you again.'

'At least give yourself a little more time,' David urged as the refugees filed out. 'This is crazy.'

'Even four days is too long,' she replied vehemently, taking another pork-stuffed bun. 'How many will die if I wait longer?'

'You know you're eating?' David acknowledged defeat. 'Eating rather well.'

'Am I?' Fronah glanced at the bun. 'So I am. I didn't have time to think about not eating.'

CHAPTER FIFTY-SIX

December 14, 1862   *Soochow*

The yellow gleam flickered with Lionel Henriques's breath. The flame flared at each deep inhalation, and light played on the green-brocade hangings of the narrow cellar beneath the silk-looms. The flame sank at each shallow exhalation, and the hidden room was suffused with artificial dusk. The sunlight trickling through the barred window high in the wall was growing pale as true dusk approached.

Though the Phoenix Silk Works on Flower Bridge Lane were only a half mile from the Loyal King's headquarters in the Garden of the Humble Administrator, hard-pressed Taiping officials made only infrequent calls. They were happy to leave the running of the works to the diligent foremen, who pursued their exacting craft exactly as they had before the Holy Soldiers came to Soochow. The officials were equally happy to follow the Loyal King's instructions to leave the conduct of trade with the Foreign Settlement to the Englishman. The Taipings were preoccupied with the new counter-offensive the Holy King was planning to divert Imperialist pressure from the Heavenly Capital – and to block the movement of the army of the Mandarin Li Hung-chang towards Soochow itself. Lionel was, therefore, doubly secure in his secret refuge from the puritanical rigour of the Heavenly Kingdom of Great Peace.

Warm, though naked between the quilted-silk coverlets that cushioned the teak opium-bed and warded off the chill of the early evening of October 14th, 1862, he felt pleasantly drowsy. He was quite content to be alone. When the light flared it shone on the altar-table bearing the exquisite gilt Buddha and the pair of Ming-yellow double-gourd vases he had rescued from the Holy Soldiers' destructive mania. He was, he mused, *almost* content to be alone. It would be good to chat in English with A. F. Lindley, the idealistic sea-captain who was a fanatical adherent of the Taiping cause. However, a few more pipes would quell that desire. The pipe ultimately quelled all desire.

Never too many pipes – and never too few. Moderation was the secret of happiness. And it was perfect happiness to float disembodied above the world, seeing its foibles keenly, yet utterly detached. At this midway point in his solitary journey towards his personal Nirvana, he was still aware of the danger of being found out. The awareness that discovery would bring summary decapitation spiced his pleasure. Soon, however, the opium fumes would waft away all fear.

The Englishman clapped his hands softly, and a small figure in a violet satin gown pushed aside the brocade hangings over the door. He extended the bamboo tube with the minuscule porcelain bowl, and the girl took the pipe on her outstretched palms. She did not turn immediately to the low table where the jar of opium stood, but sat on the side of the bed and polished the pipe's silver mouthpiece with the front-panel of her long gown, which was slit to the waist.

Her golden legs, just beginning to assume the curves of womanhood, were competely exposed. Lionel languorously stroked her petal-soft thigh, and she smiled down at him. His fingers crept up her narrow hip to the barely perceptible incurve of her waist, and her lips parted. When his hand slipped across her flat abdomen to rest on the hairless delta between her thighs, she leaned forwards. Her rosebud breasts peeped through her scooped neckline, and her dew dampened his questing fingers.

'*Pu-hsing!* . . . No, it won't do!' he said regretfully in Chinese, but continued in English, since she would not understand even if he could express the thought in her language. 'Moderation in all things, my little gem. Mustn't overdo it. At any rate, I'm not sure I could again so soon. Just another pipe now.'

Although her breathing was rapid, the girl submissively knelt before the low table. She twisted a bamboo skewer in the opium-paste and then twirled the dark-brown blob over the miniature hurricane-lamp. With indolent pleasure the Englishman watched the opium melt into a black pellet. The girl inserted the pellet into the pipe's minute bowl, leaving an air-channel when she withdrew the skewer. Unlike tobacco, opium would not burn of itself, but had to be consumed by an open flame.

Lionel propped himself on his elbow. Holding the bowl inverted over the gourd-shaped glass-shade, he inhaled for some thirty seconds. The sweet and acrid smoke suffused his lungs. After a single slow expulsion of breath, he inhaled profoundly again. Nails tapping rhythmically against the frame of the bed, he lay back while the girl prepared another pipe.

Discipline, Lionel reflected, was everything – or almost everything. He waited with divine patience while his acolyte unhurriedly repeated her rite. When the pipe was ready, he drew short, deep breaths in time to the tapping of his nails. Self-discipline was all important, self-discipline and moderation.

He refused another pipe, for the twelve he had already smoked were just right today. He closed his eyes and felt his mind detach itself from his body. All things were possible, he mused, if one knew how. The Taipings believed they had purged all the 'devil's goods' from Soochow, the city of pleasure. But small quantities of gold still procured the pleasures essential to his well-being.

Should they surprise him, the Taiping lictors would punish him severely. They would charge that he had corrupted the girl, who was just twelve, as well as her eleven-year-old sister. But truth refuted such moralising. He had actually introduced the two girls to ecstasies they would never otherwise have experienced. Not only the benign raptures of the pipe, but the pure sensual joy they could only know before their bodies were bloated by maturity. A conscientious guide through the realm of pleasure, he always ensured that they smoked just the right number of pipes. Never too many – and never too few for perfect joy.

A man cut off from all civilised society was entitled to his harmless diversions. He had fled the Foreign Settlement after Fronah had discovered his passion for pre-pubescent girls and the drug the Chinese called with fitting reverence 'the great smoke'. Some day, he would return to her and to Shanghai. Ironically, his pleasures were peccadilloes in Shanghai, but capital crimes in the Heavenly Kingdom – a few seconds' work for the headsman's sword. Such hypocrisy! Some Taiping Kings, he felt certain, indulged themselves covertly in the great smoke as well as overtly in their harems, though the solace of a single pipe or a single female was forbidden to all commoners.

The last wisps of tension left Lionel's body, and his mouth curved in the content bestowed by superior knowledge. His senses were preternaturally acute, and his mind was preternaturally alert. It was simple to distinguish the essence from the dross when one's perception was so elevated.

Footsteps clattered – and voices buzzed in the distance. He was not alarmed, since the few lictors who visited the silk works rarely inspected the cellars where the bolts were stored. Besides, they could never discover his secret chamber. The entrance was cleverly concealed, while the fumes drifted through the window set high in the wall but low in the embankment of the canal that flowed beneath Flower Bridge. He had no cause for uneasiness, much less alarm.

Lionel Henriques blinked mildly and smiled in welcome when Aaron Lee wrenched aside the hangings over the door. The failed Mandarin's features were contorted with urgency, and his high-bridged nose jutted in his lean face. But Aaron was often devoured by urgency, for he could not shake off his demons and surrender himself to enjoyment.

'Hello, Aaron,' Lionel said. 'You know . . .'

'Lionel,' Aaron broke in, 'listen to . . .'

'. . . your greatest fault,' the Englishman continued placidly, 'is you can't let go. You must learn to relax or you'll kill yourself.'

'*You'll* kill yourself if you don't listen.' Aaron shook Lionel's shoulder. 'The lictors are taking inventory. You've got five minutes at most.'

'Don't fuss. They'll never find my little room.'

'Get up, man, get up!' Aaron shouted. 'If you're too sodden to worry about your neck, I'm fond of mine.'

The girl had already scurried off. Finally alarmed, he dressed frantically while Aaron pried the window open with a pole. Together they bundled the opium paraphernalia, the quilts, the Buddha, and the Ming vases into the hollow concealed by six loose bricks. He was, the Englishman reflected complacently as Aaron darted out of the room, by no means foolhardy, for he had carefully prepared that hiding-place.

Opening a ledger and taking up a steel-nibbed pen, Lionel seated himself at the altar-table where the gilt Buddha had stood. Would a lictor, he wondered, look too closely at his pin-point pupils? Could those young fanatics still recognise the distinctive opium odour compounded with burnt sugar and clay, which hung in the room?

'The barbarian is working on his accounts.' Aaron's Officials' Language was quite intelligible, though Lionel understood others with difficulty. 'Not the inventory. Just the trading accounts. There's no need to disturb him.'

'Why hide himself underground like a mole?' The rustic patois was barely intelligible. 'Are barbarians afraid of light? We'd better have a look, anyway.'

'As you wish,' Aaron replied. 'But who can say why barbarians behave strangely? Anyway, he can only gabble a few words in a civilised language.'

Three lictors clutching the short swords that were their badge of office entered the room. Looking down from the heights to which the great smoke had borne him, Lionel was indignant at his sanctuary's profanation by their squat bodies in green tunics and their lumpy features peering between long, greasy hair. Wisely suppressing his anger, he remained silent.

'You see, not a single bolt in here.' Aaron was conciliatory – and condescending.

'Ask him,' demanded the senior lictor, 'why he hides himself like a bear in a cave?'

'He says the sun irritates his skin. Besides, commercial transactions are unbelievably complex. He needs absolute quiet.'

'They're dim-witted, these barbarians,' the lictor laughed. 'Phew, there's a funny smell in here.'

'Some ointment for his skin, I believe. The barbarians use all sorts of strange medicines.'

'What a stench!' the lictor exclaimed. 'Just for form's sake, though, we'd better have a look around.'

Lionel's pen creaked in his tense finger. His makeshift hiding-place could not withstand a determined search. The manic vigour that was as much the drug's gift as tranquillity possessed him, and he braced himself to dash for the door.

'As you wish,' Aaron said patronisingly. 'By the way, the Chief Lictor said he might call. I know you'll be glad to see him.'

The lictors glanced at each other through their matted hair. The senior nodded, and they turned to leave. As their footsteps receded, Lionel trembled with relief and heard snatches of Aaron's elaborately casual remarks.

'Just two bolts, you see. Damaged goods, though one would hardly notice. We'd destroy them otherwise.'

Lionel clasped his arms on the table and rested his head on his hands. Repeated spasms convulsed his body. When Aaron returned ten minutes later, he raised his head wearily.

'Never again,' his brother-in-law declared. 'This has got to stop. I'll never again . . . but it was funny.'

'Funny?' the Englishman asked dully. 'What's happened? How did you . . .'

'The older one worried me. He was close to guessing, though he'd never smelled opium in his life.'

'How did you get rid of them, Aaron?'

'The Holy Soldiers are all incorruptible, of course.'

'Of course!' Lionel echoed the ironic observation. 'Beyond doubt!'

'The silk I offered them. They wanted to grab it and get out before the Chief Lictor arrived.'

'The Chief Lictor?' Lionel was again fearful. 'He's coming, too?'

'Not really, but they didn't know that. Look, Lionel, this can't go on. Next time, I won't . . . can't . . . protect you. I've put up with your foolishness for Fronah's sake. But never again. You've got to stop.'

'I'll try, Aaron. I'll really try.'

'Trying's not good enough. The Taipings are getting worse all the time. The more desperate they are, the more fanatical they become.'

'Desperate? Why, the Heavenly Kingdom still holds most of the east coast, not to speak of the entire south. Perhaps Shanghai won't fall now, not with all that foreign support. But we can still win without taking Shanghai.'

'Lionel, the pressure on Nanking is growing every day. Unless the Loyal King can break that siege it's only a matter of time before the Heavenly Capital falls. And Soochow? You know how vulnerable Soochow is.'

'What do you want to do? Make a break?'

'Into the hands of the Imps? They'd lop off my head in a minute. The game's not played out yet. The Taipings still have a small chance, but I'm worried.'

'Whatever you say, Aaron. I'm with you.'

388

'That's fine, but, meanwhile, you've *got* to stop your little games. If they catch you, don't look to me for help. I'll be busy saving my own head.'

'I will. I'll give both up . . . the smoke and the little darlings. From this day on, I won't touch either one.'

Aaron looked dubiously at the tall Englishman, who was again marked by his addiction. His grey skin was stretched over his patrician features because opium destroyed his desire for food. Soon, his emaciation would proclaim his vice to anyone less obtuse than the country bumpkins he had just barely deceived.

Lionel *would* try, Aaron felt, for his friend was an honourable man. But it was hard to believe he could succeed in throwing off his addiction a second time.

CHAPTER FIFTY-SEVEN

June 3, 1863   *Shanghai*

'Look sharp now, young fellow!' Russells' junior tea-taster exclaimed. 'That doesn't happen every day. You can tell your grandchildren you saw a Mandarin of the First Grade, the Governor of the richest province in the Manchu Empire, carried in state through the streets of the Foreign Settlement.'

The tea-taster was happy to break into the newcomer's account of the inconclusive clashes between the Union and the Confederacy in the first war ever fought entirely with deadly modern weapons. Though his country's future was at stake and Confederate commerce raiders were hampering trade, the new griffin had repeatedly regaled a bored mess with his second-hand report. The tea-taster wanted to enjoy the late afternoon sunshine on Broadway, rather than listen again to a tale more lurid with each telling.

Besides, the news was months old when it reached Shanghai, and the battlefields were far away. The Mandarin Li Hung-chang, Governor of Kiangsu Province and Commander-in-Chief of the Army of the Huai, had, however, just returned from the battlefield of a civil war that lapped the Treaty Port.

Impelled by curiosity, the tea-taster had once visited the South City to see the Mandarin's palanquin escorted by lictors carrying swords and bamboo staves. The banners, the uniforms, and the lanterns had impressed even his Yankee scepticism. It was, however, virtually unprecedented for the Mandarin to visit the Foreign Settlement.

'It's a small procession, only two flags, and a single attendant Mandarin. But it's worth seeing, isn't it?'

'If you say so.' The griffin was determined not to be impressed. 'Where's the grand high panjandrum going?'

'They're turning up Yuehtung Road,' the old hand mused. 'Nothing there except some tenements and . . . yes, it must be.'

'Must be what?'

'Be patient, youngster, and all will be revealed. Let's stroll along behind and see where he stops.'

Proper in white drill and straw-hats, the Americans followed at a respectable distance. Not for them the crude curiosity of the Chinese, who turned, gawked, and trotted alongside the gubernatorial procession.

'Damned if I wasn't right!' the old hand exclaimed when the litter-bearers halted before an unpretentious three-storey house. 'He's definitely calling on the Witch of Endor.'

'The Witch of Endor?' the griffin asked. 'You've got some comical names out here all right. Who's the Witch of Endor?'

'Why, that little Jewish girl, old Saul Haleevie's girl. They've been calling her the Witch of Endor since she began driving everyone crazy begging for the refugees' kids. Believe it or not, she's got more than four hundred tucked away in those tenements her father gave her. Old Saul's no Shylock. Everything else she squeezes out of the taipans.'

'From old Griswold?' The griffin had endured a scarifying interview with his taipan regarding his travel expenses. 'That old son of a bitch is the tightest Yankee I ever met . . . And you know how Yankees are.'

'One myself, young fellow. Griswold kicked in gladly. It's easier than holding out, though she'll be back to twist his arm again. Everyone kicks in, even the French. And that's saying something. She's a holy terror. By God, she even got the Chinese to put up a little. And that, young fellow, is a certifiable miracle.'

'What does she look like? I guess middle-aged and skinny. Anyway, she can't be much to look at, your Witch of Endor. Those do-gooding females never are.'

'You know, I've never seen her. She doesn't get about much. But I heard she's a scrawny little thing. Though hardly middle-aged, still a long way from thirty.'

The Mandarin Li Hung-chang stepped lithely from his palanquin, the silver crane of his grade shimmering on the breast of his official robe. The barbarians' ways, he reflected without rancour, were truly peculiar, while their failure to comprehend the fundamentals of etiquette was extraordinary. Still, he was in a sense their guest today, and he felt little resentment at his hostess's failing to greet him as he strode towards the open door of the tenement.

'Your Excellency, I am abjectly apologetic.' Fronah Haleevie Henriques hurried into the road and curtsied. 'An emergency prevented my waiting

390

outside my unworthy dwelling to greet you. Though my offence is unpardonable, I beg your indulgence.'

The Mandarin was astonished by her command of the Officials' Language. Shanghai sibillants marred her accent, but they were no worse than his own Anhwei burr.

'Young David told me he would not be needed as an interpreter.' He repaid her Chinese courtesy by using his aide's foreign name. 'I crave your pardon for my scepticism.'

Fronah curtsied again to acknowledge his compliment, and motioned him to precede her. But the tall Mandarin stood a few moments longer exchanging courtesies with the small woman, leaving the two Americans gawking across Yuehtung Road at the slight figure in the plain fawn dress with the restrained hoop skirt. Over the vee of braid on the bodice dangled her only jewellery: a disc of white *tsui-fei* jade on a fine gold chain. Though Fronah's face was no longer drawn, her skin was taut over her delicate bones. Her olive cheeks were flushed with excitement, but her light-brown eyes sparkled with suppressed laughter at the rituals of Confucian etiquette.

She would never again be the reckless girl with whom he had romped across the countryside, but she would, by the grace of God, never again be the haggard woman for whom he had almost despaired. David smiled at the notoriety her fierce concern for her orphans had won her. A termagant, the foreigners called her, a virago. Even his indomitable chief had been reluctant to call on the foreign lady whom the junior Mandarins she badgered described in tones of awe tinged with horror. Still, it was policy, as well as courtesy, to thank Fronah for her assistance to the refugees. Besides, the Mandarin had a small matter of state to discuss, as she would discover.

When the door closed, the griffin turned indignantly upon the Old China Hand.

'A scrawny hag, you said!' he exclaimed. 'Old fellow, you must be blind. She's a looker if I ever saw one. She's only a girl, but, by God, she's a beauty.'

*

The Mandarin preceded Fronah into the reception-room, which was sparsely furnished because she had sold what remained of the rich furniture after the vandalism. She needed every penny, since she found it almost impossible to turn away a child in need.

'*Pu kan tang* . . .' she replied when the Mandarin complimented her on the neat three-decker beds in the dormitories. 'I am unworthy of praise. Actually, Your Excellency, I feel terribly inadequate. So many children need help, but I can help so few.'

'Mrs Henriques, you're an example for us all,' the Mandarin insisted. 'Aside from my fondness for your brother, that's why I had to call upon you.'

'You compliment me too highly, Your Excellency.' She led him into the

391

school-room where older children were copying passages from the elementary Classics. 'Compared to what still needs to be done . . .'

'I've also come to shame my own people because a foreign lady is doing what they fail to do. I understand you've even got silver and food from Chinese merchants.'

'Mostly David's doing, Your Excellency.'

'It's remarkable what appeals for old time's sake, my father's sake, can accomplish, sir,' David interjected. 'Particularly when I appear in official dress.'

'So I gather, David. Mrs Henriques, I see the children are studying the Classics.'

'I feel they should learn what they can. Later, they must be useful . . . to themselves and to China. I trust I don't presume in teaching them the elementary Classics.'

'Quite frankly, I'm of two minds, Mrs Henriques. But, I'll take the tea you offered. Perhaps you'll tell me how you came to this work . . . why a foreign lady cares so much for our unfortunate children.'

The Mandarin's effusive praise was almost embarrassing, and his fine features were lit with good humour. None the less Fronah felt a premonitory chill at his hint that he did not wholly approve of her educating her charges.

Had the Mandarin come to demand that she curtail her charity? He could not command her, since she was not a Chinese subject and the Foreign Settlement lay outside his jurisdiction. He could, however, command David to stop helping her. Moreover, he could withdraw his sponsorship and create obstacles.

She could not imagine why the Mandarin should wish to send her children back to their hovels or why he should honour her with his presence and his compliments if that were his intention. Whatever the subtle Mandarin wished, she resolved, she would carry on her work.

Fronah was, however, charmed by his easy graciousness. When they sat on hard chairs in the bare reception-room, she told him of her initial resolution and her subsequent difficulties. She was totally candid, since the amahs, stiff with awe as they served tea, could not understand the Officials' Language. The Mandarin's good humour grew as he ate the delicacies of his native Anhwei Province, which David had advised her to prepare.

'I was playing, Your Excellency, only playing until the refugees broke in,' Fronah began. 'When I had only thirty-five children and the house was beautifully furnished, I was only pretending. But after the day the mob stormed the home, I was committed to looking after hundreds.'

Her father had been appalled at the prospect of Fronah's devoting her life to a 'parcel of dirty brats'. She knew that his love for herself clashed with his own concern for the refugees, and she had easily talked him into continuing to help her. It was more difficult to convince her mother that she was not throwing her life away.

Fronah's conviction that God had meant her for this task sustained her in those confrontations. Her conviction that she was finally performing the important deeds of which she had dreamed as a girl emboldened her to storm the citadels of the taipans who, alone, could provide the support she required.

Dr William MacGregor generously gave all the time he could spare from his hospital, and he badgered the importers to donate medicines. His fellow missionaries did not approve of his enthusiasm – and they were bitterly hostile to Fronah. Margaret MacGregor explained: 'No one likes competition, you know.' Fronah then understood that the Christian missionaries resented her breaching their near monopoly on charity. Besides, they believed she wished to convert the children to Judaism.

She had repeatedly explained that she was not concerned to save the children's souls, but only their bodies and their minds. In any event, she told the incredulous missionaries, Judaism was not proselytising religion. They would themselves to damned, eternally damned, she finally snapped, if they prevented her succouring the needy. Their hostility naturally flared higher, and they spoke maliciously of her terrible rages.

She could endure being called a shrew, but the suspicion rampant among the refugees themselves was wounding. Like all barbarians, they whispered, the benevolent lady was sly and deceitful. She only pretended she wouldn't drench the children with magical water and transform them into barbarians. Why should she wish to help children who were not of her own people? Why, for that matter, should the barbarian merchants give money to house and feed Chinese children?

Obviously, the lady and the merchants were hatching a clever conspiracy. They would undoubtedly sell the children into bondage once they were fattened up and taught to be useful slaves. Besides, everyone knew the barbarians prized the eyes, tongues, livers, and hearts of Chinese babies to make elixirs of eternal life.

Most painful was her loneliness. Her devotion left hardly time enough for essential tasks – and none for society. Yet she had no choice. It would not only be cruel, but wicked to rescue children from squalor and, a few months or a few years later, thrust them back into wretched hovels. She knew she must follow her lonely road for the rest of her life.

Fronah paused, abashed by the naked candour with which she was speaking to the man she had met only an hour earlier. She understood David's devotion to his chief. The Mandarin Li Hung-chang not only inspired trust, but invited confidences.

'I'm not complaining, Your Excellency,' she said. 'It's just that you asked . . .'

'I understand. I honour your efforts, but I have come to ask you to give them up.'

'Your Excellency . . . I . . . I feared perhaps . . .' She faltered, then regained her composure. 'I thought you might have something like that in

393

mind. My answer, with great respect, is No. I won't abandon these poor children, who . . .'

'It's not quite what you suspect, Mrs Henriques,' the Mandarin smiled. 'I have a greater task for you . . . one even better suited to your talents. At least, hear me out.'

'Please forgive my vehemence, Your Excellency. I'll listen, of course. But I can tell you, I will *not* . . .'

'You were disturbed when I remarked that I was not necessarily pleased with your educating these waifs, weren't you?' he asked tangentially. 'It's not your teaching them the simple Classics that worries me. It's educating too many children all over China solely in the Classics. The Classics have their uses, but their study is preventing even more important education.'

'More important than the Classics, Your Excellency?' Fronah was astonished by the view of a man who, like his ancestors for ten generations, had qualified for an official career, the *only* career for a Chinese gentleman, by demonstrating his mastery of the Sacred Books of the Confucian state-creed in the Civil Service Examinations. 'What could be more important than studying the Classics?'

'Mrs Henriques, the Classics are all right – as far as they go. Certainly young boys . . . even girls perhaps . . . must study the elementary Classics if they're to learn to read and write. Of course, they'll never become Mandarins. Who's to support them during decades of study? But isn't it ridiculous that my young friend David must study years more to pass the Master's and Doctor's Examinations and win high official rank? The Classics, young lady, have become a straitjacket for the best minds of China.'

'A straitjacket, sir?' David asked. 'How else can we discipline young minds? How else can men prove their fitness to administer the Empire?'

'A straitjacket, David, which warps young men's minds . . . stultifies the best talent in the Empire. We live in a new era. Men like yourself are needed, men with Western learning gained through foreign languages.'

'You'd do away with the Civil Service Examinations, Your Excellency?' Fronah asked the blunt question David could not ask. 'What would take their place?'

'Not abolish the Examinations, young lady. That is, not entirely and not just yet. China must move forward slowly. But China must move forward.'

'By what means, Excellency?'

'Foreign powers can now virtually dictate to us. They are strong because of their science and industry . . . their discipline, too. Otherwise, European armies would not scatter our troops. We must be just as strong. We need steamships and warships, quick-firing cannon and telegraph lines. We must develop our mines, build railroads and arsenals to make China powerful and independent of bar . . . ah . . . foreign pressure.'

'A great prospect, Your Excellency.' Though she sensed she was expected only to listen and to agree, Fronah wished to bring the Mandarin

394

back to his original theme. 'How would you alter education to serve that purpose?'

'Foreign affairs should be a regular course of study. The Examinations should test candidates for office in their knowledge of outside nations. We further require schools to teach mathematics, physics, geography, and engineering. Their students could not possibly study the Classics as well, not in one lifetime. But those students must be given the opportunity to rise in the Civil Service. That's where you come in, young lady.'

'Your Excellency, I have no knowledge of such things.'

'One day soon I shall memorialise the Throne with these proposals . . . in a few years when I'm a Viceroy. Meanwhile, I mean to make a start here in Shanghai, where I can command. The key to Western learning is foreign languages. Few men possess the knowledge of both Chinese and foreign languages necessary to teach my young Mandarins. Most such men are employed in their countries' diplomatic service or the Maritime Customs. There are fewer women, but you, young lady, are one, perhaps the only one.'

'What do you propose, Your Excellency?'

'I am setting up a school of foreign languages. I'd like you to organise the English department for me.'

'Your Excellency, I am honoured far beyond my deserts by your proposal.' Fronah almost giggled at the thought of a little Jewish girl from Bombay teaching English to the future rulers of China. 'I am overwhelmed, but I fear I . . .'

'I considered my proposal for a long time before putting it to you,' the Mandarin Li Hung-chang said. 'In fairness, you should take a little time to think about it. Though I know you're not concerned about money, the recompense would be generous. And you would hold a unique position of honour in my province. Later, a unique position in the Empire. We are ruled by a young and intelligent Manchu lady, the Junior Empress Dowager. Why should a young and intelligent foreign lady not assist in reviving China's power with learning? I need your help, Mrs Henriques.'

'I'll consider your flattering offer most seriously, Your Excellency,' Fronah answered slowly. 'But I feel I should warn you now that I . . .'

'You know, Mrs Henriques, whatever you decide, I won't change.' The Mandarin rose to leave. 'I won't interfere with your children's home if you refuse. But, please, do not refuse. I offer you far more important work.'

Fronah curtsied as the Mandarin Li Hung-chang returned to his palanquin. Exultation bubbled in her veins. She had always dreamed of playing an important role in the world, though opportunities were few for women. The Mandarin was offering her an opportunity to realise her dreams. But how could she desert her helpless children?

CHAPTER FIFTY-EIGHT

The Shanghai climate was vigorously demonstrating why it was reviled for its capriciousness. The night was unseasonably warm after a week of icy rain interspersed with sleet and hail. At her rosewood desk in the morning-room of the villa called Lo Wo, the Nest of Joy, Fronah Haleevie brushed a bead of perspiration from her forehead before her steel-nibbed pen returned to the bond paper.

She had considered changing the name of the villa that was her father's wedding present. Infected by the universal superstition of China, she almost believed her home was inauspicious because its name challenged fate. However, the Chinese, who hated innovation, would have gone right on calling it the Nest of Joy, while the foreigners, who affirmed their devotion to progress, would have been almost equally loath to propitiate fate. The raw city, which prospered amid instability, loved its ready-made traditions, perhaps because it possessed so few traditions.

The Nest of Joy indeed! She could finally smile at the irony. Her marriage had been singularly lacking in joy, except for two-and-a-half-year-old Judah Haleevie-Henriques. She loved her son, and she was charmed by his quick intelligence during the few hours she spent with him. She delighted in Judah all the more because her devotion to the welfare of hundreds of less fortunate children kept her apart from him so much.

She wondered whether her devotion to her husband had, perhaps perversely, been enhanced by his absence of two years, three months, and eight days. Although she would find it hard to forgive Lionel for deserting their infant son, she could force herself to forgive him for deserting herself. She would try to welcome him with joy when he fulfilled the promise reiterated in his infrequent messages and returned to her. Though there was, in the meantime, no joy in her wedded state, she had found a certain contentment in her lonely life.

The tinkling of the strings of glass-beads hanging in the open French windows to the terrace to deter flies was a pleasantly muted accompaniment to her deliberately muted emotions. Summer was long past, but she kept forgetting to have the beads taken down. She neglected her own home for the children's home, and she was now neglecting the children's home for the commission the Mandarin Li Hung-chang had thrust upon her earlier that week. Only she could execute it, he had said, generously allowing her a week to prepare a summary in English of the Memorials, despatches, private letters, and intra-office memoranda regarding the campaign he had pressed against the Taipings for the past eighteen months. Since a month would clearly be insufficient for the task, he had laughed, he would allow her a full week – but no more.

She was often exhausted by the contending demands of Judah, the orphans, and her work for the Mandarin. Her pleasant exhaustion was, however, alleviated by her knowledge that she was doing significant – indeed extremely important – work. She retied the belt of her red-velvet dressing-gown with the gold-mounted garnet buttons and the white flare of ermine at its cuffs and neckline. She was content, though the extravagant dressing-gown and the cream satin nightdress with the lace inserts she wore under were her most frivolously feminine garments nowadays.

She rubbed her eyelids with her fingertips, sighing in annoyance at the coals burning in the marble fireplace under the scroll-painting by Ma Yüan. She should have told Old Woo, the number-one houseboy, she didn't need a fire, though he felt glowing fireplaces belonged as immutably to November as the chestnut-hawkers in the streets. Really, she should not allow her housewifely instincts to plague her with trifles when her brain was heavy with fatigue.

Still, the houseboy's zeal for fires was no more annoying than his failure to remove the bead-screens. She was comforted by both the light chiming of the glass-beads and the soft glow of the coals. When she stared into the flames, ruddy highlights danced on her cheeks.

She was still three months away from her twenty-fifth birthday, but Fronah's features displayed a new maturity in the diffused light of the oil-lamp she preferred to the harsh gas-lights on the walls. Her full lower lip was sensuous, and the slight fullness around her jaw was provocative. Yet her mouth was firmer and less vulnerable than it had been a year earlier. Her chestnut hair with the russet glints was combed off the high, narrow forehead she had once disliked – and concealed – because it was unfashionable and, she felt, unfeminine. The minute crease between her dark eyebrows was imperceptible in the fire's glow.

Noticing her rubbing that infinitesimal blemish, her mother had assured her that it was only visible when she was tired. Besides, it proved that she was no longer a light-minded girl, but a grown woman – yet not a painted doll like most Chinese ladies. She was certainly no painted doll. Nowadays she often forgot the film of face-powder that enhanced the charms of almost all the foreign ladies of Shanghai. She rarely had time for the artful touches of pigment they dared, despite the disapproval of the Queen-Empress Victoria.

None the less, Fronah knew she was attractive. The large brown eyes that looked out from her mirror were not only alluring, but assured. She knew she was more attractive than the flighty girl or the besotted bride she had been a few years earlier.

The foreigners, she feared, considered her a strange, desexed creature, somewhere between a Jewish Joan of Arc and a fanatical Florence Nightingale. They would be surprised by the pleasure she took in her undeniable attractions. Few would believe that frivolity still bubbled beneath her grave demeanour. None would imagine that she sometimes ached with physical longing. Not only a female fanatic like herself, but all ladies were assumed to be above the passions of the flesh, which only debased common women felt.

In all her life, she had been deeply attracted to only three men. First, of course, the unspeakable Iain Matthews. She could not remember the face she had once thought the epitome of masculine beauty. But she could still feel his hands tearing at her clothes and the grass springy beneath her under the plane trees. Her feeling for Gabriel Hyde, she now acknowledged, had been far stronger than she would admit at the time. But Gabriel had left her for another war, hardly concealing his disgust at her self-induced illness. Lionel Henriques was the only one, she assured herself, the one man to whom her heart and her body were pledged, the one man who should command her love.

Lionel was also the only man with whom she had truly made love, though she had never known the raptures at which novelists hinted. Fronah dismissed that disloyal thought from her mind. Such wild transports occurred only in the fevered imaginations of novelists, not in life.

If she could forget the little girls at Old Mother Wang's, she would be happy when Lionel returned. However, she admonished herself, she must get back to work.

Whatever else, she possessed engrossing occupations. The Mandarin Li Hung-chang had originally appeared content with the compromise she suggested. She would not abandon the children's home, where six hundred girls and boys were growing up sturdy and healthy, rather than dying – or surviving maimed by malnutrition. Instead, she would give half her time to the School of Foreign Languages. Ignoring the missionaries' hostility, she had recruited three of them as teachers. Their Chinese was serviceable, though not up to her own. Their English was presumably far better than hers, though she sometimes wondered. At any rate, her reports of the progress of the young officials and the younger scholars, who were the Mandarin's protégés, seemed to satisfy him.

Two months ago the Mandarin had, however, summoned her from the classroom to complain that his Translation Bureau was in disarray. David had found two Cantonese and one Shanghailander who wrote passable Chinese and claimed a reading knowledge of English. Their translations of works on geography, strategy, and mechanics were hardly polished, the Mandarin said. Worse, he who could 'superficially at least' grasp most subjects, found their sense elusive. In fact, he added, many passages made no sense at all. Drastic changes were required if the practical benefits of Western learning were to flow from the Translation Bureau to his armies and his new arsenals.

He would not ask Fronah, he said, to undertake the translations herself, since she insisted that writing with precision, not to speak of grace, in literary Chinese was beyond anyone not rigorously trained in the Classics since the age of four. He would, the Mandarin said, only ask her to compare the Chinese versions to the original English to ensure that they were accurate.

Fronah reluctantly agreed, equally disturbed and amused at the way the courtly Mandarin was taking over her life. Yet she enjoyed being close to power, and she knew how important her work was to the essential modernisation of the Manchu Empire. Moreover, Saul Haleevie benefited greatly because both his son and his daughter were protégés of the Provincial Governor. She had, however, resisted the Mandarin's most recent commission until his normally urbane tone became sulky and menacing.

The foreigners were the key to suppressing the Long Haired Rebels because of their power, the Mandarin contended, and the key to the regeneration of China because of their science. But all foreigners except an overworked handful were ignorant of Chinese. (Fronah smiled at the word overworked.) It was therefore necessary to make reliable information – and the official viewpoint – available in English. It was essential to conduct *hsüan-chuan*, as he called *propaganda*, a concept learned from the Jesuits of Zikawei, whom he sometimes employed for their French and German.

Who, he asked rhetorically, was ideally fitted for that task? Certainly the young woman whose heart was given to China could translate brilliantly from formal Chinese into moving English. He would happily excuse her from all other duties if she would only undertake that vital task. Since such propoganda was even more important to China's future than the few children for whom she cared, he would even relieve her of that burden. He would close down the children's home if the double responsibility was too much for her.

Fronah yielded, though she hated being manipulated. Her domineering father had manipulated her until the near-disaster of her marriage convinced him that he must allow her to shape her own fate. Still, however irrationally, she sometimes felt abandoned by Saul. She hated being manipulated, but she grudgingly respected – and liked – the wily Mandarin because he knew his own mind and invariably got his own way.

However, she was accomplishing nothing by brooding as the hour drew close to midnight and the street noises died. The room was silent except for the tinkling of the glass-beads in the breeze from the terrace and the hissing of the coal she had absentmindedly thrown on the fire. It was better to work than to brood, and she had much work to do. She restlessly poked the fire and added another shovel of coal before taking up her pen again.

'After the withdrawal of the Chung Wang, the Loyal King, to defend Nanking in the early autumn of 1862, the operations of the Long Haired Rebels in Su-Fu Province, as they call the territory from Soochow to the coast, were commanded by the Mu Wang, the Disciple King,' she wrote. 'With the parallel withdrawal of all foreign forces to Shanghai in late

October, the Great Pure Dynasty's offensive was conducted solely by the Mandarin Li Hung-chang, Governor of Kiangsu Province and Commander-in-Chief of the Army of Huai. Besides that force of more than 50,000, the Mandarin commanded the Ever Victorious Army, some 5,000-strong under its new general, the American Henry Burgevine.

'The Disciple King reorganised his numerically superior forces and took the offensive at the end of October 1862, ambushing a flotilla of troop-junks on the Grand Canal. The Mandarin Li Hung-chang thereupon took the field to direct the counter-offensive personally. On the 3rd of November, the rebels withdrew in disorder. After that decisive victory, the initiative passed to the forces of His Imperial Majesty, the Tung Chih Emperor, where it has remained.

'All was, however, not harmonious in the Imperial camp. The freebooter Henry Burgevine was not the man his slain predecessor and compatriot Frederick Townsend Ward had been, but was . . .'

Fronah wondered how frank she dared be. Her chief had casually told her that he must appear in a good light if his propaganda were to win foreign support. Not only the Imperial cause must be painted sympathetically but, also, he himself, since he was best suited by his natural talents and his good relations with the foreigners to save the Dynasty.

The Mandarin would not, she assumed, object to her depicting Burgevine's true character. But it would not do to reveal his own calculations too clearly, for he would only strike out the offending passages when David sight-translated her English for him. If he did not trust her judgment, he would not have forced the assignment upon her. But he trusted no one entirely except his two younger brothers.

Burgevine, she recalled, had protested when ordered to lead the Ever Victorious Army to Nanking to join the protracted siege the Viceroy Tseng Kuo-fan was slowly closing on the Taiping capital. He would not march, the American declared, unless the substantial arrears of pay due his men were immediately made up. Jealous of the praise accorded the Chinese generals of the Army of Huai, he also resented the appointment of a Royal Navy captain as the Mandarin's chief-of-staff.

Her chief would certainly not object to a frank account of Burgevine's pettiness and flagrant insubordination. But, she feared, he would not approve of an equally frank account of his own astute handling of the foreign powers that revealed the secret strategy outlined in his private papers.

The Americans were taken up with their own civil war, the Mandarin calculated, and were no longer a significant force in China. He neither feared the Americans' interference nor looked for the Americans' assistance – not even to balance their cousins and rivals, the British. He distrusted and feared the Russians, whose activity was increasing. He distrusted Russia because she had two centuries earlier been the first European power with which China came into conflict. He feared Russia because she was China's neighbour. He, therefore, followed the counsel offered by Sun Tze, the supreme strategist, in the fifth century B.C.: 'Align with the distant power, but be wary of the neighbouring power!'

The Mandarin accordingly rejected the proffered aid of three Imperial Russian warships, just as Prince Kung had rejected Russian arms and advisers for his Peking Field Force. He would rely upon the British for whatever foreign assistance he required. Since Anglo-Russian rivalry was even more virulent after the Crimean War, the implicit threat to call in the Russians would ensure Britain's good behaviour. He would, finally, utilise the insignificant French forces if he needed them. He did not take the French seriously.

'Burgevine . . . was a trial to his superiors,' Fronah wrote again after reluctantly concluding that future historians' perspicacity must illuminate her chief's brilliant diplomacy. 'His erratic handling of a near mutiny on January 3, 1863 tried the Mandarin Li Hung-chang's patience greatly. The mutineers barricaded themselves inside Sungchiang, the headquarters of the Ever Victorious Army, and threatened to sack the city. They swore they would slay all Imperial officials and join the rebels if the two months' arrears of pay they claimed were not immediately forthcoming. Telling his men he was already buying their food from his own pocket, Burgevine promised payment within three days. He then rode to Shanghai to confront the merchant Tankee, once Frederick Townsend Ward's father-in-law and still the Imperial Government's paymaster for the Ever Victorious Army.

'Takee, who had embezzled that pay, agreed to send funds to Sung-chiang by motor-launch. The craft steamed away from its pier only to tie up again around a bend in the stream. The money was returned to Takee's godown.

'Discovering that duplicity, Burgevine stormed into the godown. After beating Takee to make him open his safe, the American siezed $40,000.

'This attack on a Chinese subject forced the Mandarin to relieve Burgevine of his command. Released from close arrest by the Mandarin's lenience, Burgevine went to Peking to demand reinstatement. But his arrogance and insubordination were obvious to Prince Counsellor Kung, who rejected his demand.'

Fronah feared digressing, but she was fascinated by the fate of the American freebooter.

'Despite pressure from some ambassadors in Peking, Burgevine was not reinstated,' she wrote. 'He thereupon showed his true colours. On August 2, 1863, two hundred foreign mercenaries under his leadership seized the armoured steamship *Kajow* in Shanghai and sailed for Soochow to join the Disciple King. Burgevine participated in the rebels' attack on a key city defended by the Ever Victorious Army under its new commander British Major Charles George Gordon, who feared that Burgevine's former subordinates might join him in the Taiping camp. But they did not.

'Although the Loyal King again assumed command of the Holy Soldiers in Su-Fu Province, they could not stem the Imperial offensive in the autumn of 1863. When the Loyal King retreated towards Soochow, Burgevine accompanied him. But even the rebels had realised that he was a hollow vessel. Sent to Shanghai to purchase munitions from those foreign merchants who persisted in trading with the Taipings, Burgevine returned with a cargo of wine.'

How, Fronah wondered, would that passage strike her father? She was virtually certain he had given up smuggling, but David felt it unwise to inquire too closely.

'The adventurer's inglorious collaboration with the rebels ended shortly thereafter,' she continued. 'On October 13, 1863, thirty-three of his foreign mercenaries deserted to Major Gordon. Burgevine secretly inquired regarding the reception he himself might receive. He received no reply.

'On October 16th, the Loyal King and the Disciple King released Henry Burgevine from their service. Having stealthily returned to Shanghai, he has for the past month been skulking in the Foreign Settlement, where he is beyond the reach of Chinese justice.'

So much for Burgevine, whom Fronah found personally repellent. Major and brevet-Lieutenant Colonel Charles George Gordon, Brigadier General in the Imperial Chinese Army, was another matter. The sapper officer combined religious fervour, which made him a hero to the missionaries, with calculation, which did not endear him to the Mandarin Li Hung-chang. Christian fervour led him to denounce vehemently the brutality and treachery of his Chinese allies; ambition led him to campaign strenuously for honours and promotion, while pretending indifference to earthly rewards.

Gordon's chief accomplishment was to reinforce the lesson her chief had already learned. Led by competent officers and equipped with modern arms, Chinese troops were as effective as European regulars. Praising Gordon highly would not only displease the Mandarin, but would also distort reality. The Ever Victorious Army was a small assault force, which was quite successful in that limited role. But the Army of Huai bore the brunt of the fighting.

Fronah regretfully decided that it would be unwise even to touch on Gordon's double-dealing. The Mandarin would not risk an open breach with the British officer, since it could lead to a diminution of British support.

The morals of foreigners in China were notoriously as lax as the Chinese corruption the same foreigners piously decried. She was none the less astonished by a spy's copy of an intimate letter from the Disciple King to Gordon. 'If you have more rifles, cannon, and other foreign goods to sell, let us carry on our normal business,' the rebel commander urged. The pietistic Englishman was not only winning renown, but receiving a handsome salary – as well as lavish bonuses – for fighting the Taipings. He

402

was also making handsome profits by selling them weapons that killed his own men.

That revelation, too, must await the researches of future historians. The austere Mandarin required a chonicle of his campaigns, not a revelation of the peccadilloes of his allies.

For the next hour Fronah covered successive pages with accounts of battles and massacres, as well as strategems and teachery. She realised, however, that she could bring her narrative to the present moment, the early winter of 1863, by summing up its complexities in a few sentences.

'Despite the courage and skill of the Loyal King, the rebels were driven back on their stronghold of Soochow,' she wrote. 'The Mandarin Li Hung-chang's leadership, enhanced by his growing mastery of Western military techniques, was decisive. The Heavenly King recited his solitary prayers for divine succour in his palace in Nanking while the power and the resolution of the Heavenly Kingdom decayed. The Taiping monarch aknowledged in an admonitory decree that his realm was crumbling because his subordinates "committed evil deeds and turned away from the truth". From generals to privates, almost all Holy Soldiers looted, the decree lamented, ignoring the divine injunction to aid the common people, rather than oppress them. Meanwhile, the tide of battle flowed inexorably towards Soochow, the chief outpost defending the Heavenly Capital at Nanking.

'Neither the fanaticism nor the tenacity of the Taiping rebels should, however, be underestimated, though . . .'

Fronah raised her pen and shook her head, feeling her exhaustion an oppressive alien presence in the morning-room. Only two days remained of the allotted week, but she was close to completing her first draft. Since polishing would thereafter go quickly, she was determined to finish it that night. Although the gold watch on her lapel read 11:53, she began writing again.

'. . . Soochow appears to be on the point of liberation from . . .'

The steel-nib halted, and Fronah listened intently. Perhaps her fatigue deceived her, but the tinkling of the glass-beads in the French windows seemed to have stopped for an instant and then resumed. Despite the new Foreign Settlement Constabulary, the influx of refugees into the frontier town had brought a wave of violent robberies – and the aged Bannermen who guarded the compound sometimes slept at their posts. Irritated by her own fancies, she repressed her fear to pick up the thread of the narrative. The strings of beads jangled harshly, and she glimpsed movement among them.

Her eyes dazzled by the light, Fronah stared at the black oblong of the French windows. No darker shape loomed in their darkness. Convinced that she had seen a phantasm of her own exhaustion, she looked down at the manuscript.

'Fronah?' a man's voice whispered. 'Fronah, I'm coming in!'

She shrieked involuntarily. Her cry was muffled by the yellow-velvet hangings, and the servants' quarters were far away. She screamed again when the man stepped through the screen of beads. Astonishment held her immobile as the dark figure moved into the circle of light around her.

Fronah stared at the features she had feared she would never again see. In the radiance of the oil-lamp, her husband's eyes were dark pits above the jutting cheekbones that dominated his pathetically thin face. His hair was tarnished with grey, and his pale lips were thin. She wanted to touch his cheek, but was still gripped by shock.

'Well, the prodigal returns.' His voice was lower, its timbre harsher. 'Fronah, I promised . . . and I've come back to you.'

She still could not speak, but sat staring at the apparition in the quasi-naval uniform. Lionel grasped her shoulders, and she felt the familiar pressure of the gold signet-ring on his little finger. But she could not respond. Despite her resolve to forgive him for Judah's sake, his long absence remained an intolerable affront. The ghastly scene with the little girls at Old Mother Wang's played itself again before her eyes against the backdrop of his face. Repelled by her immobility, his arms dropped to his sides.

'Lionel?' she finally asked incredulously. 'It is really you? After all this time . . . so suddenly?'

'None other, my dear. I'm sorry I startled you, but it was the only way.'

'Lionel!' she cried. 'Oh, my darling!'

He grasped her shoulder again, and she babbled incoherently in his arms. His lips were cold on her forehead, a hard oval against the bone. Her tears stained his blue-serge jacket, and the brass buttons hurt her breasts.

'There, there,' he murmured. 'That's my good girl. It's all right, my dear. There, there!'

More like a nanny comforting a frightened child than a lover – the unwanted thought was discordant. None the less she leaned back in the circle of his arms and raised her face. His lips were harsh when he kissed her mouth. Beneath her fingertips, his cheeks were brittle and dry as paper.

'Lionel! Oh, Lionel, I've waited . . . dreamed so long of . . .' Fronah gently disengaged herself. 'Let me look at you.'

Above the choker-collar her husband's face was burnt dark by the sun. The planes of his cheeks were harder and assertively masculine. But a grey cast underlay his tan, and his pupils were abnormally small. Even when they looked into her own, his light-blue eyes were distant.

'Are you ill?' she asked. 'You're not well, Lionel, are you?'

'Nothing to worry about, my dear. It's not been all cakes and ale, of course. Deuced rough at times. But I'm fine, I assure you.'

'Are you sure? But I mustn't plague you when you've just come back.' She reached out and smoothed his hair, subduing a flicker of revulsion as the shameful tableau at the procuress's intruded again before her eyes. 'I've got so many questions. So much to tell you, too. But there's no rush. We'll have lots of time to catch up.'

'Well, actually, Fronah, not quite. We don't have all that much time. This'll be a quick visit, I'm afraid. Of course, I'll . . .'

'What *are* you saying?' She persisted, though she knew he hated being cross-questioned. 'I don't want to press, but, tell me, why the uniform? And why come so stealthily . . . so late at night? Only a quick visit, you said? No more, my dear?'

'I'm afraid so, Fronah. You see, I've learnt something about loyalty. I must be true to my word. So, I'm afraid . . .'

'What *do* you mean? What of your word to me . . . your loyalty to your son?' Her determination to welcome him for Judah's sake was shaken by his familiar evasiveness. 'You *must* tell me, please!'

'Actually . . . well, you see, Fronah . . .' he stumbled. 'I can only stay . . .'

'I'm sorry, Lionel.' She tried again, though he was not helping her forget the past. 'I know I shouldn't cross-question you. But you must see Judah if you've got so little time. Come and see our son. Then you can tell me why . . .'

'Another time, I'm afraid. I've only got a few moments.'

'Then tell me now.' If she could suppress her ghastly memories, how could he refuse to see his son? 'Please tell me.'

'I will, if you'll give me a minute.' Somehow, his asperity cheered her. 'If I see Judah, the baby-amah'll know. And I can't have that.'

'Why, Lionel? Why all this stealth?'

'As you've gathered, I can only stay a moment. Really, I shouldn't have come. There'll be the deuce to pay . . . for you, for myself, too . . . if this visit gets out. It's for your protection . . . and my own, I'm afraid.'

'My protection? Yours? Why on earth? We're in the Foreign Settlement, you know. Whatever you've done, you're safe here . . . beyond the reach of the Chinese. Why, Henry Burgevine's swanning about . . . not a hair touched after *his* behaviour. But my protection, you say?'

'Yes, my dear. I haven't left the Taipings, as you've undoubtedly gathered.'

'Your loyalties?' she responded dully. 'That's what you meant, is it? You're still tied to the rebels?'

'That's what I meant. There's a splendid chap called Lindley. A rough diamond, a sea captain, you see. I've grown quite fond of him though he's not my . . . our . . . kind of person. Has a Portuguese wife in Macao, probably half-caste. But he's been a good friend and . . .'

'I'm sure Mr Lindley's quite wonderful. But, please Lionel, get to the point. You're tormenting me.'

'Perhaps better if I hadn't come, though I had to see you. But I will get to the point. We're going to seize the *Firefly*. Lindley's in command. She's a fine little gunboat, well armed and well armoured. We're taking her at two this morning, then we're sailing her to Soochow.'

'You're mad, Lionel, mad!' Fronah exploded. 'What's the point? Even if you're not killed . . . not captured and tried for piracy . . . you're fighting for a hopeless cause. The rebellion's certain to be crushed. Another year, at most, and it'll be all over. The Heavenly Kingdom's finished, Lionel, finished!'

'By no means, my dear. It's just beginning again. A new spirit is waking, and we'll . . .'

Fronah automatically refuted his zealotry. He was talking nonsense, she knew. Perhaps he, too, knew it in his heart, though she thought not. Whatever he truly believed, she could not force him to face reality in the few minutes he had granted her after their long separation.

'Enough of politics. We could talk all night and get nowhere.' Her laugh sounded contrived to herself. 'Tell me, my dear, about . . . about something else.'

'Yes, Fronah, what?'

'You've changed greatly in many ways. Have you . . . that is . . . are you also . . .?'

'You mean my . . . ah . . . the opium and the . . . ah . . .'

'Yes,' she prompted, 'that's what I mean.'

'I've really changed, Fronah, believe me,' he lied evenly, remembering that he had briefly overcome his unconventional tastes. 'That's all over now. I only want to come back to you . . . to be with you. Just as soon as I can.'

'I'm sorry, darling.' She wanted so much to believe him. 'So sorry to bedevil you with my questions and my foolish fears. Perhaps you're right about the Taipings. But let's not talk any more. We've got so little time.'

Lioned had feared it would come to that. He truly cared for Fronah, but not that way. He suppressed a shudder as she unbuttoned his jacket and laid her palm against his chest. Her hand crept around to stroke his back.

He cared, but not that way. Though more finely drawn, Fronah was still far too fleshy for his taste. Her hips were too rounded and her breasts to full. His flesh was repelled. He closed his eyes to pretend she was lissom, barely nubile. But she smelled like a grown woman: those rank juices he detested. Pressing against him in the satin nightdress was the gross body of a grown woman.

'Fronah, the servants,' he protested. 'Should we really?'

Avid after her long deprivation, Fronah did not sense his revulsion. She gave herself to her husband, believing his reserve arose from shyness and, perhaps, guilt. Hungry for love, she did not notice his reluctance.

'Be quiet,' she whispered. 'Only be quiet. Be quiet and love me.'

When they lay naked on the silk carpet before the fireplace, she twisted and turned, caressing him with her entire body as she never had in the past. Despite his revulsion, Lionel was inflamed by her ardour. He joined with only infinitesimal restraint in the mingling of their limbs, and his hands played over her thighs and breasts.

Fronah shuddered when his fingertips found her. She shuddered profoundly, her body arched like a drawn bow, and she groaned in ecstacy. She shuddered again and sighed deeply. Then she lay quiet for a moment.

'Now!' she cried an instant later. 'Now! Come into me, my darling.

Fronah's arms and legs encircled Lionel, pressing him deeper into herself. Her feet clasped his buttocks, and her nails raked his back. Her eyes were closed, and her mouth was slack in the firelight. She stiffened again. A more profound shudder racked her, and she was borne upward on the crest of the most overwhelming sensation she had ever known. When she screamed repeatedly, he, too, found release.

Lionel began to dress after lying beside her for a minute. Fronah stretched languorously, shameless in the ruddy glow that bathed her naked body. It was, she reflected almost lazily, even more moving because he had to leave her so soon. She felt joyously abandoned, a wanton courtesan bidding farewell to an ardent lover, rather than a long neglected wife finally fulfilled.

'You'll be back?' Her whisper was an affirmation, rather than a question. 'You'll be back? . . . Soon, my darling?'

'Of course I'll be back! I told you I'd come back . . . And I did. I'll come back again just as soon as I possibly can.'

'To stay, darling? This time to stay?'

'This time to stay,' he swore. 'All our lives.'

The glass-beads jangled, and he was gone while his promise still hung in the air. She pulled her red-velvet dressing-gown over herself and lay in a golden reverie. He had come back. And he had proved that he loved her. He would return again to stay, and all would be well with them all their lives.

She was also warmed by his steadfastness to his new cause. The zealot he had become was more manly than the schemer she had married. If he were as steadfast in his devotion to herself, she could wait patiently for this man of hers to return again. He would be steadfast – and she would wait.

She did love Lionel, she realised, not Gabriel Hyde. The spark that had leapt between the American and herself sprang from strain and fatigue. Of course she loved Lionel. He was the father of her son, and she had always loved him.

When the fire began to sink, Fronah finally stirred. She slipped into her dressing-gown and sat, arms clasped around her knees, gazing at the embers.

When the embers began to die, doubt ruffled Fronah's euphoria. He had not *said* he loved her. Yet, she assured herself, he had *shown* that he had loved her, conclusively proved his love. She had never before known utter physical and emotional exultation. It must have been the same for him after their long separation.

She reproached herself for her imaginary fears. What kind of woman was it who was never content, but always questioning? There was no need for him to speak, for he had proved his love beyond all possible doubt.

Yet, she wondered, *when* would he – when *could* he – return to her? If the civil war were greatly prolonged before a final Taiping victory, as he believed, it could be years before they lived together again. If the Imperial forces were soon victorious, as she believed, he could be a hunted fugitive unable to reach the sanctuary of the Foreign Settlement – or even barred from its safety.

Fronah sighed, almost regretting that Lionel's passion had shattered her cool self-sufficiency and reawakened their love. Yet she knew beyond doubt that God would keep him safe for her.

CHAPTER FIFTY-NINE

The Night of December 4–5, 1863   *Soochow*

'The past is too much with us Chinese,' Aaron Lee mused aloud, gazing at the arrow-straight camp-fires of the Ever Victorious Army on Tiger Hill north-west of the walls of Soochow. 'The past is a crushing burden, which bows our shoulders and forces our eyes down. We cannot see the future, and we can hardly see the present.'

'You're a philosopher tonight, Aaron.' Lionel Henriques's opium-ravaged voice rasped, and his mind was fogged by the many pipes he had smoked through the seemingly endless December day. 'Why so pensive?'

'It's the end of an era, Lionel, the last hours of the Heavenly Kingdom. Tomorrow'll be a grey day. We Chinese will wear the Manchu queue for a while longer, perhaps a long while. I won't give up urging you to come with me, you know.'

'Desert? At this late date? I'm afraid not, Aaron. It's too late, much too late for me.'

'And Fronah? What of my sister, Lionel? You'll desert her?'

'Not forever, Aaron, I promise you. You see, I believe you're wrong. The Heavenly Kingdom's not finished, not by a long shot. Soochow may fall . . . all right, Soochow *will* fall to this siege. But it's only an incident. The Taipings *must* win. And I must stay with them. Some day I'll go back to Fronah. Whatever, she'll manage. I never saw her more in control.'

'You're condemning my sister to misery,' Aaron protested. 'For years she could be neither widow nor wife.'

'She'll manage, not like a Chinese lady. She can always divorce me . . .

become a gay divorcée. Besides, it may be too late for Fronah and me. Sometimes I'm afraid it's all over with me, anyway.'

'I don't understand you, Lionel. When you came back two weeks ago with *Firefly*, you were bursting with hope. I never saw you so optimistic. You were certain we'd hold Soochow and then strike back. You were bubbling . . . positively bubbling . . . about your future with Fronah. What's gone wrong, my friend?'

'That was two weeks ago, and a lot's happened. Even *Firefly's* not herself anymore, but *Taiping*.' The Englishman evaded the question. 'But my affairs are a bore. Tell me, why your fascination with the queue? I never knew anyone hang a weighty historical thesis from a rope of hair.'

'I'll be wearing the queue again tomorrow,' Aaron said dolefully, 'though I hate it.'

Impelled by his duty to his family, the only absolute imperative he knew, Aaron Lee was determined for his sister's sake to probe the Englishman's mood to its murky depths. His brother-in-law was heavily melancholy – and not only because he had been smoking heavily since his return from Shanghai, careless of the danger of retribution from the remaining zealots among the Taipings, led by the incorruptible Disciple King.

He would have the truth out of Lionel yet, and he would persuade Lionel to go over to the Imperial camp with him. With Taiping resistance crumbling amid internal dissension, the Manchus' standing offer of amnesty was their only hope of safety, perhaps their only hope of life. He had learned how to deal with his brother-in-law, never straightforwardly, but always indirectly – as the foreigners believed Chinese always behaved. He therefore allowed himself to be diverted by Lionel's question regarding the queue.

'Maybe it's an obsession with me,' Aaron admitted. 'But just imagine: the Russians conquer England and decree that no Englishman may wear his normal clothing. Only, say, the Russian blouse. They also decree that every Englishman must shave his forehead and braid his backhair into a plait like a common sailor.'

'You do look better with your hair dressed like a gentleman. But it's a small thing.'

'A small thing? It's vile and unnatural, I tell you. Monstrous! For more than two centuries, no Chinese wife has seen her husband as God made him, only disfigured by the barbaric hair-style of a primitive tribe. Father and son look away in shame at the symbol of racial humiliation both wear. It's sinful, a distortion of nature.'

'What about foot-binding, Aaron, that distorts nature violently? Hurts like the devil, too.'

'Somehow, Lionel, I can't imagine marrying a woman with big feet. Men like it, and ladies are proud of their golden lilies. Besides, the Manchu women don't. Foot-binding's not a foreign atrocity.'

'All sounds a bit metaphysical to me. Any rate, you'll soon be wearing the queue again. How do you square that?'

'I've got no choice. Why die for a forlorn cause? I can only revenge myself for the injustice to my father by changing the Confucian system from within. And David's letters say his Mandarin is open to change.' Aaron returned to the attack. 'But there's nothing for you here. The Taipings are finished. Come with me tonight.'

'We'll see, old chap.' Lionel remained evasive. 'By God, it's a beautiful night, isn't it?'

They stood on the ramparts of the Water Gate, the keystone of the intact defences of the most beautiful city in China. Lying on the shore of Tai Hu, the Great Lake, amid a lacework of waterways segmented by the Grand Canal, Soochow was like Venice, an amphibious metropolis, half-aquatic and half-terranean. Cargo vessels did not unload outside the walls as at other Chinese cities, but poled into the centre of Soochow on the network of internal canals.

The Water Gate was, therefore, the strong point of the defensive walls that had grown around the metropolis long before the birth of Christ. Lionel looked down upon an inverted ziggurat of ingenious complexity, a watery fortress with many interior walls pierced by enormous sluice gates. Silver in the moonlight, that internal water-course frequently struck off at right angles, elsewhere almost doubled back on itself. The cargo vessels following that zig-zag channel were always under the weapons of the guards on the walls that overlooked its entire length.

That defence against a water-borne attack was superfluous that night. The Imperial armies closing on the city under the Mandarin Li Hung-chang's personal command were unlikely to strike at the Water Gate. Even their modern cannon could not breach the medieval walls. Their enemy's overwhelming numbers could alone overwhelm Taiping resistance. Moreover, there was a whiff of treachery in the night air. Betrayal would not strike through the Water Gate, but would seep through the walls themselves. Too many otherwise inexplicable incidents during the past week, too many Imperial attacks on weak points which fell just short of their objectives, had demonstrated that some Taiping leaders were conspiring with the Imps.

Lionel did not know his brother-in-law's precise role in the machinations he sensed. But Aaron had told him he was in communication with his younger brother David, *aide de camp* to the Imperialist general. The spy had just revealed that he expected the dénouement of the plot within the next twenty-four hours.

Yet the web of treachery his brothers-in-law were spinning seemed almost superfluous when Lionel Henriques looked down from the crenellated Water Gate upon the massive enemy dispositions. On Tiger Hill lay the encampment of the Ever Victorious Army commanded by Colonel Charles George Gordon, the fanatical Christian determined to destroy the equally fanatical Christian Taipings for his own glory – and profit. Its battle flags were arrayed near the White Pagoda, which had stood for more than a thousand years above the grotto where the King of the feudal state of Wu, the founder of Soochow, was reputedly entombed in a cavern concealed by a flowing stream. The yellow camp-fires like rows of stars in the clear night would, in any event, have revealed the bivouac of the Ever Victorious Army, the assault force of the Mandarin Li Hung-chang.

The Army of Huai ignored such protocol, despite the Mandarin's enthusiasm for Western weapons and Western tactics. The fiery dragons of the Chinese army, which was armed chiefly with swords and spears, though stiffened with cannon-platoons and rifle-companies, writhed across the landscape where Chinese soldiers had clashed for more than two millennia.

Lionel had not trembled when the Mandarin arrived twelve days earlier to take personal command of the Imperialist armies. Despite the near awe with which Fronah spoke of her chief, he was not deeply impressed by the prowess of the Manchu's Commander-in-Chief. The Englishman had, however, been plunged into despair four days earlier when the Loyal King withdrew from the city he loved above all others. Nanking was also threatened, and it was imperative that the Taiping Commander-in-Chief return to direct the defence of the Heavenly Capital. Lionel felt a presentiment of disaster as the Loyal King rode north-west with a small escort, leaving the defence of his beloved Soochow to the Disciple King.

That lesser Taiping commander was a soldier of renown, a true believer and a true hero, as the Englishman had learned on the battlefield. But he possessed neither the strategic genius nor the supernal valour of the Taiping Commander-in-Chief. The Disciple King was, moreover, embroiled in a personal dispute with his deputy, General Kao Yung-kwan, whose given name with nice irony meant Eternal Magnanimity. That sly scoundrel commanded the loyalty of the seven chief Taiping field commanders. Water-veined Soochow was hardly secure in the keeping of the Disciple King and the Eternally Magnanimous General.

Lionel's journey into despair had begun even before the Loyal King's departure. Inspired by his ardent countryman Captain Lindley, he had exulted when the captured gunboat *Firefly* evaded Colonel Gordon's pursuit ambushes to reach the Great Lake. He had shared Lindley's belief that Gordon's Ever Victorious Army could be countered by a Loyal Faithful Auxiliary Legion – commanded by foreign officers, armed with foreign weapons, and deploying two foreign gunboats.

Despite the Loyal King's support, the Faithful Legion could never defeat the hypocritical Gordon. Competent foreign officers could be found neither among the mercenaries already serving the Heavenly Kingdom nor in Shanghai. Few gentlemen fought under the banner of the Taipings who, perforce, recruited their mercenaries among deserters, the sweepings of the foreign settlement. Finally *Firefly* had no support, and sending a single gunboat against the enemy flotillas was suicidal. Rechristened *Taiping*, she was withdrawn to Wuhsi on the Long River, and the Faithful Legion was defeated before it put a single soldier into the field.

411

Too many similar disappointments during more than two years of service with the Taipings had frayed Lionel Henriques's spirit. His reluctant reaffirmation of his love for Fronah had rent his spirit.

He now knew that he loved his wife and was deeply concerned for her happiness. But his treacherous flesh shrank from her, and his spirit recoiled from the irksome responsibilities of matrimony. Since God had not made him to live with a mature woman, Fronah frightened him.

Immersed in depression, the Englishman barely heard his brother-in-law's urging him to defect to the Imperialists. As they descended from the Water Gate and walked towards the Garden of the Humble Administrator for the conference the Disciple King had summoned, Lionel Henriques's mind was further confused by the excess of opium he had consumed during the past week. Arrogantly detached, his consciousness soared above the besieged city – and marvelled at his concern with such transient matters as war and marriage. A moment later, that vision faded – and he felt himself small and vulnerable, a blind mole cowering in the last intact tunnel of a collapsing burrow.

Aaron and he were a strange pair, Lionel reflected. Jewish by descent, they served the most extreme Christian sect on earth. The Englishman was determined to remain true to the fanatical creed that sought to overthrow alien rule in a nation alien to his loyalty. But he was faithfuly by default. At thirty-nine, weary of change, he felt his life was over. The Chinese patriot was planning to desert his fellow patriots for the barbarian oppressors. He did not believe the Manchus offered hope to his suffering nation, but he believed the Taipings offered no hope whatsoever.

The metropolis through which they walked mirrored their confusion. No longer did the four-foot-wide lanes between wooden buildings or the bridges arching over canals silvered by moonlight resound to the tread of uniformed men and women. The troops were on the city walls, and the occasional lictor warming himself over a minuscule fire glanced incuriously at them.

The Household Guard of the Disciple King slouched indifferently before the main gate of the Garden of the Humble Administrator. Hardly looking up from his New Testament, a sergeant waved them through the crimson arch. They walked unchallenged under the crooked boughs of bare trees towards the palace near the dragon-head Mountainview Tower where the Loyal King had planned his offensives against Shanghai. Admitted after a cursory glance, they joined the thirty-odd staff officers waiting in the anteroom for the generals' dinner to end.

Framed by the circular moon-gate of the entrance hall, like actors on a stage, the seven generals led by the Eternally Magnanimous Kao were sipping tea with the Disciple King. Their gaudy robes enhanced the theatrical effect, as did the fires in the coal braziers, which alternately illuminated them and obscured them with shadow. At the head of the oval formed by ebony chairs, the Disciple King's throne stood on a low dais. His square face was tense under its gold-filigree head-dress, and his gestures were emphatic.

'The generals are parleying with Gordon,' Aaron whispered. 'The Magnanimous Kao's planning to save his skin and his gold by delivering Soochow to that other righteous Christian warrior.'

'And Gordon'll be richly rewarded,' Lionel replied bitterly. 'He'll protest he doesn't want a thing. But he'll take everything he can get so as not to offend the sensitive Orientals.'

The generals rose and gesticulated broadly, their voices reverberating unintelligibly through the anteroom. The Disciple King gripped the carved arms of his throne and thrust his head forwards.

'No! Never!' he bellowed. 'We'll all die in Soochow if it comes to that. But I'll never surrender!'

Ringing clear in the anteroom, his words shocked the staff officers. Many had suspected treachery, though only Aaron Lee knew its roots. Though all feared dissension among their leaders, they were appalled by the disintegration of the flinty discipline that had carried the Holy Soldiers to victory and sustained them in reverses.

'*Mei pan-fa* . . .' The Eternally Magnanimous General Kao argued, his large head rigid on his long neck. 'There's no other way. We must save ourselves to fight the Imps again another day.'

'Even your treachery's double-edged!' the Disciple King exploded. 'But I . . . I will *never* surrender!'

A stocky figure wearing a scarlet and green robe stepped from the rank of generals confronting their commander. Lionel recognised him as Brigadier General Wang An-chun, a pleasant southerner with whom he had occasionally chatted. Respectfully smiling and respectfully silent, he crossed the six-foot distance separating him from the Disciple King. Moving with the muscular delicacy of an acrobat, he flicked a dagger from his sash and thrust the blade underhanded into his commander's abdomen below the breastbone.

The astonished Disciple King bellowed in anger. The assassin pulled his arm back and struck again. His cry cut off by the thrust, the commander slumped forward. His powerful hands scrabbled on the arms of the throne, and he shrieked in agony. Slipping off the polished wood, his fingers clawed the air. Finally still, his body toppled to the floor, crumpling within its embroidered robe. His filigree crown tinkled on the flagstones amid the blood pumping from his torso.

Flashing crimson in the braziers' glow, the generals' daggers stabbed the dying commander while the staff officers stood paralysed by shock. Through the circular moon-door, the spectacle seemed unreal, a skilful pantomime. Lionel half expected the dead commander to rise and bow with the drama ended. He shouted in horror when the Magnanimous Kao knelt in the puddled blood to hack at the Disciple King's throat with a triangular blade.

413

Drawing their swords, the staff officers surged forward. A thicket of pikes halted them. The personal guards of the mutinous generals forced them back. When the officers huddled again in the anteroom, the Eternally Magnanimous General Kao addressed them.

'I command now!' he proclaimed. 'Tomorrow I'll send the head to the Imps, one head to save all our heads. I regret that price, but it's the only way. Tomorrow, we pretend to surrender on the terms of the English Colonel. We can trust his word, not like the Chinese running dogs of the Manchus. We'll surrender, but we'll fight the Imps again, I swear. Now return to your units.'

*

The price of the generals' safety was far higher than the Magnanimous Kao had reckoned, Aaron reflected as the night sky began to pale over the ramparts of the Water Gate. Not just the life of the Disciple King, but the lives of thousands of Holy Soldiers. The traitors had not yet sent their commander's head to the Imperialists nor opened the gates of Soochow. But the slaughter had already begun. Some five thousand of the garrison were old Taiping warriors from the southern provinces. Enraged by the assassination of the Disciple King, whom they had followed for a decade, those veterans hurled themselves at the troops guarding the assassins.

Most of Lionel Henriques's gunners were southerners, and most had joined the attack on the Garden of the Humble Administrator. But the Englishman still refused to acknowledge the inevitable, or, acknowledging the inevitable Imperialist victory, he refused to act upon it. He still rejected Aaron's pleas to defect.

Lionel was wilfully deaf to the mutters of his remaining soldiers, who stood to their guns though they knew their steadfastness was in vain. They would, they swore, hurl hundreds of Imps into the thirty-three Hells before gladly ascending to the eighteen Heavens described by their Heavenly King. Knowing that the promise of the barbarian commanding the Ever Victorious Army had decided the traitors to surrender, they further swore to send many barbarians to the barbarians' own Hell.

The hewn-stone of the battlements was luminous grey, and the soldiers' yellow tunics glowed pale against the brightening sky. Dawn was hardly an hour distant, and Aaron had to be gone before dawn to save himself. When the Army of Huai began pounding Soochow at sunrise, probing the gates the traitors had promised to open, escape would be impossible. None the less Aaron was impelled by his duty to his sister and by his affection for his brother-in-law to a final effort to persuade the obdurate Englishman.

'It's all over!' he argued. 'I can't say anything new, but just look around. You must save yourself, Elder Brother, for Fronah's sake as well as your own. Besides, you can't rejoin the Loyal King in Nanking if you're dead.'

'It's good of you to trouble, Aaron.' The Englishman was as casual as if

414

courteously refusing a small gift. 'I'm deeply grateful for your trouble. You couldn't trouble more if I were really your brother.'

'You are, Lionel. You are my true brother, though you'll never understand. Just do it. Come with me before . . .'

'I'm sorry, but I can't run away again. I've been running all my life.'

'Why not, for God's sake? Fight another day if you must.'

'I don't really care any more about fighting. It's all gone glimmering. But I must stay if there's to be any meaning to my life. I can't again betray . . .'

'You're betraying Fronah and the boy. Your son and my nephew. Don't they matter to you?'

'Not really, I'm afraid. You see, Aaron, my friend . . . my brother . . . it's all gone glimmering.'

'Glimmering? I don't understand.'

'I'll try to explain. I owe you that. Really, I owe you so much more.'

'Then be quick! There's so little time!' Aaron warned when Lionel paused in thought. 'You love my sister, don't you?'

'I . . . I suppose I do . . . in my own way. I told you it was all over between us. I'm no use to Fronah any more, you see.'

'I don't see at all. A live husband's far more use than a dead one.'

'Not this husband. It's almost indecent talking this way. I can only say . . . I can't match with Fronah, emotionally or . . . ah . . . physically. She's too much for me.'

'Do you want to die?' Aaron despaired of understanding the Englishman's circumlocutions. 'Do you want to kill yourself? Isn't the opium quick enough?'

'Actually, the opium's kept me going, Aaron. But let's not drag this out. Just take it as read. I can't desert with you, and I can't go back to Fronah yet. Perhaps someday, but . . .'

As embarrassed as Lionel by the unexpressed emotion, Aaron abruptly put out his hand. His brother-in-law shook it briefly.

'Goodbye, Aaron,' he said. 'I'll see you in Shanghai.'

Behind the tall Englishman in the yellow tunic and the black trousers, his gunners were stirring. Their angry mutters giving way to menacing silence, they moved towards the two officers.

'One barbarian's no different from any other,' one declared. 'All the white-skinned devils have betrayed us.'

'Revenge, brothers!' another cried. 'Revenge the Disciple King on the barbarian and the Chinese running-dog!'

'That's torn it!' the Englishman said flatly. 'Move now!'

Aaron grasped Lionel's shoulder and thrust him towards the narrow stairwell that wound down the sally-port. The Englishman drew his sword and wheeled.

'God help me, I'll cut you down if you touch me again,' he threatened. 'Go now for God's sake, if you wish to live. I don't want to die, but if I must . . .'

'You can't control them, you fool,' Aaron shouted. 'Come now. We can both . . .'

'I can control them, you know. Any rate, we can't both . . . For God's sake, go!'

Aaron reeled under his brother-in-law's shove. He stumbled into the mouth of the stairwell and halfway down the first flight before he could check himself. The stone blocks scraped his outhrust hands, and the dark passage seemed to suck him down. But he heard Lionel's voice raised in command and entreaty.

'*Gno-gei dau* . . .' the Englishman promised in pidgin Cantonese. 'Now, lads, we'll hold off the Imps together. We'll revenge the Disciple King together.'

Raucous shouts responded, dominated by one voice: 'How can we believe a white-skinned devil?'

'You can because we've been together for years. And we'll die together if it comes to . . .'

Aaron turned the corner of the stairwell, and Lionel's voice died in mid-syllable. He knew he could not affect the confrontation on the battlements. Whatever was meant to happen would happen before he could clamber up the steep stone steps. He had failed in his duty to his family by failing to save his brother-in-law, but that duty also required him to save himself.

When Aaron stepped through the sally-port onto a glacis strewn with corpses in the uniforms of Imperial Braves, pink light tinged the eastern sky. On the ramparts of the Water Gate towering sheer sixty feet above him, no human form was visible – and no man spoke. The green muzzles of cannon gaped mute.

CHAPTER SIXTY

December 6, 1863   *The Imperial Camp before Soochow*

Men had often changed sides before the siege of Soochow. The Manchus encouraged Taiping officers to turn their coats by a standing amnesty and bounties determined by the number of their followers. The Heavenly Kingdom of Great Peace offered to defectors not only absolution for past sins, but substantial rewards. A great number had gone over to the enemy once. Many men had crossed the lines twice or thrice, drawn by the promise of rewards and promotion – sometimes driven by quarrels with their superiors and restlessness. Some officers, highly valued for their prowess or their influence, had flitted between the ranks of the Holy Soldiers and the Imperial Braves five or six times.

The Eternally Magnanimous General Kao was, therefore, by no means remarkable in expecting a generous reception after opening the gates of Soochow. It was hardly more remarkable that he planned to rejoin the Taipings subsequently. He was only remarkable – and foolhardy – in declaring that intention to his murdered prince's staff officers.

On the morning of December 6th, 1863, Aaron Lee had already made a smooth transition to the Imperialist camp after hearing that avowal from the chief assassin some thirty-two hours earlier. His transformation into an officer of the Army of Huai was accelerated by the service his brother David had rendered to the Mandarin Li Hung-chang – and the generous donations his adoptive father Saul Haleevie had made to the Mandarin's war chest. In a society where family solidarity was *the* pre-eminent virtue, their contributions weighed almost as heavily in his favour as his own espionage for the Imperialists. In one sense, they weighed more heavily because they demonstrated that his family was both competent and wealthy.

Since the Mandarin valued subordinates who possessed those sterling attributes, he had commissioned Aaron immediately. Having commanded a battalion of Holy Soldiers, the new major obviously understood the new tactics developed during he protracted civil war. Moreover, his mastery of the English language would, if necessary, enable him to serve as a liaison officer to the contentious foreign leaders of the Ever Victorious Army.

The Mandarin Li Hung-chang was eager to penetrate the minds of both his enemies and his allies, so that he could manipulate them. Sun Tze, the ancient master of strategy, had repeatedly stressed the necessity to understand the hidden motivations of both one's enemies and allies, though he was concerned with other Chinese – or neighbouring barbarians. The Mandarin believed that Aaron Lee, like his brother David, understood the mysterious mental processes of the new barbarians from over the seas, an insight, he acknowledged, that eluded himself. He was also grateful to Aaron for first-hand evidence regarding the intentions of the Eternally Magnanimous Kao, though his insight into the minds of his fellow Chinese had already warned him that the betrayer of Soochow would not hesitate to betray the Army of Huai.

Shortly after eight in the morning, Military Mandarin of the Fifth Grade Aaron Lee and recently promoted Civil Mandarin of the Sixth Grade David Lee sat chatting on a knoll overlooking the Commander-in-Chief's pavilion. Both wore blue tunics and trousers, the field uniform of the Army of Huai. Aaron was happy that he, the older brother, was finally senior in rank to David – as the Sage Confucius enjoined that age should be superior in a harmonious society.

Aaron's service with the rebels had ironically qualified him for field rank in the Military Mandarinate of the Great Pure Dynasty, while good fortune and outstanding service would in time enable him to transfer to the more highly regarded Civil Mandarinate. Aaron felt he had finally come home. Though he admired their dedication, he had never been comfortable among the Holy Soldiers. However irrationally, he was emotionally committed to the Confucian Mandarinate, which he considered corrupt and unjust – and he was determined to rise in its hierarchy.

The Commander-in-Chief approved of Aaron's ambition. He preferred to employ men impelled by the same motives as himself. The brothers' conversation might, however, have disturbed even that open-minded official. After catching up on the personal and family events of the past two years, they were discussing the radical changes they hoped to see in the rigid Confucian system.

'We agree, then,' David said. 'Odd, isn't it? We've reached exactly the same conclusion, though we were so far apart.'

'Not odd at all. First-class minds naturally take the same paths, even far apart,' Aaron replied with a rare flash of humour. 'Anyway, the Taipings are a dead loss. The only way we can avenge our father is the most refined way. We've got to work from inside to alter the Manchus' cruelties and absurdities. Since we can't destroy the Dynasty, we must destroy its injustice. And, some day . . . soon I hope . . . bring the old man back. He's well, you say?'

'Well and keeping busy.' David enjoyed repeating again the news in the infrequent letters their father was permitted to write. 'A senior foreman in the Emperor's Jade Mines. And allowed to trade a little on his own. He'll never get rich, but it keeps him busy.'

'He's lived just fifty years this month . . . We've got to get him back. You've talked to the chief?'

'Not yet, Aaron! My Mandarin's a funny chap. I've got to wait for just the right moment. After we've won, I think. After you've distinguished yourself.'

The brothers discussed their hopes for several minutes and concluded that they could soon petition the Imperial Court for a pardon. Their services to the Dynasty, past and future, should incline the compassionate young Empress Dowager to grant that petition. Remembering that the Imperial Concubine Yehenala had cajoled the Emperor to commute their father's death sentence, they assured each other she would certainly be merciful to Aisek Lee, now that mercy was wholly within her own power.

'And Lionel?' David asked again. 'You've no idea, I suppose?'

'David I can't possibly tell you whether he's dead or alive. Maybe we'll know today or tomorrow. But he was a husk when I left him, a hollow man. I am sure of one thing. He's no use to Fronah . . . And he never will be.'

'Well, I reckon she's found her own way. She'll grieve for Lionel if he's dead, but she's set on her own strange way. You'd think a young woman'd want her own family. Yet she seems reasonably happy . . .'

David broke off as his orderly approached. No more than their subversive political ideas did he wish their family concerns to become the talk of the camp.

'Sirs,' the orderly reported, 'the Commander-in-Chief summons you to the surrender ceremony.'

The standard of a provincial governor whipped between the banners of the Army of Huai and the Great Pure Dynasty before the field-pavilion of the Mandarin Li Hung-chang. The peaked and compartmented tent, whose green and crimson expanse covered two hundred square yards, was really a nuisance, his chief had confided to David, but 'useful to impress fools'. However, the *aide de camp* suspected that the Mandarin enjoyed the regal pomp, which he merited. The Mandarin was seated on a folding chair before the pavilion, while his personal troops were drawn up in three ranks to form a square whose fourth side was the pavilion.

'I still don't see why the boss let Gordon set the surrender terms.' Speaking English for privacy, Aaron returned to the question he had been worrying all day. 'It makes no sense to me.'

'The traitors approached Gordon first. Then the boss thought the Taipings would trust a foreigner.'

'Damned fools!' Aaron snorted. 'But it worked.'

'At least Gordon is gone, finally withdrawn with the Ever Victorious Army. The boss was livid, you know. Gordon demanded all the kudos for victory because of his diplomacy, believe it or not, as well as his generalship. Also two months' bonus for his men and a guarantee the boss would honour the amnesty he promised the murderers. What gall! Demanding that an Imperial commander-in-chief swear to honour *his* word as a Christian gentleman!'

'Sometimes these Christians are impossible, David. As Father Saul says, who can figure them out? What did the boss do?'

'Anything to get rid of Gordon for a while, he said. He bribed the Christian warrior with a month's pay and assurances that his personal achievements would be mentioned prominently in despatches. Also swore that all Taipings who surrendered would be treated as they deserved.'

A procession was moving towards the Imperial Camp through the morning sunlight under the grey walls of Soochow. The tunics of their escort of Holy Soldiers and the robes of the eight traitor generals were scarlet and yellow, the colours of the Chinese Ming Dynasty, which the Taipings had once pledged to restore to power. Aaron wondered if that affront to the Chinese Mandarins of the Manchu Ching Dynasty was deliberate bravado. Certainly, the Eternally Magnanimous General Kao in the lead appeared negligently self-assured. His watermelon head nodded on its slender neck as he chatted with Brigadier General Wang An-chun, the first assassin.

The brilliant array moved slowly over a plain littered with the detritus of battle. Men and horses sprawled in the wanton abandon of death amid discarded guns and swords on the scarred earth. Flaming gold and crimson in the sun's rays, the procession seemed like a flame leaping from the conflagration that enveloped Soochow, where spires of smoke rose high above the city-walls.

The Magnanimous General Kao nodded insouciantly to the Mandarin Li Hung-chang as if greeting a casual acquaintance, even an inferior. He neither kowtowed to the Imperialist Commander-in-Chief nor bowed, but nodded off-handedly. He might have been the victor, negligently acknowledging an insignificant enemy, rather than a defeated general surrendering after murdering his commander.

'Well, I opened the gates just as I said,' he remarked. 'Your people should have no trouble now. I've given you the fortress of Soochow.'

'And you expect?' the Mandarin Li Hung-chang asked curtly.

'As I agreed with your tame barbarian, the barbarian you hire to do your fighting. The rewards promised.'

'I know of no rewards,' the Mandarin replied, 'except one unimportant matter you apparently believe . . .'

'By God, we were promised gold! And what's this minor matter?'

'Your lives, Kao. I was saying when you interrupted that you apparently laboured under a misapprehension. My servant Gordon warned me you would claim he promised to spare your lives. I regret that is not possible. Allowing murderers and traitors to live would corrupt my army. Your existence is a reproach to my conscience. However . . .'

'Your joke is in bad taste, Governor Li,' Magnanimous Kao protested shrilly. 'No man of honour can renege on a sworn promise. I cannot believe it!'

'You will, Kao,' the victor said lightly. 'You will, I assure you.'

The Mandarin Li Hung-chang chopped his right hand down on his knee, and his personal guard engulfed the escort of Holy Soldiers. The eight Taiping generals stood alone in their garish robes in the square of blue-clad troops. Groups of three soldiers, each led by an executioner flourishing a broad scimitar, closed on the rebel officers. Two soldiers thrust each Taiping general to his knees, while a third pulled his long hair forward over his forehead. Eight scimitars flashed high in the sunlight and fell simultaneously.

The Mandarin watched until blood no longer pumped from the severed necks. Eight heads lay in crimson pools, their features frozen in incredulous terror. Some had dropped neatly a few inches from their trunks. Others had fallen wide when the inexperienced executioners' assistants pulled their hair too hard. The assassin Wang An-chun's face grinned ingratiatingly beside his flexed knees, and the Eternally Magnanimous Kao's enormous head was cradled in his outstretched arm.

'I regret the necessity,' the Mandarin murmured to David. 'But it was mercifully quick, a minute from sentence to execution. Bury them together, then trot horses over the grave so no one will know where they

420

lie. The Disciple King's head . . . his body if you can find it . . . despatch him to Nanking for burial. And, David, send all the troops into the city. Soochow must be scourged!'

*

As dusk crept over the plain, the Les brothers stood again on the knoll overlooking the Imperial camp. A mile away, Soochow glowed red against a darkening horizon. The most beautiful city of the Yangtze Delta was being scourged by bloodshed, arson, and pillage as the Commander-in-Chief had ordered.

The Western part of David's mind wondered at his chief's apparent inconsistency: savage summary execution and an unmarked grave for the traitors who had ensured victory, but honourable burial for the Taiping prince who had been his implacable foe; exquisite Soochow ravaged by a sensitive Mandarin who loved poetry and painting. But the troops would have sacked the city of silk and slaughtered both its garrison and its populace whatever the Commander-in-Chief ordered. The spoils of one of the richest cities in China were their rightful reward.

'Remember the South City burning almost ten years ago?' Aaron asked. 'Very like this, wasn't it?'

'Only not so big, and not so many rebels killed. The last report was twenty thousand dead.'

'Not so much looting, either?'

'Well, the South City is smaller.'

'Tell me, Little Brothers,' Aaron demanded. 'Did you know he was going to kill the generals? And you didn't tell me!'

'Aaron, it wasn't my secret, but the chief's. He trusts you, too. But not absolutely . . . not yet.'

'My God, I'm so weary of killing.'

'A little while, and it'll be over. But you've got to fight harder than ever if we're to win a pardon for . . .'

'I know that, David.'

'Is there any chance Lionel's survived?'

'Maybe he got away. Maybe we'll know otherwise when we search the Water Gate. But I doubt it.'

421

CHAPTER SIXTY-ONE

'I think I've cleared up most of the mysteries.' Fronah offered her father a paper-bound pamphlet, and, looking down at the flagstone terrace beside her long-chair, added: 'Though there's one . . . one mystery about which I . . . I wonder if I'll ever know the answer.'

'You mean, I suppose, about . . .' Saul Haleevie uncharacteristically did not finish his thought.

'Yes, Papa,' Fronah replied after a moment. 'The terrible mystery of Lionel. Oh, God, how I wish I knew. It's nine months now, and, sometimes I'm afraid he . . . But that would be too much to bear. At least, I can still hope.'

'It's an enigma, my dear.' Saul's response was infinitesimally delayed. 'No word . . . no sign at all. But we're still trying to find some clue. I've made so many inquiries . . . And I'm still trying.'

'I know that, Papa, and I'm grateful. I can only wait . . . and hope.' She paused and resumed with forced cheerfulness. 'But aren't you going to look at my *magnum opus*?'

Saul slipped on his black-rimmed reading-glasses in relief, opened the pamphlet, and read the title-page aloud: '*An Account of the Suppression of the Late Rebellion in the Manchu Empire, Relating Particularly to the Army of Huai under the Command of the Earl Su Yi, Mandarin of the First Grade Li Hung-chang, Governor of Kiangsu Province. Compiled in English by F. Haleevie-Henriques from State and Private Papers Made Available by the Said Governor, as well as Documents seized from the Rebels of the so-called "Heavenly Kingdom of Great Peace" and the Confessions of Certain Taiping Wangs or "Princes". Published by the Kiangsu Translation Bureau at Shanghae in September, 1864.*'

Saul looked up quizzically while reading the beginning of the Preface: 'This account has been prepared on the author's own responsibility and does not represent an official Chinese view. The author is herself responsible for any errors or omissions *despite* the constant guidance of the Mandarin Li Hung-chang.'

Saul removed his glasses and cocked an eyebrow interrogatively while polishing their lenses.

'I think I've made it quite clear,' she said defensively. 'As clear as I could. I want the reader to know I couldn't write *exactly* as I wished, since the Mandarin was looking over my shoulder. But he's very clever. He gave me a lot of leeway because he knows nobody'll believe his propaganda if it's too one-sided.'

'It is an official view, isn't it?' Saul persisted.

'Well, not quite. Call it semi-official, if you must. Why don't you read the final chapter first? I've made it clear there. Besides, you may find something new in it. The rest you already know.'

Adjusting his glasses on his high-bridge nose, Saul began reading the final chapter: '*The Collapse of the Rebellion from the Fall of Soochow on December 6, 1863 to the Execution of the "Loyal King" on August 7, 1864 after the Fall of Nanking*. This account, written with the generous assistance of the Chinese authorities, must unavoidably reflect an official point of view, despite the author's striving for objectivity and her use of Taiping documents.'

Saul Haleevie felt paternal pride in his daughter's accomplishment and her concern for historical accuracy. Though forced to use veiled language, she had candidly warned her readers that she was not a free agent. He wished he could be as candid with her, but regretfully concluded once again that it would be unwise.

'I didn't want to overstate the role of the foreign forces, particularly the Ever Victorious Army.' She was still defensive. 'Under Frederick Townsend Ward or Charles George Gordon, I'm convinced it was helpful, but *not* decisive. It certainly wasn't indispensable, no matter what they say in the Treaty Ports. Besides, Colonel Gordon acted very strangely after the execution of the Taiping generals.'

Her father did not reply, but sceptically read aloud the passage she indicated: 'Colonel Gordon maintains that he guaranteed the conspirators their lives in return for surrendering the city. He is justly proud of his diplomatic skill, which undermined Taiping resolve. He has, therefore, rejected the Mandarin Li Hung-chang's explanation that the execution was necessary because the captives plotted new treachery and insolently demanded major alterations in the terms previously agreed.'

Saul glanced up as if to ask precisely what case she was trying to make before reading on: 'Colonel Gordon was not present when the traitors gave themselves up. The following day, he returned to the Imperial camp and he behaved most intemperately, making fantastic threats and allegations while flourishing his pistol. He was with difficulty prevented from intruding violently upon the Mandarin Li Hung-chang, who was planning the next stage of the campaign with his staff. Finally, Colonel Gordon was prevailed upon to withdraw. He did so only after writing a note which consisted of the single word: *Treachery*!

'During the following month, the British officer seconded to the Chinese service raged in public at his Commander-in-Chief. He demanded that the Mandarin Li Hung-chang restore Soochow to the rebels and, further, resign the governorship of Kiangsu – as if that faithful official were to be penalised for committing a foul in a football game. Otherwise, Colonel Gordon threatened, he would marshal the Ever Victorious Army to reconquer all the territories taken by the Army of Huai, including

423

Soochow, and restore those territories to the rebels. He subsequently demanded that the Mandarin Li Hung-chang be executed. These threats were not only mutinous, but vainglorious.'

'You think Gordon couldn't have carried them out?' Saul asked. 'That's not what they were saying in the settlement.'

'It was nonsense, Papa, patent nonsense,' she responded. 'Look here, the Ever Victorious Army was only five thousand strong. How could it fight the Army of Huai, ten to twenty times larger? Besides, Gordon was an officer in the Imperial Army, sworn to obey his superiors, above all the Mandarin. Anyway, if the Mandarin had cut off his army's supplies and pay, he'd have faced a mutiny, just like Henry Burgevine. But the settlement cheered Gordon's bravado.'

'A sham, then, Gordon's indignation?'

'Papa, why should he have been so emotional about a parcel of murderers if he didn't stand to gain from his performance? Anyway, many Taiping officers were loyal, not like those treacherous generals.' Fronah paused and looked down at the wedding ring on her finger. 'When I think of Lionel . . . Lionel staying at his post even when Aaron wanted him to desert . . . Oh, Papa, I'm *sure* he escaped and he'll come back soon.'

Saul Haleevie removed his glasses and again polished the lenses with his linen handkerchief. It would not only be unwise to tell her now, but dangerous. If her hopes were destroyed, she could again suffer mortal depression. He had talked at length with Aaron and David before deciding not to tell Fronah that they had searched the Water Gate and found Lionel Henriques' gold signet-ring on the hand of a body so charred it was otherwise unidentifiable. Though Sarah questioned their decision, she promised not to tell Fronah. Some day, Saul conceded, it might be necessary to show his daughter her dead husband's half-melted gold ring, but not just yet.

'That's a good point about Colonel Gordon,' he observed instead. 'That he happily served under the Mandarin again after making such a fearful row. You don't think you've been *too* sarcastic? Here, where you write: "The British officer obviously realised later that he had mistaken his Commander-in-Chief's presumed pledge to preserve the traitors' lives. Colonel Gordon is an honourable man. Since he is concerned with his honour, rather than his glory, he would not otherwise have served again under the Mandarin, whom he had denounced as a butcher. He would not have been mollified merely because Li Hung-chang publicly exonerated him of blame and presented him with a most substantial honorarium, as well as the Yellow Riding-Jacket, the Manchus' equivalent of an order of chivalry." Isn't your irony a little heavy?'

'Perhaps,' she conceded. 'But I've explained that the Mandarin knew – from Aaron incidentally – that the Taiping generals intended to repudiate their surrender and go back to the rebels. Besides, he couldn't give in to their demands. They were insolent, as well as treacherous. They refused to disband their forces, and they "required" him to commission them as

Manchu generals. They also "informed" him that they would retain control of half of Soochow "to quarter their troops". It was a mock surrender.'

'Come now, Fronah, don't get swept away by your own propaganda,' Saul chided. 'What do you really think?'

'I suspect the arguments on both sides are largely nonsense,' Fronah smiled. 'Gordon was piqued . . . And the chief was furious.'

'You know, they said on the Bund that the Mandarin was behaving normally, putting the interests of his family above everything else. There were really no more than fifty thousand Holy Soldiers in Soochow, they say, not two hundred thousand, as he reported. The Taipings were no threat, and the Generals were already Li Hung-chang's prisoners, so there was no need to execute them immediately. They're saying the Mandarin decided to kill the generals because he wanted no hostile witnesses to his sack of Soochow.'

'Certainly, greed was a factor,' she conceded. 'But the argument's not really convincing. He looted Soochow unmercifully. But he was entitled to the spoils of war by European law, as well as Chinese custom. I really don't know why he killed them out of hand.'

Saul dangled his reading glasses between his thumb and forefinger and suggested wryly: 'Maybe it was just blood-lust, even if the Mandarin's not a Christian. Blood-lust and revenge.'

'The Mandarin's a bundle of contradictions, you know,' Fronah said defensively. 'If he's so greedy why didn't he march to Nanking in mid-December? Five times the Empress Dowager ordered the Army of Huai to Nanking. Five times! I saw the Rescripts. But he pleaded that his troops were exhausted.'

'Not very gallant, that. Why didn't he? Not enough spoils in Nanking?'

'The contrary,' Fronah flared. 'His troops' exhaustion was a pretext. The chief feels indebted to the Viceroy Tseng Kuo-fan for pushing him forward. He didn't march because he didn't want to steal the Viceroy's thunder.'

'Chivalry among generals . . . *Chinese* generals?' Saul goaded. 'But what about the fall of Nanking? We haven't heard that much about it here.'

'The *only* hero was the Loyal King,' she said meditatively. 'Otherwise, almost everyone behaved badly. But it's all in my account.'

Saul read aloud the paragraph she indicated: 'The Holy Soldiers still fought fiercely, but the Taipings' spirit was flagging. None the less, the Heavenly King, wholly isolated from reality, harshly rejected the advice of the Loyal King to send his heir, the Junior Lord, to a safe refuge.

'"Since you're afraid of death," the Taiping monarch stormed at his Commander-in-Chief, "you're certain to die soon!"

'Though the Heavenly King apologised, he commanded his troops to hold the Heavenly Capital to the death. More than four thousand Imperial Braves died as counter-mines destroyed thirteen tunnels undermining the city-wall. However, Nanking was totally surrounded. No reinforcements could pierce the screen of Imperial troops, and all provisions were running out.

'The Heavenly Kingdom was in chaos. Corruption, in theory extirpated, flourished as avaricious officials struggled to preserve their wealth and their lives. Only one Taiping prince remained faithful. Though the Heavenly King declared that the people could live on "sweet dew," meaning grass and weeds, the Loyal King fed them from his own stores of rice until those, too, were exhausted. He also permitted non-combatants to depart. However, that act of mercy caused great loss of life as men and women struggled to be among the hundred and thirty thousand civilians who finally escaped.

'On June 1st, 1864, the Heavenly King died at the age of fifty-one of an unknown illness aggravated by malnutrition. He had relied upon prayer alone, refusing to take either food or medicines. Though his son, the Junior Lord, formally succeeded, the spirit of the Heavenly Kingdom of Great Peace died with its founder.'

Saul broke off to light a cheroot. When he was comfortably wreathed by smoke, he observed: 'It's awe-inspiring, isn't it? The wrath of God. Even in the Bible, there's nothing quite like that much slaughter.'

'It's almost impossible to conceive,' Fronah agreed in subdued tones. 'I've reckoned that more than forty million died in the rebellion, not only soldiers, but innocent men, women, and children. I feel very small when I worry about . . . about what could have become of Lionel. But no need to read on. The rest of the tale's soon told. The Taipings held out for another month and a half under the inspired leadership of the Loyal King. On July 19th, after a last counter-attack failed, a gigantic mine demolished a great stretch of the city-wall. The Loyal King couldn't hold the tens of thousands pouring through the breach and retreated to save the Junior Lord. The Heavenly Capital finally fell after more than a decade. Not so long as Troy, perhaps, but one of the longest sieges of history.'

'And then the sack, eh?' Saul asked.

'Naturally, Papa.' Fronah smiled wryly. 'The Viceroy Tseng Kuo-fan and his younger brother took immeasurably more booty than the Mandarin had at Soochow. Both became multi-millionaires in a twinkling, and twenty of their generals became millionaires. Even colonels . . . a hundred or so . . . acquired fortunes worth hundreds of thousands of pounds sterling. And some people criticise my chief! But the saddest part was the end.'

'Your hero, the Loyal King, Fronah?'

'Yes, Papa, the one man who comes out of the tragedy untarnished. I wrote about him with complete fairness. I told the Mandarin otherwise no one would believe his propaganda. Why don't you read the end? It's short.'

'Even his enemies honour the Loyal King for his courage, his warcraft, and his devotion throughout the conflict and, particularly, at its close,' Saul read aloud again. 'Knowing the Holy City doomed, the Loyal King

426

concealed the Junior Lord in his own palace, which was defended by a thousand of his personal bodyguard. Since he could not break out through the heavily guarded gates, the Loyal King dressed the Junior Lord, himself, and a few hundred followers in captured Imperial uniforms and rode boldly through the breach in the city-wall. However, he first exchanged his own powerful charger for the tired nag on which the Junior Lord had been mounted.

'That decrepit animal fell behind, and the Loyal King found himself alone in a hostile countryside while his master rode to safety on his own favourite mount. Seeking refuge in a ruined temple, he was discovered by villagers. They took his sword and his purse before turning him over to the Imperialists for a large reward.

'After composing a lengthy confession, which purged his soul, the Loyal King was executed by the Viceroy Tseng Kuo-fan on the 7th of August, 1864, at the age of forty. The Viceroy took that summary action because he feared the redoubtable Loyal King might escape – or be rescued by his faithful followers – and rally resistance that would wreak misery on the land for many more years.'

'That is *piffle*, the only outright piffle in my entire account,' Fronah declared bitterly. 'I wrote it on the Mandarin's express instructions. He wished to defend his mentor, though most of the Viceroy's adherents have left him in disgust. That hasty execution was, of course, due to the sack of Nanking. The Viceroy reported to the Imperial Court that it was "a barren city, regrettably stripped by the rebels of all treasure, except for one gold seal and two jade seals". He dutifully forwarded those baubles to Peking.'

'I don't see the connection,' Saul said.

'Papa, even the Imperialists admit the Loyal King was totally honest. If he'd been sent alive to Peking, as the Court ordered, he would have revealed the immense treasure the Viceroy stole, including the Emperor's proper share of the loot. So the Viceroy killed the Loyal King – against Yehenala's direct orders. The Court had to accept his accounting because he had destroyed all contrary evidence. Yehenala swallowed her disappointment and created him a Marquis "in recognition of his exemplary services". Well, it was no worse than Lord Elgin's looting and burning the Summer Palaces, was it?'

'So the new day dawns a bit grey, doesn't it?' Saul smiled apologetically at his own pessimism. 'Nothing's really changed, has it?'

'That's too cynical, Papa,' she protested. 'The mass slaughter has ended. I feel we'll all see better days. If I only knew, one way or the other, about Lionel, I could be happier too, Papa. But who knows when . . .'

'You know, my dear . . .' Saul Haleevie was tempted to tell Fronah of her husband's death, but drew back because he could not risk throwing her into renewed depression. 'You know, I'm doing all I can to find out.'

427

BOOK FOUR

March 7, 1872 – January 13, 1875

THE RESTORATION

CHAPTER SIXTY-TWO

David Lee's eyes strayed involuntarily to the peacock. Silver rondels gleaming on its iridescent tail-plumes, the turquoise bird was frozen in flight towards the sun-disc in the corner of the square of rank. The pristine embroidery was bright, almost garish against the worn fabric of his black surcoat. That ceremonial garment should not have been hanging on the door of the rosewood wardrobe, which was severely plain in the style of the Ming Dynasty which the conservative gentry of Northern China preferred to the ornamented furniture of the progressive South. He would need the surcoat for the banquet the foreign merchants of Tientsin were tendering that evening to the Mandarin Li Hung-chang, Viceroy of Chihli, the Metropolitan Provinces surrounding the Northern Capital. But there was no reason to hang it out at six in the morning.

The blatant display of his new insignia as a Mandarin of the Third Grade was unseemly when his chief clerk had brought him confirmation of his elevation only the previous day. Still, he could not remove the surcoat and offend the old fellow, who was even more cock-a-hoop than himself over such virtually unprecedented promotion at the age of thirty-four. As David knew so well from his own experience, a Mandarin's elevation not only enhanced his subordinates' prestige, but enriched them. *When the senior official's dog barks*, the folk maxim said, *even Heaven listens*! Besides, his clerk could not understand the perverse modesty he had learned from protracted association with barbarians.

It was only twelve years since he had worn the crested bird of paradise of the Ninth Grade – and surreptitiously preened himself in every shining surface from mirrors and windows to lacquered chests and rainwater puddles. His wife of three years, who was a Chao of Kaifeng like his paternal grandmother, would be overjoyed that he now ranked with – but above – a major general in the military hierarchy. She would also complain in her next letter because she could not sew his new insignia on his surcoat herself, but he was so overworked that she was better off in the ancestral Lee family mansion in Shanghai. The opportunity to reclaim that confiscated property for a derisory price had been a reward for his service to the Grand Mandarin Li Hung-chang – one of many privileges.

Only a fool would, however, allow unremitting good fortune to make him complacent. Though he was alone, David composed his features in piety. Neither must he allow pride in worldly advancement to distract him from his morning devotions.

He reverently recited the last phrase of the Hebrew prayer and sipped his green tea before unwinding the black-velvet bands that bound to his forehead and arm the phylacteries, small leather boxes holding texts from the Bible. Ever since his marriage was solemnised by the Jewish rites, he had been diligent in saying the morning prayers learned from Saul Haleevie years earlier.

Until the present age, no practising Jew had been a senior Mandarin for more than three centuries. In this enlightened era, which men already called the Tung Chih Restoration of China's greatness, his faith was no particular obstacle. A few Christian Mandarins were also advancing, descended from converts made when Jesuit influence was strong at the Ming Court.

Heavy knocks shook the door, and David resigned himself to the barber's rough ministrations. They were all clumsy, these big-boned Northerners, but the churl with the razors, scissors, and ear-picks was particularly ham-fisted. However, Northerners were also good-natured and forthright.

'*Kung-hsi*! . . .' The barber glanced meaningfully at the new insignia, and David knew his charge had just doubled. 'Congratulations! Not bad for a young fellow like you. Not bad at all.'

No obsequious flattery here, David reflected as the crescent-shaped blade scraped his cheeks, skidding dangerously near his ear. Instead of the elaborate courtesy of his southern countrymen, this brash greeting, which assumed that they were equals. On the other hand, a subtle Shanghai barber would quadruple his charge to celebrate his patron's promotion.

While the barber twirled his ivory ear-pick, a manservant brought a zinc hipbath into the bedroom. Two scullery boys bearing canisters of steaming water entered while the stubby scissors trimmed the hair in his nostrils, and a third carried a glowing brazier on a bronze tripod. When the grinning quintet withdrew, David lowered himself into the hipbath.

He could not linger in the warm water this raw morning in early March, 1872. The day would be arduous and long. He would not, however, forgo his bath, though the Northerners were direly amused by his bathing four times a week. They, who hardly immersed their hands in water that often, considered the practice undoubtedly unhealthy, probably effeminate, and perhaps perverse. The soul-soothing ritual of Shanghai's bath-houses were unknown in Tientsin, the northernmost Treaty Port, though the Kiangsu Provincial Association had already introduced that luxury to the Northern Capital, eighty miles away, when his brother Aaron spent so many agonising months there seventeen years earlier to buy commutation of their father Aisek's death sentence.

Recalling his own recent visit to Peking, David towelled himself dry and slipped into his cotton underclothing before pulling on his padded-silk

432

trousers and tunic. He would not wear a fur-lined robe indoors, though the soft pelts were warm. Soiled by ink and food, his colleagues' robes exuded a revolting fusty smell after the long winter. Though his fastidiousness amused not only the servants but his colleagues, David Lee religiously observed the personal cleanliness he had learned from his adoptive father. Their Mosaic creed required them to be pure in body as well as soul.

Still musing, David walked briskly across the courtyard to his office. Most foreigners were not as meticulous, though they were cleaner than the Northerners, particularly the slovenly Manchus. Whether they were wealthy Princes of the Blood Imperial or crippled former Bannermen cadging a living from door to door, one was well advised to stay upwind of Manchus. They stank not only of their own sweat, but of greasy half-raw meat and fermented mare's milk.

The Empress Dowager Yehenala was the only Manchu of either sex who bathed daily. Sitting naked on an unpainted chair, she would chat animatedly with her ladies-in-waiting while maidservants washed her with scented soap and rinsed her with warm water tinctured with fragrant oils.

Yehenala was unique, and, despite his Western scepticism, David was virtually mesmerised by her. After granting the Mandarin Li Hung-chang a private audience a month earlier, the junior Empress Dowager had graciously assented to receive his personal suite. With five other privileged Mandarins, Saul Haleevie's adopted son had kowtowed before the silk-gauze screen that obscured her gorgeously attired figure. The filmy fabric barely concealed the features of the small woman who at thirty-six exercised absolute authority over the world's most populous empire. However, the screen decorously maintained the fiction that Yehenala modestly administered the government on behalf of her fifteen-year-old son.

Even if she had not just raised his chief from Associate Grand Chancellor to Grand Chancellor, the highest position in the Mandarinate, David would have been profoundly impressed by the first female autocrat to rule the Great Pure Dynasty. Her searching questions and quick understanding would have been extraordinary in an emperor twice her age. Her vivid personality made him forget that she was a half-educated Manchu female, who had come to power almost as much by luck as by intrigue. He saw the embodiment of a resurgent China.

When his chief clerk entered, David was transported from his memories of the Throne Room of the Six Western Palaces in the Forbidden City to the reality of his own austere office in the yamen of the Viceroy of Chihli.

'Your Honour!' The clerk bowed, so low he almost dropped the sheaf of files clutched to his thin chest. 'May I again offer my heartfelt congratulations on your amply merited promotion?'

'Come off it, Old Liu,' David laughed. 'Next you'll be calling me Your Excellency.'

'I expect to address Your Honour as Your Excellency in a few years

433

time.' The clerk's white goatee bobbed. 'Your Honour's merits ensure further rapid promotion.'

'Old Liu, that's enough,' David protested. 'I'm just lucky. I've never held a substantive independent post, but I've been promoted far above my merits. Except for the chief's kindness, I'm of no importance.'

'You mustn't say that, sir.' The clerk was shocked. 'The chief of the secretariat of the most powerful Chinese in the Empire himself possesses extraordinary ability. Otherwise, the Mandarin Li Hung-chang would never keep Your Honour by him. Not only rare distinction, but outstanding bravery . . .'

'That's more than enough, Old Liu.' David was impatient, though he knew the clerk was sincere. 'What have you got for me this morning? My conference with the chief is put forward to half past seven. I'll have to be quick if I'm to get any breakfast.'

'There is the matter of the Maritime Customs dues, Your Honour. The barbar . . . the foreigners' remittance are later and later. It has been suggested that . . .'

David grinned at the bureaucrat's slip of the tongue. He alone in the bloated secretariat habitually referred to the outlanders as foreigners, rather than barbarians. Virtually alone among China's rulers, the same practice was followed by his chief, who was beyond doubt the most powerful official, Chinese or Manchu, in the Ching Empire. It was for the time being necessary to deal with the foreigners as equals, the Mandarin insisted, rather than inferiors. The natural disdain nurtured by calling them barbarians, which they were of course, could impede delicate negotiations. David automatically corrected his clerk before turning to the Mandarin's business, which concerned not only the administration of the Empire's premier Viceroyalty, but military dispositions and commercial interests throughout East China.

The practised administrator dealt with casual ease with the problems already sifted by his staff. Certain matters would be digested for consideration by the Mandarin Li Hung-chang himself, either because of their intrinsic importance or because they touched upon his current preoccupations. David could dispose of most himself after returning from his regular morning conference with his chief.

He was, the young official reflected, himself among the twenty most powerful men in China because of the latitude the Mandarin allowed him. Since they thought alike on major issues – particularly the need to modernise the administrative, commercial, military, and industrial structures – there was no danger that he would abuse that trust. Moreover, the Mandarin shared the spoils of office so generously that the chief of his secretariat could not be temped to seek private profit. David's colleagues delicately referred to such enterprises as 'private ventures', but he forthrightly called them 'graft'.

The routine matters presented by David's clerk demanded little concentration. His thoughts dwelt instead on his own influence upon the gradual revision of the archaic and unjust Confucian system. He was gratified most profoundly not by his powerful position, but by realisation of the plans he had made with his brother before the gates of Soochow some eight years earlier. Aaron, now Deputy Chief Justice of Kiangsu Province and a Civil Mandarin of the Fourth Grade, was becoming more conservative as he increased in wealthy and dignity. But he, too, strove to vindicate their father by reforming the judicial process.

That abstract enterprise was progressing, though slowly. Yet Aisek Lee was not an abstraction but a being of sinew and bone, the progenitor of his own sinew and bone. At the end of 1872 his father would have lived fifty-eight years, fifteen spent in exile. He was by Chinese reckoning close to sixty, the age at which, the Sage Confucius had declared, a man should be free from wordly care. It was essential to win his father an Imperial Pardon, and that vindication could not be long delayed if Aisek were to enjoy his remaining years among his grandchildren.

The Tung Chih Emperor would come of age in late April of this year, sixteen by Western calculation, but seventeen by Chinese. The occasion would assuredly be celebrated by a general amnesty. What better occasion to swing the Mandarin Li Hung-chang's immense influence behind a petition pleading for pardon for Aisek Lee?

David instructed his clerk to have the servants bring his breakfast. He would eat at his desk while considering his approach to the Mandarin. Though he could be more devious than any other man in the Empire when he wished, the Mandarin had learned from the foreigners that directness was often more effective than deviousness. As the manservant placed a tray on his desk, David decided he would be forthright, candid – and brief.

*

'I've been expecting you to bring it up again.' The Viceroy of the Metropolitan Provinces and Superintendant of the Northern Ports nodded. 'Since it's important to you, it's important to me. I want to keep my right-hand man happy so that he'll serve me better.'

'Then it's finally the right time, sir, the Emperor's coming of age?' David pressed. 'This time, you'll sponsor the petition?'

'David, you have no need of me.' The Mandarin spaced his words economically. 'With your new rank, you can petition the Throne directly. You have my permission, and your eloquence is striking. But I will *not* sponsor the petition, and I would strongly advise you not . . .'

'Why, sir, why?' David did not conceal his irritation. 'For years you've been advising me to wait. Now, when the perfect opportunity turns up, you tell me to go ahead on my own. But you won't sponsor the petition. Why not, sir?'

'Because I would do myself no good pressing a hopeless petition.'

435

Apologetic laughter dinted the Mandarin's cheeks, but his fine eyes were wary. 'As you've seen, we can accomplish much by a show of deference . . . by calculated delay . . . by deliberate misunderstanding. But you know the tactics as well as I.'

'I do, sir.' David grinned despite his dismay. 'They need you too badly to cross you when you've made up your mind. That's why I thought . . .'

'Only in major matters, David. I can even be wrong occasionally in matters of state and still survive. But I cannot be less than infallible in small matters. Your father's pardon is, unfortunately, a small matter. I cannot allow myself to sponsor an appeal that is certain to be rejected.'

'Rejected, sir?' David felt like a schoolboy pleading for an answer to a foolish question. 'Why in the name of Heaven would the pardon be rejected?'

'You know as well as I do. You'd be telling me if it were someone else's father. Your petition would be rejected out of hand because it touches on filial piety.'

'Filial piety? What's that to do with . . .' David's voice trailed off as logic asserted itself.

'You see now, don't you, my boy? The *most* delicate subject to the junior Empress Dowager at this moment is filial piety. She *cannot* show mercy to one convicted of gross filial impiety. With the Emperor coming of age, she's full of doubts and fears: will he continue to obey her or will he strike out on his own? He's a young man, and the sap's rising. Besides, he's like his father, unfortunately, in his . . . ah . . . ambisexuality and his . . . ah . . . mingling with the humblest of his subjects . . . even harlots, actors, and transvestites.'

The Mandarin curled his powerful fingers around a porcelain teacup and continued: 'You know, I believe that he's kicking up an unholy fuss right now. He doesn't want the young lady Yehenala's chosen to be his Empress, but prefers Niuhura's choice. Not because Niuhura sponsors the girl, but because Yehenala does *not*. Anyway, he's cutting up rough. Yehenala, our patroness, has good reason to be worried about her son's disobedience. And you want her to pardon an abominable act of filial impiety!'

'Abominable, sir? If any man was ever solicitous of his mother's welfare, it was my . . .' David paused, abashed by his own naïveté. 'I'm sorry. I appreciate your candour, sir. Now there were a few matters on which I'd be grateful for your comments. First, the Customs dues are . . .'

'Hold on, my boy.' The Mandarin threw back his head and laughed. 'Your apology's accepted. But I won't leave you without hope. Heaven knows, this matter's dragged on too long, as I'm sure you'd be the first to agree. After the Imperial marriage, perhaps . . . without question, after the Coronation, which can't be put off more than a year, no matter how Yehenala stalls and the astrologers dither. After a year, no later I promise, I'll ram the petition through whatever the cost . . . unless it acutally

436

imperils my own position. If for some reason, we can't get a full pardon, we'll just bring your father out. I imagine you can see that he's not apprehended again.'

'I'm grateful, sir, deeply grateful. Naturally, I'd prefer vindication, but if . . .'

'You'd rather have your old father with you, wouldn't you? I'm glad that's settled.'

'I've taken too much of your time with my affairs, sir. Now the Customs dues are very tardy. I would propose . . .'

'Deal with it, David. Refer to me only if there are major difficulties. Customs dues are important, I grant you. Money's always important, isn't it? But is there anything of overwhelming importance this morning?'

'Not really, sir, though one or two matters could become . . .'

'That's fine. It's time we had a long chat, a *tour d'horizon* I'm told the foreign diplomats call it. You've got to know my thinking, and I'm always interested in how your mind works. A good Chinese mind, almost first-class despite the streak of . . . ah . . . foreign illogic. I'm not complaining, mind you. It's one of the qualities that make you invaluable to me. One day, perhaps, you'll elucidate for me the extraordinary variety of foreign religions, including the creed you and my occasional business associate Haleevie profess. But not today, my boy. Today, I intend to meander.'

David grinned and moved his chair closer to the rosewood table with the scrolled legs that served as the Mandarin's desk. The honey-gold surface was bare except for a black-lacquered tray bearing a celadon tea service. As his chief poured the bitter black fluid into the minute moss-green cups, David studied the older man.

His affection for *the* Mandarin, as Gabriel Hyde had always called Li Hung-chang, was constantly increasing, as was his admiration, which verged upon reverence, for the first Chinese to establish a virtually independent and virtually impregnable stronghold under the Manchus. The Mandarin's confidence was immense. He was supported by the Army of Huai, which had accompanied him to Tientsin in 1870 in defiance of the Dynastic Law that permitted a viceroy to bring only a small personal guard to a new post. He was also secure in wealth greater than that possessed by any other individual except the Empress Dowager or, perhaps, the dying Viceroy Tseng Kuo-fan, from whose faltering hands he had received the overlordship of the Metropolitan Provinces.

The Mandarin's struggles with the jealousy of lesser men while carrying out policies that infuriated the conservatives and occasionally took the Court aback had hardly touched his strong face. However, the moustache that concealed his upper lip was lightly touched with grey, and his widely separated eyebrows knotted when he was tired. His features otherwise appeared blander than they had been when David met him a decade earlier. The humorous quirk of his cheekbones was more marked, though time and weight had padded the lines of laughter around his eyes. His big frame covered by a royal-blue padded-silk long-gown with an enormous *shou* – longevity – ideogram embossed on its breast, the Mandarin was gigantic in physique as well as achievement.

He had passed virtually unscathed through his greatest personal crisis – and emerged even more daring. In 1865, a cabal of jealous Mandarins had impeached him for corruption, which, they alleged, merited the death penalty. Fortunately, their Memorial over-reached itself, ridiculously charging that he had misappropriated 40 million *taels* from the internal customs dues of Kiangsu Province. Since that sum almost equalled the entire revenues of the Empire, a detailed accounting of Kiangsu's finances convinced the Censorate that the indictment should be dismissed. Besides, the Viceroy Tseng Kuo-fan had persuaded the Empress Dowager that his protégé's talents were essential to the Dynasty. The malicious charge apparently raised hardly a ripple in the Mandarin's career.

But David knew that months of desperate manoeuvering had been required to clear his chief's name. Only because the major charge was not merely fallacious, but ludicrous, had they managed to cover up a squeeze far beyond the limits the Court would normally tolerate. The Mandarin's tax-collectors had taken a heavy toll of every tea-house, gambling parlour, pastry stall, and barber shop, as well as exacting extortionate grain and land taxes. His appointees manipulated the revenues of Kiangsu, while he controlled the Shanghai Customs dues and monopolised both the purchase and the production of foreign weapons.

David considered his chief's self-aggrandisement necessary. Nor was his conscience unduly troubled by the substantial benefits he and Saul Haleevie derived from their intimacy with the Mandarin. Since Li Hung-chang, Earl of Su Yi, which meant Reverent Fortitude, was truly indispensable, it was fitting that he should make his personal position impregnable by building a wall of personal wealth around himself. Let irrepressible satirists make rhymes heavy with innuendo and elaborate puns, which asserted: *The Earl's rats glean, and the Empire grows lean!* Let even the children repeat the canard: *Every cock that crows for Li Hung-chang is sleek!* Better calumny and riches than penury and impotence.

'Have you considered exactly how Yehenala can rule us all so imperiously?' the Mandarin asked abruptly. 'Do you really understand how the woman works?'

'Her position, sir, is unchallengeable.' David's deliberate obtuseness encouraged his chief's candour. 'The Imperial power . . . precedent . . . the reverence due her position.'

'You needn't play games with me, boy.' The Mandarin smiled delicately and glanced at his subordinate under ostentatiously raised eyebrows. 'If you don't trust me, how can I trust you? Too much cleverness is . . . However, I'll tell you what you already know.'

David smiled placatingly. For the second time that morning, he felt like a clumsy schoolboy.

'How can a small woman exercise such great power? The foreigners ascribe infinite cunning and implacable ruthlessness to our Imperial mistress. But it's really quite simple. First, she unhesitatingly flouts any Dynastic Law that doesn't suit her. Never before has there been a *female* autocrat of the Ching Dynasty. Her mere existence is a violation of Dynastic precedent.

'Then, there's that bravo, the Baronet Jung Lu. Everybody knows their relationship, but no one dares say a word, not even the Censors. If it came to it, even I'd champion him because he's on our side in his thick-headed way, even if he only thinks of guns – and thinks those guns drop from Heaven. But his guns always support Yehenala, his guns and my guns.

'Moreover, she terrifies the Imperial Princes by stringently enforcing Dynastic Law upon them. Even Prince Kung's had his rough passages with her, particularly after he connived in the execution of her eunuch An Hai-teh. But even Kung, despite being presiding Justice of the Imperial Clan Court, cannot oppose the death sentences she imposes. Yehenala rules the Imperial family with terror.'

'Clearly, sir!' David said forthrightly. 'By punishing her enemies savagely, she reduces potential enemies to submission. As for my trusting you, sir, I . . .'

'Forget it, my boy.' The Mandarin waved his big hand negligently. 'I wouldn't talk this way to you if I didn't trust you completely. But Yehenala must also command the willing obedience of the Mandarinate, which is overwhelmingly Chinese. So she stresses the Confucian virtues, above all, the subject's inalterable duty to obey the Throne. Filial piety requires the Emperor to obey her – and the Mandarins, too. Filial piety, I said.'

'Your point is taken, sir. And I'll hold you to your promise.'

'Do that, David. Now, her biggest problem. Since the Manchus are degenerate, she must depend on *Chinese* viceroys and governors to administer the Empire. Men like the old Viceroy, the Marquess Tseng Kuo-fan, who is, sadly, not long for this world, and men like myself. She needs us, and she's forced to tolerate our power in the regions, power so great we could challenge the Throne if we wished. She suspects our motives and our connections with the foreigners, also our autonomous armies, our modern arsenals and factories. So she heaps us with honours and, mostly, gives us a free hand.

'But she also incites the conservatives to attack us. Think of my impeachment, our constant battle to introduce new ways. She gives us power with one hand and checks us with the other. Her overwhelming imperative is not the good of the Dynasty, but retaining her own power. Perhaps she thinks she *is* the Dynasty.'

'I suspected you weren't just ruminating this morning, sir,' David interjected. 'What's to be done?'

'The Emperor will be claiming his birthright soon. Probably this year, at the latest next year. Furious and hard pressed, Heaven knows what she'll do. Perhaps unleash the conservatives, undermine my position, turn her back on progress. Anything to preserve her power.'

'We can't keep the Emperor from claiming his Throne or keep him amenable to his mother's orders,' David said. 'What's to be done?'

'I've been thinking. Remember, she's a woman, a frivolous woman, as well as a vindictive woman. The answer may be to divert her.'

David poured tea into the celadon cups. The Mandarin extracted a long bamboo pipe with a brass mouthpiece from his felt boot, where he had learned to keep it during his campaigning days.

'Divert her?' David asked when the pipe was glowing grey and smoke drifted before his chief's slitted eyes. 'She won't retire. Why, she's not even thirty-six *sui* old. Yehenala will never be content to play at being Empress Dowager like Niuhura. But even you can't give her a realm of her own to rule.'

The pinch of tobacco in the small brass bowl was already consumed. The Mandarin did not refill his pipe, but laid it on the crimson-lacquered tray. His movements were deliberate, as always when he was struck by a new idea. Knowing he was impulsive, he had once told David, he could not let his impulsiveness lure him into hasty decisions.

'You *have* learned,' he finally said. 'I'm grateful for your suggestion.'

'My suggestion, sir?'

'We will give her a realm of her own. Prince Kung can presumably keep the Emperor from behaving too outrageously, and we'll give Yehenala a new domain. She's always mourned the Summer Palaces. Let her rebuild them and rule them as her private realm. It's work enough for a lifetime. She'll rise to that lure, as long as she still believes her word is still the last word in the Empire.'

'A double lure!' David exclaimed. 'Revenge on the barbarians and an everlasting monument to her own glory.'

The Mandarin smiled complacently. However, David Lee knew he was employed not to flatter, but to question.

'But can it be done?' he asked. 'To outwit Yehenala at the core of her existence, her own power?'

'They said I couldn't sort out the mess after the Tientsin Massacre, didn't they? Two years ago, when I took over this Viceroyalty, war with the French looked inevitable. After the northern bumpkins sacked the Convent of the Sisters of Charity and slaughtered the nuns. Mind you, they had provoction. After that imbecilic French consul fired at them, they naturally tore him apart. All the wise men said our alternatives were stark: either surrender or war.'

'It almost came to that.'

'But we pulled that one off. For the first time, we used gunboat diplomacy against the foreigners. With Tientsin encircled by my Army of Huai, the French fleet offshore was powerless. So we compromised; neither surrender nor war, though the French thought they got what they

440

demanded. The same strategy will work again. Yehenala's position is threatened, and we must see that she retires gracefully like the French. But she must think she wants, above all, to throw her energies into building her monument for eternity – even though she doesn't yet know that's what she wants.'

'How, sir?'

'Not so fast, my boy. Leave it to me for the moment. There's no rush, though I am getting to be an old man.'

'Hardly, sir,' David reassured him. 'It's not a month since your fiftieth birthday. As you reminded me, the Sage said: *At fifty I clearly knew the will of Heaven.*'

'Actually forty-nine by Western reckoning, which I, somehow, prefer.' A flicker of vanity animated the Mandarin's smile. 'But old enough to see clearly that our doings are sometimes rather sordid.'

'Sordid?' David protested. 'But they're necessary!'

'I didn't say they weren't necessary. You know, David, I don't do these things for myself. I'd really prefer to retire to my estates in Anhui and write verse.'

'Retire?' David was alarmed by the conventional valetudinarian sentiments from his apparently tireless chief. 'But *you* can't.'

'You're quite right. I'm necessary, perhaps, unfortunately, essential. I needn't remind you that China now faces a crisis *absolutely* unprecedented in three thousand years. We thought we'd seen everything, but our ancestors never saw anything like the implacable advance of the foreigners by way of India through south-east Asia to China. Also the Russians in the north and the Japanese in Taiwan. Without Western guns and ships – and the will to use them – China will be swallowed up. Never have we Chinese faced such acute peril. Heaven, it appears, has chosen me to arm our countrymen. Even more important, to teach them they must abandon their arrogance and learn new ways if China is to survive entire, not disjointed like a dead chicken. Self-strengthening is our only hope.'

David had frequently discussed the Empire's peril with his chief and his colleagues. They were making progress under the Mandarin's guidance, though, perhaps, not yet satisfactory progress. Not for three thousand years, which meant during all her recorded history, had China faced such overwhelming peril. It was unprecedented, and lack of precedent made his compatriots nervous.

'However, enough meandering.' The Mandarin's mood altered. 'Let us not talk, but do something about it. I want a detailed report on the building of the new fort at Taku. Never while I'm Viceroy of Chihli will foreigners again force open the port of the Capital.'

'The Taku fort.' David made a note. 'And, sir, the China Merchants Steamship Company. You told me to remind you.'

'Yes, we must have approval immediately. Draft a letter to Prince Kung for me. Your parent Haleevie is ready to assemble the capital?'

'Yes, Sir. It will, as you require, appear to be only Chinese capital.'

'Good. We must carry our own goods, not the foreigners. Only Haleevie would I trust to collaborate.'

'The arsenals, sir?'

'I've been neglecting them, haven't I? Abstract the reports for me. Shanghai, I assume, runs reasonably well. There's talent in Shanghai. But the arsenal in Nanking is a problem, I fear. Also the shipyards. The two steamers that turned turtle, I'll never forget them.'

'It goes better now, sir. However, I'll have abstracts prepared. Incidentally, the apprentice shipwrights are ready to leave for France and Germany.'

'And my long-term project? The youngsters I'm sending to America?'

'Preparing to leave for Hong Kong. Mothers wept, even fathers, at parting with boys of twelve or thirteen, but twenty have received their passports.'

'It's necessary, David, the only way. They must attend secondary schools before entering that University. Ya-lu they call it?'

'Yale, sir.'

'Yale, of course. But those seeds can't bear fruit for a decade or more. I must have my iron-clad ships for my navy now. What of that young American officer?'

'Gabriel Hyde's been most helpful at Yale, sir. I've just written again inviting him to visit. Sent the passage money and the honorarium as you instructed.

'Good, David, good. I like that young man. He'll help me get my ironclads. But, David, we have so little time!'

CHAPTER SIXTY-THREE

October 12, 1872   *Shanghai*

The insistent rhyme popped unbidden into the head of Gabriel Hyde, Captain, USN, retired, as the ocean liner *Empress of China* of the Royal Mail Steamship Line, two days out of Kobe, was driven by her single big propeller and the wind in her square sails towards the China Coast he had not seen for almost a decade. No profound thoughts and no poignant emotions. Just the catchy jingle that warned sailors of typhoons: *June, too soon. July, stand by. August, it must. September, remember. October, all over*.

The prow of the *Empress of China* cleft the green waters of the East

China Sea beneath his feet in mid-October. He need not fear that the *tai-feng*, the great wind, would swoop out of the clouded dawn sky.

He had virtually grown up in China – and had certainly come to manhood there. For more than eight years, from the time the callow Lieutenant who was just past twenty-three stepped ashore on the Bund until the embarcation of the seasoned thirty-one-year-old Captain in the Imperial Water Force, he had fought in the civil war of the land that lay just over the horizon. He had seen and endured much between that departure in 1863 and this return late in 1872. But China had put her stamp upon his formative years. Whatever he had now become, his mind and his spirit had been shaped by those tumultuous years in a land where he had at first felt totally alien.

He was today no longer as confident of his maturity and his powers as he had been when he left Shanghai more than nine years earlier to fight in his own country's civil war. A little less certainty and a little more wisdom? Perhaps! None the less, at forty Gabriel Hyde felt he was coming home.

His seamen's eye automatically noted that the choppy waves were subsiding and the steamer's yawing giving way to a roll as the offshore swell lifted her hull. The green water was tinged with silt, so that the foam curling from the prow no longer sparkled white. Pale yellow in the dawn, the bow wave reminded him of the golden spray spewing from the paddle-wheels of the flotilla that had carried the army of the Mandarin Li Hung-chang past the Heavenly Capital a decade earlier.

The *Empress* crossed a clearly delineated line, a visible frontier on the surface of the ocean. Green and white-capped on one side, the water was darker and less turbulent on the other. Heavy with alluvial soil, the sea was suddenly tawny. The land was reaching out to embrace the steamer and to claim him again. To welcome the prodigal? Perhaps, though he did not know what he expected from this impetuous voyage into his past.

He had, Gabriel mused, had a good war, as the British said. His lieutenant's commission restored because the Union desperately required trained naval officers, he had fought with Admiral Farragut at Mobile Bay. Rising rapidly to commander because of his experience, he had commanded a fast cruiser hunting Confederate commerce raiders in the Pacific. But he had come no closer to the coast he was now approaching than the Sandwich Islands, which the natives called Hawaii. Promoted to captain, he had commanded one of the iron clad rams that were the pride of the US Navy. In 1865, when General Robert E. Lee surrendered at Appomatox, he was superintendent of the Naval Shipyard at Newport News.

Weary of bloodshed after more than a decade of battle, he had declined the Navy Department's invitation to stay on and had gratefully retired. He had not had a good peace, though it had begun most promisingly.

Realising that all he knew was war, he had enrolled at Yale University to study English literature and Chinese history. He had within a year found himself no longer a rather elderly student, but a young professor teaching

443

strategy and Chinese history, since the little he knew was more than any instructor knew. Those first years in New Haven had been restful emotionally as well as physically, which was precisely what he wanted, and communing with America's best minds had been stimulating, which was also what he wanted.

His contentment was crowned by his marriage to Jane Bewley, the twenty-six-year-old daughter of his father's law partner in Salem. After the first galvanic shock when their bodies and minds joined, their life together was serene. That idyllic repose, too, he had wanted.

Yet he had become restless even before Jane's death shattered the idyll. Though the great trees on College Green still delighted him when their leaves opened green in the spring and flamed russet in the autumn, the regular succession of the northern seasons was, somehow, enervating. The long New England winter was onerous and the brief heat of summer tantalising. Jane's gently humour had, however, reconciled him when the measured courtesy of academic disputation grew irksome. His colleagues' passions were entirely intellectual. They were born spectators, happy to watch while others acted and happy only to comment – sometimes profoundly but quite often vapidly.

Jane's death had shattered whatever pleasure he had still found in academia. Still tormented by guilt, after more than two years, he recoiled from remembering how she had died. She had been his sheet-anchor. When the cable parted, he had thrashed about like a schooner blown on a lee shore. He had briefly returned to the Navy, commanding a capital ship for six months before realising that the dull routine of peace was stifling him. He had then travelled in the Far West, sending despatches to the *Hartford Courant*, until he was appalled by the crude life of a wilderness stained by the blood of hundreds of thousands of hapless bearded bison and thousands of bewildered painted Indians.

He had, therefore, been delighted to assist the Mandarin Li Hung-chang when David Lee's first letter reached him through the pretentious Cantonese called Yung Wing, who was himself a Yale man, the first Chinese to graduate from an American university. Yung Wing was a favourite in New England not only because of that unique attainment, but because he had later purchased an entire machine-tool plant for the Kiangnan Arsenal. Yankee manufacturers were still looking forward to much larger purchases after enthusiastic reports from Shanghai. They did not know that the lathes, planers, drill-presses, and forges were meant to be copied, not supplemented. The Chinese, quite logically, saw no reason to buy expensive equipment abroad when they could, they believed, make machines that were just as good at home.

David Lee's second letter, tersely official, though softened by an affectionate postscript, had reached New Haven in late May. Gabriel was intrigued by the invitation to confer with the Mandarin Li Hung-chang, now Viceroy of the Metropolitan Provinces. Having run through the gold accumulated in Shanghai, which Jane had called his 'Chinese hoard', he had also been attracted by the munificent remuneration the Mandarin promised. After a leisurely journey broken by extended stays in San Francisco, the Sandwich Islands, and Japan, he was finally arriving in mid-October.

The water was even darker when *Empress* entered the mouth of the Yangtze, leaving low Chungming Island to the starboard. The distant banks were apparently unaltered by time. Stubby pagodas rose above riverside shrines, and Gabriel saw the flash of a monk's saffron robe. Spirals of smoke drifted from cooking fires in farm-houses built of baked-earth bricks, the more prosperous distinguished by tile roofs instead of straw-thatch. The pungent tang of burning wood mingled with the acrid odor of dried fish seething in oil, and tears came to his eyes when he smelled the heavily saline soya sauce. Even the ammoniacal stench of night-soil was not offensive, but evocative to the returning prodigal.

When the *Empress*'s bows swung slowly to port to enter the Hwangpoo River, Gabriel knew he had finally come home. His pulse quickened in response to the abode of his young manhood, where intense beauty revealed itself amid squalor. He wondered at the emotion evoked by the commonplace scene. A few hundred yards across, the Hwangpoo seemed cramped after the broad Yangtze, and the muddy water rippled as dark as Navy coffee with a dollop of condensed milk. The *Empress* gave way to a squat tug towing a clipper, which obscured his view of the city.

As the unwieldly convoy passed, Gabriel was dazzled. Breaking free of the confining clouds, the morning sun gleamed on the long wall of white structures lining the Bund. In the nine years since he had last seen Shanghai their number had quadrupled, as, it seemed, had their size. Great buildings stretched from the British Consulate, close-set pillars shining beneath its peaked roofs, past the mock-Oriental Customs House to the French Consulate flaunting its minute tricolour.

Groves of masts swayed above scores of vessels anchored in the stream: clippers and paddle-wheelers; sleek steam-frigates and heavy-hulled mer-chantmen; a covey of salt-junks from the gorges of the Long River; even a few lorchas, which appeared archaic with Chinese sails furled above old-fashioned European hulls. Cargo-lighters scurried among that stationary fleet like black water-beetles.

At seven in the morning, the Bund, already clotted with traffic, was clangorous with an overwhelming din. Pony-traps twisted between drays hauled by strings of coolies. Above their chanting, he heard the agonising squeals of unlubricated Chinese wheelbarrows, which carried passengers and goods in enormous baskets on either side of a high central wheel. Sedan-chairs swayed agilely through the throng among the bobbing of the bright yellow hoods of two-wheeled carts drawn by men trotting between their shafts.

Like enormous gum-drops hurled by a playful giant, those carts lent a

445

new gaiety to the commercial Bund. Gabriel had already seen them in Kobe, where they were called *jinrikkisha* – man-power carts – though the Chinese called them *hwang pao-che* – yellow hire carts – or *yang che* – foreign carts – because they came from abroad, India originally. Foreigners called them rickshaws, a corruption of the Japanese name for the conveyances recently introduced by earnest missionaries, who were distressed by the humiliation and the strain sedan-chairs inflicted on their bearers. Was pulling a two-wheeled vehicle like a two-legged pony, he wondered, really more dignified or less onerous than carrying a sedan-chair?

Whatever the merits of the rickshaws, progress was inevitable – and irresistible. He could already see how rapidly the Foreign Settlement had grown during his absence. Behind the Bund lay tens of acres of new buildings along new streets, while the foreign population was almost five thousand, including many more ladies, a remarkable increase from less than a thousand a decade earlier. God alone knew how many hundreds of thousands of Chinese now lived in the Foreign Settlement and the French Concession, as well as the old South City. Instead of returning to their native towns when the Taipings were finally crushed, most refugees had remained in Shanghai, while many additional Chinese were still pouring into the expanding metropolis. Banks, industry, and trade lured the well-to-do, while the poor sought employment in the prosperous city. The mercantile city founded only three decades earlier was one of the five busiest ports in the world.

Gabriel instructed the purser to send his luggage to Willards Hotel before he was whisked to the Bund by a gleaming company launch. How different, he reflected, from the grubby sampans that formerly carried passengers ashore. The Settlement even possessed a real hotel to replace the improvised boarding-houses or the enforced hospitality of business associates that had previously housed newcomers. Willards was a grandiose name for an establishment he had heard was small and utilitarian, though reasonably comfortable. Its namesake in Washington, DC was the favourite of politicians, while John Wilkes Booth had brooded in its opulent public rooms before assassinating President Lincoln. However else it had changed, Shanghai remained pretentious, concealing its deficiencies behind its bravado.

Gabriel Hyde was suddenly beset by misgivings. Should he have returned, he wondered, to this once familar city, which was so greatly altered? He had not, of course, expected everything to be the same. Nor would he wish it to be unchanged. No one could halt progress, as he had reminded himself a few minutes earlier, and he would be the last man to try. Despite personal disappointments, he was a buoyantly optimistic American who rejoiced that progress was remaking the entire world – much to its improvement. None the less, he felt himself a bewildered wraith from the past. What, he wondered again, was he really seeking?

Gabriel waved at a coolie lounging between the shafts of a cadmium-

446

yellow rickshaw and, drawing a few phrases of Shanghainese from the well of memory, directed him to Szechwan Road. He had written from New Haven to tell Saul Haleevie he was returning – and written again from Honolulu to report that he had booked passage on the *Empress of China*. Saul would, of course, have already known of the ship's arrival.

*

'You must come and stay with us,' Sarah Haleevie insisted. 'We've got plenty of room nowadays. But Willards is terrible, a flea-pit . . . a cockroach farm. Some Yankee . . . what do you call it . . . bosun who married a Chinese girl opened Willards. He knows as much about house-keeping as I do about . . . about bosuning.'

Sarah's tawny hair was streaked with silver, but her fair skin was virtually unlined. Unlike some foreign women, she had not become stringy, haggard and sallow in the cruel climate. Her birdlike movements were, perhaps, a shade slower, but still graceful and vigorous. She must, he calculated, be close to fifty-three, but neither had she grown fat and blowsy, as did other women coddled by amahs and tempted by ingenious cooks. Sarah was not vain, but she was proud.

Saul beamed while his wife fussed over the American almost as she did when Aaron or David brought his family home. Though he was hardly the patriarch he had once hoped to be, they now had four grandchildren. Originally reluctant to adopt the boys, Sarah seemed to love her Chinese grandchildren as much as she did Fronah's son, Judah. Well, he conceded, almost as much.

'Of course you'll stay with us, Gabriel.' Saul nodded emphatically. 'I never dreamed of anything else.'

'Well, if you're sure I won't put you out,' the American agreed. 'I know I'll be happier here.'

The matter, he realised, had been decided even before his arrival. He was deeply moved by their unhibited embraces and their spontaneous hospitality. He had, he felt again, truly come home. Perhaps it was atavistic, the blood of his remote Sephardic ancestors responding to their warmth, where the inhibited Yankee side of him was made suspicious – or, at least, embarrassed – by their sentimentality. But Saul's welcome was irresistible. The merchant was also as decisive as ever, more decisive, if anything, as if success had increased his inherent self-confidence. Perhaps too self- confident, he had already revealed that he was building a new house on Bubbling Well Road.

'Not a mansion,' he said. 'Just a little bigger and more comfortable. No need to live over the shop all our lives.'

The passage of a decade had silvered Saul. His russet beard was streaked with grey, while his skin was finer and paler. As he probed his boiled egg, blue veins twitched on the backs of his hands. Though his dark-blue suit

447

was incongruous, his innate authority had increased with age. Saul must be about fifty-seven. Somehow, that didn't appear as old to Gabriel as it would have ten years earlier.

'So, Gabriel, you're going to work for the Grand Mandarin, are you?' the merchant asked unnecessarily. 'He's got half China working for him. What does he want from you?'

'As far as I can tell, he wants me to create an entire navy. He's in no hurry, but I gather will allow me a month or even two.'

'He wants a navy from you,' Saul laughed. 'And from me a steamship line. Next week if possible.'

'A steamship line? Your friends at Butterfields and Jardines won't be too happy.'

'They're not to know I'm involved, Gabriel, but you're practically a member of the family. Besides, we were once partners in crime, weren't we?'

'Why the secrecy? The Mandarin usually makes a great hullabaloo of his doings.'

'Officially, it's a Chinese government-sponsored enterprise with the participation of private capital. Fortunately, Haleevie and Lee is also a Chinese firm. Of course the Mandarin will run the China Merchants Steamship Company – and take his own profits, too. But there's no reason why foreign vessels should monopolise coastal and river trade.'

'I can't argue with that.'

'But the real opposition's not from the foreign shipping lines. The Chinese owners of junk fleets and their tame Mandarins argue that thousands of native craft will be bankrupted by the CMSC.'

'Is that true, Saul?'

'Perhaps, though David's worked up reams of statistics to show that the Company will only take trade from the foreign lines and native craft won't be touched. But CMSC is going to be very big.'

'Can they do it, Saul?'

'Who knows?' The merchant shrugged. 'I'm confident enough to put some money into it myself. As long as he calls on experts like you. But the rush bothers me.'

'The Mandarin rushes everything, I gather.'

'What can you expect? He's trying to make a whole new world: arsenals and factories . . . shipping lines and telegraphs. Maybe soon railroads, though the opposition's strong. Iron-works and schools . . . Mandarins appointed without studying the Classics . . . students going abroad. He wants to remake not only China, but the Chinese.'

'I wonder,' Gabriel said. 'Changing China and the Chinese is like shifting the earth in its orbit.'

'Remember, Archimedes said he could move the earth with a long enough lever if he could find a fulcrum. It's a new world already. Look at the little Japanese, how fast they've come along. If the Japs can do it, the Chinese certainly can.'

'Gabriel, tell us about yourself,' Sarah interrupted. 'What have you been doing all these years? And where is your wife? You couldn't have escaped all those clever American girls. You're too attractive.'

The American found himself telling the Haleevies far more than he had imagined he could tell anyone. It seemed natural to confide in them, churlish to be secretive. He even told them of his wife Jane and her death, though he could not tell even them how she had died.

'Now tell me more about yourselves,' he broke into Sarah's sympathy, which he could not endure. 'What's Fronah up to? Still a spitfire? And Lionel, how's he?'

'Didn't David write to you?' Sarah asked.

'Of course. He said Fronah had recovered from her anorexy. Also she was well and happy.'

'Lionel's gone, Gabriel,' Saul said. 'Fronah's reasonably happy and very busy, but Lionel's gone.'

'Gone, leaving her alone?' The American was startled by his own indignation. 'The rapscallion's deserted her, has he?'

'We don't know,' Saul prevaricated. 'We only know he disappeared after the Imperialists took Soochow in '63. Never a word since then.'

'Is he dead?' Gabriel asked bluntly. 'How did Fronah bear it?'

'It was a long time ago,' Sarah said. 'She's happier now, and very busy.'

'What is she so busy about?'

'Working for the Grand Mandarin like everyone else,' Saul laughed. 'Also running orphanages and schools. You won't see her for a while, though. She's looking into the Translating Bureau in Nanking. She took Judah with her. Judah Haleevie we call him now, just Haleevie. He's eleven, Gabriel, and he'll soon be a man in the Jewish religion.'

'I'm delighted, Saul. I look forward to seeing Judah . . . and Fronah. When will they be back?'

'Not for several weeks,' Sarah said. 'I almost forgot. She asked me to tell you how sorry she was she couldn't put off her trip. And she's looking forward to seeing you again.'

Gabriel Hyde was surprised by his disappointment at learning that Fronah would be away so long. It had been years since he'd given her more than a minute's thought. For the first time in almost a decade he remembered their parting in Dr William MacGregor's hospital.

CHAPTER SIXTY-FOUR

Although the Tung Chih Emperor had come of age in April, the Empress Dowagers Regent still continued to 'administer the government behind the screen' in mid-October of the year 1872. They would only relinquish that responsibility when the Emperor was crowned in the Hall of Great Harmony and rode, attended by Princes, Grand Chancellors, Ministers, and Senior Censors, along the Imperial Way to the Temple of Heaven to report his accession to his Imperial Ancestors. The Court Astonomers were, however, still poring over their tables of divination and casting their horoscopes to determine the most auspicious day for the Coronation.

The senior Empress Dowager, Niuhura, properly addressed as Tzu An, Maternal Tranquillity, was anxious for that splendid ceremony. She doted on the young Emperor, who was candidly affectionate with her, though she was his mother only by convention. His actual mother, the junior Empress Dowager Yehenala, properly addressed as Tzu Hsi, Maternal Auspiciousness, did not direct the Court Astronomers to delay the Coronation. But those courtiers knew her wishes and procrastinated to ensure the continuing flow of her lavish presents.

The junior Dowager desired the postponement not only because of her personal insecurity, but the Empire's insecurity. She clung to power because she feared her numerous enemies would strike when she was no longer impregnably armoured in absolute authority – and because she loved power. She was also moved by concern for the welfare of the Empire, for she was not wholly confident that her son would attend to her wise counsel after he ascended the Dragon Throne.

Yehenala knew he was not yet fit to rule at sixteen and a half. Though her pleas irritated and alienated the Emperor, she begged him to overcome his indolence and his frivolousness. He must, she stressed, give up his carousing and attend to his duties and his studies. Neither cheered by his response nor heartened by his progress, she suppressed her natural desire to see her son crowned. She waited in hope, prayed to the Goddess of Mercy to enlighten him, and encouraged the Court Astronomers to procrastinate.

Meanwhile, Yehenala and Niuhura sat behind the screen to listen to the deliberations of her counsellors, intervening firmly whenever necessary. The thickness of that screen varied with the occasion and her own sentiments towards the officials concerned. A favourite like the Mandarin Li Hung-chang would be granted the honour of looking upon her countenance through gauze of gold that was almost transparent. A formal sitting of her chief ministers would see heavier panels behind which their Imperial mistresses were dark outlines. On one terrible day in 1865, the Emperor's uncle, Prince Counsellor Kung, the Senior Grand Chancellor, and the president of both the Imperial Clan and the *Tsung-li Yamen*, the Office of General Affairs Dealing with Other Nations, had faced a screen so thick he could barely hear Yehenala's voice.

Kneeling penitently to expiate the sins of corruption and arrogance the Senior Censors had levelled with her encouragement, Prince Kung edged forward to hear better. Peering through a crack between the panels, the Chief Eunuch Little An Hai-teh warned that the Prince Counsellor was threatening their Maternal Majesties. When Yehenala screamed, the eunuch guards streamed into the Throne Room to restrain the Prince. Raging at his temerity, Yehenala stripped him of all his offices and titles. She had restored them after a month, time enough for him to realise that, however high-born, he was still her servant – and for her to realise that she could not administer the government without him. But she had not restored the title Prince Counsellor.

Despite subsequent clashes between the Tao Kwang Emperor's sixth son and the Hsien Feng Emperor's former concubine, Prince Kung was seated before the dais of the Minor Throne in Yehenala's reception-chamber in the Six Western Palaces in the late afternoon of October 15, 1872. She could receive him informally, even rolling up the screen, as long as her eunuchs were in attendance. Her mainstay, Little An, was tragically gone, and Yehenala would not forgive the intrigues that had led to his death. Though she could never again repose full confidence in her brother-in-law Prince Kung, the junior Empress Dowager permitted him to sit. The Baronet Jung Lu, General-Commandant of the Peking Field Force and Vice-Minister of Works, enjoyed her total confidence. Without Jung Lu to sustain her, she would truly be alone amid her enemies. Even now, though unchallengeably first in authority in the Great Empire, she faced a predicament beyond her control.

'The arrangements have all been re-examined, have they not, Kung?' she asked coolly. 'We wish nothing untoward to mar this joyous occasion.'

'As far as a man can be, Majesty, I am certain,' he replied carefully. 'Unless Heaven intervenes, all will proceed as smoothly as slipping a silk jacket over a silk robe.'

'If only Heaven . . .' she mused faintly, and he leaned forward. 'However, that is neither here nor there. Nothing, absolutely nothing, must go wrong. We wish to welcome Our future daughter-in-law with the warmest maternal affection. Candidly, she was not Our first choice, but We, naturally, bowed to Our son's preference. Heaven grant that . . .'

'I am certain, Majesty, Heaven will bless the union. Aluta is a fine girl, and her background is impeccable. Hardly a year older than His Imperial

Majesty and great-grand-daughter of Prince Cheng. This brilliant marriage will heal the rifts in the Imperial Clan. Your Majesty is wise to . . .'

After years of abasing herself before the former Emperor's whims, Yehenala now found singular gratification in saying exactly what she thought. Besides, Prince Kung's droning complacency was eroding her precarious self-control.

He knew she had opposed the marriage until her son's febrile stubbornness had convinced her that she must give way. He also knew that healing rifts in the Imperial Clan was not dear to her heart. If she forgave her avowed enemies, her hidden enemies would become even more audacious. She also detested mingling her blood-line with the blood-line of Prince Cheng, who had conspired with Prince Yee and the Assistant Grand Chancellor Su Shun to deprive her of the regency – and her life. Pursued by her vengeance, Prince Cheng had hanged himself. A pity she couldn't force Aluta to commit suicide.

'Quite so,' she murmured. 'A union blessed by Heaven!'

'Would Your Majesty speak again? I could not hear Your Majesty clearly.'

'I said a union undoubtedly blessed by Heaven.'

'Undoubtedly, Majesty,' he parroted, his hypocritical smile baring his oversized teeth. 'It will assist His Majesty in carrying forward his policy of self-strengthening for the Empire.'

'His policy?' Yehenala asked, coldly, her anger rising. 'Your policy, perhaps. Our policy, certainly, but *not* his. And, Kung, Our servants do not raise their voices to Us. Nor do they demand that We repeat Our words or grin at us.'

'I am abjectly contrite, Majesty,' the Prince declared. 'I merely wished to be sure I'd heard correctly. Your Majesty mumbled.'

'Mumbled? You dare say We mumbled!' Yehenala said furiously. 'You speak to Us as if you were Our equal. Who do you think you are?'

'Majesty, I am the senior Grand Chancellor, president of the Office of General Affairs, and chief justice of the Imperial Clan Court,' he replied evenly. 'I am also Prince Kung, the Respectful Prince, the title my father gave me when I learned to curb my arrogance. I am the sixth son of the Tao Kwang Emperor.'

'Learned to curb your arrogance? Hardly! I can strip you of all your ranks and titles . . .'

'Your Majesty may strip me of my appointments, even deprive me of my princely rank. But one thing no one can alter. I shall remain the sixth son of the Tao Kwang Emperor.'

Yehenala smiled narrowly, and her jewel-sheathed nails tapped the crimson peonies on her circular fan. Prince Kung returned her stare, his large head under the upturned sable-brim of his hat twisted, as always, to one side by the great wen on his cheek. She laughed, and the jade pendants in her ears tinkled.

'You're absolutely right, Kung.' Yehenala leaned forward, and her fan almost touched his shoulder, the most affectionate gesture she could allow herself. 'You will always remain the sixth son of the Tao Kwang Emperor *unless* We require you to hang yourself for disrespect. Then you would, presumably, be the former sixth son of the Tao Kwang Emperor.'

Prince Kung was untouched by fear, for he knew her moods too well after a decade of collaboration punctuated by emotional and political storms. She would not laugh if she meant her threat to be taken in earnest. She would be icily dignified if she intended to intimidate him, as she had learned she could not. Nor could she condemn him to execution and bring the structure of her power down about her ears. She obviously wished to charm him, not to frighten him. In spite of his resentment, she was succeeding.

'We are old friends, Kung,' she said, still chuckling. 'Too long to let minor differences affect our friendship.'

'I am honoured, Majesty.' He smiled cautiously. 'If Your Majesty wishes me to hang myself with a silken cord, I shall comply immediately. Your Majesty will allow me the silken cord?'

'Nonsense, Kung, nonsense!' The peony fan hovered above his shoulder. 'We would never dream of condemning the pillar of the state. Why, We would restore the title Prince Counsellor this afternoon if it would do any good. Since Our son must be enthroned very soon, the title would lapse. You know We are profoundly appreciative of your services to the Sacred Dynasty. You know We were only teasing you.'

'I am grateful, Majesty, since I did presume. I allowed myself not to feel fear.'

'All right, Kung, We take your point. We shall not tease you any more.' Her smile faded, and her voice grew hard. 'But you *must* stop intriguing with Niuhura and the barbarians against Us. You may think Our power will soon be eclipsed. But, remember, *Our* son will ascend the Dragon Throne. And, remember, *Our* son is always obedient, a model of filial piety.'

'Who could doubt that, Your Majesty?'

'That matter of Our Chief Eunuch, Little An Hai-teh, that was not well done, Kung.' Her tone was jagged with resentment. 'You and Our beloved Elder Sister Niuhura forced Our hand. It was such a small matter. He only acted like a child, journeying to Hangchow in state . . .'

'As is forbidden to eunuchs by Dynastic Law, Majesty,' he reminded her. 'No eunuch may depart from the Forbidden City unless accompanying the sovereign. Otherwise they would meddle in provincial affairs, perhaps establish a secret espionage network, even a private army like the Embroidered Cloaks – the enormities that plagued the Ming. Dynastic Law simply safeguards legitimate power. Besides, Little An was a fool to travel in Imperial state. The governor of Shantung did well to arrest him.'

'But he should not have been condemned to death. You tied Our hands, you and sweet Niuhura between you. You contrived that We could not intervene.'

'I am grieved by Your Majesty's sorrow.' Prince Kung's voice was devoid of emotion. 'None the less, I welcome the opportunity to discuss the matter, as I have not been permitted to in the past. The arrest? I approved, but I did not initiate it. The execution? I did not wish it, and I certainly did not intrigue with the august senior Empress Dowager to force Your Majesty's hand. But the eunuch had to die. Otherwise, Your Majesty would have been the laughing stock of the Empire. For Your Majesty's protection, it was necessary that . . .'

'Enough, Kung.' Her fan sliced the air. 'We understand you. We almost believe you. And We know you understand Us. But now We must attend to the business of the state. Our son has for some weeks been pressing Us to authorise the reconstruction of the Summer Palaces, beginning with the Garden of Crystal Rivulets. He is filial, as We said. He wishes the Garden to be completed as a present for Our fortieth birthday some two years hence.'

'I had heard rumours of His Imperial Majesty's enthusiasm.'

'We have almost decided to allow him to proceed.' she added. 'Supervising the great work will be a practical apprenticeship in statecraft for Our son. He must learn how to manage men.'

'A capital idea, Majesty.' Prince Kung did not feel it necessary to reveal that he and the Mandarin Li Hung-chang had planted the seed of that ambition in the Emperor's fallow mind and diligently cultivated its growth. 'It will also impress the barbarians.'

'The barbarians? Of course, Kung, you understand their twisted minds.'

'Not entirely, Majesty.' Always, Prince Kung, mused, the barb in the compliment like the thorn beneath the rose petals: only an equally twisted mind could, presumably, comprehend the barbarians' tortuous mental processes. 'But it must demonstrate the Empire's new vigour when we restore the ancient glories the barbarians wantonly destroyed. Even they must see that the self-strengthening decreed by Your Majesty is proceeding magnificently. I should like to contribute twenty thousand *taels*, as would the Mandarin Li Hung-chang.'

'The ever reliable Li Hung-chang. We shall authorise Our son to proceed and thus learn statecraft.'

It would also keep her out of mischief, Prince Kung reflected. If she devoted her own energies to the reconstruction, which was her dearest wish, she should have less time – and, perhaps, less inclination – to meddle in affairs of state after the Coronation. The Mandarin Li Hung-chang was truly canny to have contrived that diversion. Too canny, perhaps. He would bear watching.

*

454

Yehenala was reasonably satisfied with the audience. She had forcefully reminded Kung that she still ruled the Empire, and she had impressed upon him that she would exercise immense authority after her son's marriage – even after the Coronation, which, unfortunately, could not be much longer postponed. Though change was inevitable, its detrimental effects must be limited.

That simpering virgin Aluta, who understood less of politics than her lion-dogs, would exert a certain influence over her son. Sleeping together and playing together like the children they still were, the Imperial couple would undoubtedly discuss affairs of state. Her son was too affectionate, too amiable, and too compliant. Always listening to outsiders when he should heed only his loving mother's counsel, he would be swayed by his naïve bride.

He had already grieved her deeply by running to Niuhura for consolation when she spoke severely for his own good and the good of his people. He was also fond of his Uncle Kung, the only male he saw regularly among thousands of palace women and Court eunuchs. Her brother-in-law, who had cunningly played upon her son's affection to win his confidence, would, moreover, remain the chief officer of the Empire after the Enthronement.

She had, therefore, forced Kung to acknowledge that his trumpery titles were held at her pleasure, and she had impressed upon him the irrevocable character of her own authority. As long as she lived, she would be the mother of the Son of Heaven. Her son would be required by both Sacred Dynastic Law and the canon of filial piety to render her respectful obedience.

Yehenala nodded complacently. She had earlier contrived that her son should propose to her, as if it were his own idea, the reconstruction of the Summer Palaces, the great work to which she had pledged herself even before she defeated her enemies and ensured her power. That project would keep the young Emperor fully occupied and prevent his interfering vigorously in affairs of state until she had completed his tutelage.

She was triumphant, but extremely tired. Raging, threatening, and charming in the course of a single audience was exhausting. However, her son would soon arrive to pay his formal respects on the eve of his wedding.

She gestured with her fan at the three eunuchs who had withdrawn to the far end of the Minor Throne Room so that they could not overhear her conversation with Prince Kung. The tallest eunuch, who was rapidly becoming her favourite, hurried towards the Throne, balancing a tray on one hand. He placed a white-jade service on the side-table and poured a thimble cup of refreshingly bitter Iron Goddess tea before kneeling to offer her a gold-flecked black-lacquer box with a white chrysanthemum inlaid on its lid.

Yehenala greedily took a handful of crystalised lotus seeds and red dates. She felt her energy return as she chewed, but she would need more

455

than sweetmeats to sustain her. She selected one of the small green pills the Dalai Lama had assured her would restore vigour immediately when he sent them from his mountain-top palace in Lhasa. A devout daughter of the Buddhist Church could not doubt the word of the Supreme Living Buddha, the pontiff of the Tibetan-Mongolian rite to which the Manchus belonged.

The green pill filled her with vitality – and heady confidence. She knew she would remain supreme, and she no longer felt the slightest revulsion from the sometimes sordid intrigue that maintained her supremacy. Power ultimately derived from armed force, but was sustained by intrigue – and she was a mistress of intrigue.

Yehenala saw that the kneeling eunuch was tall and good-looking, not podgy and wizened like most eunuchs. Cobbler's Wax Li, they called Li Lien-ying because he had been apprenticed to a shoemaker when ambition moved him to sacrifice his manhood in order to enter the Corps of Imperial Eunuchs. He was sixteen when he submitted to the knife, old enough to have attained his full growth. He further possessed the same affectionate nature and intelligently calculated greed as her executed favourite. Although no one could replace Little An in her heart, she already felt she could trust this Cobbler's Wax Li – *almost* as she had trusted Little An. She could confide in her new favourite as she could in no other human being, because he knew he was utterly dependent upon her. A pity that such a handsome man should have neutered himself, but, if he had not, he would not be kneeling at her feet in the Minor Throne Room.

'Bring the Baronet Jung Lu to me tonight *before* the wedding procession arrives.' Yehenala leaned forward to whisper. 'Use the new secret way.'

When the double-doors opened, she waved the eunuch away. The Emperor had left his attendants outside, and Yehenala's eunuchs also withdrew. Mother and son, the relationship was sacred, as was their privacy, though the eunuchs would undoubtedly listen at the closed doors.

Yehenala's heart went out to the plump figure in the Imperial-yellow robe embellished with four Imperial dragons and the twelve symbols of temporal power. Though she had sent a message urging him not to dress formally for this intimate meeting, he wore the golden Dragon Robe. Was that attire, she wondered fleetingly, intended to parade his independence? She banished the suspicion. He was a good lad, who only wished to pay fitting homage to his mother before his wedding.

The Tung Chih Emperor kneeled at the foot of the Minor Throne and touched his forehead to the Turkestan carpet in a kowtow to his Maternal Auspicious Ancestor. He was very like his father, Yehenala realised anew when she motioned him to the chair below the Throne. The same eager expression beneath the same sparse eyebrows, as well as the same generous mouth, which could become querulous when he was thwarted. He carried himself with the same pride as his father had as a young man. His Imperial dignity was, moreover, not so much marred as complemented by the anxiety in his sensitive eyes and his obvious wish to ingratiate himself.

The boy, she knew to her sadness, had inherited his father's physical weakness, as well as his father's predilection for low company. Still, he would be stifled if he immured himself in the Forbidden City, forgoing his incognito visits to the pleasure quarters, whose painted transvestites were as dangerous as the warp-footed Chinese courtesans. However, he would find wholesome recreation with his concubines in the rebuilt Summer Palaces. The chit he was marrying might even keep him from straying too often, as she herself had restrained his father. She only hoped he had also inherited her own steel, as well as her piety and her devotion to virtue.

'I've been praying for your happiness with . . . ah . . . Aluta,' Yehenala smiled and spoke in the familiar style. 'All the portents are auspicious. I'm certain you'll be very happy, treasure.'

'I'm grateful, Mother.' He had apparently not noticed her involuntary hesitation before speaking the name of his bride. 'You're very good to me . . . to us. I know the Goddess of Mercy listens to your prayers.'

He was understandably nervous a few hours before his wedding. Besides, he could not help feeling awe in her presence. Yehenala exerted her charm, and he responded readily. They chatted for several minutes, while she sipped Iron Goddess tea and he cracked pumpkin seeds between his prominent front teeth.

'This is how it . . .' Yehenala stopped when she realised that he was already speaking, a courtesy she would offer no other human being.

'. . . it should always be, I was saying, Mother.'

She laughed in delight when he completed her sentence. The omens were indeed auspicious. Even the peasants in the millet fields knew that immense good fortune followed when two close relations spontaneously uttered the same sentiments in the same words at the same instant.

'My treasure, now I *know* you'll be very happy.' She paused, unwilling to mar this perfect moment, but was compelled by her duty to continue: 'And I *know* you'll behave so as to make your people happy, the Dynasty strong, and the Empire harmonious.'

'You're not going to preach at me today, Mother?' he protested. 'Can't we just laugh and talk . . . today of all days?'

'Today of all days, treasure, I must speak seriously with you. That's why it is prescribed . . . your formal call . . . so that I can share wisdom with you.'

'All right, Mother, if you must.'

'But, first, your idea of rebuilding the Summer Palaces,' she temporised. 'I'd be very happy if you took it in hand. I've spoken to your Uncle Kung, and he's promised to contribute twenty thousand *taels* out of his own pocket. Others, I'm sure, will . . .'

'As well as government funds, Mother?' He was as quick as herself or his late father in money matters. 'Perhaps a substantial contribution from your Privy Purse, as well?'

'Of course, treasure. Though not *too* substantial. I must live, after all, and

457

prices are shocking. Heaven knows, I live frugally, but somehow the money just vanishes.'

'Not too substantial, Mother, but not too small,' he insisted. 'After all, it's like a wedding present. And I'll give you the Garden of Crystal Rivulets for your fortieth birthday.'

'Agreed,' she smiled. 'If you promise you'll pay more attention to your studies. I've found the best scholars in the Empire to teach you. No more yawning in your tutor's faces or playing sick. How I wish my father hadn't been too poor to give me . . .'

'You write beautiful Chinese, Mother,' he lied, for one out of ten of her ideograms was always wrong. 'No one would ever know you didn't have the best tutors. And your Manchu . . .'

'Anyone can write Manchu, treasure. But there's also this little matter of your visits to the Flower Quarters. You must curtail them. Heaven knows what disease you might catch.'

'I'll try, Mother,' he promised grudgingly. 'But it's so boring in the Forbidden City. Day and night nothing but duty and ceremonies. I might as well be a monk.'

'And the opium and the eunuchs, treasure. After you're married, after today, you mustn't touch either. Word gets around.'

'That's too much.' He was turning surly. 'A pipe now and then or a handsome eunuch for a change. One is entitled to one's innocent amusements.'

'No longer, treasure. And I wouldn't call twenty a day a few pipes. You'll go the same way as your poor father if you're not careful.'

'My poor father was hounded by the barbarians you're so anxious to cultivate.' His voice rose. 'And how do you know how many pipes I smoke? Of course, you've got spies everywhere . . .'

'Treasure, *everyone* knows,' she replied contemptuously. 'No one can keep a secret in the Forbidden City, above all not the Emperor. You *must* stop the nonsense or . . .'

'Or what, Mother? And don't say *must* to me.'

'I'll say *must* as often as I think it necessary. Or, as I was about to say, Heaven will punish you . . . as Heaven punished your father.'

'My father suffered and died not because Heaven, but because . . .'

He checked his tongue. No more than Yehenala did the Tung Chih Emperor wish to open an irreparable breach between them: she because she loved him and needed him; he because he still loved her and feared her greatly. Though she now ignored his slip, she would, he knew, never forget that he had come to the verge of accusing her of murdering his father.

'Not because of Heaven, but because of evil men,' he resumed doggedly. 'And I've learned to protect myself from plotters.'

'You've learned to protect yourself!' Yehenala laughed in cold amusement. 'As the lamb has learned to protect itself from the tiger.'

'And please don't say *must* to me. It's not fitting.'

458

'Only I, my little treasure, I will say *must* to you whenever it's necessary as long as I live. And you shall kowtow to me as long as I live, even when you're crowned Emperor. Not only because of my position, but to demonstrate your filial piety. An Emperor who is not filial would be the final affront to Heaven. And I say you *must* not touch the pipe or the eunuchs . . . or Heaven will certainly punish you.'

'I'll try, Mother,' he agreed reluctantly. 'I'll try hard, I promise you.'

'A sacred promise before the Imperial Ancestors?' she pressed.

'All right,' he conceded. 'I promise solemnly before the Imperial Ancestors.'

'That's better, treasure,' she purred. 'Much better. You know I only keep on at you because I love you. You could be a great Emperor . . . equal to Kang Hsi or Chien Lung . . . if you only try.'

*

That evening the bride Aluta left the mansion of her father, who had been created a duke because he might soon be the grandfather of an Imperial Heir. Preceded by Prince Kung and the Minister of Finance, the ceremonial go-betweens, the bride departed at precisely 11:30, a quarter past the double-hour of the horse, the auspicious moment determined by the Court Astronomers. The cumbersome wedding procession would require two hours to traverse three miles of boulevards strewn with golden sand before reaching the moated Meridian Gate of the Forbidden City, where the Emperor waited to receive his bride.

Aluta was shielded from the eyes of the vulgar by the Imperial-yellow curtain of the golden palanquin borne by sixteen court eunuchs. Bannermen from the eight flag-corps of the decadent Manchu Army were posted along the route before screens erected to prevent any commoner's seeing the Imperial bride. The soldiers had warned all householders to close their shutters so that they would not be tempted to profane her with their curiosity.

Prince Kung bestrode his mount with conscious dignity, since he knew that thousands of eyes were watching. What, as he had quizzically asked the new duke, would be the point of the splendid display if no one saw it?

Twenty bands marched in the procession, the yellow plumes in their hats like golden links joining its segments: eunuchs in crimson and yellow robes carrying Aluta's dowry, each piece of furniture, jewellery, and clothing displayed on its own platform; several hundred eunuchs swaying great paper lanterns, some painted with flowers, other shaped like mythical beasts; wave after wave of shimmering silken banners; cavalrymen on horses caparisoned in Imperial yellow; and seven-tiered umbrellas embroidered with the phoenix that was the symbol of the Empress.

As the head of the procession approached the immense Gate of Heavenly Peace, the chief portal of the Imperial City, the mounted musicians of the Imperial Guard pounded their kettle-drums and blew their conch-horns. Those ancient Manchu war instruments proclaimed the union of two pure Manchu bloodlines and reminded the subject race that no Chinese woman might ever be called into the Forbidden City. But the fireworks that soared above the three gold-tiled roofs of the Gate of Heavenly Peace were wholly Chinese in inspiration. The common people, who were, of course, *not* watching, as Prince Kung amiably observed, deserved that spectacular entertainment.

In the secret room in the Six Western Palaces, the Baronet Jung Lu held Yehenala's hand as the rockets cast their brilliance over the Forbidden City. Tears runnelled her makeup, but she did not touch her handkerchief to her cheeks. She pointed unspeaking to the sky. Above the Meridian Gate, an enormous purple orchid was unfolding. *Lan*, the former Emperor had often called her, 'orchid'. An identical display had lit the sky over the Hall of Supreme Harmoney on the evening of the banquet celebrating the present Emperor's *Man Yueh*, his first full month of life. Prince Kung had remembered.

Yehenala turned and pressed her face against Jung Lu's chest. For the first time in years, she sobbed without restraint. The Empress Dowager wept for her son and for her youth.

CHAPTER SIXTY-FIVE

November 7, 1872   *Shanghai*

Gabriel Hyde had returned by rickshaw from the official shipyard that was tentatively constructing a small gunboat. Although he was fascinated by the shipwrights' adroit use of ancient Chinese tools to build a modern craft, he was pleased to escape the din. No shipyard was restful, but a Shanghai shipyard outdid all others in clangour, if not efficiency. He would spend several weeks with the eager foremen upon his return from Tiensin, where he was summoned to confer with the Mandarin Li Hung-chang.

He would also hire a pony-trap from Smith's Livery Stables. The bumpy ride behind a coolie sweating between the shafts of a rickshaw was not only uncomfortable, but distasteful. Although he could bear being carried in a sedan-chair, he acutely disliked sitting at ease behind a man trotting like a horse. Though the do-gooders believed the new conveyance enhanced human dignity, the coolie's dignity was not enhanced by his being transformed into a draught-horse, while the passenger's dignity was hardly enhanced by his jiggling precariously on two spindly wheels. Besides, rickshaws were chancy. Driven by their competitive spirit – and hope of bigger tips – the coolies raced through crowded streets, often smashing their flimsy vehicles or tossing out their helpless passengers.

Bathing in the Haleevies' luxurious guest bathroom, the American whistled 'Marching Through Georgia'. The baritone chorus, 'We'll sing it as we used to sing it when we marched from Atlanta to the sea!' resounded from the Italian tiles as he towelled himself. To be fair, he ran through 'Dixie' while slapping bay rum on his face and dressing in his steel-gray suit: the jacket high-waisted with grosgrain lapels, the lighter gray trousers cut tight.

'Only a simple family meal, Gabriel,' Sarah Haleevie had said, flushed by her culinary activity. 'Just Fronah, Judah, and ourselves. They'll be glad of some decent food after the Chinese muck they've been eating.'

Since his hostess was obviously not planning a simple meal, Gabriel felt it proper to dress for the occasion. He was looked forward to seeing Fronah, who had returned the previous afternoon from Nanking – and resuming their comfortably jocular relationship. He remembered the uninhibited girl he had first met with fondness, while he was ashamed of his callousness towards the young matron who, he believed, was feigning illness. She had, of course, been very ill – with a disturbance of the mind just as painful as a bodily complaint.

'Look away, look away, Dixieland!' Still singing, Gabriel loped across the veranda into the garden.

The autumnal nip of the early November twilight recalled New England in September. The concentric circles of Saul's prize roses still flaunted their orange, white and red blossoms, and a few pink flowers lingered furtively on the spear-leafed oleanders. It was an evening to make a man sing.

Curiosity drew him towards the Nest of Joy, though he hesitated to intrude upon Fronah. Remembering her vanity, he knew she would still be primping.

He might run into young Judah, the eleven-year-old grandson Saul praised with embarrassed enthusiasm. Gabriel had last seen the lad, who was a unique prodigy if his grandmother Sarah spoke true, as a robust three-year-old. What, he wondered, had the union of the sparkling Fronah with the cold Lionel Henriques produced? Saul had conceded, pride overcoming his normal reserve, that the boy 'shows promise . . . definite promise . . . of someday being a worthy heir to the business.'

Gabriel felt old at the thought of meeting Fronah's son. She was, after all, seven years younger than himself. But, if he was old, he was still pretty vigorous.

A shadow drifted across his dark blue eyes. Jane's boy, his boy, would be four years old if he had lived. What, Gabriel wondered, would it be like to have a son of one's own? One thing was reasonably clear. He would probably not be in Shanghai today if . . . if things had turned out otherwise. He would certainly not be alone in Shanghai. Despite the Haleevie's embracing hospitality, he was for a moment terribly lonely.

He shivered and forced himself to appraise the garden. The spruces that towered above him had been spindly saplings when he last walked among them. The ivy that draped the terrace like a living green curtain was not even planted if he remembered aright, while the rhododendrons that thrust emerald against the sky had been dwarfs.

He slipped behind a thick spruce after glimpsing a figure in a spreading dove-grey skirt standing on the terrace, apparently also appraising the garden. He did not wish to intrude, but he had already caught her eye.

'Gabriel, it is you, isn't it?' The light voice that could grow provocatively throaty had not altered. 'Stop hiding and come and say hello.'

Sheepish at being caught out, the American mounted the steps to the terrace. Though he paused a few feet from her, Fronah stepped forward and craned to kiss his cheek. Her hand lingered for a moment on his shoulder, and the light fragrance of violets filled his nostrils. He remembered the musky perfumes she had formerly worn as she smiled with frank pleasure.

'It's so nice to see an old friend,' she said. 'Come and sit on the bench. You're looking very distinguished, I must say.'

'I'm sorry, Fronah,' he apologised. 'Didn't mean to intrude. I was sure you'd still be getting ready. You know you've hardly changed. You're the one who's distinguished, not . . .'

'You mustn't say distinguished to a lady.' Her smile was as warm as he remembered, though no longer archly coquettish. 'I'm not that old yet. But is doesn't take me as long to dress nowadays.'

'Damned pretty, then. And if you can get that effect in a short ime, you've even cleverer than you used to be.'

Gabriel disliked the heavy gallantry as he uttered it. Why, he wondered, did he fall automatically into the half-mocking banter that had been their way more than a decade ago? Perhaps because she had really not altered greatly. Her accent was still hauntingly musical, though without the chi-chi lilt he had teased her about when they met at the Fourth of July ball more than fifteen years ago. By God, it was seventeen years. She couldn't have been more than sixteen then.

'Perhaps I have learned a little,' she said. 'But you *are* distinguished. I like that touch of grey above your ears.'

'Thanks, Fronah. Though I could do without reminding I'm a little worn around the edges.'

She had changed, he saw, when he sat beside her on the bamboo bench with the raw-silk cushions. Since time did not stand still for any man or any woman, she would naturally have changed. That truism was none the less valid for being well worn. She had, however, changed so subtly that he had failed to note the transformation in his first pleasure at seeing her again.

No single aspect of her appearance or her demeanour had altered sharply. However, her features were finer and grave in repose, while her manner was no longer ingenuous. That was, again, to be expected. Yet he felt she was a totally different person from either the feckless girl he had first known or the neurasthenic young wife he had originally pitied and finally almost despised. She only faintly resembled the wan and beautiful lady framed by the dingy window of the hospital in the godown.

He would, of course, not wish her to be still that woman, whose touch has sent a shock through him. Certainly, Gabriel smiled at his own absurdity, he would not want her to be pale and wan. Nor would he wish to experience again that flare of passionate feeling. She had been very ill, and he he had been disoriented after his wounds. Neither had been fully responsible at that moment.

'You're pensive, Gabriel,' she said lightly. 'Is it such a shock seeing what I've become?'

'If it's a shock, Fronah, it's a pleasant one. I was just thinking . . . thinking of the past.'

'Let's forget the past, Gabriel. Let's just remember we were good friends and hope we'll be good friends again. Except for that, let's make a compact to forget the past.'

Gabriel smiled. He had finally discerned the essential distinction between the Fronah of ten years ago and the Fronah of today. This young woman was decisive and self-assured, where the other had been impulsive and stubborn. She had, however, regained her sparkle and her wit.

She had also warned him off. Quite clearly, she did not ever wish to discuss – much less seek to rekindle – the spark that had leapt between them in the hospital.

'Your father tells me you've become a very important young lady,' he said. 'High in the counsels of the mighty.'

'Hardly that, but I do keep busy. And I believe what I'm doing is of value.'

'What is the Mandarin like nowadays, Fronah?'

'Terribly grand, and terribly imperious, and not above lining his own pockets. Not above . . . what do you Americans call it . . . carpet-bagging. He's also wholly devoted to China . . . to building the new modern China. Fortunately, those two pursuits don't seem to conflict.'

Her astringent humour had not deserted her, though even her dress declared her new dedication. The dove-grey Italian silk of the high-cut bodice was set off by no more than a flare of cream-lace cuffs just below her elbows. Only the costly fabric and the ostentatiously simple cut distinguished it from a dress a superior servant might wear. Though no housekeeper would flaunt the triple strand of black Caspian pearls that circled her slender throat and spilled across her rounded bosom.

Her pearls were as good as a sign reading *Noli me tangere* or, more prosaically, 'Keep off the grass!' She must know he would remember that the necklace had been her husband's gift. However devoted to her orphans

463

and her work for the Mandarin, she also tacitly proclaimed her devotion to the vanished Lionel Henriques.

'We'll have lots of time to talk about politics.' Fronah's slender fingers twined among her pearls. 'Tell me now what's been happening to you all these years.'

'Another war, Fronah. A lot of shooting – and even more pointless waiting. Not so different from fighting the Taipings. A few years of teaching at Yale University and a few years of wandering. I was out of sorts, a little down on my luck, when I got David's letter. So, I thought why not try China again? China's always interesting and, quite frankly, lucrative.'

The eternal mercenary Fronah concluded, and her not wholly unpleasant tension began to dissipate. He was really just a carpet-bagger who had come to China for the spoils. Yet his rapacity had not marked his open features. The laugh wrinkles at the corners of his dark-blue eyes and the creases in his forehead were startlingly white against his ruddy sailor's complexion. Although his face was slightly fuller, the clean line of his jaw was sharper and his full mouth was more vulnerable. He had, she concluded, been tempered, perhaps refined as well. But he was still an adventurer looking for plunder in an alien land he really didn't care a fig about.

'Besides, it's something I can really get my teeth into.' Gabriel looked into the distance. 'Great things are happening here, and I want to be part of them. Like you, I believe I can do something of some value. Also, I couldn't stay away from China.'

Inexplicably nervous again, Fronah felt tension rise within her. The sensation was somehow pleasant, though disquieting.

He must be married. If he were planning a long stay, why had he left his wife behind? She had not wanted to ask, but her omission, she realised, was more pointed. She was curious, and she was fond of him. But she told herself she felt no more than curiosity about an old friend and no more than fondness for an old friend. At any rate, her inquisitive mother would know all about Gabriel after almost three weeks.

'Judah!' She called through the French windows. 'We mustn't keep Grandmama and Grandpapa waiting. Stop fiddling with your ship-models and wash your hands.'

'I'm coming, Mama,' the boy's voice answered. 'Just a minute.'

Fronah was pleased to have broken the tension. Judah could be a useful foil. She was also pleased that she had not slipped and called the American 'my dear' from old habit.

'Gabriel,' she said impulsively, 'I know we'll do great things together.'

He smiled, and she was blushing – as she knew to her great annoyance, she had not blushed for years. Had he, she fretted, taken the wrong meaning? She had only wanted to express her confidence that their work for the Mandarin Li Hung-chang, which would probably overlap, was certain to result in great achievements.

'For China, I mean,' she blurted. 'We'll do great things for China.'

Her precipitate disavowal, she realised, had made matters worse. Still, he must understand that she was offering him friendship, no more. It was just as well that he was, as her mother had told her, leaving for Tientsin tomorrow.

CHAPTER SIXTY-SIX

January 16, 1873   *Shanghai*

Sarah Haleevie clucked severely. Her forehead knotted in annoyance, she pondered before speaking.

'You must try harder, dear,' she finally chided. 'Your brothers are doing so well, but you're looking strictly sickly again. You mustn't give up.'

The bare-limbed cattleya in the emerald pot did not respond. The orchid did not even have the grace to look ashamed of his nakedness among his neighbours' opulent cream-white flowers. Though the mid-January morning was overcast and the sky was ashen above the glass conservatory, most of her orchids and bird-of-paradise plants were bright with blossoms amid the feathery ferns.

Sarah still felt foolish when she talked to her plants, as the article in *The Ladies' Companion at Home and Abroad* urged. The author of the gardening column was, however, quite certain. Every plant, even a great oak, she insisted, benefited greatly from conversation. Denied attention, they felt neglected and sulked like abandoned children.

Though Saul chuckled meaningly when he surprised her conversing with her orchids, most were thriving – and she *would* keep talking to her beloved flowers. Two days ago she had caught him urging his roses to surpass themselves next spring.

'Every day it's more like a jungle here,' Saul grumbled behind her, perhaps summoned by her thoughts. 'Still chattering to your darlings?'

'Of course. How would you like to be alone in the dark with never a friendly voice?' She saw that he wore his black-alpaca office jacket and carried a heap of files and newspapers. 'But what are you doing here so early in the morning?'

'Then buy them spectacles,' he suggested casually. 'I just thought I'd take a cup of tea with you.'

'Saul, is there some news?' Sarah persisted. 'Good news? Is Gabriel coming back soon? Maybe David or Aaron coming to visit?'

'There is news,' he replied. 'You remember I wrote a few months ago to tell the Khartoons it was time to cut our connection? Well, they've agreed.

I just got a letter from young Solomon Khartoon. He's sending a new manager out. I'll get him started, but in six months we'll be on our own.'

'That's good, Saul, that they're not making difficulties. But you don't look happy. Is young Solomon asking too much for his share of the old godown?'

'His terms are stiffish, but not as stiff as I'd feared.'

'Then why's your face so long? Oh, Saul, it's wonderful news. We should be celebrating, not . . .'

'I'm not sure,' he said abruptly, 'I can find the money.'

'Not find the money? How ridiculous. You reckoned young Solomon couldn't ask more than a hundred fifty thousand *taels*. And now it's less.'

'Actually seventy-five thousand *taels*, maybe ninety with incidentals. Say thirty thousand sterling.'

'But you're afraid you can't find the money? You're talking as if we were paupers. Why two tenements in the American Settlement would bring more. And you must have a dozen.'

'A few dozen, actually, Sarah.'

'Then what's the trouble?'

'There are no buyers whatsoever for land or houses. The bottom's dropped out of the market. I could, maybe, sell five or six tenements for ten or fifteen thousand *taels*, but I'd have to be lucky.'

'I don't understand, my dear. No funds and no market for property when Shanghai's never been more crowded? Only a week ago you told me not to worry about how much we were spending on the new house. You must've put a quarter of a million *taels* into Jade House already.'

'You also kept adding. A billiard room and a music room. Five or six parlours, I lose count. Tennis courts and a swimming pool for the grandchildren. The biggest conservatories outside Kew Gardens. But Bubbling Well Road will be the finest residential area in the Settlement. And, if it's ever finished, Jade House will be the finest residence on Bubbling Well Road.'

'If it's ever finished, Saul? How can you talk that way? You know I never wanted to move . . . but you insisted.'

'Sarah,' Saul said irritably, 'let's not start that debate again.'

'My dear, what *is* wrong? I haven't seen you so disturbed since you finally told me about your troubles with that rascal . . . with Lionel's silver loan, God rest his soul. But you managed all right in the end.'

'After you and I talked it over. It was brilliant, your idea to re-finance in London, where money was cheaper. So simple I never thought of it. And Samuelsons helped, as you said. A man of honour he was, old Samuelson.'

'Why can't you do the same now? You've still got very good relations with Samuelsons after all the trouble Lionel caused you in their name.'

'I can't, Sarah, not this time. Young Samuelson is a good lad. Funny how many sons I seem to deal with nowadays with the fathers gone. But young Samuelson's honour isn't involved in *this* mess. Besides, I've got no collateral.'

'No collateral, Saul, with all your property? What else is it?'

'This time even your lightning inspiration can't find a way out.'

'Tell me, Saul, what is this terrible business? Don't keep dodging around the barn.'

'Judah Benjamin's just failed. Your old crony's husband is for the high jump. It's still a muddle, but there's talk of legal proceedings. Just one matter among many – fraud against Sassoons for a quarter of a million *taels*.'

'Saul, I must go to Rebecca Banjamin. How awful for her!'

'It is terrible, but first hear me out. Benjamin owes me nearly two hundred thousand *taels*. That's seventy thousand sterling I'll never see.'

'It's not Rebecca's fault, and I will go to her. But, Saul, that's probably the biggest loss we've ever taken.'

'Undoubtedly the biggest, my dear, with no hope of ever seeing a copper. We could weather that, not easily, but we could . . .'

The merchant stopped in mid-sentence as the lean houseboy brought in the silver tea-service on an oval tray encircled with silver roses and placed it on the round marble table. Though he scoffed at Sarah's belief that the houseboy understood English perfectly and Hebrew well, he was taking no chances today. Yet if every Chinese in the Settlement did not already know of the scandal, all would by nightfall.

'I may have to resign from the Municipal Council,' he declared gloomily when the door closed behind the servant. 'It may be the only honourable thing.'

'Now you're really talking nonsense,' she chided. 'It's not the end of the world yet. Besides, how could the only Jew on the Council resign?'

'That's just it, my dear. I may have to resign *because* I'm the only Jew. The whole community will be smeared by this scandal. I can smell anti-Semitism rising like a black fog.'

'Next you'll be talking about pogroms. Pogroms in Shanghai! My dear, you know you see everything too black when a few things go wrong at the same time. Sit down and tell me straight out, instead of talking like a Jeremiah. We'll think of something. We always do.'

'Always in the past.' Saul wrapped himself in his gloom. 'But not this time.'

'Don't be so dramatic. Let's start at the beginning. Why is there no collateral for a loan?'

'When somebody pulls a keystone out of a foundation, even an immense building comes toppling down.'

'I'm tired of smears and black fogs and toppling buildings,' she exclaimed. 'You always say most men panic when they should be getting things straight in their minds . . . if they really understood their problems, they'd be half way to solving them. Stop hovering and picking at my orchids. Sit down and drink your tea and let's get things straight.'

Smiling at her vehemence, Saul subsided into a cane-chair, fished a

Burma cheroot from his pocket, and struck a Lucifer. When the cheroot was alight, he poured a cup of tea and stirred in a dollop of strawberry jam. When the tip of the cheroot glowed and smoke wreathed his head, he spoke with forced calmness.

'All right, point by point. First, Benjamin's failed. The two hundred thousand he owes me is a bagatelle beside his other bad loans. Four or five million, most to the banks. Then his fraud against Sassoons, opium valued at more than a quarter million *taels* sold twice . . .'

'I'm so glad we got out of opium,' Sarah interjected. 'You see, it's a judgment.'

'My virtue hasn't kept me clear of this mess. But do you want to talk or listen?'

'I'm sorry. I'll listen.'

'To finish with Benjamin, though there'll undoubtedly be more. Second, without funds he can't develop his property, maybe a twentieth of the land in the Settlement. And he can't sell it off – no matter how cheap. So much land's up for sale no one'll buy. Third, share prices have tumbled, and the Chinese investors are panicking . . . throwing everything onto the market and driving prices through the floor. I was hoping to float a stock issue to set Haleevie and Lee up properly, perhaps ten percent of the capital. But I can't now. Fourth, I'm badly overextended what with Jade House, pledges for the new synagogue, and my investment in the China Merchants Steamship Company. Fifth, Derwents is very shaky, and I've got co-operative ventures with them. Finally, I can't find even ninety thousand *taels* to cut loose from Khartoons, but I can't go back on my word now. So Khartoons'll be in competition with us. Thank God Aisek doesn't know. Just imagine what he'd say . . . Aisek Lee.'

'I know who Aisek is, dear. But what would he say?'

'That I've made a fool of myself without his guidance. He was always more reckless than me, but he pretended to weigh every move.'

'Aisek's not going to appear tomorrow morning, is he, Saul?'

'Hardly. David's still trying for a pardon, but there's not much hope. God forgive me, but in a way I'm glad.'

'Glad, Saul? Glad your friend isn't coming back from exile?'

'Has it ever occurred to you that Aisek can claim half of everything we own if he comes back?'

'Half your debts, from what you say. But he's got no legal claim. You . . . we . . . own everything outright legally.'

'Maybe no legal claim, but I have a moral obligation to Aisek. An obligation I can't repudiate, even if I wanted to. It would ruin me with the Chinese merchants. They know I took his property over so it wouldn't be confiscated.'

'You never could repudiate it, Saul. So then?'

'If he came soon, I'd have to make good. I'd have to sell everything . . . try to sell on a plummeting market. If Aisek returns, he could beggar us.'

Leaving her plants, Sarah slipped behind Saul, placed her arms around his neck, and kissed the top of his head. She poured herself a cup of tea and sat at the table.

'Saul, aside from Aisek's returning, which he won't, what's the worst that can happen?' She pointlessly stirred her unsugared tea. 'Will we be paupers without anywhere to live or anything to eat?'

'We're a long way from that,' he acknowledged. 'But six months or a year from now, when my bank loans come due, there's danger of bankruptcy if the markets all stay depressed.'

'Will they?'

'Perhaps not,' he pondered. 'But there could also be total panic.'

'Why don't we worry about what *could* happen when it happens? Meanwhile, let's stop pouring money into Jade House. Even put it up for sale as it stands. I don't need the finest residence in the Settlement. Also call whatever loans you can collect and cut down our charitable contributions, even the synagogue. God will hear us just as well in the old one.'

'All right, Sarah,' he conceded. 'I'll stop building on Jade House, but I won't put it on the market when no one'll buy at a realistic price. Anyway, if I did, everyone would say I was going under too. Also, I can't stop our charities. My credit's just that: what people think. If I retrench too heavily, they'll think I'm finished – and I will be.'

'Also, please Saul, write your brother Solomon in London and ask him to see Samuelsons. Maybe he also has a few pennies to spare.'

'I need three to four hundred thousand *taels* to tide me over,' the merchant mused. 'Say a hundred to a hundred and fifty thousand sterling.'

Sarah laughed. 'You see, Saul, it's not so bad. I remember when a thousand pounds was a fortune to us. Whoever thought we'd have that much?'

'My dear, in London a butler gets maybe £90 a year. A hundred and fifty thousand's hardly a bagatelle.'

'And you're not a butler. Also, you can tell Solomon and assure Samuelsons the situation here is fundamentally sound. If Judah Benjamin owns a twentieth of the land, you own more. So you can tell them there's collateral.'

'I suppose we own about ten percent of the settlement,' he said hesitantly. 'So, I can tell them we're sound at rock-bottom.'

Sarah leaned across the table and kissed his lips. Sitting back, she poured two cups of tea while Saul reclaimed his cheroot from the blue porcelain ashtray.

'So it'll be all right, won't it?' she insisted. 'Nothing to worry about?'

'Hardly nothing, Sarah, and it won't necessarily be all right. We'll need a lot of luck.' He spread two newspapers on the marble table. 'Remember I said I smelt anti-Semitism? Listen to what the *Shanghai Courier* has to say: *It was a boast of Judah Benjamin that the Rothschilds, the Sassoons, and the Benjamins would finally exercise predominant influence on the finances*

469

of all the world, while all Indian banks and all foreign banks in China would come under their complete control. Besides, what of the shadowy figure of Saul Haleevie, the great independent? With his collaboration, a Hebrew consortium could hold complete dominion over Shanghai. If they only knew how I was struggling!'

'You're not shadowy, dear. You're rather substantial. I must cut down on those heavy lunches.'

'It's not funny, Sarah. Not when the *Cathay Post*'s being Biblical: *First verse: And Benjamin in obedience to the word of his God Mammon came down from the land of his forefathers, leaving kith and kin, and without goods or chattels settled in a strange land among strange people. Second verse: And the God Mammon was pleased with his servant Benjamin and gave strength to his hand, so that he waxed fat and prosperous. Third verse: But Benjamin later displeased his God Mammon, so the He forsook His servant Banjamin, for Benjamin had done some snivvey (Hebrew untranslatable) things. Fourth verse: And Benjamin lost all his flocks and herds: and his vineyards and houses had monkeys in them.*'

Saul ground the stub of his cheroot against the blue porcelain bowl and searched his pockets for a replacement. Finding none, he placed his palms on the marble table.

'Don't laugh, Sarah,' he said. 'It's the stench of anti-Semitism.'

'I'm sorry, dear, but it is funny. Child's play from grown men. Snivvey, a Hebrew word! Besides we've faced real anti-Semitism before, and survived it. Now, I'm going to see Rebecca Benjamin.'

CHAPTER SIXTY-SEVEN

April 16, 1873   *The Yangtze above Chungming Island*

Wing-and-wing, Fronah reflected happily, was a lovely way to describe the set of the small cutter's sails. The big mainsail, stretched between the gaff two-thirds up the mast and the main-boom at its foot, bellied out vertically on the right side. She must remember to call it starboard, as Gabriel did. On the port side, the wind filled the Genoa jib, which was supported by the boathook he had thrust into the brass eyelet for the sheets, the ropes controlling the jib.

The cutter was running before the wind, which blew behind them. The sails really did resemble the snowy wings of an enormous swan skimming above the muddy surface of the Long River. It was almost like flying, their gliding downstream towards the sea. The silence was accentuated by the creaking of the rigging and the hiss of coffee-coloured foam along the cutter's canary-yellow flanks.

Fronah leaned back against the deckhouse and stretched her legs out on the teak bench of the cockpit. Tucking her rebellious skirts under her ankles, she looked fondly at Gabriel, who appeared unaware of her scrutiny. His eyes flickered from the sails to the green and red wisps of silk tied to the stays supporting the mast, while he guided the cutter with slight movements of the tiller. He was otherwise immobile, completely relaxed in white-duck trousers and a blue shirt, his feet bare.

His gaze momentarily left the sails, and he grinned when the wind ballooned her skirt. The white dimity, sprigged with scarlet that matched her satin sash, billowed to reveal her bare knees. She laughed as she subdued the wind-blown fabric, though she should have been embarrassed. During the three weeks since his return from Tientsin, they had regained the easy camaraderie they knew before Lionel Henriques arrived in Shanghai to charm her parents – and herself. She was no more discomfited at her skirts' indiscretion than she would have been had Gabriel been a favourite uncle, a rather young uncle.

'You used to have a dress just like that one, didn't you?' he asked. 'I remember you wore one like it at Jardines' picnic in the summer of '56.'

'It's the same frock, Gabriel. I couldn't find anything else for boating. But Maylu found this in the back of my cupboard.'

Suffused with quick affection for Gabriel because he remembered the old frock. Fronah did not boast of her pleasure at discovering that it still fitted her. She could not, of course, tell him she was doubly pleased to find she didn't need even the light summer corset of lace, silk, and slivers of whalebone she had once worn under that frock. She felt deliciously unfettered and free.

When Margaret MacGregor's messenger told them that she and her physician husband could not, after all, join them, Gabriel had proposed abandoning the outing. But Fronah had insisted that they go ahead without their chaperones, rather than waste the beautiful Sunday and the bulging picnic basket.

'The old devil-may-care, Fronah?' Gabriel had laughed. 'I don't want to . . .'

'I don't care what the gossips say,' she had replied firmly. 'Besides, you're not planning to rape me, are you?'

'You *are* forthright, aren't you?' he had said, reluctantly casting off the mooring lines. 'I'd just be happier with another man to help if the weather changes. But, honestly, I'm not planning anything drastic . . . despite the temptation. You're looking wonderful.'

Despite Gabriel's automatic gallantry, she felt completely comfortable with him. She was spontaneously happy – as she had not been for longer than she could remember – while the cutter flew down the Long River towards Chungming Island. Gabriel had spoken of the wind's veering in the afternoon to carry them home, but she was not concerned about such technical matters. She was, she knew, quite safe with him.

Gabriel would never possess Lionel's inborn self-assurance and effortless superiority, which made other men appear gauche. Nor could his black hair, deep-blue eyes, and straight nose ever move her as had Lionel's aquiline fairness. Still she felt utterly tranquil with Gabriel – as she had never quite felt with Lionel.

Why, she wondered, had she ever thought the dark American dashing? He was a rock of dependability, not an irresistible cavalier. He was a soldier of fortune by profession, but not by nature. He went to war as matter of factly as a banker went to his office. No, Gabriel was hardly her ideal of a fascinating lover, though she had been drawn to him when she was a romantic girl. After the battle of Soochow Creek ten years ago, he had been a wounded hero and she a pale angel of mercy! Those stock figures were as remote from reality as they were distant in time. The spark that had leapt between them would never flare again.

Yet somehow she was not pleased that the Mandarin Li Hung-chang had kept Gabriel so long in the north. True, the administration of the Viceroyalty of Chihli had been disrupted for months by the coronation of the Tung Chih Emperor in February, when even Yehenala's wiles could no longer prevent the Court Astronomers' designating the auspicious day.

'Tientsin was like a three-ring circus,' Gabriel had explained. 'So much to do before I could come back and potter around the new Shanghai shipyard: mounting cannon on the new Taku Fort, which will drive off any assault on Peking from the sea; testing the new high-speed gunboats; drawing up specifications for the big ironclads that'll be the striking force of the North China Fleet; and training their crews.'

He had, Gabriel admitted artlessly, been reluctant to leave when the Mandarin ordered him south again. And, much as he enjoyed being with Fronah, he was not totally unhappy about his imminent return to Tientsin.

'The atmosphere's electric,' he mused. 'We're doing great things, just as you said. I've never seen such hard work and buoyant optimism in China. Your brother David's cock-a-hoop. And he's optimistic about his father. The Mandarin's promised to get him a pardon, and, this time, he's really pressing.'

'I'd love to see Uncle Aisek again,' Fronah said. 'It's been so long. When . . . if he does, you must come, too. Papa will give the biggest party Shanghai's ever seen.'

She was slightly piqued at Gabriel's readiness to depart again. For the past three weeks, his undemanding company at dances and dinner parties given by hostesses who previously despaired of enticing her had given Fronah much pleasure. Though not exciting, he was reassuring – and he tempted her to lively frivolousness. It was delightful to feel attractive and pampered, yet pressed by no emotional demands. She would be very sorry when he left.

472

Still, he would be returning regularly to Shanghai, which was the focal point of foreign influence in China. Gabriel's chief utility to the Mandarin was dealing with the foreigners and their deadly inventions. Fronah stretched contentedly, her eyes half-closed.

'It's lovely, Gabriel!' she exclaimed when the cutter slipped around a junk struggling upstream. 'I've never seen such perfect weather.'

'Glad you came then?' he asked. 'Even if we're going to scandalise the old biddies?'

'I told you I didn't care. Just look at that vista.'

The morning sun warmed her bare arms and glowed on the ripples of the broad Yangtze, its heat not yet oppressive in mid-April. The villages on the banks were Chinese toytowns, and the junks were story-book galleons under a sky of blue taffeta tufted with cotton-wool clouds. Though a black thunder-head hovered above the rim of the horizon, its theatrical menace was drifting away.

Apparently as lazily content as herself, Gabriel spoke little. Their normal banter was suspended, her occasional acerbity and his habitual jocularity muted. They exchanged a few words as they sipped the mild punch, which poured cold from a sweating earthenware jug. Twice he warned her to duck as he jibed around bends, and the mainsail slammed across the cockpit on its heavy boom. He then allowed her to hold the tiller while he transferred the Genoa jib on its long pole to the opposite side. The cutter was still running wing-and-wing, its sails spread vulnerably before the following wind.

'Fronah!' he exclaimed urgently, and she came fully awake. 'Take the tiller. Just keep her straight.'

Gabriel pattered to the foredeck and released the pole that held the jib out from the hull. The starboard sheet coiled around his hand, he hurried back to the cockpit. With disciplined haste he pulled in the sheet and secured it around a wooden cleat.

'A squall,' he explained, taking the tiller. 'It'll hit us in a minute. Keep your head down.'

A black shape raced across the Long River, the wind-driven rain churning the muddy water. The river was placid beyond the squall, which bore directly down upon them. Fronah shivered in the sudden coolness, though she knew she was safe in Gabriel's hands. His bare foot controlling the tiller, he reeled in the mainsail-sheet with both hands.

Fronah struggled to rise from the bench, which canted sharply as the cutter tilted to starboard. Grasping the tiller with his left hand, Gabriel frantically tugged at the mainsheet, which appeared to be snagged against the mast.

'Down!' he shouted. 'Get down, damn it!'

The mainsail swung across the cockpit, crashing when the taut sheet checked its momentum. The massive boom hurtled so close it ruffled Fronah's hair. The entire cutter trembled, and she was flung into the well

473

of the cockpit. Sprawled on the floorboards, she watched Gabriel wrestle with the sheets and the tiller as the boom swung out of control. Half a minute later, the centre of the squall had passed. Both sails taut to starboard, the cutter raced towards a wooded inlet.

Fronah was startled, but not alarmed. She picked herself up and perched on the port-side bench, which reared high as the cutter heeled under the weight of the wind.

'Get down, I said!' Gabriel screamed at her. 'Get down, damn it! And stay down!'

Startled by his vehemence, Fronah slid on to the bench. Clinging to the cockpit's coaming, she watched as he eased the sheets slightly. Their wild charge across the stream slowed, and the cutter rose marginally upright.

'I'm sorry!' His voice was harsh with tension. 'We've got to anchor.'

'But the wind's dropping,' she protested. 'Why must we . . .'

'Be quiet, Fronah!' he commanded. 'Just be quiet and stay out of my way. Do as I say, damn it!'

She was astonished by the abrupt alteration in the sailor who had weathered many storms far more violent than this passing squall. His clenched lips were twitching; his face was whiter than the sails; and his eyes blinked tremulously. His hand quivered on the tiller, his knuckles whitened by the strength of his grasp.

Unspeaking, Gabriel guided the cutter into the shelter of the inlet. When the prow rounded a bend, he steered towards the wooded shore, released the tiller, and scurried to the foredeck. Fronah was for the first time alarmed. It was mad to abandon control of the craft.

But the bow swung to point into the wind, and the wind-starved sails flapped quiescent amidships. As the cutter's forward motion ceased, Gabriel flung the anchor overboard. He jerked hard on the line to make sure it would hold. Apparently satisfied, he released the jib-halyard, and the sail slid down to the deck. Still unspeaking, he gathered in the jib and secured it before lowering the mainsail.

He did not speak until the stiff canvas was furled around the heavy boom. Fronah wisely remained silent, though she marvelled at the contrast between his unhurried competence and his stricken expression.

'You'll find brandy in the cabin locker,' Gabriel finally said. 'Could you bring it up?'

He raised the green bottle to his lips and gulped hard. After taking a second long draught, he corked the neck and wiped his lips with the back of his hand. Red splotches gleamed on his cheekbones as his normal ruddy tan slowly returned.

'I'm sorry Fronah,' he apologised. 'Very sorry I was so rough with you.'

'It doesn't matter,' she assured him. 'But what's wrong? It wasn't that dangerous, was it? I didn't have time to be afraid.'

'There was no need to be afraid. It was nothing . . . just a baby squall.'

'Then why . . . why were you so shaken? Why did you . . .'

'I said I was sorry, Fronah, and I am.' Tension still edged his voice. 'But if you want the truth, I was frightened, damned scared.'

'It must've been dangerous. Otherwise you wouldn't . . . I know you've seen much worse . . . far more dangerous storms. And David says you hardly turned a hair in the fighting.'

'Not so he could see it,' the American laughed shakily. 'I've been scared to death before, but afraid to show it. Only once, though, was I as frightened as just now . . . out there.'

'Why, my dear?' The endearment slipped out. 'Won't you tell me? Of course, if you'd rather not . . .'

'What the Hell, Fronah! I might as well. But, first, let me have a tumbler for my brandy. Why not get one for yourself? It's chilly here under the trees.'

Despite the dappled shadows cast on the still water by the foliage, it was actually warmer inshore than on the river. But Gabriel was still shivering. She poured him a generous brandy and took a small one for herself. He drank half at one swallow while she sipped. The spirits were warm in her throat, but his shivering hardly subsided.

'Couple of years ago near Marblehead,' he began jerkily. 'Jane . . . my wife Jane . . . we were sailing a cutter like this one. A beautiful day without a cloud. I was cocksure. I damned well knew the weather'd keep perfect. Just a calm steady breeze from the south-west and a light chop, but nothing to worry about. I didn't even bother to check the forecast. I was a great sailor . . . And I knew.'

Gabriel took a pull of his brandy, and Fronah marvelled at his precise description of the weather conditions. Though he was still trembling, his professional instinct over-rode his agitation.

'She . . . Jane . . . was carrying a child, about six months along. I laughed when she worried about going out. Damned heavy lead keel under you and one of the best small-boat men in New England at the helm, I told her.'

He looked into his brandy and was silent for half a minute.

'It happened in the second hour,' he resumed slowly. 'A damned big squall, not a little fellow like this one. I fought it single-handed for maybe an hour and a half. I got reefed down, and even set the storm-jib. Only God know how I got the cutter pointed into the wind alone. Jane kept down with a rope tied under her arms. She was taking it in her stride, laughing and saying I hadn't just been boasting. I really was the best small-boat man in New England. The wind began to drop, and I reckoned everything was all right . . . even if I had been a damned fool.'

Fronah laid her hand on his. He was trembling, and his eyes were wet. Sitting very still, she waited for him to continue.

'I reckoned it was all over. Still a bit rough, but nothing to worry about. So I asked her to ease the jib-sheet. Out of nowhere a gust swooped down on us and practically knocked the cutter over. Naturally, the boom swung.

It grazed her head and . . . and knocked her overboard. Oh, I hauled her back by the line secured under her arms. But . . .'

'Don't talk about it any more, my dear.' Fronah put her arm around his neck and drew his head down to her breast. 'You're just torturing yourself.'

'I might as well, seeing as I'm almost through. I never told anyone the whole story before. Not that I . . . I asked her to ease the sheet. Jane never regained consciousness, after the miscarriage. It was a boy, they told me, a boy, but she never knew, though she opened her eyes, those wonderful brown eyes, and looked at me . . . so serene for a few seconds. A day later, she . . . she died. All because of my stupid arrogance. All my fault!'

He was muttering incoherently. She pressed his head closer and felt his tears seep through her dimity bodice. She stroked his hair, her hand lingering on the nape of his neck. It was dangerous, instinct warned, to feel such intense sympathy, but she ignored that small voice. Like her orphans, he was hurt and bewildered. He needed comforting, and she could comfort him, she alone.

Her free hand stroked his back. He trembled and pressed closer, his arms reaching around her. Just as naturally, she unbuttoned her bodice so that she could feel his cheek against her breasts. He clasped her tighter when she tried to slip out of his grasp.

'Just a moment, my darling,' she soothed him. 'Just let me loose for a moment.'

Fronah drew her dress and shift over her head. She lay down beside him on the bench and opened his shirt. He looked up and gasped at her nakedness.

'Oh, Fronah,' he whispered hoarsely. 'Oh, my darling. But it's not . . . we shouldn't . . .'

'Hush, my love, hush,' she crooned. 'Just be quiet and . . .'

They came together naturally. She felt no great ecstasy as he came into her, only comfort and peace. When he shuddered and lay still, she drew his face to her breasts again. Gazing into the sunlight, she stroked his hair and murmured endearments.

'Oh, Fronah, my darling.' His arms tightened around her. 'Fronah, my love, I've wanted . . .'

He pushed himself up against the teak coaming, but his arms still clasped her.

'This is terrible.' His eyes were shadowed. 'I shouldn't have . . . I never meant to . . . Fronah, I'm so sorry.'

'Don't be sorry Gabriel,' she said slowly. 'I'll never be sorry. I think I've wanted this to happen for a long time.'

476

CHAPTER SIXTY-EIGHT

July 14, 1873   *Shanghai*

'Why I celebrated the French Republic by gulping all those bubbles, I don't know.' Saul Haleevie complained. 'I don't approve of republics, and I'm not fond of the French.'

'Your position, my dear,' Sarah Haleevie laughed. 'The French would be hurt if a Municipal Counsellor didn't appear. Besides, I rather like champagne.'

The merchant prowled the veranda, grumbling each time he passed his wife, who was placidly pushing a needle through her embroidery. The oppressive Shanghai weather intensified his irritation on the evening of Bastille Day, the 14th of July, 1873.

He was tired, but he was not sleepy. He was hungry, but he had no desire to eat. On Szechwan Road cats switched their tails nervously, and dogs yapped protests against the muggy atmosphere that permitted them neither to sleep nor to prowl.

'Let's take a stroll,' Saul abruptly suggested.

'It's too hot, dear,' Sarah replied. 'I'd melt.'

'Well, I'm going to . . . All right, let's take a drive and get some air.'

'If you must,' Sarah sighed, 'I'll come along.'

'The young boy finally gave in.' Saul was slightly more cheerful after taking a decision, however trivial. 'About time, too.'

'What young boy, Saul?'

'That Manchu boy, the Emperor. He's finally received the Ambassadors after delaying for months after his Coronation.'

'I see, Saul.'

'Everybody's satisfied and nobody's satisfied. The Ambassadors have finally seen the Son of Heaven. And they didn't kowtow, but just bowed. Believe it or not, they joked with each other in his presence. Can you imagine ambassadors joking before Queen Victoria?'

'So the Manchus came out badly?'

'Of course not.' Saul's tone was heavily ironic. 'His Majesty received the barbarian ambassadors in the Kiosk of Purple Brilliance, where envoys from tributary peoples like Vietnamese or Koreans are normally received. The *Peking Gazette* set the whole thing in perspective. Being the oldest journal in the world it is, naturally, the most mendacious. The *Gazette* reported: *The barbarian envoys were so awe-strucken they trembled and dared not look upon the Imperial countenance.*'

'Well, that's that. How long have they been arguing about this audience?'

'Since 1860, arguing about nothing. Finally, the ambassadors can report they didn't kowtow. And the Manchus can tell themselves the Emperor wasn't humbled but graciously overlooked the barbarians' bad manners. May God keep us from all monarchs and all ambassadors.'

'A moment ago, Saul, you were denouncing republics.'

'God defend us from presidents, too.' He grinned. 'From everyone who meddles with honest merchants.'

*

The pony-trap rattled westward on the cobblestones of Bubbling Well Road, passing cross-streets called after the provinces of the Empire. Chinese families lounging on cane chairs obstructed the footpaths, their faces wan in the lamp-light trickling through open doors. The normally frenetic city was stifled by the heat. Though the smart trot created a breeze, Sarah touched the groom's arm when he raised his whip to slash the pony's sweaty haunches again.

'Mafoo, more better go more slow,' she said. 'No wanchee makee pony dead.'

Saul smiled at her pidgin, wondering again why a woman who spoke four languages well could not master Shanghainese. His smile faded when she turned to question him.

'Saul, why are you so edgy? The business? Aren't things getting better?'

'So how could business be better?' He shrugged in self parody. 'What can I say, Sarah? It's not disastrous, but that's about all.'

'You're worried about Samuelsons' loan?'

'Naturally, but I'll manage somehow. I had to buy out Khartoons, and I'll have to make good. If only property would begin moving . . . prices come off the floor.'

'Is there any hope?'

'There's always hope, but right now nothing else. There's also hope for Aisek Lee's pardon. David writes he's very hopeful, but needs funds for bribes. How can I not give, even if I'm paying for Aisek to come back to ruin us?'

'You must, of course.'

'Sarah, that's enough. Let's not discuss business on an already depressing night.'

'I've been wanting to talk to you about Fronah,' she said, 'If I must take this pointless drive . . .'

The merchant's daughter, like his business, was a subject he preferred to avoid.

'Maylu's overjoyed, you know.' Sarah's genius for indirection still amazed him. 'She hasn't seen Fronah happier in years.'

'I'm glad Maylu's also happy. At least two people're happy about this . . . this . . .'

'I'm happy, too, Saul. Gabriel's so good for her she's a new woman.'

'And Judah? Must my grandson see his mother behave like a . . .'

'*Your* grandson' innocence isn't sullied. They're grown-ups, Saul, and they're very careful Judah doesn't know.'

'I'm glad of that at least.'

'Saul, you should be happy Fronah's come alive again. How can you be so . . .'

'So I'm happy. You want me to sing a little song, perhaps dance a jig? Maybe I should make up their bed?'

'Stop it, Saul,' she rejoined. 'You're acting jealous . . . as if she was your sweetheart, not your daughter.'

'I'm supposed to jump with joy because my daughter's having an affair with a Gentile?'

'Saul, we must show her the ring . . . Lionel's ring!'

'So she can marry Hyde?' He looked at her in astonishment. 'Are you crazy tonight?'

'Not so she can marry Gabriel. It's still too early . . .'

'Too *early* when they're . . .'

'Much too early!' Sarah was undeterred. 'She must be sure. As long as she thinks Lionel could be alive, she'll never know how she really feels. Oh, Saul, it's her last chance for happiness. We should have told her years ago.'

'Things just slipped along. Maybe we should have years ago, but not now. Let her think Lionel could be alive – and let her believe that she can't divorce him. Let her, God forbid, have affairs with a dozen Gentiles, but not marry . . .'

'Saul, please stop talking like a fool.' Sarah silenced him. 'Stop indulging yourself.'

Despite his indignation, Saul was cowed by her vehemence and remained silent.

'You've got to listen. Fronah's happiness is at stake, any hope she has for happiness. You know, just any man won't do for her. Gabriel's the first one . . . the only one . . .'

'That oaf . . . what was his name? Yes, Iain. What about . . .'

'She was a baby then, but this is serious. She has your conscience, my dear. If you don't show her the ring, she'll never be free to know how she really feels. Then, perhaps, she won't want Gabriel. Perhaps, she will, but . . .'

'I don't want a Gentile son-in-law, Sarah. That's flat.'

'The Jewish son-in-law you . . . we . . . picked was no bargain, was he?'

'Think of the scandal, Sarah!'

'If she marries him? I don't understand you sometimes. Their affair, it'll come out some day. And that'll be a real scandal. Marriage isn't a scandal . . . if she finally decides to marry him. I think he already want to, but she isn't so keen. There's Lionel and . . .'

479

'You say you think.' Saul laughed for the first time. 'That means you know. I'm glad he's an honourable man. But think of the scandal in our community. My credit's bad enough as is. With a Gentile son-on-law, they'd . . .'

'Saul, forget business. We're talking about your daughter, not cotton piece-goods. Besides, the children . . . any children . . . would be Jewish.'

'I know, Sarah. I'm not a fool.'

'Then you'll show her the ring?'

'I'll think about it,' he conceded. 'I hate to interfere, but I'll think about it.'

'*Not* telling her is interfering, Saul. And, when you say you'll think about it, I know you mean you'll do it.'

'Don't count on it, Sarah. But that's enough for now. We're almost there.'

'You haven't promised, Saul,' she pressed.

'In six months, if they're still together, I'll tell her. Right now the shock could throw her into his arms. In six months, I promise.'

The built-up cross-streets had given way to open fields intersected by paths. The pony-trap approached a cluster of bonfires, torches, and lanterns, which flared on a long two-storey building sheathed with bamboo scaffolding. Sarah counted nine windows on the ground floor of the central structure and nine more in each of the wings behind the balustraded balconies of the first floor, while beside the pillars of the portico French windows opened from the ground floor on to a marble terrace. Three wide stairways descended from the terrace to an open expanse cluttered with the debris and the shacks of the builders.

'It's beautiful, dear,' Sarah gasped. 'But I never expected . . . You said you stopped work.'

'Otherwise it would be finished by now. I've just started again, but it'll be ready by Yom Kippur. I promised you Jade House . . . and I'm giving you Jade House.'

'Saul, this is really crazy.' She slipped her arm through his and held it close. 'It's beautiful, but it's crazy.'

'I had to start building again,' he explained defensively. 'It gives a lot of men work and . . .'

'Then business, it's really better?'

'To tell the truth, Sarah, business is worse . . . much worse.'

'Then why, Saul? Why put all this money into Jade House when . . .'

'I *have* to. If I didn't build again, everyone . . . the banks, Jardines, Derwents, everyone . . . would be certain Haleevie and Lee was following Benjamin into bankruptcy. Now they'll believe I've got funds they've never even heard of. And they'll carry me longer.'

'Then it's a bluff?'

'Yes, Sarah, it's a bluff, a great big bluff.'

480

CHAPTER SIXTY-NINE

The summer brutality of the Shanghai sun had not abated in the late afternoon. The aggressive rays pierced the reed-screen covering the window and cast alternating stripes of radiance and shadow on the broad bed. When the breeze off the Hwangpoo tossed the screen, light played on the feminine and masculine clothing heaped on the rosewood chest at the foot of the bed. On the blue-and-white Tientsin carpet, a high-heeled pink slipper and a gauzy shift lay beside a white shirt with the arms turned inside out.

Some five months after their discovery of each other on the anchored cutter, Fronah and Gabriel were still gripped by 'almost indecent passion and haste', as she would laugh. They strove to conceal the intensity of their feeling in public – and naïvely believed they succeeded. When they were alone, they yearned to touch each other. Light caresses invariably led to more profound embraces despite the frequent danger of interruption, though that danger spiced their love-making. They were, however, often alone, since Fronah was her own mistress in the Nest of Joy.

That September afternoon, her son Judah was intently studying Hebrew in his grandfather's office. Knowing her father would keep her son far beyond the appointed two hours to continue his initiation into the mysteries of trade on the China Coast, Fronah had told Maylu she wanted to nap. Beaming with conspiratorial delight, the concubine swore she would keep the servants from disturbing her Little Lady's rest.

'Young Saunders finally produced the photograph.' Gabriel traced the curve of her hip with his fingertips. 'Not a bad likeness of the cutter, I'd say.'

'You beast!' Fronah threw off the sheet and darted across the bedroom to scrabble in his coat pocket. 'You know I want to see how you came out.'

'I like you that way, darling.' Gabriel grinned at the naked figure bending over the rosewood chest. 'Even better than in your new green dress.'

'That frock is pretty, isn't it?' She stopped searching for a moment. 'Oh, Gabriel, it's so nice to be foolish and only think about frocks sometimes.'

'You've improved,' he said complacently. 'No doubt about it.'

'All due to you, of course?'

'Well, I deserve a little credit, don't I?'

'My darling, you deserve *all* the credit.' She was grave for an instant. 'It's really lovely . . . you and me, together. But where's the damned picture?'

'You're beginning to sound like a hard-case Yankee bosun, my sweet. Try the inside pocket.'

Fronah studied the sepia print, remembering that they had posed for two hours in the cockpit of the moored cutter before the young English photographer was satisfied. Ten years after first seeing a daguerreotype, she still marvelled at the extraordinary likenesses captured on the glass plates inside the big wooden box with the glaring lens.

'It's very good of you, Gabriel,' she finally pronounced. 'Though I wish he'd caught your dimple. But I look a mess.'

'Well, at least the boat looks good. She didn't have to smile. Don't be silly, darling. It's a beautiful picture of you.'

'You really think so, Gabriel? Isn't the tip of my nose too round? Perhaps it's not too bad. I do want one.'

'I've asked young Saunders to frame a copy for you. This one I'm taking with me. Now stop admiring yourself and come back to bed.'

'Have you got another present for me, Gabriel?' She played the coquette, holding the photograph before her nakedness in a parody of modesty.

'My other present'll take a few minutes more to be ready. Maybe less if you really want it . . . and help it develop. But come back to bed anyway. I want you near me.'

Fronah laid the picture on the side-table and slid down on to the bed. Throwing off the sheet, Gabriel pulled her head down on his shoulder.

'We're shamelessly abandoned, aren't we, darling?' she chuckled. 'But very comfortable.'

'Maybe it's superstitious, but I sometimes feel we're just too comfortable. I'm tempting fate, taking without giving. Welcomed in your parents house when we . . . and welcomed in your bed. I don't give much in return.'

'My darling, you give me everything, everything I've ever wanted in my bed – or out of bed.' Fronah's tone lightened. 'As for the parents, keep your eyes open when you go north. A few really good porcelains would be much appreciated. Of course they know about us. I won't pretend they're *both* overjoyed, but they understand. They're not medieval, you know.'

'I hate leaving you again, Fronah. It's bound to be several months.'

'I'm not overjoyed myself, you know. But what can we do?'

'You *could* come with me.'

Fronah wriggled free of his arm and sat up against the pillows. Picking up the photograph, she studied their images before replying.

'Gabriel, my darling, *you* are being foolish now, How could I leave my work? Even if I could, think of the scandal.'

'Maylu's practically running the children's home. And the Grand Mandarin says he's got plenty for you to do in Tientsin. So why not come? The scandal? Everyone already knows about us.'

'And they're understanding . . . very discreet. But it's not the same thing. Going north with you would be a public declaration. Open defiance would be improper.'

'You're always saying you don't care about propriety.' He paused and, heavily casual, added: 'You *could* marry me, you know. That would satisfy propriety.'

'Gabriel, you know I can't,' she protested. 'I've explained so many times. I've still got a husband, even if I don't know where. And there are . . . other things.'

Gabriel sat up abruptly and reached for his cheroot case, almost knocking over the earthenware water-jug on the sidetable. He deliberately lit the brown cylinder and vigorously fanned out the match, simultaneously trying to subdue his surge of anger.

'For God's sake, Fronah, be sensible!' he finally exploded. 'Lionel can't be . . . For God's sake, Fronah, he *must* be dead after all this time. Besides, he's deserted you.'

'Perhaps he is, but I don't *know*. And I can't divorce him. Under Talmudic law, a wife can't divorce. Only a husband. It's unfair, but there it is. Besides, there's the British law. It would be difficult, almost impossible, I'm told.'

'You've enquired then? I'm glad that . . .'

'Of course I have, Gabriel. What do you take me for? But it's a very big step. And there are other reasons.'

'What other reasons?' he demanded brusquely. 'What are these other reasons? Fronah, I can't bear to think about losing you.'

'And I couldn't bear losing you, my darling. I think it would be the end of me. Let's talk about it very seriously when you come back. We couldn't now, anyway. Even without the complications, we couldn't get married in the two days before you go.'

He nodded curtly and morosely blew a plump smoke-ring. He was angered by her evasiveness, but, he cautioned himself, he must not give way to his anger. His violent temper had decisively altered the course of his life once. He must not allow that to happen again – and, perhaps, blight the greatest happiness he had ever known by losing her. He nodded curtly for the second time and forced himself to remain silent. When she ran her fingertips along his arm, he smiled despite his anger.

'You won't catch me so easily,' he said. 'You can't have your other present till I'm good and ready. Anyway, you're just trying to change the subject.'

'That same old present? Who needs it? Of course I'm trying to change the subject. You know you never told me why you left the Navy all those years ago. Everybody thought you must be a secret agent for the Americans.'

Gabriel looked at her in frank astonishment. She truly did not know, he realised, and she was justifiably curious.

'By God, I thought all Shanghai knew about my contretemps,' he exclaimed. 'I'm amazed that you . . .'

'Then tell me, even if I'm the last to know.'

'A commander named Staughton on the *Susquehanna* kept riding me. Nothing I did could ever satisfy him. To hear him talk, you'd think I made a complete mess of all my duties. One day he reached the limit.'

483

'What was that, darling?' she prompted.

'He forced a confrontation by calling me a vile name. Maybe I acted stupidly, but I was very young and very hot-headed. At least, I didn't strike a superior officer. That's what he wanted. But he'd made a tactical error . . . insulted me in front of two other officers. In my rage, I did the only thing I could. I challenged him . . . forced a duel with cutlasses.'

'Of course, you weren't hurt. How could you be?' Fronah remembered her brother David's admiration for her lover's lethal skill with the heavy naval cutlass. 'What happened to Commander Staughton?'

'I only pinked him. Thank God I had the sense to let him off lightly, though I wanted to kill him.'

'Then what was the crime?' she persisted. 'Two gentlemen . . . well, one gentleman and a cad . . . fought a duel. Honour was satisfied, and no one was badly hurt. Why did you leave the Navy?'

'You could say,' he smiled, 'the Navy left me.'

'I don't understand, Gabriel.'

'Duelling between officers is forbidden. It's a court-martial offence to force a duel on a senior officer.'

'I never heard you were court-martialled.'

'No, I wasn't. The Navy was too embarrassed because of the insult. The Commodore didn't want to rake the matter over. So they didn't try me, but compromised . . . placed me on "extended leave".'

'What was the insult, Gabriel? Why was the Navy embarrassed?'

'It still rankles, Fronah. I know it's stupid, but it still rankles. I couldn't take it lying down. He called me a pushy kike . . . a dirty, lazy Jewish swine.'

'How ridiculous, Gabriel! Why were you insulted? If somebody called me a filthy Hottentot bitch, I'd just laugh.'

Gabriel laid his cheroot in the ashtray and stared at her in astonishment again.

'You mean you don't know, Fronah? I always assumed you knew. My mother was Jewish. She was a Poole from the old Sephardic family.'

'That's funny, Gabriel. I know it was terrible for you, but I can't help laughing. It *is* funny. All along, I thought . . . It's very funny.' She finally controlled her frenetic laughter. 'So that's why you were so curious about my name at the ball, when we first met.'

'Of course. And it never occurred to me you didn't know. All these years, I never thought to tell you. Those other reasons for not marrying me? Were they because . . .'

'Yes, of course. I never dreamed you were Jewish. I suppose you're not really, but technically you are because your mother was. If it were your father, no. You see . . .'

'I know about Hebrew matrilineality, my dear. Who knows better that Jews are very practical about bloodlines and property? A father could . . . conceivably or inconceivably . . . be anyone. But there's no doubt who the mother is. So a Jew is anyone born of a Jewish mother.'

484

'You *are* well informed, darling.'

'And it makes a difference, even to you? I can see that your parents would . . . but to you, too. Then there's no real obstacle now.'

'I'm afraid it did make a small difference to me, Gabriel,' she confessed. 'It's not enlightened, I know. But it made a difference. And to my parents, of course, it . . .'

'Then it's all right, now, isn't it? Promise you'll marry me, darling.'

'My love, I want to. I really want to. But there's still Lionel . . . what's become of him. I don't know whether I'm a married woman or not. But I promise I'll think hard about it. When you come back, we'll see . . .'

'That's not good enough. Promise me now.'

'I can't. Really I can't. But when you come back, I'll certainly . . .' Her words trailed off. 'Right now, I want something else from you. I'm glad you want to make me an honest woman. For now, just make me a contented woman.'

Her arms twined around his neck and pulled him down into the pillows. He turned joyously to her and slipped his arm around her back.

'Give me that present now,' she whispered. 'I want it now.'

Just before she herself was ignited by the passion she had kindled, Fronah sensed she would not tell her parents of Gabriel's revelation. She did not know quite why, but felt she would not. She was still puzzled as his eager hands dispelled all coherent thought. Perhaps, though, she was frightened.

CHAPTER SEVENTY

October 8, 1873

*The Imperial Jade Mines
Kansu Province*

The rotund figure in the sheepskin coat leaned towards the fire burning under the gridiron, his blunt fingers holding charred bamboo chopsticks. When the strips of mutton crackled brown, the long chopsticks swept them into an earthenware bowl containing a sauce pungent with dried chillis and thick with peanut paste. He shovelled the mixture into his mouth and bit a chunk off a long bun studded with sesame seeds. Still chewing, he sipped the powerful sorghum spirits called *bai-garh*, white and dry, from a cracked cup.

Aisek Lee sighed with satisfaction and laid his chopsticks down. He lit his pipe after stuffing its minuscule bowl with shredded tobacco. Replenishing his cup, he sipped and smoked in replete silence. The stunted Moslem who owned the eating-shop offered another helping of grilled mutton, but the exile waved him away.

'*Chih-pao-la . . .*' he said in the rough Mandarin that was the *lingua franca* of the frontier town. 'I'm stuffed full. Couldn't eat another mouthful. But thanks, old fellow.'

'It's nothing, sir,' the Moslem replied. 'I'd only hate to see a gentleman of your standing go hungry.'

'No danger of that, old fellow,' Aisek grinned. 'Though my standing's hardly very high.'

'The chief foreman of the Imperial Jade Mines,' the cook said humbly, 'is undoubtedly a gentleman of high standing.'

'If you say so,' Aisek grinned. 'But there's them that'd disagree. We're all in the shit together out here.'

The wind, cold off the snow-dusted hills, teased the canvas flap covering the entrance to the clapboard shop. Aside from the glow of the fire, banked low to conserve fuel, the smoky interior was dimly lit by hanks of wool floating in saucers of sheep grease. Neither their acrid smoke nor the reek of sheepskin garments half-cured in urine troubled Aisek Lee after nearly two decades in the frontier town among the hills where the Imperial jade was mined by exiles like himself.

He was, he reflected, as comfortable as he could be. He no longer was riven by the longing for his family or the revulsion from his primitive surroundings that had afflicted him until he learned to ignore both his anguish and his discomfort. He was finally reconciled to the graceless existence inflicted upon him by the previous Emperor's clemency. Despite his sons' occasional encouraging letters, he no longer indulged in the folly of hoping that his exile would be ended by a second act of Imperial clemency. Since he must spend the rest of his days in the wild north-west, he must simply endure its barbarous way of life.

Meanwhile, there was comfort in a full stomach, a glowing pipe, and the warming *bai-garh* – and the solace from the Uigur girl who waited in his felt yurt. He had lost count of the number of willing girls he had known. Though he enjoyed their bodies and their solicitude, he had never had the heart to enter into a regular liaison like most of his fellow exiles. Still yearning after Maylu, he could not bring himself to live permanently with a tribeswoman, though the practice was sanctioned by both law and custom. At least, he grinned, the ardour of his succession of young girls kept him young – and he could still satisfy them.

The twisted wool wicks flared when the wind flapped the canvas strip over the doorway. In the glare, Aisek's round face, seamed with fine wrinkles, glowed copper-red. Even his massive bald head was burnt bronze by the sun and the wind of the arid frontier province, some 2,000 miles from the refined pleasures of his native Shanghai. Broadened by years of hard labour, his shoulders were powerful under the greasy sheepskin coat, which he wore with the pelt turned inward. As chief foreman, an eminence attained because of his skill in accounting, he no longer toiled in the mines – and he lived as comfortably as a civilised man could among barbarians.

The canvas flap swept open, and a wizened man wearing the unadorned round cap of a *yamen* clerk entered the eating-shop. Aisek glanced up incuriously, while the Moslem cook bowed and scrambled to set out eating utensils for the newcomer. His minuscule establishment was rarely honoured by the governor's minions in the evening, since they preferred the comfort of their stone-built quarters in the *yamen*. The clerk ignored both the proprietor's abject greeting and the proffered food.

'*Ni, chia-huo* . . .' He addressed Aisek curtly, for the voluntary exiles of the *yamen* staff naturally despised the exiled criminals. 'You, fellow, come with me. His Excellency urgently requires your presence.'

Aisek resignedly knotted the strings of his coat and followed the runner into the night, which glittered with a tracery of stars. Shuffling through the dusty street, he wondered uneasily why the Governor had summoned him at such a late hour. Some irregularity in the accounts, perhaps. But he had meticulously ensured that no possible irregularity could be discovered. Although his accounts were in perfect order, he felt a thrill of apprehension as he entered the courtyard of the *yamen*. Taken to the Governor immediately, he was fearful. That bumbling Mandarin of the Sixth Grade habitually kept his convict charges waiting to demonstrate his power, for he had himself been assigned to the wilderness after the discovery of clumsy peculation his superiors thought not worth a formal trial.

'Sit down, Mr Lee, please sit down.' The Governor's pinched face contorted in forced amiability. 'A gentleman like you, there's no need to stand, even in my presence.'

Aisek was struck by acute fear. He had never in the past been invited to sit in the Governor's presence. Such courtesy from a strenuously rude official must portend trouble; the Governor was playing with him before pouncing like a terrier on a cornered rabbit. Had the incompetent *yamen* clerks actually broken the secret of his accounts? Though that was virtually impossible, Aisek's hands trembled on his knees as he waited for the Governor to speak.

'Honoured Mr Lee,' the vindictive official began, 'I take no pleasure in . . .'

Aisek sat silent, determined not to reveal the near-terror he felt at being addressed with elaborate courtesy by a man who normally treated him like a despicable slave.

'I take no pleasure at the prospect of being deprived of your valued services, honoured Mr Lee,' the Governor continued. 'But I feel great pleasure at being able to give you this communication from His Honour, Mandarin of the Third Grade Lee Dawei, despatched from the *yamen* of His Excellency the Mandarin Li Hung-chang, Viceroy of Chihli.'

The Governor passed a cloth-wrapped packet across his desk. He motioned for silence when Aisek offered his thanks and reverently slipped a scroll from its casing of Imperial-yellow silk. The Governor rose and bowed to the document.

'A rescript from His Imperial Majesty, the Son of Heaven.' The official's tone was unctuously respectful. 'A copy is being prepared for you. The Sacred Decree is, however, quite straightforward. Briefly, it has pleased His Majesty to grant you a full pardon in cognizance of certain irregularities in the proceedings that condemned you and in recognition of the outstanding services the Mandarins Lee Ailun and Lee Dawei have rendered the Sacred Dynasty. The Lord of Ten Thousand Years is, further, graciously pleased to ensure good auguries in this the year of his Coronation by this act of clemency.'

Astonished that the hope he had so long denied himself was realised in an instant, Aisek could not speak. He bowed his head to hide the tears that started in his eyes.

'You are free to return to your home whenever you wish, you know,' the Governor added. 'Even tonight if it pleases you. The Mandarin Lee Dawei's packet, I am informed, contains funds for your journey.'

'I'd like to be home by the end of the eleventh month,' Aisek finally declared. 'But it will take a week or two to wind up my small affairs here. Then I'll depart with joy.'

CHAPTER SEVENTY-ONE

December 28, 1873   *Shanghai*

The steel-blue gaslight glaring from the pillared portico of Jade House spilled on to the lawn that sloped gently for two hundred yards to Bubbling Well Road. Above the marble terrace six giant lanterns swayed in the light breeze, the giant *shou* – longevity – ideograms emblazoned on their oiled-paper skin gleaming scarlet. Hundreds of smaller lanterns flaring yellow in the December night outlined the three domes crowning the portico and sketched with strokes of fire the peaked roofs and the balustraded balconies of the long wings. The mansion was a fairy-tale castle – spun of light and air rather than stone and mortar.

'It's barbaric,' Fronah remarked to Gabriel as dusk gave way to night. 'But everybody for miles around will know the Haleevies have moved in.'

Nervously stroking his silvered beard, her father pretended he had not overheard that tart comment. He was almost sinfully proud of his new dwelling, though he wondered where he would find the money for the builders, not to speak of this night's extravagance. He could not now also worry about his daughter's mercurial temper.

He should, he supposed, already have told Fronah of her husband's death at the siege of Soochow ten years earlier – and shown her the proof: Lionel Henriques' misshapen signet-ring. But the six months' grace he had claimed from his wife had not yet expired. Nor did he believe the American, who had returned from Tientsin three days earlier, was Fronah's last chance for happiness as Sarah contended. He was, perhaps, unenlightened by the lax standards of cosmopolitan, mongrelised Shan-ghai, but he could not welcome a Gentile son-in-law.

His newest, grandest, and perhaps ruinous possession, Jade House, was illuminated for the coming New Year, Saul told himself, not for Christmas. It was ironic that a Jewish mansion in China should be *en fête* for the European New Year. The year 5634 of the Hebrew calendar had begun on September 22, 1873, while the Chinese would not hail the thirteenth year of the reign of the Tung Chih Emperor until February 17, 1874. However, the brilliant display also celebrated a far more important occasion.

'Sarah, it's just as well we built big,' Saul remarked defensively as he and his wife left their daughter and her lover. 'We could never have squeezed the whole family into the old house on Szechwan Road: Aaron, Judwei, and their three youngsters; David and Lochi and their two; plus Maylu and old Aisek. Not to speak of Judah, his mother, and her fancy man.'

'You always wanted to be a patriarch, Saul.' His wife ignored his scathing reference to the American. 'Enjoy it while you can.'

'While I can is correct,' he answered bitterly. 'You don't need to remind me we're balanced on a knife's edge.'

'I only meant we might never have them all together again, Saul. So, please, don't think about anything else tonight. Don't think of the expense or the business. Just enjoy it.'

Fronah and Gabriel remained beside each other on the lawn, though a little apart. The letters they had written during his three-month absence were long, intimate, and often passionate. But that exchange had not slaked their desire to tell each other everything from domstic trivia through their work for the Mandarin Li Hung-chang to speculation on the future of China. Those unsatisfying letters had actually intensified their need to confide in each other at first hand.

Gabriel had returned three days earlier to a tumult of words and a near surfeit of caresses, for the lovers were undisturbed in the Nest of Joy. Despite Saul's muttering, Sarah had already asked Judah to Jade House. Fearful of marring the joy of their reunion, the American had not raised the issue that was foremost in his mind until that morning, when they moved to the mansion, where their rooms were far apart in deference to Saul's sensibilities.

Since Fronah was as reticent regarding that vital question as she was otherwise forthcoming, Gabriel finally asked flatly what she had decided about his proposal. She had, she replied, thought about little else, which was quite true. She had, she added, asked her father about the Talmudic law and had made further inquiries at the British Consulate, which was quite untrue. The Talmud, she continued, made no provision for an abandoned wife, which was flatly untrue, while the Consul had advised that a divorce must be sought in London, perhaps of Parliament. That might even be true.

'So, you see, darling, it's impossible just now,' Fronah concluded. 'If only I knew about Lionel . . . knew *definitely*.'

'Well, Fronah, we'll just rub on as we are for a while.' Gabriel's tone was edged with anger. 'But we can't go on indefinitely. No, I'm not threatening . . . not yet. But I'm damned well going to find out what's really happened to Lionel Henriques – even if I have to take China apart brick by brick.'

Fronah felt a thrill of feminine triumph at that fierce affirmation of his devotion. She also felt contempt for herself. Why, she wondered, was she playing such a devious game? She took no malicious pleasure in tantalising Gabriel, but ached for his obvious distress. Perhaps she was afraid of committing herself. Perhaps she was simply perverse.

She feared he would soon force the issue, compelling her to leave her sanctuary of deception. Would she, Fronah asked herself, take a firm decision if the alternative were losing him? She simply did not know, and the mystery of Lionel's fate clouded her mind. She was, none the less, as content as she could be when tension hung almost palpable between them.

Gabriel Hyde watched his mistress's parents stroll along the marble terrace. Despite his anger, he smiled at their linked silhouettes, black against the lanterns' flare, which symbolised connubial joy for him, as paired mandarin ducks did for the Chinese. At least, as Fronah had assured him, they now knew he was Jewish by Mosaic law and, therefore, no longer opposed his suit. Determined to cut through the thicket of legal complexities that prevented their marriage, he was as content as he could be when her manner was so inexplicably strained.

In the reception hall Saul dutifully admired the scarlet poinsettias and the cacti that fringed their fleshy segmented leaves with purple flowerets only in December. Jade House was also bright with the albino and purple cattleyas among the orange bird-of-paradise flowers and the pastel tuberoses Sarah had brought into bloom in the three greenhouses where six gardeners were constantly at work. Her triumph, however, was the azaleas flaming orange, yellow, and crimson in jardinières along the mahogany-panelled walls of the dining hall. She was delighted at forcing them to flower out of season because her Chinese sons loved azaleas.

It all took money, Saul fretted, a great deal of money. He had promised Sarah not to think of the cost of Jade House tonight, and he would keep his promise – after some quick calculations. The outlay was at least 750,000 *taels*, almost a quarter of a million sterling, well over a million American dollars. Beside that immense sum, the staff's wages might appear trifling, but they were a continuing drain. Although a senior houseboy received less than two pounds sterling a month, the wage-bill was frightening because of the number he employed: twenty gardeners and grooms, as well as an indoor staff of fifty. Chinese labour was proverbially cheap, but not on that scale.

He strove to forget the expense when they strolled through drawing-rooms, sitting-rooms, and parlours adorned with silk wallpaper hand-painted in France – and furnished with antiques gathered throughout Europe. The Persian and Central Asian carpets alone represented an outlay of fifty thousand *taels*.

Bemused by the multiplicity of reception-rooms that the architects considered essential, he reckoned that he could comfortably entertain four times the two hundred-odd quests invited to tonight's banquet. Comfortably? Well, he wouldn't be particularly comfortable, but even that horde could almost lose itself in Jade House.

Despite the mahogany-panels glowing in the harsh light of gas-lamps hung with scarlet ribbons, the dining-hall was more intimate. Twenty round tables set with Chinese services for twelve almost filled it, though the enormous hanging scroll painted with a single vermilion longevity ideo-gram dwarfed the tables.

Saul shuddered when he thought of the extensive and expensive preparations in the three kitchens. The Sunya Restaurant had provided cooks to produce Chinese dishes for all the Chinese guests and most foreign guests. In the kosher kitchen his own cooks were preparing ritually slaughtered beef, lamb, and poultry, as well as the mock-sausages of soya-bean curd he loved.

Sarah and he had finally agreed they must serve non-kosher food, despite the additional cost of chinaware they could not use after it had been contaminated by eels, shrimps, and lobster, not to speak of snake, deer's sinews, and pork. At least the grapes, peaches, and figs came from his own greenhouses. But, he calculated gloomily, each hand-raised peach cost an eighth of a *tael*, four times as much as the mangoes shipped on ice from Malaya.

Saul Haleevie straightened his shoulders under his tail-coat and laughed softly. He might well be on the verge of bankruptcy. If he went down, he would certainly make a grand splash. His spectacular foundering would be long remembered, even if Jade House were later to be called Haleevie's Folly.

The great mansion was, however, an approriate setting for this celebra-tion. He owed the guest of honour more than he could repay in two lifetimes. Yet that guest could add so greatly to his financial burden as to crush him.

*

Aisek Lee had played no role in the firm of Haleevie and Lee since his arrest for the abominable crime of filial impiety more than nineteen years earlier. Sarah contended that the bribes Saul had poured out for Aisek's

491

defence actually exceeded their monetary debt to the Chinese merchant. She further maintained that they had lavishly repaid whatever moral debt they owed him by adopting his sons Aaron and David – and supporting them during their years of study for the Mandarinate.

Aisek was primarily responsible for their prosperity, her husband reminded her. Aisek's property, which Saul had claimed as his own to prevent its being confiscated by the Mandarins, was the foundation for the prodigous expansion of Haleevie and Lee. Since the firm's wealth was inseparable from his own, he could no longer distinguish what was Aisek's from what was his own. Calculating rigorously, he might find he owed Aisek far more than he could pay in his present difficulties. The most practical – and most just – solution was to make over to Aisek half of everything he possessed. That distribution could, however, mean half his debts if he were forced to sell in the present depressed market.

The crisis Saul had foreseen for some time was now upon him. Mercifully, the confrontation he dreaded had been delayed, for Confucian courtesy precluded his partner's forcing the issue only a week after his return. He would not do so, Saul believed, until he had fittingly celebrated his birthday. This 28th day of December, 1873, Aisek Lee, born in 1814, was sixty years old by Chinese reckoning. He had attained the age when, the Sage Confucius declared, no slander or rumour could trouble his serenity.

Aisek was happily preoccupied by his reunion with his sons and his concubine Maylu, as well as by meeting his son's families. He had not alluded to business matters directly, though he had observed – apparently casually, but ominously in Saul's judgment – that his old partner was obviously prospering mightily. Delighted with his five grandchildren, who were by Chinese law and practice Saul's grandchildren, rather than his own, and cushioned by the luxury of Jade House, the returned exile was apparently incurious regarding the affairs of Haleevie and Lee.

'Naturally, I can't live on your bounty forever,' Aisek had replied that morning when Saul observed that he must return to the firm as an equal partner. 'I'll find something of my own, though I'm in no hurry. Anyway, the firm doesn't need two taipans.'

That generosity had confirmed Saul's sense of obligation – and heightened his foreboding. Aisek obviously possessed no more than the clothes and the mementoes he had brought back from his penurious exile. Without capital, he could do nothing in Shanghai, and, after two decades, he was out of touch with current business practices. The Chinese merchant would undoubtedly be a burden for the rest of their lives, but Saul resolved that he would bear the burden gladly – if it did not crush him.

Aisek was, moreover, his partner, not his pensioner. He could hardly expect his partner to live in less splendour than himself, but he could hardly build another Jade House. Nor could he sell the mansion and divide the proceeds. He could not even sell the house on Szechwan Road in the depths of the depression, but had been glad to rent it to Khartoons' new manager. Yet Aisek must soon discover the reality behind the glittering facade of opulence. His partner was too shrewd for his present uninquistive goodwill to endure indefinitely.

Saul Haleevie smiled with conscious effort as he looked around the crowded dining-room. The loud conversation and the rattle of utensils was giving him a headache, but he had to smile. He could not allow the leaders of Shanghai's chief communities – Europeans, Jews, and Chinese – to see that he was gravely worried. Besides, he had to show a cheerful face to Aisek.

He smiled across the round table and lifted his cup to his partner. After the waiters cleared away the final dish, the noodles whose length symbolised long life, the inevitable Chinese ceremony was to be enacted. Saul shuddered at the medicinal *mao-tai* spirits and held his cup upside down to show that it was empty. Aisek grimaced in delight and filled his cup for another toast. Though his round face was flushed pink beneath its web of fine wringles and his bald dome was wet with perspiration, he offered still another toast to his partner.

The returned exile brushed food particles from his blue-silk jacket and turned his chair towards the open space beneath the great scroll displaying the longevity ideogram. Beside him, Maylu glowed in a mauve-satin gown embroidered with mandarin ducks and scarlet peonies. She sponged an imagined stain from her black-satin cuff, where tiny butterflies flitted among minute roses. Overjoyed at her man's return, the concubine was ecstatic at her belated acknowledgement as Aisek Lee's chief wife, who was his only wife as well. Maylu oscillated between childlike glee and the aloof dignity that befitted the first lady of the banquet.

Turning her own chair, she sat primly beside Aisek for a moment. But her high spirits were irrepressible, She waved gaily to Fronah, who was seated at the adjacent table, and lifted her cup in a toast.

'I never understood till this moment what Maylu went through all those years alone,' Fronah whispered to Gabriel. 'She put such a good face on it. She seemed cheerful, but she was always alone.'

'Alone,' Gabriel asked quietly, 'though she had you and the boys?'

'I know now she was always really alone.' Fronah's brooding mien was lightened by a gamine grin. 'Especially at night.'

Gabriel wisely said no more.

'Sa-law Sa-ha, lai . . .' Aisek gesticulated expansively. 'Saul, Sarah, come and sit beside us. It's as much your night as ours.'

When the Jewish couple flanked the Chinese couple, David and Aaron led their wives and children into the open space beneath the scroll. Both wore black surcoats over Mandarins' robes with hoof-shaped cuffs and skirts embellished with many-coloured billows. On David's breast shone the peacock of the third grade, on Aaron's the wild goose of the fourth.

The older brother, who was junior in official rank, but senior in familial authority, had pondered the propriety of their wearing their Court garments. As a judge, he was naturally proccupied with the law, which was virtually obsessed with the forms of Confucian propriety. He had finally acceded to David's argument that the ritual celebration of their father's sixtieth birthday permitted them to wear their surcoats to honour – and delight – him.

Aaron had been less amenable about the manner in which they should pay their respects. Although Aisek Lee was the father of their flesh, he had declared, Saul Haleevie was their legal father. By consenting to their adoption, whatever the circumstances, Aisek had renounced all claims upon his sons, whose names should properly be inscribed on the ancestral tablets of the Haleevie family, rather than the Lee family. David pointed out that the Haleevies kept no ancestral tablets, though Saul had written their Hebrew names in his great-grandfather's Bible. David further contended that they must kowtow to Aisek as if he were still their legal father. Aaron had regretfully ruled that kowtowing would be most irregular.

David then suggested that Saul and Sarah, their legal parents, should sit beside Aisek and Maylu, who, though not their mother, was owed reverence as their actual father's chief wife. Aaron was not amused and remained obdurate until David advanced a second proposition: they were still known as Lee, though they should legally be called Haleevie. Aisek Lee therefore merited their respect as the eldest member of the Lee family. A year older than Saul, he was the most senior in the family hierarchy. Although Aaron lacked David's pawky humour, he had laughed and agreed that they were not only permitted but required to pay profound respect to their 'uncle' Aisek Lee, who was, in effect, their 'father' Saul Haleevie's elder brother.

Emulated by their wives and children, the two Mandarins knelt and touched their foreheads to the Azerbijan carpet three times. After rising, they again fell to their knees and again touched their heads to the carpet three times. Upon the third repetition, the nine-fold prostration to their ancestor was complete.

The brothers then offered Aisek their presents. They did not touch him, since public display of affection was improper. Besides, they had already embraced him and rubbed their cheeks against his in private, even the bashful grandchildren.

'Saul, we are one family, are we not?' Aisek asked softly in his idiosyncratic mixture of Shanghainese and pidgin while the guests applauded. 'Just as we are one house in business, Haleevie and Lee. What is mine is yours, and what is yours is mine. Is that not true?'

Saul nodded automatically, striving to keep his features from mirroring his dejection. Why, he wondered miserably, had Aisek chosen this joyful moment to bring matters to a head? Despite his partner's benevolent air, exile had apparently made him hard and unfeeling.

'I know you spent a fortune on my defence, but you did take over my properties,' Aisek continued implacably. 'You sent me money in Heaven-blasted Kansu, but you've prospered greatly, haven't you? And your prosperity was built in great part on my property, was it not?'

'Aisek, I won't . . . can't . . . argue with you,' Saul said resignedly. 'You're entitled to half of all I own, though, I fear, it may be half my debts. Naturally, I'll sell Jade House and all my other holdings, but the market's heavily depressed. Still, I should get something . . .'

'You go too fast, Saul,' his partner chided. 'I've questioned not only my sons, but others. I know how straitened you are despite your outward prosperity. You'll not find me greedy, but only anxious for justice.'

'I'll sell everything and settle, as I said. I'll assume the firm's debts. I can't do more, can I?'

'Yes, Saul, you can! You can do much more!'

'What do you suggest?' Saul snapped. 'What do you want of me?'

'We are one house, as I said. You can buy now, when values are depressed.'

'Buy you said? Not sell? Aisek, I'm afraid you still don't understand. There are *no* funds . . . none whatsoever. How can I . . . we . . . buy?'

'*Yü ju chin*,' Aisek murmured.

'I'm sorry,' Saul replied in exasperation, 'but I don't understand.'

'I said jade is like gold, an old proverb. I didn't entirely waste my abundant time or my small talents in Kansu. I did a little trading, and I lived frugally. What could I buy in the wilderness? My stocks of jade were acquired openly and above board, though naturally with a little oil on the wheels. Briefly, that jade is worth some five million *taels*, perhaps more depending on the market. As you know, in hard times like these, Chinese buy jade for security. Shall we say roughly two million sterling? We'll begin paying off the debts. But not so fast that we arouse too much curiosity. And we'll buy land. Weren't you thinking of a cotton-mill? Other opportunities will certainly arise. We are one house, you and I – one family and one house.'

CHAPTER SEVENTY-TWO

February 17, 1874   *The Garden of Crystal Rivulets*
                                       The Summer Palaces near Peking

The lamas' saffron and magenta robes spilled like fallen berries over the marble platform and down the stairs leading to the Pavilion of Precious Clouds. Their heavy cassocks left their left shoulders bare despite the biting cold of the morning of February 17, 1874, the first day of the first month of the thirteenth year of the reign of the Tung Chih Emperor of the Great Pure Dynasty. The monks chanted sutras as grey-gossamer incense fumes swirled from their silver censers set with coral and turquoise. The black smoke of firecrackers drifted above the snow-spangled slopes of the Fragrant Hills to the west of the Garden of Crystal Rivulets.

Wearing the new surcoat over his best official robe and an expression of great solemnity, Mandarin of the Third Grade David Lee listened to the Buddhist prayers for the Imperial Family. The Sanskrit words, rendered phonetically – and meaninglessly – into Chinese ideograms, were entoned by Tibetan and Mongolian lamas who knew no Sanskrit and little Chinese. When he offered a prayer in Hebrew, David mused, he knew exactly what he was saying to the One True God.

Despite his distaste for the half-pagan liturgy, he was suffused with patriotic pride. After their long suspension, the resumption of the lama rites at the Pavilion of Precious Clouds testified to the resurgence of the Great Pure Dynasty, which foreigners called the Tung Chih Restoration.

He could again be proud to be Chinese. The Empire was recovering from its protracted humiliation by the foreign powers, which had begun with the First Opium War in 1840, intensified during the indecisive Arrow War, and culminated when the rape of the Summer Palaces in 1860 brought the Second Opium War to an ignominious conclusion. He could be doubly proud to be a senior Mandarin of the Ching Dynasty. Though the Manchus remained half-tamed savages who practiced barbaric rites, they ruled according to sound Confucian principles.

Actually a political and moral code, rather than the religion many foreigners thought it, Confucianism was itself forcefully adapting to the new age – just as Aaron and he had envisioned a decade earlier. Moreover, the material basis of Chinese civilisation was being vigorously modernised. Factory chimneys were rising, while railways would soon thrust their shining paths across the ancient land. Telegraph wires were already carrying urgent messages short distances, and paved roads were speeding transportation.

Most important in a hostile world, the Dynasty's reorganised military forces would soon be powerful enough to repel any new intruder. Mortars, cannon, and modern breech-loading rifles armed both the Baronet Jung Lu's Peking Field Force and the Mandarin Li Hung-chang's Army of Huai. Gunboats with steam engines patrolled Chinese waters, and armoured cruisers were to join the fleet. China would soon stand alone and unafraid.

Perhaps incongruously, the symbol of the new China in David's eyes was the Pavilion of Precious Clouds, beside which he stood among other Mandarins attending the Empress Dowager Yehenala and the Tung Chih Emperor. The people called it the Bronze Pavilion. Cast in the middle of the last century for the Great Chien Lung Emperor, it was a masterly amalgam of Chinese artistry with European technology. Damaged but not destroyed by Lord Elgin's conflagration some thirteen years earlier, the refurbished structure now towered over the intense activity that was rebuilding the Garden of Crystal Rivulets in the western quarter of the great structures of the site of the Summer Palaces near Peking.

Quintessentially Chinese in conception, the Bronze Pavilion triumphantly demonstrated Chinese artisans' mastery of European techniques originally learned from the Jesuits. The two-tiered roof with its long tiles and the partitions scrolled with water-chestnut patterns, as well as the peaked pinnacle and the nine-dragon plaque, were just like a traditional pavilion's. Unlike a pavilion of wood and stone, the 200-ton bronze structure would endure as long as Wan Shou Shan, Myriad Longevity Mount, which it crowned.

On the adjoining terrace, the golden palanquin of the Empress Dowager stood before a stack of raw beams that were to be the skeleton of an exact replica of the Tower of Buddha's Fragrance. Between the Imperial-yellow curtains that hid her from men's eyes, Yehenala watched the lama rite imploring Heaven to grant her longevity. Beside her palanquin stood the martial figure of the Baronet Jung Lu, the unicorn of a full general rippling on his chest. As the General whispered intimately through the silk curtains, David concluded that their affair was proceeding smoothly – unlike his sister Fronah's fraught relationship with Gabriel Hyde.

And why should it not? The General-Commandant of the Peking Field Force took immense pains to please his capricious Imperial mistress, who had raised him to that dignity. Yehenala held not only Jung Lu's career, but his life, in her soft palm. All men knew of their illicit love, but not even the most fearless Censor dared remonstrate with them as long as they did not violate propriety in public.

David chuckled, remembering the common jest about the conventions of England, which were almost as stringent under the prim Queen-Empress Victoria as the immutable taboos of the Manchu Court: 'You can do anything you want in Blighty – as long as you don't do it in public and frighten the horses.'

There was little danger of Yehenala's and Jung Lu's misbehaving in public and frightening the litter-bearers. They had ample opportunity to behave as they wished in the privacy contrived by the immensely powerful Chief Eunuch Li Lien-ying, who was called Cobbler's Wax Li by the irreverent and the Lord of Nine Thousand Years by the indignant.

A short distance from his mother's palanquin, the seventeen-year-old Tung Chih Emperor sat on a golden throne among his own entourage. David paid homage to the plump figure with the vacant expression as his sovereign, but was not impressed by the youth himself. Second only to intrigue as the Northern Capital's chief occupation, remarkably accurate gossip reported that the Emperor had recently almost committed his gross indiscretions in public. He had certainly frightened his Ministers.

None the less the Imperial mother and the Imperial son were not at odds or they would not have appeared together for the lama rites. The youth was certainly paying more attention to both his studies and his duties as he had promised his mother he would. He was, unfortunately, also bewildered by the domineering Yehenala's antagonism to the young Empress he had married a little more than a year ago. He was neglecting his wife to frequent the Flower Quarters, transparently disguised as a minor Manchu nobleman. He therefore suffered severely from the plum-poison sickness, the euphemism for syphilis. His sovereign the Tung Chih Emperor, David reflected irreverently, was at least as confused as his sister Fronah.

His mother, the gossips said, preferred that he debauch himself with Chinese harlots and transvestites rather than pay his attention to his ladies. That was almost certainly a canard. Even Mandarins who resented the absolute power of a female had invented stories to discredit Yehenala. David respected her because she was, however grudgingly, a prime mover of China's rapid progress.

As David watched, the Emperor strolled alone towards his mother's golden palanquin. He bowed respectfully before speaking, and he listened attentively to the reply through the Imperial-yellow curtains. A small hand with long fingernails sheathed in blue enamel darted out so rapidly David almost disbelieved his eyes and patted the youth's shoulder. While not a flagrant violation of Court Etiquette, that gesture of maternal affection in the sight of others was highly irregular – as Aaron might have said.

The spectacle David saw when his eyes ranged across the landscape proved that mother and son were united by a common purpose. The seven hundred acres of the ravaged Garden of the Crystal Rivulets had become a vast construction site, where hosts of coolies hauled building materials for armies of craftsmen. Never before had David seen such abundant energy expended on any public enterprise.

Almost two years had passed since the Mandarin Li Hung-chang conceived his stratagem of engaging Yehenala's excessive energy in rebuilding the Summer Palaces so that professional administrators like himself could reconstruct the nation undisturbed. Both Yehenala and the Emperor were now convinced that it was their own idea. The Mandarin had, unfortunately, convinced neither the conservatives, who opposed him in most matters, nor the moderates of his own camp – not to speak of the radical intelligentsia, who flourished in the sanctuaries of the Treaty Ports. Such lavish expenditure on an unproductive project was denounced by some who believed the impoverished should receive that money and by others who demanded that it build factories and buy armaments. Moreover, Yehenala still intervened capriciously in affairs of state, though perhaps not quite as frequently. But the Mandarin had reconciled some of the differences between the Empress Dowager and the Emperor in their mutual passion for building.

David Lee joined the stream of Princes and Mandarins flowing down the hill to the shore of Kunming Lake behind the Imperial palanquins. As the representative of a regional potentate among the grandees of the central government, he hung back from the front rank. As the representative of the Empire's premier Viceroy, whom he could not demean by excessive modesty, he placed himself firmly in the second rank. Yet these pompous Imperial inspections were tedious despite their political significance. David was bored, and his thoughts wandered.

A month after leaving Shanghai, he was still distressed – and bemused – by the tension between his sister Fronah and his friend Gabriel, both of whom he loved. When the great family party at Jade House dispersed, Fronah had returned with her son Judah to the Nest of Joy, while Gabriel had moved his belongings to Willards Hotel. Though the lovers still spent their free time together, that separation was symbolic of the rift that divided them.

David alone knew all the ramifications of their disagreement. Fronah and Gabriel had confided in him individually, while he and Aaron had brought the news of Lionel Henriques's death to Saul Haleevie.

Fronah did not know that she was a widow because Saul still stubbornly refused to tell her – and thus free her to marry Gabriel. Saul did not know that Gabriel was Jewish by Mosaic law because Fronah would not tell him – and be forced to a decision when her father withdrew his opposition to the American.

His sister, David reflected, was playing a dangerous game. She was lying to her lover, assuring him that she had already told her father he was an eligible suitor. That fact – and Fronah's duplicity – might emerge in conversation between Saul and Gabriel. The merchant's secret was more secure. His wife would not betray it, though she thought him wilfully wrong-headed. Filial piety bound his adoptive sons not to reveal Lionel Henriques's death, though they were distressed by the impasse.

Gabriel Hyde had found that Fronah was telling the proximate truth regarding the obstacles to divorce under British law. He had not asked Saul about the Talmud's provision – or lack of provision – to free an abandoned wife. He was unlikely to do so, since he trusted Fronah. Besides he would not embarrass her by approaching her father, the only authority on Jewish law in the Foreign Settlement to whom he could decently appeal.

David winced when he recalled his torturous evasions of the American's enquiries regarding Lionel Henriques. Without lying outright, he had conveyed the impression that Aaron and he had searched in vain for any evidence regarding the Englishman's fate after the fall of Soochow. He could in honour no more reveal Saul's secret to Gabriel and his sister than he could tell his adoptive father that Gabriel was Jewish.

Saul's attitude was unreasonable, but logical within the framework of his prejudices. Fronah's attitude, David concluded in exasperation, was irrational and self-destructive. If she wanted Gabriel, she should take him. If she did not want him, she should dismiss him.

David bowed abstractedly to the Imperial palanquins and wished he could force Fronah to behave sensibly. He sensed that she was afraid of the responsibility of marriage after one disastrous experience. He knew that she was also afraid of losing Gabriel. Her opposed fears cancelled each other, leaving her frozen in indecision.

Fronah was not only a capable and mature woman, who badgered taipans to support her children's home and efficiently carried out the Mandarin Li Hung-chang's assignments. She was also, in part, still a timorous girl, who had always been indulged and protected. Instinctively looking to her father to solve her problems, she was equally afraid of defying Saul or gaining his consent, which would require her to decide for herself.

David lifted his hand to scratch his head in perplexity. His fingers touched the upturned sable rim of his Court hat surmounted by a golden finial crowned with the sapphire of his rank and the peacock-plume decoration awarded for bravery against the Taipings. He dreaded the formal banquet the Emperor was to give later that day for a thousand Princes and Mandarins. The forced jollity would be exhausting, and the coarse drunkeness of the Manchus would be revolting. He would himself have a splitting headache the next morning.

Yehenala and Niuhura were to give a banquet for the court ladies. The women would not drink as strenuously as the men, but they would still drink. Probably, Yehenala alone would remain relatively sober, for her excess was not wine, but food. Her brigade of cooks had invented an extraordinary variety of fanciful dishes for the Grand Court Banquets of the junior Empress Dowager.

Though he found bear's paws stringy, greasy, and tasteless, they were respectable because the Sage Mencius had mentioned that dish with approval. What, David wondered, would the sages of antiquity have made of the ostentatious extravagance of camel's hump, rhinoceros's liver, elephant's trunk, scaly ant-eater, and crushed baroque pearls? Those grotesqueries would appear on the Empress Dowager's table among even more disgusting Manchu delicacies to fill out the full two hundred fifty-four courses. Just thinking of that excess was almost enough to drive him to kosher food, though he considered the Hebraic dietary laws somewhat archaic in this modern age.

The golden palanquins of the Empress Dowager and the Emperor had arrived at Künming Lake, where state barges waited to carry them back to the Northern Capital. The conflict between that son and his mother, David mused, was a reflection in a crazed mirror of the impasse between his sister and her father. Both pairs were bound by deep love, and both were tormenting each other.

Determined that her son must be a paragon among Emperors, Yehenala could not relax the domination that prevented his attaining maturity. Since she would not even allow him to live affectionately with his wife, the resentful Emperor fled to the dangerous pleasures of the Flower Quarters. That convoluted revenge and his mother's concern might well destroy him.

500

Manchus, even Chinese, after all, behaved as illogically as foreigners. Perhaps all human beings were equally irrational when moved by violent emotion.

CHAPTER SEVENTY-THREE

June 19, 1874   *Shanghai*

THE COMPLETION OF THIS HOUSE OF WORSHIP [the gold inscription on the black-marble plaque declared in English, Hebrew, and Chinese] WAS MADE POSSIBLE BY THE GENEROUS SUPPORT OF MESSRS AISEK LEE AND SAUL HALEEVIE OF THE HOUSE OF HALEEVIE AND LEE. Smaller script beneath read: *This plaque was unveiled by Saul Haleevie on June 19, 1874 on the joyous occasion of the bar mitzvah of his grandson, Judah.*

Entering the vestibule in haste, Gabriel Hyde glanced at the plaque before easing open the double doors to the hall of worship. He accepted a purple-striped prayer-shawl and a black silk skull-cap from a stooped verger and tip-toed among the benches occupied entirely by men. Slipping into a seat, he draped the shawl over his shoulders and placed the skull-cap on his head.

The service was almost over. He had just managed to keep his promise to thirteen-year-old Judah to return from Tientsin in time for the confirmation that recognised Fronah's son as a grown man in Israel.

The bright June morning could not penetrate the synagogue, since curtains were drawn over the windows in the dome with the scalloped gold lip around its base. The gas-lamps were turned up only half-way to avoid glare. In the glow of the gas-lamps, Gabriel saw the rabbi standing on Judah's right. Behind the altar draped with white satin, open gilt doors revealed the purple-velvet curtains of the Ark of the Covenant, which housed the sacred Torah, the Scroll of the Law. His prayer-shawl draped over his Sabbath robe, Saul Haleevie beamed beside his grandson. Grave in his blue suit, Judah was chanting in Hebrew from a prayer-book held in both hands. Apart from his blond hair and his grey eyes, the youth was an unbearded replica of his grandfather. The same thoughtful features were dominated by the same finely arched nose. He glanced towards the balcony where the women sat with shawls covering their heads, and his wide mouth quirked in a half-smile.

With a nod of thanks, the American took the open prayer-book his neighbour offered. He began reading at the place indicated by his

501

benefactor's long index-finger, pleased that he still remembered the angular Hebrew letters. The pronunciation was quite different from that taught at Bowdoin College, but he could follow the sonorous prayer.

Gabriel turned to look up at the women's balcony. Fronah sat beside her mother in the front row. The lime-green tissue-silk of her bodice beneath the familiar treble rope of black Caspian pearls contrasted with Sarah's orange kaftan worked with silver arabesques. Fronah fluttered her finger-tips and pursed her lips for an instant. He smiled before turning to face the altar.

Aaron and David's Mandarin casques bobbed in the front row beside Aisek's massive head, which was crowned by a black cylinder with a fluted top somewhere between a chef's toque and the stiff-winged biretta of a Ming Dynasty Grand Secretary. Glancing around the congregation, the American saw a number of familiar faces among a Jewish community that had quadrupled during the past decade: Judah Benjamin, Moses Elias, the Gubbi brothers, and Carl Weinstein. Among new acquaintances he recognised Joshua Nathan, who had replaced Saul as Khartoon's manager in Shanghai, and the young prince of the regal Sassoon family, who was called Eddie. Some of the bearded faces with their well-fed curves and their assertive noses were too full-blooded for Gabriel's spare Yankee taste, while the ascetic faces with hooded eyes like Old Testament prophets were almost frighteningly intense. Another part of him responded thirstily to their zest for life and their confident piety.

'Grandfather and Grandmother, Mother, Uncles, and Friends.' Judah spoke in English. 'I am deeply grateful that you have all come to see me initiated into the community of the descendants of Abraham, Isaac, and Jacob. As I survey this tabernacle dedicated to the worship of the Creator of the Universe, I am proud to be a man in Israel. No longer a child, I am deeply grateful to my family, who . . .'

Judah spoke with feeling and had obviously given much thought to his words. But these valedictory orations were always much the same, the immutable *vale atque ave*: bidding farewell to childhood and hailing the challenge of manhood. Could the boy, Gabriel wondered, possible realise that a man's life was a succession of such epochal transitions? Even a thirteen-year-old as intelligent as Judah could hardly appreciate that he was crossing the first of many great divides, which would not be smoothed by formal rites and public admiration.

A half year earlier, he himself had passed his fortieth birthday, a deep river studded with perilous rocks, while Judah was crossing a shallow brook tumbling over smooth stones. Fronah was herself approaching her thirty-fifth-year, half the alloted three score and ten. He had known her since she was sixteen, but had *known* her in the Biblical sense, Gabriel smiled, for little more than a year.

Yet he had always loved Fronah, he realised, above all other women he knew, indeed above all possible women. He smiled again as he recalled

502

that he had for years thought his affection was avuncular. Avuncular? Hardly! She had always been – and always would be – the most fascinating and perplexing, the most irritating and alluring woman in the world to him. To his shame, he could hardly recall poor Jane's features. Fronah's piquant, tawny-haired image floated before Jane's fair serenity in all his reveries.

Perplexing and irritating? Fronah was worse than that. She was infuriating. This time he must overcome her stubborn elusiveness. If she rebuffed him, he would leave her – though he wanted nothing less in all the world. He'd be damned if he would allow the present impasse to persist indefinitely.

Only his protracted absences, the American speculated, had forestalled the confrontation that could blast all his hopes. He had left Shanghai in late February, returning for a few weeks in April before the Mandarin Li Hung-chang summoned him again to Tientsin. Only because the Chinese considered family obligations sacrosanct was he not still in North China. When requesting leave to attend his nephew's confirmation, David had remarked that the American was virtually a member of his family. The Mandarin smiled knowingly and finally allowed Gabriel to catch the coaster from which he had just disembarked.

He could no longer postpone the confrontation. He had promised the Mandarin he would return after a week, and he had used Judah's bar mitzvah to obtain the brief leave because he was resolved to have an answer from Fronah. He wanted her to be his wife, and he wanted her beside him, rather than a thousand miles away at the end of a capricious courier service. He was too old to scurry back and forth like a romantic twenty-year-old.

If her fear of losing him overcame her apparent fear of the obligations of marriage, he felt, Fronah would at last commit herself. Possibly, her horror of irrevocable commitment would prevail. She, who was so self-sufficient, might choose to stand alone rather than marry him. Well, he would just have to risk it.

'We thank Thee, oh Lord, for the speedy resolution of the conflict between our fellow guests, the French, and our Chinese hosts,' Judah was declaiming. 'We thank Thee, also, for the peace that has during the past few months succeeded the rioting and slaughter which provoked bitterness between foreigners and Chinese throughout the Empire. In Thy infinite wisdom, Thou hast . . .'

Looking down from the women's balcony, Fronah's eyes strayed from her son's portentousness to her lover's immobility. She reached out her hand as if she could touch his black hair across the distance, and her pulse fluttered. After their long separation, she knew that she loved Gabriel totally and desired him urgently. She wanted to put her arms around his neck and press close to him.

Fronah glanced sideways to assure herself that her mother, still intent on

Judah, had not noticed her emotion. She smiled self-deprecatingly. It was quite unseemly, such youthful fervour in the mother of the tall thirteen-year-old who was today a man in Israel. But she could not help her ardour. No more, unfortunately, could she help her indecisiveness. She despised herself for prevaricating, but she could not help that either.

Possibly her vacillation would drive Gabriel away. He was not a patient man, despite the nearly saintly indulgence he had displayed for almost a year. However, he was not growing cold towards her, but the contrary. Yet his recent letters had been impatient. If she did not make up her mind soon, she might find herself alone again.

Judah was a delight and, sometimes, a comfort, but he had never truly belonged to her. His affection usurped as a child by her mother, Maylu, and the amahs, he now spent most of his time with her father. Immersed in his studies and fascinated by commerce, Judah was detaching himself from her. She would not be a clinging mother, but whom else could she cling to?

Sarah Haleevie glanced curiously at her daughter. Fronah had drawn herself upright, and her mouth was set in resolution. Sarah looked down at Gabriel's bent head and smiled. But her eyes were troubled.

She would say 'Yes,' Fronah decided abruptly. She would accept Gabriel and worry about the consequences later. She could do no less in fairness to him, as well as herself. She would agree today to marry him.

But there was still the spectre of Lionel. Could he have survived, as she now half-feared? It was not likely. If only she knew definitely, she could stop her wavering. She had not asked her father, but she was virtually certain that the *Talmud*, which provided for all eventualities, must provide relief for a wife so long abandoned. Re-marriage for a woman in her equivocal position was difficult under British law, but the obstacles were not insuperable. She could, Fronah told herself, be the mistress of her own fate – if only she could make up her mind.

'. . . these many blessings Thou hast seen fit to bestow upon us.' Judah was approaching his peroration. 'And we thank Thee, oh Lord, for our family's renewed prosperity after a time of anxiety. We thank Thee, also, for the renewed prosperity and vigour, as well as the assured hope of a glorious future, Thou hast vouchsafed to this land, where we are guests.

'We pray that Thou willst continue to look after Thy chosen people like an all-wise father, wherever they may be, however distant from Jerusalem they may find themselves.' Judah looked at his Chinese uncles. 'Finally, we pray that the people of Israel in this far land, whether new arrivals or dwellers in China for tens of generations, will always be as one.'

*

The luncheon at Jade House to celebrate Judah's coming of age was quite informal, unlike the banquet that had celebrated Aisek's sixtieth birthday. But it was far larger. More than four hundred guests drifted through the

504

reception-rooms of the mansion towards the mahogany-panelled dining-hall, where long tables offered a spectacular buffet. Consuls and army officers of six nations greeted Mandarins and Chinese merchants. Naval officers and foreign Commissioners of the Imperial Maritime Customs chatted to European ladies in flower-sprigged summer frocks. Though Maylu held court attended by Aaron's and David's embarrassed wives in a secluded parlour, no other Chinese ladies were present.

Saul Haleevie had exchanged his Sabbath robes for a white linen suit. He was simply more comfortable dressed like other men, he told himself, though he had, of course, not altered in any fundamental aspect.

He remembered the awkward supplicant who had begged Her Britannic Majesty's Consul, the almighty Rutherford Alcock, to intercede for Aisek Lee almost twenty years earlier. Alcock, now Minister to Japan, would probably not recognise him today as the alien in the robes of Baghdad who had pleaded in clumsy English. Jubilantly accepting his distinguished guests' congratulations, Saul himself hardly recognised that awkward figure in the self-assured magnate he had become.

He fingered the metallic lump in his jacket pocket, knowing he would have to show Fronah her husband's signet-ring this afternoon. Sarah pointed out that his six months's grace had already lasted a year. If he did not tell Fronah today, Sarah said implacably, she would do so herself. Though it was his responsibility to break the impasse his animus against a Gentile son-in-law had created, she would consider herself released from her pledge of silence.

The powerful merchant irresolutely watched his daughter chatting with Samuel Moses on a chintz-covered sofa. He hated to reveal to Fronah that he was not only less than omnipotent, but somewhat less than wholly honourable. Yet his sin was only an omission, and he resented the guilt he felt as he approached the sofa.

'My dear, I hate to disturb you,' he interrupted. 'But your mother needs some help.'

Sammy Moses rose with alacrity. He not only understood that domestic matters required his hosts' attention, but he was, Saul saw with gratification, still a little afraid of his former employer.

'What does Mama want?' Fronah asked lightly.

'It's not your mother, Fronah. I've got something to tell you . . . something important.'

'It must be important if it can't wait till the party's over,' she laughed. 'What's so pressing?'

'It's waited too long, your mother says. Let's go into the library.'

Puzzled by his terseness, Fronah followed her father through the throng. Her mother was talking animatedly with Gabriel Hyde. He touched Fronah's arm to remind her they would soon be alone together. Sarah glanced from her daughter to her husband and nodded smiling encouragement to Saul. Her smile was, however, strained.

Fronah looked at her father in surprise when he locked the teak door of the library.

'Now,' she demanded. 'what's this great mystery?'

'Sit down, my dear,' he directed. 'Please sit down.'

As she settled into a red leather armchair, he stared abstractedly at the crammed bookcases reaching to the plaster roses of the cornice. Vaguely apprehensive, Fronah waited.

'You know I told you we couldn't find out about Lionel . . . your husband . . . what happened to him.'

'Yes, Papa. I know you tried hard.'

'Well, it wasn't true,' he said gruffly. 'It wasn't then, and it isn't now.'

'Not true? What do you mean? What's not true?'

'Lionel . . . he . . . I *do* know. He's gone, Fronah, gone.'

'I know he's gone. If that's all you . . .' she began irritably. 'Do you mean you finally know *where* he's gone? You've heard from him? Why didn't he get in touch with me? But you know where he is?'

'Fronah, I've known since the beginning of 1864, more than ten years ago,' he said tonelessly. 'Your husband was . . . was killed at the siege of Soochow. Aaron and David . . .'

'How could you have known so long and not told me?' she flared. 'It's just a trick you're playing. Mama's put you up to it because she's so keen for Gabriel. Please tell her I'll make up my own mind in my own time. Tell her not to try to . . .'

'Fronah, it's no trick. Aaron and David, they found his . . . they found Lionel. He was . . . was gone.'

'How could you be so underhanded . . . keep it from me all these years? You're just saying what you think is best for me. I don't . . . I can't believe you. If it's true, why didn't you tell me sooner?'

'We didn't want to shock you . . . didn't want to make you worse. You were still sick, remember.' Saul placated her. 'Believe me, dear, Lionel is dead. You're free to marry your . . . your friend Gabriel. He's a good man, I suppose, for a Gentile. But Lionel is unquestionably dead. Ask David if you don't believe me.'

Fronah sat staring at the gold-leaf lettering on the vellum-bound *Decline and Fall of the Roman Empire*. Gibbon, what a funny name, she thought inconsequentially, an eminent historian called after a monkey. The title dissolved into a yellow haze of tears. Faint sorrow contended with relief in her heart. It all seemed so long ago, and she was now free to marry Gabriel – *if* she wished.

'I *will* ask David,' she finally said. 'I think I believe you, Papa. But I want to know how . . . how he died. Papa, how *could* you keep it from me so long?'

'In the beginning it was necessary . . . for your health. Afterwards, it was somehow never the right time. Your mother's convinced I was wrong.

'I'm sorry, dear, very sorry about Lionel . . . and not telling you. I'm a stubborn old man, maybe a foolish old man.'

Fronah rose and linked her arm through Saul's. Standing on her toes, she kissed his cheek.

'Not foolish,' she said softly. 'But certainly stubborn. That's where I get it from, I suppose. And that's all there is to tell?'

'Aaron can tell you more. Aaron found . . . this after the battle.' He handed her the misshapen ring. 'Aaron was very fond of Lionel, you know.'

Fronah's fingertips traced the incised coat of arms on the tarnished gold. When she turned away, Saul pressed his handkerchief into her hand. He stood beside the fireplace, irresolutely fingering the books, while she dabbed at her eyes.

'Please leave me alone for a minute,' she finally asked hoarsely. 'I don't know how I should . . . how I really feel. But I'll be all right, I promise you.'

His tall frame stooped, Saul Haleevie unlocked the teak door. As he straightened his shoulders to meet his guests, he heard the key turn in the lock. His wife, he saw, was still talking with Gabriel Hyde. His eyes sought Aaron and David among the throng, for he needed his adopted sons.

Fronah sat unmoving in the red-leather chair, her hands clasped in her lap. Her expression was calm, though tears stained her cheeks. She finally knew that Lionel had died among the fanatical Taipings. The unhappy man who was her husband and the father of her son had met death alone amid the horrors of the sack of Soochow. She would probably never know who killed him, the Taipings or the Imperialists.

As if that mattered after all these years! She smiled ruefully. It mattered not at all to Lionel, and it hardly mattered to herself.

What of herself? She was a widow, free to marry Gabriel. Yet her new freedom did not matter terribly at the moment.

*

When Saul astonished Aaron by asking for a large brandy in the early afternoon, his wife was still chatting with Gabriel Hyde. They had bantered for some time, he praising her grandson's maturity while she feigned modesty she did not feel.

'Gabriel, tell me,' Sarah asked idly.'Do you read Hebrew? I was watching you in the synagogue. You seemed also to feel at home.'

'My dear Sarah, everyone studied Hebrew . . . along with Latin and Greek . . . at Bowdoin College.' The American's negligent manner concealed his shock. 'Though your pronunciation's different from that we . . .'

'I see now. So that's the reason.'

'Of course, Sarah.' Gabriel was pricked by guilt at his own deviousness. 'That's the reason.'

'It's hard to explain, but I had the feeling it was all familiar to you,' she explained. 'Most Gentiles find our services strange and . . .'

'Not to me,' he relented. 'I'm hardly unaccustomed to the synagogue. My uncle David used to take me on the High Holy Days.'

'Your uncle? Oh, a friend of the family. Like the Chinese, you called him Uncle?'

'Not quite, Sarah,' he replied. 'Uncle David was my mother's brother.'

'You're joking, Gabriel. How can that be?'

'Simply because they had the same mother and father.' Suddenly annoyed, he demanded: 'Didn't Fronah tell you my mother was Jewish?'

Sarah hesitated for a tell-tale moment. Recovering, she smiled self-deprecatingly.

'Of course she did. I just forgot. I'm getting old, and sometimes my wits wander.'

'Or perhaps *she* forgot, Sarah.' Gabriel's flat tone masked her rising irritation. 'Perhaps she *just* forgot.'

'Maybe that's it. Maybe she forgot. But it doesn't matter now, does it?'

Joy swept aside Sarah's confusion. Saul could no longer object to Gabriel who, she assured herself, had been her own favourite from the beginning. If only they had known when they pressed Fronah to marry Lionel Henriques. It was too late for regrets, but it was not too late for Fronah and Gabriel.

'That's wonderful, Gabriel,' she exulted. 'Now you two can marry. Oh, Gabriel, I'm so happy. And I know you and Fronah will be wonderfully happy. So much happier than she was with Lionel.'

'A minute, Sarah.' Gabriel was, in turn, confused. 'I'm flattered, but there *is* one small obstacle. What about Lionel . . . her husband?'

'Husband? She has no husband.' Sarah was imprudent in her jubilation. 'We've known for years that Lionel was killed at Soochow. It was terrible . . . all alone among the Chinese. Never mind, though. The important thing is you and Fronah can get married. There's no obstacle.'

'No obstacle at all, really?' Gabriel asked in cold anger. 'You mean she could have married me at any time?'

'That's right, Gabriel, no obstacle at all.' Her normal acuity failed in her delight. 'It's wonderful.'

Sarah did not realise that her unthinking enthusiasm was confirming the fallacious impression she had already given the American. He was firmly convinced that Fronah had known for a decade of Lionel's death at Soochow. He had a few minutes earlier learned with acute irritation that his mistress had not told her parents of his Jewish blood as she said she had. He now concluded with mounting anger that she had also concealed her knowledge of her husband's fate from him.

The twofold deceit enraged Gabriel. He knew that Fronah was inclined to cut the truth to suit her own comfort, but he could never have imagined that she would unabashedly prevaricate regarding such vital matters. No, not prevaricate! That euphemism was far too kind. She had lied outright, not once, but twice, the American concluded in fury.

Fronah could have overcome her father's opposition to her marrying a presumed Gentile with a few words at any time during the past year. Moreover, she should have revealed Lionel's death when he asked her to marry him. Up to that moment, her widowed state was, perhaps, her own concern – to be kept secret if she wished. However, after he proposed marriage, she was bound by honour to tell him.

He could only conclude that she had never had any desire to marry him – or any interest in him beyond a brief affair. Otherwise, why should she have dissimulated so shamelessly? She did not love him, he decided, but was only playing with him. Perhaps it had amused her to pretend to consider his proposal though she had no intention whatsoever of accepting him.

Gabriel Hyde was profoundly wounded. His pride and his self-esteem were shattered. Though he had schooled himself to curb his violent temper, his fury made him virtually incapable of rational thought.

'Mrs Haleevie, I'm the one whose memory is going.' His sudden formality surprised Sarah, for he had not called her Mrs Haleevie in years. 'It's a shame, but I've just remembered the training exercise at the Arsenal. I only got leave by promising to report on it.'

'You're going right now? But you've just got here. Well, if you must. Anyway, we'll see you this evening.'

'Please tell Fronah I'm sorry I forgot my appointment.' Behind his unruffled demeanour, Gabriel was inflamed by rage at having been so callously manipulated. 'Tell her I'm very sorry and . . .'

'Yes, Gabriel?' she prompted. 'What else shall I tell Fronah?'

Perhaps he should not leave abruptly in anger, he cautioned himself. But his rage peremptorily rejected that counsel. Why should he endure further humiliation?

'Nothing else, Mrs Haleevie,' he said. 'Just tell her I'm sorry. Tell her I'm terribly sorry about . . . about everything!'

CHAPTER SEVENTY-FOUR

September 11, 1874   *The Garden of Crystal Rivulets*
                                      The Summer Palaces near Peking

The lieutenant of the Imperial Guard seated himself gingerly on the pile of untrimmed cedar beams, propped his feet on a rough-hewn marble block, and wiggled his toes. He was grateful for the break in his monotonous rounds, though for little else. The rigid-soled riding boots that enabled mounted archers to stand erect in their stirrups for surer aim, were cumbersome when a man was on foot. The burdensome footgear was, unfortunately, prescribed for the full-dress uniform required by the ceremonial duty he was performing.

Patrolling the Imperial Precincts of the partially rebuilt Garden of Crystal Rivulets was classified by the Guard's Manual as direct attendance upon the Emperor, though the Lord of Ten Thousand Years might be miles away in the Forbidden City. The onerous watch on the ruins of the Summer Palaces was assigned to the most junior subalterns. That duty required the officer of the day to stumble by the dim light of lanterns swinging in the hands of his resentful men among the building materials that littered the construction site and the excavations that yawned like tiger-traps.

The subaltern was as resentful as his grumbling subordinates, though a diversion had come their way in the mid-September dusk. The responsibility suddenly thrust upon him promised no possible reward, but certain disgrace if anything went amiss.

A half hour earlier, the Tung Chih Emperor had disembarked from his barge at the pier of the Pavilion of Auspicious Twilight, heralded by a bustle of eunuchs and a clatter of troopers. Ten minutes later, his nineteen-year-old Empress Aluta arrived amid a rustle of ladies-in-waiting. Except for the indispensable five eunuchs admonished to sit unspeaking and unmoving in the lower storey of the Pavilion, the entire entourage had been summarily dismissed by the Emperor, who desired the privacy denied him in the Forbidden City. Before reluctantly withdrawing, the colonel commanding the Sovereign's Bodyguard had tapped the subaltern on the shoulder.

'Over to you, Lieutenant,' he said. 'His Majesty doesn't know your unit's here. If anything happens . . . or *he* discovers you hanging around . . . you're for the high jump. You hold the life of the Dynasty in your hands tonight. Keep close watch, my boy, and think of the honour.'

Skulking among paint-pots, bricks, and timber in the bare garden of the gutted Hall of Jade Billows was not the subaltern's idea of honourable duty. Besides, his feet ached, and itched. Though damnably thirsty, he did not dare take a pull on the flask that dangled at his belt. To be caught with spirits on his breath tonight would mean a scarifying reprimand even if nothing went wrong. If the slightest incident occurred, he could pay for that transgression with his head. Honour indeed!

He yawned and scratched his sweaty chest under his heavy tunic. The evening was close, and a half-toppled wall blocked the light breeze blowing off Kunming Lake. He looked with yearning at the light flickering through the shades enclosing the rear terrace of the Pavilion of Auspicious Twilight. As the dusk deepened, he saw the yellow loom of the lanterns on the front terrace over the water.

Some Manchus had all the good luck under Heaven. That fellow on the front terrace, who was exactly his own age, eighteen years and five months, was undoubtedly lolling in a silk-cushioned long-chair and sipping wine with the lovely Aluta. The Emperor had so many women that he'd just sent away a score of the most beautiful ladies in the Empire. And all because he'd picked the right father. Well, the subaltern grinned, the Emperor hadn't been quite so clever in picking his mother, who made his life a misery. Even so, he wouldn't mind changes places with that fellow. While he sat lonely and bored on a pile of rough timber that cut into his buttocks, he heard his sovereign's tenor voice raised in glee.

The Tung Chih Emperor of the Great Pure Dynasty was actually looking over the balustrade at Kunming Lake and shouting at his Empress. He did not care who overheard him, for he had learned how intimidating Imperial rage could be. Not only his mother could awe her most courageous subjects and subdue her most vexatious counsellors by a display of fury. Unfortunately, even his most ferocious anger could not alter his predicament that night.

'Not a single penny did We get from the entire mess,' he shouted indignantly. 'Not a single shaved silver *tael* or one Shansi copper cash with a dirty great hole in the middle.'

'No one blames Your Majesty for the scandal,' Aluta soothed him. 'Your Majesty's honesty is a byword throughout . . .'

'Every son of a turtle-bitch in Peking says the opposite, Aluta,' he exploded. 'And do stop all that Majesty rubbish or you'll get smacked. Speak like a woman to a man. Say "you," not "Majesty".'

'As Your Maj . . . as you wish,' she replied docilely. 'If you'll come and sit beside me and drink a cup of *mao-tai*. It'll help you relax.'

'*Kua* . . .' he slipped into the self-pitying term reserved for the Emperor. 'This Orphan relax tonight? The whole damned world's against me. And the Gods are laughing with spite in Heaven.'

'All you wanted, my love, was to give *her* a nice present for her fortieth birthday. Everyone knows you were just being a filial son. But *she* . . .'

'We . . . I . . . I won't have you speak that way about the Empress Dowager, Aluta. My mother had nothing to do with this mess. Why she . . . she . . . ah . . . she . . . ah . . .'

The Emperor sputtered and pinched his nostrils with his thumb and forefinger. None the less the sneeze exploded into his hand and recurred six times. After carefully examining the slime dripping from his fingers, he wiped them on the tail of his silk-gauze robe, just below the nine dragon-circles scrolled in gold thread.

'Seven times,' Aluta counted. 'Everyone knows that Heaven sends seven sneezed for luck. My mother always says . . .'

'I don't give a damn what your mother says, Aluta. The stink of paint and wood-shavings always makes me sneeze. At least there's no blood in the snot tonight, but my mouth feels like a sewer. Even a puff of tobacco would taste like dried cow-dung. By Heaven, I could use a pipe of the great smoke . . . just a whiff of opium.'

511

'Maj . . . You promised, my love, remember. If you start again, Heaven knows what *she'll* . . .'

'All right, Aluta, I won't. But there's nothing like opium to ease my pains.'

The Empress's narrow face was anxious beneath its coating of rice-powder. Her fingers trembled against her pale-violet skirt, and the cut-silk phoenixes fluttered on her bosom. By Heaven's peculiar grace, which transcended Dynastic Law, she loved the wayward youth to whom she was married. Far more than his violent moods the violent pains that afflicted him frightened her.

'Are you feeling ill again?' she asked. 'Is the pain very bad? Maybe we should go back right now.'

'It's not that bad, Aluta. Just the usual headache. And those damned spots on my chest are prickling like seven devils. You've got a couple of opium pills, haven't you?'

'Of course, my love. They don't watch me so closely.' She handed him ten small black pellets. 'Only a few, though they are medicine. But no more pipes of opium. If *she* finds out . . . if Your Maj . . . your uncles find out . . .'

'What more can they do?' he sneered. 'What new humiliation can they heap on me? Anyway, let's forget it for now . . . Just look at that.'

High above the pale gold ripples of Kunming Lake, the declining sun and the new moon glowed together in the western sky. Beyond the promontory jutting from Myriad Longevity Mount, where the Bronze Pavilion shone emerald in the flare of torches, the first stars of the night sparkled over the lonely pagoda crowning Jade Springs Hill. In the distance, the Fragrant Hills were russet by moonlight.

'The most beautiful sight in the Empire!' The Tung Chih Emperor was for a moment lifted out of his self-absorption. 'You know, I said I was rebuilding the Park of Radiant Perfection for my mother. But every emperor since Kang Hsi has had the Park for himself. Take a good look. You'll probably never see it again. I know I won't . . . It's not fair.'

'The work's going so well, my dear. You're doing a wonderful job, supervising almost every day. You've showed you're a true emperor, proved you can manage thousands of men in a great enterprise. How can you say you'll never see it again?'

'The scandal, Aluta. They forced me to promise to stop building. All because a rascally Cantonese contractor and some crooked barbarians stole a few pennies. Well, actually five or six million *taels*. My mother's damned Chief Eunuch, Cobbler's Wax Li, was in it, too. Now they're making me stop, and I couldn't . . . couldn't bear to see it only half-completed.'

'My poor darling. How could they? I wonder if *she* . . .'

'It's nothing to do with my mother, Aluta,' he snapped. 'Do stop calling the Empress Dowager *she* and *her*. She's the cat's mother. My

512

mother's the Maternal Auspicious Ancestor, not *she*. I did want it finished for her birthday.'

'Sometimes,' Aluta ventured, 'I think *she*'s trying to tear us apart.'

'Aluta, that's not true. She wants only the best for me . . . for both of us. Even if I can't bear her always telling me what to do. No wonder I run away to the . . . the . . .'

'The Flower Quarters, you mean? If that's the only way you can get away from *her*, I don't mind. But sometimes I think *she* hates me . . . even hates you.'

'Sometimes I think so, too,' the Emperor confessed. 'It's not true, of course. My mother only wants the best for me . . . always after me to persevere in my studies and to . . . to behave better.'

'Does she? I wonder. But she's right about one thing. You must persevere. You must show you're a great emperor.'

'Much chance I have with everyone after me all the time. Aluta, I get so tired, and sometimes, the pain's terrible. I feel so sick and . . .'

The Empress rose and joined him at the balustrade. She lifted his hand to her cheek. The Emperor stooped and laid his head on her bosom.

A faint scratching on the door to the interior of the Pavilion intruded, harshly imperative, into their silence. The Emperor straightened his shoulders and rasped a single syllable: '*Lai!* . . . Come!'

An elderly eunuch in an orange robe cautiously opened the door. Fearful of his master's temper, he knelt and presented on upraised palms a cylindrical packet encased in Imperial-yellow silk. The youth who reigned over the world's largest empire scowled in dismissal. He stood tapping the silk-casing against his palm as the door closed.

'So it's come,' he said bitterly. 'Just read *this*, what they demand I sign.'

Aluta slipped the scroll from its casing. After staring incomprehendingly at the columns of black ideograms for a minute, she handed it back to him.

'I'm afraid it's too much for me,' she sighed. 'The Officials' Language is too high flown. Please read it to me, my love.'

'It's not so bad . . . on the surface.' He scanned the document with difficulty. 'I restore my uncle Prince Kung to his offices, and I order the reconstruction of the Summer Palaces to stop, for the good of the people in these unsettled times and to conserve the resources of the Empire. It's all put so elegantly, I could almost believe it *was* my own idea.'

He shouted, and the eunuch returned with a tray bearing a single brush in a jade holder and a malachite inkstone filled with vermilion pigment. The Emperor brushed his signature on the Decree and thrust it at the eunuch, who scuttled away.

'Damn Prince Kung!' the Son of Heaven exploded. 'Damn Prince Kung and damn Prince Chun, too. Chun's even worse. Just because he's my uncle twice over . . . my father's brother and married to my mother's sister . . . he thinks he can make me do whatever he wants. Sometimes, I swear, he thinks he's the Emperor, not me.'

The Son of Heaven could not believe that the younger Prince Chun had reluctantly agreed with his forceful older brother, Prince Kung, that they must curb their nephew's excesses. Prince Kung was himself originally almost as reluctant. The Mandarin Li Hung-chang's stratagem had appeared so brilliant: to divert the Empress Dowager, above all, and the Emperor, as well, to the reconstruction of the Park of Radiant Perfection. In the beginning, the Emperor was fascinated by the project – and even Yehenala was less domineering. However, Prince Kung reproached himself, he should have anticipated that large scale graft would mar the enterprise.

The Imperial uncles could disregard the Memorial presented a year earlier by a zealous Censor who contended that the immense cost strained the Dynasty's resources. When the public learned of the wholesale embezzlement, the Princes could no longer stay their hands. Since their Imperial nephew ignored their private remonstrances, they had submitted a formal petition imploring him to 'halt the reconstruction temporarily'. The petition had also begged the Emperor to rise above the corrupting influence of his eunuchs, because both his studies and his duties required greater attention.

They might as well bring it all into the open, Prince Kung had said fatalistically. It would probably do no good, but it would certainly do no good not to try.

The Princes, therefore, further counselled the Emperor to take more exercise in the open and to curtail his drunken carousing, as well as giving up opium and forsaking the Flower Quarters. They did not reproach their nephew with the common knowledge that a Chinese harlot had infected him with the plum-poison sickness. However, they warned circumspectly that his precious life would be in peril if he did not follow the strict regimen prescribed by the Imperial Physicians.

The young Emperor had raged when he received that petition. He would, he swore, never abandon the restoration of the Park of Radiant Perfection until it again shone in the splendour created by his ancestors. He scoffed at his uncles' concern for his studies, his duties, and his health, screaming: 'They are treating Us like a schoolboy, not a crowned Emperor!' In his fury, the Tung Chih Emperor dismissed Prince Kung from all his offices.

'It's getting monotonous,' that resilient statesman shrugged to his young brother. 'Being batted back and forth between Yehenala and the lad like a shuttlecock. Sometimes I suspect you and I are the only sane ones in the family. Our father must have had the gift of foresight. Why else give me the title Kung Chin Wang, the Respectful Prince? But even my respectfulness is wearing thin. Ah well, we'll see what happens next.'

A month later, the Emperor signified his gracious approval of his uncles' humble suggestions. Even he realised he could not rule without their support. He, therefore, endorsed the Decree directing that all building cease immediately.

'*She'll* be furious!' Aluta pursued her own preoccupation. 'She wants this birthday gift more than she's ever wanted anything else. I wonder what she'll do. I wonder if . . .'

'I'm damned sure of one thing,' the Emperor replied. 'She'll make my life miserable. Somehow, it'll all be my fault, even though her pet eunuch was in it up to his neck. She'll blame me and bully me and . . .'

'Just stand up to her, my love. If you stand up to her, what can she do?'

'Anything she damned pleases. I'm the Emperor, but *she* is the Maternal Ancestor. It's no different after my Coronation. She still pulls the strings. Between bribes and threats, she's got half the Court jumping every time she whistles. Even Niuhura always goes along with her in the long run. You, too, for all I know. You, too, for all your pretty ways.'

He bellowed, and the frightened eunuch appeared.

'Call the Imperial Barge,' the Emperor commanded. 'Get the damned thing here right now!'

'Where are you going, my love?' Aluta asked anxiously. 'Can I come? What can I do to help?'

'You know damned well where We are going,' he screamed. 'And you can do as you please. We are fed up with being bullied by women.'

'Your slave never dared raise her voice to Your Majesty,' Aluta sobbed. 'How Your Majesty can think . . .'

'We'll think what We please, woman. And We'll go where We damned well please. We're going to the Willow Lane . . . to respectful, obedient women who don't plague us. Screw the uncles! Screw *her*! And you, too, woman!'

CHAPTER SEVENTY-FIVE

November 28, 1874   *Shanghai*

'You can't expect too much too fast,' Saul Haleevie warned. 'It'll happen in its own good time . . . Chinese time, which is different from our time. It'll go on, even though that Manchu lad is ailing. He won't last forever, I hear.'

Fronah smiled wryly at her mother, who was squinting at her embroidery hoop through the tortoise-shell reading-glasses she would wear only in the privacy of the family. Sarah was determined to depict faithfully her favourite slipper orchids, which flaunted its amber and saffron in the pallid late-November afternoon. Though the conservatory was warm under its glass roof, coals glowed in the cast-iron fireplace framed by flower-patterned tiles. Sarah returned her daughter's smile and glanced with affectionate amusement at her husband.

515

Saul never referred to the Lord of Ten Thousand Years in distant Peking as the Tung Chih Emperor, but always called him 'the young fellow up north' or 'that Manchu lad'. Perhaps, Fronah mused, he found that name difficult to pronounce; or perhaps he would feel decrepit if he so explicitly acknowledged that the sovereign of the world's largest empire was a youth some four decades younger than himself. Still, she was more tolerant of others' idiosyncracies, even her parents', as she herself grew older.

'My diplomat friends are worried about what . . . who . . . comes next.' Saul was oblivious to his women's amusement. 'The lad can't last more than another year. Since he had to give up on the Summer Palaces, he's been wilder than ever. The young fellow spends all his time carousing in the . . . ah . . . Flower Quarters.'

He looked sharply at his daughter, who was staring abstractedly at the spray of orchids and automatically ruffling the sheaf of letters in her lap. When she looked up and smiled, he felt she was accusing him.

'Look, Fronah, I've said I'm sorry a hundred times,' Saul apologised explosively. 'I'm very sorry I didn't tell you about Lionel earlier.'

'It doesn't matter, Papa,' she replied evenly. 'Certainly you should have. But it wouldn't have made any difference.'

'For God's sake, Fronah, do as you want,' he rumbled. 'You will anyway, I know.'

'Saul, that's all over now,' Sarah interjected. 'It's up to Fronah and Gabriel. Just leave her alone. Don't keep after . . .'

'It's all right, Mama,' Fronah said quietly. 'Honestly, it doesn't matter. And I don't mind any more.'

'Well, then, I was saying,' Saul resumed, 'unless we understand how the Chinese look at time, we can't see why they don't understand progress. For them . . . even Aaron and David, sometimes . . . time doesn't move forward in a straight line, but around in circles. How can they progress when there's no place to go?'

Fronah, who had felt time urgently nudging her between the shoulder-blades during the past few months, tried to concentrate. Despite her interest in her father's theories, intellectual discussion could not divert her from recalling the vicissitudes of her own life.

When she regained her composure and rejoined the bar mitzvah reception after her father told her Lionel was dead, she had looked around eagerly for Gabriel Hyde. Her mother informed her that he had left in haste after suddenly remembering an essential duty.

'Gabriel said to tell you he was sorry he had to go,' Sarah had explained briefly. 'Very sorry.'

When her lover did not appear that evening or the next morning and sent no message, she had demanded that her mother repeat the entire conversation.

'So you let it slip that I hadn't told you he was Jewish?' she snapped. 'That wasn't very helpful.'

'Fronah, be reasonable,' Sarah replied. 'How was I to know? I only discovered it myself by accident.'

'I suppose that's true, Mama. But what else happened? He might have had to dash away. But to disappear and send no word, that's not like him at all. What else did he say?'

'Nothing, except that he was very sorry, my dear.'

'And what else did *you* say, Mama?'

'I think I gave him a wrong impression,' Sarah confessed. 'I was so happy and excited I didn't watch what I was saying. I talked about Lionel then. I'm afraid he thought . . . might have thought . . . you knew about Lionel all the time.'

'Mama, that's terrible. How could you? If he thinks I was keeping that secret, no wonder he's angry. I must see him. I'm going to Willards Hotel right now.'

Though eager to be helpful, the desk-clerk could offer Fronah little comfort. Captain Hyde, he said, had departed for Tientsin that morning. No, the Captain had left no message. And he had taken all his belongings, even the trunk of summer clothing he normally deposited in the box-room.

Fronah berated herself for her own deceitfulness. She was bitter at her father's secretiveness, and furious at her mother's indiscretion. She was, above all, infuriated with Gabriel for his headlong departure.

She would not, Fronah decided, communicate with him. She would not humiliate herself by offering laboured explanations like a naughty school-girl. Why couldn't he trust her? How dare he rush away without even asking for an explanation? But she loitered near the front door when the punctual postman knocked at the Nest of Joy each morning.

In mid-August, when she was half-resigned to never again hearing from Gabriel, his long anticipated letter finally arrived. Dated July 18th from Dairen in Manchuria, it had been inordinately delayed.

'My dear Fronah [the semi-formal salutation was chilling], I have been meaning for some time to write to thank you and your parents for asking me to Judah's bar mitzvah – and to apologise again for my unavoidably hasty departure. However, my duties have been both heavy and engrossing.

'The Mandarin Li Hung-chang has made me a Military Mandarin of the Third Grade. David's nose is a little out of joint, I'm afraid, though he still takes precedence over me because of his earlier date of rank and being on the civil side. The Mandarin has promised me command of a cruiser and, in the meantime, has appointed me deputy commander of the entire North Sea Fleet with the substantive rank of commodore. I find it fascinating – and trying – to endeavour as tactfully as possible to guide my Chinese commanding admiral, who happens to be the boss's son-in-law.'

That vein had continued for two pages. Not a word of either affection or reproach until the final paragraphs. which read:

'This letter is difficult to write, as you will understand. I trust you will pardon the consequent stilted tone, as well as my precipitate departure, which was impelled by acute disappointment.

'I have, naturally, not discussed whatever once lay between us with anyone else. David, always the discreet gentleman, has not inquired. However, he is obviously distressed. I do not believe that any other, even your brother who is my closest friend, should be privy to the events which revealed how tenuous were the ties that formerly bound us.

'Matters are now clear to me from your mother's inadvertent revelations, for which, I beg you, do not reproach her. I winkled them out of her with somewhat ignoble cunning. At any rate, I now understand that you can have no wish to proceed as I had hoped. Whatever you may *believe* you feel, your behaviour has revealed your *true* feelings.

'I ask your pardon for having pressed you, and I shall not trouble you further with my unwelcome attentions. Perhaps we shall encounter each other when duty next brings me to Shanghai. I cannot say when that is likely to be. Yours faithfully, Gabriel.'

Hers faithfully, indeed! The irony stung, although Gabriel, his puckish humour in eclipse, had obviously not intended it.

She was a little comforted by the stilted manner he deplored when she re-read his letter for the first of many times. He must have been intensely moved if he had retreated into schoolboy formality. Besides, his sense of the ridiculous would have prevented his setting down the double meaning of the closing if he did not long for her.

Gabriel had unwittingly revealed his true wishes, Fronah concluded. He had also revealed her most profound wish to herself. She yearned to see his open yet faintly sardonic features and to hold his square hand. By rejecting her peremptorily, Gabriel had forced her to acknowledge to herself that she wished to marry him and live with him all her life. Her fears dissolved – and she knew beyond doubt that she loved Gabriel and wanted him – and would never again waver.

Getting Gabriel was another matter. She could not overwhelm him with protestations of love. The more vehement she was, the less likely he was to believe her. His Yankee scepticism would tell him the pendulum of her emotions had once again oscillated wildly – and must inevitably swing back.

She therefore waited a week before composing a letter that almost matched his feigned detachment, thought not, she assured herself, his stilted tone. She owed him an explanation, she wrote, as well as an apology for letting him believe she had told her parents he was Jewish, though that was now irrelevant to herself. She explained her mother's confusion, which led him to conclude that she had known of Lionel's death for many years. He would undoubtedly judge her father's secretiveness extraordinary. But she had truly not known until the day of the bar mitzvah. She had mentioned neither love nor marriage, though she signed herself: 'Love, Fronah.'

His reply, which reached her five weeks later, expressed relief that she had not deceived him regarding her widowed state. He was also glad the other matter now appeared as trivial to her as it had always appeared to him. He sent her his deep affection, though not his love, and he hoped to see her on 'the most friendly terms quite soon'.

The long gaps in their communication were almost intolerable when Fronah felt so pressed by time. However, she allowed herself three days for reflection before replying to Gabriel's second letter. Striving to convince him, she acknowledged her previous terror of responsibility and her almost wilful vacillation. But, she assured him, all her foolish reservations had now totally vanished. Her single over-riding desire was to be with him again – and to prove her steadfast love to him.

Almost seven weeks in transit, Gabriel's reply arrived on October 28th. His language was, thank God, no longer stilted, though it was still guarded. He was, he wrote, too old to play childish games. He valued her affection deeply, and he returned it sincerely. But he wondered whether their mutual affection could serve as the foundation for anything more than lasting friendship. It was, he feared, too late – almost certainly too late for him and probably too late for her. He pointedly neither spoke of coming to Shanghai nor invited her to visit him.

This time Fronah did not hesitate. She, too, was weary of playing games, and she was frightened.

She wrote immediately to tell Gabriel that she wished to marry him, 'going wherever you go, my darling'. Unless he forbade it, she would come to Tientsin, ostensibly to visit her brother David and his wife Lochi. She ached to be with him – and to prove to him that her emotions were no longer whirligigs. But she would not force herself on him against his wishes. Her letter closed: 'My deepest love always, Fronah.'

She now waited for Gabriel's reaction, which could not reach her until a month after the posting of her own. Her mental review of their exchange having taken no more than two minutes, Fronah tried again to concentrate on her father's discussion of the divergent Chinese and Western concepts of time.

'Since the Chinese consider time circular and, therefore, eternal,' Saul Haleevie reiterated meticulously, 'they are truly convinced that the human race is immortal because men repeat and prolong the existence of their ancestors – at present and in the future.'

'Also they count the years in cycles of sixty years, instead of centuries.' Fronah's interjection elicited an approving nod from her father and a puzzled glance from her mother. 'A cycle goes round and round forever, while our century goes from the past through the present into the future – without repetition. I've never heard Chinese say:"That was three or four cycles ago." Not the way we'd say, "Three or four centuries ago." Their cycles don't progress, but whirl forever in the same place like an eternal Catherine-wheel.'

'I was coming to that,' Saul said. 'Now, you see . . .'

'Besides, they number their years by the emperors' reigns,' Fronah continued eagerly. 'They'd have to count back by reigns to work out how long ago something occurred. But they don't bother. They say "late in the Han Dynasty" or "about the middle of the Tang". They know the Han came first, but have no real idea . . . no visceral appreciation . . . of just how much earlier.'

'So the forward progress of time and, therefore, the urgency of time is a Western concept,' Saul agreed. 'It means nothing to the Chinese.'

'Yet they've always kept precise historical records.' Fronah automatically championed the Chinese. 'The most detailed and accurate of any civilisation.'

'Because the word becomes the reality,' Saul added. 'That's why the Chinese revere the written word, much like the Jews. For the Jews, the word represents the transcendent reality of God. For the Chinese, the word *is* God . . . or Heaven. But we were speaking of time.'

'It's the same concept, really, Papa. Man is the centre of the Chinese universe, while time doesn't progress. Man must therefore put fixed marks on the whirlpool of eternity by precisely recording his own doings.'

'You're getting rather metaphysical, aren't you dear?' Sarah jibed, though she normally enjoyed their intellectual acrobatics. 'This waiting must be going to your head.'

'I've made up my mind, Mama. I'm going to him. He *must* agree.'

'It's not very ladylike, my dear. You can't throw yourself at . . .'

'Ladylike be damned!' Fronah exploded. 'Unless he flatly says no, I'll . . .'

'You're right, Sarah.' Saul ignored the women's interchange. 'We mustn't get too abstruse, but be practical. The linear bias of the Judaeo-Christian mind is incomprehensible to the Chinese. The year 5635 of the Hebrew Era or 1874 of the Christian Era, neither has real meaning for them. But our calendars are also only a convenience, and God's world *is* eternal. Maybe they're more realistic by not bothering with artificial eras.'

'You said practical, Papa,' Fronah laughed. 'But you're getting even more abstruse.'

'All right, let's really be practical. The Chinese find Western science very difficult. How can they measure weights and volumes, distance and area if they can't measure time? But technology, industry, and commerce depend on precise measurement. I never press them for absolute precision because it just makes them uncomfortable.'

'That's why Chinese politics seem so peculiar to Westerners.' Fronah added eagerly. 'They have infinity . . . *literally* infinite time . . . to intrigue and squabble. If something doesn't work out this year or the next, it'll work out eventually. If Old Wang isn't around himself to see it, his children, his grandchildren, or his great-great-grandchildren will be. And he'll be there in them, the same Old Wang in all the new Young Wangs forever.'

'You're always defending your Chinese, Fronah,' Saul chided. 'You make them more patient and philosophical than any human being can be. If I followed your thinking in business, we'd be bankrupt tomorrow.'

'Always the business, Papa. What, then, in your practical terms?'

'Jews, too, are patient. We've had to be. But Jews are also hot-headed, jealous, and violent. The Chinese are the same . . . only more so. Sometimes the most impatient people in the world. Old Wang wants what he wants right now. They live in the eye of eternity, but an eager Chinaman's got less patience than a wild bull . . .'

'And he's more dangerous,' Sarah laughed. 'But enough, Saul. My head's spinning and . . .'

A tap on the door cut off the discussion more effectively than Sarah's protest. To her surprise Fronah saw Old Woo, the lean number-one houseboy who had served her since the departure of the reluctant pimp, Lao King, thirteen years earlier.

'Very sorry!' Fumbling under his jacket, Old Liu spoke in pidgin in deference to the elder Haleevies. 'One piecee letter have come. I savee maybe very big pidgin, so hurry bring Missee.'

Fronah took the light-blue envelope. She no longer marvelled at the servants' knowledge of her affairs. A hundred letters, including foot-square envelopes heavy with official seals, might be left for her return. But Old Woo knew unerringly that *this* letter was urgent.

She turned the envelope over in her hands, almost afraid to open it. Though she had not hoped for such a prompt reply, the flap was marked: 'Commodore G. Hyde, North China Fleet, Tientsin.' The address was written in Gabriel's Spencerian script and in her brother David's distinctive ideograms, as well. The red seal that identified 'North Seas Fleet Official Correspondence' explained its speedy arrival. If Gabriel were in such haste, it should be good news. Perhaps, however, he was anxious to forestall her threatened visit.

'Open it, child,' Sarah directed impatiently. 'What's inside won't improve by keeping.'

Fronah reluctantly slipped her forefinger beneath the flap. She peeled it away gradually as if it would be desecration to tear it. She unfolded the stiff blue notepaper and smoothed the creases on her knee. Finally, she could put off reading it no longer.

'Fronah, my dearest [the salutation was, at least, not discouraging], I have read your last letter over and over again. Quite candidly, I am of two minds. I don't quite see an assured future for us together, though I know I care for you profoundly.'

Fronah smiled in delight at that acknowledgement. The faint line between her dark eyebrows grew deeper as she read further.

'I will not come to you again, though perhaps I should. I simply cannot rush back and forth, even though the better part of me demands that I should.

521

'However, I must be brief to catch the despatch boat: Come to Tientsin if you wish. If you truly mean what you have written, by all means come to me.'

Fronah gasped in delight, but she frowned again as she read again: 'I must, however, tell you candidly that I have not made up my mind as to the future. I cannot make up my mind now, and it is more than likely that I shall not be able to make a firm decision even when I see you.

'I love you more than I have ever loved anyone. But, somehow, I am afraid. I, too, fear marriage. If we married and . . . [the next line was scored out] . . . something happened to you, it would be the end of me. I could not bear another – and greater – catastrophe.

'This may sound foolish to you. In part, it does to me. But let me be as clear as I can: I now distrust my own feelings. And, to be cruelly candid, I distrust yours as well.

'Besides, I am a bird of passage. Perhaps I am simply not suited to the married state. I cannot, I fear, provide the stability which a woman is entitled to expect, or the security even a woman as competent and self-sufficient as yourself must require.

'But come to Tientsin if you wish. Come, however, with the understanding that I can make no commitment. No commitment or promise *whatsoever*. Indeed, I fear a marriage between us is *most* unlikely. But come if you wish. All my love, Gabriel.'

Fronah carefully returned the letter to its envelope. She smiled and nodded in reply to her parents' interrogative gaze. Later she might tell them that Gabriel was indecisive and that he had virtually rejected her – if she told them anything more than that she was going to Tientsin. She had made up her mind, and she would not alter her decision. Since he had not forbidden it, she would go to Tientsin, though she feared she would be desperately disappointed.

CHAPTER SEVENTY-SIX

Peking
Night of January 12–13, 1875   *The Forbidden City*

The wasted figure was more majestic in death than it had ever been in life. The cheeks, once plump with self-indulgence, were haggard, and the rice-powder that covered the smallpox scars accentuated the lines scored by suffering. The Tung Chih Emperor of the Great Pure Dynasty, who had mounted the Heavenly Dragon after reigning for thirteen years and ruling ineffectually for less than two, appeared to have worn himself out in arduous service to his people, rather than mindless dissipation.

He was better served in death than he had been in life. His elders, who had failed to curb his self-destructive excesses, had laid him out in Imperial splendour. A half-hour after his passing, his corpse was arrayed in the golden Dragon Robes of Eternal Longevity. His head was raised by a pillow to face south as an emperor must when he looks upon his subjects or awaits the Supreme Dragon that will convey him to his first audience with the Jade Emperor in Heaven. Born amid glorious omens in the year of the dragon, 1856, he had slipped quietly away at the beginning of the double-hour of the dog in the waning days of the year of the dog, by Western reckoning just after eight in the evening of January 12, 1875.

The Tung Chih Emperor died surrounded by the Imperial Family and the Senior Counsellors of the Manchu Dynasty, who has known for several weeks that their sovereign must quite soon mount the Heavenly Dragon after living on earth for less than nineteen years. Though his strength was already sapped by dissipation and by the harlot's plum-flower poison, he had rallied briefly against the further affliction of smallpox. However, his end was manifestly close when he suffered a sudden relapse. The Mandate of Heaven would undoubtedly soon pass to a new sovereign.

Afterwards, the Empress Dowagers wept. Despite their grief, his uncles were abstracted. This death would precipitate a grave crisis. Both Prince Kung, the sixth son of the Tao Kwang Emperor, who was the deceased Emperor's grandfather, and Prince Chun, the seventh son of the Tao Kwang Emperor, were preoccupied by their own sons' claims to the Imperial succession. The lesser Imperial Princes and the Grand Chancellors, as well as the Senior Ministers and the Senior Censors of the Great Pure Dynasty, were equally uneasy. The decisions to be taken tonight would determine not only the future of the Manchu Empire, but their own fate.

Only the Baronet Jung Lu, General-Commandant of both the Peking Gendarmerie and the Peking Field Force, wore the face of conventional sorrow. His mind was easy, for his troops were already executing the precise commands of his Imperial mistress Yehenala. The Baronet was not enthusiastic about collaborating with the powerful units of the Army of Huai which the Mandarin Li Hung-chang, Viceroy of the Metropolitan Provinces, had despatched to the Northern Capital when the death of the Son of Heaven was obviously imminent. However, those reinforcements would be useful, perhaps decisive, while their presence in Peking further demonstrated his mistress's foresight.

The Imperial Guard would assuredly rally to Yehenala in any crisis. The guardsmen loved the junior Empress Dowager for her lavish presents, which filled the purses of troopers as well as generals, while their chivalry was touched by her fragile beauty. None the less, the Guard was too enmeshed in palace intrigue to be absolutely reliable and too familiar to the courtiers to intimidate them effectively. Besides, the Imperial Guard were the troops of the Dynasty, not uniquely Yehenala's own, while the forces of the Baronet and the Mandarin were entirely and solely obedient to her will. In any event, she planned to avoid a crisis.

As thorough as she was decisive, Yehenala had not only summoned reinforcements, but had already deployed them in overwhelming force. The same brain that had outwitted the usurpers led by Prince Yee and his dupe Prince Cheng some thirteen years earlier was again working to preserve the Sacred Dynasty. Yehenala's intelligence and Yehenala's resolution had crushed that conspiracy, not Prince Kung's. Besides, her brother-in-law, the Senior Grand Chancellor was unlikely to support her tonight.

The Empress Aluta, widowed a few months before her twentieth birthday, now sobbed by the Tung Chih Emperor's bier. The grand-daughter of the treacherous Prince Cheng was oblivious to the swearing of the eunuchs who squabbled over the late Emperor's personal belongings. In her desolation, she did not even hear the consoling murmurs of her ladies-in-waiting. Except for those few personal attendants, the bereaved Empress was alone beside her husband's gorgeously attired corpse.

At half-past the double-hour of the dog, not quite a full European hour since the last breath expired from the Emperor's lungs, the other actors in the death scene had already withdrawn. A Grand Conclave of Imperial Princes, Grand Chancellors and Senior Ministers of the Manchu Dynasty was summoned by Yehenala, who had with Niuhura again been invested with the authority of Regents by her dying son.

Though the Tung Chih Emperor had mounted the Dragon, the people of the Northern Capital did not hail a new Emperor. His subjects did not know of his death, and he had designated no successor. No throngs cried: 'Ten thousand years have passed! Hail the New Lord of Ten Thousand Years!'

Crouched beside her husband's bier, the Empress Aluta was virtually oblivious to the political impasse. Apart from her grief for the Tung Chih Emperor, whom she alone had loved unselfishly, the widow felt only the one emotion. Though she was not certain, she suspected that she was pregnant. It hardly concerned her that her unborn child would have the strongest claim to the Dragon Throne if it were a boy. She wept because the child would be fatherless – if she could bring herself to live long enough to bear the unfortunate creature.

'Ten thousand years passed in an instant!' Aluta sobbed to the still figure. 'We never dreamed it would be so short, My Lord. I should have been kinder to you. I should have curbed my wicked tongue. Ten thousand years are already gone!'

The greedy eunuchs did not hear her plaints, and her young ladies-in-waiting instinctively drew back from the Empress's passionate grief. Her ungovernable sorrow transcended not only the lamentations expected of all bereft wives, but the unsupportable desolation of a widow who had profoundly loved her husband. Deprived at once of her beloved and the purpose of her existence, she keened with the abandon of a woman who could not believe in tomorrow's ever coming. There could be no tomorrow

524

for her. Not daring to touch the cold hand that had caressed her, the Empress Aluta wept alone.

*

The sandstorm wailed outside the green-tiled and vermilion-columned facade of the *Yang Hsin Tien*. That name dedicated the Hall of Ceremony just south of Yehenala's Six Western Palaces in the Forbidden City to the development of the intellectual faculties and the elevation of the moral faculties. Some foreign Sinologues, presumptuous in their limited knowledge, called it the Hall of Mental Cultivation, which was not wholly inadequate. Others called it the Palace Where the Heart is Nourished, which was simply ridiculous, though *Yang Hsin* did mean literally, though misleadingly, nurturing the heart. A little knowledge could be totally deceptive, reflected the muscular officer who wore the uniform of the Army of Huai with the leopard of a major general on his tunic. Besides, the deliberations of the Grand Council would tonight be neither intellectually cultivated nor morally elevated.

Despite the portentous events in train around him, David Lee's wry humour was not subdued. Neither was his capacity for wonder. He marvelled that circumstances had made him a major participant in the selection of the next Emperor of the Great Pure Dynasty.

His function had been strictly prescribed when he left Tientsin with the crack battalions of the Mandarin Li Hung-chang's Army of Huai. Unless matters began to go wrong, he was not to interfere, but was to allow the troop commander to follow the instructions of the Empress Dowager. If the plan faltered, he was to take command and act as he believed best.

The torches lighting the forecourt of the Palace of Intellectual Cultivation and Moral Elevation rattled in their iron brackets as the gusts struck them. Their glare was obscured by the miniature whirlwinds of ochre dust swirling on the marble terrace. The gale storming out of the steppes of Central Asia through the passes of Manchuria and over the Great Wall to harry the Northern Capital cloaked the stars and hurled gouts of sand into the faces of the soldiers surrounding the Palace. The mid-January night was achingly cold and cavernously dark in the Forbidden City.

David pulled his fur-lined cloak around himself and shouted to the Baronet Jung Lu over the screaming of the wind. The General-Commandant nodded and summoned a messenger. A few minutes later, the watchfires ringing the Palace flared high as the soldiers poured oil on their flames. Above all, the troops were meant to be seen. The menace of the halberds and spears glinting in the hands of the sinisterly hooded infantrymen must strike every member of the Grand Council. The counsellors had already seen the long rifle-barrels and the gaping cannon-muzzles that commanded the approaches to the Imperial City.

When the last of the twenty-five Princes and Chancellors entered the

525

Hall, David Lee and the Baronet Jung Lu followed. Behind them marched units of the Peking Field Force and the Army of Huai numbering almost a hundred. Within the palace dedicated to the higher virtues of peace the cold, metallic reality of power must command the eyes of the conclave. The great doors clanged shut, and other platoons took station outside the portals. They were charged to prevent any interference with the deliberations of the Grand Council – and to prevent any counsellor's leaving before it had taken the decision required by the Empress Dowager.

The troops deployed in the Forbidden City were, David knew, the visible cutting edge of the tens of thousands of armed men who stood on the alert throughout the Metropolitan Provinces to support Yehenala. As the Mandarin had observed when giving David his orders, she was the best simulacrum of a man the effete Manchu race could now produce. Despite her obduracy and her ignorance, she at least dimly perceived the direction in which the Great Empire must move. Since she was the best – indeed the only – tool they could use to shape a powerful and independent China, they had no choice but to support her.

What would the Empire be like today, he wondered, if Yehenala had found in the Hsien Feng Emperor a man who could curb her wild spirit, employ her great talents, and fulfil her as a woman, rather than a weakling who could not even survive? The dashing Baronet Jung Lu, who stood beside him, was a man of straw, a Manchu savage with a mouth full of nonsensical gallantry and a head full of antiquated bravado. It was not remarkable that he was Yehenala's choice, for he would never defy her.

'*Chien lu chih chiung*!' his chief had said regarding Prince Kung: 'The Kweichou donkey has reached the end of his tether.' The folk-saying referred to the tale of a donkey in rugged Kweichou Province, which frightened off a marauding tiger by braying and kicking – until the tiger realised that the noise and the fury were no threat to itself and devoured the donkey.

The Mandarin was bitter at the Imperial Prince who was the chief officer of the Empire. He still resented Prince Kung's repudiation of their well-wrought plan to divert Yehenala's energies to the reconstruction of the Summer Palaces and simultaneously engage the Tung Chih Emperor's enthusiasm in order to wean him from the dissipation that was killing him.

Well, the Emperor was dead, and Yehenala was resurgent. Tonight, she would play the tiger to Prince Kung's donkey.

General the Baronet Jung Lu and temporary Major General David Lee took their stations at the entrance to the council chamber. Their squads of troopers armed with rifles, swords, and revolvers, Yehenala had already explained reasonably, were present to ensure that the deliberations of the Conclave would not be interrupted. But the counsellors knew the soldiers were the spearhead of the great army she had mobilised throughout North China.

The ebony thrones of the Empress Dowagers faced each other beneath the carved green-and-red squares of the ceiling, which framed an embossed and gilded dome. Panels of olive-green gauze fringed with Imperial-yellow hung from the painted beams before the thrones to honour the convention that the Dowagers 'administered the government behind the screen'. But the panels were not lowered to conceal their faces. Yehenala was determined to dominate the Grand Conclave by her naked personal force as much as her armed force.

Court Etiquette, however, required Niuhura to open the Conclave. While the Senior Empress Dowager spoke, Prince Kung, the Chief Grand Chancellor, was surprisingly quiescent. He stared at his hands, which were clenched on his knees, as if the outcome were no particular concern of his.

'We have summoned this Grand Conclave tonight because We and our younger sister, the junior Empress Dowager, consider the selection of the next Emperor a matter of extreme urgency,' Niuhura declared in her high, sweet voice. 'In times of peril and disorder like those which now . . .'

The rote preliminaries were as un-dramatic as actors rehearsing a play for the hundredth time. The twenty-five grandees who sat beneath the eyes of the Empress Dowagers already knew there were only three candidates for elevation to the Dragon Throne.

The most suitable by the most orthodox interpretation of Sacred Dynastic Law was Pu Lun, a great-grandson of the Tao Kwang Emperor. Since that infant was a member of the generation of the Imperial Family that followed the deceased Tung Chih Emperor, he could, as a collateral descendant, offer the Ancestral Sacrifices essential to ensure the tranquillity of that sovereign's restless soul. The other candidates were tangentially eligible: the adolescent son of Prince Kung; and Yehenala's nephew, the three-and-a-half-year-old son of Prince Chun. Both those Princes were, however, grandsons of the Tao Kwang Emperor, like the Tung Chih Emperor himself. Since they belonged to the same generation as the deceased Emperor, they could not perform the Rites of Filial Piety for their first cousin.

That apparently theological provision, David Lee reflected, was actually quite pragmatic. It was intended to ensure that the Dragon Throne did not pass from an elder brother to a brother or a first cousin who was almost as old, since youthful vigour was desirable at the beginning of a new reign. It further deterred princes of the same generation from assassinating the sovereign. The rule simultaneously expressed profound reverence for Heaven and intelligent distrust of men.

Niuhura concluded her remarks. As always Prince Kung's ally, the Senior Empress Dowager proposed the election of the Chief Grand Chancellor's son despite his formal disability. Yehenala frowned. An emperor who was almost of age to rule would be a catastrophe at this critical moment in the Dynasty's history. The Empire must be directed by mature adults seasoned by great experience, not by a raw youth.

She frowned, despite Prince Kung's protesting – as he was in honour

527

bound to protest – that his son was unworthy of the Dragon Throne. The infant Pu Lun, he contended, was the only qualified candidate because only a prince of his generation could offer sacrifices to the spirit of the deceased Tung Chih Emperor.

'Not suitable at all!' Yehenala intervened. 'Pu Lun is the son of the son of an adopted son of the Tao Kwang Emperor. There exists no precedent whatsoever for placing upon the Dragon Throne a child who is not of the direct Imperial bloodline, but only the descendant of an adopted son.'

'Majesty, a valid precedent exists,' Prince Kung improvised. 'Think of the Cheng Tung Emperor of the Ming Dynasty.'

'And think also of the Ching Tai Emperor of the Ming, who was the same man,' Yehenala sneered. 'Even if it is true that he was secretly adopted to please his predecessor's favourite concubine and not just Court gossip, as I suspect, that is a pernicious precedent. His reign was not only filled with disasters, but was interrupted by a year's captivity among the Mongols. He spent almost seven years incarcerated within the Forbidden City before he won back the throne from his younger brother, who usurped power while he was a prisoner-of-war. You may, perhaps, recall that he then took the new reign name, becoming the Ching Tai Emperor. Do you actually *want* to bring disaster on Our Dynasty, Kung?'

David Lee smiled to himself when Prince Kung was so swiftly impaled upon his own contrived precedent. His smile broadened when he considered Yehenala's almost equally specious riposte. He coughed and raised his hand to conceal his disrespectful amusement.

Yehenala had naturally not volunteered the further information that the reign of that Ming Emperor was blighted at its inception. When he ascended the Dragon Throne as a child, his grandmother had ruled as Empress Dowager Regent – in violation of that Dynasty's precedents. Apparently ignorant of that episode in the history of the Chinese dynasty that had preceded their own, none of the Grand Counsellors attacked Yehenala's vulnerability. Or perhaps they were not ignorant, but did not dare attack her directly.

Prince Kung remained conspicuously silent. He had known he was speaking *pro forma*, just as he had spoken *pro forma* when he argued against the elevation of his own son, who was unquestionably the best qualified candidate. His head cocked to one side, he glanced without hope at the great plaque on the wall, which exhorted: CHUNG CHENG JEN HO: JUSTICE, BENEVOLENCE, AND HARMONY.

'It is Our opinion that only one candidate is qualified both by Heaven's approbation and the exigencies of human affairs.' Yehenala continued. 'We cannot spare the services of Prince Kung. If his son, who is a worthy lad, were selected, the most capable counsellor We possess would be forced to retire from public affairs. Since a father cannot kowtow to his own son, Prince Kung would have to withdraw from the service of the

Dynasty. We esteem Prince Chun as highly, but he is ill. He has confided to Us that he wishes to withdraw from active political life.'

Prince Chun looked up in mild surprise. He had not been feeling well, it was true, but he had not until that moment known that he wished to retire.

'We, therefore, propose Tsai Tien, the son of Prince Chun.' Yehenala looked sharply at Niuhura. 'With the assent of the Senior Empress Dowager, the Grand Conclave will now vote.'

The twenty-five Grand Counsellors glanced from Niuhura's resigned expression to Yehenala's imperious stare before regarding the plaque that exhorted them to practise justice, benevolence, and harmony. Their eyes turned finally to the armed troops at the door.

The vote was slow and not entirely to Yehenala's satisfaction. Despite the menace of the soldiers, seven counsellors, led by Prince Chun and Prince Kung, voted for Pu Lun, the only candidate of the appropriate generation. Three voted for Prince Kung's adolescent son. The remaining fifteen haltingly cast their ballots for Prince Tsai Tien, Prince Chun's three-and-a-half-year-old son, who was Yehenala's nephew.

Smiling demurely in her triumph, the Junior Empress Dowager congratulated the Conclave on its wise selection. She declared that she would adopt the new Emperor as her own son, so that Prince Chun's services would not be lost to the Dynasty, an action she could equally have taken on Prince Kung's behalf. Moreover, the new Emperor's first-born son would be posthumously adopted by the Tung Chih Emperor, whose soul would be at peace when sacrifices were offered by that filial descendant. Adoption was quite acceptable to Yehanala, David Lee reflected, when it suited her purposes.

The Baronet Jung Lu slipped out of the Palace as soon as the voting was completed. He mounted his horse, and the ready squadron closed around the waiting Imperial-yellow palanquin. Pulling their cloaks around their heads to protect themselves from the driven sand, the squadron cantered through the Meridian Gate of the Forbidden City into the Imperial City and passed through the Gate of Heavenly Peace into the Tartar City. Buffeted by the wind in the deserted streets of the Northern Capital, the cavalcade rode to Prince Chun's mansion to escort the new Emperor of the Great Pure Dynasty to the Dragon Throne.

'We would suggest, Elder Sister, that Prince Kung, the best loved uncle of the former Emperor, is the most fitting person to take charge of the obsequies for Our beloved son.' Yehenala spoke directly to Niuhura. 'We cannot think of a more capable man to discharge that duty. It may, also, help to assuage his grief.'

That sacred duty, David Lee mused, would also keep Prince Kung out of the way while the infant-Emperor was consecrated

*

The Baronet Jung Lu brought the new Emperor to the bier of his predecessor at the beginning of the double-hour of the monkey, three in the morning of January 13, 1875 by European reckoning. His mother, who was Yehenala's younger sister, unloosed his clutching arms from her neck and set him on his feet. Encumbered by his heavy metallic-brocade Dragon Robe, the round-faced child knelt weeping in bewilderment before the powdered corpse clothed in the golden Dragon Robe of Longevity.

His reign would be called Kwang Hsü, Brilliant Beginning, Yehenala decided, watching the child who was of her own blood, perform his first duty as Emperor. This nephew, now her adopted son, she would train better than she had the son of her own womb. He would grow up strong in body and mind to reign as a truly great Emperor. Intensive tutelage was obviously essential – the more protracted the better.

Thank Heaven, she reflected, for the Mandarin Li Hung-chang. He had backed her when she and the Dynasty required his support most desperately – and he would be richly rewarded. Above all, she thanked Heaven for the Baronet Jung Lu's devoted love. Without Jung Lu, she could never have accomplished so much all these years. Pray Heaven he would stand behind her for many years to come.

She had not wished to impose her will on the Conclave, she told herself, any more than she had wished to assume the burden of supreme power in the beginning. However, these perilous times demanded firm rule – and she was manifestly the only member of the Imperial Family who possessed the requisite decisiveness. If she had not asserted her will in the past, the barbarians and the rebels would have destroyed the Sacred Dynasty. If she had not acted decisively tonight, the feuding factions within the Court would subsequently have come into armed conflict – and the Manchu Empire would have splintered into anarchy.

She could not simply shrug off the burden Heaven had laid upon her frail shoulders. She had previously temporised with the barbarians, but she would stand up to them in her new regency, just as she would resume the reconstruction of the Summer Palaces to provide a fitting sanctuary for her old age. Never wavering from the traditional verities and virtues, the Empire would wax prosperous and strong under her resolute hand during the decade and a half before the Kwang Hsü Emperor came of age.

Always aware of a handsome man, Yehenala smiled at the young officer of the Army of Huai who wore the leopard of a major general on his chest. David Lee bowed deep. Twice he had been privileged to look upon the Manchu lady, now thirty-nine years old, upon whose will the fate of his country now depended entirely. Upon her whim, as well. She was already forty by Chinese reckoning, the age at which the Sage Confucius had known himself free of all temptation. She was certainly not beyond the abundant temptations of absolute power or personal indulgence.

The Tung Chih Restoration had, formally at least, just ended with the death of that unfortunate Emperor. Would men soon praise the continuing

530

Kwang Hsü Restoration of China's greatness under the aegis of the Empress Dowager, who was now wholly at odds with her former Prince Counsellor Kung? Would the ancient grace of Chinese civilisation in harmony with the vigour of Western technology create as era of benevolence and justice, as the great plaque in the council hall exhorted?

The unselfish contributions of a score of foreigners like his sister Fronah and his friend Gabriel gave much hope for that happy outcome. The dedicated services of enlightened younger Mandarins like himself, who sympathised with the foreigners' ways and the foreigners' passion for trade, would strive towards that magnificent goal.

David Lee rendered silent gratitude to Almighty God and to Heaven, the concepts that were virtually one in his mind. He thanked the Divinity profoundly for assigning him a major part when his country confronted such enormous opportunities and such stirring challenges. He also prayed for divine favour to overcome the great dangers that stalked the future.

Nala of the Yehe Clan, once the Virtuous Concubine and again the Emperess Dowager Regent, was also preoccupied with the future. Would she, in truth, ever feel justified in laying down the heavy burden of responsibility she carried? She hated that burden, she told herself, although her foolish detractors believed she delighted in exercising supreme power. Would she ever in good conscience be able to pass it to the new Emperor?

She did not know. She simply did not know.

CHAPTER SEVENTY-SEVEN

January 14, 1875   *The Gulf of Pohai off Taku Bar*

The teak panelling of the owner's cabin groaned as the *SS Keelung*, the pride of the China Merchants Steamship Company, pitched in the long swells reaching into the Gulf of Pohai from the coast of Tientsin. The crashing of the waves from the North China Sea against her square stern was subsiding as the rage of the wind declined. The big paddle-wheeler no longer quivered in every plank as she had when her prow smashed into mountains of water that seemed as unyielding as granite. The shutters protecting the portholes had been taken down earlier that morning, and the drab light of the northern winter dyed the opulent furnishings with a grey patina.

Fronah gratefully watched her amah pack the two big steamer-trunks for disembarkation. She had been ashamed of her terror at the height of the gale. But the gruff Scots captain and the laconic Down Easter from Maine, who was the first officer, both assured her that only a fool would have been unafraid. Did she think, they asked, they weren't frightened? Did she think *Keelung* would have put into Tsingtao for refuge if the danger from the storm had not been overwhelming? The voyage, which should have taken five or six days – no more than eight even in rough winter seas – was entering its third week on January 2, 1875.

She was delighted that today would see its end. She had been disappointed at spending New Year's Eve in storm-whipped waters, bereft of the childlike pleasure she usually took in the festivities that bade farewell to the departing year, and, far worse, deprived of Gabriel's anticipated presence at the celebration. She yearned to reach Tientsin. The voyage had been both frightening and dull.

She was not diverted by the officers' attentiveness to the solitary female who occupied the crescent-shaped suite directly under the bridge. A privilege had, for once, not been accorded her because she was Saul Haleevie's daughter, but because she was the guest of David Lee, chief of the secretariat of the Mandarin Li Hung-chang, Viceroy of Chihli, Superintendent of Trade for the Northern Ports, and the effective owner of the China Merchants Steamship Company. Since she travelled as Mrs Henriques – for the last time, she prayed – the officers had not known that she was the daughter of a major stock-holder in the line.

Not Gabriel, but David had replied to her message that she would sail on the *Keelung* after ensuring that the children's home and the language school would function smoothly during her absence. David's message had taken the same curious route as her own: by the new telegraph lines for short distances and by mounted courier between the stations. Acknowledging her message, her brother had added, as if by afterthought in taut telegraphese: COMMODORE HYDE ALSO HOPES WELCOME YOU BUT MUST REPEAT MUST PROCEED KOREA FIFTH JANUARY.

Fronah was nonplussed by both the curt injunction and David's signature. Gabriel must naturally go where directed by the Mandarin, she consoled herself. It was less consolingly that he apparently did not wish to appear to sponsor her visit. Since Gabriel was ordered to Korea, the delay occasioned by the gale was doubly irksome. They must, above all, meet again *now*, not later. The beginning of the new year was the auspicious time, she knew, superstitious as a Chinese maidservant poring over her horoscope.

She would, Fronah resolved, go with Gabriel to Korea even if they could not marry before the trip. But he decision was not hers, she realised with dismay. She would go with him *if* he wanted her to, just as she would marry him *if* he chose. It was galling to be completely dependent upon someone else's will, even Gabriel's. Not only *where* she would spend the next few weeks, but *how* she would spend the rest of her life rested entirely with the man who had been her devoted lover before her own capriciousness drove him away.

532

That dependence was, curiously, also comforting. Having submitted totally, she could no longer direct her own fate. The time for coquettry and hestitating was past. Feminine wiles would only put him off, and humiliate her. It was entirely up to him now.

Would Gabriel already have made up his mind one way of the other? She did not believe so, and she knew that he would *not* have decided upon marriage. She only prayed that he had not decided *against* marriage.

For perhaps the fiftieth time, she unfolded his much-creased letter and re-read his equivocal words. At least, there could be no doubt about his love. But could he overcome his doubts about himself, as well as his doubts about herself?

A sharp rap on the cabin-door interrupted Fronah's ten thousandth retracing of the circles in which her thoughts had been whirling for weeks. She admitted the first officer, whose long face bore a patronising smile.

'Cap'n MacFarlane presents his compliments, Ma'am,' the Down Easter said. 'He wonders if you'd care to come to the bridge. We'll be making our landfall on the new Taku Fort in an hour or so. But the fishing junks are coming out, and they're well worth seeing the first time.'

Content in her anonymity, Fronah felt it would be ungracious to tell the young man that she had already seen more junks than he would ever see. Let him think she was a newcomer to China who had never seen a fleet of Chinese vessels, much less sailed up the Long River on a black smuggling junk.

Captain MacFarlane was heartily welcoming when she climbed the varnished ladder to the bridge, which was built near the bows in the new fashion. The wheelhouse sparkled, its wood bright and its brass fittings gleaming. The Chinese quatermaster at the teak wheel as tall as himself was manoeuvring *Keelung*'s white bows through a school of junks. Their red and blue paint faded and their bows frail amid the grey-green waves, the brave junks made her throat ache.

'A beautiful sight, Mrs Henriques, isn't it?' The Captain was courtly. 'But I wouldn't go to sea in a junk for a year's pay.'

No, Captain, Fronah thought, you wouldn't. And you shouldn't. You probably couldn't bear it, master mariner though you may be. Every helmsman in that fleet knows more in his bones about the winds and the waves that you'll ever know with all your machinery and your chronometers. They are *real* sailors. They respect the power of the Goddess of the Seas, but they are not afraid.

She was startled by her passionate advocacy of those sailors. Perhaps she was, as her father charged, too deeply committed to China and the Chinese.

'Now that's odd,' the Captain said. 'A man-of-war, obviously, but showing some queer signal-flags. Very odd. Care to have a look, Mrs Henriques?'

Fronah took his binoculars and adjusted them to her eyes as Gabriel had taught her. The angular side-wheeler was as awkward as old *Mencius*, Gabriel's first command, though much larger than that makeshift river-gunboat. The rigging, Fronah saw in the wavering circle of the lenses, was festooned with scarlet bunting.

'Damnedest thing I ever saw,' the first officer exclaimed. 'Dressed all over in red. And damned if she isn't . . . I'd swear she's flying a commodore's pennant.'

Fronah's heart turned over in her breast. She had always thought it was only a figure of speech, but she felt her heart jump.

'Must be some Chink holiday,' the Captain observed. 'Damned unseamanlike. But the heathen have got some strange ways.'

The Chinese quartermaster moved the wheel minutely, his face heavily impassive.

'She's coming up fast, Cap'n,' the first officer volunteered. 'Must be bustin' her boilers. She's in one big rush.'

'She's also flying a proper signal, Mister.' The Captain strove to steady his old-fashioned brass telescope. 'Can you make it out?'

'No. Cap'n, not yet. Just a minute though. Yeah, she's flying: *Heave to. I wish to board.*'

'The devil with that!' the Captain swore. 'We're already badly delayed. Mister, I won't stop for a Chink gunboat.'

As the squat vessel drew close, freshnets of spray broke over the windows of her wheelhouse. *Mencius*, Fronah remembered, had provided no such protection against the elements.

'She's Chink, all right,' the Captain said curtly. 'Maintain course and speed. I'm not stopping for some Chink tomfoolery.'

The warship cut in front of *Keelung*, urgently lowering and rehoisting her signal-flags to ensure that they were seen. When the big steamer ploughed ahead, a signal lamp winked imperatively.

'Morse in English,' the first officer reported. 'She's making: *Obey my order! Heave to!*'

'Maintain course and speed,' the Captain repeated.

A puff of smoke drifted from the gun on the warship's prow, and a spout of water rose fifty yards in front of the steamer.

'Shot across the bows, Cap'n,' the first officer said conversationally. 'Guess she means business. Guess we're stopping for the Chink tomfoolery.'

'Slow engines,' the Captain ordered. 'Put her into the wind.'

Fronah scrutinised the big gunboat through the binoculars. A Chinese crew was clustered around the long gun on the prow, and Chinese sailors were hoisting a small boat out on its davits. Those scarlet flags, she pondered, they were unusual. The blurred circle of her binoculars shifted to the enormous banner streaming beside the tall smokestack. It was emblazoned in gold with a stylised ideogram, which she could not quite read through the wavering binoculars.

534

'Holding us up like this,' the Captain grumbled. 'It'd better be damned important.'

'It is, Captain, it is!' Fronah thrust the binoculars at him. 'It's damned important, I promise you. Damned important!'

The officers watched in astonishment as she scrambled down the ladder to the deck, heedless of her flying skirts. While the captain grumbled, the emblem on the great banner had resolved itself into the double-*hsi*, the twofold-joy ideogram that symbolised weddings and connubial bliss. Fronah had also glimpsed an officer wearing a blue uniform and a white cap striding towards the small boat handing from its davits. She could not distinguish his features, but the officer walked with Gabriel's assured tread on the pitching deck.

Fronah stood at the rail of *Keelung* beside the open gate through which the sailors were lowering a Jacob's ladder. She willed the small boat to dance faster over the waves. But she already knew, and her heart leaped again.

He *had* made up his mind. Only Gabriel would have flaunted that bravura banner, the old Gabriel she loved. Had there ever been a more ostentatious proposal of marriage? Every man on the gunboat must know why their barbarian commodore was flying the double-joy ideogram. He would never have hoisted the signal if he were not absolutely certain of his own mind. He trusted her, and he wanted her – or he would not be proclaiming his intention of marrying her.

Fronah bridled for an instant. Perhaps he was *too* sure of her. The next instant, she smiled. He had every reason to be sure of her.

The small boat was a bobbing cockleshell at the foot of the towering side of the steamer. The officer in blue swung on to the rope-ladder and began to climb slowly, fending off the ship's planking with one hand. Fronah bit her lips in fear. The ladder was so frail, and the steamer was pitching violently. She wanted to shout at him to go back, but her voice would never carry over the wind.

His head down, the officer struggled up the rungs – for hours, it seemed. Only when his cap, miraculously still secure, was level with the deck did he raise his head. Fronah saw Gabriel smiling at her as he pulled himself through the railing, and she stepped forward.

0116006